SO-AUN-788

MATILDA'S STORY:

The California Years

A Biographical Novel

By Jacquelyn Hanson

To Elaine
Now enjoy the
rest of Matilda's
story — Sincerely
Jacquelyn Hanson
July 2015

Glenhaven Press   Mission Viejo - 2003

MATILDA'S STORY: The California Years
A Biographical Novel
by Jacquelyn Hanson

Published by:

 GLENHAVEN PRESS
24871 Pylos Way
Mission Viejo, CA 92691

All rights reserved. Printed in the United States of America

Copyright 2001 by Jacquelyn Hanson

First Edition

First Printing – August, 2003
1   2   3   4   5
Publisher's Cataloging in Publication Data
Matilda's Story: The California Years – a Biographical Novel

Bibliography: p
Biographical novel based on the life of Matilda Randolph.
Early Sacramento County History
Pioneer Life 4. Genealogy- Gardner and Elizabeth Ann Randolph
descendants
Library of Congress Catalog Card Number 2003094241
        Hardcover ISBN 0-9741279-0-6
        Paperback ISBN 0-9741279-1-4

Typeset with Quark
Font 12 pt. Times New Roman
Cover Art by Studio II

DEDICATION

This book is dedicated to Mia
Jacquelyn Hanson, great-great-
great granddaughter of Matilda
Randolph – and the most
beautiful baby girl in the world.

Also by Jacquelyn Hanson

Matilda's Story

Susan's Quest

Katlin's Fury

Note from the Author

When *Matilda's Story* ended in 1867, with her marriage to my great-grandfather, I thought I was finished with Matilda, and was going to turn my attention to her father, Gardner Randolph. This book is the result of so many readers demanding to know what happened to Matilda after 1867.

This book continues her story until her 69th birthday in 1905. As with *Matilda's Story*, the story has been fictionalized, but is based closely on fact, primarily family stories augmented by actual newspaper accounts.

Since Matilda spent the rest of her life in the community of Hicksville, this book is not only her story, but the story of those who surrounded her and were an integral part of her life. I have tried to give a realistic picture of life in a farming community in South Sacramento County in the last thirty years of the nineteenth century.

Of course, continuing research into Matilda's life led me to more information, and a few errors in *Matilda's Story*. Steve Hoover of Elk Grove pointed out that chukars were introduced into the U.S. in 1924, so Sinclair could not have shot one on the trek out in 1864. We had just rousted a flock when following Matilda's trail and did not check further.

My chemist brother Robert informed me, after the book was in print, that pig fat does not make good candles, the melting temperature is too low, so I must ask forgiveness for the reference in Chapter Three.

My great-uncle always said James and Delilah Burleson (Betsy Ann's sister and her husband) went back to Alabama in 1832 and then into Texas in 1835 where James Burleson took part in the Texas War for independence in 1836. He did do that but he did not take Delilah. I discovered through some Burleson descendants that Delilah died in McLean County between the birth of her last child in 1828 and James Burleson's second marriage to Malinda Sevier in 1832.

I also learned that Minerva's daughter Anna was born in 1857, and that the infant who died at birth was probably born in 1866 when Minerva died.

I closed *Matilda's Story* with her marriage to Alfred Wheelock at her home in Hicksville. Subsequent research revealed they married in Sacramento at the boarding house of Mrs. S. Maddox.

In researching for *Matilda's Story: The California Years,* I am indebted to Pat Johnson of the Sacramento Archives, Helen Rydell of the Santa Barbara County Historical Society, Debbie Mastell from the San Joaquin County Historical Society, Mary from the Sloughhouse Area Genealogical Society, Kathy Alvie of the Lakeport Museum, and Eugenie Olson of the Galt Area Historical Society.

The Internet led me to many helpful newly discovered relations. On the Tovrea line, Gladys Brandstoettner and Christy Vanderkieft. For the Burlesons, Steve Deitz, Mary, Dan Burleson, Inez Mack, and Estelle Blake. For the William Frye/Elizabeth Goforth connection; Betty Henderson McCauley and Nina Waldrip. I owe thanks to Nancy Smedley, Norma Loew, Marc Doty, and Martha Anderson for their help with Wendell Crose. I am indebted to JoAnn Hornby and Charles Rutter for helping me trace the family of Caroline and Eli Robertson, and Nancy Lohbrunner and Robert Hoadley for their help with the Latourettes. For the Stringfields, I am grateful to Glen Atwell, Melissa Barker, Emily Baker, Shirley Rinderkraft and many others who contributed to the Stringfield family forum. For the Randolphs, Billie Harris and Sherrell Buchanan and all of the others of the Randolph family. Kira Rickabaugh provided additional information on the Dyers.

Benjamin Carnahan not only provided information on the Dyers, he solved the mystery of Goldie.

Special mention must be given to Marian Randolph, wife of my third cousin, Leonard Randolph. Len is a descendant of Matilda's brother Will through his son Bud and grandson Walter. Marian has made her extensive research available to me, for which I am very grateful.

Margaret Bender, granddaughter of D.K. Stringfield and Maggie Randolph provided me with a number of treasures in the form of letters and pictures from her grandmother's trunk, including a picture of D.K.and their wedding certificate.

The late Ken McKean, of Wilton, son of my father's good friend Charlie McKean, and great-grandson of Alec Blue, provided details on the local MiWok history.

I must also thank Nora Shellenbarger and Kathleen McKenzie for helping me wade through reel after reel of microfilm of old newspapers. Madelyn Valensin and Ruth Pratton also supplied me with helpful information on the early days of Hicksville.

My fellow writers at the Saddleback Writers Guild again helped me by patiently critiquing page after page of the manuscript. And I must thank my publisher, Sid Freshour for his help in getting the book ready for the printer.

Many thanks are due to Michael Nudi for all the work he did getting the manuscript into Quark for me.

My grandson, Philip Brown, is my computer guru, and without his help, the book would never have been published. And I must thank my son Jayson and his wife Michele for giving me my beautiful granddaughter, the reason we all try to preserve our family history.

PROLOGUE

For those who have not read Matilda's Story, Matilda Randolph was born in McLean County, Illinois, July 19, 1836, the tenth child and fourth daughter of Gardner and Betsy Ann Randolph.

When she was eighteen, the family migrated to Kansas. There she married Lewis Baldwin and bore four children, John, who died young, Mary, Elizabeth, and Lewis, born two months after his father's death. The slavery-anti-slavery issue raged around her, followed by the Civil War.

In 1863, her husband was killed in a well accident. In 1864, as a widow with three small children, she, with her parents, brother Sinclair, and brother Britt and his family, crossed the Oregon-California Trail to join other family members already living in California. There she settled in Hicksville where she would remain for the rest of her life

In 1867, at the end of *Matilda's Story*, she remarried, to Alfred Wheelock. And on June 19, 1867, *Matilda's Story: The California Years* begins.

Chapter 1

June, 1867

"UNTIL DEATH DO us part," Alfred intoned in a solemn voice. "Until death do us part," Matilda echoed, a little breathless, gazing deep into Alfred's sparkling hazel eyes. Caught up in the emotion of the moment, she did not hear the minister pronounce them man and wife. She only realized the ceremony had concluded when Alfred swept her into his arms and kissed her soundly to a rousing, if undignified, cheer from Mary.

As soon as the newlyweds turned from facing Reverend Anderson, Mary and Elizabeth launched themselves into Alfred's arms, showering his face with kisses.

"Now you really *are* our papa," Mary announced, hugging his neck. "Forever and ever."

Elizabeth added her agreement with equal enthusiasm, also throwing her arms about his neck. Alfred's face began turning red as the two girls tightened their embrace.

"Girls, girls, you're strangling him." Matilda, feeling it time to intervene, peeled the children off and set them back on their feet. "I'm glad you're so happy he's your father now, but give him a chance to catch his breath. You'll have plenty of time to show him you love him."

1

With a smile, Betsy Ann herded the children off to the side. "Let the grown-ups talk for a minute."

Alf enthusiastically shook Alfred's hand. "Congratulations, Partner. You've got yourself a good woman." He added, with a mischievous glance at Matilda, "Even if she is my sister." He hugged Matilda when she swung at him. "And you've got a good man, 'Tilda. Take good care of him."

Matilda laughed. "I plan to."

"Mama!" Mary's voice attracted Matilda's attention. "Why do we have to stay with Grandmama and Uncle Alf?" The blue eyes rebuked her. "Why can't we go with you and Mr. Wheelock to San Francisco, now that he's our new papa?"

"Sweetheart, we've discussed this many times. You're almost eight years old. You have to stay home and help your grandmama take care of Elizabeth and little Lew for me. Your new papa and I will be back on Saturday. From then on we will do everything as a family." She held up a hand to stem further protests. "And you have to help your grandmama get everything ready for the big party, remember?"

To herself, Matilda thanked Heaven Mary and Elizabeth had grown so fond of Alfred. Of course, she thought, love for him coursing through her, anyone who knew him could not help loving such a kind, gentle, considerate man . . . .

Mrs. Maddux smiled. "I have prepared a small repast to celebrate the wedding. After all, it's not often I get the honor of being hostess to such a special occasion here in my humble boarding house."

The Reverend Anderson chuckled. "Blame my tight schedule. They wanted to get married this weekend, but I have to leave Friday for San Francisco, and tomorrow I had another wedding to perform. When Mr. Wheelock approached me, this was the best arrangement we could make."

Matilda smiled graciously as he kissed her hand. "It has worked out just fine, Reverend Anderson. We are going to go ahead and have the reception as planned on Sunday, and we will take our honeymoon trip before instead of after."

"Thank you for your understanding," he said. "Now, let us join Mrs. Maddux at her table. As one of her most regular diners, let me assure you, she lays a magnificent spread. With the bumper crop of blackberries this year, she has made a wonderful compote, and makes a very tasty blackberry cobbler."

She certainly has a lovely home, Matilda thought, as they wended their way into the elegant dining salon, admiring the beautiful wood finish on the banister, the fine marble of the fireplace mantel, the imposing chandelier that hung over the elegant polished table. Her feet sank into the rich carpet with its intricate pattern. Red velvet draperies covered the windows. A damask tablecloth adorned the table, set with fine crystal goblets and china plates.

The house, located on 2nd Street between 'P' and 'Q', was only two blocks from the magnificent Crocker mansion. Matilda could not help thinking Mrs. Maddux must be quite wealthy to possess such a large home with such rich furnishings, wondering why she felt the need to run a boarding house.

As though reading Matilda's mind, Mrs. Maddux smiled. "My husband died last year, and, although he did leave me some funds, I felt I should use the space in this big house to supplement my income. I am very selective about my clientele. I know many widows prefer to live on what their husbands leave for them, but I have seen many of them either lose the money through poor investments, or use it up and be left destitute. This way, I can keep my independence. And it gives me something to do. So many ladies spend their days doing useless things to while away the time.

"Besides," she grinned, "I love to cook, and am proud of my culinary achievements. It's nice to have an appreciative audience."

Reverend Anderson laughed. "And a bachelor like me is a very appreciative audience indeed."

An hour later, Alf loaded four jars of blackberry compote, Betsy Ann, and the three children into the buggy for the return trip to Hicksville. Matilda and Alfred prepared to go to their hotel.

"See everybody Saturday," Matilda embraced Betsy Ann in a fond hug. "Mother, be sure you get plenty of help getting ready for the reception Sunday. Don't try and do it all yourself."

Betsy Ann grinned as she climbed up beside Lew on the front seat of the buggy. The two girls sat in the back. "Not to worry. Already got all the jobs laid out."

"She does, too," Alf chuckled as he climbed into the driver's seat. "You should have seen her doling out orders to Polly and Sarah. Even got Abe's new housekeeper some chores to do." King snorted, anxious to get moving. "See you Saturday. Watch you don't take the 'Pox in San Francisco. I hear they've got an epidemic going."

"We'll be careful," Alfred promised. "Now that I've found my dream girl, I'm going to take good care of her." They waved as the buggy drove off down 'P' Street, the two little girls in back waving as long as they were in sight.

"Now, Mrs. Wheelock," Alfred said, smiling down on

her fondly, "shall we go to our hotel?"

Happiness swept over Matilda in a wave. "As you wish, Mr. Wheelock."

The afternoon sun had begun its descent into the west, painting the cloud bank along the horizon with the reddish-purple glow of sunset, when the hired buggy deposited them in front of the Golden Eagle Hotel on 'K' Street. Matilda had wanted to spend her first night with Alfred in the famous Golden Eagle.

They walked arm in arm into the lobby, their feet sinking in the plush carpet.. Matilda had never known carpet could be so thick. And she had thought the carpet in Mrs. Maddux's home was plush! Her feet sank even deeper in this one.

"Hello, John," Alfred greeted the young man behind the counter. "My dear," he drew Matilda forward, "this is John McGinnis, recently promoted to Chief Clerk here at the Golden Eagle."

Matilda extended her hand. "Pleased to meet you, Mr. McGinnis."

"The pleasure is all mine, Mrs. Wheelock. I wish you every happiness. Alfred here is a fine fellow."

Matilda tossed a merry glance at Alfred. "Thank you. I think so, too."

"What he's not telling you," Alfred said with a grin, "is that he is a newlywed himself. Congratulations."

"Thank you." Mr. McGinnis waved the bellboy over and handed him a key. "Enjoy your stay with us. I'll have coffee sent up in plenty of time for you to board the *Yosemite* in the morning."

Matilda gasped when she saw the size of the room he ushered them into. The red velvet draperies were tied back with gold braid to reveal white organdy covering the window, which the young man opened to allow the evening breeze to cool the room. A love seat, its cushion covered with the same fabric as the draperies and the counterpane, sat in front of the window. A small table stood by the wall at the end of the bed. A lamp with red roses painted on the shade lighted the area by the two cozy reading chairs. A door opened onto a room with a big claw-footed bath tub.

"Oh, Alfred!" She stared at the luxury surrounding her. "Even a private bath? Can we afford such extravagance?"

Alfred turned from escorting the grinning bellboy out of the door and swept her into his arms. "Of course, Mrs. Wheelock. Nothing but the best for *my* wife," he murmured against her hair. He tilted up her chin and kissed her gently on the lips with a wicked grin. "I think I am going to enjoy married life."

Matilda blushed.

The following morning, the smell of coffee tickling her nostrils awakened her. Alfred sat on the bed beside her holding a cup of steaming coffee. He looked down on her with laughing eyes.

"I don't wish to disturb your beauty sleep, my love, but if we are to catch the *Yosemite* for San Francisco, we had best be getting on our way. I had the bellboy bring us a pot of coffee and a couple of biscuits. We can get a real breakfast on the steamer."

Matilda stretched luxuriously on the silken sheets, savoring each movement. She sat up and accepted the coffee he offered her. "You're right. We must get started." She smiled at him across the top of the cup. "I think I could get used to this."

Forty minutes later they stood on the dock and watched the *Yosemite* swing in to tie up. Shouts from the sailors echoed as lines were tossed to the hands on the pier, the loops secured to the bollards. Muscles strained to pull the boat alongside against the constant tug of the current, which tried to carry the steamer on down the river. Matilda admired the skill of the men who made the whole job look so easy. In minutes, the little craft was secured, the gangplank in place. Passengers who had come down from Marysville streamed ashore. Cargo handlers lifted off barrels and crates, and others loaded on more.

Matilda stood watching all the activity around her in fascination when she felt Alfred take her arm.

"Come on," he murmured into her ear. "If we don't get on board pretty soon, we'll be left standing here. The captain only stays long enough to off-load the cargo and passengers and take on the next batch. They're always in a hurry."

"Of course." She pulled her attention back to Alfred and he assisted her across the rickety, swaying gangplank and onto the deck. She recalled discussing with Annie how the *Yosemite* had blown her boiler the previous October. Fortunately, she had sunk in shallow water and not sustained serious damage. The owners had her back in service in a remarkably short space of time.

Vague memories of others of the many stories she had heard about boilers blowing and ships sinking and passengers being killed ran through her mind. All because captains, always anxious to make better time than rival captains, tried to stoke the boilers too hot.

She did not voice her fears to Alfred. She forced her thoughts away from such a morbid subject and moved with Alfred to the rail opposite the dock, away from the crowd.

7

The morning already promised a hot day, although it was not yet eight o'clock.

With a blast from her horn, the *Yosemite* swung out into the river. The current caught her bow and aimed her downstream. Matilda gasped in excitement. She was finally going to see not only the fabled city of San Francisco, but the Pacific Ocean as well. She thought of the thrill of the previous night, and anticipation shot though her. Not only would she see places she had only dreamed of seeing for so long, she would see them in the company of a man who loved her, a man she adored in return.

Her new life was just beginning.

Chapter 2

June, 1867

ALFRED AND MATILDA stood arm in arm at the bow of the *Yosemite* watching the farms on both sides drift by. She felt a twinge of sadness that all of the Indian villages were gone. Alf had told her how they had dotted the river-banks, with naked children playing in the water and women washing clothes. Thousands of Americans swarming all over the land had changed their whole way of life.

As they progressed down river, they swung into a side stream. "Why do we leave the main river?" she asked Alfred, who stood beside her looking down at her indul-gently. He's humoring me, she thought, knowing her lack of sophistication amused him.

"Because it cuts about ten miles off the journey. They even call it 'Steamboat Slough' because the steamer cap-tains learned the trick shortly after they started plying the river. The main river swings in a wide loop." He pointed out a flock of ducks taking off ahead of the steamer's prow. "Not near so many of them now. When I came up the first time, in '49, you could hardly see the river for the ducks and geese." He shook his head. "Too many of them have gone into duck dinners."

They watched the birds in silence for a few minutes, then Alfred said. "Speaking of dinner, for a dollar we can get something to eat."

Matilda, too excited to think of eating, shook her head. "Oh, no. We might miss something if we go into the cabin to eat." She looked about, hoping she was not too obvious as she checked out the other female passengers, halfway looking for Bridgette, or one of the other ladies who 'worked the river' as Annie had told her. She blushed, hoping Alfred did not guess the reason for her scrutiny. "Besides, it's probably hot and stuffy inside. It's much pleasanter here."

Alfred nodded. "As you wish. Wait until we get the othr side of the Carquinez Strait. A little hot and stuffy might feel pretty good."

"What is the Carquinez Strait?" Matilda asked, feeling very ignorant in the presence of such a well-traveled and well-educated man. She could only hope she did not disappoint him.

"That's where the San Joaquin and the Sacramento Rivers join to go into San Pablo Bay, then to San Francisco, and out into the Pacific. All the rivers of the valley, from the Feather in the north to the Kern in the south drain out through the Carquinez Strait." He grinned. "Lot of water goes through here. We're making good time at the moment, for the tide is with us. When it turns, the engines will have to work harder."

Visions of blowing boilers again intruded into Matilda's mind, and she pushed the thought aside. Instead, she focused her attention on the outline of Mount Diablo, becoming larger as they moved down the river. "Why did they name the mountain Diablo?" she asked.

"Spanish governor gave a land grant to a fellow named Pacheco back in '27, and he called it Monte de Diablo. I suspect because it is an extinct volcano."

"Alf told me that. Do you suppose he's right? Is it really extinct?"

Alfred chuckled. "Well, we will certainly hope so. Before the Spanish granted the mountain to Pacheco, it was called after the Bolbones Indians, who lived here before the Spanish came."

"And lost their land to the white men," Matilda concluded, thinking of her Pottawatamie friends, and of other Indians who had seen their ancestral lands taken from them as more and more whites moved into the area.

"That seems to be the way it works out," Alfred shrugged. "Look," he pointed. "You can see a small herd of deer through the willows on the bank."

From the Sacramento River, they entered Suisun Bay, and Alfred advised her they would soon be entering the Strait. "Will start to get cooler soon after we get through. Wind comes up from San Francisco. After the Strait, we enter San Pablo Bay. The Napa, Petaluma, and San Rafael Rivers all feed into the bay. It's one big bowl."

The sheer cliffs of the Strait rose on both sides of them. Matilda, impressed with the width of the river, gasped, "It must be a mile wide!"

"Easily," Alfred agreed. "Remember how much water has to go through each year."

As they steamed into San Pablo Bay, Alfred tried to point out the different rivers, but the tules and trees were so thick it made discerning the mouths of the rivers difficult. Matilda shivered as the wind became cooler, and Alfred pulled her shawl out of the valise and tucked it around her solicitously. "Your coat is in the trunk. I hope you won't need it before we arrive."

"Will it really get that much colder? After all, it *is* summer."

Alfred smiled down on her. "Remember what Mark

Twain said when we went to that lecture he gave in Sacramento?" He quoted, "'The coldest winter I ever spent was one summer in San Francisco'."

Matilda laughed. "I thought he just said that to be funny. I never dreamed he really *meant* it." She pulled the shawl tighter. "But I am beginning to see what he was saying."

"We can go inside if you get too cold. I don't want you to take a chill."

"I'm sure I will be fine," she assured him, then looked off to the port side of the little vessel. "Oh, look, how lovely." Two rocky crags stood in the water, just offshore, and the afternoon sun turned the rocks to a golden red.

"Those are the Sisters. The next two, coming up, are the Brothers. The big island on the starboard side is Angel Island. There's an army base there now." As they moved around Angel Island, another lone island came into sight "That's Alcatraz. It used to be an army base to protect the harbor, but in 1861, they turned it into a military prison."

Matilda stared at the bare mass of rock with the stark walls of the prison visible on the top. "What a lonely, isolated spot!"

Alfred nodded. "Virtually escape proof. Between the currents and the sharks and the fifty degree water, not much chance of a swimmer making it to shore." He pointed "Just beyond the island is the Golden Gate. The current would just sweep any swimmers out to sea, even on an incoming tide."

Matilda shuddered, but said nothing more. She stared at the isolated island and tried to suppress her horror at the thought that anyone could be imprisoned there. A strange feeling of sympathy swept over her.

They stood clinging to the starboard rail and watched the famous passage to the Pacific loom before them. A sailing vessel came between the golden cliffs under full sail as they watched. The sun behind her outlined the sleek lines of her hull and the billowing sails testified to the strength of the wind behind her.

Matilda stood transfixed, fascinated to see the fabled Golden Gate at last. A bank of fog stood just behind the ship, seeming to chase it though the opening. The mist clung to the hills on both sides of the fabled passage, moving slowly across the water.

Alfred put his arm around her. "As soon as that fog reaches us, it will be even colder. You really should come inside the cabin. We will be tying up at the pier soon."

"Oh, no," Matilda shivered, tucking her chin deeper into her shawl. "Then I would miss my first view of the city."

Alfred just shook his head and held her tighter.

When the *Yosemite* reached the pier, Matilda eagerly watched as the city emerged from the fog that enveloped it. Beside her, Alfred laughed.

"Quite a change from when I landed here in '49. Then there were only two piers, now there must be fifteen. Most of us scrambled ashore over the clay banks at Clark's Point, and the boys that helped carry luggage wanted two whole dollars." He waved his arm in a wide sweep. "Now the entire area where we landed is completely covered with streets and houses. They've filled in the whole bay!"

Matilda smiled. "And instead of a boy running to carry your bag, we have a whole line of hacks and omnibuses, all trying to get us to go to their particular hotel."

"We're going to fool them," he advised her. "We are going to stay at a small boarding house run by the widow of an old friend, up on Telegraph Hill. It's the best view of the city and the bay, even the Golden Gate. Met them after I picked up the *Capital* in Panama. They had come from Boston, around the Horn. He planned to set himself up as a merchant in San Francisco." Alfred chuckled softly. "I told him I was on my way to get myself some gold in those fabled hills. I can still hear him saying, 'gold digging is a young man's game. Lots of easier ways to get gold than to dig for it.'"

"I trust he succeeded?"

"Oh, yes, he did quite well. Built himself and his wife a spacious home up on Telegraph Hill, because she always enjoyed watching the ships come in. Being from Boston, I guess the sea was in her blood. They had no children, so when he died, three, four years ago, she opened her home as a boarding house, but only to a few, select guests, people she knows or who are referred to her by friends. I'm sure you will enjoy meeting her. She's very well read and well educated. And the world's biggest gossip. If there is any news to be had, she will know it." He chuckled. "In fact, I suspect she takes in guests so she will have people to share her stories with. Quite a lady."

"And her name?"

"Don't laugh. It's Charity Boone. Her husband told me her two sisters were Faith and Hope. Her mother was a staunch Presbyterian. Her family came over from Scotland in the 1830's. I guess that why her mother chose those names."

Matilda laughed in spite of his admonition. "I know how that goes. I had a sister named Temperance, but she was named for Mother's sister, Temperance Stringfield. The Stringfields were Methodist, through and through."

A blast from the steamer's whistle drowned any reply Alfred might have made, and dock handlers came racing down the pier to receive the mooring lines from the crewmen. In moments, the ship was secure, and passengers streamed ashore. Crewmen piled baggage and trunks out on the pier for passengers to collect. Captain Van Pelt came out of the pilot house to wish them a good trip.

"Good having you folks with us," he said as he bowed over Matilda's hand. "Will you be returning with me?"

"No, we are booked on the *Chrysopolis* for Saturday morning."

"Then I look forward to seeing you on another voyage. Captain Woodward will see you have a good trip back up the river."

"Thank you, Captain." The captain turned to greet another departing passenger and Alfred secured their small trunk. He immediately unlocked it to retrieve Matilda's warm coat.

She snuggled into it gratefully. "And to think I told you I surely would not need this!"

He laughed. "I'm afraid I know San Francisco weather a little better than you do. I knew you'd need it. Come on, I've engaged a hack to take us to Mrs. Boone's. I think he was impressed when I gave him the address. I guess she really does have an exclusive clientele. He'll probably think I'm rich, and expect a big tip."

Matilda's eyes widened. "Can we afford to stay in such an establishment?"

"We can, because when I wired her and told her I was coming on my honeymoon, she insisted we stay as her guests for no charge."

"Can we take advantage of her like that?"

"She'll love every minute of it," Alfred assured her. "She was thrilled to find I have finally married. She said she had given up all hope for me, sure I was a confirmed bachelor." He smiled at Matilda and squeezed her hand. "I

15

told her I just had to wait for the right woman to come along."

Happiness washed over Matilda as she returned his smile.

An hour later, their hackman turned his horse left off Battery and headed up Filbert Street. As the street grew steeper, Matilda gasped. "Is it safe to go up such a steep hill?"

"Relax," Alfred reassured her. "These horses climb these hills all the time. How else would people get to those houses up there?"

Matilda said no more, but clung a little tighter to Alfred's arm as they wended their way higher and higher until at last they stopped in front of a magnificent house with a spacious porch overlooking the bay. The house looked warm and inviting, its three stories rising to what seemed, to Matilda, unbelievable heights. Gabled windows faced the street. An iron rooster stood atop a weathervane on the very peak of the roof.

"Are you coming, or do you want to just sit there and stare?"

Matilda started, and realized Alfred was holding his hand out to help her alight. "Sorry. I was just so taken with the house. I've never seen houses as tall and narrow as these. Why do they build them this close together?"

"Because land is very dear. They build up instead of out. You'll have plenty of chance to admire them. We'll be here for two days."

A dignified lady in her late fifties, dressed in a black silk dress, emerged from the front door onto the porch. Her bright blue eyes sparkled and the bun of white hair bounced up and down as she nodded cheerfully. "Alfred, my dear boy. It has been far too long since I have seen you. Come and give an old lady a hug. And introduce me to your charming bride. Leave the trunk. Charlie will take it up to your room."

Alfred paid the hackman, and the man turned the horse and drove off. Alfred, Matilda clinging to his arm, mounted the three steps to the porch and embraced Mrs. Boone. Matilda next felt the silk clad arms envelop her in a warm hug.

"So this is the lucky young lady who finally captured the heart of the confirmed bachelor." She stood back and the bright eyes scrutinized Matilda. "I must say she was worth waiting for."

"Thank you," Matilda stammered, not knowing quite how to respond to such open speech.

Alfred just laughed. "You'll get used to her, my dear. San Francisco ladies are much more forward than they are in the country."

"Now, you saucy boy, you know I am the perfect lady, not like that Lillie Coit."

"Lillie Coit?" Matilda looked blank. "Who is she?"

"Lillie Hitchcock Coit," Alfred advised her. "Daughter of the wealthy Hitchcock family, who takes great delight in shocking the local society ladies."

"Such as by going to bars and smoking cigars," Mrs. Boone added, shaking her head. "The latest is she has become the mascot of the Knickerbocker Company #5, a volunteer fire company." Mrs. Boone ushered them in and signaled to the maid to take Matilda's coat and hat. "Let Clara take you to your room to freshen up, then come back here and we'll have a cup of tea while I tell you about her latest escapade."

17

Matilda found their small trunk already in the spacious room. A big four poster bed stood on one side. An armoire, its doors ajar to invite its use, greeted her as she entered. A colorful screen, with a scene she recognized as Lake Tahoe from the top of Johnson's cutoff, walled off one corner. A marble topped table with a kerosene lamp sat next to the bed.

"Towels on the commode next to the basin, along with some of that new-fangled cleaning paper of Mr. Cayetty's." The maid's voice brought Matilda out of her trance. "Behind the screen," she added. "Bath room down the hall. Ring for me when ye're ready to bathe, and I'll bring ye hot water."

"Thank you." The maid departed and Matilda hastened behind the screen. The facilities on the steamer had not encouraged their use. The 'new-fangled' cleaning paper the maid referred to was soft and felt wonderful. She wondered vaguely how expensive it was. She grimaced. Don't get too accustomed to luxury, she reminded herself. This trip will be over all too soon.

She washed her face and hands and dried them on the thick, lilac scented towel, then walked to the window. The fog covered most of the bay, but she could see the tops of the cliffs outlining the Golden Gate, and watched the setting sun bathe them in its golden light as it settled into the purple clouds in the distance.

Alfred came up behind her as she stood there, her hand on the rich red velvet draperies, put his arms around her, and buried his face in her red-brown curls. "Wait until the fog lifts, my love," he said. "The view from here is magnificent. They put a signal tower on the top of this hill so they can let the town know when a sailing vessel or a steamer comes through the Gate. If it's not too foggy, the top of this hill can be seen from almost anywhere in town."

He turned her to face him and kissed her soundly. She still could not get used to the emotions he could arouse in her. "And now, Mrs. Wheelock, are you ready to go listen to the tales of San Francisco? Mrs. Boone can hardly wait to get a new audience for her stories."

Matilda took a deep breath to get herself back under control and laughed. "Yes, Mr. Wheelock, I think a cup of tea and a little gossip is just what I need."

Chapter 3

June, 1867

MRS. BOONE'S EYES sparkled as she watched the newlyweds enter the little parlor hand in hand. "Does my heart good to see him head over heels in love," she chuckled softly to Matilda. "Way he looks at you, a body would think there was no other woman in the world."

Matilda did not know how to answer such a comment. She met Alfred's eyes and he looked at her with such adoration that it took her breath away.

"There isn't," he declared firmly. "She is a treasure beyond compare."

Embarrassed, Matilda blushed and, to cover her confusion, glanced about the room. A magnificent silver tea service sat on the marble-topped table. A little spinet piano stood on one side of the room. Mrs. Boone occupied one of the red velvet covered sofas. Alfred and Matilda sat opposite her on the other. Clara, the maid, hovered nearby. Mrs. Boone poured three cups of tea into the delicate china cups. "Sugar? Milk?" Matilda nodded, and Alfred shook his head. Clara took the cups and distributed them, then offered delicate sugar cookies on tiny china plates.

Mrs. Boone took a sip of the fragrant tea, and launched into her first story. "Lillie, believe it or not, went to Warner's Bear and Monkey House down at Meigg's Wharf in North Beach. Actually, it's on an alley off of Francisco

Street, sort of a combination saloon and museum. I understand he has a parrot there that utters the most vile string of profanity at the slightest provocation. Can you imagine a lady going to such a place?" She shook her head. "They call it the Cobweb Palace, because Abe Warner swears it's bad luck to discommode the wretched spiders, so the webs have been undisturbed since he built the place. Such nonsense." She shuddered. "Collecting dust all this time. Makes a body sneeze just to think on it.

"Anyways," she rattled on, "Lillie was telling me she was there one afternoon when a little boy came by with a whole bag of peanuts that he kept tossing to the bear. The bear, of course, was real happy, but the monkey, who was on a chain with a real long line, he got frustrated with the bear getting all the peanuts, and came up by the boy, who was leaning way out over the edge of the bear pit, and swiped across the boy's face with his paw, leaving a long line of scratches. I declare, I don't know what that boy's mother could have been thinking, to let him go alone to such a place. Wonder is the monkey didn't scratch out his eyes." Mrs. Boone shook her head. "Told me all about it, Lillie did."

Their hostess paused, and Matilda, beginning to feel a little short of breath just listening to the narrative, inhaled deeply.

"Oh," Matilda said, "I'm sure the boy heard about it when he got home, with those scratches on his face." She felt a certain amount of sympathy for the mother, for she could see her own daughter Mary doing the same thing, and probably leading three or four of her friends in as well.

"I haven't seen you since the mid-fifties," Alfred interposed, "when the Sydney Ducks and the Vigilante Committee were keeping things lively, and the Vigilantes hung Supervisor Casey for shooting James King of

William. Seems real peaceful now."

Mrs. Boone nodded her head in vigorous agreement. "Those Sydney Ducks did cause a lot of problems, all right. Mr. Boone had to pay them what they called 'protection' money every week. Merchants that didn't pay got their establishments burned. Disgraceful behavior, but it did put a lot of pressure on the city to have a good volunteer fire department."

"I understand the plan now is to have a paid fire department," Alfred said.

"Yes, as a result of that ruckus back in '65. Three volunteer fire departments got into a contest to see who could get to a fire first. They got into such a fight that the building burned to the ground, and there were a lot of injuries, even got some of them killed."

Alfred chuckled softly. "Yes, a full-time paid fire department would solve that problem. And where is Joaquin Murietta's head these days?"

Matilda gasped. "Head?"

Alfred nodded. "Yes, the rangers tried to get money for the head to pay for the expedition that caught him."

"It was at a bar for a while," Mrs. Boone said, "then the so-called Pacific Museum of Anatomy and Science bought it and put it on display." She sniffed with scorn. "Museum, indeed. It's nothing but a thinly disguised peep show. By rights, it should be shut down."

"Then it won't be on our list of places to visit," Alfred said.

Matilda shuddered. "I should hope not. To cut off the head of a dead man, even one as notorious as Joaquin Murietta! How horrid. And what a grisly thing for anyone to want to see."

Mrs. Boone smiled. "So, no head of Joaquin Murrieta.

Where *do* you plan to take your lovely bride, young man? What *does* she want to see?"

"The Pacific Ocean," Matilda replied promptly. "I want to look out and know the next land is Japan, and stand and watch the waves wash up on the shore."

"That's easy enough. I'll have Charlie run you out there in my gig. If you only have one day, you won't have time to take the new horse-drawn rail cars, although that is an experience in itself. Are you going to take her to Woodward's Gardens? Mr. Woodward just opened them last year, and I understand they are quite spectacular. I hope to make it over there myself someday soon. You should also take her to the Mercantile Library. They have a magnificent copy of Audubon's Birds that you really should see."

She chattered on. "And the new assistant Librarian is a charming young lady, Sarah Gunn. Her father is the city's Assessor of Internal Revenue, and she is quite bright, but there is a great deal of opposition to her appointment, libraries being such a bastion of men. I hope she stays by her guns and keeps the position, but I fear she may yield to the pressure and return to teaching school. She has the loveliest black hair which she wears in long ringlets down her back. All of the young men ogle her when they come to the library."

Matilda again took a deep breath, wondering how Mrs. Boone could keep up such long speeches without running out of air. During the brief pause, Clara announced supper was ready to serve in the dining room.

After a delicious meal, Matilda and Alfred retired to their room. Matilda, behind the painted screen, changed into her robe and nightgown while waiting for Clara to fill the tub in the bath room down the hall with hot water.

While they waited, Matilda commented to Alfred on Mrs. Boone's loquacity. "I swear, she never stops to breathe!"

Alfred laughed. "If you think she was bad tonight, don't get her started on the Terry and Broderick duel and the Chivalrists. She can go on for hours." A rap on the door interrupted them. "Sounds like your bath is ready." He gave her a quick hug. "Go have a nice, relaxing soak. You're going to have a busy day tomorrow."

She woke to the smell of coffee and sat up, momentarily confused to find herself in a strange spot. Sunlight shone through the window. Beside her, Alfred slept on, breathing softly through slightly parted lips. Smiling fondly at him, she slid gently from between the covers and pulled on her robe. From the window, she had a marvelous view of sun sparkling on the waters of the bay, and on the golden cliffs of the Gate.

At a tap on the door, she admitted Clara, who bore a tray with a pot of coffee and two cups, with lumps of sugar in a small bowl and cream in a silver pitcher.

"Morning, Mrs. Wheelock. Breakfast will be in thirty minutes." She set the tray on the table beside the lamp.

"Thank you, Clara. We'll be there."

Taking a cup of coffee, she held it under Alfred's nose. When his eyes opened, she laughed softly. "Good morning, sleepy-head."

His eyes opened and a grin spread across his face. Without a word, he set the coffee cup on the table and swept Matilda into his arms.

They reached the breakfast table to find their hostess seated at the head of the table, the blue eyes as bright as ever. "Sit down, sit down. I have arranged for Charlie to take you

25

to Woodward Gardens. It will be a lovely day, so my cook is preparing a basket lunch for you. They have places in the gardens for picnics. When you have seen enough of the Gardens, Charlie will drive you out to Land's End to view the Pacific. He should get you back here in time for supper, as you will want to retire early if you are to catch the *Chrysopolis* tomorrow morning." She fixed her bright eyes on Matilda. "I do wish you could stay longer, my dear. It seems as though you just arrived. I will miss you."

Matilda smiled. "Thank you, Mrs. Boone, we appreciate your generous hospitality, but we do have to get back. My brother is meeting us at the dock in Sacramento on Saturday evening to take us home and we have the whole neighborhood arriving Sunday for our wedding reception."

"I understand you have the Pox here in San Francisco," Alfred said. "The Sacramento papers had several articles on how severe it is. We were warned to look out for it."

"Yes, although I don't know why more Americans are not vaccinated against it. In Scotland, most people used Dr. Jenner's method, and very few take the Pox anymore." She lifted her left sleeve. "See? I have the scar on my arm to prove it, so I don't have to worry. There are doctors here in San Francisco who advertise they will give the vaccine. I tried to get Clara to get vaccinated, but she is afraid. So many people think the vaccination will give you the Pox, but experience in Scotland proved otherwise."

She grinned. "We have 50,000 Chinese people here in the city, and very few of them have taken the Pox, for I understand that in China, they protect themselves by inhaling the exudate from the pustules of those who are suffering from the disease. I understand the process works the same way as Dr. Jenner's."

Matilda gagged and Alfred chuckled softly in sympathy.

"Doesn't sound too appetizing, does it?"

"The fact that many white men did take the Pox probably only added to the resentment against the poor Chinese. There is a lot of conflict between them and the white laborers as it is, Pox or no Pox. Angry workers have even burned some Chinese homes and businesses, and have driven them from their jobs. Disgraceful, absolutely disgraceful. Mr. Boone would turn over in his grave if he could see it. He always liked dealing with the Chinese. Said they were more honest than many of the white men he had to contend with."

Plates of thick ham, fried eggs, and biscuits appeared on the table. Dishes of strawberry and blackberry jam accompanied the biscuits. Matilda, whose usual breakfast was a bowl of oatmeal, looked at the mountain of food with dismay.

"Eat, child, eat," their hostess encouraged her. "You are going to have a busy day."

Matilda tried to put the Chinese method of preventing Pox out of her mind and sank her fork into the inch thick slab of ham on her plate.

Chapter 4

June, 1867

AFTER BREAKFAST, Charlie brought the gig to the front porch. Alfred helped Matilda into the seat and climbed up beside her. Clara handed Charlie the picnic basket and he put it on the seat beside him.

"Have a wonderful time," Mrs. Boone said, sending them off with a flourish. "If you want to know anything about San Francisco, ask Charlie. He knows even more about what is going on than I do."

"That's a large order," Alfred murmured to Matilda as the gig started forward. Charlie pulled the brake tight as the horse started down the hill at a smooth trot. Matilda said nothing, but clung tightly to Alfred's arm with her left hand and the rail with her right.

Alfred patted her hand in reassurance. "Relax. I'm sure Charlie has been up and down this hill many times."

Feeling somewhat better, Matilda nevertheless heaved a deep sigh of relief when the horse reached the bottom of the hill and turned right onto Battery. "How far is it and how long does it take to get there?" she asked their driver.

"'Bout three miles, give or take a tad. Take about an hour, it will. Got to cross Market Street, then head up Mission to 13th Street. Streets in good shape now, since McCauley got all them prisoners at San Quentin to put cobbles on a lot of the streets. Takes longer in bad weather, of course." He maneuvered the gig skillfully around a parked cart, and added. "Maybe Emperor Norton will be holdin' court down on Market. He hangs out there a lot."

"Emperor Norton?" Matilda felt extremely conscious of her ignorance. Perhaps she should have made more effort to learn about San Francisco. "Who is he?"

"Feller name of Joshua Norton who come from South Africa in '49. Had about $40,000 in cash on 'im, and made a fortune in real-estate , then lost it all in '54 tryin' to corner the rice market. Kind of disappeared for a bit, then surfaced in '59 and proclaimed himself Emperor Norton I. Goes about makin' proclamations, like anyone caught usin' the term 'Frisco' for San Francisco is guilty of a misdemeanor and subject to a $25 fine." He chortled with glee. "Newspapers have had a field day, some of 'em makin' up their own proclamations and crediting 'em to him."

"Sounds like the poor man is unbalanced," Alfred offered.

"Yep, I 'spect he is, but he's harmless. Fact is, one time he cooled down a bunch of hotheads as was demonstratin' against the poor old Chinese by standin' in front of the mob and reciting the Lord's Prayer. Has even printed his own money, and the local merchants accept it, humorin' him."

"That's a good trick if you can get away with it," Alfred murmured.

"Ain't it? I'd wind up in jail if I tried it. Only time he ever got mad was one time Ed Jump drew a cartoon that showed him at a table with Bummer and Lazarus, and called it 'the three bummers'. They say he took his walking stick to the window that displayed it, declaring he was no 'bummer'. Cartoon became a hit all over San Francisco."

"I think I saw that," Alfred said. "Bummer and Lazarus were two stray dogs the city took on as mascots, even getting them exempted from the leash laws," he explained to the bewildered Matilda. He turned to Charlie. "I heard that Lazarus bit a boy and someone poisoned him. Is Bummer still around?"

"Nope. Got himself kicked to death couple of years ago. Sheriff arrested the fellow who done it to keep him from gettin' lynched." Charlie turned the gig up Market Street. More and more rigs surrounded them now, so their driver had to pay more attention to his maneuvering. "But they say his cellmate punched him in the nose, so there was some justice in it." He waved to another driver, "Mornin' Abe, an' a fine mornin' it is. The Emperor on duty today?"

"Just up Market a bit, keeping his eye open to be sure the police is on the job and all the streets be in good repair," his acquaintance replied over the clatter of hooves and creaking of harness leather. "In rare form he is, too. You takin' the lady and gentleman to meet 'im?"

"Not today," Charlie replied. "On our way to Woodward's, we are. No time for side trips, as these folks have to go back up river tomorrer."

"And a rare fine place it is to visit. Good day to ye, folks, milady. Enjoy yer stay in our fair city." He tipped his hat to Matilda and turned his rig right at the next intersection.

Matilda watched wide-eyed as a horse drawn trolley loaded with passengers rolled smoothly towards them on two steel rails that ran down the center of the street. She had heard of the horse trolleys, but had never seen one.

"Look," she turned to Alfred, awe in her voice. "What a smooth ride they must have. No ruts or bumps or holes to bounce over."

Charlie agreed with her observation. "Yep," he said, "gettin' right popular, they are. City fathers want to extend 'em all the way down Market Street."

31

They crossed to Mission Street and turned right. Charlie pointed out a building on their left, on the southeast corner. "That there building, that was bein' built when the quake hit in '65. Knocked down two thirds of the entire front. Did a lot of damage to the Custom House, too. Quite a shaker, it were. Not hardly one buildin' in the city as didn't get some damage. Even the City Hall. One lot, down at 7th and Howard flooded so much a flock of ducks settled in just like it was supposed to be there." He chuckled. "Mark Twain, he were here then, workin' as a reporter for the Alta California, and he had a lot to say about it."

"I'll bet he did. He's never at a loss for words," Alfred agreed.

Shortly after they reached their destination and Matilda could only gape. Never in her life had she seen such a magnificent building. It reminded her of pictures of castles she had seen in books. Three sets of steps led up to a wide, spacious building at least three stories tall. Four spires framed the dome on the top. A fountain stood by the entry to the steps, a Chinese style pagoda by the top row.

Matilda stopped at the foot of the steps where Charlie dropped them off and stared. Alfred took her arm with a grin. "Quite a place, isn't it? Charlie will pick us up at two to take us to the beach." He took his watch out of its fob and consulted it. "Ten after ten. We have just under four hours, and from what I understand, we have a lot to see. We had better get started."

By the time they reached the entrance, after climbing more steps than Matilda had ever climbed before in her life, she was gasping for breath and had a stitch in her side. Alfred paid their twenty-five cents admission, and they entered through the massive portal and emerged onto the grounds.

They passed by a wall with a fresco depicting, according to the sign, various scenes from the ancient city of Pompei. Matilda stared at the wall, read the text, and shook her head.

"Can you imagine," she murmured to Alfred, "how terrified those poor people had to have been when they realized all that ash was covering their city?"

Alfred shrugged. "From what I have read of it, most of them suffocated, probably in their beds, never realizing what happened."

Matilda only shuddered and turned from the gruesome scene to enter a room with a large coin collection from all over the world. From there, they found vast collections of zoological specimens, and a magnificent collection of Japanese minerals. Matilda's favorite was the room filled with exotic ferns.

"Ready for the outdoor exhibits?" Alfred asked as she raved over the plants. "I understand they have a large collection of sea life."

Two large ponds boasted a number of seals and sea lions, along with many kinds of birds, including the ubiquitous seagulls, which she considered noisy, rapacious, and dirty. The Marine Aquarium contained many different species of fish, including one tank with a school of handsome brook trout.

Alfred stood beside her as they watched the trout swim lazily about. "Makes me wish for a hook and line." He consulted his watch again. "If you want to see the animals in the Zoological Gardens, we had better get moving. I understand we have to go under a tunnel that goes beneath Fourteenth Street. The whole Park is over six acres. Are you up to seeing it all?" He patted her hand solicitously. "I don't want you to wear yourself out."

"Remember I keep house for Alf and run after three children all day." Matilda laughed. "I'm tougher than you think. Let's see it all! Lead the way."

They emerged from the tunnel to find themselves among pens containing camels, deer, and buffalo, and many varieties of domestic fowl, some with brilliant plumage. They passed the bear pit, and Matilda felt a twinge of sympathy for the poor bear who paced from one side of the enclosure to the other. Small boys throwing him peanuts reminded her of the story Mrs. Boone had told of the little boy at Warner's. She glanced about and smiled. No monkeys here to try and snatch the peanuts from the bear.

The laughter of children rang out as they climbed on the monkey bars and slid down the slide. She felt a bit dizzy as she watched a group of boys on a big wheel which spun faster and faster as the bigger boys kicked.

Returning to the main grounds, they skirted a large pavilion with many seats surrounding the center arena. "I understand they hold acrobatic feats, dances, and skating tournaments here," Alfred told her. "Judging from the number of people around, this must be a one of San Francisco's main attractions."

Matilda's feet had begun to hurt, and she also felt the urge to find a commode. Alfred seemed to sense her fatigue, for he guided her to a table under a wide sycamore tree and set the picnic basket on it. He motioned to a small building next to the wall. "If you need it, there it is. Then let's see what Mrs. Boone's cook has tucked into that basket. Judging from the weight, there has to be a lot of food in here." He consulted his watch again. "One o'clock. We have an hour to eat and rest a bit before we meet Charlie."

When Matilda returned to the table, Alfred had laid the tablecloth and napkins. On the tablecloth lay two boiled potatoes in their jackets, two ears of corn, a mound of fried chicken, several dill pickles, and a small basket of sweet biscuits. A pot of honey stood beside the biscuits.

"What a feast," Matilda laughed. "Does she really expect us to eat all this? Thank you for setting the table."

He smiled and handed her a glass of lemonade. "Been a bachelor for so long I got used to waiting on myself. Eat hearty. We don't dare take any of it back with us."

To her amazement, Matilda found herself ravenous, even after the huge breakfast she had consumed. She dug eagerly into the delicious chicken, fried to perfection and seasoned with delicate herbs. When they had eaten everything, she brushed the crumbs from the last biscuit off her fingers while Alfred stowed the napery, dishes, and honey back into the picnic basket. Small birds squabbled over the crumbs they had dropped.

Matilda looked up from watching the birds to see Alfred smiling down on her with the gentle indulgent smile she had come to love.

"I thought you said you would not be able to eat for a week after breakfast.." He chuckled softly.

At two o'clock, Charlie picked them up and headed the buggy west. They crossed many busy streets, and, after about an hour, the buildings became sparser and sparser until they crossed only sand dunes. When they crested the last dune, the vast Pacific Ocean lay before them. The fog had not yet started to come in, although it stood a few miles off the coast, as though lying in wait. Sun sparkled on the rolling combers that crashed on the shoreline. White froth lined the sand where the waves departed.

Matilda strolled along the beach, stopping to look out over the vast expanse of water disappearing over the horizon. Impressed, she could not take it in all at once. She had never even imagined anything so magnificent.

She picked up several seashells of the many that lay along the waterline. One, in particular, differed from the others. A spiral shell, it had a pure white exterior with a brilliant pink interior. Alfred came up to stand beside her, smiling down on her as she admired the array of shells in her hands.

"I'll take these back for the children," she told him, displaying her collection. "But this one will be mine." She held up the small pink and white gastropod. "I will keep it forever as a remembrance of our honeymoon, and of my first trip to see the Pacific Ocean." She smiled and stared out across the undulating ocean. "Do you suppose my little shell came all the way from Japan?"

Alfred laughed. "More likely from about forty feet offshore, but if you want to pretend it came from Japan, it's all right with me." He took her arm. "Charlie says the fog will be moving in soon, and we have to get back. We have to get up early tomorrow if we are going to catch the *Chrysopolis* back to Sacramento."

Matilda stood for another moment, savoring the view, then turned back to where Charlie waited. "You're right. We don't dare miss the steamer. We can't miss our own wedding reception."

"To say nothing of how mad Alf will be if he drives all the way to Sacramento to meet the steamer and we aren't on it!"

Chapter 5

June, 1867

SURROUNDED BY neighbors and well-wishers, who swooped down on the heavily laden tables of food like a swarm of vultures, Matilda could not help but think of her wedding to Lewis, back in Kansas in '56. Then, half of the neighbors refused to attend because of her father's pro-slavery stance. Here in California, with the controversy far behind them in both time and distance, no one any longer knew or cared who had been for or against slavery.

"Sammy, you can't eat that many cookies! Put some of them back." Will and Polly were present with their whole brood, and Polly's voice scolding her three-year-old son interrupted Matilda's thoughts and she laughed softly. Some things never changed. She remembered that long ago day in Kansas when it had been Michael Polly chastised for snatching food before everyone was ready to eat. Tears stung her eyes as she thought of dear, handsome Michael and the accident that had, just six months before, so tragically ended his young life. Mary still often wept over the loss of her favorite cousin.

Matilda glanced to where Johnnie Wall stood with his father, John. She sometimes caught a look on his face of infinite sadness, like the whole scene replayed itself in his mind. As if he again felt the shotgun go off in his hands, and again saw the gaping wound in Michael's side as his life's blood poured out onto the field in spite of Johnnie's efforts to stop the flow with his bare hands. She knew it had to be very hard on the boy, to know his carelessness had cost the life of his best friend.

She turned her mind from it. Today was a happy day.

Bill Frye came up to where she and Alfred stood greeting their guests. "Congratulations, old man," he said, shaking Alfred's hand. "Envy you, I do. Fine woman you've got."

"Thank you, Bill. I think so too."

The man moved on and others came to offer best wishes. The Cantrells, both Derby and Mitchell, with their families, Billy Bandeen and his wife Jane, with their five, from John down to two-year-old Henry in tow, Mr. Butler, even 'Uncle' Billy Hicks. All of the family, of course. Matilda thought, with a smile, how fortunate she was to have such a large and close-knit family.

Poor widowed Abe stood nearby with his four little ones around him, Charlie just barely walking, clinging to Laura's hand. Tears sprang into Matilda's eyes as she thought of Minerva, wishing her sister could have been with her at this special time. Britt and Sarah, with their three. Young Gardner was a grown man already, and talking of joining his great-uncle Sevier Stringfield in Santa Barbara.

Her eyes traveled to where Alf, Tom and Sam, the family's perennial bachelors stood, talking with great animation about the latest news from Mexico.

"They've tried Maximillian and sentenced him to death," Alf reported. He shook his head. "Poor man. Napoleon just placed him on the throne in Mexico City and left him to his fate. He never had any idea what he was getting into."

"Serves him right," Tom growled. "France got no business trying to set up an empire here in North America.

President was right to tell him so, too. Napoleon would do better to pay closer attention to his Prussian neighbors. Bismarck is adding one German state after another to his empire. Napoleon may think Benedek's defeat at Sadowa last July was due to the man's incompetence, but most folks realize it was because the Iron Prince had breech loading rifles on his side, against the muzzle loaders the Austrians were still using. And if Napoleon thinks France is not in Bismarck's plans, he's got his head in the sand. He's going to trick France into attacking, and Napoleon is hot-headed enough to make it work. This business with Maximillian is just one sign of the man's arrogance."

"Maximillian must be quite popular with the ladies," Sam offered. "He's right handsome, from what they say. I hear sixty ladies have interceded to plead for his life, although I doubt it will do any good. Mexico's folks are pretty mad at him. Not as forgiving as we are. I hear the folks back in Washington are getting ready to release Jefferson Davis from prison."

"Might as well," Sam growled. "No point in blaming the whole thing on him. Best to put the whole thing behind us and get on with putting the country back together."

"That Reconstruction Act's probably not the best way," Alf said. He wiped the sweat from his forehead with his big, red handkerchief. "Lot of folks resent the way it's being handled."

Sam sighed. "Shame Lincoln got himself killed that way. He just wanted to let the States re-join the Union, peaceful like. Would probably have been a whole lot better way to handle it."

"Johnson is trying to do what Lincoln wanted. Just getting himself in trouble with the Senate doing it. Lot of those hotheads are out to make the South pay, and Stanton is egging them on. It can't lead to any good."

Matilda smiled as she listened. Men always had such firm answers for even the most complex questions, and always seemed so sure they were right. She found herself wondering if any of the three would ever marry. Betsy Ann frequently scolded them for staying single.

Mr. Cootes, the schoolmaster, approached her. "Please allow me to offer my best wishes, Mrs. Wheelock," he smiled, taking her hand. "Mary has been chattering for a month about her new papa. She has been so excited that she could hardly be persuaded to write her sums the last few weeks of school." He turned to watch the two little girls for a moment. "Even sedate little Lizzie seems to have caught some of Mary's excitement."

"Oh, dear," Matilda sighed. "I do hope that by the time school starts again, some of the novelty will have worn off, and she can concentrate on her schoolwork." She knew, even though Mr. Cootes was too polite to say it, that scholarship was not high on Mary's list of priorities. She glanced over to where Mary teased George Douglass as he tried to impress her with his prowess with a top. Again. As young as she was, she seemed to delight in tormenting the boy. He and his parents had been among the first to arrive, probably at young George's insistence.

Seven-year-old Ada, daughter of Derby and Hannath Cantrell, stood watching from a respectful distance. Mary seemed to enjoy Ada's company, and they spent a lot of time together at school. Matilda hoped the friendship between Ada and Mary would continue to blossom. Ada's gentle manners and polite, proper behavior would, Matilda hoped, be a good influence on madcap Mary.

She sighed and turned to greet George and Henry Putney and Henry's wife Rhoda, with their two children. "So glad you could come," she said, putting Mary out of her mind. After all, she had all summer to persuade Mary of the wisdom of learning to read and cipher. And she could only hope that as Mary grew older, she would develop more lady-like manners.

Denis Moroney tuned up his fiddle, and called out to the assemblage. "Time for the bride and groom to dance!" He struck up a lively version of 'Turkey in the Straw', and soon many people danced merrily around in the space beside the tables.

Alf stood to one side, saying nothing as Alfred swung Matilda into his arms and began a lively dance. Matilda knew that Alf, being a strict Methodist, did not approve of dancing, but went along with the party atmosphere. Mr. McGuirk added his fiddle to the impromptu concert.

An hour later, with everyone worn out by the heat and the dancing, people sat around in the shade of the magnificent oak trees that surrounded Alf's home and sipped lemonade and ate the cakes and cookies that appeared after the hams and eggs and roasts had been devoured.

Matilda could not help overhearing a heated discussion between Rhoda Putney, Jane Bandeen, and Hannath Cantrell. Mrs. Putney, one hand on her rambunctious two year old son George, was telling the other ladies about the latest news on women's suffrage.

"I declare," she said vehemently, "that Lucy Stone is going to set the whole country on its ear. Been touring Kansas of late, according to the paper, saying women have the right to the elective franchise. Even predicts the right will be extended by this year's legislature."

"Oh, my," said fifteen year old Jenny Dixon, who everyone predicted would become Mrs. George Putney when she was a little older. "Will they really?"

"Do you suppose women are ready to handle voting?" Jane Bandeen asked. "That crowd that hangs around the election booth is such a rowdy bunch."

"Nonsense," Rhoda retorted. "Of course we are ready. We are just as capable as the men, for all of their declarations to the contrary. Feminine weakness indeed! I'd like to see any man who can keep up with a good woman. And if women were voting, the crowd would probably not be nearly as crude. Women would be a good influence."

Matilda smiled to herself as she listened. If that group of women ever agreed on anything, it would be worthy of note in the history books. She could not help thinking of her friend Sarah Williams. Sarah would agree with Rhoda Putney. She could hear Sarah saying those exact words. And, Matilda thought, with a little laugh, Sarah would be just the woman to prove it. She would have to write to Sarah. She smiled, thinking how much the description of Lillie Coit's exploits would amuse Sarah.

Alfred came up to Matilda with the Haskin Swains in tow. "Mr. Swain says that business about the Chabolla land grant is starting though the courts."

Swain nodded and grinned. "Soon as we get the title clear, me and Amanda have decided you young folks should have that two hundred acre piece just across the road, by the schoolhouse. You're just the kind of neighbors we want."

"Thank you, Mr. Swain, Mrs. Swain. We look forward to it."

The Swains moved on. Matilda smiled at Alfred. "Does this mean we'll be having our own place soon?"

Alfred grinned wryly. "Never known courts to move very fast. We'll rent those 80 acres from Mr. Short for the moment and save our money. When, and *if*, the Swain

property comes up, we'll be ready."
Matilda laughed. "That's probably the best."

Chapter 6

June to July, 1867

ONE WEEK LATER, they had settled into the little house on James Short's property, about two miles east of Alf's. Matilda bustled about preparing supper. She looked out of the kitchen window and saw Alfred sharpening the blade on the plow they had purchased from Denis Moroney. She smiled fondly as she watched. Being married to Alfred was as wonderful as she imagined, and the children adored their new father. All three sat in a circle around him, staring solemnly while he worked. Jake lay with his head in Lewis' lap. It seemed hard to believe her baby was almost four years old. As he had matured, the boy and the old dog had become as inseparable as Jake and Lewis' father had been.

The memory of that day in Kansas when Lewis Baldwin had ridden into her life on White Star, the beautiful golden horse just a two-year-old, Jake a puppy riding in the saddlebag, flashed through her mind. It seemed so long ago.

White Star stood by the corral fence watching the whole operation. Matilda felt again the little twinge of guilt that had stabbed through her when they sold White Star's two colts, but the price the dealer had offered was one they could not refuse. They needed so many things to get started in farming. The plow Alfred worked on, for example. And a horse to pull it. White Star could not pull a plow, and neither could Four Stockings or Long Legs. No, they had needed a good sturdy farm horse, and the big Clydesdale was perfectly suited for the job.

She smiled as she thought of Mary's response to the proposed swap. Matilda had been sure Mary would be upset, but the gentle Clydesdale, who Mary promptly dubbed "Big Ben", won her heart as the skittish Four Stockings never had. All three children would ride him as he plodded along, their feet sticking straight out to the side on his wide back.

The evening was so pleasant after the almost unbearable heat of the day she decided to get out of the stuffy kitchen and join the rest of the family enjoying the cool evening breeze. She pushed the pot of stew to the back of the stove to simmer, and took the biscuits out of the oven.

Walking from the back door to the front of the barn, she cut across the garden and noticed that every swish of her skirt sent clouds of grasshoppers jumping in every direction. She recalled a recent article in the *Daily Bee* stating the grasshoppers were becoming a major problem. She stopped for a moment and watched the voracious insects devour the leaves on the bean plants. As she saw the speed with which the leaf disappeared, she remembered similar hordes of the creatures swarming down on the grain fields in Kansas.

Mary and Elizabeth saw her coming, and ran to meet her. Mary swatted at the grasshoppers with her hat, sending them hopping off in every direction, while Elizabeth squealed in distaste.

"Silly, they're only grasshoppers," Mary admonished her sister. "They won't hurt you. All they bite is grass."

"But they are so - - so *squiggly!*"

Matilda laughed. "Your sister is right, Lizzie. They are

perfectly harmless." Unless you are depending on a crop for a living, she thought, with a twinge of dismay, wondering how serious the multitude of ravenous insects would become. She shrugged. Nothing she could do about it. Might just as well not worry. Maybe they would not get any worse. She thought of the letter from John's wife Mary Ann in Kansas, telling about the swarms of grasshoppers in '66, fortunately after Matilda had left for California. Then the creatures were so thick wheels slipped on the roads from the thousands and thousands of crushed bodies.

She smiled. If Lizzie thinks these are squiggly, she thought, I wonder how she would have reacted to what Mary Ann had described.

They reached Alfred's side as he rose to his feet and stretched, stiff from bending over the plow for so long. "Best I can do with it. It should be sharp enough. We got it for a good price. I think Moroney looks upon it as a wedding gift."

Matilda laughed. "Maybe so. The biscuits are done, and the stew is simmering. Ready for supper?"

"Always ready for your delicious stew, my love. You have a real talent for making beef and a few vegetables taste like a feast worthy of a king."

Matilda blushed. Alfred always had such a pretty way with words. "Go on with you. Come in and eat before the biscuits are cold and the stew burns." She paused at the corral fence to give White Star her lump of sugar and hugged her neck before following the rest into the house.

They ate in companionable silence. After the stew and biscuits were consumed, Matilda brought an apple pie from the pie saver, and drew the metal milk jug up from the cool water in the cistern and refilled the pitcher.

Alfred's eyes glistened as she put a wedge of apple pie in front of him. "Sure never ate like this when I was a bachelor," he said with a sigh of pleasure as he sank his fork into the golden crust.

Mary looked at him over the rim of her milk glass. "Can we go to Hicksville for the fireworks next Thursday? Can we? Can we? Please say we can." She wiped the milk mustache from her upper lip with the back of her hand.

"Use your napkin, dear," Matilda sighed automatically, as she did almost every meal. Elizabeth daintily wiped her lips with the linen napkin with a smirk at her sister.

Mary paid no attention to either her mother or her sister. Her whole attention was on Alfred, waiting for his response.

"Of course, my dear," he assured the child. "We have to celebrate our first Fourth of July as a family in style. I understand Mr. Cootes has promised to give the oratory, and the church choir will sing. Moroney and McGuirk have agreed to play the Star Spangled Banner on their fiddles." He smiled at Matilda. "Won't be quite as fancy as the brass band they always have in Sacramento, but it should be fun."

"My friend Addie Cantrell will be there, of course," Mary announced. "Since her Daddy is playing in the program too, the whole family is coming." She smiled smugly at her sister. "Addie told me she wants me to be her best friend. You haven't got a best friend."

Elizabeth's lip jutted out and tears filled her eyes. "Mama, why don't I have a best friend?"

Matilda hastened to play the peace-maker. "You will, darling, just as soon as you go to school this fall."

Alfred smiled in gentle patience at the interchange between the sisters and continued outlining the plans for the celebration. "The gentleman providing the fireworks is coming out from Sacramento. I understand he is bringing some of the best that can be purchased in Chinatown. And the Chinese have some very spectacular fireworks."

By early evening on the day of the celebrations, the oration and musical events over, and after several readings by local talent, Matilda sat on a log and sipped a cool glass of lemonade while waiting for the sun to sink low enough in the west for the fireworks display to begin. She watched Mary and Ada chattering away under a nearby oak tree. Hannath Cantrell joined Matilda, who moved over to make room for her friend.

"Warm day," she sighed as she sank gratefully onto the log. "My feet are killing me." She followed Matilda's gaze to where the two little girls sat on the dry grass. Mary chattered away like a magpie, her arms waving for emphasis. Ada sat and listened, taking in every word in awed silence.

"I'm so glad Mary and Addie get along so well. Addie gets lonely at home, being the youngest the way she is." Hannath hesitated, and Matilda felt Ada's mother had something that bothered her. She waited.

"Addie's not strong," she finally blurted. "I worry about her all the time. She tires easy, and gets real short of breath if she tries to run and keep up with the other children." Tears sprang into her eyes. "I tried to tell myself it was just because she was so much younger, but I finally took her to Dr. Oatman in Sacramento. He said she has a weak heart, and sent me to Hotz and McDonnell's Apothecary to get a tonic for her. They recommended Hegeman's Cod Liver Oil, and Dr. Henley's Grape Root Bitters."

"And have they helped?" Matilda felt a twinge of dismay. If Ada were to die, Mary would be devastated. And after losing Michael and Sinclair and Minerva, Mary

49

already felt God hated her, taking so many she loved from her. She pulled her attention back to Mrs. Cantrell's words.

"They don't seem to do anything at all," she sighed. "The child tires so quickly, and never seems to be rested, no matter how long she sleeps. I've thought about taking her to see that Dr. Reud, who says he is one of those new homeopathic physicians." She shrugged her shoulder expressively. "Can't hurt, I guess."

Matilda murmured a non-committal response, thinking what Betsy Ann would say. She had grudgingly conceded some doctors were getting wiser in their treatments, but remained skeptical of the whole profession. Matilda suspected some of her mother's herbal remedies would probably be as effective as the two Hannath had mentioned, the composition of which was mostly alcohol.

Hannath rose. "We had planned to stay for the fireworks show, but I told my husband we had best not keep Addie out after dark. I so fear the night air will harm her, with her already weak heart." She start gathering her brood for the trip home.

Matilda watched as Hannath took Ada's hand. Her heart ached for her friend, and she silently thanked God her own three were so healthy.

Summer drifted by, busy with harvesting, gardening and canning the produce from the garden. News of the progress of the Central Pacific Railroad drifted in. The schooners *North Beach* and *Columbia* arrived in Sacramento laden with railroad iron destined for the western end of the road, which continued its march eastward.

Alfred reported the progress to Matilda. "All those skeptics as have been saying it's impossible to build a road over the Sierras are going to have to eat their words."

"What about in the winter?" Matilda asked. "They get an awful lot of snow up there. Won't it cover the tracks?"

"Judah's original plan was to build snow sheds over the tracks at the points where the snow is the worst. I'm sure that's what they'll do. It's the only practical solution. Beats trying to tunnel through all that rock." He shook his head in sorrow. "Poor Judah. His lifelong dream was to see that railroad built. Shame he took the yellow fever crossing Panama and died before he could see his dream fulfilled. Such a young man, only 37, and with such a brilliant mind."

"It's not built yet," Matilda said, with a touch of skepticism.

Alfred laughed. "You're right. But the money is there, and so is the motivation. California is such a rich state, and Mexico has not yet forgotten that it once belonged to them. Besides, the Panama Route takes so long. And there is always the danger of taking yellow fever on the Isthmus, witness poor Judah. Besides," he added, "now they've got all of those Chinese to do the work for only about $28.00 per month. They are doing all the dangerous work. Believe me, it's just a matter of time."

Matilda felt his optimism a bit premature, but said no more. She thought of the poor Chinese being lowered by ropes over the steep cliffs to chip away the granite and plant the explosives. She shuddered at the thought.

Alfred sat reading the paper. Matilda took out her sewing basket. The children seemed to always get holes in their stockings, and she spent a lot of time darning them. This was Matilda's favorite time of the day, the children in bed, the dishes done, and just the two of them sitting together in companionable silence. She would sew or knit while he read, sometimes aloud to her, and frequently commenting on the current events in the newspaper.

She had just shoved the darning egg into one of Mary's stockings - Mary always, for some reason, had three times as many holes as Elizabeth - when Alfred started to laugh and reported on the article he was reading.

"The steamer *Yosemite* ran hard aground on the Hog's Back, and was stuck there for over twelve hours before they got her off." His eyes twinkled as they met hers. "I'll bet Captain Van Pelt was fit to be tied. He always prided himself on always being on time, and he wound up over twelve hours late."

Matilda laughed. "I'm just glad we were not on her when *that* happened. We would have missed our own wedding reception."

"And there is an outbreak of diphtheria in Nevada," he continued, in his usual practice of keeping her abreast of current affairs. She appreciated him doing so. It showed he thought of her as an intellectual equal, not as "the little woman" to be kept in ignorance as many men did. But this last bit of knowledge dismayed her. Diphtheria was such a frightening disease. So many families had lost children to it.

"Well," she said in an attempt to make light of her fears, "I hope it stays in Nevada." Her thoughts flew to Ada Cantrell. Betsy Ann had always said that if a child survived diphtheria, it would be prone to a weak heart. But if the child already suffered from a weak heart, like Ada?

She shook her head. Don't borrow trouble, she told herself firmly. She forced a bright smile. "And what else is happening in the world?"

Chapter 7

August, 1867

ADA CANTRELL DIED less than two weeks later, at the age of seven. Alfred brought the news to Matilda, his face solemn as he glanced across the yard. Mary pushed Elizabeth to and fro in the swing that Alfred had hung from the branch of the huge live oak tree in the front yard. Happy laughter from the two little girls floated across the yard as the watching Lewis clapped his hands and cried, "Higher! Higher!"

"Oh, no," Matilda whispered. "Hannath so feared for the poor child. How are we going to tell Mary?" Tears rolled down her cheeks as she met his eyes and read the sympathy there.

"We are fortunate ours are so healthy." He took her in his arms and stroked the red-gold curls. "The services will be the day after tomorrow. I suggest we wait until the two younger ones are asleep before we tell Mary. It would be best to tell her alone."

Matilda sighed. "You're probably right. But I dread it." Unbidden memories forced themselves into her mind. Memories of Mary's reactions when she learned of the death of her Uncle Sinclair, then her cousin Michael. Of course, Matilda recalled, Mary had handled Minerva's death with a maturity beyond her years.

"Mama, what's wrong?" Mary met Matilda's eyes over the top of her cup. "You haven't laughed once. You and Papa Alfred usually talk and laugh at supper."

Startled by Mary's perspicacity, Matilda was mute. Mary continued. "It's Addie, isn't it?"

Matilda could only gasp, and Mary went on to say, "I knew she was bad sick. She told me. She said her mother took her to a doctor and the doctor said she had a weak heart. Her mother wouldn't tell her, but Addie knew she was going to die soon." Tears filled the blue eyes. "She told me not to feel bad when it happened, because then she would be in Heaven with Jesus."

Matilda did not trust herself to speak. Alfred responded for her. "Yes, Mary, Ada is now in Heaven with Jesus."

Mary nodded, her little face solemn. "And I told her when she got there to give my love to Uncle Sinclair and Aunt Minerva, and Michael, and Grandpa." She looked from one silent face to the other, then burst into sobs. "But, Mama, she was my best friend! How could she leave me?"

Matilda gathered the stricken child into her arms as tears coursed down her own cheeks. Memories of losing her friend Agatha Templeton that long ago day in Illinois raced through her mind. Remembering her own agony at the time, she could think of no words to comfort her grieving daughter.

"Hear tell Ben and Will Wilder's brother Ase died a few days back," Alf commented to Alfred and Matilda as they prepared to enter the little church for the services for Ada Cantrell.

"Saw that in the paper," Alfred replied. "Shame, must have been only about fifty. Be hard on Ben. I know they were close, and been through a lot together."

Alf nodded. "Yep, fellers at the Hotel were just talkin' about it the other day. Say he was walking back in from the field and just grabbed his chest and keeled over. Probably dead by the time Ben reached him. They carried him in the house and sent one of the hands post haste for Doc Dunscomb, him being the closest Doc, even though he don't maintain his practice, being in poor health like he is. Doc came fast as he could, but Ase was gone.

"Shame it is. Sorry to hear it. Should go by and pay our respects to the widow. Was thinking about it, but when little Ada died, it put all other thoughts out of my head, since Mary was so distressed about losing her friend."

Matilda remained silent. Her thoughts reverted to the Wilder family. Ase had been so supportive to Ben's wife. Poor Elitha had not only lost her parents in that horrible winter with the Donner Party, but she had put up with her ill-fated marriage to that dreadful Perry McCoon. And Ben had been involved in the miners' squabble that cost Jared Sheldon his life. She knew that weighed heavily on Elitha as well, for the Sheldons had befriended her. She sighed. I must go and see them, she thought, but not just yet.

At least, she thought, they were spared all of the ruckus over the Chabolla Land Grant. The Wilder land, just a mile and a half down the Cosumnes River from Billy Hicks' bridge, was a part of the Cazadores Land Grant, and the ownership of that was not disputed. She chuckled to herself. At least, not yet.

The services for Ada were short and solemn. Hannath had, over the minister's objections, insisted that Ada's young friends be included in the ceremony. At the end of the sermon and the eulogies, four little girls, including Mary, walked slowly down the aisle and placed a flower on the little wooden box. When the men lifted the coffin from its bier, the girls followed it from the church to the grave site. Children were usually not even brought to funerals. Matilda's eyes overflowed as she watched the somber procession. What a lovely way to bid farewell to Ada.

Life resumed its usual pace very quickly. Harvest was in full swing, and Matilda kept busy preparing the midday meal for the harvest hands. The heat settled on them with a vengeance, and every day the dust rose in great clouds and swept over everything, penetrating every crack and fold.

"Heavens," Matilda exclaimed as she shook the dust from a clean table cloth she had just removed from the linen chest. "Even folded up and in the chest it has dust in it. I will be so glad when the rains start!"

"Then you'll have to contend with the mud," Alfred grinned, looking up from the wash basin where he rinsed the worst of the grime off his face and arms.

She laughed. "You're right, but at least the mud won't fly through the air."

"I worry more about fire," Alfred fretted. "We still have three more fields to do, and that wheat is dry as tinder. One spark and the whole harvest will go up."

"Don't think about it. Think about the State Fair. The girls have been excited about going for a week now."

"Ever since I told them I would take them to see that mammoth ox, Orizaba Babe. The owners brought it from Kentucky just for the Fair. Guess they've been winning prizes with it all over the country. Arrived in Sacramento on the *Chrysopolis*. Weighed in at over 3000 pounds. That is some ox, let me tell you. Can't even picture one that big in my mind. Sure would have liked to watch them get him on that steamer."

"We'll have to be sure and see it. I'm going to enter some more of Minerva's needlework. The Blue Ribbon she won last year is little Laura's pride and joy. She has it hung up in the parlor and tells everyone that was for her Mama's embroidered tablecloth. I thought maybe this year I would try with some of her needlepoint."

"And you, my love? What are you going to enter?"

Matilda shook her head. "Maybe one of Mary's stockings. It seems that's all the needlework I have time for."

Chapter 8

December 1867 to July 1868

"OH, MAMA, THE tree is so beautiful." Mary's blue eyes sparkled as she helped Matilda string another row of popcorn around the festive green boughs. Alfred had ridden White Star to Placerville to fetch it, declaring since this was his first Christmas with a real family to call his own, he felt it should be extra special.

"Mama! Lew keeps eating the popcorn," complained six-year-old Elizabeth, who sat meticulously stringing the fluffy white kernels with a big darning needle. Although two years younger than Mary, Elizabeth had the patience required for stringing the popcorn, which Mary did not.

"Don't worry," Matilda soothed. "We can pop more. Besides, I think we almost have enough. We don't want to overload the poor tree." She smiled on the little tableau. When Lewis had been killed that long ago day in Kansas, (could it be over four years already?) she thought her life had ended. She had never dreamed she would find such happiness and contentment again.

But Alfred proved over and over again that she could. Thoughts of his quiet manners, his elegant speech, his gentle smile, his steady, unvarying love, all welled up in her heart until it almost overflowed. They had their own home, albeit rented, but had set money aside for when the Swain property would become available. Among their stock, they had the two horses, White Star and Big Ben, six milk cows, eight other cattle for meat, fourteen hogs, and assorted chickens to provide them with eggs and chicken dinners. The garden had flourished, giving her a whole winter's supply of beans and corn to can. The bushes from the nearby creek gave them plenty for not only fresh blackberries and cream, but a number of jars of compote shared the shelves in the basement with the beans and corn. Potatoes and winter squash lined the corner opposite from the shelves with the canned goods, hams and bacons hung from another.

She smiled indulgently at the happy children. Yes, life was good.

March brought the news that John McCauley had bought 'Uncle' Billy Hicks' land at a sheriff's sale. Alfred shook his head as he relayed the information to Matilda.

"Told Hicks not to borrow money from McCauley. I tried to warn him. That McCauley's a real sharp one."

"But Uncle Billy is his stepfather-in-law! How could he take advantage of the poor old man like that? Won't his family be upset?"

"He pulled a sly trick. Assigned the mortgage to that friend of his name of Lloyd Tevis. Tevis and his bunch have been pulling shady land deals all over California. Hear they got a whole bunch of land down in Kern County with some of their slick political maneuvers. By assigning the mortgage to Tevis, McCauley can say his hands were clean of the affair. So when the land came up at a Sheriff's auction, McCauley could buy it fair and square."

"It still sounds like a mean trick to me," Matilda muttered.

Alfred shrugged. "Uncle Billy is left with only about 1100 acres of the over 10,000 he got when he came here in

'43 and got his Mexican land grant. Real shame. He was down at the Hicksville Hotel drowning his sorrows in a bottle of whiskey, telling anyone who would listen all about it."

"Mr. McCauley has all of that land down in Forest Lake. And I understand he has a home in San Francisco. What does he want with more?"

"You and I don't understand it," Alfred replied, "but to people like him, it's a game, to see how much you can grab and hold on to."

"And his wife and son and daughter are still in Europe?"

"That's what I understand. He goes back and forth. Guess he doesn't trust anyone else to keep his empire going here."

"My," Matilda marveled. "Imagine not only going to Europe, but being able to go back and forth."

Alfred eased himself into his favorite chair and lighted his pipe, getting ready to settle down with the paper. "Guess he went for his health the first time." He chuckled. "He was a rabid Southern supporter, and during the War years, that didn't set too well with a lot of folks."

"No, I don't imagine it did." Matilda well remembered the hostility between the Jayhawkers and the Border Ruffians in Kansas during the years leading up to the War. And all the squabbles between the likes of Whitson and Kress and other abolitionists and her father.

She also knew her Aunt Delilah's son, James Randolph Burleson, Jr., had served as a farrier for the Confederate Army with the Texas Lancers, and poor Josh Tovrea, her sister Temperance's widower had died of wounds he received fighting for the Union in 1862. His brother John had been wounded at Shiloh, but recovered. And to have Josh and Temperance's only son Henry die at Marietta, Georgia just two years later. Her parents had been torn between their loyalty to the South and their objection to dividing the Union. She sighed. "I just hope the country can put all that animosity to rest."

"It's going to take a while," Alfred remarked dryly, "especially in the South. Stanton and his bunch are determined to punish them for starting the War. Johnson tried to get rid of Stanton so he could let the South rejoin as if nothing had happened, to reduce the animosity, as Lincoln wanted. All it got him was brought up on impeachment charges."

Matilda sighed and picked up her mending basket. "Well, I guess there is nothing we can do. I'm just glad it is so far away. What else is happening in the world?"

In mid-July, Betsy Ann had Alf drive her over for a visit. She shared a letter with Matilda from Jim Burleson's wife Amanda, saying Matilda's Uncle Jim had died on July 1 in Ford's Prairie, Texas.

"Amanda is his fourth wife, I might add," said Betsy Ann wryly, "in case you have forgotten. He always was a good-lookin' man. I remember when your Aunt Delilah died, he had ladies coming around before the poor girl was cold in her grave. The second one now, Malinda Sevier, he married her in '32, then took her and the young-uns and went back to 'Bama in 1835. She was some relation to the friends of my father, the one he named your Uncle Sevier after. Poor child had to follow him into that god-forsaken place in Texas, in Fayette County, all sagebrush and cactus and rattlesnakes. Then she died too. After that, he married Sibra, then Amanda."

"Heavens," Matilda sighed. "I would think he'd have had trouble remembering which wife he was talking to." Matilda had never met her Uncle Jim, but he had always seemed such a dashing and romantic character. After all, he had been a Colonel in the famed Texas Rangers, and helped Texas win her independence from Mexico. Fortunately he had not been at the Alamo twelve years later when Santa Anna decided to reclaim the territory.

"Got a letter from your sister Sarah, too, all the way from Bloomington. Amazing," Betsy Ann was saying. "Only two weeks for her letter to get here. What is the world coming to? Soon's that train gets through, we'll be a-gettin' mail in even less time." She emitted a deep, heartfelt sigh. "Probably just as well your father is in his grave. He hated trains, kept moving west to get away from them. Anyways, Sarah says Temperance and Josh's daughter Sarah Rebecca, has finally decided to tie the knot. Happened last April, but Sarah just found out about it from Becky's grandmother Tovrea. Married a feller name of John Moore, some cousin of Julia's." She chuckled. "Guess they want to keep it in the family. Was beginning to think she was going to be an old maid. She is over twenty-six years old." Betsy Ann looked at Matilda shrewdly and abruptly changed the subject. "And you, young lady, are you in a family way again?"

Matilda had to laugh at her mother's uncanny ability. "Well, I think so. It's a little soon to tell for sure. It would be nice to have a son for Alfred. I haven't said anything to him yet. I wanted to be sure first. Probably be born around the end of February, first part of March. And I don't think Pa would have had to worry about the train coming through Hicksville. If that Obed Harvey has his way, the train will go through to the west of here. Alf and Alfred both say he is talking to his friends Huntington and Crocker and Stanford and that bunch, trying to get them to bring it across that swamp land of his at the edge of the high tide line." She laughed. "Guess he wants to be as rich as Mr. McCauley. But they will have to drain a lot of water before it can become much of a town."

"What will be, will be," Betsy Ann shrugged, her mind obviously not on the coming of the train. "You just be sure and take good care of your health. We want Alfred's son to be a healthy one."

"Yes, Mother," Matilda agreed, and laughed softly. "Even if his first son is a daughter."

She told Alfred two weeks later, as she was sure by then. He swooped her into his arms and kissed her soundly.

"That's wonderful news, my dear. Now you really will have something to tell my father the next time you write to him. I am sure he despaired of me ever presenting him with a grandchild." He led her to a chair. "Now," he said, his voice full of concern, "you must take good care of yourself."

She laughed. "You are as bad as Mother. I'm fine. I've had four healthy babies without a hint of a problem with any of them. I'm sure I can manage one more. Relax and read your paper." She handed him the two week old copy of the *Daily Bee*. "Did you see that article on Colonel John Chivington, that horrid man who massacred all those poor innocent Indians at Sand Creek a few years back? It says he married the widow of his son Thomas. Lecherous old man."

"Just getting around to reading that?" The paper rustled as he turned the page. "The latest is that her parents objected to the marriage so much that they put a notice in the paper announcing that their daughter married him over their strong objections."

"Good for them." She laughed merrily at the news. "Any chance you could take me to Elk Grove tomorrow in the buggy? I'd like to go. The Shaffer's just lost little four-year-old Ella, and I made a pie to take to them. And I really should get some flannel to start making some baby clothes. It's been so long since Lew was born I don't have any baby things at all. I left most of them in Kansas with Caroline, and what I did bring, I gave to Minerva for little Charlie and he wore them out."

"We can do that if you'd like. We finished the last field today."

"Good. The children can stay with Mother at Alf's. She enjoys them, and they mind her so much better than they do me."

"Everyone obeys your mother," Alfred said with his soft chuckle. "Even the hired hands jump when she speaks. She sure has a way about her." He rose and stretched. "We're going to have a busy day tomorrow. Better get to bed."

The following day, the children with their grandmother and her sad duty at the Shafer residence completed, Matilda happily browsed through the yards of flannel at Elk Grove's one dry goods store. The variety of colors and material never ceased to amaze her.

"Got enough?" Alfred asked. "Not expecting triplets, are we?"

"Go on with you. You just don't know how many clothes a baby can go through in the in the course of a day. Why, I remember - - "

A loud scream interrupted her. With a little gasp, she clutched the package of flannel to her breast as Alfred ran to the door. She followed at his heels, the clerk right behind her. They reached the street as a double team of horses drawing a wagon loaded with sacks of wheat bolted past. A young man clung desperately to the reins, yelling, "Whoa! Whoa!" to no avail. As Matilda stared in horror, the older man fell from the seat, and the two wheels on the right side of the wagon passed over his body. The wagon went on down the street, with the young man still struggling to regain control of the team.

Matilda did not move. Nor did the body lying in the street.

The clerk beside her gasped. "Why, it's Mr. Adams, it is. Is he killed?"

A crowd gathered about the fallen man. The young man who had been at the reins returned on foot, running as fast as he could, crying out, "Pa, Pa, you okay? I got 'em under control now. We kin go on to the mill . . . ." His voice trailed off as he stared at his father's body. One of the bystanders took his arm and led him away.

Alfred led Matilda back inside the store and ushered her to a chair, out of sight of the gathered crowd and the pitiful heap lying so ominously still in the dusty street.

The clerk came back inside as well, wringing his hands and shaking his head. "Absalom Adams, owns a place out east a' here. Got a wife and six young'uns, he do. That's his oldest boy as was drivin' the wagon." He peered at Matilda anxiously. "You all right ma'am? Sorry you had to witness that, ain't somethin' for a lady to see. Do hope it don't drive you into a decline."

Matilda laughed, a shaky little laugh with no humor. "Thank you for your concern, but I suspect I am a little tougher than I look." She turned to Alfred. "I think I've had quite enough excitement for one day. Let's go home."

Chapter 9

September to November, 1868

MATILDA AWOKE suddenly, not understanding what had awakened her. She turned carefully in the bed, not wishing to disturb Alfred. His gentle, regular breathing reassured her. She smiled softly, unable to keep from comparing Alfred's quiet sleep to the lusty snores she remembered from Lewis.

Slipping carefully from between the sheets, she thought perhaps she just had to use the chamber pot. After all, she was three months pregnant, and even though little Lew would soon be five, she could remember many nightly trips during her previous pregnancies. When she stood, she glanced out the window to see a bright red glow against the skyline to the north, in the direction of the community of Sheldon.

Her gasp of horror brought Alfred awake instantly, and he hurried to her side. "Fire," he muttered softly. "And a big one, too."

She followed him to the porch. They stood arm in arm in the cool evening air and watched as the flames leaped higher.

"Got to be a building," he said. "No field fire would send flames that high."

"Oh, how dreadful," Matilda murmured, keeping her voice low so they did not waken the children. "What time is it?"

Alfred entered the house to check and returned, stuffing his shirt into his trousers, to announce that it was just 11:00 PM. "Seems like it should be a lot later. What woke you up?"

She shrugged. "I don't know." Her eyes fixed on the leaping flames. Her thoughts raced to the people that may have been in the building. Noticing he was fully dressed, she asked, "Are you going to go? It could be a long ways."

"I suspect it's around the Sheldon area. If it's much farther, it's a really big fire. I'll go as far as Hennessy's Hotel. That's the biggest building I can think of in the area. If it's farther away than that, I'll leave it to Sacramento's efficient Fire Departments."

"Do be careful. It's dark to be riding." The harvest moon had just begun to rise. "The moonlight should be much better soon."

He kissed her quickly. "I'll ride by starlight. White Star is so surefooted we shouldn't have any problem."

She watched him stride away, and, a few minutes later, saw him ride off. She stood, anxiously watching the flames, until she began to shiver. Thinking she would not help anyone if she took a chill, she returned to the little bedroom and crawled back under the covers.

But she did not sleep. Her eyes kept flying open to the sight of the leaping flames through the window pane. When at last the fire diminished until it no longer glowed against the night sky, fading into insignificance in the brightness of the brilliant harvest moon, she thought she would drift off, but the thought of Alfred out there, possibly in danger, kept her awake.

When dawn finally broke, she heard White Star returning with Alfred. She quickly pulled on her robe, shoved her feet into her slippers, and ran to meet him. Weariness showed in his face as he dismounted and came to hold her in his arms. His hair and clothing reeked of smoke, so she knew he had been near the fire.

They stood for several moments. Glad he had returned safely, she was content to wait until he was ready to tell her what had happened. Finally, he released her. "Suppose you make us some coffee while I take care of White Star. Then I'll tell you all about it."

Over a steaming cup of coffee, he explained what he had found.

"It was Hennessy's Hotel, just as we suspected. The reason it looked so big is because the Sheldon Hotel went up too. Actually, it started there." He shook his head. "Just real fortunate no one was killed. Those staying in the hotels barely escaped. Lucky the night clerk was alert, not sleeping like he usually is."

"Probably because it was still a little early," Matilda remarked dryly. "If the fire had started at two in the morning, everyone, including Jeremiah, would have been sound asleep."

Alfred nodded. "Most likely. As it was, most of them got out with their lives, but not much else. Several were in their nightshirts, and lost all of their clothes and belongings. Many of the folks that stay there are workers who don't have any other home, so all of their worldly possessions were burned."

"Poor souls," Matilda murmured. "Is anyone helping them?"

"Oh, yes, the ladies of the community had already gathered and were giving them coffee and biscuits, along with spare blankets and clothes. The Odd Fellows have said they will help them too."

"How terrible, to lose everything." Matilda shuddered
at the thought of losing all of her possessions. The booties
Minerva had made for Baby John, her lock of Lewis' hair,
the painting of herself and Baby John. To lose everything
in a fire must be a frightful experience.

"Do they have any idea how it started?" She suddenly
remembered she had not asked that question.

"Started at the Sheldon Hotel. Rippon Kelly, the owner,
lives there. He said he heard the fire crackling and ran to
see what it was. The woodshed by the side of the building
was a mass of flames, and he could smell the skunk oil.
Looks like someone poured the oil over the wood and set
fire to it."

"You mean someone set the fire on purpose? Deliberately
destroyed Mr. Kelly's fine hotel? And ran the risk of killing
people, too? What if everyone had been asleep?"

Alfred shrugged. "Maybe he set it early enough, figuring someone would be awake. Rip dashed through the hotel
yelling for everyone to get out, and they just ran. But the
wind picked up some embers and carried the fire next door
to Hennessy's before anyone could do anything. Jeremiah
heard all the commotion at Kelly's, and ran to see what was
going on. He looked up and saw his own roof starting to
burn, so he scurried back inside to wake everyone up and
get them out." He shook his head. "Miracle no one died."

"I just hope they find the monster who started it. We
sure don't want someone like that running around loose.
Does Mr. Kelly have any idea who it might have been?"

"He says probably someone who owes him money, hoping his ledger would get burned up in the fire so he would
have no proof of the debt." He shook his head. "But that
was just a guess. No one saw or heard anything, so we may

never know." He gave a prodigious yawn. "And neither one had any insurance, and both men are poor, so they may not even be able to rebuild. They have lost everything."

"What a shame." Matilda rose to her feet. "You're exhausted. Lie down and get some rest. We'll let the law find the horrible man responsible for this dire deed."

When time passed and no suspects appeared, talk about the arson fires died down. The weather turned cold, and early rain promised a wet winter. The children began to talk with great animation about Halloween, and the costumes they were to wear for the neighborhood pageant.

Matilda, however, was more concerned about the reports of smallpox.

"It's been raging in San Francisco for four months," she fretted to Alfred as she cleared the supper dishes from the table. She had sent the children to get into their night clothes to prepare for their baths and bed, so she and Alfred were alone. She did want the children to sense her fears. "Do you think we should get vaccinated? Dr. Blackwood in Sacramento advertises a safe and reliable vaccine. Do we know anyone he has treated?"

"That the Doc with the office on 'J' Street? Down by the waterfront?" When Matilda nodded, he shrugged. "No one I know of. Guess we would have to make some inquiries."

"I wish you would. Smallpox frightens me. Mrs. Boone sounded so sure that vaccination was such a good idea." The thought of Mary and Elizabeth taking the disease, their beautiful skin ravaged by the ugly pustules, made her cringe. "If there is any way to be sure the children never take it, we owe it to them to try."

"We can always try the Chinese method," Alfred suggested with a wicked grin.

Matilda shuddered. "No, thank you. I prefer Dr. Blackwood's"

"And if the American doctors who object are right? What if we give them the disease by having them vaccinated?"

"We need more information,' she announced firmly. "Find out if anyone who has been vaccinated has taken the Pox. Surely he has a list of the people he has seen."

"Do you really think he is going to tell me about any patients of his that have died?"

She shrugged. "Probably not, but it's a start. I know some American doctors still oppose the procedure, but according to Mrs. Boone, it's been used successfully in Scotland for a number of years."

"Guess a body should pay some heed to that. Don't know how long the experience of Dr. Boylston will continue to haunt us. After all, that was clear back in the early 1700's. And if you recall, the majority of those he vaccinated survived. Most people tend to forget that."

"I know." Matilda sighed. "My mother says the disease is caused by bad diet and poor hygiene habits. My father used to say it was God's will."

Alfred added two more plates to the stack waiting to be washed. "Maybe vaccination is God's way of telling us to learn how to take care of ourselves. Today's paper said they have eighteen more deaths in San Francisco. And one lady who came upriver on the *Yosemite* with some kind of a skin condition wasn't allowed to disembark until the doctors assured the dockmaster she did not have smallpox."

"How can they be so sure?" Matilda demanded. "One man got clearance from the doctors in Petaluma and he turned out to have the Pox after all."

"That's probably why the papers are encouraging everyone to become vaccinated. I think it's just a matter of overcoming a lot of fear and superstition." The whistle of the kettle on the stove interrupted him. "Are we having tea?"

"No," she laughed. "That's for the children's baths. Bring in the tub, please, while I finish these dishes."

"Your wish is my command."

"Go on with you." She flapped the dishtowel at him. "Mary, Elizabeth! Are you ready?"

She put the last plate in the cupboard as Alfred appeared, tub in hand. "Put it in front of the stove. We don't want the children to take a chill."

Obediently, he arranged the galvanized wash tub in front of the kitchen stove, which glowed with a pleasant warmth. Matilda emptied in one pot of hot water, then followed it with the water from the teakettle.

Alfred watched her preparations, then suggested. "Maybe we should get one of those new rubber bath tubs."

"What?"

"Yep," he grinned. "Read about it in the paper. Latest invention, they say. It's portable. A lady can fold it up and store in her satchel to take with her. Great for traveling. It has a special appeal for ladies, because then they don't need to share the bath room with the other occupants of the hotel."

"Or wait in line for them to finish. You men think ladies take a long time! That man at Mrs. Boone's was in the bath room for over an hour. Thank goodness I had gotten in ahead of him."

"Yes, another advantage." He nodded in agreement. "Plus you always know who has been using it before you. I've had some fellow travelers I'm not sure I'd want to follow into the tub." He paused. "Of course, some of them have probably never bathed in their lives."

73

Matilda shuddered.

The day before Halloween, while Matilda put the finishing touches on Mary's costume for the neighborhood pageant, Alfred looked up from his paper and chuckled.

"Wait until Alf hears this one. 'September 19: London has given women the right to vote.' What do you suppose he will have to say about that?"

Matilda laughed merrily. "Plenty, I'm sure, We used to have some real discussions about it, let me tell you. And I've heard all of the arguments about how it's against feminine nature, and how women are too emotionally unstable to vote rationally." She bit off the thread at the end of the seam she had just finished with more force than the action really required. "I've told him I've noticed a lot of emotional and irrational behavior on the part of men, too, when they get to talking about politics."

She took a deep breath. "How about that southern Senator who ranted and raved about how Negroes were too ignorant to vote? When he found out they planned to vote for him, they were suddenly intelligent and qualified!"

He nodded his agreement. "I sadly fear that when politics is the subject, rational thinking is something that is never even considered."

One clear, cold evening in November, Matilda returned to the parlor after bedding down the children to find Alfred waiting for her. He was dressed warmly, and held her coat and scarf.

She met his dancing eyes with a puzzled look. "Are we going somewhere? We can't leave the children."

"Just into the back yard, but it's chilly outside. Come

on." He helped her into her coat and wrapped her scarf around her head and neck. "I want to show you something spectacular."

Puzzled, she followed him out into the night. The moon had not risen, and the dark velvet blue of the night sky sparkled with thousands of points of light. As she looked up into the star-studded vault, a streak of light flashed across the sky, followed by a second, then a third.

"Oh," she gasped, as the streaks continued to light up the night sky. "I've seen meteors, but never so many. What is it? "

"It's the Leonids," he explained. "They come every year around the fifteenth of November. They seem to come from the constellation of Leo, hence the name. The astronomers predicted they were going to be especially spectacular tonight, so I thought it would be fun to watch them for a while together. It's fortunate we have such a clear night."

They sat together on a log and leaned back against the side of the house, watching the show until Matilda started to shiver.

"Enough," Alfred commanded. He rose and pulled her to her feet. "We don't want you taking a chill, especially in your condition." He hugged her and kissed the tip of her nose. "We can watch them again next year if you enjoyed the show."

She stifled a yawn. "Maybe next time we can include Mary and Elizabeth."

As she snuggled under the quilts and nestled close to Alfred's warm body, she thought again how much she loved him. He knew so much. She still stood somewhat in awe of his wisdom and knowledge. As she had so many times before during the past year, she thanked God again for sending her such a fine man.

The baby moved within her, and she wrapped a protective arm around her abdomen. She listened for a moment to Alfred's quiet, even breathing, then murmured softly, "Baby, you are going to have a wonderful father."

Chapter 10

December, 1868 to February, 1869

CHRISTMAS OF 1868 found the whole family in Matilda and Alfred's house for the celebrations and dinner. The break in the weather that had allowed them to see the meteorite shower so clearly had vanished, and the cloud cover returned, along with incessant rain. Intermittent showers of increased intensity pounded on the roof at periodic intervals. Water poured off the eaves, and ran in little rivulets across the yard, making new paths toward the creek to the north of the house.

Polly and Sarah took charge of the kitchen and made Matilda sit in the parlor. Since she had reached her seventh month of pregnancy, and her feet tended to swell when she stood for too long, she did not object. She held Will and Polly's year and a half old son on her lap. His eyes were as big as saucers as he stared at the little tree with the wrapped packages underneath.

He's too young to understand, she thought. When he's older, we'll tell him why his name is Michael, but we call him Bud. Tears stung her eyes as she thought of Michael, who would have been eighteen just a short time ago had his young life not ended so tragically just two years before.

She forced her thoughts from it and looked around the room at her loved ones. Dear Abe, with his four. How he had managed without Minerva, she would never understand, but he had resolutely refused to marry again.

"I've been married, 'Tilda," he said sadly when she had mentioned yet another neighborhood lady who would like to have become the second Mrs. Dyer. "I know it's hard, not having a mother for the children, and little Laura has had to grow up pretty fast. She tries so hard to be mother to the younger ones. But somehow, the idea of someone taking Min's place . . . ." His eye filled with tears and he fell silent.

At the time, Matilda had patted his hand in understanding. As she watched him, she remembered the conversation. Poor Min. Her life had been so short, but she had been blessed with a fine man, and had shared a wonderful love with him.

Laura and Mary were both nine, and patiently tolerated the presence of seven year old sister Elizabeth as they set up their own Christmas dinner for their dolls in one corner of the room. Will and Polly's daughters Susie, eight, and Maggie, six, watched from a respectful distance. Polly's Mary, age ten, and Anna, eleven, had been called into the kitchen to peel potatoes. Will and Charlie, along with Sammie and Lewis, played on the back porch under the watchful eye of ten year old Frank, assigned, over his objections, to care for his little brothers and cousins.

The men sat around the parlor discussing events of the day. Will and Tom occupied the new sofa that dominated the little room. Matilda had made the needlepoint covers for the horsehair cushions herself. The other men pulled in kitchen chairs or sat on the floor or on boxes.

Matilda noticed her brother Britt's hairline had begun to recede, and a sprinkling of gray showed in his dark locks. He was, after all, she calculated quickly in her head, fifty years old. His daughter Sarah, at 28, had married recently to a quiet young man, Jack Morrison, who said not a word as the men talked. Her other brothers, Will, Tom, Sam, and Alf, had plenty to say.

Alfred sat a little apart, on the chair Gardner Randolph had brought across the prairie from Kansas. He listened, Matilda thought, with some amusement to the conversation. She recognized the little twinkle, the slight crinkling around his eyes. He was very polite, but secretly amused.

The discussion centered around the coming of the Central Pacific Railroad south from Sacramento towards Stockton.

"The logical route," Sam declared firmly, "is through Hicksville and Liberty. After all, the stage follows that route now. There are established towns, with Post Offices already. Makes perfect sense."

"Makes sense, yes," Will agreed. "But Obed Harvey owns all of that land west of Liberty. He wants the trains to go through his land. Make him even richer."

"Why, in God's wisdom," Sam declared, "would any logical builder want to go through all that swamp land when they've got a smooth road to follow?"

Will shrugged. "I don't think logic is going to have anything to do with it. Harvey's good friends with Stanford and the rest of that bunch. He's trying to use that friendship to get the line to go where he wants it. And looks like odds are good he'll be elected a State legislator in the '70 election. Stanford and Crocker and the rest want to stay on his good side. He gets the legislature to threaten to block them from doing something they want, and they do what he whatever he says."

"Politics in action," Tom muttered. "And the towns of Hicksville and Liberty can go straight to Hell."

"Watch your language, Tom," Sam murmured, with a glance at Matilda and the little girls.

"Sorry," he muttered. "But it just isn't right."

"Right or not," Will commented, "It looks likes that the way it's going to be. The engineers are already surveying about a mile west of Hicksville."

"Too bad Harvey didn't drown in the wreck of the *Central America*," Tom grumbled.

Will grinned. "Guess he almost did. I hear he floated for nine hours on a hunk of wreckage before he got rescued."

"Bet he pushed off anyone sharing with him," Tom muttered, half under his breath.

"Now, Tom," Will chided his brother, "that's only rumor. No way anyone could ever prove such a thing. No point in slanderin' the man unfairly."

"Right," Sam agreed. "Him threatening to use his influence as a legislator for his own personal gain is slander enough."

Will only shrugged his shoulders expressively. "That's politics."

Tom's sense of humor returned and he chuckled. "Anyone care to bet he only serves one term? Just long enough to be sure he gets his way?"

Betsy Ann interrupted the conversation. "You men get started on politics you can go on forever. Sam, lift the goose out of the oven and get to carving. Rest of you go wash up and get ready to eat. And get those young-uns in from the porch before they catch their death of cold and get 'em fit for the table."

The rains continued through January. Alfred reported that McCauley had filed suit on January 18 against Obed Harvey and Haskell Swain to clear the title to the Chabolla Land Grant.

"Soon's it's settled," he told Matilda, "Swain says if he wins he'll sell that 200 acre piece to us. Then we'll have our own land. Our very own land! No more paying rent, even to as good a landlord as Jim Short." In his exuberance, he gathered her into his arms in a bear hug. The baby kicked in protest, and they both laughed.

Another burst of rain thundered down on the roof. Alfred looked up and scowled as they listened to the pouring rain. "Doesn't stop raining soon there's going to be so much water we'll never get the wheat in the ground."

"Alf says the paper is reporting the Sacramento River is rising. Do you suppose the Cosumnes will go over?" Visions of raging water rushing past the house brought back vivid memories of her struggle against the flood waters of the Big Blue with Baby John strapped on her back. She shuddered as she recalled that long ago day in Kansas when she and Lewis had lost their first home.

Alfred kissed the tip of her nose and reassured her. "Alf says if it does, it won't reach the house. He says this piece of land was high and dry in the floods of 1861. I was up in Placerville, but I remember how folks talked about it being one big lake from Hicksville to Liberty."

She sighed. "I certainly hope he's right. I'd sure hate to see everything we own floating down Laguna Creek."

The rains continued, with the danger of flooding reported in the papers more and more. By early February, the threat seemed more imminent. Matilda tried not to think about it. Alfred sat reading the newspapers while she settled into her chair with her mending basket. With less than a month to go in her pregnancy, she found herself tiring more easily. Her feet seemed to swell more than she remembered with the first four.

Her mother assured her it was not unusual, and treated

her with one of her lobelia concoctions, lobelia and lobelia seeds steeped in apple vinegar designed "just for a woman in a family way" as Betsy Ann put it. The bottle stood on a shelf in the pantry, and Matilda faithfully and valiantly swallowed a spoonful every morning, as vile as it tasted.

Alfred was deep in the newspaper. " 'Crime is on the increase in San Francisco,'" he read. "I do hope it doesn't affect Mrs. Boone."

Matilda laughed, remembering the colorful old lady with affection. "I'm quite sure Mrs. Boone is capable of taking care of herself."

Alfred nodded in agreement. "You're probably right. No criminal in his right mind would think of tangling with her." The paper rustled as he turned the page. "Here's a big article on the conspiracy to assassinate Lincoln. Guess the writer is not that impressed that the court let John Surratt loose. Jury hung 4 to 8 to release him, in spite of 80 witnesses for the prosecution, so I guess the judge didn't have any choice except to let him go."

"How could any jury do that? Surely he was as deeply involved as the others! After all, the plotting was done in his mother's house. And didn't several people say they saw him outside of the Ford Theater that night? Several people who knew him well? If he was as innocent as he claims, why did he run off to Canada and then over to Europe?"

"Oh, I'm quite sure he was as guilty as the ones they hung. The writer of the article seems to think so, too. Guess the difference was, his mother and the other three they hung were tried by a military court, and the son by a civil one." He shook his head soberly. "The law that said civilians couldn't be tried in military courts wasn't passed until 1866. Unfortunately, the law came one year too late to save Mary Surratt." He chuckled. "At least she will go down in history as the first woman to be hung by the Federal Government."

"I'm sure that knowledge was small comfort to her as the hangman put the noose around her neck." Matilda shook her head sadly. "Such a shame. But it's hard to feel too sorry for her. If she and Booth and that bunch of conspirators hadn't killed poor Mr. Lincoln, this terrible mess in the South with that horrid Reconstruction Act would never have happened."

Alfred shrugged. "You're probably right, but unfortunately, we can't change what has already taken place. It's going to take a long time for the land to heal, I'm afraid." He laid the paper aside, picking up the next one. Matilda smiled. Someday, she thought, we will get the papers on a daily basis, instead of picking up several days' worth at a time.

"'Kerosene oil being used in New York City is highly explosive'," he read. He looked at Matilda across the top of the paper. "No wonder that fire started so fast at the Sheldon Hotel. I told you Rip said he smelled skunk oil where the fire started. Dangerous stuff." He returned to the paper. "And someone else cautions against the use of poisonous hair dyes." He grinned at Matilda. "Guess we will never have that problem. No woman ever had more beautiful hair than you. Certainly no need to ever risk your health to change it."

Matilda blushed and smiled. Alfred always said such nice things. She thought again how fortunate she was to have such a thoughtful husband.

He rose to his feet and yawned. "Come, my lovely bride, I think it is time we retired."

The next morning, she woke up early, and lay quietly

beside Alfred, listening to his soft, even breathing. She often awoke before anyone else, and treasured these moments of quiet. Soon the children would be awake, and the hustle and bustle of the day would begin. The pink glow of early dawn had just begun in the eastern sky. She put her hand on her abdomen, reassured by the active movements of the baby inside. She smiled. He (or she) should be born soon. Her mother had said the last week in February or early in March. She could hardly wait to place Alfred's first child in his arms.

As she lay there thinking of the coming baby, her heart missed a beat as the unmistakable roar of rushing water reached her ears.

Chapter 11

February to March, 1969

MATILDA TOOK a deep breath and forced down her panic. She remembered Alf's words, and Alfred's reassurances, that the water would not reach the house. Still, she had to know. If they had to get the children out, they might have to begin quickly. The barn was on higher ground than the house, so White Star and Big Ben and the cows should be fine. Not like poor Priscilla when the Big Blue tore the barn off its foundation and carried it down the river in seconds.

She closed her eyes and shuddered at the memory of the despairing cries of the doomed animals. She had come so close to losing White Star at the same time. If Lew had not chosen that day to help Abe fix his plow . . . . She let the memories trail off and eased herself out of the bed, pulling on her robe in the chill of the room. Time to stoke up the fire anyway, she thought, even if that roar is not as ominous as it sounds.

Hurrying as fast as she could without waking Alfred or the children, she forced her footsteps to the back porch and opened the door. She gasped when the cold air struck her, then stood transfixed in horror. Benign little Laguna Creek had turned into a raging torrent. Beyond it, water covered the land as far as she could see. She took some comfort from the knowledge that the water would have to rise several feet to reach the place where she stood.

She continued to watch the water, waiting for the level to rise and threaten her sanctuary. She did not even notice she had started to shiver until Alfred came up behind her with a shawl and wrapped it around her.

"Come inside. I've got the fire going good. You have to get warm. Think of the babe." He turned her aside, pulling her riveted stare from the raging water. "It won't get much higher, I promise." Then he chuckled. "And I'm sure Mary will be delighted when she learns there is no way to get past the flood waters to get her to school."

Matilda laughed. "You're right. Elizabeth will be disappointed, for she loves school, but Mary will be praying every night for the flood to continue." She smiled, a little grimly. "And I'm sure one reason she dislikes it so much is because Elizabeth is a better student. Mary has never said anything, but I suspect the fact that Elizabeth is already the superior reader bothers her."

"We, I imagine, will just have to get used to the idea that Elizabeth is our scholar and Mary our, well, whatever."

"Go ahead and say it," Matilda agreed with a wry smile, thinking not only of Mary's lack of interest in scholarly pursuits, but her equal lack of interest in domestic chores. "Mary is our rebel." She held her hands before the little Topsy stove, soaking up the warmth. "I suspect Mary was born fifty years before her time. I can see her being the first woman in the State Legislature."

Alfred laughed merrily, "And if she had been in the Legislature now, the Central Pacific would go though Hicksville and Liberty. I can't see Obed Harvey outmaneuvering our Mary. I can even see her shouting down Leland Stanford!"

Two weeks later, the water still covered much of the land

the Cosumnes had flooded when it leapt over its banks on that memorable February morning. Matilda rose and began to build up the fire in the big iron stove, preparatory to getting breakfast for the family. She checked the water again, to find, to her dismay, that it still covered as far as she could see to the south and west. Some hills emerged to the north and east, but so far, the roads remained covered. She could not keep from chuckling at the thought that the flood had slowed down the railroad construction. The tracks had reached the Cosumnes River just before the water overran the banks, and had been halted ever since. They want to build over swamp land to make Obed Harvey happy, she reflected grimly, let them see what it is like.

She sighed. Another day the children could not go to school or even go out of doors. She sighed again, more deeply, reluctant to admit even to herself that she grew weary of having everyone underfoot all day. She knew one reason for her lack of patience was the approaching birth. Even her mother had assured her that little things would irritate her more now. She thanked Heaven for Alfred. He could always get the children to settle down by reading to them, or telling them stories of his experiences coming across the Isthmus of Panama in '49, and tales of his gold mining days up in Placerville. She had to admit she still enjoyed the stories herself, especially when he recounted the roof blowing off of his canvas hotel the night he stayed in Mud Springs on his way to the diggings.

With a soft chuckle, she thought of how he always seemed to know when she had reached the end of her patience. As she reached across the stove to pick up the tea kettle to refill it, a sudden spasm of pain started in her back and crossed to her abdomen. At the same time, she felt a rush of water down her leg. Oh, my, she thought with a sudden panic.

My waters have burst. And Alfred can't get across the flood to reach Mother at Alf's. Who's going to help with the birth? She shrugged her shoulders expressively. Well, she thought, I guess it will have to be Alfred. He's going to get a little more introduction to fatherhood than he planned.

Leaving the half full kettle on the stove, not daring to risk pumping water to fill it, she returned to the bed and lay down beside Alfred.

He woke up and lay an arm across her. "You're shivering. Did you let yourself get cold? Have you been outside watching the creek again? It's gradually going down. Another week and all the roads should be at least passable, if not easily." His hand slid to her abdomen just as another spasm rolled across. He sat up and gasped, his eyes widening. "The babe! It's coming. But . . .but. . . I might not be able to get your mother here. The water is still too high, to say nothing of the mud after the ground being soaked for two weeks. What are we going to do?"

She smiled up at him. "You're going to have to be the one. The pains are coming too fast for anyone to get here." She grimaced as another contraction seized her in its grip.

His face revealed his panic. "But I know nothing about delivering babies! What if I do something wrong?"

With a serene smile, Matilda reassured him. "You'll do just fine. I've had four already, remember? And I've helped my mother birth many more. I'll tell you everything you need to know. Now, get the fire stoked good and get it warm in here. The north wind is starting, and we need to have the room warm for the babe." She shivered at the thought of the cold winds that always howled down from the cold northern climates every March. "And fill that tea kettle. We'll need some warm water to bathe the baby in."

Mary's face appeared around the door jamb. "Mama,

what's wrong? We saw you get up and start the fire, then go back to bed. You never go back to bed."

Elizabeth's head popped up below her sister's, her eyes wide. Matilda had to laugh at the expressions on their faces, in spite of another contraction sweeping across her womb. "The new baby is coming, girls, and you will have to help your father. Mary, go get the baby clothes we made and . . . ." She paused and gritted her teeth as another wave of pain washed over her, then continued, "and get some of them nice and warm to dress him in. Elizabeth, keep Lew entertained. Go on," she ordered, when neither girl moved, just opened their eyes wider. "Now!"

Both faces disappeared as the girls scurried to obey. Matilda's contractions were almost continuous, and the urge to push the baby out almost irresistible. Alfred had better hurry back, or she would have to deliver the baby herself. She sighed with relief when he returned, his face as anxious as ever.

"I have the teakettle on, and the kitchen is getting cozy. Mary is warming the baby clothes, she said you told her to. What . . . ."

She put a finger on his lips to stop the flow of words. "Just . . ." she caught her breath, then went on, "just bring a warm blanket to wrap the baby in. And hurry back."

An hour later, Carrie Belle Wheelock was born. Alfred proudly carried the infant girl to the kitchen to bathe. When he returned, Mary was with him, walking very slowly, her new baby sister cradled in her arms. How thoughtful of Alfred, Matilda thought, to let Mary bring the new baby to me. With a smile, she took the infant and put the tiny face to her breast. Alfred leaned over and kissed her gently.

"Thank you for a beautiful daughter, my love," he whispered, his voice husky with emotion. Tears stood in his eyes.

Happiness washed over Matilda in a wave. She stroked Alfred's cheek, then caressed the soft fuzz of reddish blonde hair on the infant's head. "Mary," she said to the child waiting so patiently by the bed, "you did a beautiful job of helping your father bathe the baby. Now go tell Elizabeth and Lew to come and meet their little sister."

Almost two weeks passed before the water went down and the roads dried enough to allow passage between Alf's home and Matilda and Alfred's.

"Credit the north wind with something," Alfred advised Matilda when she grumbled about the cold wind penetrating to her very marrow. "It's blown away every rain cloud, and is drying out the roads quite rapidly. I wouldn't be surprised if Alf doesn't bring your mother over today or tomorrow."

Matilda agreed. "As soon as Alf can get a buggy through, Mother will have him drive her. I'm sure she has been fretting, knowing little Carrie here was so close to due when the river went over."

Her prognostication proved correct. Shortly after midday, Alf appeared with Betsy Ann beside him on the seat of the buggy.

While Betsy Ann oohed and aahed over her newest granddaughter, Alf raved about a Methodist preacher he had gone to the Seventh Street M.E. Church in Sacramento to hear the previous Sunday. "Bishop, he is. Name of Henry Marvine. Never heard a more inspiring sermon in my life. Ever have a son of my own, I'm going to name him after Bishop Marvine, I am. Fine man. Be a good one for a growing boy to look up to as his hero."

Alfred chuckled. "If you want a son to name after the

good bishop, you had best be thinking of a wife, Partner. Got anyone in mind? Several widow ladies that come to mind would no doubt be happy to fill the position. You are, if I recall correctly, pushing forty. Time you were thinking about getting hitched, if you want to have a son."

"Now, don't rush me. Plenty of time left." He grinned. "I'm still a young man."

The next contingent to arrive was Will and Polly with their brood. Sam rode beside the buggy on his horse. Everyone was anxious to see the new baby, and assure themselves that all was well with Matilda after almost three weeks of isolation by the high water.

"Fortunately, we had plenty to eat," Matilda laughed, when questioned how they had fared. "And Mary was delighted to have such a long vacation from school. Elizabeth is fretting about catching up, but I'm sure she will have no problem. No one else could get to school either."

Everyone crowded into the little house, for the cold wind made sitting on the porch unpleasant. Fortunately, Matilda had a big pot of stew simmering on the stove, so Betsy Ann and Polly set about adding more vegetables and making biscuits. The men, as usual, sat around discussing politics. The Cuban Revolution was very much on everyone's mind, having so recently begun.

"Looked for a while like de Cespedes and his bunch were going to win easy," Sam declared. "Then Spain sent over a bunch of soldiers. They were under orders to take no prisoners, so I guess it was a pretty brutal affair. Papers were decrying it, demanding to know how enlightened Europe could allow such barbarism on the part of Spain to occur without protest."

"Just hope we stay out of it," Will declared. "It's no concern of ours, even though there is talk of us taking over

Cuba." He dismissed Cuba with a wave of his hand and returned to more local affairs. "I hear the County wants to install a system of levees to help drain some of the Delta, create more farm land. Also, help drain some of the water away faster when we get floods like we just had."

"I don't know," Sam opined. "Seems to me, whenever men start fooling with nature, the results are bad. Look what happened to the rivers when they started washing down the hills to get at the gold."

"Oh, but this will be different," Will assured him.

"We'll see." Sam remained skeptical. "We'll see.'

Matilda put Carrie in her crib and joined the women in the kitchen to put the finishing touches on the midday meal. As she saw the women working while the men sat and discussed current events, she recalled an anecdote she had read in a recent paper.

"Polly," she asked her sister-in-law, "Why, when God took a rib and made Eve, didn't he take another and make her a servant?"

"I take it this is a joke," Polly responded, scooping a ladle full of the simmering savory stew from the kettle and pouring it into a bowl. "Okay, I give up. Why?"

Matilda laughed. "Because Adam never came whining to Eve with a stocking to darn, a collar string to be sewed, or a glove to mend."

Chapter 12

March, 1869

BETWEEN THE NORTH wind and the sunshine which poured down every day, almost as though trying to apologize for the many days of rain, the land dried rapidly. To Matilda's relief, the children had returned to school.

Alfred reported that the fields were solid enough to plant. He loaded the seed into the seeder borrowed from Matilda's brother Will and prepared to get his fields in as quickly as possible. She accompanied him to the barn and stood stroking White Star while she watched him pile the sacks of wheat beside the bin.

"Lucky for us Will is closer to the river, and his ground is still too muddy to plant," Alfred commented, folding up the sack he had just emptied into the bin. "Planting will go a lot faster with this fancy seeder of his. Should see about getting someone to help me, so's I can be sure and finish before Will needs it back. Go a lot faster with one man driving and another keeping the bin full."

"Maybe one of Will's sons can help you. Or maybe Chase."

"Would liked to have had Gardner. He's a good worker."

"From what Sarah says," Matilda laughed, "he's so taken with Santa Barbara he's trying to get the rest of them to join him."

A low growl from Jake, lying at her feet, brought their attention to a young man walking into the yard from the road.

"Hush, Jake," Matilda reassured to old dog. "The young man looks harmless."

The young man heard her remark and chuckled softly. "Yep, perfectly harmless. Lookin' fer work, I am. Any chance you folks could use a hand for a few weeks?" He stuck out his hand to Alfred. "Name's Absalom Shaw, but most folks call me A.B." He twisted his mouth into a wry grin. "Absalom is too much name to pronounce."

"Agreed," Alfred returned the boy's smile and gripped the proffered hand. "Alfred Wheelock. My wife, Matilda."

"Pleased to meet you."

"And," Alfred continued, "we were just discussing how I could use an extra hand. Where you living?"

A.B. hesitated. "Well, sort of nowhere. Came out from Ohio with my folks in '49, to the gold fields. They died in the cholera epidemic in '50. Silas Whitcomb, over Georgetown way, he took me in and they raised me. I been workin' for them up until Silas died, just recent-like. Mrs. Whitcomb, now, she's got the place for sale. Tired of farming, wants to sell out and go back to where her family is, back East somewheres. She told me I could stay as long as I wanted, but I didn't like to be beholden to her, since she really didn't have no work for me to do, seeing as how she has two other hands there as can do everything as needs doin'."

"We'll fix up a place for you in the barn. It's snug and cozy. Weather should be pretty mild from here on out."

"That'll be just great, Mr. Wheelock. Now, we'd better get to work. What do you want me to do first?"

Alfred laughed at the young man's eagerness. "I guess

you can start by hitching Big Ben to the seeder."

"And I'll ring the bell when dinner is ready," Matilda added. "Did you have breakfast, A.B.?"

"Lady at the first place I stopped give me a couple of biscuits. I'll be fine until dinner time." He offered a shy smile and reached down to scratch Jake's ears. "But I'll be more than ready to eat by then. Meanwhile, with wheat sellin' for $1.40 a hundred, we'd better get this crop in." He turned and headed for the barn, Jake at his heels.

"Looks like a nice young man," Alfred commented, as he and Matilda watched the two of them stride off.

Matilda laughed. "Obviously Jake has accepted him."

When the three of them sat down for the noon meal. Matilda looked more closely at their newly hired hand. The persistent cough, the slight flush on his face, the translucent appearance of the skin over his cheek bones, all reminded her of her sister Temperance before she died of consumption. She feared this young man also suffered from that dreaded disease. She said nothing, but resolved to ask her mother the next time she saw her. Betsy Ann would know the best medication to prepare for him.

"Hoping to save enough to get a place of my own," the young man was explaining to Alfred, in between bites of biscuit and ham. "Courtin' a young lady as lives down on Lower Stockton Road, just a piece down from the Whitcomb place. Haven't popped the question yet, but me an' her, we have an understanding, we do. Just got to get some money She's tryin' to help, sews real pretty, she does, and takes in sewin' for the neighbors."

"Working as a farm hand is not a way to get a great deal of money fast," Alfred advised. "Maybe you should consider some other line of work."

"Like farmin'. Like being in the open air, love horses. Friend of mine, name of Brickell, George Brickell, he and his brother, they took jobs up at the Gold Hill Mine. Pays real good, according to George, but I can't see me workin' underground all day, so I decided not to go with 'em."

Matilda thougt, if the boy really does have consumption, working underground in all that dust in a mine would be the death of him. As these thoughts ran through her mind, a spasm of coughing racked A.B.'s frail frame.

Alfred apparently noticed it too, for he said, "Dust from the seed must be bad for you. This afternoon, you drive the team and I'll ride on the seeder and re-fill the bin."

"As you wish, Mr. Wheelock."

Betsy Ann recommended Chamomile tea, a decoction of elecampane, and the yolk of an egg beaten with a table-spoon of honey. Matilda faithfully plyed A.B. with these, and he dutifully swallowed them. Whether he felt they would help him or whether he merely took them to humor Matilda he never said and she never asked.

At breakfast one morning towards the end of March, Alfred brought up the subject of a recent newspaper article. "Seems," he advised his listeners, "that Californians are being urged to write to their representatives in Congress to press Washington to grant a pension to John Sutter for his role in helping save immigrants that got themselves strand-ed trying to cross the Sierras."

Matilda spoke up. "I remember one story of how the immigrants not only ate the supplies he sent, but the mules he sent them on, and the two Miwok boys who took them."

"That was an awful thing to do, but I hear he didn't always treat his Indian helpers too well."

"I guess he treated them about as well as the Spaniards

that came before him, or the miners that came after."

As the conversation progressed. Matilda saw Mary's and Elizabeth's eyes grow wider, and felt it time they departed. "Girls," she ordered, "Go and get the eggs gathered before you have to go to school." When they hesitated, she added, "Now!"

The two men continued as though the interruption had never occurred. "I hear he never paid the Russians for Fort Ross. And they say he never paid his bills. If his son hadn't come out and straightened up his affairs, he'd have lost it all anyway." A.B. shook his head. "But when the settlers came, they settled on his land and stole his cattle. So much for gratitude for sending the supplies that saved their lives."

"So Will Daylor giving him the money to bring his wife and family actually saved him, by bringing the son to handle his financial affairs, although I'm sure he didn't see it in that light at the time."

"I remember Will Daylor. He died in the same epidemic as my folks. That was a terrible time. Lotsa people died, even doctors. Dr. Morse came by when my mother died. I was only ten, and my father had died the week before. When he saw I was alone, he took me to Silas Whitcomb."

He closed his eyes for a moment. Matilda felt a pang of sympathy for the little boy A.B. had been when Dr. Morse found him.

He pulled himself together and grinned boyishly. "Don't think Daylor thought he was doing Sutter a favor. He did it to get even with Sutter for having Micheltorena jail him because they were both after the same Injun girl. 'Scuse me, Miz Wheelock, if that gives offense. Jared Sheldon went down to Monterey and bailed him out. Micheltorena, he thought it was funny. He just laughed and released Daylor right away. Sutter's wife had been wantin' to join him, but he kept puttin' her off, sayin' he didn't have money for their passage from Switzerland." He chuckled. "From what they tell me, she's a real termagent."

He rose from the table. "Thank you again for the breakfast, Miz Wheelock. You're a right good cook. Mr. Wheelock, here, he's a lucky man."

Alfred grinned and agreed. "Get Ben ready to go. I'll be out in a moment."

As the boy departed, Matilda expressed her concern again. "He reminds me so much of Temperance just before she died. I don't think he feels as well as he wants us to believe."

"You're right. He tires very easily. I try to have him do the things that require the least effort. I don't know what else we can do."

Matilda sighed and started gathering the breakfast dishes and carrying them to the sink. "Mother says avoid fatigue, be sure he gets plenty of fresh air and wholesome food, and take the medicines. Other than that, all we can do is pray."

Alfred carried an armload of dishes to the sink and filled the teakettle with water from the hand pump and set it on the stove to heat. "It could be worse. He could have gone to work in the mine with his friend George. Or he could be in Cuba."

"Cuba?"

"I understand the revolution is getting more violent all the time. The rebels have started burning plantations. A former Confederate officer, name of Rudolph Pate, is leading the revolutionaries."

"Didn't he get enough during our own war? I know I sure had enough, with all of the problems between the Border Ruffians and the Jayhawkers, and that horrible massacre Quantrill led in Lawrence."

"That's right, you were in Kansas then. I was out here, and we only heard about it. But I understand Cuba is asking the United States to recognize them as an independent country."

"And are we going to do it?"

Alfred shrugged. "Who knows? They are arguing it out in Congress now."

"Will we wind up at war with Spain? I hope not!"

Alfred shrugged his shoulders and took her in his arms and kissed her. "Right. We'll hope not. I'd better get going, or A.B. will think he has to finish that last field by himself."

By the end of March, even A.B. could no longer deny he was seriously ill. Matilda had Alfred make up a bed for him in the kitchen, close to the stove so he would not get chilled at night. Betsy Ann was called for consultation, but she could add nothing except comfrey poultices to the treatments already in use. Jake had grown accustomed to sleeping with the young man in the barn, and refused to leave his side, howling dismally if locked away from him. The old dog shared the bed with A.B., who seemed to take comfort in his presence.

"Never had a dog of my own, Miz Wheelock," he smiled weakly, stroking the silken head. Jake responded by licking the boy's chin. "Never knew how much company a critter could be."

Matilda turned her head to hide the tears in her eyes, for she knew the boy was dying. She remembered the comfort the dog had been to her when Lewis had been killed. "Jake is very good company," she smiled. "It's his specialty."

In the end, it was Jake who told her when A.B. died. Carrie had been fussy in the night, and Matilda had fallen into an exhausted sleep. Jake's mournful howl woke her just before dawn. She pulled on her robe and lighted the lamp by the bedside. As she approached A.B.'s cot, Jake came to meet her, whining softly. The light from the lamp fell on the boy's still face, and she knew his short life had ended. The home he and his sweetheart had been saving for would never be.

A few days after A.B.'s funeral, Alfred opened the paper and read his funeral notice to Matilda. "Gives no next of kin, or anything. Makes me feel sad we never made any inquiries as to who his sweetheart was. Wish we could have told her. Will be a real shock to her to read it in the paper."

"I asked him. He didn't want her to know he was ill. Said he wanted to tell her after he was better." Tears rolled down Matilda's cheeks. "I couldn't bring myself to tell him he was never going to get better. I feel so bad. I wish I had insisted so she could have told him goodbye."

"His friend that went to Gold Hill Mine fared no better. There's a big article on that terrible fire at the mine. Over 30 men were killed. Didn't A.B. say his friend's name was George Brickell?"

"Yes."

"Says George was trying to get his brother out, got him on the elevator, but he fainted and the brother's arm got torn off."

"How dreadful!"

"Yes, and George himself died the next day."

Matilda only shook her head.

Chapter 13

April to November, 1869

THREE WEEKS AFTER A.B.'s funeral, Alfred rode back from Billy Bandeen's place with a puppy in White Star's saddlepack. When Matilda saw the flop-eared little dog peering over the edge, her heart missed a beat. The animal looked so much like Jake had when Lewis rode up to the cabin that long ago day in Kansas.

She struggled to get her breathing back under control as Alfred dismounted and lifted the puppy from White Star's pack. He handed it to Matilda, and the little fellow immediately lavished her face with doggie kisses.

Matilda laughed and grimaced as the rough tongue lapped at her face. "What a darling," she managed to gasp. "The children will love him. He looks like Jake did when he was a puppy."

"That's what Billy says. His bitch whelped about six weeks ago, and several of the pups looked so much like Jake that he figured that sly old dog had come calling."

"Jake! At your age, that's a long way to travel." Matilda looked over at the old dog lying on the porch watching them. He raised his head as she spoke his name and thumped his tail. "Did you ever see such a look of total innocence?" she laughed to Alfred. "Maybe he's not as old as we thought he was."

She stroked the puppy's soft ears as he cuddled against

her neck. "Well, Little Jake, the children will love you. And you can play with them. Mary was just complaining that Jake was getting too old to run after a ball."

Mary appeared on the porch, followed closely by Elizabeth and Lewis. Mary let out a squeal at the sight of the puppy in Matilda's arms and rushed to take him. Soon all three surrounded the little fellow and he wriggled all over himself trying to kiss three faces at once.

Alfred joined Matilda and put his arm around her. She leaned her head against his shoulder as they watched the little tableau.

"How thoughtful of you," she murmured. "The children adore him already. I was wondering how we were going to deal with the children when . . . when . . . ." She could not bring herself to say it. Her glance fell on the silent old dog watching from the porch and her eyes filled.

Alfred, with his usual perspicacity, sensed her feelings immediately. He hugged her closer and kissed the top of her head. "Wasn't so much my idea as it was Billy's," he grinned. "He wanted me to take all three of the ones that looked like Jake. I told him I'd better start with one."

The papers reported the smallpox epidemic was subsiding, much to Matilda's relief. Jake seemed to rally, even tolerating the puppy cavorting around him.

All the talk about the railroad and the Cuban Revolution took Matilda's mind off of the smallpox epidemic and her concern for Jake. Sam and Tom came to help Alfred build an extension on the barn. At the mid-day meal, Matilda listened as they put forth their conflicting opinions.

Sam felt the United States should step in and settle the whole affair. "Got two expeditions of volunteers going down there already," he opined. "England and France think we should step in. Those Spanish soldiers are killing everyone they see. Time someone stopped it."

"None of our affair," Tom argued. "If we got involved in every little squabble in the world, it would drive us into bankruptcy. Volunteers want to go help, let 'em, but officially I say we should stay out of it."

Alfred shrugged. "I understand the Cubans are already unhappy because the Senate refused to back the rebellion. Somehow, I can't help but feel the world is getting smaller. Why, already there's only a few more miles of track left before the East and West will be connected by rail. Then what used to take so many long, hard weeks to cross can be crossed in a few days, and in relative comfort." He laughed and glanced at Matilda. "At least, you don't have to walk."

"That should finish the steamer route," Sam grinned. "There's already talk of dropping the price in half. Old Aspinwall has been gouging folks long enough."

"I suppose if the price is low enough, some will still go by steamer, although Britt swore no one would ever get him on another boat. Guess he was seasick half the time."

"Bet the crossing of the Isthmus is a lot easier now they've got the railroad through." Alfred chuckled. "No more spending the night in a hammock with the dogs brushing their fleas off on you."

Laughter at the memory of Alfred's stories of the crossing went around the table. Tom volunteered that Leland Stanford was going to help drive the last spike in the road himself, and planned to leave soon for the big event.

Sam grinned. "Fancy him trying to drive a spike! Bet he can't even hit it."

Summer passed quickly. The harvest was a bountiful one, and the men were all in good spirits. The last spike had been driven, and trains regularly crossed from one side of the continent to the other.

Matilda returned from a visit to Will and Polly to report Polly had an ice box. "Will bought it for her from David Bush's shop up on K Street, between Second and Third. She says the milk stays sweet for several days. Much better than just keeping it in the cistern, or the cool box." She looked over at Alfred who seemed deep in his paper. He did not respond, so she said no more.

Three days later, he put three hogs in the buckboard and took them to the market in Sacramento to sell. When he returned, he hurried into the kitchen where Matilda stood by the sink scrubbing turnips. He put his arms around her and kissed the back of her neck.

"Come with me, I have a surprise for you." He picked up the towel and dried her hands. "Come on."

Mystified, she followed him out and saw the little ice box tied onto the back of the buckboard. "Oh, Alfred!," she cried, thrilled to think she would now have one of her own. "I love you." She threw her arms around his neck and kissed him soundly.

Giggles penetrated her exultation and she turned to see three solemn faces staring at them. Undismayed, she cried to the children, "Look! We now have our own ice box!"

They enlisted Alf's help to offload the newest acquisition and install it in a place of honor in the kitchen. Alf teased her. "Now you can start complaining just like Polly does, that the ice is melting too fast, and that the pan keeps overflowing and spilling water out onto her clean floor."

As the men wrestled the recalcitrant box into place, Alfred reported that when he was in Sacramento, he had been told that Mrs. Whitcomb sold her place over in Georgetown. "Got $64,000 for it, according to what they say. That's $15 an acre. Good farm land."

"I'm sure A.B. would be happy to know she got enough so she will be fixed for life, after all she did for him." Matilda's heart ached as she remembered the boy they had come to love in the short time he had been with them..

Determined not to let the sorrow get her down, she took Alfred's arm and leaned her head against his shoulder. "How about taking the children to see Dan Castello's Circus and Abyssian Caravan, whatever that is? It's going to be in Sacramento for a week in the middle of July. I'm sure I can get Polly to watch Carrie for me, especially if we take Mary and Susie. It's only a dollar apiece, and they've got wild animals and all kinds of birds and reptiles. Even an elephant show. I've never seen an elephant up close." She paused for breath. "And children are only fifty cents."

Alfred laughed. "You win. We'll go to the circus."

Alf shook his head. "Could have warned you, Partner. When she gets a notion in her head, you don't stand a chance."

Matilda swatted him with the dish towel.

The last rails between Stockton and Sacramento were laid with great fan-fare, and Tom decided to join the celebrants Thursday, August 12th, on the first train to cross on the new tracks. He came to dinner the following Sunday and told Matilda and Alfred all about the experience.

"Train left Sacramento precisely at nine o'clock, right on time, and had to have been the largest train ever. Had 39 cars, and two locomotives. Three fire engine companies joined in the celebration, along with the Union and Cornet bands, and a band of military music. You never saw such goings on as when the train left Front Street and rounded the corner onto 'R' Street, headed out. At least three thousand people crowded on board, hanging from all of the doors and windows, even off the end. Everyone waving and cheering and flapping handkerchiefs."

"Must have been quite a sight," Alfred agreed.

"When we got to Galt, they had crowds of people waving, and the blacksmith had hauled his anvil out and was banging away on it. In Stockton, we were greeted by a sea of handkerchiefs and hats. I swear, everyone in town turned out to greet that train."

"When do they start regular service?" Alfred asked.

"End of August. Leaves Sacramento every day except Sunday at 6AM and gets into Stockton at 9:00. Imagine! All the way from Sacramento to Stockton in only three hours. And it comes back to Sacramento in the afternoon."

Matilda recalled her father's hatred of railroads, and her thought, so long ago as a girl in Illinois when the Illinois Central came through, that no matter how hard her father fought, progress would not be stopped. She thought of the changes that had taken place in such a short period of time, and wondered what the next twenty years would bring. She looked down at the sleeping baby girl in her arms and smiled. "Carrie, darling, you are going to grow up into a world of marvels."

After Tom left, Alfred commented dryly, "So it looks like the new town of Galt will be a success. I'm sure Harvey is cheering it on."

"Why on earth did they name it Galt? " Matilda queried. "I'd have thought Harvey would want to name it after himself. After all, it is his town."

"They tell me his buddy, John McFarland, asked him to name it after his hometown of Galt, up in Canada, and persuaded Crocker to go along with the idea."

"If he misses his hometown so much, why doesn't he go

back?"

Alfred shrugged his shoulders expressively. "Who knows? They say he got out to escape some bad memories, an old sweetheart or something." He grinned. "That would explain why he seems to be a confirmed bachelor."

Matilda shook her head. "So we abandon two perfectly good towns to build a new town to make Obed Harvey rich? And if McFarland wanted to get away from his memories, why name the new town after the one he left?"

He chuckled. "Sam says he probably left two jumps ahead of the law, but that's just Sam's theory. I've never heard anything but praise for the gentleman. He's got a fine place west of the new town, 1800 acres, grows a fine wheat crop. He put up that big two story house back in '59. "

"And Liberty?"

"Talk is they are going to move a lot of the buildings from there to the new town. I hear Calvin Briggs bought that hotel Fugitt had Sawyer build for him back in '59 and is having it moved to the street that faces the tracks."

"Chism Fugitt will be fit to be tied. Liberty is his town."

"Some are saying he wants to start another Liberty, call it New Liberty, just down the tracks from the Galt Station."

Matilda only shook her head.

Summer drifted into fall. The fire in the Gold Hill Mine finally burned itself out, after several months of belching smoke that could be seen for miles. Spain sent 20,000 more troops to Cuba in an attempt to quell the rebellion. The United States offered to pay Spain a fair price for the island.

Carrie mastered the art of rolling from her back to her stomach, and began her first attempts at crawling. Alfred watched her struggles and warned Matilda. "Bet she's going to be an early walker."

Matilda sighed. "I just wish a could use my Pottawatamie cradleboard. It's so much easier than having to use one arm to carry her."

He chuckled. "I'm afraid you would scandalize the neighborhood, my dear."

The first frost struck the first of November. Jake's joints had become so arthritic he could barely move. Matilda made up a bed for him beside the kitchen stove so he could be warmer.

Tom saw her one evening applying comfrey poultices to the old dog's swollen joints. He could barely move anymore, and she had to carry him outside twice a day to relieve himself.

"You know," Tom told his sister, as gently as he could, "You'd be doing the old fellow a favor if you would let one of us put him down." She made no reply, and he continued. "I know it would be hard for Alfred, but Sam or I could do it for you."

Tears filled Matilda's eyes and coursed down her cheeks as she stroked the bony head. "No," she whispered. "As long as he's not in pain, I want to keep him as long as I can."

The end came quietly two weeks later. Matilda had risen early, as usual, to stoke the fire before the children rose to prepare for school. She approached Jake's bed and knelt to pet him. He made a feeble effort to raise his head, then, with a little sigh, closed his eyes. He took one long, shuddering breath, then relaxed back against her hand.

Alfred found her there, stroking the silken head, silent tears streaming down her face.

Chapter 14

March to September, 1870

SPRING CAME EARLY in 1870. The fields burst alive with wild flowers. Mary and Elizabeth gathered handfuls of poppies and lupine, and put a bouquet on Jake's grave every morning. Little Jake happily trailed along as they performed their solemn ritual.

Matilda watched the touching scenario each day, glad the children had Little Jake, but also glad to see they remembered the original Jake. The pain of losing the faithful old dog had eased somewhat, but he had been so much a part of her life for so long she would always miss him. White Star still looked about for him each day. Matilda did not know how to explain to the old horse that Jake was gone. She stroked the golden muzzle, noted how much had faded to gray, and the realization that she would soon lose White Star as well twisted her heart.

Carrie had turned one on the first of March and, true to her father's predictions, had begun walking at the age of nine months. She was a tiny child, much smaller than the older three had been at her age, but seemed healthy and strong. A placid child, with hazel eyes like Alfred, and a sunny smile that also reminded Matilda of him.

The winter had been busy one, and mercifully mild. The Cosumnes River stayed within its banks. Alfred and Matilda paid $19.24 in property taxes on their two wagons,

16 cattle, two horses, and the hogs and chickens. A railroad station was built just west of Hicksville, with a dance hall, a store, and a saloon. John Brewster was named the first Postmaster for the new Post Office in the town of Galt.

The family gathered for Carrie's first birthday party. After the single candle had been blown out, with a little help from Mary, and the cake eaten, the men sat around to catch up on the winter's news and gossip.

Sam chuckled that his prediction about steamer prices had come to pass. "Down to $100 for First Class, $50 for steerage. Far cry from the $300 and $150 Aspinwall was getting when the only choice was the steamer or that miserable jolting dusty sleepless ride by stagecoach." Tom had gone as far as Carson City on the stage and had sworn off of long stage rides forever. "Bad enough to go from here to Sacramento City," he had declared.

Matilda, remembering the stage passengers she had seen on their trip out in '64, was inclined to agree.

Tom glanced from Matilda to her brother Alf and back and grinned. "I see Utah has joined Wyoming in giving women the vote. And they say Colorado will soon follow."

Alf muttered a comment about what was the world coming to, but Matilda only exclaimed, "It's about time! Doesn't the Constitution say 'all citizens'? How can they justify excluding fifty percent of them from voting!"

Tom, who always enjoyed the debates between Alf and Matilda, fanned the flames. "I read the Ladies for Women's Suffrage Association has held its first meeting in Sacramento, at the Pioneer Hall. Judge Foote's wife Rosa is one of the founders. Got a whole group of the leading ladies of Sacramento society. I understand David Bush's mother is the President. Lawyer Henry Starr's wife is another member of the group, and Doc Nixon's wife as well."

"I understand it's supposed to come up for a vote in the House of Representatives this month. We'll see if they go along with it." Tom shrugged. "I'll bet they defeat it. Not a one of them has backbone enough to vote for it."

Alfred, ever the peacemaker, interceded. "Did anyone else notice that John Sutter's son has been named the U.S. Consul to Acapulco?"

Spring ceded to summer. True to Tom's prediction, the House of Representatives dealt another blow to Women's Suffrage by defeating the bill to allow women the vote. Busy with canning the summer fruit and vegetables, tending her garden, and keeping up with an active Carrie, Matilda put the whole subject out of her mind.

In August, Sacramento initiated the first streetcar service in town. Alfred told Matilda the service planned to extend as far as the proposed site of the new County Hospital. "That should settle some of the complaints folks have been making about building it so far out of the city."

"We'll have to take a ride, to visit Annie. I am almost ashamed to confess she hasn't even seen Carrie yet. And little Annie is almost old enough to start school!"

"I hear her hat shop continues to do well, in spite of several competitors."

Matilda laughed. "Of course. Annie has enough determination to handle any amount of competition."

September saw the opening of the school term, and she watched Lewis stalk off proudly with his two sisters, Little Jake trailing along behind. Matilda hoped the new school teacher would tolerate the dog's presence, for he and Lew had become inseparable since the death of Jake. She watched them go with mixed feelings. Mary is almost eleven, she thought, and Elizabeth will be nine in December. It seemed such a short time ago they were babies. Mary already showed signs of blossoming womanhood. She sighed, suspecting Mary would be a handful.

September also brought a letter from her brother John's wife in Kansas. Mary Anne's letter was short, grief in every word.

"Scarlet fever has swept through our little community, and George, Nora, and Edwin took it. In spite of the best medical care, George died on August 9, and Nora two days later. George was just three, Nora eighteen months. Edwin seems to have recovered, but does not have his strength back. He's only two months old, but when he cries, he sounds so feeble, and his lips turn blue. The doctors say it may have affected his heart. We are all praying for his recovery.

"I do hope this letter finds all of you in good health. Give my love to Caroline when they arrive. I'm so glad they are going by train. The journey will be so much easier on them all, with baby Till just a few months old. They call her Till, as Matilda Lavina seems such a big name for such a little girl. I worry about Carrie. She says she feels fine, but I don't think she has recovered her strength after Till's birth, and she still has a persistant cough.

"I so fear she may have consumption and will die like Tommy and Temperance did. I mentioned it to Eli before they left, and he is worried as well, but said all he could do was pray for her. He also said she should probably not have any more babies. I know he was very disappointed this last baby was another girl. He had been so hoping for a son.

"John says he is glad Washington has decided we should not get involved in that horrid war between France and Prussia. Napoleon III is saying France will win because God is on their side. John says Bismarck says God is on the side of the army with the biggest batallions, and, in this case, the biggest batallions are Prussian. I just hope it is all over quickly. Didn't we just have enough war in this awful rebellion?

> *"Love to all,*
> *"Mary Anne*

As Matilda finished the letter and folded it to tuck away to read to Alfred that evening, Mary and Elizabeth came bursting into the house, fresh with the news of their day, both talking at once and, as usual, on different topics.

"Mama," Mary complained, "that George Douglass was pulling my hair again! He even told me he had dipped it in the inkwell. I just knew I would get ink all over my new pinafore." She scowled. "You have to get the teacher to move him to another seat."

Elizabeth added her comments, obviously not interested in Mary's grievance. "Teacher says I am the best reader and speller in the class, and she wants me to be in the Spelling Bee she's going to have for the Christmas Pageant."

Lewis trotted in behind the girls, Little Jake at his heels, both of them leaving muddy prints. "Mama," he wailed, "I didn't mean to get my good school shirt dirty, but Little Jake put his paws all over me." He displayed the front of his once white shirt, now covered with paw prints.

Matilda sighed. They had obviously been by where the horse trough overflowed. They always managed to walk through the one place on the way home from school where they could find mud in September.

Carrie chose that moment to awaken from her nap with a wailing, "Mama."

She shook her head in exasperation, then her frustration vanished as she remembered the sad news in her sister-in-law's letter. She laughed at herself. Instead of wondering how you are going to cope with all of this chaos, Matilda Randolph Baldwin Wheelock, you should be thanking God all four of yours are so healthy. She knew the schools were closed in Yuba City because of an epidemic of scarlet fever. Yuba City wasn't that far. Steamers came down river from there every day, and could easily bring in an illness.

Frightened at the thought of how quickly she could lose one or all of her precious children, she opened her arms and tried to gather all three at once. Little Jake wriggled in his efforts to be included in the embrace.

"Oh, my darlings, I love you all so much." She gave each one a kiss before releasing them with a final fond hug.

Mary's blue eyes met her mother's. "Does this mean you'll get the teacher to move that horrid George Douglass away from behind my desk?"

Chapter 15

September 1870 to August 1871

CAROLINE, ELI, AND the girls arrived the third week in September. When Matilda and Alfred, along with the rest of the family, met them at the Arno Station, Matilda was shocked to see how thin Caroline was. When she embraced her sister, she could feel the bones in Caroline's ribs. Remembering the robust, healthy sister she had left in Kansas only six years before, she could not keep from thinking how quickly her sister Temperance had faded.

She mustered a bright smile, with a leaden heart, "Now that we have you in California, we are going to fatten you up and dry out those lungs."

Caroline responded with a faint smile. "All I want to do now is find a bed and lie down. I feel like I could sleep for a week. Thank goodness for Becky and Sally. If they hadn't taken care of the little girls, I don't think I could have made it."

Sam enveloped her in a bear hug. "I'm taking you home with me. And if you want to sleep for a week, you can sleep for a week. Buggy's right over here. All aboard!"

True to her brother John's predictions, France fared poorly in her war with Prussia. By spring of 1871, Paris had capitulated to Bismarck's forces, and starvation was reported rife throughout the city.

Alfred nodded grimly at the news. "John was right. God is on the side of the army with the biggest battalions. Maybe Napoleon should have checked out the size of Bismarck's forces before he jumped into such a war."

"I thought Bismarck captured Napoleon at the battle of Sedan, last September," Matilda exclaimed. "Shouldn't that have ended the war?"

"You'd have thought so, but I guess a bunch of people in Paris ousted him as Emperor and declared themselves a Republic. So the war went on."

Matilda only shook her head at such foolishness.

Closer to home, the new County Hospital had opened in Sacramento in February to great fanfare, including speeches from some of the leading politicians. All of the indigent patients were moved out to the modern facility, and even given new clothing to mark the event. Fortunately, the streetcar service had proven so efficient it had quelled all complaints about the distance of the hospital from the city proper.

Caroline did seem to regain some of her strength, and even Eli felt there was possibly some hope for her recovery. Only Becky and Sally remained pessimistic.

"If we'd come here two years ago, when she first started getting sick," Becky opined, "we might have been in time. Now?" She just shook her head.

Spring of 1871 also found Matilda pregnant again.

"This will be our son," she told Alfred confidently, thrilled at the prospect of having a boy for Alfred at last. She did not tell him the nausea was so much worse than with the others, sure it would pass in time, and knowing he would worry.

He grinned. "I won't tell you to take care of yourself. With four children to run after, there's not a chance." He took her in his arms and kissed her soundly. "Maybe some day we'll be rich enough to hire someone to help you. Like the McCauleys. I hear that daughter of theirs, Alice, the one that caused all the ruckus in San Francisco by singing *Dixie,* married an Italian Count last month, name of Gulio Valensin, or some such outlandish name. From what the fellows say, he's the son of a wealthy banker named Moise Valensin."

"Sounds like just the son-in-law for John McCauley. Lots of money. Are they going to stay in Italy, or are they going to come over here to live?"

Alfred shrugged. "No one seems to know for sure. I guess she's having a great time there with all the high society balls and such. She sure won't find that kind of life style around here."

Matilda laughed. "Not likely. She will find the fancy balls around here pretty mild after Italy."

"Old man McCauley is bringing his wife and son George back to stay. I hear they have built a right nice place down on their Forest Lake property, just south of Galt. Been buying out all the folks around him."

"Maybe they will bring a touch of culture to Galt. Goodness knows it could use a little." Matilda rose.

Alfred grinned. "Boy just turned 18, but I hear old man McCauley refers to him as 'an educated fool'. Doesn't sound like he thinks too highly of his only son."

"Probably because the poor young man hasn't learned how to swindle his family out of property yet. I'm sure if he listens his father will teach him. Call the children. Supper's ready."

Shortly after they received the news of Alice McCauley's marriage, Matilda made her weekly visit to her brother

Sam's to visit Caroline. Since her sister was now bed-ridden, and really had no friends in California, she looked forward to family visits. In the back of Matilda's mind, the knowledge that Caroline was dying refused to leave her completely.

Caroline greeted her with a bright smile, and they talked about the children as well as the neighborhood gossip, including the Valensin-McCauley nuptials. Then she confessed she had some bad news to impart.

"I received a letter from John and Eli's grandmother. She says that Tommy's son John died on February 5, at the age of 24. Here, read it." She handed the letter to Matilda who scanned the page and read:

> *"Poor boy spent two years in a Confederate prison camp, and never regained his health. Guess the conditions and food in the camp were real bad. He moved to San Antonio after the War, and that's where he died. Eli had his brother's body taken back to Randolph's Grove, and buried in the Stewart Cemetery. He felt John would want to be buried with his parents."*

Matilda remembered the little boy who had stood so bravely fighting the tears at his mother's funeral, holding his brother Eli's hand, trying to be strong enough for both of them. Poor Susan had died so young, leaving John and Eli just seven and five years old. Susan's family had taken the boys to raise, so Matilda never really knew them. But it saddened her to hear he died so young.

That evening, she reported the news to Alfred. "That makes three of our family lost to that dreadful conflict," she murmured. "My sister Temperance's widower, poor Josh Tovrea, died from a wound he got in '62 fighting for the Union Army, their son Henry died in '64 in Marietta and now John Evans is a casualty as well. I guess we should be glad that Josh's brother John recovered from the wound he got at Shiloh"

He nodded. "Yes, that tragedy was repeated far too many times. This was a war which should never have happened. And we certainly hope nothing like it ever happens again."

"Caroline showed me the letter today. She seemed in good spirits. I know she is glad to be here with the family. She doesn't mention her health at all, but it concerns me." At the smell of burning from the kitchen, she jumped to her feet. "My bread! I forgot about my bread."

Dizzy at the sudden movement, she swayed for a moment and Alfred took her arms to steady her, concern in his eyes. "Are you all right?"

She shook off the giddy feeling, not wanting him to worry, and anxious to save the bread. "Of course. Just lost my balance for a moment."

Alfred chuckled softly as she dashed from the room.

June merged into July, bringing the worst heat Matilda had ever seen. Day after day the temperature hovered between 95 and 100 degrees even in the shade. Her feet swelled so badly she could barely stay on her feet to prepare meals and care for the children. Even good-natured little Carrie seemed affected.

Alfred came in from the fields mopping his overheated forehead and poured himself a cool glass of water from the bottle in the much appreciated ice box. He sighed with satisfaction as he quenched his thirst and grinned at Matilda. "Drought is so bad, they tell me the river above Sacramento is so low they can't take any barges up. Only going to get worse, too, because there won't be any rain until at least October."

Matilda sighed. They retreated to the porch and the relative coolness from the slight breeze from the delta. Matilda sank into a chair, glad to be off of her aching feet.

"Also hear Obed Harvey and his wife have a little girl. Born July 3. Named her Genevieve." He peered at Matilda's face, concern showing in his eyes. "Your feet are swelling again, aren't they? Are you taking the Chamomile tea your mother recommended? "

Matilda attempted to smile, but it was a dismal failure. "The tea does seem to help a little, but this heat is just wearing me down. I'm sure as soon as the hot spell breaks, I'll feel better. The heat waves usually only last a few days. I've never had any trouble with babies before." To take his mind off his concern for her, she smiled and said, "I was reading an advertisement from a company in New York. They say they have a magnificent collection of photo lantern slides from Yosemite. I've heard so much about Yosemite it would be fun to see the pictures."

He grinned and hugged her. "Wouldn't you rather go there and see it for yourself?"

"Oh! Could we?"

"Well, not until you have this baby and get well, but yes, there are now regular excursions to see the wonders. There is even talk of preserving it, so no one will build in it and cut down the trees."

In August, she received another letter from Sarah Williams, as full of life and vigor as ever. Sarah's lovely face rose in her vision as she read her words.

"*My shop continues to thrive. All of the high society ladies here in St. Louis patronize us. I have hired three more girls as seamstresses, and my mother is happier than ever with three more to fuss over. Two of the girls came from Sweden, and don't speak very much English. Watching them trying to communicate is so funny sometimes I have to leave the room to keep from laughing out loud.*

"*I have expanded, and now have three more rooms in the back to give the girls a place to sleep. Fortunately Mother loves to cook, and keeps them all fed. One of the Swedish girls is trying to teach her some Swedish recipes, but I don't think they'll ever get her to accept* ludefisk. *It smells too much like rotten fish. But they have taught her to make what they call* lefsa, *a pancake made from potatoes, which is very tasty.*

"*The papers have been reporting the results of a study by a German scientist, a Dr. Hertzmuller, who says that unmarried ladies live ten years longer than married ones, which has convinced Mother, (who, I must admit, is throughly enjoying her widowhood), and me that we are wise to remain single.*

"*He also states that green tarletan dresses contain enough arsenic to kill a man. I sure hope it doesn't rub off on the seamstresses, for green tarletan is very much in vogue this season. Every lady in town has ordered at least one dress made from it. "But here is my big news, Susan Anthony and Laura DeForce Gordon are scheduled to speak at a suffragette meeting at the Congregational Church in Sacramento this December, and I am coming with them! The ladies of the Sacramento Women's*

Suffrage Society have invited us. It will give us a chance to see each other again.. It has been far too long.

"Poor Miss Anthony. She started themovement at the insistance of a number of wealthy women, and got herself into debt for over ten thousand dollars. Only two of all of those women gave her any money. So now, since California groups pay her two thousand dollars for each speaking appearance, she is going to spend more time out there. She was in San Francisco in January, and was so well received she accepted the invitation from the Sacramento ladies to return to California in December.

"Of course, some agree with General Grant, that the Sixteenth Amendment is not necessary, because the Fifteenth Amendment already gives women the right to vote, since it says 'all citizens', and no one questions that women are citizens.

"Mrs. DeForce Gordon is a lawyer, and was actually admitted to the Bar, a real bastion of male superiority. When she defends a case, hundreds of spectators try to crowd into the courtroom just to see her in action. From what I understand, she is quite talented, and very successful.

"Like Dr. Mary Walker. She has a flourishing medical practice, but she is constantly being harrassed. Three men tried to fool her, and came into her office feigning illness, wanting her to cure them. She said she could, but insisted on her five dollar fee first. They stared at each other for a while, then fled, one by one. When the last man got *up and ran, she called after him 'It'll take smarter men than you three to fool me!' The friend who reported this is still laughing over it.*

"*I hope this letter finds you and your entire brood in good health. Your Mary sounds like me when I was growing up, and I am looking forward to meeting her. Your Alfred seems a charming young man. Maybe if I meet someone like him I may change my mind about remaining a spinster. But from my observations, men like him are rare.*

Love to all,
Sarah

Matilda chuckled as she finished reading the letter to Alfred and looked up to find him blushing.

"My, what did you tell her about me?"

She smiled. "Only that you were the kindest, most thoughtful, most intelligent and most wonderful man in the world."

He grinned as he swept her into his arms. "I hope she is not too disappointed when she actually meets me." He kissed Matilda and released her. "Do you suppose," he mused, "that Sarah will recruit our Mary as a Sufraggette?"

Matilda laughed. "Can't you imagine what Alf would have to say if she did?"

Chapter 16

August to October, 1871

THE HEAT CONTINUED through August. Matilda's brother Sam came by at dinner time with a letter from their sister-in-law in Kansas. Alfred, of course, invited him to stay to share the meal with them. Matilda teased Sam as she shooed him to the back porch to wash up. "Thank you for bringing the letter. You always seem to arrive just as we are sitting down to eat. Alfred, love, please call the children in. Mary and Elizabeth are in the barn. Lew went over to play with Henry Bandeen, but he is supposed to be home for dinner." She tried to ignore rumors she heard that all was not well in the Bandeen household.

Sam laughed. "He spends so much time with Billy's boy he's going to start talking with a Scottish accent."

"I hope not, but Henry is only a year older than Lew, and it's good for him to have a friend of his own age. Mary," Matilda sighed, as the two girls both tried to wash up at the same time, "don't jostle your sister. There is plenty of room for both of you at the basin." A loud wailing reached her ears, and she ran around to the front of the house to find Lewis carrying Little Jake, sobbing and stumbling as he struggled along under the heavy load, for the dog had almost reached his full growth.

Frightened, she ran to Lewis and relieved him of his burden. Little Jake, obviously uninjured, much to her relief, happily tried to lick her face and she grimaced, closing her eyes against his eager ministrations.

Lewis threw himself at her and buried his face in her apron, continuing to sob. Her soothing words had no effect and he continued to wail. "For heaven's sake, stop your blubbering and tell me what has happened," she finally exclaimed in exasperation.

Alfred appeared at her side and gathered the boy into his arms, calming him as he carried him to the back porch where he placed him gently on his feet and washed his tear-streaked face.

Matilda handed the puppy over to Mary and knelt by the still weeping Lewis. "Sweeheart," she urged softly, "we can't help you if you don't tell us what's wrong. Take a deep breath."

It took several moments, but the racking sobs finally ceased, and the story came out in bits and pieces. "Henry says - - , Henry says - -." Sobs threatened to take over again, but the boy gulped several times and continued. "Henry says," the words came in a rush, "that someone is poisoning all the dogs in the County, and that - - that - -" His voice broke. He glanced up at this mother and took another deep breath. "That Little Jake is going to die too!" The wails broke out anew.

Behind her, Matilda heard Sam chuckle. "Boy got it part right. There is a dog poisoner at work in Sacramento. Has poisoned three or four dogs, and there is a reward of $100 in gold out for anyone who catches him. Bandeen boy must have heard that and decided the man is out to kill every dog in the County."

Matilda sighed and shook her head. "Assure him we will take care of Jake and get him calmed down. My biscuits will be as hard as bricks!"

126

When all settled down and everyone was busy eating stew and biscuits, Matilda took a few moments to open the letter from Mary Anne, almost forgotten in the excitement. In it Mary Anne reported the death of little Edwin on August 13.

> *"His heart never recovered from the scarlet fever. He just grew weaker and weaker until his lips were blue all the time, and he finally just stopped breathing. Poor little mite was only fourteen months old. But I do have some good news. We will have another baby next January.*
>
> *"Do hope this letter finds you and all of your family in good health. Do take care of yourself. You never had dropsy before with your children. Maybe Alfred is right, this should be your last one.*
>
> *"A tornado went through last week and took a neighbor's barn and shattered it into pieces.*
>
> *"John was re-elected circuit judge, but I think he is beginning to tire of Kansas weather. He has been talking about following the rest of the family out to California, so maybe we will be seeing you before too long.*
>
> *"Do hope the California weather is helping Carrie regain her health. She tells me Eli has taken some time off from the church to be able to stay with her. It's about time, after he hauled her all over Kansas going from church to church. That was as hard on her health as the Kansas weather.*

Matilda folded up the letter and announced, "Mary Anne and John are expecting another baby in January. And John is thinking of maybe joining us in California. I guess watching a neighbor's barn smashed by a tornado convinced him." She said nothing about Edwin's death. She would tell Alfred and Sam after the children left, not knowing how they would take the news. Fortunately, they had never met their small cousin, born after the family left Kansas for California.

Sam filled his plate for the third time with a happy sigh. "You sure are a good cook, little sister. Bachelor like me doesn't eat this good very often."

Matilda laughed. "Only every time you can find an excuse to come here or to Polly's at dinner time. Maybe you should get married. I'm sure there are plenty of candidates."

"Sally, has taken over my whole house, so I have to admit I do eat better at home now." Sam's eyes glistened at the slab of apple pie Matilda set in front of him. "Tease her, tell her she's gonna be an old maid, but that there are plenty of eligible males out here. However, she says she never going to get married."

"She's only about fourteen. She'll probably change her mind when one of the handsome neighbor boys comes courting. And don't get too comfortable. If Caroline does get well enough, Eli may take another church and they'll be gone."

"Sally says even if he does, she and Becky are going to stay with me." He grinned. "Meanwhile, until Sally learns to make as good an apple pie as yours, I'll make my rounds. Read in the paper they want to save Sutter's Fort from being demolished to extend 'M' Street. Some say it should be saved because of its historical significance. Others say they want to make it into a kind of Woodward Gardens like the one in San Francisco. Gardens, swimming baths, dancing hall, skating rink, maybe even a shooting gallery, with lots of space for picnics. Got a group together that's trying to raise the money they'll need to do it."

"That would be wonderful. Woodward Gardens was very impressive." She glanced at Alfred, who nodded and agreed. She looked at Sam, a glint in her eye. She could tell Sam recognized the look at once.

"You want something, little sister." It was a statement, not a question, which confirmed to Matilda that he had interpreted the look correctly.

She laughed at his perspicacity. He knew her so well! She and Alfred had discussed the State Fair, and agreed Matilda should make no attempt to go, not as swollen as her feet were, and as easily as she became fatigued. They had decided to approach Sam.

"Sam, Alfred and I will be unable to take the children to the State Fair this year, but they'll be so disappointed if they can't go. Will and Polly can't go either, since Polly's next baby is due soon as well."

"And you want me to take them." Sam grinned.

Mary's eyes grew round. "Oh, Mama, we have to go to the State Fair! Please, Uncle Sam, please take us." The two girls ran around the table and embraced him, begging.

Finally he threw up his hands. "You're ganging up on me, but you win. And I suppose Polly will expect me to take her brood as well!"

Samuel Alfred Wheelock joined the family at dawn on the morning of October 4, 1871. The birth had been a hard one. When Matilda fainted, Alfred had sent Mary rushing to Billy Bandeen's to ask him to fetch Dr. Nester out from Sacramento. Fortunately, the doctor was at home and came immediately.

By the time he arrived, Matilda had regained consciousness, but had to remain flat on the bed or dizziness threatened to overcome her again.

When Dr. Nester placed the tiny blond bundle in her arms, she gave him a tired smile. "Thank you so much for being here. My other births were so easy I never thought of having a problem."

He patted her hand. "I'm just glad I was able to help. The dropsy is why you had so much difficulty. Experience has shown me that it frequently gets worse with subsequent pregnancies. You and Alfred have a fine boy to go with your lovely little girl. I strongly recommend you have no more children. Another pregnancy might cost you your life." He smiled down on her. "And we wouldn't want that."

"You're right, we wouldn't." She nodded. "Alfred says the same thing." She managed a little laugh, in spite of her fatigue. "He also says I have my hands full with five." Thinking of some of Mary's antics, and how active they all were, she added, "And I am inclined to agree with him!"

Betsy Ann came from Alf's to help Matilda until she could get her strength back, full of advice as usual, and armed with various remedies guaranteed to put Matilda back on her feet in no time at all. Fortunately, Sam was a quiet, non-demanding baby, similar to Carrie. Not at all like Mary and Lewis had been, Matilda recalled with a chuckle.

Betsy Ann, as always, was full of gossip. "They say that Brigham Young just got in a shipment of ten cases of silk dresses and cashmere sweaters for his thirty wives. Thirty wives! Can you believe that? I swear, I'll never understand how the man gets the notion that he should have so many wives. What about the young men who can't find a wife because the Elders have taken all the women? Then he has the nerve to say he does it because it's his duty, and that the expense of keeping up all of these wives is his penance."

She snorted in derision. "Cashmere sweaters and silk dresses indeed!"

Matilda, who had never owned either of those luxuries in her life, and knew very well she had no prospects of ever owning one of them, had to laugh at her mother's indignation. "Well, I'm sure silk dresses and cashmere sweaters for that many wives don't come cheap."

"There's even talk of putting Young on trial because folks are saying he ordered a murder some years back."

Matilda remembered Sinclair telling her about Eph Hanks and the "Destroying Angels" when they passed through Salt Lake City. "Oh, but that was years ago. Surely no one is going to try and drag that up."

Betsy Ann shrugged expressively. "Guess some of the man's folks figure it's worth a try. Young says he welcomes a trial, and is sure he will be exonerated."

"Since the majority of the jurors will probably be his followers, he's probably right."

Betsy Ann was off on another topic. "Wasn't that fire in Chicago a terrible thing? Chicago not that far from Bloomington. Bet Sarah will have something to say about it. Lots of folks have been holding benefits to send money back to help them out. Preacher last Sunday took up a collection." She chuckled. "He said if folks put buttons in the plate, would they be careful not to break off the eye, 'cause then they couldn't be used. And would you believe that even with him sayin' that, they still wound up with five buttons in the plate?"

Matilda could not keep from laughing. "Maybe the folks figured people in Chicago would need buttons!"

Sam stirred in his little bed, and Betsy Ann scooped him up with a practiced hand, deftly changed his diaper, and handed him to Matilda to feed. "And did you hear about all those folks that took their money out of the Sacramento Saving Bank? Rumor was the Bank lost money in the fire, and was liable to go broke. All over the papers, o' course, so now every thief and his brother knows they've got the money stowed away at the house. Dang fools. Even the papers are warning 'em to watch for thieves."

While Matilda digested this bit of information, Betsy Ann rambled on. "And poor Governor Bigler is still hangin' on. They say he's close to death this time, but I remember they said the same thing last August when the ascites was so bad that they took three gallons of fluid out of him.." Betsy Ann shook her head. "And I'll bet not a one of these fancy doctors has sense enough to give him Chamomile tea."

Her sister Sarah's letter came a week later, and, true to Betsy Ann's prediction, was full of news of the fire. Matilda read it to Alfred that evening after supper.

> "The fire in Chicago was terrible. It burned for days. We could see the flames in the sky from here in Bloomington. So many people lost everything, and were fortunate to escape with their lives. Some say it started in a barn, and maybe a cow kicked over a lantern, but Albert says that is ridiculous. The fire started past midnight, and no one would have been milking at that time. And no one is going to leave a lighted lantern for the cow. He says it was probably a tramp who bedded down for the night in the barn and set the fire to heat some coffee.
>
> "Many folks are holding benefits all over the States to raise money to help the poor souls. They even say folks as far away as California have been raising money."

Alfred interrupted with a chuckle. "Sacramento has raised a fair sum, but Wes's folks down Stockton way say they planned a big benefit there and nobody came."

"I guess not many in Stockton care to send their hard-earned money all the way to Chicago," Matilda remarked dryly, and returned to Sarah's letter.

> *"Four ladies from the Congregational Church went to this old farmer outside of Bloomington and asked for a donation. He grumbled and said he didn't believe a word, that it was all a Republican plot to get money out of folks, and that the fire never happened, it was all a hoax.*
>
> *"When they persisted, he looked at these finely dressed ladies slyly and told them if they really wanted something, they could dig up his field of potatoes and give them to all of those supposedly starving folks. Much to his surprise, the ladies came back the next day with a wagon and spades and proceeded to dig up every last one of his potatoes. So the joke was on him."*

Alfred grinned. "At least they could probably use the potatoes more than the buttons that wound up in the donation plate."

Chapter 17

December 1871

"LISTEN, I CAN hear it!" Matilda shivered in the damp air and peered down the tracks, trying to discern the approaching train through the dense fog.

"He'll be moving slow, since he can't see more than a few feet in front of him, this blasted fog is so thick." Alfred put his arm around her. "Are you sure you're not getting chilled? I'm so relieved you seem to have recovered your usual bloom of health after little Sammy's birth, but we don't want to take any chances."

These past two months Matilda had felt better and better every day. She smiled at Alfred. "Mother swears my recovery is due to the comfrey and raspberry teas, but Dr. Nester says he has observed mothers usually recover quickly from the dropsy once the baby is born."

She and Alfred had also agreed to take his advice. No more babies. But she continued to follow her mother's recommendations, more to keep the peace than in any real faith in the remedies. At least the raspberry tea was pretty tasty, and with enough sugar she managed to swallow the comfrey tea.

"I'm just glad Lizzie was born so Polly has milk to feed our little Sammy while we go to Sacramento with Sarah tomorrow. I can hardly wait to hear Miss Anthony. I understand she is a very good speaker." Matilda thanked her lucky stars Sam was such a docile baby that Polly readily agreed to keep him.

Another blast from the train's whistle drowned Alfred's response and caught her attention. She ran to the edge of the platform. The train's light now shone through the fog. Excited at the prospect of seeing Sarah again after so long, she tried to remember how much time had passed. Good heavens, it had been over twenty years.

Matilda could not stand still. She strode up and down the uneven planks, peering at the light as the train materialized through the mist.

Sarah planned to spend the afternoon with Matilda, then they would take the train to Sacramento on the morrow. Alfred would accompany them, for, as he said, he might just as well since it still had not rained, and the ground was too hard to plant. Miss Anthony and Mrs. DeForce Gordon were scheduled to speak in the afternoon and again in the evening. Matilda planned to return home after the afternoon meeting. She did not wish to be away from the children overnight. Her mother had cautioned her that if she was away from Sam for very long, her milk would dry up, in spite of the dill tea Betsy Ann insisted she drink to keep up her milk supply. "Then what would the little mite eat?" she had prophesied grimly.

Matilda had grumbled to Alfred, out of her mother's hearing, that if she had been a cucumber, she had enough dill in her to become a pickle.

As the train huffed and chuffed to a halt with a blast of steam and screech of brakes, Matilda wondered if she would recognize Sarah. After all, they had not seen each other since the summer they were fourteen, when Matilda made that fateful visit to the ferry crossing to visit Sarah, and they made their clandestine trip to the slave auction.

At the memory of that long ago adventure, the vision of the little boy she had given the piece of rock candy rose in her mind, and she wished she could know whatever became of him. He would be a grown man now. She hoped freedom had brought him happiness, and that he had been able to find his mother again.

She shook her head to vanquish the specters of the past, thankful that dreadful period was behind them, when her eyes fell on a tall, sophisticated young woman in a striking green dress alighting from the steps onto the platform.

Matilda was suddenly conscious of her plain calico dress and her own lack of the sophistication Sarah so plainly possessed. Would Sarah be disappointed in her?

If she was, she showed no sign of it. With a cry of "'Tilda! 'Tilda, my love, it has been ages," Sarah flew across the platform and smothered Matilda in a bear hug. She kissed her on the cheek, then held her at arm's length and looked her up and down.

"Well," she finally declared, "married life must agree with you. And after how many children? Five? No, six, if I recall. I declare, you look just the same as when I last saw you."

Matilda laughed. "Same old Sarah. I'm afraid I am a little thicker in the middle. But you look absolutely beautiful. Is that one of those green tarlatan dresses Dr. Hertzmuller said contain enough arsenic to kill a man?"

Sarah's hearty laugh boomed across the platform as Alfrd accepted the carpet bag and two bandboxes the conductor handed down. Conversation ceased while the train started up in a cloud of steam and rumbled down the tracks as it slowly gathered speed. After the noise and dust settled, Sarah offered her hand to Alfred. "You must be the wonderful young man who has made Matilda so happy. I declare, she positively glows."

With Matilda and Sarah arm in arm, Alfred tagging along behind with the luggage, the little party moved to the buggy where Big Ben waited patiently. Sarah stroked the big horse's soft neck while Alfred stowed the bags, then accepted his assistance to climb up on the seat beside Matilda. "And White Star? Do you still have the famous White Star I have heard so much about? And I can hardly wait to meet Mary. From what you have written, she must be an interesting young lady."

"White Star spends most of her time lying in the sun or secure in the barn. Her joints are getting painful, and no one rides her any more." Matilda's heart gave a twist as she realized White Star would not be with her much longer, but she brushed the thought aside. "Mother is at home with the children. They are all anxious to meet you. Much to my brother Alf's dismay, Mary has announced she is going to be just like you."

Sarah's contagious laughter rang out again as the buggy started down the bumpy track and she grasped the arm rest to steady herself against the swaying motion. "Is Alf as anti-suffragette as ever? I have so enjoyed your letters describing your discussions with him."

"Oh, yes, worse if anything. He says voting is against female nature, and women will get more like men if they vote, and it will even steal men's masculinity from them and men will get more like women. I can't quite follow his logic, but I guess he's not the only one to think like that."

Alfred grinned, but made no attempt to join in the discussion as Sarah sighed, "Oh, yes, that's one of the things we have to battle all the time. Just wait until you meet Miss Anthony. She is a real bundle of energy. And such enthusiasm for the Cause.

"Did you meet Emperor Norton when you went to San Francisco on your honeymoon?" Sarah asked. "He has been all over the Eastern papers recently. He announced he was going to Washington to attend the reception for the Russian Grand Duke Alexis. He said he fears the Russian would be offended if he did not extend his hospitality."

Matilda laughed. "No, we decided to spend our time at Woodward's Gardens instead, but from all I have read and learned since, I wish we had taken advantage of our chance to meet him. We were very close to where he was holding court. Charlie, our driver, offered to take us to hear him."

They reminisced over the years that had passed since their last meeting.

"Weldon is married now. Married a young lady just seventeen years old. Met her on a trip back to Kansas. Had begun to think he was a confirmed bachelor like Alf and Sam."

"Little Weldon! I haven't seen him since he was six years old. What an adorable little boy he was. And always so solemn." Sarah's green eyes sparkled, set off by the emerald green in her dress. The dress may be full of arsenic, Matilda thought, but it certainly brings out the color in those magnificent eyes. The sleek black hair showed no hint of gray, as rich and thick as Matilda remembered it. The black hair was such a contrast to the almost porcelain skin and those striking eyes. Matilda again felt the same pang of jealously she had felt when she first saw Sarah, that long ago day in Illinois when Sarah and her family had arrived in Randolph's Grove.

Their arrival at the Wheelock home twenty minutes later created a small sensation. The two girls came running out, Lewis at their heels, followed by Betsy Ann, Alf, and Sam.

"Land sakes, child," Betsy Ann murmured as Alfred helped Sarah and Matilda down from the buggy. "You've really grown up into quite the young lady!" Sam and Alf stood behind their mother, both, Matilda thought, tongue-tied by the sight of Sarah's beauty. They just gaped and finally managed to shake hands with a mumbled "Howdy."

Matilda suppressed the urge to giggle at their obvious response. *I wonder if Alf is going to tell her what he thinks of Suffragettes now that he has actually seen Sarah. I'm sure he never expected her to be so lovely, from all people have been telling him about how strange women who were Suffragettes became. Almost,* she thought, *like he expected her to have three legs and a tail.*

Mary took one of Sarah's hands, Elizabeth the other, and they led her into the house. "You have to see the tea sets our papa gave us," Mary said.

"And the dolls with real china heads," Elizabeth piped up. "And our new baby Sammy, he's only two months old. And our sister Carrie. She was two last March. We had a real party for her, with two candles on the cake." She scowled at her sister. "But Mary blew out the candles. She didn't let Carrie do it."

"Then we will take you to the barn and you can meet White Star." Mary ignored her sister's comments. "She's getting old, so no one rides her any more. Her knees are bad, and she might fall with us," the child opined with all of the wisdom of her twelve years.

"And then we're going to have my birthday cake tonight after supper. I will be ten tomorrow, but Mama says since she and Papa are going to Sacramento with you, we have to have my birthday celebration today." Elizabeth scowled. "But Papa says I can't have my present until tomorrow. He's got it hidden high up in their bedroom. He says I have to wait until I am really ten, because the present is only for ten year old girls." She tugged on Sarah's hand. "What do you suppose it could be?"

"And you are going to sleep in our bed, and we get to sleep on the floor in Mama's and Papa's room, just like Mama says it was when we came out from Kansas in the wagon." Mary stuck her tongue out at her sister. "You don't remember that, 'cause you were just a baby."

Elizabeth ignored her sister, and pulled Sarah out of the house, heading for the barn. "Come on. You have to meet White Star." Lewis trotted along behind them.

When Sarah had completed the tour with the children and returned to the house, she sank into a chair and accepted the glass of lemonade Matilda offered and laughed and laughed. "'Tilda darling, I don't know how you do it. I am worn out after twenty minutes. I never knew children could ask so many questions."

"If you think the girls are bad, just wait until Sam and Alf get back from doing the chores. They want to know all about Miss Anthony."

After supper, Alfred built up the fire in the little heating stove, for the damp night air sent a chill though the room. Elizabeth blew out the candles on her birthday cake, and everyone pronounced it delicious. After the last crumb disappeared, Matilda tucked in the little ones and sent the older girls to bed so the adults could talk. She suspected both Elizabeth and Mary would have their ear to the door, for they had heard so much about Susan B. Anthony that they were as curious as Sam and Alf.

"You must know Miss Anthony well." Matilda opened the conversation as she served coffee to the gathered party, and passed around a plate of her sugar cookies. The ones the Pottawatamies liked so well, she thought with a smile, remembering the chief who always came to the door in Kansas begging for a 'coo-kee'.

"I met her in 1869, when she and Elizabeth Cady Stanton formed the National Woman Suffrage Association. They condemned the Fourteenth and Fifteenth Amendments as blatant injustice, because they allowed only men to vote, specifically saying 'male' citizens." She paused. Her audience did not move. "But I was more interested in their stand advocating easier divorce and calling for an end to discrimination in employment and pay. I couldn't help but think if my poor mother had been able to divorce that worthless man I unfortunately had to call my father her life would have been much easier. But with the difficulty women had getting work, she was afraid she would not have been able to take care of me and my brothers."

"I heard Miss Anthony was active in the anti-slavery movement as well," Sam interjected.

"Yes, she participated in the Underground Railroad." Matilda recalled some of her father's comments about abolitionists with a smothered smile. "In fact, when they held their first meeting, back in 1848, Frederick Douglass was the only man who attended their convention that had the courage to come out for Suffrage." She chuckled softly. "He said since the ladies were so interested in the anti-slavery movement, and fought so hard for him and his fellow negroes, the least he could do was support them in their fight to get the vote. He was made an honorary member of the society, and has been an honored guest at every meeting he has been able to attend ever since. He has spoken on a number of gatherings."

Sarah's hearty laugh rang out. "Miss Anthony was a rebel at an early age. She always had an independent spirit. When a child, she asked her teacher why he taught long division only to the boys. He told her that all girls needed to know was how to count the egg money and read the Bible. She refused to accept that reasoning, and made sure her seat was close enough to the group of boys that she learned long division as well."

Matilda laughed. "I'll have to tell that story to Mary. Maybe it will inspire her to take more interest in learning long division."

"It's worth a try," Alfred chuckled, "but I suspect it will take more than that to get our Mary interested in learning her sums."

A faint smothered snicker that had to have come from Elizabeth told Matilda the two girls listened. Scuffling sounds also told her Mary had responded. She smiled to herself. Time to put an end to the conversation. She rose to her feet with a yawn,

"I'm sure Sarah is tired. She's had a long day. Alf," she turned to her brother, "We will be catching the first train tomorrow. We'll leave Ben and the buggy at the station Can you come and take him to your place for the day? We will be returning on the evening train. It leaves Sacramento at 6:45, so we should be at Arno Station by a little after seven." They had discussed this, and decided that since there would be a full moon, returning after sunset would be safe enough, so they would not have to leave the children overnight.

"Alfred going with you to be sure Sarah here doesn't turn you into a raging suffragette?" Alf grinned, dodged the sofa pillow she threw at him, and ducked out the door. He stuck his head back around the corner and said, "See you tomorrow. It'll be foggy in the morning, so start early. Nice to see you again, Sarah. Sleep tight."

Alf's prediction for fog proved correct. When Matilda looked out the next morning, she could not see as far as the road. The tops of the trees were obscured by the mist, and she shivered as she stoked the fire. She felt a momentary qualm at the thought of taking little Sammy out in such damp, cold weather, but Polly could not bring all of her brood to Matilda's house, so she had to take him over there. Betsy Ann would stay with the older children, but only Polly could feed Sam. She brushed aside her fears and busied herself preparing breakfast.

The smell of sizzling bacon and brewing coffee soon brought the others gathering around. Matilda held little Carrie on one hip while she turned the bacon with her other hand. Sarah stood back and watched the hustle and bustle as everyone prepared for the day. She finally shook her head and exclaimed, "And people have the nerve to say women are too nervous and too easily fatigued for the vote! They obviously have no idea what women go through every day. And all of that nonsense about women's physical weakness. 'Natural fragility!' What nonsense."

Matilda laughed. "I hear some say women could vote more than once because we can hide the ballots in our voluminous sleeves." She held up her free arm. "Do you see a sleeve I could hide a ballot in?"

Betsy Ann took Carrie and started feeding her from the bowl of porridge Matilda set on the table. Alfred took his seat as Sarah and Matilda placed the bacon, eggs, and biscuits, along with a pot of honey, on the table. Sarah poured the coffee.

Alfred watched the two women with a twinkle in his eye. "Did you know one writer even believes allowing women to vote will jeopardize the nation's security?" He grinned.

"Could even lead to war, he says."

"That's not the worst," Sarah exclaimed, handing him a cup of the steaming coffee. "Others say that those of us in the women's movement suffer from mental disorder, that all women are prone to hysteria, that many of us in the movement are hysterics, and are mentally ill. And would you believe it was a doctor who said that? Wait until you listen to Miss Anthony. If there is a saner person in this world, I would like to meet her."

"I don't wish to intercede in the discussion," Alfred said mildly, rising from his seat and draining the last of his coffee from his cup, "but if we are going to get Sammy to Polly's place and catch our train, we had better get started."

They arrived at the platform, Matilda a little breathless from hurrying, a good ten minutes before the train pulled up. To her relief, the fog thinned, and visibility had improved markedly by the time they set out. Sammy accepted the journey with complete aplomb, and did not even wake up during the ride to Will and Polly's, or when Polly took him from Matilda's arms.

"The train trip out from St. Louis was very interesting," Sarah said when they had settled in their seats. The train started with a jerk that threw them against the seat back, and chugged on its way with a loud shriek from the whistle. "We came through long wooden tunnels which, they tell me, are to protect the trains from the snow," she continued when the sound of the whistle faded and they could hear again. "I saw very little snow, just some on the mountain tops, but they told me sometimes it gets high enough to cover the sheds."

"Oh, yes," Alfred nodded. "This has been a very dry year. The snows haven't started yet, and it's already

December. But it's very unpredicatable. The year the Donner Party was caught, the first snow came in September."

In a remarkably short span of time, the train pulled into the station in Sacramento and they alighted. Matilda could not help but marvel at how much more quickly they could make the journey by train than with a horse and buggy. Alfred insisted they hire a driver to take them to the meeting, although both Sarah and Matilda said they could walk. But when they pulled up in front of the Congregational Church, she was glad they were in a buggy, for dozens of men swarmed around the building, some heckling the ladies as they entered.

Alfred escorted them to the door. Matilda saw him look around the crowd filling the pews. A dozen men were interspersed throughout the women, which seemed to give Alfred the courage to stay, and the three of them took seats.

"Aren't you to be one of the speakers?" Matilda whispered to Sarah. "Should you be sitting back here with us?"

Sarah shook her head. "No, I stay in the background, arrange schedules, get rooms in hotels and such. I leave the speaking to women like Miss Anthony and Mrs. Gordon. Wait until you see Miss Anthony. She's over fifty, but she's as dynamic as a young woman."

The audience hushed as three women entered from the side and took their seats on the dais. A thrill of excitement shot through Matilda as she recognized Miss Anthony.

Alf or no Alf, she thought, this was a day she would never forget.

Chapter 18

December 1871 to February 1872

AFTER SARAH'S DEPARTURE, Matilda wondered how life could so quickly return to its normal routine. Sarah's visit, like a tornado blowing through, left everyone a little stunned by her presence.

Alf grumbled for days about Suffragettes, but everyone ignored his complaints and they also soon faded.

The rains began shortly after Sarah's visit. By December 21, the area had received almost six inches, and people along the American River had to be evacuated to escape the flooding. As Alfred doffed his muddy boots and hung his sodden coat on a peg on the porch, he smiled at Matilda, who hovered with a dry blanket to wrap around him.

"Going to make that reporter from the Bee eat his words. Remember his article on the anniversary of the 1861 flood?"

"Oh, yes." Matilda took a towel and began gently drying Alfred's hair. "The one who said the levees were so strong now, and the city streets raised to a level where they no longer need to fear floods. He dared the floods to 'come and try our bulwarks' is how he put it, I believe."

He nodded. "Another major storm is moving in, and I suspect he may regret his challenge to the elements."

She seated him in front of the fire and brought him a cup of hot tea. "I'm just glad we are high enough we don't have

147

to worry."

Christmas was a cheerful affair, in spite of the continuing downpour. Spirits were dampened by the news that Caroline definitely suffered from consumption, and her condition worsened daily. Matilda remembered how quickly her sister Temperance had died of the same disease once she started to go down.

Sam announced over his third slice of mince pie that not only Sally, but her sister Rebecca as well planned to stay with him after their mother died. All, even Betsy Ann and Dr. Nester agreed it was just a matter of time.

"Becky and Sally say that if Eli hadn't insisted on staying in that dreadful climate for so long, and hauled the family all over Kansas, never letting poor Carrie get really settled anywhere, their mother would not be dying. They've all heard stories about folks with consumption who came to California and got well."

"Didn't help A.B. any," Matilda remarked dryly. "I don't know what they expected Eli to do. After all, the Methodist Church assigned him to the different parishes, and he could hardly refuse them. He did come to California as soon as they approved his transfer. And what about the three younger girls?"

"Eli won't be able to drag them all over, going from place to place as a circuit rider. And both Becky and Sally say they want to keep the children with them."

Alf chuckled. "You ready to go from being a bachelor to being responsible for house full girls? How old is Becky? She can't be more than fifteen or sixteen."

"She was born in '55," Matilda said. "She's sixteen and Sally is fourteen. But Belle and Minnie are only six and four, and Baby Till isn't a year old yet."

"Well, 'Tilda," Sam told his sister wth a grin, "I shouldn't have to bring my shirts over to you when I need a new button."

"Yes," she agreed tartly. "And you should eat better at home so you won't have to show up here so often for dinner."

On the 29th of December, another storm struck, this one full of thunder and lightning as well as rain. Matilda sighed as she reassured the children and the cowering Jake.

After comforting the children and finally getting them into bed, she returned to the parlor. "When will this wretched rain stop?" she sighed to Alfred, who sat by the fire reading his paper.

He looked up and smiled. "A month ago we were complaining because there was no rain. God must think we can't make up our minds what we want."

Matilda laughed in spite of her exasperation. "I suppose we should appreciate the rain. I am glad we don't seem to get droughts here like we had in Kansas. Once we went seventeen months without rain. I remember that terrible time very well. All the streams and wells dried up. People from all over the States were sending barrels of food. Sarah sent us a lot of apples from Illinois, and were we glad to get them! Everything in Kansas turned the same color as the dust, which blew around us every day, and covered everything. That drought was what made Tom and Abe decide to come to California in '60."

"Doesn't sound like a pleasant experience. I'm glad I was already here. California has had some dry years, but never anything as bad as that." Alfred grinned and opened his paper. "I see the Metropolitan Theater is showing Whittier's play, Moll Pitcher, about the fortuneteller of Lyon. Mrs. Stewart is playing the lead role. Do you suppose we could persuade your mother to stay with the children so we could go? They have a matinee so we could catch the 6:45 train back home."

"That would be fun," Matilda agreed. "I hear Mrs. Stewart makes a very good Moll Pitcher. Sufficiently eerie to convince the audience she really is a witch."

"And this is a good time to go. Can't get on the fields to plant. Too wet." The paper rustled as he turned the page. He read for a few moments, then chuckled. "Wisconsin papers report a man with smallpox was buried alive. His sister protested at burying him so fast, and had him dug up." He grinned. "I understand the man is now recovering."

Matilda gasped. "How could they not know he still lived? Didn't they lay him out for a while, or hold a wake, or anything?"

"Seems Wisconsin has a law that says smallpox victims have to be buried right away, to keep the disease from spreading. Guess the minute he looked dead he was in the ground."

"He's lucky his sister was around, and insisted on double checking."

"Perry McCoon wasn't that fortunate."

"Perry McCoon?" Matilda knew Elitha Donner had been married to him, but she had heard nothing more, except that he was a drunkard and mean, not only to Elitha, but to his first wife. In fact, rumor suggested he had beaten his first wife to death, but no one made any effort to prove it. California had been a pretty lawless place at that time. .

Alfred nodded. "He was killed, or so everyone thought, when his horse threw him in a race, back in '51. They buried him, then some years later, they went to dig him up, to move him, I guess, I'm not sure just why, and they discovered he had turned over and moved, so he had to have

150

regained consciousness and found himself in his grave."

"How dreadful," Matilda shuddered. "That should never happen to anyone, even a terrible person like Perry McCoon."

"Guess it used to happen fairly often in the past," Alfred said. "That's where the custom of holding a wake came from. Everyone would sit around and watch the casket for several days to see if the dead person was going to show any signs of life." He paused, then added, "And they even started tying a string to a person's hand when they buried him, and ran the string to a bell on top of the grave. Then if the person moved their hand, it would ring the bell and they could dig him up. Even had someone in the graveyard all the time to listen for the bells."

Matilda shuddered.

The weather continued cold, miserable, and foggy, with one storm after another. A neighbor died on December 30, and was buried in the Hicksville Cemetery. Alfred and Matilda attended the services. Matilda shivered as she stood on the frosty dead grass that covered the ground, watching the haze of fog shift among the tree tops. Her mind reverted back to the funerals of her father and nephew Michael in the same miserable weather.

Another letter came from her brother John's wife Mary Anne, in which she related John talked more and more of coming to California.

> *"We lost so many cattle in the last storm, as did all of our neighbors. The papers reported that Kansas had more cattle die in that storm than were slaughtered during the entire last harvest season. I don't know what we would do if we did not have*

John's salary as Circuit Judge. It does not pay well, but at least it pays the taxes. Thank goodness we had a good garden last year, so I canned a large supply of beans and tomatoes, and the potato and turnip harvests were good. Plus, we have been eating a lot of beef.

"*Our big news, of course, is that Lilly May joined the family on January 6, and she is a beautiful baby. She is growing like a weed, and is as healthy as any mother could wish. She is going to look just like our precious lost Nora.*

"*I read about an article published in the Boston Journal of Chemistry, a new way to make this tough beef tender enough to eat. I really had to try something, for none of the children could chew it. Rub each piece with a little salt and pepper, and a lump of sugar. Put it in a heat-resistant earthen jar with a little water, lay on a thick piece of buttered paper, and press down the cover. Bake it for four or five hours. It comes out tender and juicy. Works for chicken and turkey, too. Try it, you'll be glad you did.*"

Matilda looked up from reading the letter to Alfred. "I'll have to take her advice. The last old hen I tried to cook had been running around the yard for so long she was so tough Mary and Elizabeth complained they couldn't eat it. Mary said it was like chewing on a piece of India rubber. Even Lewis didn't like it, and you know he'll eat anything."

"By all means, try it. Can't hurt." Alfred smiled. "Have heard so much about your brother John. He sounds like a man I would like to meet. Maybe one more Kansas winter is all it'll take. Don't tell him about our floods. I understand

Sherman Island is still completely under water, and the entire crop has been destroyed. Also, Knight's Landing has lost thousands of acres of grain."

"I just knew putting so much faith in these levees was a mistake. Tom said it was a bad idea."

"I guess some others agree with him," Alfred nodded. "Bunch of fellows cut the Parks' levee at Butte Slough. Guess the cattlemen didn't want the land reclaimed for crops, wanted to keep it free to run cattle on." He shrugged. "They say over a hundred masked and armed men surrounded the levee watchers and coraled them in the house under guard while they did the destruction."

"That's a terrible way to solve a dispute. What if someone had gotten shot?"

"Paper says the Levee Commission is going to rebuild it. It was a big levee, eighty feet wide at the base and twenty-five feet high. That's a lot of dirt to haul. They're making a law against destroying levees. It's before the legislature already."

"I would think destruction of property is already against the law. Why do they need a special one?"

Alfred chuckled. "Guess the lawyers found a loophole."

Matilda shook her head and changed the subject. "Did you see where General Sheridan is going to take the Russian Grand Duke Alexis on a buffalo hunt out of Fort McPherson? We came through Fort MacPherson on our way out in '64. It's on the North Platte. Chief Spotted Horse is going to be invited to come along as his escort." She laughed. "I wonder if they will invite Emperor Norton to come along as well!"

Caroline died on February 12, with Matilda holding one hand, the grief-stricken Eli the other. She said nothing, just gave Matilda a faint smile and stopped breathing. Matilda, who had been matching her breaths to her sister's, inhaled deeply. Eli buried his face in his wife's breast and wept inconsolably. Matilda watched with the tears streaming down her face.

They buried Caroline next to their sister Minerva, another who had tragically died young. Eli's voice broke several times as he led the eulogy, telling friends and neighbors what a good wife and mother she had been, and the help she had been to him.

Sam was the first to send a shovel full of earth raining into the grave. He joined Matilda and stood beside her as the last echos of the clods landing on the coffin faded away. He swallowed thickly and Matilda saw the tears spring into his eyes. "Hard to think Carrie's gone," he murmured. "Seems like just yesterday I stood up beside Tommy the day they got married."

Matilda put her arms around him and their tears mingled. So many thoughts of her sister flooded her mind. The stories shared in whispers in the big bed in Randolph's Grove after their parents slept. The time she caught Caroline with Tommy Evans in the barn after Temperance's funeral while Tommy's wife Susan was still alive. The glow in her sister's eyes when she finally married her beloved Tommy, only to have him die four years later from the same disease which had now claimed her life as well. She was only 37, Matilda thought, as she wept against Sam's shoulder. It's not fair. And she's leaving those five girls motherless.

She pulled back and met Sam's eyes. "We'll just have to do our best to take Carrie's place."

Chapter 19

March, 1872

"MAMA, I DON'T feel well. I don't think I can go to school today."

Since Mary frequently tried this ploy to skip school, and Matilda had fallen for it only to have the child miraculously recover in a remarkably short period of time, this comment was greeted with some skepticism by her mother. But a hand to Mary's hot forehead told Matilda the child did have a fever.

Elizabeth, beside her, also looked up through feverish eyes. "I don't feel good either, Mama. I felt bad yesterday, but didn't tell you because we were having a special reading test at school, and I didn't want to miss it."

"You went to school with a fever? You could have become seriously ill." Panic welled in Matilda's breast, as she thought of Mary Anne and John losing little Will and Nora so close together. She remembered reading that chicken-pox was prevalent in the county and her panic eased a little. If they had chicken-pox, they were not in serious danger. "Has anyone else at school been sick?"

"Teacher said Henry Bandeen had the chicken-pox. He came back to school with ugly spots all over his face. Ugh!" Mary shuddered. "And yesterday two of the Blue children did not come, and neither did George and Melvina Putney."

155

"That settles it then," Matilda sighed. "You two have the chicken-pox. And I suppose Lew will get them as well. Stay in bed. We'll let Lew stay home too. I'll bring you some barley soup and your grandmother's lobelia tea."

Mary wrinkled her nose. "That tastes awful. Can't we have catnip tea instead?"

"Your grandmother says lobelia is the best. Your Uncle Alf is coming to help your papa with the planting. Since she is coming with him, we had better take her advice. She and I are going to block that new quilt I just finished piecing for your bed." Matilda chuckled. "Just cross your fingers and hope she doesn't insist on giving you any of that Number Six compound of hers to make you sweat and bring out the rash." Matilda shuddered at the memory of her own experiences with that particularly vile mixture.

Carrie came running into the room and, with her usual enthusiasm, jumped up on the bed with her two big sisters.

Matilda snatched Carrie before she bounced more than twice. "Come on, Carrie. Your sisters don't feel like playing this morning. You can come and help me get them something to eat."

Betsy Ann arrived mid-morning, and confirmed the diagnosis. "Have to get them to sweat, to bring out the pustules. Eruptions don't come, fever goes inside. Get more of that lobelia tea in them. Stay bundled up, you two," she commanded the two girls, who cowered under the covers.

Matilda smothered a smile. She knew they feared their grandmother would order something even less palatable, but Betsy Ann seemed content, and returned to the kitchen. She put Carrie's breakfast on the table while Matilda nursed Sammy. "Keep 'em bundled up warm, keep the soup and lobelia tea going. I've plenty of Golden Seal to put on the eruptions when they come. Don't let 'em scratch those bumps, or they'll leave scars. Not as bad a smallpox, but if they don't scratch, should not mark 'em at all."

The old woman bustled about the little kitchen, refilling the tea kettle, and getting hot water out of the reservoir on the side of the stove to start the dishes. "Got a brief note from Weldon. Says he's going to stay in Missouri, as his new wife wants to stay close to her family. Also says their first baby is due in in July."

Matilda smiled and lifted Sammy over her shoulder, patting him gently on the back. "It's about time. He's 28 years old." Sammy let out a contented burp. "Married life seems to agree with him. Was beginning to think he was going to be a confirmed bachelor like Sam, Tom, and Alf."

Dishes clattered as Betsy Ann began the breakfast clean-up. "Grow up fast, they do," she sighed. "Seems like only yesterday A.M. and Amanda brought the poor little mother-less mite in and laid him in my arms. Now he's a man grown and going to be a father." She chuckled softly with a sly glance at Matilda. "Won't be long until Mary gets over her tomboy ways and starts wanting to wear fancy dresses to attract the boys." She scowled. "But she'd bet-ter not think about lacing herself up in one of those whale-bone corsets. Those things are bad for the lungs. Won't let the air flow in and out like it ought." She shook her head, "Why, the papers had an article not long ago about a girl in Utah who died because she insisted on lacing her corset too tight."

Matilda laughed. "I think that will be a while yet. A tightly laced corset would keep Mary from climbing the trees." She put Sammy in his little bed, and he kicked and waved, cooing happily. She went down to the root cellar and came back with an apron load of potatoes which she began to peel. Same thing over and over, she thought with a sigh. Just get them all fed breakfast, get the dishes washed, and it's time to start on dinner. Not only Alfred, but her brothers Sam and Alf would be coming in ravenous very shortly.

When the men entered, Alfred went to check on the two girls and reported them sound asleep. Lewis sat at the table, waiting for his dinner. While he waited, Matilda prodded him to practice his sums, since she had allowed him to stay home from school along with his sisters. She checked his forehead for fever. If Henry Bandeen had chicken pox, chances were very good Lewis would take them as well. They were inseparable.

"Talk is they're gonna close the school until the chicken-pox runs its course," Sam reported. "Half the 31 pupils are absent. Swung by Will and Polly's. Maggie and their Sam have it too,"

"Guess they might as well shut her down," Alf agreed. "Not much sense keepin' it open with only half of the young'uns there." He settled into his seat and reached for a biscuit, slathering it with butter and honey.

Matilda set the bowl of potatoes on the table, and another bowl filled with the green beans she had canned the previous summer, then set the meat out on a platter. She watched somewhat anxiously as the men dug into the meat. She had decided to try Mary Anne's recipe, and had been baking the tough beef since early in the morning.

She almost laughed out loud when Sam started to saw through what he thought would be a tough chunk of meat and his knife went down to the plate almost immediately. The startled expression on his face made the extra work worthwhile.

Alfred noticed Sam's reaction and smiled. "Well, my

love, I see you have achieved another culinary miracle."

Sam only grunted and began to talk of current events. "See where David Bush is pushing that new composition pipe of his. Says it's better and cheaper than either lead or iron. Was thinking of trying it. Want to run a pipe from the well out to the next field down so's I don't have to lug water when I've got the cattle down there."

"Been hearing the doctors have some concerns about that fancy new pipe," Betsy Ann opined. "Say it causes all kinds of health problems. Even heard about the conductor on one of the streetcars had a stroke of apoplexy they say was caused by the new pipe."

"Folks have been having apoplexy for years, long before the new pipe. How can they be so sure that's the cause?" Alfred looked skeptical. "I sometimes think they just look for something to blame. Some are afraid of anything new."

Matilda was inclined to agree, but said nothing.

Sam changed the subject. "See that fight between McCauley, Swain, and Harvey over who gets 'Uncle' Billy's land is going through the courts again. It's been going on over three years now, since Janaury of '69. They say there was over 200 defendents when they started, and the number keeps increasing. Got so many papers now it takes a box a foot deep to hold 'em all."

Alfred nodded. "Guess it was quite a holding when Micheltorena gave it to Chabolla back in '44. Hear it covered over 35,000 acres, all the way from McConnell's Ranch down to Dry Creek."

"Good thing Abe got us all to file those deeds making us joint tenants, back in '68," Sam said. "Thought it kind of silly, myself, at the time, but Abe learned from losing his land once before." He took another big bite of biscuit before continuing. "Chabolla's wife Josefa sold her share to

Govers and he sold it to "Uncle" Billy Hicks. That's the land McCauley is trying to get clear title to, after pulling that little trick of assigning the debt to that scoundrel Tevis, then buying it at the Sheriff's sale."

Matilda remembered Alfred telling her about that particular ploy, and felt again the surge of indignation that had swept over her when she had first learned poor old 'Uncle' Billy had lost his land, over 14,000 acres.

"Feeling is, Judge McKune is going to render a judgement soon." Alfred's eyes met Matilda's. "And as soon as the title is clear, Haskin and Amanda Swain are going to sell us that 200 acres down by the schoolhouse."

Matilda returned his smile, thinking of the bag of gold coins so carefully stored beneath the bed, ready for the big day. "Then we will have our own home at last."

"One thing for sure, you move in there, the youngsters won't have far to go to get to school." Sam grinned and turned to his mother. "You sure these girls have chicken-pox and not smallpox? I hear they've got smallpox in San Francisco and Sacramento."

"We'll know for sure in a day or two, when the pustules erupt," Betsy Ann opined. "But they're not bad sick, so it's a pretty good chance it's chicken-pox. Especially since half the youngters at school have taken it. Haven't heard of the Pox anywheres around here." She grinned wryly and added, "At least not yet."

Matilda again thought of the wisdom of getting every-one vaccinated, but knowing her mother's strong opinion of anything associated with doctors, she said nothing, just began clearing the dishes from the table.

Alf drained the last of his coffee and rose to his feet. "Back to work, men, or we'll not get that field finished by dark." He chuckled. "And so Weldon is happily married and soon to be a father. Next thing you know, Sam here will be tying the knot."

Sam snorted. "With five women in my house already? You think I'm crazy enough to add another? Becky has taken the whole affair in hand. Place is so tidy now I can't find a thing."

Recalling what his bachelor quarters had looked like before Caroline's daughters had joined him, Matilda could only admire Becky's determination to take her mother's place and make a nice home for herself and her sisters. A big job for a seventeen-year-old girl.

As Betsy Ann predicted, the girls recovered quickly. Lewis followed them one week later. By the end of March, it seemed apparent Carrie and Sammy would not become ill, and Matilda sighed with relief. The cold north winds blew down as they did every March, but with five children and a busy household, she scarcely noticed.

As a reward for being so good during their illness, Matilda took the girls on a visit to Annie Hurd's hat shop in Sacramento for new Easter bonnets.

As the girls looked at all the sample bonnets, unable, as usual, to make up their minds, Annie bounced little Sammy on her knee and marveled at how fast Carrie had grown.

"Speaking of growing," Matilda smiled, "I can't believe little Annie is eight years old. Doesn't seem possible it's been that long."

Annie laughed. "Not only eight years old, but she's helping me in the shop. She has such a gift for arithmetic. She can already make change better than I can. She is going to be a real help to me." Her eyes filled with tears. "Ben would have been so proud of her."

Matilda patted Annie's hand in sympathy. "I'm sure,

wherever he is, he knows what a fine daughter he has."

"There's another Hurd family here in town. He's a local businessman. Morgan Hurd. I wondered if he might be kin to Ben, and if so, maybe Annie would have some family." She shook her head. "We couldn't find any relationship, but of course, since Ben was an orphan and never knew any of his folks, it made it hard to make any connections. All he knew was they had come from England."

"Mama," Mary's voice interrupted. "Lizzie says she wants the blue flowers, but she didn't want them until I said I wanted them."

Matilda hastened to play the peace-maker. "Now, girls, I'm sure there are enough blue flowers for both of you."

"But I don't want her hat to be like mine. And I want the blue flowers!"

Annie interceded with a chuckle and settled the dispute. "You can both have blue flowers, and I promise the bonnets will be very different."

As Matilda and her brood prepared to leave, Annie escorted them to the door. "Remember Bridgette DeLusi?"

Matilda laughed, remembering the tall, graceful woman who had come into the hatshop on one of Matilda's earlier visits, the one Annie had told her "worked the steamers", then had to explain to Matilda what "working the steamers" meant. "Of course. Does she still have the same – er – occupation?"

Annie giggled. "Oh, yes, but she's got another little girl now. Named her Agnes."

"How in the world can she take care of another child?"

"She doesn't. She gave the little girl to the Catholic Orphans Home for the nuns to raise. Goes by and sees her regular, and gives money to the nuns to help run the orphanage, so they are quite glad to have the child. They get so many children with no financial assistance at all." Annie glanced at the two girls and told Matilda in a low voice. "I will say this for Bridgitte's "profession". It pays well."

On the train ride back home, Matilda thought about poor little Agnes DeLusi. She wondered what kind of life the child would have. She shrugged. She had her own to raise.

Three days later, at 2:17 on the morning of March 26, she awoke to the crash of dishes hitting the floor. She felt the bed rocking, and sat bolt upright in the bed. Alfred gasped in alarm beside her. As the rocking continued, the lamp beside the bed crashed to the floor and shattered.

"Earthquake," Alfred muttered beside her, jumping out of bed. Frightened cries from the children rang out from the other room. Sammy slept peacefully in his little bed.

"Come on," he urged, as crockery continued to crash in the kitchen. "We have to get the children out. Get your slippers on," he ordered sharply as she leaped to her feet. "There's bound to be glass all over the floor where that lamp broke. Thank God it wasn't lighted."

By the time they got into the children's room, the shaking had stopped. Moonlight streamed in the window, lighting the room enough for Matilda to see both girls sitting up in bed, their eyes wide.

"What was that, Mama," Mary gasped. Elizabeth clung to her sister, mute with fright.

"It was an earthquake, girls, and it just knocked some things off of the shelves. It's all right now. It's stopped. You can go back to sleep."

Alfred found a candle, and came into the room holding it before him. It cast eerie shadows on his face, but allowed her to see that Lewis and Carrie had slept through the whole event. She looked around the room. A stack of clothes the girls had left on a trunk had been knocked to the floor, and the lamp had fallen over, but not broken. She quickly set it upright so no more oil would spill. She looked around, but could see no other visible damage.

"You didn't put the clothes away like I told you to. Now you will have to pick them all up and re-fold them tomorrow."

"Yes, Mama," Mary quavered.

Matilda gave both girls a reassuring hug, for they were both still pale, then turned to go back to her room. Alfred trailed along behind her.

As she passed through the door, she heard Elizabeth whisper to Mary, "I told you we should have put those clothes away yesterday."

Mary, who despised folding clothes, grunted in disgust. "Dumb earthquake!"

Matilda rose at six, and went into the kitchen to survey the damage. Many of the dishes on the shelves had fallen, and most of those that fell appeared to be broken. With a sigh, she began to clean up the mess. One of the casualties was a teapot she and Lewis had received for a wedding present from the Dahlbergs, their neighbors back in Kansas. She gathered the pieces. Maybe she could glue them back together. She would not be able to brew tea in it any more, but she could put it on a shelf and keep it as a memento of that long ago wedding day, from another life and another lifetime in a far different world.

As she swept up the worst of the mess, the first after-shock struck, and she grabbed the sink to keep from falling as the floor swayed beneath her feet. Many of the dishes that had not fallen with the first shock now followed their brethren.

After the shock wave passed, she took a deep breath. Alfred came running in from the bedroom, stuffing his shirt into his pants. He looked so startled and so disheveled that suddenly the whole thing struck her as funny and she started to laugh. He took her in his arms and they laughed together. "It is a mess, isn't it," he murmured into her hair.

They turned to see Mary standing in the doorway watching them. "Mama," she said solemnly, a tremor in her voice, "do you suppose God is trying to shake us off the world?"

Chapter 20

March to May, 1872

MATILDA SPENT the whole next day cleaning up the mess. She sent Alfred to the basement to check the damage there, afraid of what she might see. In her mind, the rows of glistening glass jars of canned beans, corn, tomatoes, peaches and pears, the jars of fig jam and blackberry compote, all stood neatly on the shelves. The contents of the basement shelves were the result of many hours of toil over a hot kettle, to say nothing of all the work involved in growing, harvesting, and preparing those fruits and vegetables. The thought of all the wasted hours if those jars were now a shattered mass was too dreadful to comtemplate.

Alfred returned, grinning. "Relax. Most of the jars stayed on the shelves, by some miracle. And many of the ones that fell are only cracked, not shattered." He grimaced. "But enough of them did to make a gawdawful mess."

"Bring up the cracked jars. I'll be able re-can some of them, like the beans, if they are not too badly damaged. The jam and the compote will be ruined." She put her hands to her temples and sighed. "The girls can stay home from school and help me."

When told of the plan, Mary eagerly agreed, but Elizabeth protested. "I told Teacher I would help her with the first graders, so I have to go." She made a face at her sister. "Teacher *depends* on me."

Mary stuck out her tongue at Elizabeth and said. "Go ahead, Smarty. *I'll* stay here and help Mama. I'm more help than you are anyway."

Matilda held up her hand and stopped Elizabeth's retort, ignoring Alfred's chuckle at the rivalry between the two. "Girls, girls, that's enough. Elizabeth, you and Lew go to school. Your teacher will probably have a big mess to clean up as well. Mary, you stay here and help me. Now, eat your porridge, all of you. We've got a busy day ahead of us. I have to get Carrie's shoes on her before she starts running around. There is broken glass all over from that broken lamp, to say nothing of the broken dishes."

Carrie, at three, was a delightful child, and entertained little Sammy while her mother and sister spent the morning putting the house to rights again. It turned out to be a rewarding time, for as she and Mary sorted through the jars of fruits and vegetables, deciding what was salvageable and what was not, it gave her a chance to talk to her oldest daughter with no one else around, For all of her lack of interest in academic studies, Mary had an awareness of the world which Matilda found amazing in a twelve year old.

"After all, Mama," she said in a lofty tone, "I am almost thirteen."

Well, Matilda thought, smothering a smile, you are twelve and a half.

"I want a Dolly Varden dress"

Startled, Matilda could only stare at her daughter.

"So don't you think I am old enough for long skirts?"

"I don't think so, Darling. Not yet." Mary was growing up. Matilda found it hard to imagine her madcap tomboy daughter wanting to wear long skirts, especially frilly ones like a Dolly Varden. "Would you settle for some Dolly

Varden towels? They have them for sale at a couple of stores in Sacramento."

"Maybe," Mary shrugged. "Do you suppose that Alice McCauley and her Count will come back here to live?" She sighed. "It would be *so* romantic to be married to a Count." She picked up another apparently unbroken jar of pickles and washed it clean. "The girls at school talk about it all the time. Melvina Putney has seen a picture of him and says he is *so* handsome, with his uniform and fancy hat." She set the dried jar on the counter and picked up a jar of peaches. "Is Uncle Weldon really married? Is it to the girl he talked about the last time he was here? A Susan somebody?"

Matilda's mind had trouble keeping up with Mary as she jumped from subject to subject. "Bilderbeck, Darling. Susan Bilderbeck," she responded. "And yes, they did get married. They have been married for some time now, and are going to stay in Missouri, at least for a while."

"I'm so glad that George Douglass won't be back after this year. Teacher says his father told him he's got enough book learning, time he stayed home to help on the farm." She grimaced. "He is sixteen, after all, and is bigger than all of the other boys."

"I'm sure his father needs him to help at home," Matilda said, knowing the senior Douglass's health had been failing, and only the oldest son, James was available to help him. The next three were girls, and Edwin was two years younger than George. She also knew George was as besotted with Mary now as the first day he saw her on the trip across the prairie. With both of them maturing, Matilda felt relieved to know they would not be together as much.

"And Henry Bandeen is sick a lot. He reminds me of Addie. Do you suppose he's going to die, Mama? He is Lew's best friend, you know."

Matilda froze in the middle of wiping a jar of tomatoes. Would Jane lose little Henry? After all she had been through with the divorce from Billy? She met Mary's eyes and said quietly, "We'll hope not."

The damage from the earthquake extended up and down the valley, and had been felt as far north as Oregon and as far south as Mexico City.

"I guess we were fortunate," she smiled at Alfred as he related the amount of devastation to her.

"Yes, a number of brick buildings sustained some pretty heavy damage. We probably won't find out the full extent for several weeks. Some folks are trying to raise money for the town of Lone Pine, down in the southern Sierras. Feller was down at the Hicksville Hotel this morning, taking up a collection. He says the quake toppled over thirty buildings and killed twenty three people, and left a lot homeless. Gets pretty cold at Lone Pine, too."

"Somehow, hearing that, losing a few dishes and some cans of beans and peaches doesn't seem so tragic."

Alfred settled into his favorite chair and opened his newspaper. "One feller in Sacramento, reporter for the Alta, jumped from his third story window in the rear of the Orleans Hotel. Landed on top of an outhouse, leaped from there to the wagon shed behind the Wells Fargo office, went through the shingles, and landed atop a covered wagon. When the watchman responded to his cries for help, he only had a few minor lacerations from going through the shingles." He shook his head. "The Orleans held together, so he'd have been better off staying inside the building. But I guess he wasn't thinking too clearly at the time."

"I can understand that," Matilda nodded. "If I had been on the third story of a brick building when all of that shaking started, I might have done the same thing."

The paper rustled as he turned the page. "Says here a man in Oregon is suing his wife's parents." He chuckled softly. "Seems they told him she was strong and healthy and she turned out to be weak and sickly."

"What?" Matilda exclaimed. "Was he buying a horse or taking on a wife?" She shook her head. "I'll bet he's not much of a husband, either."

"Speaking of sickly, I hear the Callahan's daughter, the one that lives down in Stockton, is suffering from consumption. They fear she's liable to die."

Callahans? Oh, yes, of course, the owners of the Golden Eagle. What Alfred had said sank in and Matilda's mind flew to her sister Caroline. Tears filled her eyes. "Oh, I hope not. Consumption is such a terrible disease."

"The Callahans are devastated. The grandson is only a few months old." Alfred shook his head. "Such a shame."

Several aftershocks struck in the ensuing weeks, but did no furthur damage. The girls proudly wore the new bonnets Annie had made for them when the whole family went to church for Easter services.

After church, the main topic of conversation was the collapse of the new building under construction by the John Breuner Furniture Company at 6th and K in Sacramento.

"Whole building just collapsed," Alf stated. "Lucky no one got killed. Ruined some thirty to forty thousand dollars worth of brand new furniture that was inside."

"Must have been damaged by the quake," Sam opined. "Just took a nudge from one of those aftershocks we've been havin' to bring it down."

"Dunno," chimed in George Putney. "I hear tell the building wa'n't any too well constructed to begin with.

Breuner just might have a claim against the builder."

"Irony is," Alf added, "they stored all the furniture as wasn't too much damaged in a shed behind the collapsed building, and the shed caught fire. Burned the whole lot."

"Sounds suspicious to me," George muttered. "Like maybe someone had it in for Breuner. Didn't want him to open his store."

"Well," Alfred grinned, "he is undeterred. He says it's time Sacramento had a top quality furniture store, and he is determined to rebuild and open just as he planned."

"Careful, Mary. Don't drop that bowl of potato salad."

"Mo – ther," Mary's voice showed her exasperation. "I am almost grown up. You don't need to keep telling me not to drop things."

Matilda, remembering many other similar occasions ending in minor disasters, bit her tongue and held her breath as Mary and Elizabeth helped carry the salad, the deviled eggs, the fried chicken, and the corn on the cob to the buggy where Big Ben stood waiting patiently to carry them to the Hicksville Cemetery for the Memorial Day picnic and annual cleaning.

"There are two pitchers of lemonade in the ice box. Don't forget them. It's going to be a hot day, and everyone will be thirsty. Here, Carrie, take this jar of pickles. I have to get Sammy."

She changed his diaper while he waved his arms and legs and cooed. He could now sit up by himself, and tried to pull himself to his feet whenever he was near enough to something to get hold of. She sighed. He would be walking soon, then she would have her hands full.

She gathered a quilt to set him on when they reached the cemetery, and carried him out to the buggy. The other children were all seated, even Carrie. Matilda swung by the corral where White Star stood, looking so alone. She and Little Jake had never developed the camaraderie the horse and the old dog had shared, and Matilda knew White Star still looked up expectantly, as if she thought Jake would appear and join her at any moment. Giving the horse the lump of sugar she gave her every morning, Matilda stroked the graying muzzle and hugged the sleek neck.

"Come on, Mama," Mary called, impatient to be off. The children always enjoyed these outings. Matilda, with one final hug, hurried to where Alfred waited to help her into her seat.

At the cemetery, as they did every Memorial Day, the men worked at clearing the grass and debris from around the graves. The women busied themselves tending the large numbers of children that scampered around and setting out the food and drink. With so many willing hands, the work went quickly, and by mid-day, all were ready to eat and gather for a good gossip.

Hannath Cantrell poured a can of the new condensed milk onto a bowl of canned peaches. Matilda watched in awe. She had heard the milk was becoming more popular. Hannath saw her watching and smiled.

"It's a marvel, especially now with so many people having ice boxes. The milk stays fresh in the can, then good for several days in the ice box after it's opened. Going to be a lot fewer children dying of second summer complaint now. And it's real help for women who don't have milk for their children."

"Or if we want a day off," Matilda exclaimed, thinking of all she had to go through to get Sammy to Polly when she wanted to go to the Sufragette meeting with Sarah. After losing John, she was so fearful of giving cow's milk to the children.

Words flew around Matilda as she stood at the table and dished out potato salad. In between scoops, she kept one eye on Sammy who sat on his quilt nearby with Carrie teaching him to play pat-a-cake.

"Terrible thing, that Cox feller shooting poor old McCabe, right there in his own saloon in Old Elk Grove."

"Yep, all he done was tell them Cox brothers to lay off the shoemaker. Guess they all musta been drunk."

"Ed Cox went back and got a rifle and shot McCabe through the window. Man never had a chance. Never even knew Cox had come back."

"Hear tell it looks like he's gonna die, too. Doctors don't hold too much hope for him."

"Hear about that terrible accident down Stockton way? Train hit a herd of horses. Engineer was injured, but the poor fireman fell off the train and was killed."

"Fell under the train. Hear he got both legs cut off when the wheels ran over him, poor feller."

"Number of horses got injured, too. Some of 'em so bad they had to be put down."

"Allus hearin' o' accidents now we got all these trains. Didn't used to kill folks all the time back when we used hosses. Why, just t'other day a Chinaman fell off the train at Elk Grove Station and got killed. Landed on his head, he did. And brakemen are gettin' hurt all the time."

Matilda finished serving the salad and walked over to her father's grave. Listening to the speakers, she could not help but recall her father's opinion of trains, and how he had fought the Illinois Central so long ago back in Randolph's Grove. She put her hand on the headstone, which read 'Gardner Randolph of Illinois' as he had requested, memories of her father washing over her.

Jane Bandeen joined her. "Did you hear that Obed Harvey asked the Board of Trustees in Sacramento to cancel the taxes he owed on some property he owns there?" Jane smiled. "They turned down his request. Guess he thought he was such a great man they would forgive him for not paying taxes."

Matilda laughed. "I can just see some of us trying that!"

Henry clung to his mother's hand, instead of joining the other children in a vigorous game of tag. Matilda remembered Mary's words. The boy did look sickly, but Jane said nothing, so neither did Matilda. Instead, she said, "Did you see that big article in the latest Harper's Magazine? They are telling all the folks back East that California is such a beautiful state that everyone should plan to visit it. They especially rave about the wonders of Yosemite. Makes me kind of anxious to see it, since we are so close."

Jane shrugged. "Guess it's a pretty easy trip for the folks from the East, now that the trains come all the way."

"They say Mr. Hutchings, who has the hotel in the Valley itself, has been giving lectures all over back East, extolling the beauty to be seen and marveled at." Matilda laughed. "They are also building a four story hotel on the San Joaquin Valley Railroad line, at Merced, the closest rail stop to Yosemite. It's going to have gas lighting throughout, and water and bath rooms on each floor. Real luxury. I'm going to persuade Alfred to take us, after the grain is harvested and before the weather turns cold.

"I'm sure the article will bring good news for all the hotel owners," she continued. "Sacramento is the logical place for anyone from the East to stop before going on down to Merced. Poor Mr. and Mrs. Callahan could use some good news. I hear their daughter just died. She was only twenty-four, and her baby only five months old."

Jane did not reply. She picked up Henry and held him closely. Matilda saw the fear in the girl's eyes, and her heart sank.

Chapter 21

July, 1872 to March 1873

HENRY BANDEEN DIED July 15, and was buried in the Hicksville Cemetery where so many of the neighborhood children lay. As Matilda held the weeping Jane after the ceremony, she could not help but think there had to be some way to prevent these tragic deaths of ones who still had so much living left to do.

Her mind reverted to reading how old Peter Cartwright had suffered from paralysis and was near death at his home on the Sangamon. He had lived for 87 years and been preaching for 68 of them. The unfairness of little Henry dying so young, like Ada Cantrell and Edna Shaeffer and so many other young ones struck her. She thought of herself losing Baby John, and her brother John and his wife losing four of their children at such tender ages.

Maybe God felt Peter Cartwright had a mission, and this permitted him to live for so long, but Henry Bandeen was such a bright little boy he could have become a great leader as well.

She had to smile to herself as she remembered the time Reverend Cartwright had come to the Randolph residence back in Randolph's Grove. Innocent child that she was, she could not understand why God had allowed the Indians to be driven off their land. She never forgot his condescending reply as he patted her head. The words rang again in her head 'Why, child, they weren't using it as God intended'. She recalled again how he had told her the land did not belong to the Indians, but to the United States Government. Right, she thought, after the government decided to take the land the Indians had lived on for centuries. The impulse to kick his shins surged through her again as it had that long ago day in Illinois. She shook her head. It's over and done with. Nothing you can do about it now. Matilda forced her mind back to the present.

Jane pulled herself together and stood back. "Thank you, 'Tilda." She smiled faintly through the tears and turned to receive condolences from Rhoda and Jenny Putney.

Matilda walked away from the group gathered at Henry's graveside over to the mound where Caroline lay, not far from Minerva and Sinclair. She thought of Temperance, buried far away in Stewart Cemetery back in Randolph's Grove, and Baby Andrew.

Some day, she murmured to herself, some day we will understand. God must have a purpose for it all.

The bumper crop of peas brought Betsy Ann to help Matilda shell them for canning. As she watched her mother's gnarled and work-worn fingers fly though the pods, she thought again of her mother's ability to accept each blow life dealt her. She's buried a husband, a baby, a son, and three daughters, Matilda thought, yet she fills her life with little joys and triumphs.

Like now. As the peas rattled into the bowl in an ever increasing mound, Betsy Ann busily quoted a Mrs. Livermore, whose advice to young ladies had recently appeared in the paper.

"And she says it's time ladies got over the notion they have to be sickly and always in the megrims in order to be attractive to men. She is so right. Why all that nonsense has been put into these girls' heads, I can't imagine. A healthy wife is what a man needs. How he thinks a sickly one can keep up with the milking and the churning, the garden and the canning, all the cooking and washing." She paused and took a deep breath. "And to say nothing of raisin' the babes! A sickly wife is just as like as not to die in childbirth and leave him with a passel of young'uns to raise."

Matilda, who had never in her life resorted to the fainting spells so in vogue among the fashionable young ladies of the present, murmured an assent. She could never think of any reason why that would attract a husband. She thought of the man from Oregon who had sued his wife's parents because she was sickly, and not robust and healthy.

"And all of these tight corsets," Betsy Ann snorted. "Compress the lungs, they do, to where they can't take a decent breath. No wonder they faint. Even likely to bring on the consumption." She chuckled and reached into the basket for another handful of pea pods and was off onto another topic. "Did you see where someone dug into Jefferson Davis's history and found out he was court-martialed while he was at West Point? Caught him smuggling whiskey into his quarters." She chuckled. "Disgraceful. And that John Surratt who got out of a well deserved hangman's noose has gotten married. Makes a body wonder what kind of gal would marry a man like that."

Matilda had wondered the same thing when Alfred read the notice to her, but made no reply. She did not need to. Betsy Ann was already off on another topic.

"Was reading that Illinois has over 700 more miles of railroad track than any other State in the Union. Your father would turn over in his grave. Never saw a man as hated railroads with more of a passion than Gardner Randolph."

"Yes," Matilda responded. "He certainly did. But I read that Kansas is the most productive State for wheat. California produces the greatest amount of wheat, but Kansas has the greatest yield per acre. Pa predicted that. Said the land was good for growing crops, and planting wheat would make a man a better living that trying to raise cattle where the weather killed them." Matilda recalled Mary Anne's letter about how many cattle the previous winter had killed in Kansas.

Memories flooded into her mind of the severe blizzard the January after Baby John was born, the storm that killed so many of her father's cattle. She closed her eyes for a moment and again saw Lewis struggling back through snow drifts with the half-dead calf slung across White Star's pommel. Matilda had lovingly nursed that calf back to health only to have it die in the flood that took the barn down the Big Blue the following spring. She shuddered as she thought again how close she and Baby John had come to being swept away by the raging torrent. Yes, she thought, California is a much pleasanter place to live.

As though reading Matilda's thoughts, Betsy Ann met her eyes and smiled. "Winter here sure a lot easier on these old bones than in Kansas." She picked up the basket and shook out the last pea pod that had been hiding in the corner. "Looks like that's the last of 'em for today. Let's get them in the pot. Got those jars ready?"

"Boiling away." Matilda wiped the perspiration from her forehead as she poured the peas into the pot of boiling, salted water waiting to blanch the peas before putting them in the jars. While the pot again reached a boil, she deftly scooped up a jar, drained the water, and set it on the counter on a towel. "Got three jars ready to go. That should hold all we've got. Any left over, we'll have 'em for supper."

"Been thinkin' of maybe moving over to Sam's place, to help out over there. Becky and Sally have their hands full with those three little girls." Betsy Ann chuckled. "Don't know where they'd put me, o' course. They got a houseful. Long as Alf's by himself, lot more room for me. Haven't seen any sign of him lining up a wife yet."

Matilda nodded. "I'm sure Alf needs you more, bachelor like he is. Becky and Sally rather pride themselves on how well they are filling in for their mother. Hear Eli is thinking of going back to preaching. Guess he finds working as a field hand for Sam is difficult for him. Being a preacher all of those years, he's not used to long hours under a hot sun. After all, he has not been well for years, poor man. And he is so depressed. Carrie told me, before she died, that he had lost his first wife only a year after they were married, and then their baby son died just a few months after his mother. And I know he took little Fanny's death hard. Maybe what he needs is to start riding the circuit again. Keep him from sitting around brooding all the time. Becky says sometimes he just sits and stares into space."

School started in the fall with an enrollment of 31 students, including one Negro girl and two Miwok boys. Much to Mary's relief, George Douglass was not among them. Along with the three Baldwins were Putneys, McGuirks, and Maroneys.

The chance to purchase the Swain property became more and more realistic as summer drifted into fall. Alfred and Matilda counted the coin hoard in the covered kettle under the bed. Their eyes met as they counted the coins again and again.

"It's not going to be enough, is it?" The price was $2250. Mr. Swain had ridden over the day before to tell them a ruling was expected soon after Christmas, and told them how much the price would be.

"We're about $1000 short. Plus, I understand the house has not been used for a long time. It will at the least need a new roof. And we'll need a well, a tank house, and a tank." He smiled and patted her hand. "Maybe I should hire out as a hand. I understand they are paying $50 a month."

"And hire someone for $50 a month to do the work you do here?"

"Or do as Alf says. He says go down to Sacramento on a Saturday night and gather up a few drunks, throw them on a steamer, and take them to San Francisco. Ships are paying $40 a head for seamen."

Matilda gasped. "That's a terrible thing to do! That's as bad as slavery. And I hear the poor men are not treated well at all. "

He laughed. "I was just teasing. What I have done is spoken to Lizzie Owens. She is willing to give us a one year loan for what we will need to pay Swain, at 1½% interest. And if we need more to make the place livable, Mr. Waterhouse might be willing to give it to us."

She sighed. "Just hate to start out with a mortgage. I keep thinking about what happened to poor old "Uncle" Billy. What if we can't pay her at the end of the year?"

"I asked her. She said if we can pay the interest, she'd be willing to extend the loan."

Matilda shrugged her shoulders expressively. "I guess we don't have a lot of choice, if we ever hope to own our own home." She smiled at him. "Pray for a good wheat crop!"

Their dream became a reality. On January 27, the Swains received title to tract #65, 191.67 acres. On March 4, 1873, Alfred signed the papers giving them title to the entire property, all 210 acres for $2250 in gold coin. He also signed a note to Lizzie Owens on the same day for the $1000 they were short.

The following day, they hitched Big Ben to the wagon and hauled over the first load of belongings.

"Are you sure you want to move in so quickly?" Alfred asked, his eyes sparkling at her enthusiasm. "Sure you don't want to wait until we get a well dug?"

"We can get by with the hand pump. I just want to get settled as soon as we can. We certainly don't want to pay rent any longer than we have to."

"Better hope it doesn't rain until I check out that roof. And I've got to get the grain off the fields before we give the place back to Mr. Short." He shook his head and frowned, a worried look coming into his eyes. "All the nice rain we got last fall made the wheat come up fine, thought we were going to have a bumper crop, but it's been so dry lately, no rain in over two months." He sighed. "And that north wind dries out what little moisture there is. Others are worried too, but we're really counting on a good crop to help us pay for this place."

The winter had passed quickly. Excitement at the prospect of their very own home dwarfed the activities going on around them.

Even the jolt of an earthquake barely penetrated her consciousness, only glad no more of her precious jars of canned foodstuffs were damaged. Even Mary and Elizabeth, busy chatting about the new house, remained unfazed by the latest tremor.

Alf came to help with the packing, full of stories of the

Modoc War. "Started last December. Several of the leaders began raiding their neighbors. They then duck back into the lava beds, which give them excellent cover. Say they won't go back to the reservation. Talk is of sending soldiers in to subdue them." He chuckled. "Writer of the article says they should be grateful for all the Government has done to make them comfortable, can't understand why they prefer what he calls the 'vagabond life'. He also goes on to say the only good Indian is a dead Indian."

"That's not true," Matilda exclaimed. "Our local Indians are very good neighbors. And white people coming in have not always treated them kindly." She thought of the many incidents where the native tribes had been driven off of their ancestral lands because white men wanted the gold underneath, or wanted to fence the prairie, and how they continued to slaughter the buffalo many of the tribes depended on for their livelihood. She remembered her three Pottawatamie friends from so long ago in Kansas. "That's a terrible thing to say."

He shrugged. "Guess if it's your cattle Scarface Charley is stealing, or your husband One-Eyed Watchman kills, you tend to look at it a little different. Kidder says his brother Melvin, from up Eureka way, served as a scout for the army during the whole affair. He was with the California Mountain Battalion at Fort Humboldt back in '63 to '65. so I guess they figgered they could call on him again."

"You can't blame the poor Modocs for not quite trusting the Government," she retorted. "I just read where Colonel Henley is in Washington right now, trying to get Congress to take most of the Round Valley reservation away from the Indians there. They were given 30,000 acres, and he wants to give 25,000 of those to what he calls "actual settlers". What does he think the original inhabitants are? Artificial settlers?"

He reached for his hat. "I'm going to the Post Office," he said with a grin. "I can see I'm going to lose this battle. You've got too much of Pa in you. You'd better not read what the good writer from the Daily Bee has to say about the Apaches."

Chapter 22

March to June, 1873

BY THE END of March, they were settled. The new house had four rooms, a fairly large bedroom for Alfred and Matilda, two smaller bedrooms for the children, and a combination kitchen, dining room, and parlor. It was located at some distance back from the main road so all of the dust from passing buggies and wagons dissipated before reaching the house. The main disadvantage was that the well and handpump were outside, meaning she had to either carry water in or go outside to wash dishes.

"That's one of the things we are going to have to do, is get the water inside," she exclaimed. "It's one thing when the weather is warm, but with this wretched cold fog, my feet are freezing even with my hands in hot water."

"Been thinking," Alfred said. "Would be a pretty easy thing to do, to add three more rooms along the back. Would give us a kitchen, a nice dining room, and this room could go back to being just the parlor. And would give us a nice bedroom for Mary and Elizabeth."

"That would be wonderful. But can we afford it? I thought the crops were not going to be as good as we had hoped."

"Probably not yet." He shook his head ruefully. "Need too many other things first anyway, and will have to pay back Lizzie Owens." He swung her off her feet in a bear hug. "But it is something to plan for, for our future together in our own home. It will be a mansion compared to most of the other houses around here."

She returned his hug with enthusiasm. She loved him so much.

The children were delighted to find the walk to school had become much shorter, with the schoolhouse visible from the front porch, as opposed to the half an hour walk they had before.

The controversy over Negro and Indian pupils in the schools barely touched Hicksville.

"Can you imagine," Matilda exclaimed to Alfred in indignation, "that someone at the Sylvan School out on the Auburn Road actually complained about the Howard children attending school with their children? Surely none of our neighbors would ever complain about Doc's daughter going to school here. I heard that Carter Jackson had to argue a bit with the school district in Sheldon, but his four children are enrolled there. "

"And brighter than many of their white counterparts, if what I hear is correct," Alfred chuckled. "I thought the State Supreme Court ruled on that. They declared the Federal law was constitutional, all right, but that it was not practical in California. Can you imagine how much it would cost if we had to build another school and hire another teacher for Doc's daughter and the two Blue children?"

"Does seem a little silly, doesn't it."

"Silly? It's ridiculous. And I can't imagine why anyone would complain if they realized all that it involved." Alfred shook his head. "Family offering the objections must be Southerners. I knew that Reconstruction Act would come back to harass us. There are some terrible things going on in the South, with all of those Ku Klux Klan members terrifying black folks."

Matilda's mind reverted to the terrible years in Kansas leading up to and including the War of the Rebellion. She sighed. "I had so hoped we could get away from all that when we came to California."

The drought and almost constant north wind continued. The air was so dry clothes clung together and hair crackled when brushed. Day after day Matilda watched Alfred worry more and more about the wheat crop. By the middle of May, the coming disaster seemed inevitable.

"Even if it does rain now, the rain itself would do as much damage as good." Alfred sat at the table with his head in his hands. "Last fall, the rains were so perfect that it looked like we were going to have a bumper crop. I was sure we would be able to pay back Lizzie on schedule." He laughed, a harsh laugh with no humor. "And with wheat selling at over a dollar per hundredweight."

She lifted his head and clasped it to her breast, stroking his hair. With a smile, she kissed him where his hairline had just begun to recede. "We will just have to pay her back next year. She did say if we can pay the interest, she will carry the principal."

"Of course." He sighed. "It's just that we need so many things, the new well, the pumphouse, the tank. And so much for our plans to build an addition to the house."

Matilda noticed Mary standing in the doorway. How much she had heard was obvious by her comment. "I guess that means I can't go away to High School when I finish the eighth grade."

Matilda had to laugh. "No, Darling, I'm afraid not. But you don't have to look so happy about it!"

Alf brought Betsy Ann over to Sunday dinner towards the end of May, and she could talk of nothing else but the so-called 'Deer Creek' sickness near Miner's Ravine.

"The fourteen year-old boy died a few weeks back, his mother and sister a few days earlier. Five others in the family have the same sickness. Seems strange only that one family has it."

"No one else?"

"No one else." Betsy Ann shook her head. "Strange. Very strange. Must be something peculiar to the place," she opined. "Some poison in the water or such."

"They are downstream from some of the gold mines. Could be something in the water," Alfred offered. "I know that runoff sure killed off the fish."

"Probably never know for sure," Alf offered. He switched to his favorite topic, the Modoc War. "Got 43 Modocs against about 600 U.S. troops. Captain Jack and his bunch killed 40 to 50 soldiers with no losses on his side. Even killed General Canby."

"I suspect the main reason for the unequal battle was the rifles," Alfred said. "Captain Jack had breech loaders while the soldiers were still using the old muzzle loaders. Army is so set in their ways. The older generals insist on staying with those antiquated rifles. Been a number of men trying to get the army to upgrade. Maybe this will convince the stubborn fools."

"Big comfort that will be to the widow of General Canby and the families of the other men killed," Matilda said wryly. "I understand that Mrs. Canby was so badly shocked to learn of her husband's untimely death that she is dangerously ill, poor woman."

"The Reverend Dr. Thomas, a Methodist minister from

Petaluma, was also killed. He had recently been appointed Peace Commissioner." Alfred added.

"I hear Captain Jack attacked the soldiers' camp wearing General Canby's own uniform." Alf grinned. "Have to admire the man. He has a sense of humor." He chuckled. "The *Daily Bee* made a suggestion. He says take all the editors from all over the country who have offered a solution to the stand-off and send them to the lava beds.

"Sounds like a good idea to me," Alfred nodded. "Have always noticed that the farther some fellows are from the action, the surer they are what should be done."

On June 13, to celebrate Mary's graduation from the Hicksville School, and a wheat harvest that looked to be at least a little better that they had dared to hope, they took the three oldest children to the circus spread out over two acres of ground at Eleventh and J Streets in Sacramento.

"The paper said they have eighteen cages of live animals," Mary declared. "And the elephant's name is Siam. Does that mean he is from Siam, Mama?"

Matilda had no idea, so she just murmured a non-commital answer, but the girls were paying no attention to her reply anyway.

"And a large open den of real lions," Elizabeth added.

"The swan chariot is drawn by fourteen camels," Lewis piped up. "I've never seen a camel." He looked puzzled. "And what's a swan chariot?"

"A chariot that looks like a swan, of course, and you've never seen a lion or an elephant either," Mary advised him loftily. "You were too little to go the last time we went."

"I've seen pictures," he declared in his defense. "Henry, before he died, showed me his stereo - - stereo - - whatever, that showed the pictures of lions and tigers and giraffes and everything."

"Stereoscope, Darling, it's called a stereoscope," Matilda reminded him gently.

"Stereoscope. His father sent away for it, since Henry was ailing so much and he wanted one. He sent for it all the way from New York. That's clear on the other side of the world," he told his sisters smugly.

The girls ignored him. "And Miss Christiane, the aerialist, walks up a single wire that goes up to two hundred feet above the ground! Can you imagine?" Elizabeth shuddered. "That's scary."

After the show, the children fell asleep in the back seat of the buggy, sated with candied apples and peanuts.

Matilda smiled at Alfred. "Thank you for a lovely afternoon. They will remember this for the rest of their lives." She laughed. "I'll never forget the look on Lew's face when the elephant took the peanut out of his hand. He looked like he was sure the elephant would take his hand too, but he stood there so bravely and didn't move a muscle."

Alfred chuckled. "Probably afraid the girls would laugh at him if he flinched." He shifted the reins to his left hand and stroked Matilda's cheek with a smile. "And Elizabeth and the monkey making faces at each other! Our prim and proper Lizzie finally let her hair down."

She glanced back at the sleeping children again, their faces still showing the stickiness of the candied apples. They were growing up so fast. Mary would be fourteen in October, Elizabeth twelve in December. Where did the time go? She watched Alfred's profile as he urged Ben along the dusty road. She smiled to herself. Thank you, God, she thought. Thank you for sending me such a good man.

Chapter 23

July to December, 1873

SUMMER STRUCK with a vengeance, and fields already tinder dry from weeks of drought and north winds turned a golden brown and crackled underfoot. As the harvest of the meager crop continued, Alfred fretted about fire.

"One spark and the whole field will go up. As sparse as it is, we need every grain. Glad we aren't any closer to the trains. Those wretched trains start fires all the time."

Matilda, carefully counting the coins from the bag she kept under the bed, looked up at him and smiled. "No point in worrying about it until it happens. Alf has his crew harvesting as fast as they can. They should be done in another week." She tied up the bag and tucked it back into the kettle, ready to put back under the bed. "We have enough to pay the interest to Lizzie Owens, at least. That will keep us going until we get in another harvest. Hopefully next year will provide a better crop."

He returned her smile. "You're right. No sense in borrowing trouble." He grinned. "I see the legislature is debating whether or not to accept greenbacks as currency instead of gold. Maybe you won't have to deal with those heavy coins anymore."

"Judging from the way they are arguing, I'm sure it will be some time before it's settled." She laughed. "Maybe I should get the children to catch gophers to add to our

193

income. I see where a man in Woodland made $61.70 collecting gopher scalps. That was the bounty for 617 of the wretched little critters. And I sure have enough of the pesty things in my garden. One of my best producing tomato vines is starting to wither, and I suspect a gopher has been at it, judging from all of the gopher holes I see."

He chuckled. "If you can persuade the girls to go after them, it's fine with me. I have a little trouble seeing Lizzie trapping gophers, but Mary would probably tackle the job with enthusiasm."

"Yes, she's still enough of a tomboy to do it. And I'm sure she can find an ally in Lew. We're going to have to keep her busy, now she is out of school."

"Between all the housework and the canning and gardening and sewing, I can't see that being a problem."

Matilda sighed, recalling some of the arguments she and Mary had over household chores. "I just wish Mary took more interest in domestic matters. She says they are boring. I'm sure she would much rather be out on the harvester with her Uncle Alf."

Alfred looked shocked. "I can just hear your anti-feminist, anti-suffragette brother's opinion about that."

She laughed merrily. "Yes, I'm sure he would have plenty to say."

"We really need a well and a new roof. And we need the new roof before winter. I went up into the attic and saw daylight in dozens of places. We can't go through a winter like that. And we need another horse. Ben is a fine animal, but we really need two. I spoke to Mr. Waterhouse and he is willing to loan us what we need on a sixty day note."

"Sixty days? That's only two months. Won't that put a lot of pressure on us to pay it back? Is he as willing as Mrs. Owens to extend the time?"

194

Voices on the back porch told them the children had returned from their excursion to the hen house, and were ready for dinner. Matilda rose and began putting plates on the table.

He nodded in understanding. "We'll discuss it later."

All five children piled through the door. Carrie proudly carried the basket. "Look, Mama. Lots and lots of eggs."

"We found a whole dozen, Mama," Mary reported. "But that old red hen got out again, and I'll bet she's setting."

Two weeks later, Matilda and Alfred sat together in the parlor. The children had been sent to bed, with some protest from Mary, who declared that since she would soon be fourteen she should be allowed to stay up longer. Matilda worked on a new piece she was preparing for another quilt. A growing family required more and more coverlets for winter. Alfred settled in his favorite chair with the newspaper.

Matilda looked up at his indignant gasp.

"I can't believe this," he muttered. "I thought we outlawed slavery in this country."

"Didn't we?" Matilda thought of the terrible tales they heard of the activities of the Ku Klux Klan down in the South. "In one of the Southern states?" she asked.

"No, right here in San Francisco."

"San Francisco? But Blacks have always been free in California."

"Not Blacks. Chinese. It says here the steamer Japan brought in 28 Chinese women and girls and auctioned them off. Got up to $450 each for the girls, $250 for the women. And I'll bet you can guess what those poor girls were purchased for."

Matilda shuddered. She could, indeed, guess what the

men buying those girls had in mind. "That's terrible. Is anything being done about it?"

"Plenty of rhetoric by the papers, but I'll bet nothing more comes of it."

"And many probably no older than Mary and Elizabeth." Horror raced through her at the thought of one of her precious daughters being dragged into such a situation. "Don't their families have anything to say about it?"

"Most of the girls are sold to the Chinese slavers by their families. Some do it to get the money, other in hopes the girls will have a better chance of survival. Many Chinese children starve to death. And the Chinese prefer sons. Girls are not highly valued like they are here."

Her horror must have shown in her face, for he murmured, "Remember when we read about the massacre in Yunnan Province, where the Emperor's soldiers fell on the prisoners and killed 30,000? Life is pretty cheap in China, which, I am sure, is why so many of them come here, in spite of all of the intolerance and prejudice they encounter. At least they can get enough to eat."

Christmas was a gala affair, celebrating not only the first Christmas in their own home, but celebrating it snug and dry under a new roof. The $1,280 loan from Mr. Waterhouse paid not only for the new roof, but for a well, pumphouse, and tank. Another sturdy Clydesdale gelding, named Charley, shared the corral with Ben, ready to pull the new hay rake the following spring.

White Star had gone to join her old friend Jake. At least that was how Matilda comforted herself when she found her beloved horse lying still and quiet in the corral, Ben standing guard over her body. As Matilda stroked the soft muzzle for the last time, she could not help but think that the last tie to her old life in Kansas was cut. The children had no real memories of that long ago time. Mary sometimes talked of the journey across the prairie, for she had been seven, but her memories of the house in Randolph were vague, and she seldom spoke of her father any more. Matilda felt guilty that she had not made more effort to keep Lewis' memory alive with the girls. If only she had a decent picture. Photography had been in its infancy at the time, and she only had that daguerrotype of herself, Lewis, and Baby John when John was only a few weeks old.

As Matilda's mind recalled the events of the past few months, Sam arrived with Betsy Ann and Caroline's girls in tow, all laden with food and parcels. Will and Polly with their whole brood arrived shortly afterwards, and the little house rang with chatter and the laughter of children eagerly anticipating the opportunity to open the many presents now stacked around the little popcorn-strung tree.

Will greeted Matilda with a hearty hug. "Merry Christmas, little sister. Hear we're supposed to have a lot of rain this winter. Good thing we got that new roof on, or you'd be floating around in here, judging from all the holes we found when we took off the old roof."

She laughed and returned his embrace. "You're not half as glad as I am."

"Hey, Sis," Tom interposed. "Did you hear our old friend Don Ray got himself the job as Postmaster in Galt? He'll be able to turn that to his advantage, I'm sure."

"If there is any way to turn it into a profit, I'm sure he'll find it," Will said wryly.

"Modocs have been real quiet since they hung Captain Jack and five of his main warriors." Sam said. "And I hear the Army generals have agreed to look at getting breech loading rifles for the soldiers."

"About time," Will nodded. "Too bad all those poor fellows had to die to wake them up."

Sam chuckled softly. "Been my observation that it usually takes something like that to wake up Congress. Guess the main objection was having to pay for new rifles when they already had all of those 'perfectly good' muzzle loaders. Sort of like saying why ride in a train when we've got all of these perfectly good mule carts."

"Maybe we will be in another war soon. There is some talk of declaring war with Spain over the *Virginius* affair." Tom took the bowl of mashed potatoes his mother handed him and put them on the makeshift table. "Spain executing Captain Fry and the other officers so summarily has not set well with some of the folks in Washington."

"Spain was within her rights. They look on the rebels in Cuba the same as we did the Rebels in the South. When we captured the *Alabama,* it was the same idea."

"We didn't execute the officers. We kept them as prisoners of war. That's very different."

"Enough politics," Matilda interrupted. "If you men want to eat, get the rest of those tables set up outside so we can get the food on them. The goose is about ready to carve."

"Good thing it's not raining," Alfred grinned. "Until we get the addition built onto the house, we don't have much room for family gatherings, at least not with a family the size of yours!"

She laughed. "Go on with you. You've got family too, it's just that they are too far away to gather."

"My sister Zilpah talked about joining me when I left for California back in '49, but she wound up marrying a neighbor fellow and moving to Ohio. She's 12 years older than me, and I suspect she felt she had to go along to take care of me." He chuckled. "Cyrene and Ansel were both convinced I had taken complete leave of my senses, dashing off to this wild country. They were so convinced that I would be murdered that they even told everyone I had been."

Matilda poked him in the ribs and teased, "Only because you never wrote a single letter telling them of your safe arrival. If you had, they would have known you still lived. What were they supposed to assume when they never heard a word?"

He grinned. "Well, you took care of that. Now they know I am alive and well."

"Come on, Mama, let's eat before the food gets cold." Mary tugged on her mother's sleeve. "And while it's so warm with the sun out."

Everyone gathered and stood around the laden table while Alf intoned a lengthy grace thanking God (it seemed to Matilda) for every blessing he could think of.

While everyone sated themselves with roast goose, stuffing, mashed potatoes, sweet potatoes, green beans, canned corn, deviled eggs, and assorted pickles and relishes, Mary and Elizabeth chattered about the reports of the recent birth of a baby boy to Count and Alice Valensin.

"Isn't it romantic?" Elizabeth sighed. "A real Count. They named him Pio, after Pope Pius. And some are saying they are going to come back here and live." Elizabeth looked at Matilda. "Won't it be exciting, Mama? To have an Italian Count for a neighbor?"

Chapter 24

December, 1874

ONE YEAR LATER, as the family again gathered for Christmas, Matilda's mind went back over the events of 1874. How could the time have flown by so fast?

It had been a busy year. After a week of cold, damp, raw weather in January, the sun had come out and the weather had smiled upon them. Not only the wheat, the but hay and barley crops, in spite of threats of rising rivers, enabled them to pay off the $1280 mortgage to Mr. Waterhouse. Although the money was not enough to repay the debt to Lizzie Owens, there was enough to pay her the interest, and she seemed content with that.

"Don't fret, Mr. Wheelock," Lizzie had smiled at Alfred as Matilda carefully counted out the coins to pay her the money. "I'd only loan it to someone else for the interest. Might as well be nice folks like you and Matilda."

The conflict over colored pupils in the Sacramento Schools continued, with Superintedant Hickson refusing to recognize supply requests from Mr. McDonald as principal because of McDonald's refusal to transfer the children to their own school. Matilda smiled at the memory of Hickson's refusal to sign McDonald's pay warrant, and the Board ordering President Tracy to do so. Then McDonald was paid, and the matter seemed to fade away. She was glad the issue had never come up at the Hicksville School, where black and Miwok and white children attended classes together in harmony.

In March, a fierce snowstorm in the Sierras left drifts up to 25 feet high, seven feet higher than the previous record of 18 feet. Trains were frequently delayed. There were even reports of the snow sheds catching on fire.

"I'm glad we don't have to cross those mountains in winter, even on a train," Matilda shivered when Alfred reported the snow level to her.

He had just grinned. "Back in Vermont, we got snow like that every winter. Now you know why I never gave a thought to going back!"

Billy Bandeen created some scandal in the neighborhood by accusing another neighbor, Thomas Mahin, of brandishing a weapon, which turned out to be a false accusation.

"Why would he lie about it, if it never happened?" Matilda asked Polly when Polly told her of the incident as the two of them worked on a quilt together.

Polly laughed. "I suspect the fact that Mr. Mahin married Billy's ex-wife might have something to do with it. I think he suspects Jane took a little too much interest in Tom even before the divorce."

"Jane?" Matilda gasped. "Why, that can't be true!" But then little things began to add up in her mind. After Henry's death, Billy had accused his wife of not properly caring for their son, almost blaming her for his death. Matilda remembered finding the poor girl in tears one day after church, and she had confessed her unhappiness at his accusations. And Mr. Mahin, one of the community's most popular bachelors, was always so kind and understanding.

She met Polly's eyes and nodded. "I guess it can be, can't it." She sighed, "It's too bad someone can't make Billy see he's never going to get Jane back. She grieved for poor little Henry as much as he did, and he still treated her so cruelly."

April brought another rash of dog poisonings in Sacramento. Recalling a trip to Sacramento in which a dozen mangy dogs had snarled at Ben's heels, she could almost understand the mentality of the poisoner, but when she thought of how dear Jake was to everyone, she found it hard to have any sympathy for the man.

She remembered the day Alf came home from a trip to Galt and told her the Liberty Post Office had closed for good on May third.

"Chism Fugitt finally had to shut her down," he said with a grimace. "Not enough folks left to pay to keep it open. Guess he got a letter from the Postmaster General telling him no more money would be coming in to keep it running." He shook his head. "He sure had hopes the town would build up again, but the railroad going through Harvey's town settled Liberty's fate. Business goes where the railroad goes. Harvey sure knew what he was doing."

Alfred added his agreement. "And I understand the town of Mokelumne Station is changing the name to Lodi, after some battle in Europe. They say the Postmaster General said there were too many Mokelumnes in the state, and they should pick another name."

Alf chuckled. "After a place in Europe? I thought the Dye family named it because there are so many Dyes in the town that folks just kept saying "'Lo, Dye" as they walked down the street."

"The Dye family can think that if they want, but the city fathers prefer to say they named it after Napoleon's famous battle site in Italy." Alfred reached for his hat. "If you're going to help me finish the chores, let's go."

Alf reached for his hat as well, and followed Alfred out

the door. "Maybe they named it after the race horse after all," he muttered as they departed.

May had been an eventful month. Not only did the Liberty Post Office close, the Brewsters lost their youngest daughter, Clara. Only two years old, Matilda recalled with the pang of guilt she always felt when another woman lost a child, while her own remained so healthy. Each time she uttered a little prayer of thanksgiving for their continued well-being.

May also brought the news that the Golden Eagle Hotel's owners, the Callahans, were being forced into bankruptcy.

"Poor old George," Alfred reported, shaking his head in sympathy. "Just never seemed to get over losing his daughter. Folks say he just sat and looked at her picture, let the business go."

Matilda's mind immediately reverted to memories of the young clerk who had waited on them on their wedding night, a young man with a growing family. "Will poor John McGinnis lose his job?"

Alfred shrugged. "Probably not. Whoever takes over the running of the facility will need a Chief Clerk, and John has been there for years."

The threat of another epidemic of smallpox, with two fatalities at Knight's Landing, finally persuaded Matilda and Alfred to ignore Betsy Ann's dire warnings of the consequences of the procedure. They and all five children were vaccinated at Dr. Nestor's office in Sacramento. Except for sore arms for a few days, no one became ill. She did have great difficulty keeping little Sammy from scratching the pustule on his arm, but it healed without incident. The relief she felt knowing her family was safe from that dreaded disease made the whole effort worth while. In fact, she had even persuaded Will and Polly to do the same for their entire brood.

As Matilda watched Mary and Elizabeth help their Aunt Polly place the food on the table, she recalled the visit of Alice and Count Valensin. The girls had chattered about it for days afterwards. Matilda had to admit they made a striking couple, dressed in the latest fashion, riding in a buggy with highly polished leather and shiny wheels. The two magnificent black horses were driven by a Negro horseman, and Mrs. Valensin's Negro maid sat beside him on the front seat.

She remembered her reaction as she recalled the McCauleys had been slave owners, and that these people had chosen to remain with the family, although they were now free and worked for wages. Their finery was almost as striking as that of the Valensins. She greeted the rumor that John McCauley planned to build his daughter a mansion on the Hicksville property he had taken from poor old 'Uncle' Billy Hicks with mixed feelings.

June had seen the death of George N. Douglass, as many had expected. He had been in failing health for several years. Since they had come out together in '64, and had remained in touch, living in the same community, Matilda and her family attended the services at the Hicksville Cemetery.

Matilda could not help noticing how his son George was now a grown up young man. She thought back. He was four years older than Mary. She counted quickly. He must be nineteen. Yes, a grown man. Well able to take over running his father's farm over at McConnell's Station, just across the Cosumnes River. His brother Lewis was two years younger, and certainly big enough to help their widowed mother. George was probably looking around for a wife. She noticed his eyes on Mary. Mary, at fifteen, looked far more mature than Matilda liked. She still thought of her as a little girl, but would soon have to face the fact that her little girl was turning into a young lady.

A letter from her sister Sarah back in Illinois told her Curtis Stewart had married. Matilda's mind flew to her long-ago romance with Curtis as she read her sister's words.

> *"Everyone had despaired of his ever tying the knot. I think most folks around here have forgotten that he was so besotted with you. No one seems to know why he put off marriage for so long. He's been considered quite the catch, successful farmer and all that he is.*
> *"Anyway, a good friend of his died, leaving a widow, Amanda. Whether Curtis felt responsible for her care, or made a promise to his friend, or if he genuinely loves her, no one will ever know. Folks have been saying it's about time he did his duty and got married, him being 39 years old, after all.*
> *"I've let the speculation continue. I never let on that I know he refused to marry for all of those years because my baby sister 'Tilda rejected him, choosing instead to go gallivanting off to Kansas."*

Matilda had read the letter to Alfred, who smiled fondly at her. "I can understand his disappointment."

Matilda blushed. "I was only eighteen! And I wanted to see more of the world. After all of those letters from Alf describing his journey, and California, how could I just spend my life in Illinois?"

He smiled gently. "Your sister Sarah stayed."

Matilda laughed merrily and rose to give him a fond hug. "You're right. I suppose if I had really loved Curtis Stewart, I would have stayed and married him."

And so, she remembered thinking, another episode of my life is closed.

Two unfortunate accidents with horses claimed the lives of two young men, one in August, the second in September. In both cases, they had been thrown and dragged to their deaths. The second was a boy of only fourteen, on the Jack Wackman ranch. Each had reminded her of the tragic loss of Sinclair. She never worried when the children rode Ben or Charley, for both were so docile. She hoped the five colts now growing to maturity would be the same. Lewis favored a pinto filly, and the two were inseparable. Matilda could only pray this one would not turn out like Devil Wind, the black horse that had killed Sinclair.

In September, they had taken the children to see a matinee performance of the Royal Marionettes. The show had included a comic pantomime of Little Red Riding Hood, and each child had received an illustrated book on the story. Between the glittering grottoes, Italian sports, fairy land, and singing by the Christy Minstrels, it had been a fun-filled two hours that the children talked about for days.

"Come on, Mama. Uncle Alf is ready to say Grace, and the food is all on the table. We're hungry." Mary tugged on Matilda's hand, pulling her out of her reverie.

When Alf finished his usual lengthy prayer, everyone ate in silence until sated, and Matilda and Polly began to distribute the slabs of mince pie.

George Hand Stringfield, Matilda's cousin, son of Betsy Ann's brother A.M., announced his plans to join his Uncle Sevier Stringfield in Santa Barbara.

"He says that's God's country." He grinned. "I guess, being as he's a preacher man, he ought to know. And Britt says he can also use another hand. He's got himself another quarter of land."

"Not going back to teaching school are you?" Will chuckled, reminding everyone of the one term private school George had run in Liberty the year before the first public school had opened.

"Not on your life," George said emphatically, bringing a round of laughter from the group. "I'll leave that to the professionals."

"I guess you and Uncle Sevier have not been able to persuade your parents to join us here in California," Matilda commented.

Tom grinned and reached for another biscuit. "Uncle A.M. is such a big man in Bloomington. Everyone respects him. Why should he come to California where he'd be a nobody?"

"Besides," Betsy Ann snorted, "Amelia has all of her family there, all except George here, the only one with enough gumption to get away. She'd never leave them."

"I've been trying to talk them into coming for a visit," George grinned. "Be an easy trip, now the trains come regular. I know if they ever spent a winter out here they'd never go back."

Alf held up his cup for Polly to refill. The hot liquid sent off a plume of steam in the chilly air. He took a sip and nodded emphatically, in agreement with George's observation. "That's why Sam and I never gave a thought to going back. Britt had to, since he'd left his family there, but one winter with no snow and no blizzards convinced me and Sam to stay. Right, Sam?"

"Amen," said Sam fervently.

Alfred smiled at Matilda, then at Alf. "I'm glad you did, Partner, otherwise I might never have met 'Tilda here. And would probably still be a bachelor."

Matilda blushed as laughter ran through the group.

Mary nodded solemnly. "We're all glad you stayed. We're glad you're our papa now."

Will finished off his mince pie with a flourish and sighed in contentment. "You fellows hear that Modoc War cost the Quartermaster's Department $335, 000?"

Sam grunted. "Lot of foolishness. Wonder how much they are going to spend fighting the Apaches."

"Anyone read that editorial in the Bee?" George asked. "He says the only solution to the problem is to kill off all of the Apaches."

That comment unleashed a storm of opinion, both for and against such a policy. Matilda listened but said nothing. The idea of deliberately destroying a whole tribe appalled her. I wonder how Pa would have reacted to that, she thought.

"How about another piece of that delicious pie, Sister dear," Will said to Matilda when the discussion of what to do about the problem with the Apaches died down. She sliced another slab and passed it to him. "Thanks, 'Tilda." He dug his fork into the flaky crust.

"Heard any more about a Hicksville baseball club?" George chuckled. "Been forming 'em all over the County. Game been taking the place by storm." He clapped Lew on the back. "Young man like you just what they need on the team."

"Hear Tom Mahin and Billy Bandeen's wife are right happy," Betsy Ann offered. "Poor little mite, she's been through some tough times. Glad she's so happy with Tom."

"She should be. He's a fine man." Matilda thought of

all of the disappointed ladies who had been setting their cap for him, but he had eyes only for Jane.

As Matilda and Polly worked on the dishes, with the help of Mary and Elizabeth, Polly confided that Will planned to borrow $7000 from Andrew Whittaker to expand their property and make some improvements.

"He has a chance to buy the next quarter of land, and wants to build a bigger barn. He also says we need a new cultivator. And with more land, we will need another gang plow." She sighed. "It frightens me to think of owing so much money. Mr. Whitaker has a reputation for not being very patient, not like Lizzie Owens."

"Will's a good farmer," Matilda soothed. "He'll make the money back."

Polly shrugged and picked up another plate to dry. "You're right. I shouldn't worry. It's just that - - what if something should happen to Will? I'd never be able to pay the loan. We could lose the whole ranch."

Matilda tried to reassure her. "Come on, Will is inde-structible. No one else could have survived getting hit like a scythe like he did!"

But as she said it, a cloud covered the sun, darkening the room. Matilda shivered in spite of herself.

Chapter 25

January to May, 1875

JANUARY OF 1875 opened with news that Dr. John Morse had died in San Francisco.

"Over 3000 people attended his funeral," Alfred looked up from his paper to report. "Whole bunch of folks from Sacramento went down in a special car rented just for the occasion . Odd Fellows, Masons, and Pioneers all sent representatives."

"A shame. He was a fine man. He contributed a lot to Sacramento in the early days." Matilda folded up the stocking she had just finished mending and reached into the basket for the next one.

"He certainly did," Alfred agreed. "I remember how he and his partners, Dr. Stillington and Dr. Higgins, took in the survivors after the flood of 1850. A lot of the sick ones died, in spite of their efforts, but many more would not have survived, if not for them. They took in all of those patients abandoned by their caretakers when Dr. White's hospital flooded."

She smiled at him. "You met him once, didn't you?"

"Yes, when I came down from the diggings just after the cholera epidemic in October of 1850. Dr. Stillington was in San Francisco when the news of Statehood arrived on the *Oregon,* on his way back East to visit his family. He sent word to Dr. Morse, to warn him that cholera had come in on the same boat as the news, with 22 cases on board. Many of them died. He felt there was a good chance someone from the *Oregon* had taken the *Abby Baker* up to Sacramento and would bring the disease into the city. And it happened just that way. A few days later the first victim was found lying on the levee in the last stages. His sons had abandoned him to die while they went on to the gold fields."

"What a dreadful thing to do," Matilda murmured.

He nodded. "Many fled the city during the epidemic, but Dr. Morse stayed at his post. Fortunately, he was not one of the doctors who succumbed to the disease while caring for patients." He grinned. "I noticed him adding brandy to the ink in his ink well and asked him why he did that. He said it was to give spirit to his letters."

Matilda laughed merrily. "He must have been a wonderful man. I wish I could have known him."

"That's not all. His partner, Dr. Stillington, added laudanum, to still any concerns his letter might cause."

A week later, fire destroyed the Western Hotel on 'K' Street between Third and Fourth.

Alf, who had been in town and watched all the excitement, reported his experiences to the family the following Sunday as everyone gathered at Will and Polly's for Sunday dinner. "Hotel a total loss," he reported solemnly. "Smoke poured out of every window and door, and flames started curling around the woodwork. Fire department tried to pour water on, but the water came so slowly from the hoses they didn't have a prayer of saving the building."

"How did it start?" Alfred asked.

"They say Charley, the porter was filling the lucine oil lamps to put in the guest rooms when they figure a match must have been accidently set off somehow. No one knows how. He came back into the room to find it engulfed in flames. The walls are covered with China gloss, which is a mixture of oil and turpentine, and they went up like a torch. Fire Department worked like fury, but it wasn't until they got the rotary pumps working that they finally started making some headway against the flames."

"Did everyone get out?" Matilda shuddered in horror at the thought of being trapped in a burning building. Alfred always laughed at her for her insistence on making him put the extra door from the back bedroom out onto the porch. She never overcame her childhood fear of fire, ever since she had stood beside Sarah Williams and watched Sarah's house burn to the ground.

"Guess three people died. Two of 'em were printers for the Union. The third hasn't been identified yet. Thought it might be a woman or a young boy, judging by the size of the bones." Alf shook his head and reached for another piece of fried chicken. "One of 'em stuck his head out the window, from the third floor. We could see the despair in his face. We tried to get him to try climbing down, and a couple of fellers set off to fetch a ladder, but he turned and ran back inside."

Mary and Elizabeth exchanged nervous glances. "Our house isn't going to burn down, is it Mama?" Elizabeth asked in a quavery voice.

"We'll hope not," Matilda assured the children. "Now you know why I always tell you to be so careful with fire."

A week later, the mysterious third person still had not been identified. George Land vowed to rebuild the hotel, which he had insured for about half of the replacement cost, but by then, concerns of rising rivers replaced the fire as the main topic of conversation.

Tom, whose land lay along Badger Creek, reported the water higher than he had seen it since the floods of 1851 and

1868. "Looks like that Injun as predicted a dry winter was a little off in his calculations." He chuckled and helped himself to his third biscuit. "I hear Sherman Island is underwater again, and so is Brighton."

"Fellows down at the station are saying folks are taking up a collection to help those flooded out by the American River, up by Marysville." Alfred chuckled. "Wasn't it a Shoshone medicine man that predicted a flood that would drown all of the white men?"

Matilda joined in the laughter. "I suspect that was more wishful thinking than an actual premonition." She remembered the lightning display of the previous October. Lightning had lighted the whole sky time after time, and been followed by a deluge of rain. Had that been the warning they should have heeded? Aleck Blue had said that early rain, especially if accompanied by a lot of lightning, indicated a wet winter.

The jolt of an earthquake jarred them awake at four in the morning on Saturday, the 23rd, and all five of the children wound up on the bed with Matilda and Alfred.

"I swear," Matilda muttered. "If the earth wiggles one more time I'm going to live in a tree!" She pushed Sammy's knee out of her ribs and struggled off of the bed. Lighting the lamp, she could see no evidence of any damage. There had been no crashing sounds of breaking glass like she had heard after the last earthquake. The shaking had not even been enough to knock over the lamp. "We never had earthquakes in Illinois or Kansas."

Alfred struggled to sit up, surrounded by five children and a dog, with Carrie's arms wrapped around his neck. "Would you rather have blizzards and tornadoes?"

"Not on your life." Matilda shuddered. "You're right, I'll take an earthquake any day over a tornado." She ushered the children off of the bed. "Come on, Mary, you and Elizabeth are too big to be frightened by a little earthquake."

"I wasn't afraid, Mama," Lewis declared boldly. "I just came because Sammy was frightened and I brought him."

"Ha!" Mary scoffed. "You were more scared than Sammy."

"I was not! I just . . ."

"That's enough." Matilda felt it time to intervene. "I think it's too early to get up, so let's all go back to sleep for a while." She escorted Sammy and Carrie back to their little trundle beds and tucked them in. "Everything is fine now, the shaking has stopped."

In February, they heard old Mike McGuire, caretaker at the Golden Eagle had died. "Poor old man had been there for years. I'm sure all of this business with the Callahans losing the Hotel bothered him more than he let on. And then the Odd Fellows Bank taking it back over and putting in yet another new manager." Matilda sighed. "I suspect he just gave up, the poor old dear."

"The paper also says the French Academy of Medicine recommends lemon juice as the most efficacious treatment for diphtheria." Alfred looked up from the paper and nodded to Matilda. "I wonder what your mother will have to say about that. She has recommended lemon juice all along, but the doctors have rejected her claim. Now she can point out that she was justified all along."

April brought a letter from Mary Anne announcing their plans to come to California.

> *"John says this latest round of grasshoppers was the last straw. People are taking up collections*

to send contributions to provide relief for people here in Kansas and in Nebraska as well. The hoppers are as bad as they were in '67 when wagons were slipping off the side of the roads, the bodies of the wretched creatures were piled so thickly.

"We had a lovely crop of corn, but it has been stripped to just stalks, before the ears even had a chance to fill. It's the same as last time. If not for John's salary as Circuit Judge, we would be as destitute as our neighbors.

"We will have to come by wagon, for to bring every thing by train would be too expensive. John is writing to Alf to see if he can take the train back here to help us make the crossing. He seemed to enjoy it back in '50, and it's a much easier trip now.

"Isn't this Beecher/Tilton trial a disgrace?", John says he cannot see why anyone of Mr. Beecher's reputation would risk it to have an affair with a girl young enough to be his daughter. I guess the saying 'there's no fool like and old fool' is as true now as it ever was. I'm sure his sister is embarrassed by the whole affair.

"The jurors are disgusted. They were promised seven dollars a day, but John says they are only getting the usual two.

"The Boston News quoted Beecher as saying the Pope is a good Christian man, and he will sing hymns with him in Heaven. John says he doubts his Holiness would say as much for Mr. Beecher, in view of recent events."

When Matilda read the letter to Alfred, he grinned. "Alf was critical of Beecher's conduct, saying no good

Methodist would ever do such a thing. But after that Methodist preacher from up north left his wife and ran off with the wife of one of his parishioners, even taking his three children, Alf has been very quiet on the whole subject."

Matilda laughed. "I remember. I wonder if his poor wife ever got her children back. I remember she was asking the authorities to help her. I'm sure she is just as happy without him, but he had no right to take her children on such a disgraceful adventure." She folded up the letter.

"Maybe if he winds up in jail, they could do to him what they do in Bangor, Maine. There they let the students from the Theological Seminary practice preaching on the inmates."

Matilda laughed. "I'm sure the inmates appreciate it."

"I'm sure they do," Alfred grinned. "The paper calls it 'cruel and unusual punishment'." Then he sighed. "We won't be much better off than John and Mary Anne if we don't get anymore rain this season. We haven't had any rain since the first of March. The wheat fields are dry enough to crackle, and the heads are only half full. They won't fill properly unless we get some more moisture to them. It's good John has some experience lawyering, for there's been an awful lot of immigrants coming west thinking there's a lot of work on the farms, but farm owners haven't been hiring anywhere's near half of them."

Matilda rose and tucked her sewing away in the basket with a yawn. "John will manage. Let's go to bed. Tomorrow is going to be a busy day." She laughed softly. "Has Lewis been pestering you for a velocipede? Ever since George Putney got one, he has been hinting that he should have one too."

Alfred grinned. "Papers are full of complaints about

boys on velocipedes knocking down pedestrians on the streets in Sacramento. They've become quite the fashion. In fact, Obed Harvey, in his campaign for State Senator, has promised to pass legislation curbing their use." "That should get him some votes. And the boys can't vote against him."

A week later, Alfred returned from driving Alf to the train to send him on his journey to help John and Mary Ann on the journey west as Matilda fed breakfast to the children, getting ready to send them off to school.

"Alf's as excited as a youngster. I think he's been in one place for too long. Needed a little change. He needs a wife, is what he needs. He's alone too much, just him and your mother there." He poked around the stove. "Any porridge left?"

The sound of a horse being driven hard caught her attention. As she froze in place, she heard Mary's voice. "Mama, Mama, come quick! Jack says Uncle Will has been kicked by a horse."

Chapter 26

May to September, 1875

MATILDA GASPED and turned to Alfred, fear showing in her eyes.

Alfred jumped to his feet. "I'll hitch up the buggy. Mary, you and Elizabeth stay with Sammy and Carrie while your mother and I find out what has happened."

Matilda quickly pushed the teakettle and the pot of porridge to the back of the stove. "Be sure Sammy eats his breakfast, Mary. We'll be back as soon as we can."

"Do you think Uncle Will is dead?" Mary's eyes were wide with fright.

The panic in Jack's voice as he spoke to Alfred convinced Matilda this was very likely the case, but she did not wish to frighten the children. With an effort, she kept her voice calm. "We'll hope not. Just pray for him."

The ride to Will's was a short one, with Jack riding his horse alongside of the buggy, babbling the whole time. "Mama went out to the barn to look for Pa when he didn't come in for breakfast. I heard her scream and went running out there, so did Will and Frank. The girls just kind of clung to each other and looked scared. When I got to the barn, Mama was sitting on the floor, holding Pa's head and rocking back and forth, wailing. That scared us half to death, and Will, he said to me, run quick and fetch Aunt 'Tilda. So I jumped on old Buck here, and headed for your place."

219

Jack paused and took a deep breath. "And he sent Frank to Sacramento for Dr. Nixon."

Alfred pulled the buggy to a halt in front of the barn. Polly's keening sounded eerie in the silence. Jack jumped from his horse and helped Matilda down from the buggy. She gathered her skirts in both hands and ran into the barn, following the sound of Polly's voice.

Her heart sank at the sight that greeted her. Will's face was gray and still, the mark of a steel hoof clearly etched on the side of his forehead. The trickle of blood had already dried. His eyes stared into space. Dead eyes, Matilda realized at once. She knelt by her stricken sister-in-law and gently persuaded her to ease Will's body back to the floor and took her in her arms.

"Come, Polly," she whispered. "We can do nothing more for him. Come into the house with me." With Alfred's assistance, she helped Polly to her feet and started to lead her away.

Alfred nodded, saying softly, "The boys and I will carry him into the house."

The funeral was a large one, for Will and Polly were both well known and well liked in the community of Hicksville. Will had served on the Grand Jury, and was one of the earliest settlers.

Polly went through the funeral in a daze. Four-year-old Lizzie clung to her mother's skirts, her eyes wide, as though she could not comprehend what was going on around her. Poor Polly, Matilda thought. Eight children and only one of them an adult. Will, Jr. was grown, but Jack was just twenty, Frank eighteen, and Sammy and Bud were just eleven and eight.

Polly kept muttering, "We owe Mr. Whittaker $7000.

How am I ever going to repay him? He'll take our home. He has done it to others. I warned Will against dealing with him. I was afraid something like this would happen!"

"Hush, Polly," Matilda soothed. "Try not to worry about it now. You've a good crop coming, and surely with Will Junior and the help of the other boys and the rest of the family, you can continue to run the farm. Sam and Alf will pitch in, and so will Alfred and I."

So once again Matilda stood in the little cemetery, listening to the birds chattering in the trees, as the dreadful sound of clumps of earth striking the coffin of yet another of her loved ones echoed through her heart.

A few days later, Alfred came back from the Hicksville Post Office full of news. "We got a letter from Alf. He and John and Mary Anne and the whole tribe got off right on schedule. The roads are so good now, they anticipate being here by the middle of September. And he says those critters are not grasshoppers, they are locusts."

"What's the difference?" Matilda asked.

Alfred shrugged. "Something to do with their life cycle. It was locusts that almost wiped out all of the crops of the new Mormon colony, back at the City of the Saints, right after they settled. Swarms of seagulls came in and ate the locusts, so they've got a statue to a seagull in the town square."

Matilda laughed. "I can see why they would be grateful. Does he say anything else? I trust everyone is in good health?"

"Oh, yes, the only other thing he says is that Lincoln's widow was declared insane by her son Robert, and he had her committed to an asylum."

"What a dreadful thing for a son to do! Poor Mary. I

know she was very distraught, but how could she help it, having her husband shot right in front of her the way he was? Surely that would not be enough to classify her as insane."

Alfred turned the letter over. "That's all he says about her. I suppose we will hear more in good time." He scanned the letter again. "He also says, " Alfred paused and frowned. "He says, I met a most beautiful young lady. My heart left my bosom in a single bound." He looked the page over again. "That's all."

Matilda smiled. "A mystery! I can't believe our confirmed bachelor has actually been smitten."

"Guess we will just have to wait and see."

The second week in June, they awoke to a loud crash. Alfred leaped from bed and ran to the door, open to catch the evening breeze the night before, Matilda at his heels, pulling on her robe. Wind whistled around them, almost shrieking in its fury. The crash had been from an uprooted locust tree which, fortunately, hit nothing but the ground. As they stood gaping at the fury of the wind, the rain began, pouring down with the intensity of a winter storm.

As though the same thought came to them at once, Alfred muttered. "The wheat. It was just ready to harvest. We were going to start next week. This wind and rain will lay it flat, and knock half the grain onto the ground."

"Thanks heavens we only owe Lizzie Owens, and she will carry us. We do have enough to pay her the interest we owe." Matilda's mind flew to Polly. "But Polly was counting on a good crop to pay Mr. Whittaker. I know she was so worried. It's all she could talk about at Will's funeral."

More than an inch of rain was to fall before the freak storm moved on, and left many fallen trees in its wake. The next day, Matilda and Alfred walked hand in hand to survey the damage to the wheat crop. Sodden heads, many empty of half or more of their grains, lay in clumps on the ground. Alfred kept shaking his head in dismay. Matilda could think of nothing to say.

Tragedy struck the little community again in July. George Putney's wife, Jenny, died on July 13 of scarlet fever, after a brief illness.

Matilda wept at her funeral. Poor, shy pretty little Jenny, to die so young. Sometimes life was so unfair, she thought, recalling her feelings when she lost Sinclair and Minerva. And Jenny's little daughter Carrie (named, Jenny had informed Matilda, after Matilda's daughter Carrie) was only a year and a half old.

"Melvina is taking care of little Carrie" Mary informed her mother in a low whisper. "And she thinks the baby has scarlet fever as well. She's very feverish, and has the beginning of a rash."

Carrie followed her mother to the grave only two weeks later. Matilda's sympathy for George swelled through her again, as did dread of scarlet fever spreading through the community, fearful for her own children. Thankfully, all of hers remained healthy.

The summer passed quickly. Fortunately, the sun came out and the wheat crop was not quite the disaster they had feared, although not the bumper crop they had hoped for. Another letter from Alf, this one from Salt Lake City, was full of news.

Alfred looked up from the letter and shook his head. "Between the fighting between the different factions of the Cherokee, and the war between the soldiers and the Indians in Nevada, they will be glad to get here and put it all behind them."

"Do you think they are in danger?"

"Alf doesn't seem particularly worried. I guess the Cherokees are fighting with each other, and the Army will keep the Indians in Nevada busy. He seems more interested in reporting what Brigham Young has to say about the Mountain Meadow Massacre. Seems he says he didn't even hear about it until three months after it happened."

"I find that hard to believe," Matilda said dryly.

"So does Alf," Alfred grinned. "He refused to appear in court, so they won't accept his testimony. Now they are saying they only took part in it for fear of offending the Indians."

Matilda only shook her head.

John and his family, with Alf accompanying them, arrived in mid-September, as anticipated. As the weary entourage pulled into Alf's place, the family, anticipating their arrival after the wire from Sacramento, was there to greet them.

They were sad to inform John of Will's death, but the reunion was otherwise a joyous one. Everyone had survived the trip in good health.

"We did spend last night at a hotel in Sacramento," John grinned. "Wanted to spend a night in a real bed and get a bath in a real bath tub, with hot water. Besides, we wanted to look our best when we arrived. After all, you haven't seen us in years. And you have yet to meet Belle, she's eleven." A pretty girl, Belle dropped a quick curtsy. "And these two shy young ladies are Lilly and Eva. They are three and two." The two little girls peered around their mother's skirts.

Polly introduced her brood, and Matilda presented Alfred, Carrie and Sammy. John greeted Caroline's daughters warmly. They, of course, remembered him well from their Kansas years.

"And Sam, my boy," John greeted his brother with enthusiasm. "Still a bachelor? With all of these young ladies fussing over you, you are probably too spoiled to ever take a wife!" He looked around. "And Mother? As feisty as ever?"

"Oh, yes," Sam advised him. "Says the rheumatics in her knees are giving her some trouble, so I have been ordered to bring you over to see her."

John and his family settled in, although John spoke of moving to Oregon for a more permanent residence.

A neighbor, Adolph Palin, was reported killed when kicked by a horse.

"Turns out he is coming along fine," Alfred chuckled. "Don't know how the rumor got started that he was dead. He says folks keep looking at him like he was a ghost. He wasn't even hurt bad, just knocked down." He turned the page on the paper. "But I do see where they have a problem with another destructive fire in Virginia City."

"Again?" Matilda exclaimed. "Someone must have a grudge against the town. Surely as much fire damage as they have had could not be all accidental."

But interest in neighbors and fire victims and Indian battles far away in Nevada were dwarfed by concerns much closer to home.

Chapter 27

December, 1875 to June, 1876

MATILDA GASPED AS she caught the profile of Mary's abdomen through her nightgown. The dim light from the kerosene lamp on the bedside table shone faintly, but enough to outline the unmistakable bulge. With a flash, Matilda remembered so many things from the last few months. The usually vivacious Mary had been strangely morose, and seemed to have lost her appetite.

"Of course," Matilda muttered. "How could I have been so blind?" She closed the door behind her and leaned against it, her legs suddenly so rubbery she feared they would not hold her. She felt a pang of guilt. How have I failed her? She's only sixteen. Who could the father be? She racked her memory. George Douglass. It had to be George. He hung around her all the time. Had they ever been alone? She thought frantically. The Harvest Hayride last August. Mary and George had been gone for more than an hour. When she returned, Mary had looked flustered, which was unusual for Mary. That must have been when it happened. Matilda counted quickly. Yes, it all fit. Mary must be about four months pregnant.

She went into the parlor where Alfred sat reading. Dear Alfred, she thought. Thank God I have him. He'll know how to handle this. Her heart swelled with love for him. Lewis had faded from her memory more and more with each day since she met Alfred. These seven years with him had been the happiest of her life.

The expression on her face must have told Alfred something troubled her. Always so sensitive to her feelings, he put his book aside and rose to take her in his arms.

"What is it, my dear?" he asked in his gentle way.

At his sympathetic understanding, she burst into tears and sobbed the whole story out against his shoulder.

He gently stroked her hair and murmured, "Why, George Douglass has been besotted with Mary for years. You've often told me how he even followed her around on the trail across, when he was only ten years old." He tenderly kissed her forehead and wiped away her tears with his big red handkerchief. "Surely he will be pleased to marry her."

"But she's barely sixteen," Matilda cried. "She's so young!" She took a deep breath to bring her voice back under control. She did not want the children to hear her. "And George has such a temper. I fear she will not be happy with him."

He smiled into her eyes and stroked her cheek with a forefinger. "The final decision will have to be Mary's," he said. "If she chooses not to marry him, then we will face whatever comes." He kissed her quickly. "Go and talk to her. There is no time to waste. If you noticed, others will also."

"You're right, of course." She sighed and blew her nose vigorously into his handkerchief. She set her jaw and entered the room Mary shared with her sister Elizabeth.

Elizabeth's regular breathing assured Matilda she slept. Mary's eyes, on the other hand, flew open when the light from the lamp in her mother's hand fell on her face. Tears glistened on her cheeks.

Matilda held out her hand. "Come, Mary," she said softly. "It's time we talked."

Mary cried and stormed, declaring she hated George. At first, she refused to marry him. When she realized the other option, bearing a child out of wedlock, was one she could not face either, she agreed.

George, of course, was delighted, and the brief wedding ceremony took place on January 17, 1876, in the parlor of Dr. Pratt, the Methodist minister in Sacramento. Only the immediate family attended.

Fourteen year-old Elizabeth had not taken the news well. "Mother," she cried, as Mary wept beside her. "How can I face my friends? They are all saying Mary is marrying George because she has to. It's so embarrassing."

"Hush, Elizabeth," Matilda said firmly. "You are not responsible for your sister's actions. If your friends blame you, they are not very good friends." She softened at the worry on Elizabeth's face. "I know this is difficult for you, my darling, but your sister needs us now. This is very hard on her, too."

As though this had not occurred to her before, Elizabeth turned to her sister and threw her arms around her. "Oh, Mary," she whispered. "I am so sorry."

Mary smiled through her tears and returned her sister's embrace. "Will you stand up with me at the wedding?"

"Of course I will," Elizabeth vowed. "But you have to let me wear the pink tarleton dress Uncle Sam gave you for your birthday."

Matilda watched the tableau a sigh of relief. Her concern that this would drive a wedge between the girls would not materialize after all. She suppressed a laugh. Elizabeth had envied her sister the dress, which suited her coloring much better than it did Mary's red hair. Men had no sense of fashion.

After the wedding, Mary and George settled into the Douglass home by McConnell Station where George had lived by with his widowed mother and younger brother since his father's death the previous May. Aside from the fact that Mary found George's mother an exacting taskmaster, life seemed to drift back to normal. Carrie moved, in great delight, from her small trundle bed into the large double bed with Elizabeth, thrilled to share a room with her big sister.

Alfred grumbled about the raise in property taxes. "Only paid $34.26 last year. I know we've made a few improvements, but not that much."

Matilda nodded in understanding. "They say they need more because they are improving the roads and adding to the schools."

Alfred grimaced."And have you noticed any improvements?"

She had to laugh. "The improvements must be in another part of the County." She settled into her chair with a sigh and reached for her sewing basket. "Did you notice how Wes Overton was hanging around Will and Polly's Mary at Christmas? Since her father was killed, I'm sure marriage looks very attractive to Mary. Polly has been having a hard time dealing with Will's death."

"Yes, I noticed. Also, I noticed Becky and Jack making calf eyes at each other. Aren't they still pretty young?"

"They are both twenty this year. Will's Mary is only seventeen, just a few months older than our Mary. But Wes is over thirty. Certainly time he thought of getting married."

"Maybe we will be having a couple of weddings pretty soon."

Wes Overton and Mary Randolph married at a quiet ceremony at her mother's home on May 5. At the reception, Jack Randolph and Caroline's daughter Rebecca Evans announced they had been married the previous week.

Mary's son, Matilda's first grandchild, was born two weeks after her cousin Mary's wedding. Mary labored long and hard. Her screams echoed through Matilda's head.

"Hush, Mary," she soothed, tears running down her cheeks as she witnessed Mary's agony. "Use your strength to push."

As the hours passed, Matilda began to fear Mary would not survive the birth. The midwife seemed helpless. George had ridden for Doctor Nixon only to be told he was out on another call and his housekeeper could give no estimate of the time of his return.

When Matilda began to despair, Alfred said, "I'm going to Alf's for your mother. As old as she is, she may be able to help. She's birthed a great number of babies and will surely know what to do."

The hour it took for him to return showed no improvement in the situation. Attempts to persuade Mary to push had no effect. As soon as next the contraction began, she started to scream, rolling in agony.

When Betsy Ann walked into the room, she immediately took charge. Matilda had never been so glad to see anyone in her life. Even Mary seemed to sense the change.

"Bring me a rope, Alfred," she called out the door to where he hovered anxiously with the pacing George. When he returned with it, she tied one end to the foot of the bed.

"Matilda," Betsy Ann's next command was to her daughter, "get up on the bed behind her. Scoot her down so her

feet can brace on the bedstead and hold her shoulders up."
Matilda scrambled to obey.

"Now, Mary," she told her granddaughter firmly, "When
the next pain hits, you clench your teeth, brace your feet on
the bedstead, and pull that rope. Pull like you've never
pulled before."

Mary, drenched with sweat, nodded and gasped, "Yes,
Grandmama."

Matilda had to smile. Even as frightened as Mary was,
her grandmother could still command obedience. Mary
arched her back as the next contraction rolled across her
abdomen and opened her mouth to scream.

"Mary!" her grandmother commanded sternly.

Mary immediately clenched her teeth and started to pull
on the rope. Matilda strained to hold her. "Pull, Mary,"
Betsy Ann ordered. "Pull and push. Push that baby out."
The pain passed. "Now relax. Rest until the next one
comes."

Mary panted in relief, and the next contraction rolled
across her abdomen. Gritting her teeth, she pulled the rope,
her feet firmly braced. Her strength seemed renewed.
Grimly silent, she concentrated on the task at hand.

On the fifth contraction, Betsy Ann grunted with satisfaction. "All right, Mary, relax. It's over." In moments, the
baby slid into Betsy Ann's experienced hands. With a sigh,
Mary collapsed back into Matilda's arms, weeping with
relief.

Matilda climbed stiffly off the bed. The silence frightened her. Why hadn't the baby cried? She approached
Betsy Ann's side and watched her laboring to get the baby
to breathe. Matilda found herself holding her own breath.
Her frightened eyes met her mother's.

"Here, you," Betsy Ann told the midwife, who had stood

silently to the side, watching. "See if you can deliver the afterbirth." She motioned to Matilda to follow and they sped to the kitchen where Betsy Ann immediately dipped the infant in cold water several times. She slapped its heels and buttocks to no avail.

Finally, she placed her mouth over the infant's and blew. A faint cry rewarded her efforts, and Matilda started to breathe again. She looked at the pallid face of her first grandchild and her heart sank. His arms and legs hung limply, and the cries remained feeble.

"Best I can do," Betsy Ann muttered. "That fool woman's incompetent. She should know how to handle frightened girls." She laid the infant across her shoulder. His head lolled. She sighed, "Well, we'll do our best."

Mary named the baby Earnest at George's insistence and over her objections. But he never developed enough strength to suck at her breast. He even had difficulty swallowing the milk Matilda and Mary expressed from her breasts and dribbled into his mouth. Dr. Nixon, who arrived just after Earnest drew his first feeble breath, could offer no help.

"Baby's probably not going to survive," he told them, as kindly as ever. "I'm so sorry I could not have been here sooner."

In spite of day and night efforts on the part of both Betsy Ann and Matilda, Earnest died on the third day after his birth. They buried him in Hicksville Cemetery next to his grandfather Douglass.

One week after Earnest's funeral, news reached them that the Hicksville Hotel had been sold, to a man named Louis Herbert who planned to re-open, with a blacksmith shop and a pump shop as well. A great deal of speculation accompanied the news, with different opinions of the effect the change would have on the community.

"Some say the reason Dick Johnson sold is he and Celestia are not getting along too well," Alf reported. "Some say another blacksmith shop will be bad for Kidder's business at his shop here on my place, but he's so good shoein' horses I can't see it affecting him too much. Guess we'll have to wait and see."

Rumbles of agitation against Chinese labor also began to circulate through the community. Matilda could only hope it did not reach serious proportions, although some of the comments she heard concerned her. She knew many people resented the hard working Chinese, who often worked for less pay than other men. They also were willing, Matilda thought wryly, to do work others felt too hard or too dangerous, remembering some of the stories of them risking their lives dangling from ropes to place the dynamite charges used to chisel the path for the railroad. How quickly men forget how much they owed those brave souls!

Matilda ignored the furor, preferring to concentrate on her home and family. Her brother Alf returned from Kansas in the middle of June, an attractive young lady with him.

"Matilda," he announced proudly, "meet my wife, Emaline. We were married May 25th at her mother's home in Kansas."

Matilda, stunned, could only stare for a moment. Why, the child couldn't be any older than Mary. How old is Alf, anyway? She calculated quickly in her mind. Why, he's forty-six. You old fox, she thought, remembering the brief note in Alf's letter, and Mary Anne's comment when she and John had arrived the previous fall, about how young Miss McFadden had enchanted Alf. So this is why you had

234

to turn around and go back to Kansas this summer. She pulled herself together and remembered her manners.

"Welcome to California, Emaline." She managed a smile, wondering why the girl looked so frightened. *Probably because the poor thing has never been away from home before.* "Shame on you, Alf. Why didn't you write and tell us so we could have given some kind of a reception?"

A smile lighted the girl's face, and the blue eyes shone through the unshed tears. "Please, Mrs. Wheelock, call me Emma."

"Of course, Emma, and you may call me 'Tilda." A surge of pity for the child swept over Matilda and she gathered her into her arms. When she did, Emma's tears came freely. Matilda looked at Alf over the girl's blonde head, questions in her eyes.

He shook his head sadly. "The rest of the family hasn't been as kindly, as you, 'Tilda. They feel Emma's too young for me. I'm afraid Mother became quite vocal on the subject. She has announced her intention to move in with Sam, saying I don't need her any longer, that she will not share household responsibilities with a child." He raised his chin defiantly. "But I love her. She's the first woman I've ever loved. You know that." He stroked the blond curls gently. "And she loves me."

"Then that's all that matters," Matilda said firmly. She put her hands on the girl's shoulders and smiled into her eyes. "Welcome to the family."

"Thank you, 'Tilda," Alf said gratefully. "I knew I could count on you. By the way, has John left for Oregon yet?"

"No," Matilda replied. "He's delayed their departure, wanting to wait until Mary Anne's baby is born in October. He says they'll go next spring."

"I sure want to see him," Alf grinned. "Want to tell him

the bill he introduced into the Kansas Legislature passed. The name of Waterville is no more. Randolph, Kansas is once again Randolph. Too bad Pa didn't live to see it."

Matilda smiled softly. "I'm sure wherever he is he is happy. I know it bothered him, losing his town like that."

Alfred arrived in from the field at that moment and Alf repeated the introductions. Obviously taken with Emma's beauty, Alfred gazed in open admiration of the pert nose, rosebud lips, and pearly skin. "Well, partner, I'd despaired of you ever marrying, but I have to say you got one worth waiting for."

They all laughed.

After Alf and Emma left, Matilda turned to Alfred. "Why did you come in so early? Are you having that pain again?"

"Just a touch," he replied, attempting to make light of it. He sat down at the table suddenly, as though too weak to stand. "Probably just a little wind in the stomach. Need some of your mother's good elderbark tea."

He did not fool Matilda. The pain showed in his eyes. She looked at the beloved face, the weathering around the hazel eyes, the slight receding of his dark hair, and her love for him surged through her. What if the pain heralded something serious? Panic seized her. What if she should lose him? She hurried to his side and cradled his head against her breast. As she stroked his hair, tears sprang into her eyes and fear touched her heart with icy fingers.

Chapter 28

July to August, 1876

"DID YOU KNOW," Alfred told Matilda one evening as he sat reading the newspaper, "that they made a law in China ordering that if the bank fails, the heads of the officers will be cut off and tossed into a corner with the assets?" He chuckled. "There hasn't been a bank failure in China for over 500 years."

Matilda had to laugh in spite of her concerns for his health. She knew he tried to take her mind off the pain she could see in his eyes. "I can see why the directors would be motivated to keep the bank solvent."

Scandal rocked the County with an investigation of complaints against Dr. White and the administration of the County Hospital. Polly, full of indignation, told Matilda about one case she knew personally.

"Mr. Sprout's poor little daughter can't walk or see or speak, her not being right since she was born. She took sick and her father took her to the hospital. She spent the night without enough cover and shivered the whole time, not being able to sleep a wink. When Mr. Sprout went to see her the next morning, he told Dr. White how the poor child had suffered." Polly paused and took a deep breath, "And do you know what Dr. White said? He said, 'What's the difference? She's going to die anyway.' Mr. Sprout was furious, and he took the child out of the hospital at once. He was just sputtering with indignation when he told me what had happened. How could any doctor be so callous about the child's suffering? Even if she's not right in her head."

Tom nodded knowingly. "Lots of stories like that came out. Coroner Wick even says often a patient would be dead for three or four days before he was called. Says bodies would be in the dead house and would be black and fly-blown, even on the verge of rotting. When he asked why he hadn't been called in sooner, the answer was they had forgotten!"

Matilda shuddered. Her appetite disappeared. "That's terrible," she cried.

"And I've heard patients are often swarming with vermin," Sam added, not to be out-done. "The wards are overrun with lice, and clothing and sheets are frequently dirty."

"Disgraceful," Betsy Ann opined. "Whole place should be shut down. One feller said he was there for four weeks and never had his sheets changed once."

Sam chuckled. "I understand the quality of the food depends on what class they put you in. The poor really get short-changed."

"Well, the Grand Jury sure was frank in its report," Tom said. "We'll see if anything comes of it. I'll bet if our Will had still been on that Grand Jury there would have been some action taken. Will would never have put up with such goings on, never for a minute."

"You're right, he wouldn't have," Polly said. "Maybe someone should investigate the Protestant Orphan's Asylum, too. Did you read about the poor little girls who ran away and took the train to Oakland? Begged to be allowed to stay, pleading not to go back to the Asylum, saying they were beaten and mistreated there. And the poor waifs only eleven and eight years old." She snorted indignantly. "Their mother is dead, and their father's whereabouts are unknown, so they have nobody to defend them. And the authorities are sending them right back! And probably to be punished for running away."

Betsy Ann nodded her agreement. "Something should be done. Have heard stories like that before coming out of that place. Good there is somewhere for the poor little souls to go, where they can be fed and housed, but they should never be abused."

Matilda glanced over at Alfred, who sat silently to one side, not entering into the conversation, which was unusual. She saw the pain in his eyes, and her heart missed a beat.

On July 19, the family gathered to celebrate Matilda's fortieth birthday. Matilda rose early. Alfred had been restless in the night, and, although he did not complain, she knew the pain in his side was worse. Betsy Ann recommended slippery elm. The comfrey poultices seemed to ease the pain a little, but it never went completely away.

She glanced over at him. He slept soundly, exhausted by the restless night, and she eased out of the bed carefully so she did not disturb him. He certainly needed his rest.

By mid-day, the clan had gathered, and the makeshift table in the shade of the big locust tree by the south side of the house bent under the weight of all the food.

Polly hugged Matilda. "My, goodness 'Tilda, you don't look forty. I swear I have many more gray hairs than you."

Tom hugged her as well. "Happy Birthday, little sister. Someone else share's your opinion of the County Hospital. I hear someone burned down their barn, with all of their hay."

She returned his hug. "The County Health Department should get after them. I hear they are trying to clean up China Slough. And they've put pressure on Drs. Baldwin, Briggs, and Hatch to vaccinate everyone against smallpox."

"Yes," he chuckled, "but the good doctors say all who can pay the $2.50 for the vaccination should still pay it."

"They had to make it available to poor people," Matilda retorted. "If the schools require all children to be vaccinated before they can go to school, there has to be some way for them to get it, if they can't afford to pay."

"Stuff and nonsense," Betsy Ann snorted. "Never known doctors to do anything to help a body at all."

The arrival of her niece Mary and Wes Overton brought more hugs and welcomes. Mary looked wonderful. Wes must be a very thoughtful husband, for Mary to look so happy. She wished she could say the same for her daughter Mary. She and George arrived soon after Mary and Wes, the difference quickly apparent. Mary looked sullen and George flustered. They've quarreled again, Matilda thought with a sigh. If only Mary had not gotten pregnant so young. She shrugged. Nothing she could do about it now.

The men gathered in a group and began discussing the latest round of Indian fighting.

"Sioux began raising a ruckus in Wyoming and Montana. Probably could have settled it, but Custer set out to make a name for himself. Rode right into the trap the Sioux set up for him at Little Big Horn.' Sam shook his head. "Shame all those men had to die because of Custer's ambition. If he had waited for General Terry, he might have won."

Tom disagreed. "If he had waited, there just would have been more men killed. The Sioux were determined to get him for massacring a village full of women and children a few months back.'

Wes started to laugh. "I stopped by Jacob Gruehler's place on "J" Street a few days back to try some of his famous Boca Beer. A bunch of the regulars were expounding on what should be done about the Indian problem. A lawyer said all the preachers of peace should be led to a conference with the 'bloody savages' as he called them, and leave them to their fate." As the laughter died down, he added, "A merchant suggested the lawyer was better fitted to betraying his clients than leading troops into battle. A liquor merchant proposed a plan to ply all of the Indians with firewater, then surround them and shoot them down."

"Full of their usual bravado," Tom interceded with a wry chuckle.

"Yep," Wes grinned. "Then a veteran of the Mexican War stood up and produced a paper. Said he was trying to recruit a troop to go to the scene of the wars, and inviting all to sign on."

"I'll bet he didn't get many takers," Tom laughed.

"Nary a one. All of the most vocal left the room as fast as they could."

By the first week of August, they could no longer deny that Alfred was seriously ill. A visit to Dr. Nixon in Sacramento told them he suffered from inflammation of the bowel, and he recommended the slippery elm, like Betsy Ann had suggested, which did not seem to help. The comfrey poultices gave some relief, but nothing but laudanum ever removed the pain completely.

Matilda watched him grow worse every day. His appetite disappeared, and she had to encourage him to take even sips of soup. His face grew thin as his weight dropped. As he wasted away, Matilda would look at the portrait of him that hung on the wall, vigorous, healthy, eyes full of life. If only she could work some miracle that would restore him to that condition. She prayed and prayed, but her supplications to God did not even slow the gradual destruction.

His spirit remained. He tried to cheer her, to assure her he would get well. "After all," he chuckled, "have to get the next crop in. Can't expect Frank and Bud to do my chores forever." Polly's boys had begun helping when Alfred's illness became so severe he could no longer work.

She smiled at him, her love for him surging through her. "The boys don't mind. It gives them a chance to get away from home. I think Will makes a hard taskmaster. He's trying so hard to take his father's place. Over here, they can take a break when they want without anyone scolding them."

On the 27th of August, as Matilda sat holding Alfred's hand, he opened his eyes and smiled. "I'm not going to make it, am I 'Tilda, my love." It was a statement, not a question.

Matilda had to admit that the last time the doctor had come by he had been unable to offer any hope, only more laudanum to keep the pain under control. The swelling of Alfred's abdomen had become more severe, and any attempt to swallow even sips of water resulted in his vomiting it back. His body burned with fever in spite of the cool compresses she kept applying to his forehead. She knew death would be the only relief he would ever have, but she could not bear to let him go. She refused to even think of a life without him.

"Please don't leave me," she whispered. Her eyes filled with tears as he slipped back into the opium-induced sleep. "Please, please don't leave me."

As she watched, the breathing stopped, and the tears slid down her cheeks.

It was over.

Chapter 29

August to October, 1876

MATILDA WENT through Alfred's funeral in a haze of pain. She scarcely heard the words of Reverend Fields as he conducted the service. She could not believe Alfred was gone. He had become such a major part of her life. Neighbors spoke to her after the services, but she later had no memory of what she said or to whom she had spoken.

That night, as she lay alone in the bed she and Alfred had shared for over nine years, sleep refused to come in spite of her exhaustion. Along with the grief at losing him came the realization that she was once again a widow with young children to care for. Panic seized her, and her heart pounded. Lewis was only thirteen, still too young to accept a man's responsibilities. Her brother Sam, bless him, could be counted on to help. She again thought how fortunate she was to have such a large and close-knit family.

"Mama?" Carrie's voice came through the thumping of the blood pounding in her head. "Mama, can I stay with you tonight?" She started to cry. "I miss Papa."

Matilda sat up in the bed and folded the child into her arms. "Of course, Darling. I miss him too. We will just have to get through this together."

As Carrie snuggled beside her and drifted off to sleep, Matilda remembered that long ago day in Kansas when she came to grips with the fact that she was a widow with three young children to raise.

She sighed. If this is the life God has decided I am to have, I had best get on with it. She forced down the panic, making herself breath slowly and deeply, and finally fell asleep.

Life went on around her. On September 25, she signed the papers naming Sam as the administrator of Alfred's estate. She could not bear the thought of doing it herself.

The papers reported a case of smallpox transmitted by a letter. The thought that the dreadful disease could travel so far frightened her, and made her more thankful than ever that Alfred's foresight had ensured she and the children were protected by vaccination.

The picture of William Land's new hotel provided a positive note, but it only reminded her of the widows of the two young men who had died so tragically. The third victim had never been identified, and each time she thought of it, she wondered what mother missed a son who never wrote, like Alfred had never written his family and they assumed he was dead.

Of course, she thought, they had never really determined if the unidentified body was a boy or a woman. She shuddered to think of the condition he or she must have been in when found.

The Wall family lost their son Edmund, thrown from his horse and killed at only 23 years of age. The rest of the family attended the funeral, but Matilda could not bring herself to go. Alfred's loss still hurt her too much to even think of going to another funeral.

News reached them that Wild Bill Hickok had been killed in Deadwood, Dakota Territory. Polly had come by and told her.

"Everyone seems to think of Hickok as a hero," Matilda commented when Polly related the news. "All I can think of is how he killed poor Mr. McCanless and two of his friends when all the man wanted was the money the stage company owners owed him for a horse he sold them. Even killed the poor man with his own gun."

Polly was a great comfort to Matilda since she, also, had been so recently widowed. Sometimes they talked, sometimes they cried. Sometimes they just sat in silence and sewed, or worked together in the kitchen. Polly seemed to sense when Matilda wanted to talk or when she just wanted companionship. They shared many a pot of tea.

It was also Polly who told her about the government giving arms to the Utes. "The Utes were supposed to help the army in their fight against the Sioux. At least, that was the army's plan. But I guess the Utes had other ideas. They politely accepted the rifles and ammunition, then some time in the night they just faded away. No one even saw them leave. The soldiers woke up the next morning and there was not a single Ute in camp." She chuckled and rose to refill the teapot from the kettle on the stove. "And all of the rifles and supplies they had been given went with them."

Matilda laughed, for the first time since Alfred's death. It felt good. "The Army should have known better. The Utes have no loyalty to the Government. Why should they? The Government has taken their lands and given only unfulfilled promises in return. I'm sure they just saw it as a chance to get all of those good rifles. And they sure can move quietly! Remember Britt and Alf telling about how they snuck into their camp and ran off the horses?"

"I guess they'll know better next time. If there is a next time." Polly rose and stretched. "I'll check the bread. It should be about ready to go in the oven."

"Check the temperature while you're there. We may have to get the oven a little hotter."

Polly moved to the stove and squinted as she checked the gauge. "I'll toss in one more chunk." She lifted the metal lid with the handle and dropped in a piece of wood from the box beside the stove, then raised the towel on the bread bowl and poked the rising dough. "Ten more minutes." She returned to the chair opposite Matilda and sat down.

"Reverend Fields told me the Alta California has reported the Methodist Church has decided to reunite the North and South divisions."

"It's about time," Matilda commented. "War between the States has been over for more than ten years."

Polly sighed. "I just wish the States could agree as peacefully. Terrible, the things I keep reading about that are happening in the South."

Matilda shook her head. "War between the States. War between the Turks and the Serbs. War between the Egyptians and the Assyrians, whoever they are. War between the Utes and the Sioux, and between the Sioux and Pawnee. Why is it men are always so eager to fight? And look at the poor Modocs. What did fighting get them? Stuck on a reservation in Missouri where half of them have died. And no wonder, in that dreadful climate, with all of that ague. I'll bet the poor Indians had never even heard of the ague until they got to Missouri. And I hear they have not been given any medical care at all. Disgraceful."

She rose and put the bread in the oven and returned with more hot water for the teapot. "And when I think of poor Josh being killed in that tragic war between the States, his brother John wounded and almost dying. Josh left poor Julia with Sarah and Henry to raise. Why, Henry was just a boy of fourteen when his father died, and after losing his mother as well."

"He was only two when Temperance died," Polly said. "Julia was surely the only mother he ever knew."

"Yes, and then he goes off and fights as soon as he's sixteen and winds up dying himself." Matilda sighed. "And in such a far off place as Marietta, Georgia. He was wounded in the battle on July 4, but didn't die from his wound until a month later. To die so young is sad enough, but to lie there and die so far from friends and family is even sadder. Why, I remember . . . " she began when Carrie and Sammie came running through the door.

"Mama, Mama!" Carrie's eyes danced. "Lew says if we keep the chickens fed and the eggs gathered, he'll take us trick or treating for Halloween in the buggy."

At the end of October, in the midst of a driving rainstorm, Sam brought by the inventory Mr. Loughran, Uncle Billy Hicks, and Mr. Short had prepared for the Court.

"You've got to look it over," he said gently, placing the paper on the table. "Anything you don't agree with we have to correct before we file." He pushed the single sheet of paper in front of her.

As the tears welled in her eyes, he attempted to cheer her with an account of an amusing incident that had occurred on the train a few days previously. "Passing through Galt it was, and ran into a whole bevy of hornets. They swarmed in through the windows and created a panic amongst the passengers. Guess the train was real crowded. Conductor says folks were running about and swatting at the hornets with newspapers and umbrellas, anything they could get their hands on, and falling all over themselves." He chuckled. "Number of them got stung, but it's a wonder no one got killed, with all of that swinging and swatting. Some even tried to jump off the train, but luckily could not get off, or someone would have been killed for sure."

Matilda made no response. She did not even look up from the paper in front of her. Sam seemed to realize she had no interest in the story. He hugged her and kissed the top of her head.

"Take your time," he murmured softly into her hair. "I'll be back for the list tomorrow."

She did not move as he departed. Carrie and Sam, under Lew's direction, had gone to feed the chickens. Elizabeth collected the last of the tomatoes in the garden. Matilda was alone. She blinked to clear her eyes and finally focused on the paper in front of her.

Nine cows, she read silently. Seven calves. Nothing about how the cows would only let down their milk for Alfred, how Frank and Bud and Lew had to struggle to persuade the cows they really could give up their milk, that they did not have to save it for Alfred.

Twenty-seven head of hogs. She closed her eyes and saw Alfred tenderly helping one hungry piglet find an open teat on his mother's belly when it seemed his little brothers and sisters had taken all the available slots. She shook her head and read on.

Five head of work horses. Ben and Charley still looked for Alfred every morning. The paper said nothing about how every day he gave them a lump of sugar, how they stood at the corral eagerly awaiting him. They still looked for him each morning, their heads over the fence, their ears forward, anticipating his arrival. How do you tell a pair of horses their beloved master was never coming back? That he was cold in his grave?

Two head of two-year-old colts. The colts Alfred had

planned to tame for Carrie and Sammie. He wanted to teach them to ride, and he wanted each to have their own horse.

Two sets of harness, three wagons, one mower and a horse rake. Can a man's life be described in a list of equipment? Nothing about their plans for the future, about the love they shared. No, just three dozen chickens, four dozen turkeys, four tons of barley, seven tons of baled hay, twenty tons of loose hay. Total $3573.00.

Is that what a man's life is worth after he's gone, she thought, with an ache in her heart? Nothing about his kindness, the patient, gentle way he helped the children with their studies, the hours he spent reading to Carrie and Sammie, imbuing in them his love for books. Nothing about the emptiness within her, the gaping hole he left in her life.

A sudden gust of wind buffeted the building, whistling around the batting, and another spate of rain poured down upon the roof.

She pushed the paper aside and wept.

Chapter 30

October to December, 1876

SAM FILED THE inventory on October 31, and Matilda tried to get on with her life. Two days before, on October 29, her brother John's wife had presented him with another daughter. They named the little girl Ora, and John began making his plans to move to Oregon the following summer.

Sammie and Carrie were not impressed with their new cousin. Instead, they looked forward to Halloween with great excitement, and carved their pumpkins with great care and a lot of help from their big brother Lew. Matilda helped them light the candles inside, and the eerie faces grinned at them from either side of the front door.

Matilda and Elizabeth made a whole batch of candied apples to give to the neighborhood children for trick or treat, as well as a number of caramel popcorn balls carefully wrapped in brown paper. Elizabeth had declared herself, at fifteen, as too old to go trick or treating. She stayed home to help her mother hand out the treats. Lew, true to his promise, took Carrie and Sammie in the buggy. With gentle, patient, and faithful old Ben pulling them, Matilda felt safe in allowing them to go. Sammie had chosen to be a ghost, and Carrie went dressed as a princess. She looked so adorable it brought a lump to Matilda's throat. How she wished Alfred could have seen her.

After Halloween, November stretched before her. On November third, the big news to hit the community was the shooting of a man in Alabama Township in a dispute over the use of a piece of land for sheep.

"Shot him at close range with a shotgun, he did," Sam reported. "Not likely the poor fellow will survive."

Matilda could only shake her head at such foolishness when Sam related the sad story. "Can you imagine killing someone over a few blades of grass?"

"Does seem a little silly, but men have been killed for less."

Matilda, thinking back, could recall a number of such incidents, and was forced to agree.

One week later, the big news affecting Hicksville was Dick Johnson's sale of the Hicksville Hotel and surrounding property to Louis Herbert. A lot of speculation on how that would affect the community followed.

"Solid businessman, he is," Sam declared. "Should be good for the whole town. Plans to open a blacksmith shop and a pump shop as well. Be good to have someone local to handle the pumping business. Getting water out of the ground is a big job. Getting harder all the time. Getting so just a windmill won't do the job."

"Hear he's working on the design for a new pump, one that will be more efficient." Alf said. "About time."

"Won't he take business from Kidder?" Matilda asked.

Alf grinned. "Kidder's got more business than he can handle. Should be better for everyone. Besides, Kidder wants to run for Justice of the Peace. If he gets that job, he'll have even less time for blacksmithing. And once he's a married man, he'll have his hands even fuller." Plans were underway for the marriage of Will and Polly's daughter Maggie to Kidder Stringfield. He had been courting his cousin for a long time, and the wedding date set for January 29, though Maggie would not be fifteen until February 11.

She did not voice her concerns, that she felt Maggie too young to marry, remembering how young Mary had been when she married George Douglass, and how unhappy she was now. But Kidder was a fine young man. He would make Maggie a good husband. Instead, she just asked, "Isn't Herbert the man as was charged with selling liquor on Election Day a few years back?"

Sam laughed. "You're right. I'd forgotten that. I think they said something about selling liquor to the Mi-Woks as well. He should make an interesting neighbor."

An epidemic of diphtheria broke out in Dixon, and a number of families lost children to it. The thought of losing Carrie or Sammie to that dreadful disease frightened Matilda.

"Oh, don't worry so much, little sister," Sam teased when she voiced her concerns. "Why don't you let me take you to Moore's Opera House this coming Saturday? I hear they have a pretty good show on now."

She thought about it. It would be good to get out. She had not been anywhere other than to church, to Sam's, or to Polly's since Alfred's illness became so severe. Her mind went back over the dreariness of the past few months and she sighed.

Her thoughts came back to the present and she saw Sam waiting for her answer. "Sorry, my mind wandered for a moment." She gave him a rueful smile. "It would be lovely, but I think I will skip it this time." On an impulse, she added, "And I don't think you should go either."

"Why on earth not?" He gaped at her, a puzzled look on his face.

"I don't know. Just a feeling I have. Please don't go."

"All right," he laughed. "I'll humor you. But a couple of my friends are going. If they say I missed a great show, it will be your fault!"

The following Monday, Matilda had just put the day's bread to rise and started on the breakfast dishes when Lew ran in, out of breath.

"Mama," he gasped. "Did you hear? Moore's Opera House collapsed last Saturday night. Everyone at the Post Office was talking about it. A whole bunch of people got killed. Weren't you and Uncle Sam planning to go that night? Aren't you glad you didn't?"

Matilda stood in shocked silence for a moment, the tea-cup she had been about to submerge in the pan of soapy water suspended in her hand. Memory of the strange feeling she had when Sam first proposed the excursion washed over her and she felt herself sway on her feet.

"Yes, Son," she responded slowly, trying to get her heart rate back under control. "I'm glad we didn't go. Sam didn't go either, did he?" A sudden terrifying thought of losing yet another brother shot through her.

"No, he's at his place. He's the one as told me first. Says he's coming over this afternoon as soon as the paper comes out. Wants to show it to you. Says your instincts might have saved his life."

She laughed, a little shakily. "I don't know why I felt we shouldn't go. It just came over me."

Sam appeared on her doorstep that afternoon, a copy of theDaily Bee in his hand so Matilda could read about the tragedy.

"Looks like only seven were killed, which is a miracle,

as many people as were there. I talked to several who were in the building when it fell. Seems it started to collapse and fell kind of slow at first, so folks had a chance to get out." He placed the paper on the table in front of her.

She read the names of the casualties. "Were any of your friends one of these?"

"One of those that died, young Bill Forster. Compositor for the Record Union. Fine young man, only 26 years old. Real shame. I knew a couple of the injured as well, but they're expected to recover."

She read on. "Are they really going to charge the owners with negligence?"

Sam shrugged. "Probably. Several folks are saying they warned the owners the building was not constructed well enough to hold the weight of so many people."

She turned the page to foreign news, wondering mildly which of those outlandish foreign countries were fighting each other when a headline caught her eye. "300,000 drown in deluge in India." Her eyes widened in horror. "Three hundred thousand? Merciful heavens. How in the world can that many people drown at one time?"

Sam read the article over her shoulder, "Monsoon season. Lots of people in India. They live all along the river, river floods, water comes in fast, lot of 'em drown. Simple as that."

She could only shake her head at the magnitude of such destruction, then added, with a little laugh, "And we thought it was bad when the Cosumnes went over its banks!"

On December 2, another wedding took place in Hicksville. "Uncle" Billy Hicks' nephew James, son of his brother Joseph, married Henrietta Fredericks of Roseville, much to everyone's surprise, for no one even knew he was courting.

"Thought he was running up to Roseville kind of often," Sam chuckled, "but he said he was looking for cattle to buy. He was looking all right, but not for cattle!"

As the year drew to a close, the children looked forward to Christmas. Matilda could not get enthusiastic over the holiday. Thanksgiving had been depressing enough. She could only think how dreary Christmas would be without Alfred, remembering the jolly Christmases they had shared in the past.

At least, she thought with a sigh, this dreadful year is almost over.

But 1876 had one final blow to deliver.

Chapter 31

January to June, 1877

THE NEWS CAME from Britt's son Gardner, in a telegram that arrived mid-day on the second day in January. The note was terse:

> *"FatherthrownfromhorseDec31stopDiedinstantly stopletterfollowsstopGardner."*

She sank into the chair and put her head in her hands. The image of her oldest brother as she last saw him filled her mind. He had kissed her goodbye when he moved his family to Santa Barbara. She remembered the twinkle in his eye, the slight receding of his dark hair, just beginning to turn gray. She felt again the deep sense of loss, of another hole in her life. She had lost Sinclair and Will, and now a horse had killed a third brother.

Alf walked in as she sat, stunned, with the telegram in her hand. Not noticing how still she remained as he entered the room, he reached for a biscuit from the stack on the plate on the sideboard and started to slather it with blackberry jam from the glass beside the biscuits. With a grin, he said, "Hear that old Colonel Pitcher has been making such a nuisance of himself that his friends want him arrested." He chuckled. "Fine thing, when a man gets to the point where his own friends . . . ." He met her eyes and stopped mid-sentence, the jam knife halfway to the biscuit. "What's the matter?"

Wordlessly, she handed him the telegram.

Setting the knife and biscuit back on the plate, he wiped his hand on his pants and took the paper she gave him. He scanned the brief message in silence. "Britt?" he finally gasped in disbelief. "Britt? It can't be!" He read the words on the paper again, as though to reassure himself he really had understood it, and turned to his stricken sister. The tears welled in Matilda's eyes and he gathered her into his arms.

"Poor little 'Tilda," he murmured against the top of her head. "As if losing Alfred wasn't enough."

He held her as she sobbed out her grief against his shoulder.

Because of Britt's death, the wedding of Maggie and D.K. was a subdued affair. Since only Sam and Tom made the journey to Santa Barbara for Britt's funeral, plans for the nuptials continued, but included only the immediate family.

The simple ceremony took place in the little Methodist Church on the grounds of the Hicksville Cemetery. Reverend Clanton performed the rites, and Alf and his wife Emma were the witnesses. After the bride and groom were presented to the small congregation, the ladies served a simple repast of cookies and lemonade. Matilda had bestirred herself and, with Elizabeth's help, made a small wedding cake.

Matilda sat in the back pew, away from the revelers, her mind going over the letter from Britt's son Chase describing his father's death. Britt had worked for Sherman and Eslund in Santa Barbara, and was driving cattle to the slaughterhouse for them. She shivered as she thought how he must have felt when he realized the horse had thrown him. She hoped it was over so fast he felt nothing. She shivered again. It was a cold, raw day, in spite of the brilliant sunshine pouring through the windows.

Carrie, beside her, asked anxiously, "Are you cold, Mama?"

She smiled to reassure the child, who had clung to her ever since her father died. "Just a little. I was thinking about your Uncle Britt. But my feet haven't gotten warm yet from the ride over here. I declare, the temperature had to have been down to freezing last night."

"Maybe you should move over where it's warmer." The big cast iron stove radiated a glowing heat, but did not seem to reach much beyond a few feet from it.

Elizabeth slid into the pew on the other side of her mother and whispered, "Mama! The other girls are saying Maggie is getting married so young because she is in a family way, like Mary was!"

Matilda glanced down at Carrie, listening wide-eyed, and shushed Elizabeth. "That's just gossip, Darling. You know you shouldn't repeat gossip."

Elizabeth shrugged. "Well, that's what they are saying. I guess time will tell. I saw their marriage license. Maggie gave her age as sixteen, that's how she could get married so young."

"You mean she lied?" Matilda gasped.

Elizabeth nodded. "She sure did. And I hear that Alice Valensin and her Count are coming back here to stay this time. I guess she is tired of living in Italy, although I think it sounds really exciting, don't you, Mama? Just imagine living in an exotic place like Italy, and going to fancy balls in villas." When Matilda did not respond, Elizabeth repeated the question. "Don't you think it sounds exciting,

Mama?"

Matilda, realizing her mind had drifted from what her daughter was saying, pulled herself out of her reverie. "What? Oh, oh, yes, of course, it sounds real exciting, but maybe now she has a child she feels she should bring him home."

"The little boy is four years old, I hear. And they named him Pio, after the Pope. I know the Pope is Catholic, but it still seems to me it would be thrilling to know such a famous man that you name your son after him."

Matilda smiled. "Lizzie, Darling, you don't have to know the Pope to name your son after him. I could have named Lew after the Pope instead of his father if I had wanted to."

"Yes, but Melvina Putney says Mrs. Valensin actually knows the Pope."

By now, Matilda had to laugh in spite of herself. "If 'Vina is your source of information, then we have no choice but to believe it."

"Will the little boy be a Count, too, Mama?"

"No, Darling. We don't have Counts here in America." She had to smile at Lizzie's enthusiasm.

The men, gathered around the stove, had no interest in local gossip. Their topics included the recent fire at Williams which, if she understood correctly, had almost annihilated the whole town, the uprising in Turkestan, wherever on Earth that was, which was reported to have destroyed 40,000 Russian troops, and a feud in Virginia City between the Hop Sing and San Sing Companies, which threatened to erupt into a full tong war and include the whole town.

She shook her head. She wished Alfred was back, to tell her about all of these world events, like he always did. Somehow, she could not find much interest in such affairs anymore.

Mary Anne, her brother John's wife, came and sat beside her. Baby Ora slept in her arms. At three months, she was a perfect baby.

"I wish we could stay here," Mary Anne confided to Matilda, "but John has his heart set on Oregon. He wants to leave this spring, as soon as the rivers are down and the snow is gone, but I have persuaded him to wait until at least July to give Ora here a chance to get a little older before we take off on such a trek."

"I wish you could stay, too. It seems like you just got here. After all, we had not seen you for such a long time. Over ten years, at least."

"Abe gives such glowing reports of how much better the farming is in Oregon. Don't have to put up with all of the mud and silt being washed down by the hydraulic mines onto the fields" She twisted her mouth into a wry grin. "Until someone finds gold on the Willamette." She glanced over at Emma as the girl laughed merrily at something said to her. "She is a lovely girl, isn't she? As you know, Alf met her when he came to help us move in '75. I'll never forget his reaction when he saw her. He was smitten. I've never seen anyone fall so hard so fast."

"Especially as old as he was." Matilda glanced over at Alf with a fond smile. "I thought he was a confirmed bachelor like Tom and Sam."

"And it looks like he's going to be a father. Emma confided to me she thinks she is in a family way. And I guess Jack and Rebecca are also expecting, so Polly will be a grandmother soon."

Matilda thought back to her feelings when Polly's son Bud was born, shortly after losing her brother Sinclair, Polly's son Michael, and her sister Minerva so close together, how new life always seemed to come to replace those lost. How each year the leaves fell and the next spring, new life burst forth. She smiled to herself, and, for the first time since Alfred's death, found herself looking forward to living, watching her children grow, and taking an interest in the world around her.

She turned to Mary Anne, still holding the sleeping Ora. "May I hold the baby for a while?"

The following June, as the temperature hovered between 105 and 115 degrees, Matilda sat in the shade of the locust tree on the south side of the house, trying to direct as much of the afternoon breeze as possible onto her overheated forehead. This stretch of heat had lasted far longer than usual. She could not recall such a spell going longer than two or three days before the high temperatures inland brought the fog in to San Francisco, and the breeze from the Delta cooled everything down.

She thought of the unwashed dishes, the unfolded clothing, the myriad of other chores she should be doing, but all she wanted to do was sit and sip on her lemonade. She rested her head against the back of the chair, closed her eyes, and let her mind wander over the events of the preceding six months. It had been an interesting time. Louis Keseberg's wife Philapha had died the end of January. Matilda remembered feeling a great deal of sympathy for the woman, for she knew she had suffered from many of the wild tales that flew around about her husband's activities at the time of the Donner tragedy, most of which were untrue or wildly exaggerated. Thinking of the Donner's recalled to her memory the stories Giles told her about the event. She was more inclined to believe him than the newspaper accounts, especially those told twenty years later, after the stories had a chance to grow more and more lurid.

The thought of Giles made her wonder again what had happened to him. She had not seen him since they parted company in Sacramento after their arrival in '64. She did hear he was guiding the soldiers in some of the Indian battles that had been occurring of late. She wondered how he would reconcile his sympathy for the Indians with the mistreatment they had suffered at the hands of unscrupulous Indian agents who used the position to line their own pockets. She sighed. Nothing she could do about it. She wondered what had become of the three young Pottawatamie squaws who had befriended her so long ago in Kansas. She still had the little ring they had given her when she departed for California.

In March, a cart ran into the dogcatcher's wagon in Sacramento, releasing all of the dogs, to the dismay of the driver and the delight of the numerous small boys who encouraged the dogs in their rapid disappearance from the scene. Sam had witnessed the whole affair and laughed until the tears ran as he described the melee to Matilda.

"Dogs everywhere," he chortled. "Must have been forty or fifty. Scattered in every direction, with boys chasing after 'em. And old man Thatcher cussing up a storm. I don't know if he was madder at the driver of the cart that hit him or the boys or the escaping animals, but one of the constables finally came by and told him some of the ladies were complaining about his language." He paused to catch his breath and grinned at her. "I thought I knew all the words, but he taught me a few even I had never heard."

March brought the news that John Lee was hung for his part in the Mountain Meadow Massacre. She still thought it very unfair, to hang that one poor man when Brigham Young himself had ordered the assault, and told them to kill every man. The letter from General Wells, dated August 19, 1857, had proven that. Young had specifically said that no one was to be left alive.

March also brought another scandal at the County Hospital, with the Board of Supervisors insisting on keeping Dr. White in spite of numerous citizen complaints and his visible incompetence. Supervisor Hopkins had introduced a resolution forbidding any County Hospital employee from using his position for political gain, aimed at some of Dr. White's extracurricular activities, but only Supervisor Blair backed him, the other five voting against him.

And a massacre of the poor Chinese in Chico led to even more discussion about what should be done about the "Chinese Problem" as the papers called it. At least the senselessness of the killings had roused the Governor and the citizens to offer a reward for the capture of the killers. But somehow, she mused, thinking about past incidents, she doubted anything would come of it.

Tom and Sam continuously talked about the war between the Turks and the Montenegrans and the Russians, but she could not bring herself to even care. Reports of Indians uprisings, the news that a tidal wave in Panama had killed over 600 people and wiped out all of the coastal towns, all seemed so far away.

Emma's baby was born in May. Alf rode up as Matilda hung the last of the morning's wash on the line to dry. One look at his face had told her what had happened. She had never seen such pride and joy in an expression before.

"Emma's had her baby," she had exclaimed, dropping the last shirt back into the basket and running to meet him as he dismounted.

"Yep." His grin widened. "Fine healthy boy. Named him Henry Marvine, after the Methodist Bishop, just like I said

I would. With a fine man like that as his namesake he'll have to be a good man too."

She smiled in remembrance of Alf's pleasure in his baby son. As she mulled these things in her mind, wishing the sun would go down so it would be at least a little cooler, Sam rode up.

"Well, I've finally pulled it off, little sister. Andrew Whitaker bought 80 acres of Will's land and will pay Polly $4,750 for it. That's almost $60 an acre. That's enough to keep her going for a while, and buy some time to pay the $7000 she owes him." He mopped his forehead with an already soggy handkerchief. "Just came from Polly's and gave her the papers. Took some negotiating, let me tell you. He drives a hard bargain. Wouldn't have bothered him at all to see Polly and the young ones out of a home. He's eager to buy some of your land as well, but so far he hasn't been willing to come up with what I want to get for you. Need enough to pay off your debt with money left over to have the extension built on the back of the house like you and Alfred had planned."

She sighed. "That would be lovely, to have some more room. I had especially hoped to have that nice kitchen."

"We'll get there, little sister. He wants more land, and I think I can get him up to twice what you and Alfred paid for it."

She jumped to her feet and ran to hug him. "Oh, Sam! What would I ever do without you?"

"I haven't managed that one yet," he laughed. "You might want to save your praise for a while. And one more thing." He put his hands on her shoulders and met her eyes. "I have filed a Homestead claim for you on the rest. If I can get that, no one can ever take the land away from you. No matter what kind of legal shenanigans McCauley tries to pull."

Remembering how hard McCauley had tried to claim all of the Chabolla Grant, she was grateful Abe had been alert to it and had them all file as co-owners back in '68. Of course, Abe had had his land taken away once, which made him more alert to another attempt.

As if reading her thoughts, Sam grinned. "I can't help but think the reason the judge went with all of the defendants in that case was almost all of the voters in Hicksville had signed it, even old "Uncle" Billy himself. Would have taken a brave judge to defy that many men who could turn him out of office at the next election!"

Chapter 32

June 1877 to December 1878

THE HEAT CONTINUED. Day after relentless day the thermometer climbed to over 100 degrees. Fish died in the river from the heat. The plants in the garden could not absorb the water fast enough, and wilted in spite of their combined efforts.

Alf rode in one hot day towards the end of June with a letter from Caroline's daughter Rebecca. She tore it open eagerly. "Do you suppose she's had her baby? What a shame Caroline did not live to see her first grandchild. I know Eli was thrilled to learn he is going to be a grandfather." She scanned the page in her hand. She looked up at Alf and her eyes danced. "It's a girl, and Becky is fine. Jack put in a page of his own, and reports 'mother and daughter doing well'. I'm so glad." She read on. "They have named her Maud Estella. Wonder where she got that name? Probably in some book."

"Bet it's cooler in Placerville than it is here," Alf grumbled, taking off his hat and wiping his overheated forehead. "Had to get out of the house for a while. Emma is complaining all the time about the heat. Says it was never this bad in Kansas."

Matilda laughed merrily. "I lived in Kansas. She can't tell me anything about Kansas heat. It was far worse there than here. You don't know what you missed, not living in Kansas. What she forgets is she did not have a tiny baby when she lived there. Heat is much harder to bear trying to feed and care for a small baby. How is the little fellow surviving the heat?"

"Better than his mother is, that's for sure. He's got a rash all over him that she says is from the heat. Be glad when the little fellow gets a little bigger. And I'd better get home, or Emma'll be mad at me for being gone so long. " He grinned. "Be good to get her back to normal."

Matilda laughed. "Let me finish hanging the last of the wash and fetch Carrie and Sammie. I'll go back with you. I haven't seen little Henry Marvine in over a week. I assume Mother is still there helping out?"

"Oh, yes, running the whole household with her usual efficiency. I don't know what I would have done without her. I know Emma didn't really like her at first, but now, I think she will be sorry to see her go home."

As Ben pulled the buggy into Alf's driveway, Matilda noticed her brother John and several men over at Kidder's blacksmith shop. She turned to her brother, who rode beside the buggy on his horse, and asked, "What is John doing?"

Alf grinned. "Getting his cattle ready to drive to Oregon. Seems they do much better on a long trek if they're shod."

"How in the world do you shoe a cow?"

"Come on, I'll show you."

She walked with him, Carrie and Sammie tagging along behind, to where the men worked. The shoes looked like little half moons, not like a horseshoe at all. The men rigged a sling under the cow and hoisted her off her feet, then quickly attached two of those little half moons to each side of the cloven hoof.

"Amazing," she said, thinking how much easier the trip

across to Salt Lake would have been for poor old Bert had they put these little shoes on him.

"Really helps if you have to cross hard rocky ground. Soft prairie not so much of a problem, rocky ones real hard on the cattle."

"And the sling?

"Cow falls over if you try to lift one foot, not like a horse or a mule. Have to lift the whole cow."

Matilda shook her head. "I'm going to go see the baby. Come on Carrie, Sammie."

Sam shook his head. "Rather watch the cows get their new shoes on. Babies are ugly, smelly, squally things."

Matilda laughed as she took Carrie's hand and walked away in the direction of the house. "You'll change your mind one of these days."

Betsy Ann hovered nearby when Matilda entered the house. Emma leaned back against the pillows looking exhausted, sweat pouring down her face in spite of the damp cloths on her forehead and neck.

"Hello, 'Tilda. How can you look so cool in this wretched heat?"

"It should break soon," Matilda soothed. She picked up the sleeping infant. "My, he has really grown. I thought he was a big boy when he was born. Alf told me he thought he would weigh nine pounds. He must be twelve pounds by now."

Emma grimaced. "Sure felt like that when I was having him, let me tell you. Don't know what I would have done without Mother Betsy Ann."

Matilda remembered how her mother had saved Mary when she had so much difficulty giving birth to Earnest. . "Yes, Mother is good." She cast a merry glance in her mother's direction.

Betsy Ann snorted and continued folding the stack of clean linen. "She thinks it's hot here. Only 95. Galt got up to 107." When she finished the linen, she replaced the cloths on Emma's head and neck. She lowered herself into the rocking chair with a sigh. "Old bones don't move as fast as they used to." She closed her eyes and leaned back against the chair. Matilda looked at her and her heart missed a beat. She had not thought of her mother as getting old, she always seemed so indestructible. But she is showing signs of her years, she thought. We'll have to treasure her while we have her.

As Matilda watched, the old lady sat up straight and declared, "Now, all those riots back in Chicago, aren't they a disgrace?"

Matilda smothered a smile. Same old mother, she thought fondly.

The heat broke a few days later, with the welcome breeze coming up the Delta cooling everything down. Even the brief afternoon shower returned. The plants in the garden responded by holding their heads high again, and everyone breathed a collective sigh of relief.

On September 21, the whole family attended the wedding of Ezra Walton's daughter Benecia to J.T. Chinnick of Sacramento. Mary and George were present as well, Mary as glum as usual. After the wedding, as everyone gathered around to eat cake and drink punch and coffee, Matilda noticed Mary and young Frank Walton. She started, for she knew he was only sixteen or seventeen, but he stared at Mary with open admiration. Mary brightened under his attention.

Matilda felt a little pang of fear. She had seen that same

look on Tom Mahin's face as he looked at Jane Bandeen before Jane divorced Billy. Would Mary do something foolish? She shrugged. Frank's still a boy. Won't be a problem for a while.

Mrs. Walton came over to chat with Matilda. "I'm so glad you came to Penny's wedding, Mrs. Wheelock. Carrie and Sammie are such good children. And Elizabeth is getting to be quite the young lady. I hear old Moses Stout's grandson, young Henry Wade has taken quite a fancy to her."

Matilda smiled. "Thank you for inviting us. Penny made a lovely bride. And Mr. Chinnick seems to be a fine young man." She laughed. "You may be right about how Henry feels, but Lizzie is only sixteen, and still enamored of Counts and Princes. I don't think she is quite ready to settle on any ordinary young man."

"Same age as my Frank." She glanced fondly at the young man who still talked to Mary with great animation. George was over in one corner deep in conversation with several men, paying no attention to Mary. The girl's sullen expression was gone, and her blue eyes sparkled.

Mrs. Walton turned back to Matilda and their eyes met. Neither made any mention of what Matilda knew both of them were thinking. Instead, Mrs. Walton said, "I hear diphtheria is starting to make the rounds again."

By November, the storms came and the epidemic went on its way. The holidays came and went. 1878 opened with the marriage on January 8 of a neighbor, Thomas McEnerney to Miss Jennie Wilson. The winter was a severe one, with heavy rains and breaks in the levees. In February, the most severe storm of the season struck, with broken levees and flooding all down the Delta. Matilda and the children huddled by the stove trying to stay warm as the rain pounded down upon the roof and the wind hammered against the walls. She thanked heaven for the new roof Alfred had wisely put on when they had moved into the place.

One of the consequences was the steamer Pioneer wound up stranded high and dry near the head of Miner's Slough. Sam, on one of his frequent trips to check on her, reported the plans to raise her.

"Captain Nickerson has contracted with a feller named Johnson. Johnson was boasting he had a hand in floating Noah's Ark off of Ararat after the Flood, so Nickerson told him to put his money where his mouth is."

"Surely Nickerson didn't believe him!"

Sam chuckled. "I doubt it, but he figgers he hasn't got much to lose."

The summer of 1878 bid fair to be as hot as 1877. The newspapers reported 77 deaths in Chicago from the heat. Fortunately, the ocean breeze from the Delta moved in and cooled everything down.

Her daughter Mary confided she expected another child in January. "I hope it's a girl, Mother," she confessed. "George wants a son, blames me because Earnest died." Her eyes narrowed. "Would serve him right if this baby is a girl."

Matilda could not repress a sigh as she recalled Mary's unhappiness in her marriage. She wished there was something she could do to help, but try as she might, she could not think of anything. Mary's situation reminded her of the Bandeen saga and she chuckled softly. Jane was certainly much happier with Tom Mahin than she had ever been with the temperamental Billy. She had visited briefly with Jane after her son John's wedding to Mary Maitland in Sacramento last March, and Jane had positively glowed speaking of how wonderful Tom was.

She thought, with a sudden fright, that maybe that would be Mary's solution. She remembered the scene between young Frank Walton and Mary at Frank's sister's wedding. She knew he very much admired Mary, thankful he was only seventeen. Matilda hoped that a baby would make life a little more satisfying for Mary, and lessen the chance that she might do something rash. Mary was so impetuous.

Elizabeth came bouncing in from a visit with Melvina Putney, full of Queen Victoria's pending marriage. "She's marrying a German, Prince Albert, and Melvina says he is very handsome." She sighed. "It's so romantic."

Matilda had to laugh at her daughter's enthusiasm. "With your dreams of Counts and Princes, you had better realize you live in America, not Europe. What about that nice Wade boy? What does he think of you romanticizing about Royalty?"

Elizabeth laughed merrily. "He doesn't know. Melvina hasn't told her swain either. But isn't it romantic anyway?"

Matilda remembered her own dreams when she was sixteen. And how her heart had jumped when her Prince had ridden up to the Randolph cabin on White Star, that long ago day in Kansas. She smiled at her daughter. "Yes, Darling, don't lose your dreams. How is Melvina's baby sister doing?" The Putneys had produced yet another child the previous May.

"Oh, 'Vina says she fusses all the time." Elizabeth grimaced. "When I have a baby, she's going to be just like our Carrie. But she also said her uncle George is getting married again in August."

Matilda's mind immediately flew to visions of Jenny and

little Carrie Putney and their tragic deaths just a few years before. "I'm glad he has found someone again. Did she say who?"

Elizabeth shrugged. "Some widow. I forget the name."

"No matter. I'm sure we will find out in good time."

Sam rode up with the mail a short time later. "Hello, little sister. Bet you're glad the heat spell has finally broken."

She smiled at him fondly. "Well, the plants in the garden certainly are. Come in and have a glass of lemonade."

"Don't mind if I do. Papers are full of all of the Indian ruckuses, all over Montana and Idaho. Before they hung that Bannock Injun Tambiago for killing one of the settlers, he told the sheriff a white man named Dempsey has been running around for more than a year encouraging all of the Indians to fight the white settlers."

"Why on earth would any white man do that?" Matilda gasped, horrified at the thought.

He shrugged expressively. "Who knows? Tambiago also said that Dempsey supplied the tribe with guns and ammunition made by the Mormons."

"Does that mean the Mormons are also encouraging depredations against settlers?" She could not help but think of the Mountain Meadow Massacre.

"Tambiago didn't know. All he knew was the guns and ammo were of Mormon manufacture." He grinned. "Maybe the Mormons didn't know what Dempsey was doing with the supplies. You know what good businessmen they are. Maybe they just thought he was an excellent customer. No way to prove one way or the other." S a m drained his glass. "Better be getting back. Am watching Tom's livestock for a few days. He went back to Santa Barbara." He grinned at Matilda. "When we went down to Britt's funeral last year, Sarah introduced him to a widowed friend of hers. Name of Mary Dooley. Our Tom was smitten. Guess they have been corresponding back and forth ever since."

Matilda's eyes sparkled. "The love bug has finally bitten our Tom? He's over fifty!"

"As they say, no fool like an old fool. At least he didn't fall for someone half his age like Alf did. Mrs. Dooley seems like a very practical lady. Wouldn't surprise me in the least if he comes back with her on his arm as his blushing bride."

When Tom returned, he did, as expected, introduce them to Mary Dooley as Mrs. Thomas Randolph. As Sam had said, she was a lovely and practical lady. Matilda loved her at once.

On August 18, the whole Randolph clan attended the ceremony in Brighton to watch the Reverend Eli Robertson join George Putney and Helen Lewis in holy matrimony. Matilda was happy for two reasons. First, of course, was that George had found love again. She knew Jenny would want that. Her eyes stung as she thought of Jenny, such a sweet girl, and so young when she died. George had waited for her to grow up so he could marry her, and then only had her for a few short years.

The other was relief at seeing Eli take an interest in life again. After Caroline's death, he had been going through the days almost like he was in a trance. The girls tried to interest him in activities going on around him, but he seemed to take part only to please them. What he needs to do, Matilda thought, is get back out on the circuit and get himself another congregation to involve himself in. Sally had taken the girls in hand, so he would be free to go.

As he pronounced George and Helen husband and wife, he looked out over the little group gathered at Mr. Bell's home. His eyes met Matilda's and he smiled. Yes, Matilda thought, he is back doing what he was born to do. Maybe now he can begin to heal.

The big news in October was the fire that burned the County Hospital. "Right down to the ground," Sam reported with a chuckle. "Luckily they got all of the patients out. Couple of 'em as was close to where the fire started got a mite singed, but the doctors reckon they'll pull through."

"Do they know how it started?" Matilda asked.

"Figure one of the chimneys in the kitchen overheated. Seemed like it started in that area anyway." He grinned. "Alf thought maybe someone had set fire to it, figuring the only way the community is going to get Dr. White out is to burn down the place, but it looks more likely the chimney is the guilty party." He paused. "But I'm sure the suspicions will continue to be bandied about. There was too much feeling against Dr. White for everyone to accept the fire as accidental, no matter what the so-called authorities say."

"Where are the patients?"

"Moved 'em all over to the Pavilion and set 'em up in temporary quarters there. Will go out for bid for a new building soon."

Matilda sighed. "That's a pretty drastic way to get rid of Dr. White. What if some of the innocent patients had been killed or seriously injured?"

Sam shrugged. "If it was an incendiary, I guess he figgered it was worth the risk."

Matilda shook her head.

At Thanksgiving, the family gathered at Polly's for the festivities. The weather had turned cold and foggy. Matilda joined Polly early in the morning to help with the preparations.

"Brr," she shivered as she hurried in from the barn where

Bud had taken charge of Ben and the buggy. Carrie followed at her heels. They huddled around the little stove in the salon for a few minutes before shedding their coats.

Polly greeted them. "Really, 'Tilda, you could have waited until the fog lifted a little. Hasn't it been cold this past week?"

"I keep thinking how we complained about the heat last July! We could sure use some of that heat now. When is Mother coming?"

"Sam says he will bring her about noon. The cold really seems to bother her. After all, she will be eighty years old next March."

"I know, and still keeps active and interested in what is going on." Matilda laughed. "You should have seen her taking over Alf's household last summer when Emma had her baby."

"She wants to be included in all the family affairs, and is looking forward to Susie's wedding this afternoon."

"Susie is marrying well. Jake Davis's brother Hamilton owns a lot of land around Mokelumne Station. Oops, I mean to say Lodi. Hard to remember when they change names like that." Matilda rolled up her sleeves and started peeling potatoes. "The mince pies are in the buggy. I told Bud he and Sammy and Lew can bring them in after they get Ben settled." She dropped a peeled potato in the pot of water beside her. "I brought some relish, and some cranberry sauce. And some jars of green beans. But I'm sure we will have enough food, by the time everyone gets here."

"We'll feed the leftovers to the wedding guests. George's new wife, Helen, is making the wedding cake."

Carrie ran off to play with her cousins, leaving Matilda and Polly alone. When sure none of the children was in earshot, Polly murmured to Matilda, "Did you see where a

Mormon gentleman married three wives all at once? At the same ceremony!"

Matilda laughed. "Maybe he wants to have a lot of children at the same time. Like the twin daughters Columbus Dillard and his wife just produced."

"And I hear poor Mr. Cassidy is still in a bad way. Can you imagine that wretch Charlie Morris going up behind the poor man and bashing him in the head with a club? He was just sitting in the saloon having a glass of beer. Didn't know Morris was even in the building. Broke his skull in two places."

Matilda shrugged. "I hear there has been bad blood between them for some time. But you're right. To come up behind a fellow and smash him in the skull with a club was a cowardly thing to do."

The children came running back into the kitchen, and conversation became general as Matilda and Polly continued preparations for the feast, assigning various chores to family members as they appeared.

As Alf droned on with his usual lengthy prayer of Grace as they sat down to eat, Matilda thought back. The year had been a difficult one, but she did have five healthy children, with a grandchild on the way. The wheat crop had been good, and the garden had produced well in spite of the heat spell. And if Sam's negotiations with Mr. Whittaker proved successful, she might even be able to build the addition on the house she and Alfred had planned. Tears threatened, but she fought them off.

The hoped for sale was completed just before Christmas. Matilda had gotten Carrie and Sammie off to school and Elizabeth and Lewis out to do the morning chores. She herself had just started to wash the breakfast dishes when Sam rode up.

The grin on his face as he waved the papers told her he had the answer she had hoped for. "It's done," he cried in triumph. "Whitaker will buy the fifty acres. It adjoins his other property, and he'll pay you $1100 for it. That's twice what you and Alfred paid back in '73. Not bad at all." He swung her off her feet in a bear hug. "Ready to start building?"

"Of, yes," she breathed. "I've been ready for ever so long."

"Sure you don't want to send part of it to England?" he teased. "I understand the poor people there are unemployed and starving."

"Absolutely not. Not one penny. If they would stop fighting wars in outlandish places like India and Afghanistan they would have more money for their people. This money is mine, and I'm going to use it to build my children a decent home."

280

Chapter 33

January to June, 1879

THE MORNING OF January 7, 1879, dawned clear and cold. Matilda sat up in bed, her breath making little clouds of mist in the cold air. She shivered and snuggled back under the quilts for a moment before rising. Carrie stirred sleepily beside her. Rustling in the kitchen told her Lew, bless his heart, was stirring the fire into life. Wrapping her robe about her, she shoved her feet into her slippers and started for the door.

"Mama?" Carrie's voice came from the bed.

"Stay warm, my sweet, until we get the stove going and the chill off. No reason to get up in the cold." Matilda hurried into the room that still served as kitchen, dining room, and salon. Not for long, she thought, thinking of the construction already underway on the new kitchen, dining room, and bedroom. She only hoped it would be finished soon, crossing her fingers that the rain would hold off until the roof was completed. The framing had been done, and the men had spent all day yesterday applying shingles. The new roof would cover not only the three new rooms, but the four original rooms as well.

"Make it stronger, plus it'll be warmer with the double roof holding the heat in," Sam had declared when explaining the plans to Matilda.

As she joined Lewis beside the rapidly heating fire in the stove, they heard hoofbeats. She looked inquiringly at Lew. "Riding fast. Can't be the workmen. Do you suppose Mary is having her baby? Your grandmother has been staying with her, sure the baby is due soon." After the experience with Earnest, Mary didn't want anyone else but Betsy Ann, rejecting the local doctors.

The question was answered in moments as George burst through the door. "Mother Matilda, Mary's been laboring most of the night, and wants you to come."

"Of course." Matilda hastened to dress while Lew hitched Ben to the buggy. "Lizzie," she called to her oldest daughter, still snuggled under the covers, "be sure Carrie and Sammie get their breakfasts and get off to school. Lew is taking me to your sister's. She's having her baby."

She took the mumbles coming from the covers as an assent and pulled on her coat and mittens. Wrapping a woolen scarf around her neck against the cold January air, she joined Lew at the buggy and climbed onto the seat.

Matilda and Mary's baby arrived at the Douglass residence at the same time. As Matilda entered the house, she heard a lusty cry. Relief washed over her at the sound. She turned to Lew with a little chuckle. "That's a healthy baby cry if I've ever heard one. Get over to the stove and get warm. I'm going to meet my grandchild."

Matilda hurried into the bedroom as Betsy Ann washed the baby. Mary rested back against the pillows, looking both exhausted and triumphant. "It's a girl, Mother." She grinned wickedly. "Just like I wanted. And I'm going to name her Mable. George wanted a boy, and he hates the name Mable." She took the newly wrapped baby from her grandmother and snuggled her close, kissing the reddish fuzz on the baby's head. "She's going to have red hair, just like mine, Mother. Isn't she beautiful?"

Matilda, choked with emotion, said nothing. She took the baby in her arms and held her. The tiny arms reached above her head, and she yawned. For a moment, the eyes opened, long enough for Matilda to recognize the same dark blue she had seen in Mary's eyes at her birth. My first grand-daughter, she thought, nuzzling the soft reddish hair. Mary's hair.

She met her daughter's eyes and they smiled. "I'll introduce Mable to her father," she said. "And I'll be very surprised if he doesn't fall in love with her at once."

Matilda carried the tiny bundle to where George stood staring out the window. He turned at her step and in two strides stood before her. "My son?"

Matilda shook her head. "No, you have a beautiful daughter." She watched the conflict in his face as he touched the tiny hand. The little fingers curled tightly around his thumb and her eyes opened. Matilda, remembering her own reaction when Sinclair had done the same thing at his birth, that long ago day in Illinois, saw the change in George.

Tears sprang into his eyes. "May I hold her?" he whispered.

Silently, Matilda placed the infant in his arms, where she closed her eyes and slept. He stood staring down at the tiny face. "My baby," he murmured. "My little girl. You are beautiful."

Matilda remained silent, not wanting to break the spell, but in her heart she rejoiced.

February brought the first really heavy storm of the season, but fortunately the construction of the three new rooms on the back of the house was nearly completed before the rains came. She listened to the downpour on the new roof as she happily moved her belongings into the new bedroom. Lizzie and Carrie would share the big back bedroom, Lew would have the small bedroom, and the little cubicle off of Lew's was now Sammie's. Because building the addition covered the exterior window, the cubicle became known as the dark bedroom. Sammie, afraid of the dark, insisted the door between his room and Lew's remain open. Lew, good natured as usual, agreed.

As Matilda smoothed the quilt on the bed, her thoughts were of Alfred, and how they had planned for this to be their own private sanctuary. Tears threatened, but she pushed them aside. Live for the future, she told herself firmly. This was what he wanted for his family, and at last we have it.

Sam became a frequent visitor. It was he who told her the County proposed buying the Hicks Bridge across the Cosumnes.

"Be good for the community," he declared. "not having to pay tolls any more. Uncle Billy is willing to sell it for $3000, which is less than its real value. Says he'll let it go for that for the good of all the folks in Hicksville. County wants the neighborhood to come up with a thousand dollars towards the purchase price. Some of the richer folks like McCauley, Butler, McConnell, and Cantrell shouldn't have much trouble raising that much. Want Cantrell and McConnell to sell them some right-of-way along the sides, as well."

"I just hope that means they'll maintain that roadway a little better. It gets to be in terrible condition in the winter. It's just a wonder no one has drowned." A burst of rain on the roof told them the promised March storm had arrived. She listened to the rain, then said, "Speaking of bad road conditions, I think you should plan to stay the night. It's going to be a miserable night to travel."

He laughed. "My very thought. Now that you have all of this extra room, you should be able to tuck in an old bachelor brother."

The March storm brought not only flooding and railroad washouts, it brought the birth of Jane Bandeen Mahin's first grandchild. As soon as the rivers receded and the roads dried sufficiently to travel, Jane came by to visit Matilda.

"He's a bouncing baby boy, I can tell you," she laughed. "They named him Merrill. He's going to be my John all over again." Jane looked marvelous, younger and prettier than Matilda ever remembered seeing her while married to the temperamental Billy. "John says he isn't even going to tell his father about the baby. He is so mad at him for threatening to cut off all of his heirs without a penny because they were so supportive of me during all the ruckus. I tried to tell him if there is anything that will calm him down it will be the sight of his first grandchild, but John will have no part of him." She took another sip of tea and smiled. "I don't think John will ever forgive him for trying to get him and Tom arrested, even though Justice Kane saw right through the ploy and threw it out of court."

Matilda refilled Jane's cup. "You have to admit things did get a little exciting for a while. But I thought things would kind of die down, once Billy moved up to Sacramento. I hear he has a lady friend, even."

Jane scowled. "I think that's what bothers John. He has heard that she keeps trying to get Billy to sign his property over to her."

Matilda pursed her lips and shook her head. "Sounds like she is after his money, not him."

"That's what John says, especially after the experiences we had with that shrew Billy married after our divorce. I told John to just go ahead and work up his farm and make his way himself. Don't look back, and don't expect anything from your father's estate. After all, he did let us keep part of the ranch in the divorce settlement, and was pretty reasonable about it." She met Matilda's eyes and smiled. "And Tom is so wonderful. I never realized how happy a person could be. I used to watch the way Alfred would look at you, and now I see the same look in Tom's eyes."

Matilda sighed. "I wish I could say the same for Mary and George."

"I thought things were better. I hear he is besotted with Mable."

"He is, but I think it's going to take more than that. Mary is just - - just so, so dissatisfied, is the only way I can explain it. I think she felt she was forced to marry George, and nothing is going to make her accept it." She hesitated. "And I fear he has a terrible temper. His sisters have made some comments that worry me."

Matilda shook her head and dismissed the subject with a shrug. "Have they awarded the contract to build the new County Hospital yet?"

Jane laughed. "Not yet. I don't know why they dawdle for so long. Everyone knows they'll give it to the Carleys. They are going to have to hurry up, or they won't get the patients out of the Pavilion in time for the State Fair."

Carley and Carley, as Jenny predicted, were awarded the contract in April. Sam told Matilda all about it when he came in for dinner after helping Lew and Frank in the fields. "Going to be two story, with six separate buildings, and modern in every respect. Will be something the County can be proud of."

He lingered over his second cup of coffee after the boys left to return to their work. "Hear young Frank is courting the Maxfield girl." He cast a sidelong look at Matilda. "Also hear her folks object. Say Frank won't be able to support her right. Say he is a nice young man, but they have higher aspirations for her, whatever her father means by that."

"Frank does have a temper. Maybe that's what worries them. He's gotten into a couple of fights."

Sam dismissed that with a shrug. "Most young men get into a fight once in a while."

"You never have. And neither has Tom or John."

He laughed. "Because I was always afraid I'd get hurt. Never much relished the idea of a broken nose!" He picked up the paper. The scene was so reminiscent of how she and Alfred used to share the news that it brought tears to her eyes. "Listen," he chuckled, "I wanted to share this with you." The paper rustled as he turned to the page he sought. "'A Good Day for Divorces,'" he read.

"What?"

"I quote: 'Isaac Harris was divorced from his gentle Amelia on the grounds of cruelty.'"

"Cruelty?"

"Yep. Paper says the defendant 'had the habit of fanning her liege lord's brow with the slop-bucket, and perfuming him with the contents thereof . . .'"

Matilda burst into laughter and laughed until the tears came. "Oh, the poor man!"

Henry Wade became a frequent visitor, and Elizabeth stopped talking about Counts and Princes. Instead, it was

Henry this and Henry that. Matilda thought, with a mixture of amusement and sadness, that Elizabeth would be eighteen in December. She's growing up.

However, she felt much better about Elizabeth and Henry than she had about Mary and George. Henry was a fine young man from a good family, grandson of old Moses Stout, a long time neighbor and good friend. She felt sure Henry would make Elizabeth a good husband.

It was an exciting summer. The whole neighborhood buzzed with rumors and speculations about the mansion John McCauley was building on the Hicksville farm for his daughter Alice and her Count husband.

Elizabeth returned from a visit with her friend Melvina Putney full of news. "It's going to have seventeen rooms, Mama," she burst out. "Seventeen rooms! Can you imagine a house that big, Mama? And for just three people. What do you suppose they will do with that many rooms?"

Matilda thought how thrilled she was when their four rooms turned into seven and said nothing.

But Elizabeth chattered away. "'Vina says they need a house that big just to put in all the beautiful things they brought back from Europe. They have a marble fireplace, and 'Vina says it's huge!"

Matilda found herself wondering how Melvina got all of the information which seemed to be at her command. Elizabeth rattled on, "And big four poster beds, and a great banquet table, and boxes and boxes of books. And they even say some of the books are in Italian and French and Spanish as well as English, and that Mrs. Valensin can actually speak and read all of those languages. Imagine being able to speak that many languages. Isn't that amazing, Mama?"

The next news to reach Matilda came from Lew. He returned from a trip to Galt to report that Galt had a new tin-smith.

"Name of Latourette, from Ohio. Says he moved to Courtland three years ago, but figgers Galt to be a more up and coming town, with more chance to build up his business. Brought his wife and family. Got the prettiest little girl, looks to be about twelve, but I'll bet she'll be a real beauty when she grows up. Name's Armedia, but everyone calls her Media. Got two boys, too, Willie's about ten, and John is just a little fellow. Going to open up his shop next to Iler's."

Matilda had to smile to herself. Lew would be sixteen soon and, apparently, just beginning to notice girls. Little Miss Latourette had obviously caught his eye.

"Got a new Doc in town, too. Name of Montague. Alexander Montague. Folks are saying he's a right modern doc, went to some fancy school in the East, supposed to be the very latest in doctoring. Everyone is talking about him. In fact, Aunt Emma says she wants him for this confinement." Alf and Emma's second child was due imminently. "Says she's tired of midwives and incompetent doctors."

Matilda chuckled. "That's because your grandmother says she getting too old to deliver babies, and told Emma she had to find someone else."

Lew's face turned solemn. "She is getting old, isn't she Mother? Last time I saw her she just sat with her hands wrapped in comfrey poultices. Says the rheumatics have started bothering her real bad."

"Yes, Son," Matilda replied softly, with a pain in her heart. "Remember she turned 80 on her birthday last March. In fact, I have already talked to Sam about perhaps moving her over here. He's beginning to worry she's going to wind up bed-ridden and he won't be able to take care of her. We talked about it while we were helping her with the papers to file for a federal pension for your grandfather's service in the War of 1812. Sam says she has been entitled to it all along. Don't know why we never filed before."

Thoughts of her mother filled her head. Eighty years old. She met Lew's worried eyes and smiled. "I guess we should be thankful we have had her as long as we have."

Chapter 34

June to November 1879

THE SUMMER PASSED quickly. News reached the little community of Hicksville of the Zulu Wars in South
Africa, and the war between Chile and Bolivia, but it did not
touch Matilda. Busy keeping the harvesting crews fed, she
reveled in the convenience of her new kitchen, with the
water pump at her new sink. She rejoiced at the extra space
now that she had a dining room and a real parlor.

In June, when Sam came in for dinner at noon, he told
her Ben Wilder had served an injunction on H.S. Crocker
and Company to prevent the publication of a particularly
lurid account of the Donner Party experiences by the
Truckee Republican.

"Says it discredits not only the folks who died, but casts
aspersions on the living." Sam shook his head. "Don't see
why they can't just let it rest."

"I feel sorry for Elitha," Matilda cried. "Must the poor
woman be dragged through the horror of that terrible experience again?" She shook her head. "It's good Mrs.
Keseberg has passed on. She certainly went through
enough, with all the accusations people made against her
husband, as ridiculous as most of them were. At least Elitha
was just a child at the time. No one can accuse her of any

atrocities. And she did lose her parents."

"Won't stop them from trying," Sam grunted. "That's why Ben tried so hard to prevent the publication."

"Surely the judge could see why he wanted to protect his wife!"

"Money talks," Sam shrugged. "The lawyers for the publisher tried to make it into a case of free speech and freedom of the press."

"But you know half the stories that circulated are wild exaggerations, or even total fabrications. Giles told me that on the trip out fifteen years ago."

"Yes, but that doesn't mean the public doesn't want to believe it." Matilda's face reflected her horror at Sam's words. "Ben says he's filing an appeal, but he doesn't hold out too much hope." He grinned wryly. "I suppose we can start a campaign to tell people not to read the book, that it is mostly a pack of lies. But that would probably do even more to convince people the story was true."

Matilda shook her head and sighed. "Let's eat. Dinner is ready. Here, carve the roast while I dish up the rest of the food. The crew will be in here any minute announcing they are starving to death." She set the platter in front of him. "How is Mother?"

Sam shook his head. "Rheumatics seem to bother her more and more. I teased her, told her she had to stay well until the new County Hospital is finished in July. Like to bit my head off, she did." He grinned and tackled the roast, jabbing the fork in to hold the meat while he sliced off slab after slab.

Matilda returned from the kitchen with a bowl of potatoes in one hand and a bowl of green beans in the other. Elizabeth followed with a platter of sliced tomatoes and cucumbers she had picked from the garden that morning.

The sounds from the back porch told her the crew would be on them shortly, so she only said, "Well, you shouldn't have been surprised. You know her opinion of doctors, even when Emma raved about Dr. Montague after he delivered little Stella."

Towards the end of July, when Matilda and Elizabeth, with Carrie's help, had finished the dinner dishes, Matilda, on impulse, asked Lew to hitch Ben to the buggy and drive her over to spend the afternoon with Polly.

"After all," she explained, "I haven't had a good visit with Polly for a long time."

Lew grinned. "Sure you aren't just curious to know how Frank's courting with Clara is going?"

She laughed at his perspicacity. "Well, that too!"

Polly greeted her with enthusiasm. "I was hoping you would come by. I was going to send Bud over with a note. Becky and Jack are coming down from Placerville on Sunday, and I want you and the children to come for dinner. Little Essie is such a darling. I wish they didn't live so far away. You're lucky Mary and George live so close so you can see little Mable growing up."

"Yes, she's six months old now, and can sit up by herself. She looks just like Mary did at that age. And you have two grandchildren right here, now that Gussie has a little brother. I think it was very thoughtful of DK and Maggie to name the new little fellow Alfred." Matilda laughed softly. "I think Lizzie and Melvina Putney were disappointed that Gussie wasn't born until April of last year. They were both so sure the reason Maggie and DK were getting married before Maggie turned sixteen was because she was in a family way."

Polly joined the laughter. "I have to admit I had some

suspicions myself."

Polly bustled about making tea, and set a plate of cookies in front of Matilda. Sugar cookies, Matilda thought, her mind flashing to the Pottawatamie chief who had been so fond of her sugar cookies, so long ago in Kansas.

"Looks like we will have a good harvest this year," she said, dismissing the memories. "The boys have been quite optimistic, bragging about how many bushels they are getting to the acre."

"Alf says we've had a good harvest here as well. Remember that awful year when the rain came so hard in June it knocked half the grain out onto the ground?"

"Very well," Matilda said grimly. "We couldn't pay Lizzie Owen because of it."

"I would like to be able to pay off the rest of what I owe Mr. Whitaker." Polly sighed heavily. "That debt weighs on me so. I do wish Will had never made any dealings with that man. I don't trust him at all."

Matilda shrugged. "Sam says he is just a good businessman."

"Maybe, but I still don't trust him." She poured the tea and changed the subject. "Isn't it dreadful about that explosion in Bodie?"

Matilda had not heard anything about it. "What happened?"

"Powder magazine blew up. Report is it killed eight men, but they can't be sure there aren't more. One of the injured had his eyes blown out and his skull fractured, so he is sure to die. Some of those closest to the blast just disintegrated into atoms. They couldn't find any trace of their bodies."

Matilda shuddered. "Their poor wives."

"They don't know what caused it, but everyone is blaming the mining company. I suppose we'll never know what actually happened, with so much devastation. Anyone who could have explained it is in a thousand pieces."

Matilda shook her head in sympathy.

"They say one woman and a child were trapped in the collapse of their boarding house." Polly shook her head. "And another miner was buried in his cabin and they had to dig him out. They felt the blast as far away as Bridgeport, some twenty miles from Bodie. I suppose it will wind up being a big political thing. Like the County Hospital. They're going to start moving the patients out of the Pavilion the end of this month and already they have removed Dr. Pyburn as the head of it. Have named Dr. Dixon instead."

Matilda knew the Board had finally yielded to public pressure the previous March and replaced Dr. White. "Dr. Dixon won't last long," Matilda commented. "He's not that interested in their little political games. He'll get thrown out just like Dr. Pyburn."

"Probably," Polly agreed as she refilled Matilda's cup. "Poor Dr. Pyburn was doing a pretty good job, but he's a homeopathic doctor, and Baldwin and White and the others are allopathic, so they brought in a lot of trumped up charges. One was of burying the body of a stillborn without proper burial permits. The other was putting his wife in charge of the ladies ward. She is a fully qualified homeopathic physician as well, so I can't see why anyone should object. They just wanted to get rid of him. I hear Dr. White is campaigning to get the job back."

Matilda gasped in horror. "Surely, after all of the problems and complaints, they would never put Dr. White back in."

"Probably why they settled on Dr. Dixon." Polly shrugged. "They'll do what they want to do. Nothing we can do about it." She changed the subject. "And how is

Elizabeth's romance with the Wade boy coming along?"

"Quite well. She is actually starting to talk about trousseaus and hope chests instead of Counts and Princes. I have high hopes. He is such a fine young man." She hesitated and took another sip of tea, then glanced obliquely at Polly. "And Frank's romance with Clara Maxfield?"

Polly shook her head. "I wish he would get that girl out of his head. I've tried to tell him marrying a girl over her family's objections can lead to nothing but trouble." She sighed. "But there's no talking to him. He's got his heart set on her."

A week later, Lew came in at noon for dinner grinning from ear to ear. Matilda immediately saw he was bursting with news.

He didn't wait for her to ask. He blurted out, "Frank did it. He ran off with Clara Maxfield. They hopped on the train to Stockton and got married by a justice of the peace there." He chuckled. "Bud says old man Maxfield is fit to be tied. He got wind of it and tried to follow them to stop it, but he was too late. By the time he got to Stockton, they were married."

"I hope he will accept Frank, now that he can't do anything about it."

"Bud says he wouldn't bet any money on it, but says he's real proud of Frank for daring to pull it off. I guess the old man is a real tyrant. Rules the whole household with an iron fist. Guess he never thought one of the girls would defy him."

Matilda sighed. "Love makes people do funny things."

"And it's a good thing Uncle John left Kansas when he did. I hear they had a whole series of tornadoes go through Randolph. Like to wiped out the whole town. Even knocked down the Methodist Church."

Matilda hosted Thanksgiving, now that she had so much extra room. She proudly surveyed the heavily laden dining room table. Mary arrived with Mable, but without George. She explained he had promised his mother to spend the day with her, but Matilda knew from the set of Mary's jaw that she and George had quarreled again. She sighed and lifted Mable from the buggy. The child was just beginning to walk, and her blue eyes and red hair were so much like Mary's.

Polly and clan had come early to help with preparations. Bud, at twelve, bid fair to look like his father. Matronly little Lizzie, at seven, insisted on helping set the table, a chore she shared with Carrie. Alf and Emma arrived with two and a half year old Harry and the infant Stella. Maggie and DK drove up soon after with Gussie and baby Alfred, followed by Sam with Sally, Carrie, Minnie, and Till.

The main topic of conversation was Elizabeth's upcoming wedding to Henry Wade, scheduled for December 11, shortly after Elizabeth's eighteenth birthday. Mary would be her matron of honor, and Carrie her flower girl.

"I'm so glad that nice Reverend Staton was named minister for Hicksville at the Methodist Conference last month. Elizabeth and Henry both like him so much. He is very pleased to have their wedding be his first in his new position." Matilda straightened one of the place settings and smiled at Polly. "Are the newlyweds coming?"

Polly shook her head. "Would you believe the Maxfields asked them to come to their house? Frank was dumfounded, but said they could hardly refuse, if the old man was willing to make amends."

"Why, that's wonderful news. I had so hoped they would

accept him."

Polly sighed. "I hope that's the reason. I guess they'd hardly invite him if they planned to poison him. I suspect it's because Clara is not well. They fear she may have consumption."

"Oh, no. Not when she and Frank are so happy." Her mind flew to Tommy Evans, and how short a time her sister Caroline had with her beloved Tommy, after waiting so long to marry him. And then to die from the dreadful disease herself not that long afterwards.

Sam came up and hugged Matilda. "You women still gossiping about Clara and Frank? Let me tell you a joke on our high and mighty Dr. Baldwin. He ignored a subpoena to appear as a witness in Court, and the judge fined him ten dollars. When he declared the fine was an outrage, the judge fined him another ten dollars for contempt." Sam chuckled. "He's always figgered himself a little above common folk. Judge gave him his comeuppance, he did."

"Well," Polly contributed, "While on the subject of doctors, you were right, 'Tilda.. Doctor Dixon didn't last long at the County Hospital. They've given the job to Dr. Laine, who, I understand, has built a new pig sty, and markedly improved the record keeping system, along with some other improvements. They even say the food is better."

"He won't last long," Matilda remarked. "If he's doing a good job, they'll find some way to get rid of him. Dr. Pyburn was doing a fine job. See how fast they threw him out? And look how long and hard they fought to keep Dr. White in the position, even after all of those complaints against him."

"Moral of the story," Sam remarked. "Keep out of politics. Did you hear they found the remains of old W.S. Bodie, the one they named the town after?"

"No! After all of these years?" Polly gaped at Sam.

"Yep. Disappeared in a snowstorm in 1859. Missing all this time, and they found his bones right outside of town. As many folks as are up there, with all the mining activity going on, a real surprise it took so long to find what was left of him."

Matilda smiled. "I'm sure he is pleased they named the town after him."

"Lot of good it did him," Lew muttered, helping himself to an olive from the dish on the table. "Are we going to eat pretty soon? Uncle Tom and his new bride just pulled in, so I think everyone is here."

His mother laughed and swatted his hand. "Yes, we're ready. Gather everyone around. I have a table set up in the kitchen for the children."

"You mean I have to eat with the babies?"

"I'm teasing. You're sixteen, and have been doing a man's work. I'm sure you qualify for the grown-ups table."

After the blessing, everyone ate until Matilda was sure there would be no leftovers. When she began serving the mince and pumpkin pie, Tom brought up the closing of the Orleans Hotel.

"Real shame," he said. "Stayed there on several occasions myself. Don't see much of that Old World flavor anymore. Sold off all of the furniture, from all 160 rooms. Some grand old antiques, including a marvelous old Mathushek piano, many fine marble top tables, lace draperies. Going to turn the building into an oil factory." He shook his head. "Hate to see such a glorious old lady sink so low. An oil factory, of all things!"

"Yes, doesn't seem right," Sam agreed. "What do you think of the report by that priest saying he had proof that Joaquin Murietta lived to a ripe old age down in Sonora?"

"If that is true, then whose head were they parading around San Francisco?" Alf asked.

"Who knows?" DK said with a twinkle in his eye. "That batch of vigilantes probably just found some poor Mexican with a mustache like Murieta and killed him," He grinned. "After all, they couldn't come back empty handed could they?"

"According to the story, his family identified the head as Joaquin's, at his request, so those chasing him would think they had their man and would stop looking for him. Apparently he lived out the rest of his life as an ordinary man in Mexico." Sam shrugged. "We'll probably never know for sure whose head that really was."

"Then all those folks who were parading that pickled head all over San Francisco didn't have Murieta after all?" Polly gasped. "How horrible."

"Enough," Matilda commanded. "One more comment about pickled heads in jars and I'm going to be sick."

Chapter 35

December 1879 to February 1880

THE MORNING OF December 11, Matilda woke to bright sunshine. As she opened her eyes and blinked, she remembered today was Elizabeth's wedding day. She yawned and stretched, working the kinks out of her back. They had both worked for several hours the previous evening in the flickering light from the kerosene lamp, putting the finishing touches on the wedding gown. What had taken the time and work was the frilled bodice and the buttons down the back. The gown itself was simple, but it seemed to Matilda she sewed on at least a thousand buttons. She had sewed on button after button while Elizabeth worked on the bodice.

But the finished gown now hung on the wall beside Elizabeth's bed, ready for the big event. All of Henry's family was coming, and by the time they added all of the Randolph clan plus all of the neighbors, for both Elizabeth and Henry were quite popular in the little community, they would have probably more people than the little church would hold. Fortunately, it looked like it was going to be a pleasant day. She shuddered to think what it could be like had it been raining.

As Matilda watched Elizabeth and Henry stand before

Reverend Staton and recite their vows, the girl looked so beautiful and so happy. Matilda could not help thinking what a shame it was her father could not see her.

Her thoughts on Lewis and the love they had shared, she wanted very much to believe Lewis was with her, that he could see what two lovely daughters they had. She remembered their all too brief life together, thoughts she had suppressed for years.

We had such a short time, Lewis my love, but they were good years. And we have three wonderful children. She glanced fondly down at Mable, who sat quietly in her lap, seeming to understand the solemnity of the affair. And one beautiful granddaughter.

"I now present to you, ladies and gentlemen, Mr. and Mrs. Henry Marshall Wade." Reverend Staton's voice brought Matilda back to the present and she realized the ceremony was over. People crowded around them, offering congratulations. The ladies of the church bustled about, setting out plates of cookies, cups of coffee, and glasses of punch.

Matilda watched as the newlyweds cut the first piece of Helen Putney's intricately decorated cake. The new Mrs. Putney took pride in her cake decorating, and found herself much in demand for all sorts of festive occasions. She turned Mable over to the attentions of Carrie. In spite of being only ten years old, Carrie took the responsibility so seriously it brought a smile to Matilda's face.

Don't think of the ones you have lost, she told herself firmly. Just be thankful for the ones you have. She picked up a cup of coffee and a plate of cake and found a seat next to several of the men who were deep in a discussion of the shooting at Elk Grove a week or so previously. She knew one of the men involved, Bill Jefferson, a blacksmith who worked for Louis Herbert.

"Jefferson always was hot-tempered," Henry Putney declared. "From what I hear, he was the one who started the fight."

"Probably drunk," Tom Riley put in.

"Probably, but not too drunk to know he was losing," Sam chuckled.

"As I understand it," Bill Frye said, "when Bill's brother thought he was losing, he started to intercede. At about the same time Bill figgered he needed stronger ammunition than his fists and pulled his gun."

"Yes," Sam said. "And shot his own brother. Lucky the shot doesn't look to be fatal. Fellers at the Post Office this morning were saying it looks like he'll recover."

Matilda, listening, could not help but wonder at men. If Bill Jefferson had not consumed so much alcohol, he probably would never have gotten into the fight that could so easily have resulted in his brother's death. She wondered if he would think of that and curb his drinking. Probably not, she shrugged. They never seem to learn.

She looked up to see Bill Frye standing in front of her. He smiled shyly at her and said, "Elizabeth made a beautiful bride, Mrs. Wheelock. And young Wade is a fine fellow."

"Thank you, Mr. Frye. I am so glad you came."

A light leaped into his eye and his smile broadened. "May I bring you some more coffee, Mrs. Wheelock?"

With a little smile, Matilda watched him cross the room to the coffee pot. She remembered his remark at the wedding reception when she married Alfred. Hicksville's most confirmed bachelor (after Sam, of course) embarking on a romance?

She dismissed the notion. We're both too old for romance.

Kitty Loughran, the teacher at Hicksville School came by and spoke briefly to Matilda. She had dismissed classes early so all of the children could attend Carrie and Sammie's sister's wedding. "I do hope you will come to the Christmas festivities at the school next Wednesday, Mrs. Wheelock."

"Of course. I wouldn't dream of missing it. Carrie and Sammie have been chattering about their roles for days."

Miss Loughran smiled. "They are such well-behaved children. And such good students! Did Carrie tell you she has been on the honor roll all term? She is so quiet I thought maybe she had not told you."

Matilda laughed. "Oh, yes. Many times. She is shy around others, but does not hesitate to remind her siblings how well she is doing. She also says Bertha Cottrell and Lizzie Herbert are her closest rivals. She is quick to point out to Sammie that he is not on the list."

Mr. Frye returned with her coffee and Miss Loughran rose. She looked from one to the other with a mischievous twinkle in her eye. "Then I will see you on Wednesday. Perhaps, Mr. Frye," she added, the twinkle deepening, "you would also like to attend?"

Matilda sighed silently. That's all I need, she thought. Kitty Loughran telling everyone I have a romance going with Bill Frye.

She did not say what she thought. Instead, she smiled, thanked him for the coffee and said, "I'm sure Carrie and Sammie would be honored to have you observe their performances."

He did attend the festivities, much to the delight of Carrie and Sammie, both of whom liked him very much. And was very attentive to Matilda, which, she knew, would stimulate a lot of gossip. She had to admit she rather enjoyed his attention. She could not imagine herself falling in love with him, but had to admit companionship was a nice thing.

Other than the death of Henry Wade's grandfather, Moses Stout, at Short's Ranch on December 22, the rest of the year passed quietly. Matilda, along with the rest of the family, attended the services for Mr. Stout, an honored member of the little community. He had even served one term in the State Assembly.

Sam stood beside her for the brief ceremony at the Hicksville Cemetery. "82 years old, he was," Sam told her solemnly. "Would have been 83 next month. He's seen a lot of changes in those 82 years. Understand he got pretty feeble towards the end, but was still able to regale his visitors with stories of how it used to be in his younger days. Even though he only served for one term, I guess it was a pretty memorable experience for him."

"I'll bet he had some stories to tell, if even half of the goings-on I hear about of the early days of the State Assembly are true. I hope someone had sense enough to write some of the stories down. They really are part of the State's history."

Sam shrugged. "Has anyone thought to write down some of the stories our mother has told? That's the problem. We are all so busy with our day to day lives we don't think about recording what's happened in the past."

"Speaking of Mother, how is she doing?"

He shook his head. "Not well. I offered to bring her today, as I know she was fond of old Mose, but she said it was too cold to go out. Her joints ache most of the time now."

Matilda sighed. "Poor Mother. After her active life, and

always so involved in everything going on around her, it must be very hard to have to remain in the house all the time." She knew in her heart the day was coming soon when she would have to bring her mother home and take care of her. A bed-ridden old woman would be too much for Sam, and Sally had her hands full with her three sisters. After all, little Till was only ten. It was not fair to expect Sally to take care of an ailing grandmother as well.

Matilda saw Sam watching her and smiled. "I have room now that Elizabeth has married. Maybe we should see about moving her over."

Sam nodded. "Yes, I believe it's about time."

January began with the death of Emperor Norton in San Francisco on January 8.

"The end of an era," Matilda sighed when Sam told her about it. "I just wish now that Alfred and I had gone to see him when we had the chance."

"Well," Sam grinned, "they say his funeral procession was the biggest San Francisco has ever seen, bar none."

"I'm glad. He certainly brought enough flair to the city that he deserved the honor."

"Did you see what the paper said? Said he was not crazy in the least bit. He was a well-educated and sensible man."

"Then why," Matilda asked, puzzled, "did he do all of those odd things?"

Sam grinned. "According to the paper, they thought he probably abhorred work. And he sure found a way to avoid it."

"So it was all an act? And all of those people fell for it?"

"Well, he did provide a certain amount of local color," Sam admitted. "He was good for the tourist trade. Gave the visitors something a little different."

Matilda had to laugh. "That he did,"

"By the way," Sam added, "did you hear they have a case of leprosy at the County hospital?"

"What!" Matilda gasped in horror. "Are they sure?"

"Yep. Man denied it at first, but finally admitted he lived for a number of years among the lepers in Bombay and Calcutta. Guess that's where he picked it up. Seems he has known he had it for seven years. Been dodging the health authorities ever since he got back to San Francisco. Had to avoid the Chinese, for they recognized the disease at once and refused to work with him." Her face must have reflected her fear, for he hastened to reassure her. "Don't worry, they've got him isolated. Worry more about the outbreak of diphtheria, which I understand has just begun."

Matilda only shook her head. "If it's not one thing it's another. I understand Chief Ouray says he and his Utes have been treated unfairly, and that if the government can't protect them, they will protect themselves."

Sam nodded. "He refuses to leave Colorado. I can't blame him. It's been their home for years, but he's the only one who can keep the Utes in line. The government better cooperate with him or they'll have more trouble on their hands."

Matilda gave up on the Indian problems and returned to one closer to home. "Have you said anything to Mother yet about moving over here?"

"Not me. Any time I say anything about her getting feeble she bites my head off. You'll have to convince her you need her help, then maybe she'll come." He rose to leave. "Have to get back. Critters will be waiting to be fed." He turned back at the door and put his head around the corner. "And how is your romance with Bill Frye coming?"

He ducked out of sight just in time to dodge the dishtowel she threw at him.

Chapter 36

January to May, 1880

WES AND ALF returned from a trip to Sacramento full of reports of a recent raid on a Chinese opium den.

"Chinatown has a number of them, as everyone knows," Wes reported. "But they usually cater only to Chinese. If only Chinese go to them, the police pretty much leave them alone."

"Disgraceful," growled Alf, staunch Methodist that he was. "They should all be shut down."

"So what attracted the police to this one?" Matilda asked.

"Some busybody reported seeing two young white girls going into Ah Fen's place, down on 'I'," Wes grinned. "The good ladies who saw them suspected it was a not a place they should be frequenting."

"No, probably not," Matilda said dryly.

"When they raided it, there were two young men with the girls, so what they had in mind when the girls drifted off into an opium daze you can probably guess," Wes added.

"Yes, I can well imagine. So what happened?"

"Police kicked the boys out, took the girls home, and shut Ah Fen down." Alf said. "He'll pay a fine, then go out and open another opium den, but will probably be a little more circumspect with his clientele in the future."

"Another thing we found," Alf said. "We met Reverend

Anderson. He's back at the Seventh Street Church again. He remembered you and Alfred very well. In fact, he's back staying at Mrs. Maddux's boarding house. He was sorry to hear Alfred had passed on, but I told him he left you your own place and two fine youngsters. Including the most beautiful little girl in the world."

Matilda laughed. "Don't let Stella hear you say that. How long is he going to stay? I would like very much to see him again."

"Oh, at least a year, I suspect. I told him I would be sure and get you up to one of his services as soon as the days get a little longer."

"Summer might as well come," Wes grumbled. "If we don't get some rain soon, won't be any crop to get in."

In mid-February, the rains began, and the farmers breathed a collective sigh of relief. In March, Polly, with Bud and Liz in tow, came for Sunday dinner after services at the little Methodist Church at the cemetery. As Polly put piece after piece of coated chicken into the hot lard in the pan, she remarked, "Did you see where Dr. Laine was accused of neglect and cruelty?"

Matilda, busy dipping tomatoes into boiling water to peel them, gasped, "Not again! I thought he was doing a good job. Did he cross some politician?"

"No, it seems three of the charges were made by a man who had been a nurse at the hospital, but one Dr. Laine had discharged because he was inefficient. When he brought the charges, Dr. Laine pointed out the man had appropriated the clothing of a deceased patient under his charge." She took a fork and began turning the pieces to brown evenly. "Then Larkin, of the *Leader*, took the stand with all kinds of demands for investigation. That paper of his is just a rag, anyway."

"I trust Dr. Laine had an answer for that."

"Oh, yes. He said Larkin was attempting to blackmail him. And this time the Board, believe it or not, backed Dr. Laine."

"I'm glad." Matilda shook her head and began to slice the tomatoes she had just peeled. "It's about time they realized a good administrator should get their support, instead of all that political sniping."

"Oh. They did. The paper reported the Board said 'Dr. Laine has acted in a humane, discreet, and gentlemanly manner with a bearing that does him honor and credit'." Polly chuckled. "Can't you just hear them saying that?"

Matilda had just poked the potatoes boiling on the stove with a fork to see if they were done when Sam arrived with Betsy Ann. Matilda's heart gave a twist as she saw her mother hobble up the driveway, as determined as ever. She shook off Sam's arm when he tried to help her. Sam met Matilda's eyes and shrugged.

Matilda hugged her. "Mother, now that Elizabeth is married, I have room for you over here. Sally can manage without you, but I can use your help."

Betsy Ann just grunted and said, "We'll see."

Matilda smiled to herself. *I've planted the seed. Now we just have to let it grow.*

April brought the worst storm of the season. As rain poured off the roof and made little runnels in the yard, she thought of refusing to allow the children to go to school.

"But Mama," Carrie protested. "I've not missed a day. I'm going to get an award for perfect attendance."

"But you'll get soaked. What if you take cold?" She did not voice her worst fear. *What if the cold becomes pneu-*

monia?

"I'll bet no one goes to school today," Lew interceded. "The creeks are rising fast. Tell you what. I'll take you in the buggy, and if there is no one else there, I can bring you back."

That settled it. Matilda bundled them warmly, with their India rubber ponchos and galoshes. And was not surprised when all three returned half an hour later.

Lew grinned. "We sat in the buggy until it was obvious no one else was coming, then came home. Whoosh, what a rainstorm! All the rain we didn't get in December and January is coming now."

As it turned out, the county received an incredible 7.24 inches of rain in less than twenty-four hours. Bridges washed out, slides delayed the trains, and the rivers overflowed their banks. It was three days before anyone went anyplace. Water surrounded them, but thankfully, did not reach them. She remembered Alf saying the houses were all built above high water.

As she stood staring out the window at the creek below the house, now a raging torrent, she also remembered what he said about the winter of 1861: One huge lake from Hicksville to Liberty.

She laughed, a little shakily, to Lew who stood beside her. "At least it's stopped. I was beginning to think it was going to rain for another forty days and forty nights!"

On May 8, her brother Sam pulled into the yard with the buggy, Betsy Ann, and all of her belongings. "Well, Sis," he announced, "Mother got the notification today that she has qualified, and will be getting her pension. So she has announced she is moving over here to help you out, since, she says, I don't need her help any more."

Their eyes met. She saw they shared the same thought.

One bright sunny day towards the end of May, Matilda said to Lew as she began clearing the breakfast dishes, "Son, it's a beautiful day for a drive. A letter came from Annie yesterday. She has asked if I can come and see her." She frowned. "She doesn't say why. Maybe it's just because I haven't seen her for so long, so I would like to go to Sacramento today. Just imagine! Little Annie is 16 already."

Betsy Ann looked up from her bowl of porridge. "You go along. Carrie and Sammie and I will do just fine."

Matilda hid her smile. She and Sam had conspired to convince Betsy Ann that Matilda needed her help. Matilda secretly suspected Betsy Ann had been a little jealous when Sally took charge of Sam's household.

"Just make sure they do their chores as soon as they get home. Sammie especially. He has a way of getting involved in a book and forgetting all about the chickens and the pigs."

"Don't you worry about a thing. We'll get along just fine. Put the water on to heat for the dishes and get these youngsters off to school. I'll wash up. The hot water makes my hands feel better."

"All right, Mother. We'll leave it to you. I'll give Annie your regards." Annie had never forgotten Betsy Ann's help and kindness when Little Annie had been born, that long ago day on the Humboldt Sink.

With Lew at the reins, Matilda felt comfortable using one of the younger and friskier horses, so they made good time, arriving at Annie's hat shop just before noon.

"Come in, come in, I was just closing for dinner so you are just in time." She shut the door and put the 'Closed' sign up. The little shop looked just like Matilda remembered it, a clutter of ribbons, feathers, and artificial flowers, with rows of finished hats on identical featureless heads.

Chattering away, she ushered them into the room behind the shop and seated them at the little table. "You're looking well, 'Tilda. And Lew! You're a grown man. It's so good to see you. Annie, come and eat, and see who is here."

A pretty girl came from the back room and smiled at the visitors.

"My," Matilda exclaimed, "you have grown up too."

Lew shyly offered her his hand. "So nice to see you again, Miss Hurd," he mumbled.

Annie chuckled softly. "Now, sit down and eat, both of you. Matilda, take this chair. Lew and Annie can use the stools. Then you young people can run down to Mr. Fisher's Confectionary for some ice cream while your mother and I visit. It's over on J Street. Annie can show you, and at the same time, you can see the lovely new cement sidewalks the city has put in. Now we don't have to watch out for the holes in the wooden walkways anymore."

When the stew that had been simmering on the little stove and biscuits she brought out of the sideboard had been consumed, Annie hustled the young people out of the door and bustled about making tea in a small china pot with flowers painted on the side. She set the tea and a slice of cake in front of Matilda, and poured the steaming tea into dainty china cups painted with the same flowers as the teapot. "Now that we are alone, we have so much to talk about." She gave Matilda a smile of conspiracy. "Remember Bridgitte DeLusi?"

"Of course." Memories of the tall, majestic woman she had seen in Annie's shop so many years ago rose in her mind. "Does she still have the same - -er - - profession?"

314

"They say she fell off a steamer and drowned."

"Drowned?"

"If she did fall off, she was probably drunk. But some say that is just rumor, that she didn't drown at all, but was just a terrible mother and ran off and left her children. Of course, she only had the two girls left. The others had all died, she said, from eating green apples."

"I find that hard to believe," said Matilda, with some skepticism.

"So do a lot of people. Anyway, Agnes is with the Catholic nuns. Maybe Bridgitte ran off because she got tired of giving money to the nuns to take care of the girls. I guess we'll never know." She chuckled softly. "And I understand her name was really Delilah Lucy. I guess she took Brigitte as a fancier name for her profession. Agnes is nine now, and a bright little thing. Her sister Mary got married at sixteen, as soon as her father died. So it's just Agnes at the orphanage."

The kettle emitted a plume of steam, and Annie rose to refill the teapot, and sliced some more cake.

"Most surprising thing that has happened," she said, returning to the table, "is a girl came from England and arrived in San Francisco. Both her parents were dead. I guess the mother died back in England, and the father on the trip to San Francisco.

"The steamer captain knew Morgan Hurd had a business here in Sacramento and thought maybe she was kin to him, since her name is Annie Hurd. Mr. Hurd had no idea of any kin in England, so he brought her here to me. She's only twelve. I couldn't abandon her, or give her to the Orphanage. I kept thinking maybe she's kin to Ben."

They sipped their tea in silence for a few minutes, then Annie said casually, "Do you suppose one of your family could adopt her?"

Startled, Matilda stared at her.

"I'm not asking you to take her yourself," Annie hastened to say. "I know you have your hands full. But I thought maybe you might know someone. She's not happy here in the city. She loves animals, and keeps asking if we can't have some chickens or a pig. And she is begging for a horse. She really needs to be on a family farm."

Matilda's mind flew to her brother Tom and his new wife. She knew they planned to adopt George Jones, an orphaned neighbor boy. Might they also like to have a girl? A girl who loved to take care of chickens would be a big help to Tom's wife Mary.

Annie, watching Matilda's face, smiled. "I see you've thought of someone."

"Yes, my brother Tom. He just recently married, to a widow whose children are grown. They are planning to adopt an orphaned neighbor boy. Why not a girl as well? Can I meet her?"

"Yes, she should be home from school soon."

So when Lew and Matilda returned home, about an hour before sunset with just enough time to do the chores, the shy, blue-eyed little girl accompanied them. Her delight at being on a farm was evident from the moment she alighted from the buggy and ran to the corral where Ben and Charley stood with their heads over the fence, waiting for them. As she stroked their muzzles, a happy smile lighted her face. She squealed with delight when Charley snuffled her neck.

Matilda smiled. "Carrie and Sammie, this is Annie. She will be with us for a while. Why don't you introduce her to the chickens and the pigs?" They had swung by the Post Office for the mail, and Matilda had a letter from Weldon's wife, Susan she was anxious to read.

Betsy Ann greeted her when she entered the house. "And how was Annie? Find out what she wanted?"

Matilda laughed. "Yes, she was given a twelve-year-old orphan she wants to find a home for."

"So I suppose you brought her here to stay with us." Betsy Ann's ability to know everything before anyone said a word had not waned with the years.

"Yes," Matilda sighed. "What else could I do? The poor little mite. I thought maybe Tom and Mary could adopt her. She loves animals, and should be a big help to Mary."

Betsy Ann nodded. "Might be just the thing. Who's the letter from?"

"Weldon's wife, Susan, talking about taking in strays. I remember when Weldon joined us."

Betsy Ann chuckled softly and shifted in her chair. "Poor little orphan feller. Lucky for him I had just lost little Andrew and had milk to spare. Skinny little thing he was, 'cause his Maw was so sickly before she died she didn't hardly have enough to keep him alive. I told her after the time she had birthin' Peter that she shouldn't have any more. After all, she had five healthy ones. But they went ahead and had Weldon anyway." She waved at the letter. "And now he's a man grown with young-uns of his own."

Matilda tore open the letter and scanned its contents. "She says they've moved back to Kansas from Missouri. Minnie is seven already, and Guy is five. She also says her nephew, a young man named John Leonard, has come from Iowa to help them out, now they have their own farm. Here, read it yourself. I have to get supper started."

Two days later, she invited Tom and Mary to Sunday dinner and introduced them to Annie. She saw Mary's eyes light up when she learned the little girl was orphaned, and knew she had made the right decision.

317

Chapter 37

June to December, 1880

"LOOKS TO BE a big fire up across the river. Close, maybe about McConnell's"

Lew's words brought Matilda running to the front door. From the end of the porch, she saw billows of brown smoke rising to the sky.

"Get the buggy and the buckets and gunny sacks. Use Charley or Ben. They are the calmest around fire. The younger ones are too skittish. Sammie, help him. I'll get Carrie." As the two boys took off on a run, she called after them. "You had better fill the buckets. There may not be much water if the fire has blocked access to the river." Not that there was much water in the river anyway, she thought. By the first week in August, it was pretty low.

She and Carrie climbed into the buggy when Lew brought it to the front of the house and they headed for the fire. She brought a basket with biscuits, cold chicken, and a jug of lemonade, knowing the fire fighters would be hungry and thirsty.

When they arrived, about twenty minutes later, many other neighbors had gathered. She saw Denis Moroney and Ed Riley swatting at the fire line with wet sacks. Lew tied Charley to the hitching post and he and Sammie each grabbed a bucket and sack and ran to join the other men and boys. Carrie and Matilda hefted the basket between them and joined Mr. McConnell's two daughters on the porch.

"Oh, Mrs. Wheelock, it's so good of you to come so quickly. We were so frightened when we saw the line of fire, but fortunately the hands got a backfire going to direct the flames away from the house."

"What about the railroad bridge?"

"They're fighting it there right now. One of the boys came back and said one of the trestles was burning."

"Is someone going back up the tracks to warn the train?"

"It was the train men that found the fire in the first place, when the Los Angeles Express came through this morning. They stopped and fought the fire, then went on to Galt. It flared up again after they left." Anna sighed deeply, her fright still not completely abated, judging from her pale face. "My father did send one of the hands up to warn the Monterey Express. He says those pilings should be checked before another train crosses."

Lew, Sammie tagging behind him, and followed by several other men, arrived to hear her words.

"Yes," he said grimly. "How the train men ever let the Los Angeles Express cross those pilings is a wonder. Two of them are so badly burned that it's a miracle they are still holding up the rails, let alone a train." He wiped his soot-stained brow, took a long drink of lemonade from the jug and helped himself to a piece of chicken. Sammie, not to be out-done, followed his brother's example with such precision that it brought a smile to Matilda's face.

"Yep, boy's right." Denis Moroney took a biscuit in his grimy hands and took a big bite. "Gonna have to replace those two pilings before the Monterey Express comes through."

"Well, since the fire is out, we may as well be getting home." She picked up the now empty basket and handed it to Lew. "Come along."

They took their leave of the McConnell's and departed. The smell of smoke still hung heavily in the air. All Matilda could think of was how close it had come to getting into Denis Moroney's wheat fields, and from there, she shuddered to think how fast it would have gone. Fortunately, much of the wheat had already been harvested, but enough still stood in the fields it could have been devastating. And if the trestle had collapsed . . .. She shrugged. No use borrowing trouble. The fire was out, and the train, while it would be delayed, would be safe.

The summer had passed quickly, everyone busy with harvesting and canning. The big news in the neighborhood was Count Valensin's construction of a racetrack on his Arno farm.

"As if that great big house wasn't enough to impress his neighbors with how important he is," Polly chuckled when Matilda told her about it. "And after losing that valuable stallion just last May."

"I know," Matilda exclaimed. "I hear the poor thing died of a rupture. Just think of the pain he must have suffered? And can you imagine a horse worth $10,000? As beautiful as she was, White Star wasn't worth anywhere near that much." She still felt a pang of loss when she thought of White Star.

Polly shrugged. "Has something to do with his value as breeding stock. Seems he had a pretty good racing record and a lot of other horse owners wanted to mate him with their mares."

"You should hear Alf on the subject," Matilda chuckled.

321

"He says horse racing just encourages gambling, which he considers sinful. Says Valensin might call himself a good Catholic, but he's a dyed in the wool sinner. And according to Mr. Herbert, the good Count is one of his best customers at the bar in the Hicksville Saloon."

"Poor Alice. She's got a man who is going to run through her father's money even before she inherits it." Polly refilled their teacups with a smile. "Although I can't see old man McCauley cutting loose with any money to support the Count's little games."

"I guess money is not a concern. Tom says he just bought another batch of horses. Says he paid up to $8,000 for ten brood mares and a three-year-old sorrel colt, all of them supposed to be out of famous racers."

Polly shook her head. "Such foolishness. If I had that kind of money, I sure wouldn't waste it on horses."

"I understand, just rumors, of course, that his wife is not all that happy about it either. She thinks the money would be better spent in cattle and farm equipment."

Polly's son Sammy entered in time to hear Matilda's last comment. He chuckled. "Some of the gambling men who hang around the Hicksville Saloon are already offering odds on how long it will be before old man McCauley throws his royalness out."

His mother sighed. "Just goes to show being rich can't buy you everything. McCauley bought his daughter royalty, but it looks like it wasn't much of a bargain." She rose and poked the bread rising on the windowsill. Apparently satisfied, she removed the protective towel and placed the loaf pans in the oven. The bread cared for, she sat back down across from Matilda. "You were right about bringing little Annie for Tom and Mary. I've never seen a child blossom so quickly."

Matilda laughed. "Yes, that has worked out very well. It's hard to believe she's only twelve. She seems so mature for one so young." She paused thoughtfully. "Although I guess she has been through so much it has forced her to grow up quickly." She rose. "I had better go. We have chores to do. Sammy, please tell Lew to collect the children and get ready to head for home."

"Isn't it a shame about poor Mr. Sutter?" News of his recent death back East while trying to get funds from the United States Government had reached them. "After all he did to save American settlers coming across the mountains, it seems they could have done a little more for him." Polly shook her head. "And those he helped forgot so quickly."

"Yes, quickly enough they started stealing his land and his cattle almost as soon as they recovered from the trek," Matilda said wryly, remembering some of the stories Giles had told her. "At least there were three bills introduced in the State Legislature to grant him a pension, even if it was just a pittance."

Lew appeared at the door. "Ready, Mother?"

"Yes." She suddenly remembered the recent letter from Sarah. "Did you hear from Sarah? She and Albert have a grocery store in Bloomington, and I guess they are doing well." She shook her head. "Sarah's the only one who stayed in Illinois, but she sounds happy. She says Lawson can't persuade Arabella to have another baby. She says since she lost Willie she doesn't want to risk going through that again. Poor little fellow was only four years old."

"It's been less than a year," Polly said. "She may feel different after the shock has had a chance to wear off."

"Sarah says she tried to tell her most women lose at least one baby," Matilda said, thinking of Baby John, so long ago in Kansas. She met Polly's eyes and knew her sister-in-law

323

thought of her son Michael, dear, sweet handsome Michael, and his tragic death. "After all, Sarah herself lost her own Elizabeth when she was twelve."

"Speaking of babies," Matilda added, "Jane Mahin tells me she has another grandchild. John and Mary have a little girl born August 4, the same day as the fire at McConnell's Station. Named her Gracie." She glanced at Lew, waiting patiently, and gathered her reticule. "And now, I really do have to leave!"

August continued with its usual hot dry weather. Several small fires were quickly extinguished. Reports that Chief Ouray was seriously ill threatened the peace talks among the Utes, but it was so far away, Matilda only heard it with minor interest. All of these Indian disputes seemed to have a way of taking on a life of their own.

Early in September, the family gathered at Matilda's for Sunday dinner. Since it was apparent to everyone that Betsy Ann grew more frail every day, they gathered frequently, wanting to spend as much time with her as possible.

After dinner, the girls were assigned to do the dishes and the adults gathered in the parlor to visit. Alf was highly indignant at Sam's report on a recent theater visit, where two notorious women of the town had the nerve to sit down beside respectable ladies. "Can you imagine the management allowing such a thing to happen? When ladies go to the theater, they should be assured they will sit with decent people, and not be wedged between fallen women from the slums of Second Street."

"I'm sure it was not intentional," Matilda murmured, thinking of Cora from her trip through Dobytown so long ago.

"Well, I should think they would be more careful. Pure women will certainly not want to take chances on being neighbors with prostitutes."

Sam, a little behind Alf, almost managed to hide his grin. Apparently thinking it time to change the subject, he said, " Has everyone heard that the Utes have signed the peace agreement?"

Not to be outdone, Tom added, "And wasn't that a terrible fire they had in Sacramento? Burned several blocks. Started in a paint shop, took out Schindler's Sash and Door Company, and several other businesses."

Matilda returned to the kitchen to see how the girls were doing with the dishes. Mary pulled her mother into the bedroom and said, almost casually, "I think I'm in a family way again."

Something in Mary's tone told Matilda this was not the happy news such an announcement usually brought. She said nothing, waiting for Mary to continue.

"This will be the last one, Mother," she said firmly. "That man is never going to touch me again." She burst into tears.

Matilda took the weeping girl in her arms and held her. She could think of nothing to say.

At the end of October, Sam came in with a wad of papers in his hand and a big grin on his face. "It's done, little sister. As of October 28, your remaining 136 acres is set aside as a Homestead. Nobody can pull any McCauley tricks. Just don't ever borrow money on it, or use it for collateral, and no one can ever take it."

"Oh, thank you, Sam. That's such a relief."

"And how is Mother?"

Matilda hesitated. "She's not doing well. This morning she decided she wanted to stay in bed "for a spell longer" as she put it. She's still there. It's not like her at all. Even when the pain in her joints was bad she would be up with the chickens and out puttering in the kitchen." She glanced toward the door. "I've been in to check on her a couple of times, and she seemed to be asleep." She shrugged. "At least she's still breathing. I know there is no point in asking her if she wants to see a doctor. She still does not trust doctors, not even Dr. Montague."

Sam shrugged his shoulders. "Not much we can do, then. Just take care of her as best we can. She is 81 years old." As if to satisfy himself, he gently opened the door and looked in at the form on the bed. He returned and sat down. "Looks like she's still asleep." He sighed. "You're right. Nothing else we can do." He changed the subject. "I hear that it looks like Frank Iler will recover after all. There was some doubt at first."

"That's the strangest thing. Did anyone ever figure out where the bullet came from?"

Sam shook his head. "Nope. Really odd, him just sitting there working away at his workbench in his wagon shop when the bullet out of nowhere hit him. Came from so far away no one even heard a shot."

Betsy Ann continued to grow weaker, spending more and more time in bed. Finally in mid-December, she told Matilda, "I think it's about time I joined your father." She sighed and closed her eyes. Matilda waited. When her mother spoke again, she talked of others she had lost. Matilda had never heard her mother speak of them before, almost like she had not wished to dwell on lost ones.

"Baby Andrew was the first time I lost a babe." She sighed. "He was never right, from the beginning, poor little mite, almost like his heart was bad. Little lips were blue all the time. Finally, one day, he just didn't wake up." She smiled at Matilda. "That's when Weldon joined us. His ma died just a few days before Andrew, and since they were kin of my brother A.M.'s wife Amanda, they brought him to me."

She closed her eyes and sighed deeply. Matilda waited.

When Betsy Ann spoke again, she talked about losing Temperance and her futile battle against consumption. "It was the one enemy I could never beat," she sighed. "I knew, when your sister Caroline lost Tommy, that she would take the consumption as well. And she did. Losing Minerva and Sinclair so close together took all the heart out of your father. At least he was spared watching Will and Britt killed by horses as well."

She met Matilda's eyes and smiled. "Got a lot of loved ones waiting for me over there. Time is coming for me to join them. Lived a long time, I have, well past my 'three score and ten'. I never was too strong on church, but I know there's a Heaven, and Gardner is waiting for me there. He was a good man, and I'm sure he's taking delight in the grandchildren that are there with him, too."

The next morning, Matilda could not rouse her. She lay flat on her back, breathing in little shallow gasps. Matilda sent Lew for Sam, Alf and Tom, and sat by her, holding her hand. The breathing became shallower, and began to have long pauses, followed by a long, shuddering sigh. Matilda continued to hold the work-worn hand, thinking how many babies those hands had delivered, how many bodies they had healed. She hoped her brothers would be in time to say goodbye.

Carrie stood by the door, watching, her eyes solemn. She seemed to know what was happening, without Matilda saying a word.

Sam and Alf arrived and tiptoed into the room. Tom followed a few moments later. "Is she gone?" Alf asked in a whisper.

"Not yet, but soon," Matilda replied. Sam sat on the other side of the bed and took his mother's other hand. Alf and Tom stood at the foot of the bed. Lew, Carrie, and Sammie watched from the doorway.

When the breathing stopped, Matilda kissed the withered cheek.

"Goodbye, Mother," she whispered.

Chapter 38

December, 1880 to December, 1881

CHRISMAS WAS followed by heavy rain, then two weeks of relentless, depressing fog. Each morning Matilda rose to slate gray skies, with visibility sometimes limited to only a few yards. The damp cold permeated the house, and penetrated her very bones. She shivered, wishing for just a few hours of sunshine.

Sam brought her the mail from the Post Office and the neighborhood news. "Hear the School Board tried to get the Health Department to waive the smallpox vaccination requirement. Says it's keeping too many children out of school."

"With all of the smallpox epidemics recently, I certainly hope they didn't relent!"

"No way," Sam grinned. "They said protecting the children's lives was more important than teaching them arithmetic."

"Good," she muttered. "If everyone gets vaccinated, maybe we can wipe out that horrible disease." She shuddered to think of Mary or Elizabeth having their lovely skin disfigured by the ugly pustules. She could not imagine why everyone did not get vaccinated. Thankfully, Alfred had agreed with her, and they were all protected.

"And the Baltimore papers have suggested a way to get rid of polygamy in Utah."

"And how do they propose to do that?"

He chuckled. "Easy. Divide the Utah Territory between Colorado and Nevada, and Utah just disappears."

Matilda had to laugh at the simplicity of the solution. "It might work, but I bet they'll never get away with it." She rose. "Are you hungry? There's some stew and biscuits left from feeding the children."

He grinned. "Can always eat some of your stew and biscuits, little sister." He settled into a chair at the table.

She dished up a steaming bowl and asked, "And how is the flooding?"

"Worse." He blew on the spoonful of stew and put it in his mouth. Breaking a biscuit into the bowl, he swallowed that mouthful and said, "Several levee breaks between Colusa and Knights Landing." He grinned. "Tom said those levees were a bad idea. I'm inclined to think he was right. And the tracks have been washed out in several places along the Feather River." He swallowed another mouthful of stew. "And our local roads aren't much better. The road between Hicksville and McConnell's Station is treacherous. Man risks life and limb to cross it when the Cosumnes is as high as it is right now."

She remained silent while he finished eating. Would this be another hard winter? One where heavy rains continued day after day? She sighed.

Sam rose to leave, then dropped one more item of bad news. "Frank's wife Clara is worse. Doc Montague says she has consumption."

In February, the Sacramento River reached the highest point ever recorded, 26 feet, six inches. Word of more levee breaks and washed out railroads reached them.

In March, the political machinations of the County Board of Supervisors finally resulted in Dr. Laine losing his contract and being replaced by Dr. White.

"Four to three the vote was," Polly declared. "So they got Dr. White back in. And Dr. Laine is such a gracious gentleman he thanked the Board for their 'uniform kindness and courtesy'. Can you imagine him saying that after the way they treated him?"

"Can't help but wonder what Dreman, Wilson, Beckley and Bailey will get out of Dr. White they couldn't get out of Dr. Laine," Matilda mused. "All the things we heard about that went on when Dr. White was in charge before, about patients not being fed, and not getting proper care, not getting clean sheets and such. Makes a body wonder where all the money went."

Polly chuckled grimly. "I don't know, but I can sure make a good guess." She sighed and shook her head, "Just hope I never wind up a patient there!" She rubbed her left breast.

Matilda had noticed that movement before, but had said nothing. This time, she asked Polly if there was a problem.

Polly grimaced. "I've got a sore on my breast. It just doesn't seem to heal."

Horrified, Matilda could only stare. What if it was cancerous? Lose Polly? Her heart sank. The two had become so close since they were both widowed. "Have you talked to Dr. Montague or Dr. Jenks about it?"

"No, I'm too embarrassed. Besides, what could a doctor do? I've been using the golden seal and myrrh, which was Mother Betsy Ann's remedy for sores, but it hasn't helped. It doesn't really hurt, it just - - just kind of bothers me is all. More just an awareness that it's there."

Matilda had no answer. Remembering Polly's comment about hoping she never had to be a patient at the County Hospital, and knowing there were no funds for a private hospital, she hesitated to urge her to seek medical care. Dr. Montague was a very modern physician. Surely he would want to operate to remove the lesion, which would mean hospitalization.

While she pondered, Polly asked, "And how is Mary doing? Isn't her baby due soon?"

"Yes," Matilda nodded. "Any day now." She laughed. "I keep waiting for Elizabeth to tell me she and Henry are going to produce an heir, but she is so busy being Mrs. Henry Wade. She is planning to go with him on the cattle drive this summer. I guess such a trip would be hard if she was expecting. Or worse if she had a small baby." Matilda hesitated a moment, then asked, "And Clara?"

Polly only shook her head.

War loomed between Chile and Peru, and between China and Japan. A movement began to consolidate all of the American railroads, and France had begun plans to build a canal across the Isthmus of Panama. But all of these events passed Matilda by. Her concerns were on Mary's baby and Polly's health.

Earl Baldwin Douglass made his appearance on April 19, 1881. At Mary's insistence, she and Mable had stayed with Matilda for the last week before Earl's birth.

When the baby's birth appeared imminent, Matilda sent Lew riding for Dr. Montague. While they waited for the doctor's arrival, Matilda tried to persuade Mary to let her send Lew for George when he returned with the doctor.

"I don't want him, Mother," Mary gasped between contractions.

"But he's entitled to know. It is his child," Matilda protested.

"We'll send Lew to tell him after," she said firmly. When Mary set her jaw like that, it was the end of the discussion. Matilda shrugged and accepted Mary's decision.

The arrival of Dr. Montague ended the conversation. He immediately took charge. Matilda, who had assisted her mother at many deliveries, was impressed by his competence. Even Mary responded to his gentle ministrations. He could not, of course, make childbirth an easy experience, but he did make both of them feel everything would be all right, and it was.

As Mary nestled little Earl, and Mable stared at her little brother in mingled awe and fascination, Matilda seated Dr. Montague at the table and plied him with a cup of tea and a piece of apple pie.

"Thank you so much for coming, Dr. Montague. We are so glad you have decided to open your practice in Galt. It's so much closer than having to send to Sacramento. There really was more work than Dr. Jenks could handle. And Dr. Harvey is so involved with politics and getting rich that he doesn't have a great deal of time to practice his profession."

He laughed merrily. "I am delighted to be here. After growing up back East, spending a winter in California has made me realize how much I hated plodding through snow." He finished the last bite of pie and drained his teacup. "Thank you. That was delicious. Bachelor like me doesn't get pie this good very often. I will just take a peek at Mrs. Douglass to be sure all is well and be on my way."

It was on the tip of Matilda's tongue to ask him about the sore on Polly's breast, but she hesitated. After all, if Polly wanted him to know, it was her business to tell him. Instead, she said, "I'm sure there are any number of young ladies who would be glad to alter your single status."

He only chuckled softly. She was sure any number of the referred to young ladies had already tried. He ignored the implication, but did volunteer one item. "Maxfield's daughter, Clara Randolph, is married to your nephew, is she not?"

"Yes, to my late brother Will's son Frank." She met his eyes. "The girl is consumptive. I know. She's dying, isn't she." It was not a question. Matilda had seen Clara recently. She had lost weight, her cheeks were sunken, the skin over the cheekbones flushed with fever. "I watched two sisters die of consumption. I recognize all of the signs."

His face grew gentle. He took her hand and stroked the back of it. "Then I will not try to deceive you. I fear she will not be with us much longer. She is not responding to any of the medications I have tried." He released her hand. "I am so sorry."

The rest of the summer and fall passed quickly. Clara died peacefully in her sleep and was buried in the Liberty Cemetery. An inconsolable Frank moved back with his mother and tried valiantly to get on with his life.

"All I can say," Polly said to Matilda as they discussed their concern for him, "is that I am glad he was strong enough to defy her father and give them the short time they had together. They were so happy and so in love." She paused, absently rubbing the same spot on her breast. The movement caught at Matilda's heart.

"Maybe," Polly went on, "God took her before the happiness faded. He must have some reason for taking her away from him so soon."

Remembering how Lew and Alfred had both been taken from her after a few short years, Matilda could only wonder. She knew it was not her place to question God, but had often thought it might not have interfered too much with God's plans for the universe to leave Alfred with her at least until Carrie and Sammie were grown. Shocked at her blasphemous thoughts, she returned her attention to Polly's words.

"Anyway," Polly continued, "he is still young and handsome. I'm sure he will find another wife after the shock of her loss wears off."

Christmas of 1881 was a solemn affair at first, but children seldom remain downcast for long. Matilda found herself taking part in the games and gift opening, trying not to think of previous Christmases and the many loved ones who now slept beneath the brown, frost-killed grass in the little Hicksville Cemetery.

Late in the afternoon, after the guests had departed and she and Carrie had begun putting things away, Bill Frye knocked on the door, several packages in his arms. He stood on the porch, a shy smile on his face. "I hope you don't think I'm intruding, but I brought a few gifts for the Yule."

She returned his smile. "Of course you are not intruding. Come in, come in." She ushered him inside and relieved him of the parcels while he shrugged out of his coat. "You are too late for Christmas dinner, but I do have some leftover ham and some pie and coffee."

He had brought gifts for Lew, Carrie, and Sammie. Lew and Sammie received folding knives, and Carrie a beautiful silk scarf with pink flowers, which she kept stroking, savoring its softness. Her eyes sparkled. The boys were speechless at the magnificence of the knives.

"Only family I ever had was my sister Elizabeth," he mumbled, "And her young-uns live so far away I never get to see them. Man gets older, he learns to value family."

Matilda's heart went out to him. "It's thoughtful of you to think of my children, Mr. Frye. I'm afraid my income does not allow me to buy them such beautiful things."

He grinned like a little boy. "One more package out in the buggy. Excuse me a moment."

He returned in a few minutes with a large bundle and handed it to her. Her eyes wide in wonder, she opened it. It was a beautiful lamp. The glass shade had roses painted on the side. She had never owned anything so lovely in her life. Her eyes filled with tears at his kindness.

"Thank you so much, Mr. Frye," she whispered. "I'm almost afraid to accept something so valuable."

"Please," he murmured, "call me Bill, and the pleasure is all mine." He took the hand she offered and raised it to his lips. Their eyes met and her heart lurched.

Could she possibly fall in love again at her age?

Chapter 39

January to November, 1882

BILL FRYE BECAME a regular visitor, and Matilda did enjoy his company. She had been lonely, more so than she had admitted even to herself. It was comforting to have someone with her to discuss the neighborhood and world news. She felt she was finally emerging from the cocoon she had wrapped around herself.

Her concern for Polly increased. Polly steadfastly refused to call in a doctor, but she lost weight steadily. She almost seemed thinner each time Matilda saw her.

After Easter Services, Matilda invited the Reverend Staton and his wife to join the family for Easter Dinner. Following the meal, and while the children sought the brightly colored eggs hidden in the grass around the house, Reverend Staton brought up the subject of the possibility of Lewis attending Pacific Methodist College in Santa Rosa for the coming fall term.

"How old is he now?" the pastor asked.

Matilda hadn't given college a thought. Money was always so scarce. "He'll be nineteen in October. But isn't it expensive to go to the college?"

"I think I can get him a scholarship. He's a bright young man. He should have the chance. He can get room and board in return for doing chores."

Bill Frye agreed. "Be a good opportunity for the boy. One year would give him a good background."

Matilda laughed. "I'm not sure he wants to leave. He is so besotted with P.H. Latourette's little girl Media. I think he's considering going into the tinsmithing business!"

Bill grinned. "Will give her a chance to grow up. She's only about thirteen or fourteen."

"I'll discuss it with him. We'll see what he wants to do." She hesitated. "I really need him here. Sammie's not old enough to do the work, and I hate to keep calling on Polly's sons."

"Nonsense," Polly interspersed. "Keeps Sam and Frank busy, and Bud is big enough now." She grinned wryly. "And Frank is becoming very attached to little Annie Hurd."

"Annie?" Matilda gasped. "Why, she's just a child!"

Polly shrugged. "A very mature child, I fear, as I am sure you have noticed. She turned fourteen this summer. And Maggie was only fifteen when she married Kidder, as Frank has pointed out to me several times when I have mentioned how young Annie is. At least she has taken his mind off of the tragic death of Clara."

Matilda sighed. "Such a shame Maggie and Kidder lost little Alfred. That diphtheria is such a terrible disease."

"Thank heavens they didn't lose Gussie as well. Several families have had more than one child die when an epidemic sweeps through." Polly closed her eyes for a moment and Matilda saw a wave of pain cross her face. Then she brightened. "Wes says his relatives in Stockton are all talking about Bob Ford killing Jesse James. I guess a lot of his family in Missouri have been friends of the James brothers for years. And I hear Frank turned himself in to the law. Guess losing his brother made him want to put that whole terrible life behind him."

Matilda laughed, "I'm not sure if that is good or bad."

The wheat fields produced a bumper crop that summer. At least all that rain had brought one good result. With the income, Matilda began to seriously consider sending Lewis to Pacific Methodist College, at least for one year. No one in her family had ever been to college. In spite of her brother Alf's intentions of making enough money in the gold fields to attend the University at Bloomington, he had never once thought of returning to Illinois. Of course, Matilda thought with a smile, after spending a winter in California, she had never thought of going back to Illinois either.

Reverend Staton had kept his promise, and Lewis had a one-year scholarship, with promise of room and board from a family in Santa Rosa near the campus.

The week he departed, thirteen carloads of wheat shipped from the Arno Station, almost twice the previous year. The temperature had finally broken. It had hovered around 111 degrees for several days.

"At least they tell me the weather is cooler in Santa Rosa," Lew grinned as he hugged his mother in a goodbye embrace before boarding the train. "It's closer to the ocean." He hugged and kissed Carrie, and shook hands with Sammie. "You two be sure and take good care of Mother, now."

"Oh, we will," Sammie assured him solemnly. "And Mr. Frye is going to help us."

Bill Frye had driven them to the Arno Station, and he listened to Sammie with a boyish grin.

A loud blast from the train's whistle drowned out any further attempts at conversation and Lew hopped aboard as the rain chugged its way out of the station, gathering speed as it went.

Matilda waved to Lew as long as she could see him. Her feelings were mixed. She was proud of him, and glad the Reverend Staton had given him the opportunity to go to college. But at the same time, it was hard to believe he was grown up and leaving her. It seemed just yesterday when he took his first faltering steps out on the Nevada desert on the long trek across from Kansas to California.

She suddenly realized she had been lost in her thoughts. The train was out of sight, and Bill and the children waited in silence. With a smile, she turned to them and said, "Let's go home."

As Bill turned the buggy around and headed back towards the Wheelock property, he commented, "Sure glad we didn't have to haul the wheat to the Galt Station. They say the bridges between Hicksville and Galt aren't safe for heavy loads. I hear there was a lot of damage done to the pilings by the high water last spring. Denis Moroney said the last load he brought across, the bridge over the Laguna wobbled so much he was sure he'd never make it to the other side. Says he's not going over it again until it's fixed."

"Aren't they going to repair them?" Matilda demanded. "Why do we have a Road Commissioner and why do they collect all those taxes if they don't do anything about a dangerous condition like a defective bridge?"

"Oh," he assured her, "they say they are going to fix them." He grinned. "One of these days."

"Yes," she agreed. "One of these days. As soon as a wagon goes through and someone gets killed."

"Probably," he chuckled. "And how is your little granddaughter doing?"

She smiled at the thought of Pearl, Elizabeth's first, and the difference between the Wade house and Mary's. "Very well. Henry is so besotted that he carries her around all the time and boasts she is the most beautiful baby in the world."

"Of course," he responded with a sly smile. "She looks like her grandmother."

"Go on with you." She swatted at him with her fan as Carrie and Sammie giggled in the back seat.

He just grinned and said, "I hear Dick Johnson bought the Hicksville Hotel from McIntyre. He plans to have a grand opening on the 31st of this month. Says it will be a free Grand Ball and supper." He gave her a sidelong glance. "I'd be right proud if you'd allow me to escort you, Mrs. Wheelock."

Her heart rose and she laughed merrily, ignoring the snickers from the children in the back seat. "I'd be delighted to attend with you, Mr. Frye. And I think it's time you started calling me 'Tilda."

The ball was a great success. Dick Johnson was very popular in the community, and noted for his magnificent parties. His wife, Celestia, made a gracious hostess. Most of the little community of Hicksville was in attendance.

Matilda had to smile at the murmur that went through the assembled crowd as she entered the room holding Bill's arm. She knew that what had been speculation among her acquaintances would now take on a life of its own.

Mr. Johnson greeted them cordially, and said what she knew most of the guests were thinking. "Mrs. Wheelock, so delightful to see you. It has been far too long. And are you going to ensnare one of Hicksville's most perennial bachelors?"

Matilda blushed, and Bill patted her hand with a grin.

"If she'll have me," he replied simply.

The next news to circulate through the little community

was the marriage, on September 7, 1882, of Frank Randolph and Annie Hurd.

It was Polly who told Matilda. "They just up and ran off to the Court House in Sacramento and got married by the Justice of the Peace," she reported. "Tom and Mary weren't too happy about it, said the girl was too young. After all, she is only fourteen."

"And the Justice of the Peace married them with no parental consent?"

Polly laughed. "Annie put down on the form that she was eighteen. She's always looked mature for her age, and no one ever questioned her."

Matilda only shook her head. Polly looked thinner than ever, and Matilda's concern for her deepened. But what could she do?

Polly was more interested in Matilda's romance with Bill Frye. "And has he proposed yet?"

Matilda laughed. "Not in so many words. But he is frequently at the house, and helps Sammie and Carrie with their schoolwork. And just last week he fixed the pump. Again." She sighed. "Says I'm going to need a new pump before too long. He says Louis Herbert is trying to get a patent on a new kind of pump he has designed, and maybe we should try it out." She smiled. "So, while he has not yet said the words, he certainly seems interested in me."

"And how do you feel about him?"

Matilda hesitated. "I'm not sure. It's wonderful having the companionship. Alfred and I were so close." Her eyes filled with tears and she blinked them away. "I don't think I'll ever love him as I loved Alfred." She met Polly's eyes and smiled. "But at our age, companionship is a good thing. And he has always been alone, especially since his only sister died. He is so happy to be part of a family."

Polly hesitated and Matilda saw the conflict in her face. Finally she spoke. "I'm dying, 'Tilda. You know it and I know it. This cancer in my breast is draining away my life." She held up her hand as Matilda started to speak. "It'll be all right. Will's been gone for seven years now. It's time I joined him. Lizzie is eleven and Bud is fifteen. I've almost got my family raised. I've already spoken to Maggie and Kidder. They are willing to take them both in. I couldn't ask you to do it 'Tilda, as your hands are full already."

"You know I'll do anything I can, Polly."

"I know, 'Tilda. Since Will died, your friendship has been the most important thing in my life. I will be sorry to leave you."

Matilda's response choked in her throat. She took Polly in her arms and held her closely. Their tears mingled.

Diphtheria marched through Galt and the surrounding communities again in mid-September, cutting its usual swath among the children. Matilda breathed a sigh of relief when no one close to her was among those cut down in this latest round. This time. What will happen next time the dreaded scourge passes through? She could only cling to her children and grandchildren with a thankful prayer that this time they were spared.

Then, on November 2, 1882, Matilda stood in the little church in Hicksville in front of the Reverend Staton and became Mrs. William Frye.

Chapter 40

December, 1882 to May, 1883

THEY LOST POLLY on December 27. Christmas had been a dreary time, for Polly had slipped into a coma just two days before the holiday, and Matilda had refused to leave her side. Poor Bill, she thought. His first Christmas as a father and family man had to be such a sad one.

She tried to apologize, but he just took her in his arms and kissed her gently. "I know how much Polly means to you. The children and I understand. There will be other Christmases. I have already promised Carrie and Sammie that next Christmas will be a day to remember."

Lew had come home from Pacific Methodist College for the holidays, and stood beside her as she watched Polly's coffin lowered into the grave, beside her beloved Will and son Michael. Lizzie clung to her brother Bud and wept during the whole ceremony.

After the services, everyone gathered at Matilda's. Polly had been very popular, and a large number of people attended her funeral.

Matilda smiled faintly to Alf. "It looks like the whole neighborhood is here. I guess we weren't the only ones who loved her."

Alf nodded. "Folks not only liked her, they admired the

way she managed to carry on, keeping her family together after Will was killed."

Sam joined them. In his hand he carried a plate piled high with ham, fried chicken, biscuits, a boiled potato, and deviled eggs. Matilda smothered a smile. Bachelors never seemed to pass up an opportunity to eat well.

"Hear our Don Ray got himself appointed Postmaster in Galt. Wonder if he'll run that like he does his other businesses. Probably be the only Post Office in history to turn a profit."

Alf grinned. "Uncle Joe Still says Don Ray is the best collectors he has ever known. All those folks as have postage due on letters at the Post Office better pay up."

Reverend Staton joined them and offered his condolences. "I know how close you and Mrs. Randolph were. She often spoke to me of how much your friendship meant to her."

Matilda's eyes filled and her throat tightened. She managed to whisper "Thank you," but could say no more.

Alf stepped in. "Say, Reverend, I hear rumors they are planning to move the parsonage from Hicksville to Galt. Are you going to be leaving us?"

Reverend Staton shook his head ruefully. "The decision was not mine. My wife and I like it here. The Conference decided that since they have built that lovely new church in Galt, the parsonage should be there."

The day after Polly's funeral, Lew rose early and went out to the barn to give Ben and Charley their morning treat of a lump of brown sugar. Matilda smiled as he returned to the house, grinning from ear to ear. He had loved the two horses since his first ride on Charley when his legs would still not reach over the sides of Charley's broad back.

"Ben and Charley are getting old, Mother," he said as he took his seat at the table for breakfast. "How long do Clydesdales live?"

"Charley is eighteen, Ben a couple of years older," she replied. "I'm sure both of them have at least five years yet. Don't worry. They'll still be here when you come home in June."

Lewis could only stay a few days. He had to be back in Santa Rosa the first Sunday in January, as the second term began the following Monday.

"Have to be there, Mother, for the first two days are exams and registration. Anyone who's not there is dropped."

"We've scarcely had time to talk," she replied. She placed a plate of eggs and ham on the table before him and poured him a cup of coffee. They were alone. Bill had gone to milk the cows and Sammie and Carrie were still asleep.

He grinned and sighed happily as he slathered jam on a biscuit. "I think the thing I miss most about home is your cooking."

She swatted at him with the dishtowel. "Go on with your flattery. Much as you like to eat, I'm sure you eat the food at the college with as much enthusiasm as you eat here. I want to hear about your classes. What are you studying?"

"English, which is pretty easy. You taught us well, Mother, never letting us use bad grammar. Geography is kind of fun, learning where all of the places the newspapers talk about are located. And arithmetic. Fortunately Miss Loughran drilled that into me. And so did Papa Alfred."

A stab of pain ran through her as she remembered Alfred patiently drilling Lewis over and over again until he had all of the basics of arithmetic mastered.

"History, of course," he went on. "And English reading." He sighed. "And penmanship." He looked up at her and grinned. "And orthography."

"And what?"

"Orthography."

"And what on earth is that?"

"Spelling and the proper use of letters, so the capital letters all go in the right places. That sort of thing."

"Oh. Just never heard it called that before."

"I did okay on my exams in English grammar and arithmetic, but I'm afraid my Latin and Greek are a little weak. Never occurred to me that Caesar's Communications would have much value for a farmer."

She laughed merrily. "I suppose you could expound on them to Ben and Charley."

"And next term we expand the elocution to include composition." He mopped up the last of his egg with a piece of biscuit and drained his coffee cup, glancing sidelong at his mother. She waited, knowing he had something on his mind.

"I was thinking." The young man paused and watched her face. "Maybe I will just finish this term and come home. My scholarship is only for one year anyway. After all," he added hastily, "the main things I wanted to learn, arithmetic and English and such, are covered in the first two terms. Then they get into Latin and Greek and Bible. I really don't see much point in learning all of that. I should get back to help you with the farm. I mean, I've enjoyed it, and made some great friends, including one fellow from Sacramento who says he's going to be a judge. And I'm sure he'll make it. He's real smart."

Lewis paused and took a deep breath, anxiously watching her face.

She smiled and refilled his coffee cup. The fascination for young Miss Latourette was stronger than she thought. "Whatever you feel is best, Son. I just wanted you to have the chance to decide for yourself."

When the train pulled out of the Arno station to return him to Santa Rosa the next morning, she watched him leave with mixed feelings. Bill stood beside her in silence, seeming to understand. A surge of gratitude for him washed over him. Good, kind, reliable Bill. She turned to him with a smile and kissed him lightly on the cheek.

"Let's go home."

The weather continued cold. Matilda wondered if the temperatures were really lower or if she was just getting older and more sensitive to the chill. She woke up one morning in mid-January and padded out to the kitchen to stir up the fire. When she looked out of the window, she saw a sight she had not seen since leaving Kansas.

"Mama, look!" Sammie had come up beside her as she stood staring at the white flakes drifting down. "Is that snow? Is it really snow? Can I go out and make a snowman?"

She had to laugh at his enthusiasm, remembering such emotions in herself as a child. "I don't think there is quite enough yet to make a snowman, but I'm sure there will be enough for you and your schoolmates to have a good snowball fight. Be sure and bundle up warmly, and wear your mittens. I remember how cold my hands used to get when we made snowballs."

Carrie joined them and stared out at the white covering the fields and trees and observed the scene solemnly. "It's beautiful, Mama. It makes everything look so clean and perfect. I'm sorry that Aunt Polly couldn't see it."

Matilda put her arms around the girl and held her closely. "I'm sure she can see it from wherever she is," she whispered.

Bill's voice boomed behind them. "Well, Sammie, my boy, are you ready for a snowball fight?"

The snow was gone by the next day, but the weather continued clear and cold. Plans to move the parsonage from Hicksville to Galt continued, and by the middle of February, the transfer was completed. The move was viewed with dismay by many members of the little community.

"Going to be moving the whole thing to Galt soon," muttered Jack Cottrell.

Mrs. Johnson echoed his sentiments. "Bad enough Harvey got them to take the railroad away from Hicksville and start up the Arno Station to compete with us.

"Trying to take all of the business away," agreed Louis Herbert.

Matilda stood a little apart from the speakers. She knew there was a lot of pressure for the businesses to move to Arno, but to Galt? Would that mean having to go to Galt for groceries and supplies? She sighed. At least it was easier with the train.

The County did fix the bridge across the Lagoon in April. She met Mrs. Herbert at the Post Office and she was very pleased.

"Cost $420.00, it did, but worth every cent," she declared. "Relief it is to know we have a safe crossing, especially as high as the water has been this spring."

"And the wonder is they didn't wait until someone got killed," Mrs. McGuirk volunteered. She smiled at Matilda. "And I hear you have another wedding coming up in your family."

Matilda nodded. "My nephew Sam is marrying my niece Carrie Belle."

"Keeps it all in the family, don't it," Mrs. McGuirk laughed. "Never got a chance to know your sister Caroline, she was here such a short time afore she died, but knew both Will and Polly well. Fine folks. Shame they were both taken so soon."

"Yes, I'm sorry Polly will not be here for the wedding. I know she looked forward to it. And encouraged them to continue with their plans. Sam has been up to Sulphur Creek, over in Colusa County. Seems they have a few gold mines going up there, and he wants to try his hand at mining. Mr. Whitaker has made a good offer on his land, so as soon as the wedding is over they'll be moving."

The wedding, May 31, 1883, went off smoothly, as Polly had wished. She had insisted they go on with their plans for a big celebration, in spite of knowing she would probably not live to see it. The whole neighborhood turned out, for both Sam and Carrie Belle were popular among the younger set.

As Matilda sat watching the camaraderie after the ceremony, she could not help but think of the changes. Sam had sold the last of the land inherited from his father, land Will had owned since 1854. Bud and Lizzie would live with Maggie and Kidder. Kidder himself talked of giving up blacksmithing and moving to a new home in Galt and going into the carriage business. He had plans for the design of a new cart he would like to manufacture.

Abe swung by to greet her, and she thought of Abe's decision to join his sister Sarah in Millwood, Oregon. She knew he planned to leave this summer. She smiled as he went on to greet others. He was still pursued by many of the local widows and single ladies, but steadfastly refused to marry any of them. Matilda thought back. 1866 was the year Minerva had died. He's been alone almost seventeen years. Laura had once told her that he kept a little shrine to his dead wife in his room, with Minerva's picture, her comb and hairbrush, and her favorite scarf, as well as some of her needlework.

"He's got to come out of it by himself, Aunt 'Tilda," Laura had said when she told her. "Some day he'll just put all of those things away and move on. Until then, Will and Charlie and I never say a word. Anna is less patient. She keeps telling him he should get married again. That she and I are not going to take care of him forever." She laughed. "Otherwise we are both going to wind up as old maids!"

Her brother Sam brought her a piece of cake and refilled her punch glass. "Beautiful day for a wedding, isn't it? Nice and warm, not getting hot yet. End of May is always a pretty time of year. And the last chance to relax before we get into the harvest season."

"What are you trying to tell me?" She sensed he was taking refuge in words to avoid telling her something she instinctively knew she did not want to hear.

"You're as bad as Mother was," he complained.

"Well?"

He took a deep breath, and said, "I've sold my place to Whitaker and Ray and am moving to Lake County to raise sheep." The words came out in a rush. "Now," he held up his hand to forestall her response, "You don't need me any more. The girls are raised, Sally will come with me. You have Bill, and Lew will be home from college soon."

"I don't trust either one of those men," she finally got out when she got her breath back. "Did they pay you a good price?"

He looked down. "It was kind of a swap," he admitted.

"How much?"

"A dollar," he finally said, abashed, as though he knew how she would react.

"A dollar? Just a dollar?"

"It was a swap. He gives me the land in Lake County, I give him my land here."

She sighed. "All right. It's your land and your money." She shook her head. "I just don't trust him, is all. I hope it works out well for you."

"Besides," he grinned. "Now that they are putting telephone lines all over, we can talk any time we want. I understand they now have long distance service between Sacramento and San Francisco. Won't be long until it's all over the country."

She sighed. "If you say so."

Chapter 41

July to December, 1883

JULY ARRIVED WITH its usual blast of heat, but also brought another physician to Galt. Dr. Nestell opened his offices on C Street between 4th and 5th, and was welcomed by the whole community.

Kidder Stringfield's brother A.M. also arrived. "Photographer, he is," Kidder announced after church as he introduced the young man. "He's a real famous in Santa Barbara."

"And what brings you here?" Matilda asked. "Other than visiting family, I mean. I would think the photography business would be better in Santa Barbara."

"Well," he grinned, "it is and it isn't. I'm not quite as famous as Kidder would have you believe. There is a lot of demand, but also a lot of photographers." His smile lighted his whole face. Matilda decided she liked this young cousin she had not seen since he was a child.

"Besides," he continued, "my health is a little delicate and I thought a drier climate might help. Kidder here assures me it gets very hot and dry here in the summer, so I thought maybe, well . . . ." His voice trailed off. He grinned ruefully. "My health was why Pa and Ma decided to leave Humboldt County in '69 and move to Santa Barbara."

And it didn't help. So you thought maybe spending a summer in our hot, dry heat would dry out those lungs, Matilda thought. She looked at him with sympathy. He has consumption. Her mind flew to Temperance, to Caroline, to Clara.

"Anyways," he continued, after a pause, "I've fitted up a gallery in the vacant lot in front of Harvey's Hotel, and will start working tomorrow." He looked at her anxiously. "I do very good work, and guarantee satisfaction. I have samples of my work available for folks to see. If you know anyone who would like a photograph, please send them to me." He hesitated a moment. "I specialize in children. And your little girl Carrie is a beautiful child."

"Thank you. We think so, too." Matilda offered him her hand, which he gallantly kissed and she smiled. "We certainly hope you do well in business while you are here. But most of all, we hope our dry climate improves your health." She couldn't help thinking of not only Caroline and Clara, but many others in the community who had not been so fortunate. How she wished they could vaccinate for consumption like they did for smallpox.

Some day, she thought as she watched the young man walk away. Some day we will be able to defeat this terrible disease.

As disappointed as she was that Lewis elected not to return to college for the second year, she had to admit, as they headed into the harvest season, that Bill really did need the help, now that Polly's sons, Frank and Sam, had married and moved from the community and were no longer available.

At the services for Mrs. Greeno, a long-time neighbor who had been ill for some months before passing away, Wes

Overton told them that Frank James had been released from prison.

"But didn't he just turn himself in after his brother was killed by that terrible Ford person last spring?" Matilda had not been bothered to learn Jesse James had been murdered. What bothered her was the fact that his murderer had pretended to be his friend. "How can he be out so fast?"

"Jury acquitted him."

"Acquitted him?" Matilda gasped. "After all of those killings and bank robberies? They just let him go?"

"Yep," Wes nodded. "Pa says one of his cousins back in Missouri took him in after they let him out. Says he's sworn to go straight, no more life of crime."

"Humph." Matilda remained skeptical.

"Seems they've always led kind of a double life. Good family men and church-goers on one hand and bank robbers and killers on the other. Guess a lot of it was Quantrill's influence." He smiled at Matilda. "I've got you folks to thank for taking me in after Quantrill's raid on Lawrence. I might have wound up part of Jesse's band."

Matilda returned his smile. "I don't think so. Not even a war could turn you into a heartless killer. Nobody with a voice like yours could ever be all bad."

They laughed and each went on to greet others.

July moved into August. The community gossip spread the word that Count Valensin had gone to Chicago to attend the horse races. His wife, the gossips also said, was not happy that he had gone.

"All apparently is not well in the Valensin household," Lew grinned as he told Matilda what he had heard. "And Willie Short is getting ready to go to Santa Rosa next week. Going to attend Pacific Methodist College. I gave him the names of some of my friends there so he will know a few people, anyway. Also told him which professors to dodge if he can." He grinned. "One old Bible professor is a real stickler."

"I know Mr. and Mrs. Short are so proud of him," Matilda said. "He plans to become a doctor."

"Should make a good one," Bill interposed. "He's a smart lad."

"And I hear they found the five young horses that got stolen from Denis Moroney a couple of weeks ago."

"That's wonderful," Matilda said.

"Where did they find them?" Bill asked.

"San Francisco."

"San Francisco!" Bill and Matilda echoed.

"How did they get to San Francisco?" Bill wanted to know.

Lew grinned. "Loaded 'em on a steamer in Sacramento and floated 'em down. Guess it was real easy. Steamer crew had no idea they were stolen."

"Is poor Mr. Moroney better?" Matilda asked. "I'm sure he's happy to have his horses back, but the last time I saw him at the Post Office, he had just had a stroke of facial paralysis. Poor dear. Half of his face just kind of hung. His eyelid drooped and one side of his mouth sagged."

Lew shrugged. "I didn't see him and never thought to ask. We'll have to make some inquiries next time."

By mid-August, harvest was in full swing. One Saturday, Bill headed in to Galt to get a look at a plow advertised in the Galt Gazette for a good price. Lew had gone over to help young Walton Journay get the new combined header and thresher of Mrs. Valensin's ready to put into service.

"This is the latest in harvesting equipment, Mother," Lew

had said as he prepared to ride off. "Walt's gonna show me how it works. Imagine only having to make one pass through the field!"

"Just be careful. Some of these new-fangled gadgets are dangerous."

"Don't worry, Mother. I'll be fine."

The corn and tomatoes both needed to be harvested, so she put Sammie and Carrie to work, promising to help them as soon as the breakfast dishes were done. Not over half an hour had passed when she heard a horse being ridden hard. She ran to the front porch. Lew pulled up in front of her in a cloud of dust as the horse slid to a halt. Coughing, she ran forward to meet him.

"Come quick, Mother. Walt's got his hand caught in the cogs and he's bleeding bad. Mrs. Valensin sent someone for Dr. Montague, but I thought you might be able to help."

Carrie and Sammie ran up, eager to find out what had brought Lewis back in such a rush. Matilda explained quickly as she put one foot in the stirrup and Lew pulled her up behind him. "Carrie, you and Sammie keep on with the corn and the tomatoes. If you get them all picked, wash up the canning jars. I'll be back as soon as I can." She wrapped her arms around Lew's waist and they were off.

When they arrived, several people stood around helplessly as young Journay moaned in pain. Lew helped Matilda down and she hurried to the injured man's side. His right hand was hopelessly trapped by the heavy cogwheels. She assessed the damage quickly. The trapped hand would have to wait for the doctor, for the hand would have to be cut away. He bled profusely from his left hand, and there, she decided, lay the immediate danger. He could bleed to death before the doctor even arrived. Lifting her skirt, she tore a strip of muslin from her petticoat and tried to stem the flow of blood from the missing thumb.

"Lost the thumb . . . ." the boy moaned. "Tried to get hand . . . ." He sagged against Matilda in a faint.

"At least he's out of pain, now" she said to Lew. "Help me hold him so he doesn't pull on his right hand and do it any more damage. Keep this hand up to lessen the bleeding." She wrapped the strips of muslin tightly around the injured hand as her mother had taught her, and, to her relief, her ministration seemed to stanch the bleeding. They could do nothing more now but try to keep him quiet while they waited for the doctor.

It seemed forever, but was actually less than an hour before both Dr. Montague and Dr. Nestell arrived. Dr. Montague greeted Matilda with a smile. He quickly assayed the situation. "Good work, Mrs. Frye," he said. "Stopping the bleeding probably saved his life."

Walton moaned as the pain from the doctor's actions stirred him from his faint. "Please get me the bottle of laudanum from my bag," Dr. Montague said to Dr. Nestell. "He is going to need it if we have to do as much surgery as I fear this is going to require."

Dr. Nestell nodded in agreement. "I think we can probably save the thumb, but the rest of the hand is hopelessly crushed. And the only way to get him loose is to amputate."

Matilda stepped back and she and Lew watched in silence as the two surgeons spent half an hour extricating the hand. Lew whispered to his mother, "He was oiling the machinery while the cogwheels were turning, and his hand got caught. He was trying to get it loose with his left hand when he lost the thumb. That was when I left and came for you." Tears stood in Lew's eyes as he watched his friend's face contort with pain.

When the operation was finally over and the patient's

hands bandaged, Matilda rose stiffly to her feet. "We had better get home, Lew. Carrie and Sammie will be anxious."

Dr. Montague introduced her to Dr. Nestell and thanked her for coming so promptly. "As I said, you probably saved his life by having the presence of mind to stop the bleeding. Where did you learn your medical skills?"

She laughed. "From my mother. When I grew up, we were miles from medical care. Anything happened, we had to take care of it. I'm just glad we were so close."

They mounted the horse and headed for home. Carrie and Sammie demanded to know what had happened. While she explained, Bill rode up.

"They've captured Black Bart," he exclaimed. "Would you believe they traced him through the laundry mark in his shirt? After him robbing stages for over eight years and no one able to find out who he was. Caught him at his boarding house in San Francisco and ...." He stopped short as he she turned to face him and he saw the blood on the front of her dress. "'Tilda! 'Tilda, my love, what happened? Are you injured? Where did the blood come from?" His glance took in an obviously uninjured Carrie and Sammie, then swung to Lew, who stood grinning at Bill's dismay.

Matilda, knowing full well what a mess she was, took pity on him and started to laugh. "We are all fine. Come in and we'll tell you the whole story."

The rest of the summer passed uneventfully. Kidder and Maggie began building a house in the new Palin addition in the town of Galt.

Bill came home in mid-September with the news that Louis Herbert had applied for a patent for his new submergible double action force pump through Webster and Stowe Patent Agency in Stockton.

"When he gets it working good, we'll have to have him install one here," Bill said. "He claims it can bring up twice as much water as the one we've got now."

Lew renewed his courtship with young Media Baldwin. "Guess the whole family will be out here some day," he told Matilda on his return from his latest visit. "Got a sister living down in Santa Cruz. On the 15th his brother John arrived with their mother. Real nice widow lady, name of Elizabeth Funderberg. P.H. and John's father died young and their mother remarried. Invalid, she is. Had a stroke of apoplexy that left her bedridden." He grinned. "She said the stories she heard about how mild winters are in California convinced her to spend the rest of her years out here."

At the end of September, the ladies of the Hicksville Church gave a farewell entertainment and ice cream social at the church to benefit Reverend Staton.

"We'll miss you, Reverend Staton," Matilda said with a fond smile. "After all, you have presided at three weddings in our family."

"The pleasure was mine, Mrs. Frye. And hasn't young Sammie grown!"

Matilda's eye followed his to where Sammie stood visiting with Frankie and Willie McEnerney. "Sammie," she gasped. "That has to be your fourth dish of ice cream."

Sammie looked up and grinned. "It's Willie's fifth."

Reverend Staton laughed. "Boys sure can put away a lot of ice cream. Is your lovely daughter going to be one of the entertainers?"

"Oh, yes, she and Sammie both. They have decided to do the recitations they have learned for the school performance next week. Said they might as well do the same ones, since they have worked so hard to learn them."

School had opened in mid-August with Miss Blanche Huber returning as teacher, much to Carrie's delight, with an enrollment of 22 pupils. On October 5, they held the recital Matilda had told Reverend Staton about, and they all went to again hear Carrie recite "Curfew Must Not Ring Tonight", and Sammie's performance of "The Child's Wish". .

Afterwards, Matilda congratulated Miss Huber on the children's performance. "You work wonders with them," she said. "I never knew how talented my children were."

Two weeks later, her brother Sam came by to tell her he planned to depart for his new home in Lake County the following Monday.

"Got my will made out. Isaac Joseph and J.H. McCune have it all witnessed and legal so if anything happens to me, property will get distributed amongst the lot of you."

Matilda laughed. "At the rate the family is growing, by the time it gets divided between all of us, there won't be much to speak of for each one. Unless you make a lot more money than I think you will raising a bunch of sheep." She hugged him. "Besides, you are going to out-live all of us, remember?"

Sam grinned. "Sure going to try." He kissed her gently on the forehead. "I'm going to miss all those good suppers I've had here. But Lake County's not all that far away. Can hop on a train and be here in a few hours. I promise to come back and visit often."

She smiled. "I'm going to hold you to that promise."

Her next visitor was her brother Alf, who presented himself at her door with a lugubrious expression.

"What's the matter?" She knew all was not well between him and Emma. Had they quarreled again?

"Emma's taking Harry and Stella and going back to Kansas to visit her folks. Says they've never seen their grandchildren, and it's time the young-'uns met their grandfolks." He grimaced. "She's been after me to take her, but it's so hard for me to get away." He sighed. "And the expense! I've been savin' to buy me some more land. Don't want to spend it on train fare."

"So if she is willing to go alone, what's the problem?"

He sank into a chair, his arms between his knees, and hung his head. "She says she wants to stay all winter." He looked up at Matilda, his eyes reflecting his fear. "What if she decides not to come back?"

"She's probably forgotten how bad Kansas winters are. She'll be back."

He grinned at that. "You're probably right. She even complains about the cold here. I guess she got the notion to go talking to P.H.'s wife Eliza. Eliza is taking her youngest son John and going back to visit her folks in Ohio. Emma and the children will go with her as far as Kansas." He sighed. "P.H. says he's glad Emma's going, so Eliza and John will have company on the trip."

The first week in December, the Reverend J.C.C. Harris preached his first sermon at the little church in Hicksville. The big news circulating was the theft of the carpentry tools from D.K. Stringfield's new home under construction in Galt.

D.K. sputtered with fury. "Brand new tools, some of 'em were. Blasted thief took the whole lot."

Maggie took Matilda aside and whispered, "The reason he's so mad is because I told him he shouldn't leave the tools there overnight and he didn't listen. "

Alf came up, his face beaming. "Got a letter from Emma," he said. "You were right, 'Tilda. She says she's had enough of Kansas winter and is leaving for home next Saturday."

Chapter 42

January to June, 1884

1884 OPENED WITH a visit from her brother Sam in the middle of January.

"Just can't stay away," Matilda laughed as she hugged him. "You must miss my cooking!"

"Sally likes it in Lake County. Says the hills remind her of Kansas. And she likes to go for walks along the lake and see the ducks and frogs."

"Never thought she would be nostalgic for Kansas."

"There's a nice young man from a couple of ranches over that has been calling. He likes to walk around the lake and talk about the wild things there. He's some kind of a naturalist."

Matilda laughed. "That's probably the attraction, not the memories of Kansas." She seated him at the table and put a piece of pie and a cup of coffee in front of him. "Bill and Lew are back out in the fields. You just missed them. But Sammie and Carrie will be home from school soon. They'll be glad to see you."

He bit into his pie with a sigh of satisfaction. "Sally tries, but her apple pie just isn't as good as yours."

"And how is the sheep business?"

"Good. Neighbor, Hi Ozmun wanted to move out, and sold me his 160 acres for $1100, so I've more than doubled my acreage. Sheep almost raise themselves, foraging on the hills. Just have to keep an eye peeled for coyotes." He laughed. "Lambing season is on us, so I have to get back. Just had a few loose ends to tie up here." He grinned. "And had to get another piece of your pie."

A week later, Lew came back from Galt and a visit with young Media Latourette full of news of the latest fire in town.

"The Bijou Saloon," he reported with a grin. "Burned to the ground, it did. Started out back, probably in some of the hay in the stable, may never know for sure." He ruffled Sammie's hair and patted Jake on the head. The dog wriggled in delight. "Some are saying maybe a tramp was sleeping in the stable and started the blaze, but if there was anyone in the place, he's long gone. And the whole building is just a mass of ashes."

Matilda sighed. "Well, if any building is going to burn, that is probably a good choice."

Lew chuckled. "That's what Mr. Latourette says. He's a rabid Prohibitionist. Says all saloons should be burned to the ground."

"But I trust he did not set the fire!"

"Oh, no, swears complete innocence. I don't think anyone suspects him. But he sure was not sorry to see it go. I told him it won't help. Owners will just start up another one someplace else."

Matilda nodded. "You're probably right. I know the Hicksville Hotel would have a hard time staying in business if not for all the money the liquor brings in." She laughed. "Mr. Herbert says the money he gets from the liquor pays for what he can't collect from the farmers for the pumps and blacksmithing work."

"And I hear they are closing the Liberty School."

"Again?"

"Say they've only got five students, and that's not enough to pay a teacher."

Matilda sighed. "Poor Chism. His town certainly is fading away."

The winter storms began in earnest. Wade Dillard and his wife lost their baby daughter, stillborn, and buried her in the Hicksville Cemetery. The usual concerns for the safety of the bridges became a topic of conversation.

The next big news to run through the neighborhood was the death of Buccaneer, a stallion belonging to Gulio Valensin.

"Worth $25,000," Mrs. Herbert told Matilda one morning early in February when she stopped at the Post Office. "Can you imagine? A $25,000 horse! Some folks has more money than sense, I do declare." She chuckled. "No wonder his wife is so fed up with him and his horses. They say the critter wasn't even off his feed. Just up and died."

By the middle of March, several bridges had been washed out, and travel became hazardous. The rain continued, and the Cosumnes River rose and overflowed its banks.

Bill came home from getting Charley re-shod full of the news. "They say the road between Hicksville and McConnell is in real bad shape."

Matilda sighed. "Someone is going to get killed on that road. Then maybe they'll do something about it."

Bill grinned. "I hear Louis Herbert is talking about running for Road Commissioner."

"Good. If anyone can get anything done, he'll be the man to do it."

The death of Mrs. John Rae headed the topics of conversation after church the Sunday following her funeral.

"Interesting lady," Mrs. Herbert declared. "Hear she took

369

care of wounded soldiers during the War of the Rebellion. And she was real active in getting the Congregational Church built. Hear she even got her sons back in New York to help her raise funds for it. She and John never had young'uns, of course, bein' as how she were a mite on the oldish side when they married. Widow, she was, when John married her. Understand she has a married daughter living up in Oregon in addition to the two sons back in New York."

"She's kind of famous in a way," said Reverend Harris, who had conducted her services. "I understand she was the lady that completed the first garment on a Wheeler and Wilson sewing machine, and even assisted in its perfection. The dress she made is on display at the company's head-quarters, and her name is on record in the Patent Office."

"She once told me she was exhibiting the machine at the Crystal Palace in New York when the building caught fire," Mrs. McGuirk interposed. "Was the last lady to leave, made sure everyone was out first." She nodded. "Sounds like something she would do. Fine lady, she was."

Reverend Harris smiled. "And it was she who worked to get the Sunday laws passed, although, unfortunately, they were repealed shortly after. At least she had tried."

June brought several changes. The pump at the ranch finally breathed its last gasp, and Matilda and Bill were forced to pay for a new well and pump.

"Talked to Herbert this morning," Bill told her. "He'll be by tomorrow."

"How much will it cost?" Matilda asked, always concerned about expenses.

"Says he'll bore the well for fifteen dollars. His new double action pump is fifty dollars. There'll be a little more for pipe and stuff. Should get by for under eighty dollars."

She sighed. "I certainly hope so.

The results were astonishing. She and Bill stood arm in arm and watched the pulsing stream of water fill the water tank on top of the pump house in half the time the old pump had taken to fill it.

Bill beamed down on her and patted her hand. "See? I told you that new pump of Herbert's is a marvel. That's why he's getting a patent on it."

Maggie and D.K. moved into their new home in the Palin tract, and D.K. rented a shop in town and began developing his new cart.

"He's so clever, Aunt 'Tilda," Maggie boasted as she talked about his plans. "He says he can make us a much better living selling carts than he ever could shoeing horses." She giggled. "And much less chance of getting kicked by a horse. He's even talking of running for Justice of the Peace. What do you think about the church at Hicksville starting a Sunday School? Now that D.K. and I have moved out, they actually are going to do it. They've been talking about it for months."

"I know Reverend Harris has been pushing for it," Matilda said. "Reverend Staton was the one who got folks thinking we might actually be able to do it. This way, we can have something at the church every Sunday, even on the Sundays when we don't have a preacher." She smiled. "Carrie is looking forward to it, but I don't think Sammie is as enthusiastic."

"How is poor Uncle Billy doing?"

Matilda sighed. "Poor dear has senile gangrene in his left foot. I know Dr. Montague has been treating him, but he says probably the only way to cure the problem is to amputate the foot. And he and Dr. Nelson have consulted and Dr. Nelson fears Uncle Billy would not survive the operation."

"So they are just going to do nothing?"

"For the moment."

Maggie shrugged. "And they say that fellow Rich that married Minnie Metcalf a couple of weeks ago is going to take over running the Arno Tavern."

Matilda nodded. "That's what I hear." She hesitated. "There are some as say he's not to be completely trusted, but I guess we'll have to wait and see."

An unexpected late season rain poured down in mid-June, with a ruinous effect on the hay and grain crops. Alf came by and stood beside her watching the rain flatten the wheat in the fields. It reminded her of that other storm in June shortly after she and Alfred had purchased the ranch, with the result that they could not pay Lizzie Owen as planned.

Alf came as close to swearing as his strict Methodism would allow. "Ding-dang rain," he mumbled. "Just as soon as I get back from Ione with that new threshing machine I bought from the Carlisle Ranch and get ready to start custom harvesting, we get this dad-burned rain."

As they watched, the clouds finally moved on, and sunshine peeked out, coloring the fields with gold. A rainbow rose in the east as the sun shone through the remaining remnants of the downpour.

"Maybe it will dry out quickly, and we'll be able to salvage at least part of the crop. Meanwhile," she suggested, "Since you can't do any harvesting today, why don't you hitch Charley to the buggy and take me over to see poor Uncle Billy. I have an apple pie to take over to him. He was always partial to my apple pie."

Alf grinned. "So is half the neighborhood. Your apple pie is legendary." He put on his hat and headed for the door.

"Get your bonnet on. Charley and I will be ready to go in fifteen minutes."

It only took them twenty minutes to get to the Hicks residence. His housekeeper greeted them warmly. "He don't get many visitors," she frowned. "Number of friends as he has, lots more should be a-comin'."

"I'm sorry, Emma. I should have been here sooner. We just get so busy with our own lives." Matilda had not really visited with Billy since his wife Sarah had died a few years before, just saw him now and then at the store or the Post Office. She was stunned to see how he had aged. She knew he was 67 years old, but recent brief glimpses of him did not prepare her for his appearance now. She could swear his face was gray.

Dr. Montague was just leaving, and greeted her warmly. "So nice of you to come by, Mrs. Frye." He beamed at Uncle Billy. "I'm sure Mr. Hicks is happy to see you."

"Sure am, 'Tilda. Please set a spell. Forgive a feeble old man for not gettin' up to greet you proper."

Matilda removed her bonnet and settled into the one chair in the room. "Alf is bringing in the apple pie," she smiled.

"Your apple pie!" His face lighted. "My favorite." He sighed. "Don't get many pleasures out of life no more." He shifted the wrapped foot on the pillow and grimaced. The smell of rotting flesh wafted over Matilda, and it took all of her strength not to gag. No wonder he didn't have many visitors, she thought. That odor would keep anyone away.

"Doc Montague says we oughta cut this foot off, but Dr. Nelson says the chloroform might kill me, that he might just as well cut my throat as cut off my foot." He sighed heavily and leaned back against the pillows stacked behind him. "Guess it don't make much difference which one kills me, the foot or the operation."

Matilda could think of no reply.

The old man rambled on. "When I think what I used to have, when I was young and strong." He met Matilda's eyes. "Had me a young wife and a son, years ago. Her name was Suzanne, and we got married in April of '48, right after I settled here. Lost both of 'em from sickness, just a few weeks apart. Not many folks know that. Only had her for a year. Never talked about it, hurt too much. Never married again until I met Sarah, but by then we were both too old to have young'uns. I suppose, by rights, since Caroline's my step-daughter, I could say I've got off-spring, but never cottoned to McCauley. Especially after he pulled that trick between him and Tevis and took most of my land . . . ." His voice drifted off and his eyes closed. Matilda waited in silence.

"Anyways," he went on, "I'm leaving the 1100 acres I've got left – out of my original 10,000 – to young Jim, my nephew. He's the only one of the lot who has always been good to me. He'll take care of Joseph, if he needs anything. And he'll be able to deal with McCauley, if McCauley tries to pull any tricks. I'm afraid if I leave it directly to my brother Joseph, McCauley will get his hands on it."

"Surely not, if your will is made out properly."

"Hope it is. Had Tom McConnell write it out for me, and he read it back. He wrote it just like I told him to. Told him I wanted it so McCauley couldn't break it. Then I had Dr. Montague sign and witness it, and called young Will Skinner in from his work to be witness as well. Tom wrote my name and I made my mark beside it. Named Mr. Furnish as executor. Doc Montague suggested naming Mr. Whitaker as well, so I did. Left $3000 to Emma for all the care she's given me, especially the last few months. Don't know what I'd'a done without her."

Alf came in as Emma Smith brought Hicks a piece of Matilda's pie. The two men spoke for a few minutes, and Matild a rose to leave.

"We will let you enjoy your pie, Uncle Billy. Please try and get well. The neighborhood would never be the same without you." She offered him her hand, which he gallant-ly kissed, and thanked her for coming.

Tears filled her eyes as she stroked the strands of wispy gray hair back from his brow and kissed him gently on the forehead. "Goodbye, Uncle Billy."

Chapter 43

June to December, 1884

MATILDA NEVER saw Uncle Billy again. He died the following Sunday, and his funeral, held on Tuesday July the first, was one of the largest the neighborhood had ever seen.

As his body was lowered into the grave, Matilda could not help wondering where the wife and child that had died so many years before were buried. Surely they had to have been buried here in Hicksville as well, for he had been living at the same place since 1847, and they had married in '48. She shook her head sadly. Since he had never told anyone, probably no one would ever know.

Tom stood beside her, mopping his brow in the heat. The sun beat down upon the assembled crowd without mercy. "And so another pioneer leaves us." He sighed. "Reminds us we are all getting along in years. I'm sure he's one of the very few left out of the Walker-Chiles Party. Even helped rescue some of the Donner folks in '46."

He glanced over at Elitha, standing with Ben. "I'm sure Elitha remembers that." He smiled wistfully. "Would have loved to have seen California in 1843. Not getting here until 1850, I never got a chance to see it before it was overrun by miners. Remember Jared Sheldon telling me what it was like. Oak trees and deer and fields covered with wild flowers, miles between settlements. Nothing between his place and Uncle Billy's."

Matilda smiled. "The discovery of gold sure changed it."

"Especially now that they have those big dredges, and are hosing down the mountains into the rivers, silting them up, killing the fish, even covering what was rich farm land with silt and gravel." He shook his head. "Legislature's going to have to do something or all of the valley will be ruined for farming."

Matilda remembered Alfred talking about the damage the hydraulic mines did to the whole area. She shrugged. "Do you suppose the Legislature will do anything to stop it? The fellows that own those big mines have a lot of money. They can buy a lot of legislators."

Tom grinned wryly. "Guess us farmers are going to have to join together and buy a few legislators of our own. Grange is fighting for us, I know."

Mrs. McGuirk approached Matilda. "Neighborhood just won't be the same without Uncle Billy," she declared. "Wonder if that new doc in town, Patterson, him as just moved into Galt from Woodland, if he might have been able to save him. I know Doc Montague wanted to cut off his foot. Wonder if they'd done it, if they might'a saved him."

"Understand it was senile gangrene," Tom said. "Ossification of the arteries, according to Doc Montague. That's why Doc Nelson was afraid to operate. Course, the last few days he was in a coma. And he'd been suffering from rheumatism for a long time as well, poor fellow." He grinned. "Of course, I suspect the fact that he was one of the best customers at the bar in the Hicksville Saloon could have contributed to his poor health."

Louis Herbert added, with a chuckle, "And Injun Alec was so depressed to hear his old friend Uncle Billy were 'adyin' that he went and got drunk and wound up in the lock-up." Matilda looked at him accusingly and he defended himself. "Wa'n't me. I never sold it to him. But the feller who did had to pay a fine of six dollars."

Kidder and Maggie stopped to speak to them. "My new cart is coming along, Aunt 'Tilda. Going to be the finest cart you've ever seen. No one else can equal it for strength, ease of use, or durability."

Maggie beamed proudly. "He's so talented, Kidder is. He can build anything. You've got to come and see our new house, Aunt 'Tilda."

"And I'm dickering with Fish Brothers to carry their new buggy," Kidder added. "Along with my cart, it will give me a good inventory."

Maggie went on. "And Frank and Annie are thinking of moving from Lake County to Vina. Frank says he doesn't like sheep, and wants to have an orchard. I guess peaches and apricots grow well in the Vina area."

"But they just got settled over there in Lake County. Will they be able to get their money out of their place?" Matilda's thoughts flew to her brother Sam, who had talked Frank into joining him.

"Oh, yes," Maggie nodded. "Uncle Sam has agreed to buy the whole 480 acres that Frank owned, and paid him $500 in gold. None of those new fancy greenbacks. So Frank and Annie will have money to buy a place in Vina. Guess Frank talked to the Gaffney sisters. Their brother Vin lives up there and raves about it." She shrugged. "Guess he should do all right."

"Well," Matilda smiled, "We'll certainly hope so. If Sam had that much gold to pay Frank for his land, Sam, at least, must be doing well."

On Thursday, July tenth, Bill came home from the Post Office bursting with news. Matilda could tell by his face when he walked in the door that something momentous had happened.

"What is it?" she asked as he hung up his hat, grinning from ear to ear.

"Our high and mighty Count almost did himself in."

"He did what?"

"Accidental, of course. Guess he's been suffering from attacks of neuralgia. Seems last evening, after dinner, he decided to treat himself with laudanum. They say he swigged down about two ounces of it."

"Two ounces! Good heavens. That's enough to kill ten men. Mother would never give more than half a teaspoon, no matter how severe the pain."

Bill grinned. "Actually, Doc Montague said it was enough to kill a dozen men. Mrs. Valensin sent for him post haste, and he came running. Lucky for the Count Doc wasn't out on another call somewhere. Doc immediately pumped out his stomach and gave him the antidote. Guess he was just in the nick of time to save his life. By what the fellows at the Post Office were saying this morning it looks like he's going to pull through." He chuckled. "But I guess it was nip and tuck there for a while."

Matilda thought for a moment. So Alice had almost lost her Count. She recalled a number of items of neighborhood gossip about how all was not necessarily well in the Valensin household, and started to laugh.

Bill gaped at her, a puzzled look on his face. "What's so funny?"

"I was just thinking that maybe Dr. Montague didn't really do Alice any favors."

The next news to circulate through the little community was that Billy Hicks' brother Joseph had challenged his will.

"Poor Uncle Billy," Matilda exclaimed when Bill told her what he had heard. The afternoon sun had taken the coolness from the house and she began opening all of the windows to catch the evening breeze that had, mercifully, sprung up from the Delta. "I swear, since they've put all of those levees in, the summers get hotter and hotter. I can remember when we used to cool off really well in the late afternoon, even get a little shower of rain now and then." She poured him a glass of lemonade. "Tell me what Joseph is trying to pull. Are you sure McCauley isn't putting him up to it?"

"If he is, no one is admitting to it. Looks like Joe is just trying to get the land away from Jim."

"Billy was so concerned someone might try and break the will. How do they think they can get away with it?"

"Are saying he was insane when he wrote it, and incompetent to make a will."

"That's ridiculous. I know he was in a coma for the last few days of his life, but Alf and I visited him just the week before. He was perfectly sane then, and knew exactly what he was doing. He had made out his will a week or so earlier."

"Are also trying to say the will was not signed by him or by any of the attesting witnesses."

"You mean he has the gall to say that Tom McConnell and Dr. Montague are lying?" Matilda gasped, aghast at the suggestion. "Two of our most upstanding citizens?"

Bill grinned and finished the last of his lemonade, wiping his mouth on his sleeve. Matilda winced. That was a habit of his she had trouble getting used to. "Guess his estate is valued at $34,000. Reckon Joe figures it's worth going after. Course, I understand he owes $17 or $18 thousand on it, so by the time that gets paid and the lawyers take their cut, there won't be much left for Joe if he does manage to break the will."

"Poor Uncle Billy," she sighed. "They can't even let the poor dear rest in peace in his grave."

The challenge was overruled, and Uncle Billy's will was admitted to probate on July 28. August brought the news that Louis Herbert had received the patent he had applied for on his new pump, and D.K. received the rights to market the Fish Brothers buggies as he had hoped.

Maggie, bursting with pride at his new business, showed Matilda the advertisement in the *Galt Gazette*. "He not only sells the buggies, and manufactures his new cart, but he does all kinds of repairs. He even makes buggies to order, if someone has a special need, or wants some extras. He's going to be very successful."

"I'm sure he will be," Matilda hugged Maggie warmly. "You have every right to be proud of him."

"And in September, he's going to file for Justice of the Peace."

The next news to rock the little community was that Alice Valensin had sued the Count for divorce. Sam had come over from Lake County for a visit, and Matilda filled him in on all of the latest gossip.

"She accuses him of cruelty, but all of the charges seem rather mild." She laughed. "To me, cruelty means hitting or depriving of the means of living, or something like that. But all she can accuse him of is having a bad temper, and ignoring her, and failure to treat her with 'due respect and consideration'."

"Doesn't sound to me like grounds for divorce."

Matilda agreed. "What folks are saying is that she wants to be shed of him before he goes through all of her money. He's losing so much on horses all the time. He just had one worth $25,000 up and die, and just spent another $10,000 buying more." She refilled his coffee cup. "She even says she has been forced to put a $30,000 mortgage on the place." Matilda's mind had difficulty grasping such high numbers. "Can you imagine? 30,000 dollars!"

"Is she sure it's not his own money he's using? I understand his father is a wealthy international banker."

"I guess he's claiming that. And also saying the ranch is community property, and his to do with as he sees fit." Matilda laughed softly. "Be interesting to see how it turns out.

"And John McFarland's niece, Annie, the one that came to keep house for him about four years ago, has been sick. I suspect it's consumption, but no one has said. Her father, Duncan, came from Canada to visit and just went back." She shook her head. "She's such a nice lady. Very active in the Grange, and does a lot of charity work. Has worked very hard to get funds for the new Congregational Church they are building. Everyone loves her."

"We'll hope for the best."

"Can you stay for a few days? Reverend Harris is preaching his farewell sermon this Sunday. He's being transferred to a church in Visalia."

"Got myself a pretty reliable hired man," he smiled. "I'm sure I can stay until Sunday."

The news reached them at church that Miss McFarland had passed away that morning.

"Understand McFarland wired his brother that she had

taken a sudden turn for the worst, and he is on his way. Unfortunately, they have no way to tell him that he will be too late to see her alive again. Funeral will be Tuesday, soon as he arrives." Mrs. Herbert shook her head sadly. "Poor man."

"At least he was here a couple of weeks ago, and had a chance to see her then," Matilda said. "It would be worse if he had not seen her since she left Canada."

Sam returned to Lake County. The following Saturday, the *Galt Gazette* carried a nice article on Miss McFarland. But as Matilda read the story, her eyes wandered to a brief notice and she gasped.

Bill looked up from his book. "What is it?"

"'Boys and girls may be had'," she quoted, "'particularly boys, for service at wages, for indenture, or for legal adoption'." She looked up in horror. "The Boys and Girls Aid Society in San Francisco."

Bill grinned. "Thinking of getting a couple?"

"No!" she exploded. "That's terrible! Buying and selling these children like they were horses."

"Guess it's pretty common practice," he shrugged. "Beats leaving 'em on the streets."

Matilda sighed. "I suppose so. It just sounds so dreadful."

In November, the Reverend T.D. Bauer took over the duties of ministering to the little flock at the Hicksville Methodist Church, South. The new Congregational Church that Annie McFarland had dedicated so much devotion to held their dedication ceremonies, but the news that buzzed around Hicksville the most was the details of the Valensin divorce trial.

Mary could talk of nothing else. She, along with Earl and Mable, spent more and more time with Matilda. Matilda feared Mary's fascination with the Valensin case might give her some ideas.

"She's trying to keep him from selling her property or borrowing money against it. She did get an injunction that restricts what he can do. But did you hear that his lawyer, that Catlin person, is making all kinds of vague accusations? Accusing poor Alice of crooked dealing. Even the judge got all out of patience with him and told him to either produce some solid evidence or shut up." She shook her head. "They might as well get divorced. After all of the accusations they have been making against each other, I can't see them ever living happily together again."

Matilda sighed. "I suppose not. It just seems a shame that with all of that money, they can't learn to get along."

Bill, who had been listening, grinned. "Problem as I see it, you got two people both used to gettin' their own way, and neither one will budge an inch."

Mary and Matilda laughed at his perspicacity. "I do believe you're right, Papa Bill," Mary said. "Alice has always gotten her way with her indulgent Papa her whole life, and, I suspect, so has the Count."

"Guess someone figures those horses of Valensin's are worth something," Bill added with a chuckle. "Someone stole his stallion Arno right out of the stable."

"No!" Matilda gasped. "And no one saw the thief?"

"Nope," Lew grinned. "Walt told me Arno was in his stall the evening before, and when he went out to feed the horses in the morning, Arno was gone. Stall door wide open."

Matilda shook her head. She wondered idly how much that one was worth. "And how are Walt's hands? Have they healed?"

"Pretty well. He kind of has to compromise, for he's got

his fingers on his left hand, but no thumb, and a thumb on his right but no fingers. But he's managing, and Mrs. Valensin has kept him on. Guess she feels a little responsible. Count was all for turning him out. Not much charity in him."

In December, Mary brought the news that John Rae had remarried, to a Miss Kate Harvey from San Francisco.

"Some folks are saying his poor wife is barely cold in her grave," Mary chuckled. "It's only been seven months."

Matilda laughed. "Maybe he figures he's getting older and doesn't have much time to waste."

"Mother!" Mary laughed. "You shock me." She rose. "I'd better get back. His highness will be wanting his supper, and he gets so grumpy if he has to wait." She lowered her voice and muttered, half under her breath, "Maybe Alice Valensin has the right idea after all."

"Mary!"

"Oh, don't worry, Mother. I haven't made any plans." She paused. "Yet. Come on, Mable. Find Earl. We've got to leave. Did you hear they appointed Mr. Rich to be the new Postmaster at Hicksville?"

Matilda gasped. "Really? And someone posted his bond?"

Mary shrugged. "I guess so. Why?"

She shook her head. "Just never could quite bring myself to trust him, is all."

Her brother Tom, his wife Mary, and their adopted son George joined them for dinner after church the following Sunday.

"Reverend Bauer gave a real rousing sermon," Tom commented to Matilda. He glanced at his wife, who nodded. "We'll miss him."

"Miss him? Is he leaving so soon? He just got here." Matilda stared at Tom.

"No, he's not leaving. We are. Have bought an apple orchard up in Oleta. Wheat turning out to be a glut on the market, and I got no hankering to run cattle or sheep. Rather farm."

"What about your place here?"

"Sold it. Lock, stock and barrel, all three hundred acres."

"And to whom?" she demanded.

With a sly glance at Bill, he grinned and said, "Bill Frye."

Chapter 44

December 1884 to April 1885

MATILDA TURNED TO Bill. "And you never told me?"

"Wanted it for your Christmas present." He looked at her fondly. "Young Lew is courtin' the Latourette gal, and I figgered one of these days he's gonna pop the question, and they'll need a place of their own."

Tom grinned at her astonishment. "We'll probably move in the spring."

"Rains have been real heavy so far this December. They say the water's as high as it was in the winter of '61 to '62." Bill shook his head. "I remember we had one big lake from here to Liberty, just a few high spots here and there. Including this house, as I recall."

"That's what Alf said. I didn't get out here until '64, so we missed that." Matilda rose and began clearing the plates from the table. "I suppose the bridges are all in their usual unsafe condition."

"Not only that, they are so bad Reverend Bauer won't be able to come for services this Sunday. No one can cross the Lagoon until the water goes down."

Matilda turned to Bill. "See? They should have left the parsonage here at Hicksville."

"Don't blame me," he chuckled. "I was as opposed to moving it as everyone else. And there are several levee breaks, luckily all south of Stockton and north of Sacramento. However, except for a few impassable bridges, Galt and the surrounding areas, like here, seem to have come though this one fairly well."

Matilda shrugged. "Winter's not over yet."

Frank and Annie returned from Lake County en route to their new home in Vina, but planned to stay until after the birth of Annie's second baby.

"She wants to have the baby here with me, and she wants Dr. Montague," Tom's wife Mary told Matilda. "I think she's just a bit afraid to go off up to Vina expecting, since she doesn't know anyone up there." Mary hesitated. "And I guess she had a bad experience when little Eddie was born. She's so young."

Annie's son was born January 26, and Dr. Montague, true to his word, was there to deliver him. Matilda had gone over to help as soon as Frank told her Annie had gone into labor, and he was riding for Dr. Montague.

"Fine, healthy boy," the doctor told a beaming Frank.

"Thanks for coming, Doc. Annie had her heart set on you delivering him, after Mary Douglass couldn't praise you enough."

He smiled. "I'm just glad all went well. I will miss all of my patients and my many friends here."

"Are you leaving us?" Matilda hoped she had not heard him correctly.

"Only temporarily. My parents are elderly, and I should spend some time with them. They live in North Carolina. And I plan to spend a year back in New York at my Alma Mater, catching up on the latest medical knowledge. The field of medicine changes quickly, and I want to learn the latest. I feel I owe that to my patients."

"But you will come back?"

"Oh, yes, even bought eleven acres of land just outside of town. My brother Alpheus and I have some ideas for truck farming we want to try." He grinned. "Can't do that in downtown New York." He picked up his bag, preparing to leave, and added, "Besides, after a winter in California, I don't look forward to the weather in New York. I'll be leaving in May. Have to collect as much as I can of what's owed me. The notice to creditors will be out in next week's paper. Dr. Patterson is talking about buying my office and moving in. He's a fine fellow. I feel comfortable leaving my patients in his care."

At the door he turned back. "And Reverend Bauer wished for me to tell everyone he has recovered from his bout with la grippe, and will be back in the pulpit this Sunday."

On Mary's next visit, all she could talk about was the damage by dogs done to Mr. McConnell's sheep.

"Anna and Mary told me all about it. They came over right after it happened. Forty of those beautiful, expensive Merino sheep that poor Mr. McConnell just bought killed by dogs. Anna said it was a sight to see. Those wretched dogs had just torn the helpless things apart. Some as they didn't kill direct were run to death trying to escape."

"Are they sure it was dogs, and not coyotes?" Matilda asked. She glanced down at Jake, lying by her feet. He looked up and wagged his tail innocently.

"No, it was dogs. Mr. McConnell and one of the hands heard the commotion and ran to find what all the ruckus was about. Moon was bright enough to see the dogs. Anna said there was at least a dozen. They both shot at them and the dogs ran off. They did manage to kill one, and now Mr. McConnell is trying to find out who owned it." Mary chuckled. "Anna says her father was spitting nails. He was so proud of those sheep, and they cost a lot, too. A number of the ones killed were ready to lamb. They, of course, were the easiest for the dogs to catch."

"That makes it even worse. He not only lost the ewe, but the lamb as well." Matilda shook her head. "What a shame."

"Mr. McConnell says dogs are worse than coyotes. Coyotes will kill a lamb or pull down an old sheep, but the dogs just kill for fun. They don't take one and eat it. They just keep on running sheep down and killing them." She reached into her mother's cookie jar and gave Earl and Mable each a sugar cookie.

"You're just full of news today. Anything else?"

"Just that young Kelsey Hobday's wife had a little boy on February 2. Named him Kelsey, of course. They say Mr. Hobday's so proud he's busting his buttons."

Mary could not seem to sit still. Matilda sensed there was more to this visit than to impart the news of the tragedy of the McConnell sheep and the birth of the Hobday infant.

"What is it, Mary?" she finally came right out and asked.

Mary said nothing for several moments, then blurted. "George wants to take the children and go to Montana. His sister Mary and her husband are there. They say he can get George work in one of the mines. He wants me to go, but I don't want to go to that awful cold place. And all of my family and friends are here. If I went with him, I wouldn't have anybody."

"When does he want to go?"

"This summer."

"That's several months away," Matilda soothed. "Maybe

he'll change his mind."

"Maybe. But what if he doesn't?"

Matilda had no answer.

Bill came back from the Post Office to report that Jim Hicks was managing his Uncle Billy's land. "They say Uncle Billy owes up to $23,000, instead of the $18,000 they first thought. Looks like Jim will have to sell to pay off the debts."

"Can Jim raise enough to buy it?"

Bill shrugged. "No one seems to know. Poor old Uncle Billy. To go from over 10,000 acres to nothing." He shook his head. "Also, talk is that the Mormons are dickering to buy land up by Sonora. Folks're saying they're thinking of moving the whole colony out here."

"Why on earth would they do that? I saw that magnificent temple and their beautiful city when we came through Salt Lake City on our way out in '64. Surely they'd never abandon that. Maybe what they're really talking about is starting another colony out here." She smiled. "I'll bet that has gone over well with the neighborhood."

Bill grinned. "Real well. They're already getting up petitions and talking about lynching the owner of the land if he sells it to them."

She laughed. "So much for freedom of religion. Too many folks think freedom of religion means the freedom to believe exactly as they do."

He grinned wryly. "I'm afraid you're right. But they'll never change." He rose and refilled his coffee cup from the pot on the stove. "Also, they say John McFarland has got Annie's sister Mary to join him to take Annie's place. She says Annie's letters raving about how much easier the winters are here convinced her."

"One winter here convinced me. And I'm sure Canada is worse than Kansas."

"Well, just as bad, at least," he nodded. "Did you see in the paper about the couple up in Roseville as shipped her mother to Los Angeles?"

"So?"

"Seems they got tired of taking care of the poor, old soul, and just put her on a train. She arrived in Los Angeles with no money and no idea where she was or why." He chuckled. "Authorities down there took her in. Don't know what they are going to do with her."

"Why, that's terrible! To just dump your own mother?"

"They say it was his idea, and I guess his wife's enough afraid of him that she didn't try to stop him."

"Humph." Matilda grunted. "I hope they hang him."

Early in March, Will's son Sam arrived from Sulphur Creek for a visit, accompanied by Caroline's daughter Sally.

Matilda greeted them warmly. "Sally, it's so good to see you. I understand you have a young man over there who may be interested in matrimony."

Sally laughed. "That's only Uncle Sam's fantasy. Matthew and I are just good friends. He's only interested in frogs. He spends all of his time studying frogs, and plans to go back East to study biology or something." She grinned. "He says he enjoys my company because I am the only girl he has ever known who is not too squeamish to pick up a frog. Actually, they are interesting little creatures." She hesitated. "I've come back because we are worried about Becky."

"Is she worse?" Matilda had feared all along that the girls would take the consumption from their mother.

"Jack's last letter convinced me I need to stay with her,

so we are on our way to Placerville. Uncle Sam will have to manage without me for a while. Poor little Essie is only eight, and taking care of a sick mother is too much for her. Becky has really never recovered her strength since she lost that baby six years ago."

Sam nodded. "I told Sally I would bring her, as I wanted to make arrangements for Belle to come home to have her baby. After listening to Annie, Belle decided she wants Doc Montague for this confinement as well. She was so pleased with him when Willie was born last year."

"She'd better hurry. He's leaving in May."

"Baby's due in early April. I already talked to Doc, and he says he'll still be here."

"Do keep me posted on Becky."

Rebecca Evans Randolph died at her home in Placerville on March 13, of consumption, as Matilda had feared. A grief-stricken Jack accompanied her body on the train bringing her to the Arno Station for burial in the Hicksville Cemetery.

"Her last wish was to be buried next to her mother, Aunt 'Tilda, so the least I could do is honor that wish." He burst into sobs and buried his face on Sally's shoulder. She stroked his hair and murmured in consolation.

"Sorry." He pulled himself together and walked away.

Sally shook her head. "I really worry about him, Aunt 'Tilda. I can hear him pacing in the night. I don't think he has slept since before she died. He just kept clinging to her hand, begging her not to leave him." Sally's eyes filled and the tears coursed down her cheeks. "We've brought Essie with us, of course. She's outside with Carrie and Sam. I'll take her back with me to Lake County. Jack has no way to take care of her except by hiring someone. Poor little thing should be with family. And she and Till have always been good friends, even though Till is a little older. I think Till has always thought of her as her own little sister."

"Poor Sally," Matilda smiled. "Are you going to spend your whole life raising the children of your relatives? I don't think Till even remembers her real mother. You are the only mother she has ever known."

Sally smiled. "Matthew has his frogs. I have little sisters."

They laid Becky to rest next to her mother and the infant that had died at birth. Another member of the family in the Hicksville Cemetery, Matilda thought. Jack sobbed through the whole ceremony, unable to speak at her eulogy, so his brother Sam filled in for him. He had to be physically restrained from joining Becky in her coffin.

Two days later, Sam and Sally returned to Lake County, taking Essie with them. Jack refused their offer to include him, and returned to Placerville.

On April 6, 1885, Raymond Lester Randolph was born to Sam and Belle, delivered by Dr. Montague as Belle had wished. And so, Matilda thought, another life comes to replace one we have lost.

Lew came bouncing in to report Caroline McCauley had put a notice in the paper. "Says she won't pay any bills not signed by her personally," he chuckled. "Guess the Count has been making too free and easy with her name around town since word got out he hasn't been too prompt in paying his just debts." He nodded. "Yep, so she put her foot down and said no more. Wondered how long it would take."

"Any more on the divorce proceedings?"

"Not yet. Coming up soon." He grinned. "They say it should be good."

Chapter 45

May to July, 1885

May was a busy month. In between gardening, laundry, canning, and all the myriad chores that seemed to be present every day, Alf brought her the news that the estate sale of Billy Hicks' ranch was scheduled for May 25.

"Lot's of folks are hoping young Jim can buy it," Alf said when he reported the news to her. "If he can raise the money. Says he thinks maybe McFarland will lend it to him."

"Mr. McFarland should be in a good mood. Sit down." Matilda poured him a cup of coffee from the pot on the stove. "I understand they just had a wedding in the family, and while he won't have grandchildren, he can look forward to some grand-nephews and grand-nieces."

"George Orr came from Canada, too. Him coming so close on the heels of Miss Mary, and them gettin' hitched so soon makes a body suspect they had some plans before she came."

Matilda chuckled. "I'm sure. Since she's only been here since February, and them getting married just three months later. And Columbus Dillard and his wife have a baby boy. This one's nice and healthy, thank goodness, after losing the last one."

"Doc Montague's leaving on the 26th, and Doc Patterson did buy his office, as we thought he might." Alf chuckled. "Doc Montague sold him the place on the condition that Doc Patterson take care of that big old tabby cat as is always sitting in his front window."

Matilda laughed. "I wondered what he was going to do about Napoleon. Most overweight and spoiled cat I've ever seen."

"And I see where Kidder has performed his first wedding as Justice of the Peace," Alf added. "A Dr. More and a Mrs. Geer." He shook his head. "Didn't know either of 'em," he grumbled. "Gettin' to be so many folks around here now, hard to remember 'em all."

"I'm more impressed with the crop of potatoes Kidder raised than any of his doings as Justice of the Peace," Lew put in. "Gave me a whole sack full, he did. Good ones, too, not mealy or wormy at all. He also says his brother A.M.'s coming back in June to spend another summer baking in our heat to try and dry out his lungs. Will be opening his photography business again."

Remembering the flush of fever on the young man's face, and his visible weight loss, Matilda feared his recovery would require more than a summer's heat would provide. She made no comment.

At the end of May, her nephew Sam returned from Sulphur Creek for another visit.

"Just can't stay away, can you?" Matilda greeted him warmly. "All of your friends are always so glad to see you. How are Belle and the new baby?"

"Just fine." He returned her hug. "Willie's so fascinated with his new little brother that he just sits and stares at him. Every once in a while he pokes him, ever so gently, as if to check and see if he is really real."

"I'm so glad he wasn't jealous. So often that's a problem with a new baby."

"Well, not yet. Maybe when Ray gets a little older and wants to start playing with some of Willie's toys. So what has been going on over here?"

"Tom and Mary are all settled into their apple orchard up in Oleta. I haven't seen it, but I understand they have a lovely home." She chuckled. "And everyone is all agog over the Valensin divorce case."

"Oh, yes," Sam nodded. "The ubiquitous Count. So what has been going on?"

"It looks like the only real issue involved is property. The grounds for divorce are based on some rather ambiguous technicalities. Most of the complaints are little minor things that usually come up among married couples from time to time. But the counsel on both sides are squabbling back and forth, and, according to the paper, their quarrels are 'chaffy, vulgar, and undignified.'" Matilda laughed. "I've almost been tempted to attend some of the hearings. That worthless husband has accused poor Alice of all kinds of odious behavior, which she, fortunately, was able to refute."

Sam grinned. "Sounds interesting. Maybe I should try and attend myself."

"Alice has proven those who spoke unkindly of her to be malicious liars. We still don't know what the outcome of the trial will be, of course, but the reporter for the Gazette minces no words about his feelings on the matter. He says Mrs. Valensin will have justice shown to her and her 'no-Count husband', as he calls him, will be taught a lesson on American justice. We'll see who is right."

"Who's the Judge?"

"McFarland."

"He's supposed to be a good one."

"Come back in a month and I'll tell you."

Elizabeth and Henry produced their second child, a son they named Henry, Junior. After the baby's birth, Elizabeth laughed to her mother. "Pearl is just barely three years old, but she fusses and coos over the baby just like a little mother. She is just fascinated with him. Holds his hand and marvels over the tiny fingers." She nuzzled the baby's neck. "Is already asking me about babies. Are they always this little, and where do they come from, and how did God know to put this baby in my tummy." She shook her head. "Her questions would baffle a Talleyrand. You should see poor Henry trying to answer them."

Matilda chuckled and took the baby in her arms. He opened solemn eyes and stared at her. "He's going to have your eyes. And you should have heard the questions you asked me when your brother Lewis was born! You were about the same age as Pearl is now."

"And how did you answer them?"

Matilda laughed. "I didn't. I let your Grandmother take care of that one."

The problems between Mary and George came to a head in June. Matilda knew from the speed of the buggy coming down the drive that something was wrong. She saw Mary toss the reins to her brother and stride up to the porch. Matilda hurried to the door to meet her.

"Mother," Mary began, her eyes dark with pain. "George has definitely decided to take the children to Montana. He says he is going to help operate a mine outside of Butte, where his sister's husband Emerson is working."

Matilda felt a stab of fear. Earl and Mable were so young,

only four and six. Would they survive the harshness of a Montana winter? Of course, she supposed many children did, but she remembered Kansas with a shudder. And losing Baby John to that dreadful climate. Unable to think of any words of comfort, she took Mary in her arms.

"He can't take care of them properly," Mary raged, breaking away from her mother's embrace to pace the room. She clenched her fists and pounded the wall in her fury. "Especially Mable. He says his sister Mary can take care of her. His sister! I'm her mother. I should be allowed to take care of her. Curse the laws which say he has a right to take her to that horrible place."

But they were powerless to stop him. The law, unfortunately, was on his side. Matilda tried to reason with him, but he stood firm.

"They're my children, by law," he announced. "If she wants to be with them, she should come with us like a good wife and mother."

But that was the one thing Mary refused to do.

A week before the scheduled departure, Mary and Matilda caught the train for Sacramento at the Arno Station to have Earl and Mable photographed. George had grudgingly consented to Mary's wish for a photograph of the children before they left. Unfortunately, A.M. Stringfield had not yet arrived from Santa Barbara, so they were going to a photographer in Sacramento.

Earl loved to ride on the train, and chattered about the anticipated train trip to Butte. "Papa says we go though tunnels and everything," he reported, excited by the prospect. "Why aren't you coming with us, Mother? It should be a fun ride."

Mable, usually happy to get a chance to ride the train, was

silent. Her eyes, so like Mary's, remained on her mother the whole time. She seemed to sense the significance of this trip.

They walked from the train station to Gregory's Photography Studio in the Lewis Building on J Street. In the mid-day sun, the heat shimmered about them. Dust from the street covered them with a fine film, sticking to skin sweaty from the heat. Mable clung silently to Mary's hand. The excited Earl looked into the windows of all the shops.

While Mr. Gregory posed the children for the photograph, Mary spoke to Matilda in hushed tones. "I can take them and run, Mother. We can go to San Francisco and hide. He'd never find us there."

"Yes he would, Mary. You'd have to work. He'd hire one of those Pinkerton detectives to find you. He could even file a complaint against you and have you put in jail." Matilda frantically used all the arguments she could think of, for Mary was just rash enough to try something. "Besides, you'd have no one to take care of them while you worked."

The photographer returned with the children. "Your picture will be ready in a few days, Mrs. Douglass. Do you wish me to put it in the post, or will you pick it up?"

Mary met Matilda's eyes. Their gaze locked for several moments, then Mary said, "I'll pick it up Friday, Mr. Gregory."

Two days later, George Douglass left for Montana with the children. Mary and Matilda saw them off at the train. Carrie stayed home. "I would just cry, Mother," she had said, "and that would make it harder for everyone."

Matilda felt none to strong herself as she watched Earl

solemnly kiss his mother goodbye. "I'll be back, Mother," he promised, "just as soon as I'm big enough." He shook hands with Matilda. "Goodbye, Grandmother."

Mable clung to her mother, weeping. Matilda watched Mary's face turn to stone as she hugged her daughter closely. The whistle blew.

"Get on the train, Son," George directed Earl. Turning to Mary, he pulled the weeping Mable from her arms. "You had your chance, Mary."

Mary stood still as a statue, the pain in her face so patent Matilda felt it. Her heart ached for her daughter. They watched the train disappear into the distance.

"I'll never see her again, Mother. I know I'll never see her again." The tears she would not shed in front of George now slid, unchecked, down her cheeks.

Chapter 46

July to September, 1885

Two days after George left with the children, Mary moved back home with Matilda.

"Mrs. Douglass thinks I should have gone with George, Mother. She never comes right out and says it, just gives little hints about 'wifely duties', and how she followed her husband out to California, leaving her nice home in Missouri, 'as a wife ought'. With her daughters married and moved out, I'm the only one left to help her around the house, but I can never do anything right." Mary slammed down the box she had just carried in.

"'Now, Mary,'" she quoted, "'I don't mean to be critical, but that last batch you ironed could have been just a tad neater' or 'I'm sure your mother taught you to make jelly proper so it sets up right' because the last batch I made stayed kind of soupy."

Matilda smothered a smile. She could almost sympathize with Mrs. Douglass. Domestic skills had never been high on Mary's list of priorities.

Mary turned to Lew who helped her carry in her belongings. "Thank you, Lew. Set that last box over there."

He grunted as he set down the heavy box. "You sure managed to collect a lot of stuff. Do I hafta take the buggy back to the Douglass's place now or can it wait until tomorrow? '

"Now, please. I promised I would get it right back. Mrs. Douglass was whining about she might need it 'can't never tell when', so go."

"Your wish, milady, is my command." Lew dodged the swat she aimed at him and headed out to saddle a horse to take with him for the ride back.

As soon as he was gone, Mary turned to her mother. "Where are Carrie and Sammie?"

"Feeding the chickens."

"Good." Her eyes narrowed. "Another reason I moved out. George's younger brother kept hinting that if I got lonely, he'd be more than happy to take George's place. And he wasn't proposing marriage." She shuddered. "Over my dead body." She hugged Matilda. "Oh, Mother, it's so good to be home!"

Lew returned from delivering the buggy, and had picked up the mail and the latest gossip on the way back. "Hear Mrs. Smith tried to get the $3000 Uncle Billy left her, but the Court only let her have $1440, so she had to settle for that."

"Poor Emma," Matilda responded indignantly. "And Uncle Billy was so positive he wanted her to get it."

"Seems the estate didn't have enough money to pay all the debts and have enough left over. They decided hers was a legacy and not a debt." He shook his head. "I'll never understand how courts figger things. At least Uncle Alf got the money he was owed for the hauling he did."

The next big news to circulate through the community was the settlement of Alice Valensin's suit for divorce against her Count. To everyone's amazement, Judge

McFarland ruled that she was not entitled to a divorce.

"Took eighteen pages of foolscap to write his opinion," Alf reported, "but he said the charges of cruelty against the Count were held 'not to be established by the Court'. In fact, he said the preponderance of the evidence went the other way." He chuckled. "I can kind of see his point. I'm sure Alice can be a little termagant when she gets her back up. He did grant her custody of young Pio, but no distribution of property was made because the marriage was not dissolved."

"I'm sure that went over well with McCauley," Bill chuckled. "I suspect Alice is going to go right on doing exactly what she wants to do, divorce or no divorce. If the Count knows what's good for him, he'll pack up and git."

Matilda grinned wryly. "And let go of all of that money? I'll bet not."

Alf shrugged. "Nothing we can do about it. Got to get home. Emma will be waiting supper for me, and she gets testy if I'm late." He rose to leave. "Hear Chism Fugitt is in a hospital in Sacramento. They say he's got inflammation of the bowel."

"Oh, no, the poor dear," Matilda cried, immediately thinking of the agony Alfred went through during the last days of his life.

"They say his daughters, especially Cecelia, are spending most of their time with him. Guess they don't hold out much hope. And I really gotta go."

Bill and Matilda watched as he hastened out the door and mounted his horse.

Bill grinned and raised his eyebrows. "Speaking of termagants."

Matilda laughed.

Chism Fugitt died on July 15, and Matilda had Lew drive them to the services. As they watched his coffin being lowered into the grave in the Liberty Cemetery, Matilda murmured to Mary. "Poor dear. He was such a good man. It's fitting he be buried here instead of the cemetery in Galt. Liberty was his town, and I'm sure his heart was always here."

"Yes," Mary agreed. "He made Galt a very good constable, but he never stopped regretting the loss of his town to Harvey and the railroad."

On August 1, D.K. expanded his cart business by purchasing the Sparks carriage, wagon, and blacksmith shop.

"Sounds like he's going to be one of the biggest businesses in Galt," Mary commented.

"He's well on his way," Lew said. "Mother," he turned to Matilda, "are Alf and Wes still planning to go hunting over at Uncle Sam's place in Lake County?"

"Yes. They want to go over to Colusa County as well, to spend some time with your cousins Sam and Belle, and hopefully bag a couple of deer. Why? You thinking of going along?"

"Can't," he grinned. "I promised Media I'd take her to a social they're having at her church. And a couple of the fellers want me to come to a surprise party they are planning for D.K. here in a couple of weeks." He held his finger to his lips as Bill walked into the room. "But I didn't tell you. Don't tell anyone else."

Matilda nodded.

"See James Marshall passed on," Bill said as he entered the room, holding up the paper he held in his hand. "Eighty-three he was. Guess he never did make it rich, in spite of all his prospecting."

408

"Give him credit," Lew said. "He knew there was gold in those hills. Some folks are now saying he found it by chance, but he wouldn't have found it if he hadn't been looking."

"I've heard that story both ways," Bill grinned. "Kind of like the stories about the Donner Party. Everyone has to make it a little better."

At the end of August, after a day of sweltering heat, Matilda and Bill sat in the shade of the big fig tree in the back of the house, sipping lemonade and watching the new pump fill the water tank. Matilda, mesmerized by the pulse of the water, still marveled at the amount the pump managed to produce. Absently sipping her lemonade, and enjoying the cool breeze that wafted over her, she realized that Bill, reading the paper beside her, had spoken.

"I'm sorry," she smiled. "I'm afraid my mind was wandering. What did you say?"

He chuckled. "You did seem to be a million miles away. I said this article says the Chinese don't get malaria because they boil the river water before they drink it."

"Really? Mother always thought the ague came from the miasma from the swamps and low standing water." She laughed. "I know on the trip from Illinois to Kansas we could never camp by the water. Always had to camp on a rise so the wind could blow the miasma away." She smiled. "Of course, it was easier to sleep because the wind also blew away the mosquitoes and those beastly little black flies that were always biting us. My brothers grumbled because they had to take the cattle back down the hill to water them."

"Guess the Chinese think the malaria comes from the water."

"I know Mother always boiled the water, to "get out the deleterious properties" was how she put it. Maybe they're right. Maybe the reason we had so little trouble with ague was because she always boiled the water. I know my first husband had a bout of it in Kansas, and Mother's father, Grandfather Stringfield, died of it back in '22."

"Paper also says Constable Phillips is keeping an eye on that Chinese opium den they are running on the south side of town."

"Good for him." Matilda frowned. "I don't approve of the attempts to drive the poor Chinese out of work and out of town, but I really don't think they should be allowed to run those opium dens."

He returned his attention to the paper, and turned the page with a rustle. "And I guess someone poisoned Dr. Montague's cat."

She gasped. "Napoleon? Why on earth would anyone want to hurt poor, old Napoleon?"

"Don't know. Doesn't say who did it." He shrugged. "Maybe Doc Patterson got tired of taking care of him."

"That's terrible," she said. "Cat never hurt anyone."

Bill rose to shut off the pump. "And I hear they're reopening the Liberty School. Guess they found more youngsters somehow. Miss Clement will be the teacher."

Matilda sighed. "I'm sure poor Chism is happy, wherever he is, poor dear." She looked at the laden fig tree. "Do you want fig preserves or dried figs? Looks like we're going to have a bumper crop."

He followed her glance, and grinned boyishly. "Both," he replied. "And fresh figs and cream for breakfast!"

Matilda's uncle, Sevier Stringfield arrived in late September from Santa Barbara for a visit, staying at his son

D.K.'s house, where the family gathered to visit. Matilda greeted him warmly. She had not seen him since her mother's funeral.

After catching up on the family news, the conversation turned to the recently reported massacre of Chinese in Wyoming Territory.

The argument among the men went back and forth. All agreed the massacre was wrong, but many felt laws to exclude the Chinese were appropriate.

"Take jobs from white men, they do," averred D.K. "Hard enough for a laboring man to get enough work as it is."

"Never would have got the railroad through the Sierras without 'em," Bill stated firmly. "They did work the white men were afraid to do. Would you have dangled over the side of a cliff to place explosives? I sure wouldn't have."

"And those opium dens," Tom said. "Disgraceful." He and Mary had come down from Oleta to see Sevier during his visit.

Matilda heard the discussion from the kitchen where she, Mary, Maggie, and several of the other women prepared dinner for the gathering. Matilda sighed to her daughter, "I just hope none of the violence spreads to here. I have had some dealings with several of our Chinese and have always found them pleasant and honest." She remembered some of the things she had learned about the Chinese conflicts from Mrs. Boone when she and Alfred went to San Francisco for their honeymoon. She had certainly hoped the problems would have been resolved by now.

She pulled her mind back as Maggie said, "Did Lew tell you about the terrible tornado they had in Ohio? I guess his young lady, Miss Latourette, said her father was real worried, because he has a lot of family there. He seemed especially concerned for his sister Sarah. Says he's real glad his mother and brother John came here when they did."

"Are they all right?"

"Yes. A letter from his sister assured him the tornado passed some distance from them."

Matilda shuddered. "I remember tornados in Kansas. They were terrible things. Luckily, they always seemed to touch down in central and western Kansas and we lived in the east part."

Maggie giggled. "Did you hear that old man McCauley almost did himself in?"

"No! How?" Her mind immediately flew to Count Valensin's recent experience. "Did he take too much laudanum like Alice's husband did?"

"Oh, no, nothing like that. Seems on his last trip to San Francisco he bought himself one of those new fancy hammocks so he could lie out of an afternoon in the shade of the oak trees and take a nap where he could get the cool breeze. He hung the contraption about nine feet above the ground and piled up some boxes to climb up to get in. All went well until he tried to turn his shoulders a bit, and the whole thing turned over."

"Was he hurt when he fell?"

Maggie giggled again. "He didn't fall all the way. He got tangled in the lines, and there he was, hanging head down, unable to pull himself up or get his feet loose. Guess he hollered and hollered, but no one heard him."

"I'll bet he was cussing up a storm."

"I'm sure he was. Lucky for him, a gentleman from Sacramento arrived looking for him on a business matter, and a search party set out. When they found him, he was beyond swearing. He was almost dead from hanging upside down all that time."

Matilda laughed. "I'll bet next time he hangs it lower to the ground."

"His wife says there won't be a next time. He piled it in a heap and set fire to it." Maggie's eyes twinkled. "The fire promptly spread into the dry grass around the house, of course, and if the hands hadn't been so quick to put it out, he'd have burned down the whole place."

Chapter 47

October to December, 1885

October opened with more rumors of Apache problems in Arizona, and reports that Jim Hicks hauled in a fine lot of corn from his operations on Uncle Billy's property.

"I'm so glad young Jim is doing well. He should be able to pay off the debt on the place and keep it, as Uncle Billy wanted," Matilda related to her nephew Sam on his next visit. "Can you stay over until the 21st? Carrie and Sammie are both performing in the entertainment the Sunday School is putting on to raise funds. It's only twenty-five cents, but we usually get a good turn-out."

Sam stood looking out the kitchen window. Suddenly he called, "Look, Aunt 'Tilda. There's a big fire in Galt. You can see the smoke from here."

She hurried to join him at the window. "Are you sure it's that far away? Could it be closer?"

"I don't think so."

At that moment, Lew came running in. He had seen the fire as well. "I'm going, Sam. Want to come?"

"Yep, wouldn't miss it. Aunt 'Tilda?"

She shook her head. "You boys will get there much faster on horses. Come back and tell me all about it." She stood mesmerized by the roiling black smoke as hoof beats headed out the drive.

She watched at the window until the smoke died to a few wisps, and returned to turning the figs drying on the racks, a chore Sam's arrival had interrupted, and waited for the two young men to come back.

They returned four hours later, grimy and covered with soot, and full of their adventure. Matilda had to smile at their excitement. A fire was as much of an occasion as a party.

"It was Iler's Blacksmith shop at 6th and C. No one in the building when it began. Started about one o'clock while everyone was on dinner break. By the time we got there, over 200 men had gathered to fight it." Lew stopped and pumped some water into a basin at the sink and washed some of the soot off his face.

"D.K. was there," Sam offered, "and John Sawyer, Will Hicks, Simon Prouty, Wes Long, almost every able-bodied man in town. But Contner's house next door to Iler's burned anyway. We tried, but couldn't save it. Did manage to get most of his family's belongings out. Mrs. Contner was so grateful she broke down and cried when I handed her the tea set off her sideboard. She said it had belonged to her grandmother. Simon and Wes were carrying out the sideboard, and I figgered the tea set might fall and break, so I took it out separate."

"How thoughtful of you, Sam." Matilda smiled. "Lew, what about Iler's fine new residence, and Mr. Latourette's home and tin shop? They were so close!"

"Iler's house got scorched," Lew replied, "but the Latourette property came through almost unscathed. P.H. had gone to Lodi, and returned to find his home almost in the center of the conflagration. He sure thanked everyone who put in all the effort to save his property, I'll tell you."

"So the only loss was Contner's house and the Iler building?

"Some folks had rented storage space on the second story of the Iler's, and they lost it all. Bartlett had some paint and stuff, and Mrs. Russell lost her furniture. I guess some fellow named Mills lost his things as well. He wasn't there, and I didn't know him."

"I hope they were insured."

"Iler said he estimates his loss at around $6000, and he had $4000 in insurance. The Contner's had a little coverage. They say the others had none."

Matilda shook her head. "And for how long have we been saying we need a fire department? Sacramento has been saved from many a disaster because they have a good fire department."

Lew grinned. "Believe me, that was the main topic of conversation as soon as the fire was out." His face turned serious. "John Quiggle was one as helped us put out the fire. He says his little nephew and namesake, Lack and Cora's boy Johnnie, is still real sick. Doc Sanderson doesn't hold out much hope for his recovery."

The Quiggle boy died on Wednesday morning, November 18. Mary heard the news from Mrs. Herbert and returned home to tell her mother.

"I know he had been ailing with typhoid fever," Mary said, "but I guess it went into his lungs, and pneumonia was what killed him. Poor little fellow." Tears filled her eyes. "He was so brave. Every time he was asked how he felt, he'd say, "Better". But he never got better. He just got weaker and weaker."

"Are they going to bury him in Hicksville next to Frankie?"

"No, Mrs. Herbert says they're planning to put him in the Odd Fellows Cemetery in Galt." She grimaced. "Guess they feel they're too uppity for Hicksville."

"So poor little Frankie will be the only one of his family at Hicksville? Seems a shame not to have any of his kin around him."

"Well, at least none of our kin can complain," Mary smiled.

Matilda had to laugh. "You're right. If there's one thing Hicksville Cemetery has, it's an abundance of Randolphs!"

At the Thanksgiving gathering of the clan, Wes Overton reported that Stockton had passed an ordinance prohibiting the Chinese to operate laundries in the city of Stockton.

"The poor souls," Matilda said, indignation in her voice. "How are they supposed to make a living?"

Wes grinned. "Pa says they just set up their operations outside of the town. Folks as have been making use of their services for years just take the clothes to them. Some of the more enterprising have set up a delivery service."

Matilda had to laugh. "They are very resourceful, aren't they?"

"Speaking of resourceful," Wes continued, "I hear Kidder has purchased Iler's Blacksmith shop. I guess after the big fire Iler didn't feel like starting over. Kidder took in young Sparks as his partner. Guess Sparks missed the business after he sold out to Kidder. Getting to be quite an enterprise."

Matilda glanced over to where Kidder and Tom were in animated conversation. "Yes," she nodded solemnly. "Quite an enterprise."

December rains brought the usual fogs and damage to the roads. As Lew prepared to ride into Galt, Matilda tried to deter him.

"The roads are in such bad condition. And the bridges are dangerous. Do you really have to go? The fog is already building."

"I'll be fine, Mother." He hugged her to reassure her. "John Quiggle and Charlie Cogswell have leased the Arcade Stable, and tonight is the party to celebrate their grand opening. I promised Charlie I'd be there."

"I don't know," Matilda demurred. "There's a hard drinking bunch as hangs around those two. I'm not sure I like you going."

"Mother!" He laughed, half amused, half exasperated at her fussing. "I can take care of myself. Remember, I am twenty-two years old. I'm not a boy anymore."

With a heavy sigh, she acceded. "All right. Just be careful. And if it gets too foggy, stay with one of your friends in town, don't try to come home."

"Yes, Mother." His tone was so comical that Mary laughed.

"Let him go, Mother. He's a big boy, and will have to learn the hard way. And Blaze is a good horse. He'll get him home no matter what state of inebriation he is in."

Lew shrugged into his coat and jammed his hat down on his head. "Go on with the both of you," and stomped out the door.

The light from the lamp showed the clock moments from striking ten. Matilda looked outside. The setting moon reflected through a dense fog. She could barely see a few feet from the house.

"Mary, the fog is building, and the moon will be gone in a few minutes. Do you suppose he is going to try and make it home?"

"Probably not," Mary shrugged. "He has a host of friends

in Galt. Surely one of them will let him sleep over. He could always go to Maggie and Kidder." She rose and stretched. "If I have to darn one more sock I'm going to scream. Let's go to bed. Leave the lamp in the window to guide him if he is foolish enough to try to come home."

Uneasily, Matilda watched out the window until the moon vanished completely, and she could see nothing. Admitting to the wisdom of Mary's advice, she left the lamp on the window ledge and went to bed.

The next morning, she rose to fog so thick she could barely see a few yards. The lamp had run out of oil during the night. She looked out of the window and, to her horror, could barely make out the outline of a horse standing just south of the house with his head down, the reins dangling. She recognized him as Blaze, the young horse Lew had ridden to town the previous evening. Her heart pounding, her eyes followed the reins through the fog, and she could barely make out a figure lying on the ground in front of the horse.

"Mary," she screamed. "Come quick, it's Lew!" She ran out the back kitchen door and to the figure lying so still on the ground. Had he been thrown? Blaze was a very gentle horse, even though young. Was he ill? Had he been injured? He couldn't be dead, please God, he can't be dead. All of the thoughts raced through her mind as she ran to her son's side.

Mary, hard on her mother's heels, pulled on her robe as she ran.

Kneeling by Lew's side, Matilda gently rolled him onto his back. A loud snore greeted her efforts and she breathed a sigh of relief. At least he still lived. Blaze nuzzled the back of her neck, and she gave a little laugh at the horse's evidence of concern. "You want me to take care of him, don't you, Blaze? You brought him home to me." She rose and stroked the horse's neck affectionately. "Now we just have to get him off of this damp ground before he takes a chill." She turned to Mary, who knelt by Lew's side. "He must have had trouble finding the house," she remarked to her daughter. "But shouldn't he be waking up?" Concern raced through her again.

Mary started to laugh. "Smell him. He's drunk as a skunk. And he's vomited all over himself." She laughed even more. "He's going to have a head on him that won't quit."

Matilda stared at Mary, puzzled. "How do you know so much about drunkenness?"

"After being married to George Douglass?" Mary snorted. "I've nursed him through many a hangover. Not everyone is a Methodist, Mother. Come on, help me get him on his feet." She slapped her brother's face a couple of times and he grunted in protest. "Get up, you booze hound. You're too heavy for us to carry. Come on, up on your feet."

"Bill is out in the barn milking. Should one of us go for him?"

"Oh, Mother, we can manage. He'll be able to walk once we get him moving."

Between the two of them, they prodded Lew into sitting up. Blaze promptly nuzzled his face in concern and knocked him flat on his back again.

"Blaze," Matilda protested, "You're not helping!" Mary burst into giggles and tugged helplessly on her brother's arm. "And you're not helping either, Mary. Stop laughing and lift."

Between the two up them, they managed to get him on his feet and, with an arm over a shoulder of each, he managed to stagger into the house where Mary persuaded her mother to lay him on the floor instead of the bed.

"Don't want him on the bed until we get those clothes off of him and get him cleaned up. You start on the clothes, I'll get the fire built up." Lew had started to shiver, and Matilda began peeling off the vomit-laden shirt.

"Phew," she said. "We'll never get the smell out. Maybe we should just burn it."

Mary chuckled grimly. "If you think that's bad, wait until you get his pants off."

An hour later, they had him cleaned, bathed, and tucked into bed where he lay groaning. Matilda brewed him some of the Chamomile tea her mother had always used for headache, and urged him to sip it.

"Can't raise my head," he complained. "Get dizzy if I do, and sick to my stomach."

"Then we'll spoon it in," Matilda said firmly. "You need the chamomile and you need the warmth of the tea." Patiently, spoonful by spoonful, she got the whole cup of tea into him, then covered him up. "Now, you need to sleep." She chuckled softly. "And when you wake up, you can tell us what happened."

The sun had begun its descent into the west, and the fog had built up again before Lew felt able to sit up and sip some soup and eat a little bread.

Matilda sat on the edge of the bed while he gingerly ate the bit of soup she fed him. She waited.

He heaved a long sigh, and smiled wanly at his mother. "You were right, Mother. No way can I keep up with those fellows. They just kept refilling my whisky glass and urging me to 'drink up'. I know it was foolish, but they kept joshing me on. When I finally got so dizzy I couldn't stand without holding on, I knew I had to get out. Charlie helped me out of the saloon and gave me a hand into the saddle. He just whacked Blaze on the rump and told him to go home." Lew grimaced. "Blaze is a good horse. I guess he got me back okay. Next thing I remember was Mary slapping me."

"Yes, he got you home, and stayed right by you all night. Lucky he did. I might not have seen you in the fog for another hour or so. We thought you had stayed the night in Galt."

"Sure hope Mr. Latourette doesn't hear about this. He and Media don't approve of drinking at all."

"Oh, I'm sure he will, bet on it. One of your good friends will be sure and tell him, since they all know he is a staunch Prohibitionist. He fought to keep those Sunday laws as long as he could."

"I know." Lew brightened. "I'll join his Prohibition Party." He grimaced. "After last night, and after as bad as I feel now, it's not a bad idea." He turned to Sammie, who stood at the end of the bed staring at his brother. "Let this be a lesson to you, Sammie, my boy. Don't let anyone talk you into drinking whiskey."

Matilda's distrust of Hicksville postmaster W.W. Rich came to a climax. The community had talked for months about his absence, now going on for six months, and had petitioned Washington to replace Rich with Veso Johnson. Matilda knew Mr. Johnson and Walt Journay's father had been fulfilling the duties during Rich's absence, but now his bondsmen were beginning to become concerned.

Mary shrugged when Matilda mentioned it to her. "Guess we'll just have to wait and see. Glad none of our family put up his bond. Did you hear that Columbus Dillard and his wife have another little boy? "

"Another one? Are they out to set a record?"

Alf came through the door at that moment, full of news. "Did you hear about the big dynamite scare in San Francisco? They caught a full-fledged nest of Nihilists who were all set to blow up City Hall. Found a whole cache of dynamite, too. Caught 'em red-handed, they did."

"What's a Nihilist?" Mary wanted to know.

"Bunch of folks as feel that existing political institutions have to be destroyed in order to clear the way for their new state of society."

"Run by them, I suppose," Mary said ironically.

"Of course. They use any means available, including anarchy, terrorism, and assassination."

"Sounds like a great bunch of fellows," Mary exclaimed.

"The postmaster leaves his bride and runs off from his post, leaving his bondsmen to pay, two of our most respectable businessmen fight in the middle of the street over fancied insults, the Chinese arm themselves in response to massacres, and now we have a group that wants to blow up all of the government buildings?" Matilda shook her head. "What is this world coming to?"

Chapter 48

January to April, 1886

THE BIG NEWS at the start of 1886 was George McCauley's marriage to Laurilla Crawford early in January. Lew, grinning ear to ear, reported the news to his mother and sister.

"Guess she doesn't have the best reputation. George's mother was real vocal in her protests against his choice of bride. The new Mrs. George McCauley took great offense at her comments and attacked her new mother-in-law."

"Attacked her? You mean she actually hit her?" Mary gasped.

Matilda could only gape.

"Yep. And Caroline McCauley not being one to take such an action lying down, so to speak, had her arrested and charged with battery." He chuckled. "Came up in D.K.'s court and he fined Miss Laurilla $50 for battery. That's a pretty hefty fine, so I'm sure there's more to it than we've been told."

"Poor George." Matilda sighed. "Now his mother is disappointed in him too? I know he's never been able to satisfy that father of his. Alice has always been the apple of her father's eye."

Mary laughed. "And the man Alice married didn't turn

out to be such a prize either!"

Lew shrugged. "The irony is, George will have to pay the fine, and all the money he has is what he gets from his folks, so Caroline will wind up putting out the money herself."

"At least she has the satisfaction of hauling her into court," Mary grinned.

Knowing Lew had just returned from a visit with Media, Matilda asked, with a twinkle in her eye, "And how are you and Media's father getting along?"

Lew gave a shout of laughter. "You were right, Mother, he did hear about my encounter with the Quiggle/Cogswell party. When I told him I wanted to join his Prohibitionist Party, he looked real pleased, and said he was glad to see I had "seen the error of my ways", was how he put it." Lew grinned. "I don't know about the "error of my ways" part, but I'm sure I never want to have a head like that on me again."

Mary grunted. "Never deterred George."

"John Quiggle is retiring from the business, so Charlie will be running the Arcade Stable by himself. He apologized for getting so much whiskey down me. Admitted the fellows had a bet to see if they could get a Methodist drunk." He twisted his mouth into a wry grin. "Have to admit they succeeded."

Matilda patted his hand and refilled his coffee cup. "Just so you remember."

Mary looked skeptical. "We'll see."

In February, the big news to hit the community was the movement up and down the state to drive out the Chinese.

Mary read the reports in the paper to Matilda. "Red Bluff is to boycott the poor Chinese. Petaluma has given them ten days notice to move out. And in Redding, the last five of them left on the 31st of January through the 'efforts of the committee.' Committee. Ha," she snorted. "I wonder what those 'efforts' were. Bunch of hoodlums, I'll bet."

Matilda sighed. "I had so hoped it would not come to this."

"And on next Tuesday, the first anti-Chinese meeting is to be held in Galt."

"Oh, no."

"Oh, yes." Mary grinned. "D.K. is going to join. Maggie says he won't let her send the laundry to the Chinese who have been doing it for her ever since she moved to Galt. She's mad. Says they charged so little and always did such a nice job. They never leave the iron on the stove until it gets too hot and scorches the clothes like I always seem to do. And when I didn't leave it on long enough, I couldn't get out all of the wrinkles, and Mother Douglass would complain about the collars not being smooth enough."

Matilda laughed. "I'll bet not being able to send the laundry out did make Maggie mad. She hates to iron as much as you do, Mary."

"Almost," Mary replied with a wry smile. "Nobody hates to iron as much as I do."

Kidder did attend the anti-Chinese meeting in Galt, which, he said, had drawn a large crowd. "Doc Harvey gave a good talk, kind of summed up the sentiment of everyone there," he reported. A number of family members, including Matilda's household, had gathered at Kidder and Maggie's home for Sunday dinner.

"He said it was pretty well expressed in the vote of 1880, over 150,000 against letting more immigrate as opposed to only 1000 for it. Even a lot of the Chinese didn't want to allow any more to come in, said there were plenty here already," Kidder continued. "Harvey says everyone agrees as to the "evil and burden of these Chinese upon our civilization and industries" is how he put it." He chuckled.

"Seems to me most businesses had no objection to opening trade with China when the treaty was passed," Bill remarked. "All they saw at that time was a huge market opening up to buy all of their stuff."

"Yes," Kidder nodded. "What no one foresaw was hordes of Chinese coming to take all the laboring jobs from white men."

"I don't see any of those white men clamoring to do the laundry," Matilda said in an aside to Mary.

"No," Mary said. "They just expect their wives to do it."

"Give Harvey credit," Lew said. "He said we should drive them out "by all lawful and legitimate means". That means just pass laws so they can't live anyplace and can't do anything to earn a living."

Kidder flushed a bit at Lew's sarcasm, then admitted, "He did say he's going to evict the Chinamen that are running the washhouse in that tenement he owns." He looked at the assembled faces and saw no agreement, so he tried no further argument. He only said, "I was elected to be the Galt Delegate to the anti-Chinese Convention in Sacramento the second week in March. We'll see what comes of that." His face relaxed into a smile. "Now, I think the ladies have dinner ready for us. Come, let's eat. Alf, I'm going to ask you to say the blessing."

The next phase of the George McCauley/Laurilla (or Lizzie, as he called her) Crawford saga came at about the same time. The paper reported she was on trial in San Francisco for the murder of two men.

"Seems she was accused of robbing a sheepherder from Gilroy of over $700 while he was at the St. David House in San Francisco." Bill grinned. "No mention of why she was there, but have heard some reports. Anyway," he went on, "witnesses say she admits killing the two men, but vehemently denies robbing the sheepherder."

"So where is she now?"

"The jury couldn't agree. Some speculated that the three that held out for acquittal were tampered with. The judge dismissed all three. She couldn't come up with the $2000 in bail money, so she was "provided quarters in jail" was how they put it."

Matilda laughed. "So she doesn't mind being labeled a murderess, but refuses to be branded a thief?"

"It would seem so."

"And apparently George didn't want her back badly enough to post her bail?"

Bill chuckled. "I suspect George has come home to Mama. Wouldn't surprise me if the next we hear is a notice of divorce proceedings."

Matilda only shook her head.

By the end of February, the weather turned mild, and farmers began getting their mowers ready for harvest. A notice announced the Commercial Hotel in Stockton had discharged all of their Chinese help.

The *Galt Gazette,* to Matilda's relief, went on record as deploring violence against the Chinese. It also reported 1400 had sailed on March 5 from San Francisco harbor, returning to China.

"But the Chinese laundrymen in Galt are still doing business," Bill reported. "Much to the disgust of many of the men, but to the delight of the women. A number of the ladies of the town have discovered how much easier life is if you can just drop off your dirty laundry one day and pick it up clean the next."

"Not only clean, but folded and ironed," Mary declared. "I'll bet if women had had the franchise the vote to exclude the Chinese would not have been so one-sided."

Bill laughed. "You're probably right. But his stand against the Chinese has gotten Obed Harvey nominated for Governor."

Kidder attended the anti-Chinese Convention in Sacramento as the delegate from Galt as he planned. At the next family gathering, he explained the results, listing what the assembly viewed as the evils arising from the Chinese presence.

"First," he declared, "their coming is an invasion, not an immigration."

"Bet the Sioux and the Pawnee felt the same way about the white men," Lew said.

"I know the Sauks and the Foxes thought so," said Matilda, remembering the Blackhawk Wars.

"The Apaches still feel that way," Bill added.

Kidder ignored the comments. "Second," he said, "they have no families or homes among us."

"And whose fault is that?" Mary asked.

"Third," he went on, a little louder, "their mode of life is so different they will never assimilate with our people."

"Is that bad?" Lew asked.

"Fourth," Kidder continued. "By education and customs, they are antagonistic to a republican form of government."

"The same government that is now getting ready to drive them out? Is that what the founding fathers meant when they wrote the Constitution?" Mary commented caustically.

Kidder ignored her. "Fifth, they maintain in our midst secret tribunals in defiance of our laws."

"Like the Masons and the Odd Fellows?" Lew asked, his face a mask of innocence.

Kidder continued without acknowledging Lew's comment. "They also felt the presence of so many males owing allegiance to a foreign government is dangerous."

"From what I understand," Bill offered, "not many of them feel any allegiance to the government of China. Matter of fact, most of them came over here to get away from the government of China. Sort of like we felt about King George."

"Plus they deter laboring men from coming to California."

"Not so you'd notice," Bill remarked. "Seems every train from the East brings a whole passel. And Galt has doubled in size in the last five years."

"All right, all right." Kidder threw up his hands. "But you do have to admit them sending a large portion of their earnings back to China is bad for the economy."

Bill grinned. "Not if the folks in China use it to buy American goods."

"And if they were allowed to bring their families, they probably wouldn't send money back to China," Matilda declared. "Now, enough politics. Dinner is ready. If I hear one more word against the poor Chinese I'm going to lose my appetite."

"Sounds good to me," Bill agreed heartily. He rose and headed for the table.

As he settled into his chair, Alf observed. "Barley's ripening early this year. Should be able to start harvesting by May."

"Did you hear we now have telephone lines connecting Stockton and Sacramento?" Mary said. "Now we can talk

431

to anyone who has a telephone all up and down the line."

"My, the world is getting smaller and smaller," Matilda marveled. "Where will it all end?"

Lew grinned and reached for a biscuit. "Charlie Quiggle is nursing a sore head. He got thrown from his buggy when it upset in a big hole in the road. And if that wasn't bad enough, while he was laid up someone ran off with both his horse and the buggy."

Chapter 49

May to July, 1886

MAY BROUGHT NEWS that the publishing house of A.L. Bancroft in San Francisco burned to the ground.

"Real shame," Lew reported to Mary and Matilda when he and Bill came in from the fields for dinner. "All of those wonderful books. Not another publisher to match it on the west coast. Will have to send East for any we want now, I guess."

"Do they know how it started?" Mary asked.

"No, but it was probably an incendiary. We may never know." He shrugged and changed the subject. "Did I tell you Mr. Latourette has been chosen to be a delegate to the Prohibitionist State Convention in Sacramento next week? He wants me to go with him."

"Are you going?" Matilda looked at her son, remembering his experience with liquor.

"Maybe. I haven't decided yet." He grinned and reached for the platter of sliced tomatoes. "Might be fun to get involved in politics."

"Should make you popular with your future father-in-law anyway," Mary contributed wryly.

Lew laughed. "He's not my future father-in-law yet. Media is still making up her mind." He added another potato to his plate. "They found Charlie's horse and buggy."

"Did they? Where?"

"Los Banos."

"Los Banos? That far away? I take it they were not local thieves."

"No one knows. They were found abandoned." He grinned. "Whoever stole them probably wanted a faster horse than that slug of Charlie's. Charlie likes old Barney because Barney is so docile and always gets home whether Charlie is able to direct him or not."

"As often as that man needs help to get home, I can see why he values the horse," Mary said caustically.

"I hear your cousin Sammie is in town from Sulphur Creek. Has he said how Jack is doing?" Matilda's concerns for her nephew Jack had not abated with time. Jack had purchased land close to her brother Sam in Lake County to be near Essie, since Essie now lived with Sally and Sam.

"Not well. He's talking about selling his land to Uncle Sam and moving back here. He can't seem to concentrate on anything since Becky died. Sally says sometimes she sees him just staring out across the fields. In fact, Essie says sometimes her father scares her. Calls her Becky and grabs her arms and stares into her eyes."

Matilda shook her head in sympathy. "The child he doesn't want instead of the woman he does. Having two children did take a lot of Becky's strength. I hope he doesn't blame poor little Essie. She tries so hard to please her father."

"It's good she has her Aunt Sally. She's a sensible young woman," Mary said. "But it's been over a year. Jack should be starting to come out of his depression."

"Sammie says he hasn't seen any sign of it yet. It took Frank over a year to get over Clara, but he had Annie to help him. Jack doesn't seem to be interested in any other woman. At least, not yet."

Matilda sighed. "Well, we can only hope for the best. Did you talk to Mr. Herbert about a new water trough as Bill asked?"

"Yep. He'll do it for $3.50. Told Bill and he agreed it's a good price, so I told him to go ahead and put it in next week. He says down at Furnish's place in Liberty, they're trying out something called deep plowing. Puts five horses on a single plow."

"What's the advantage to that?" Mary wanted to know.

"Tills the soil deeper." Then he chuckled. "Wouldn't do any good here. They get more than a couple of feet down and they hit hardpan!"

Two weeks later, Lew returned from a trip to Galt with a copy of the latest Galt Gazette. "You'll like this one," he told his mother. He quoted, "Stringfield and Sparks will shoe horses on and after Monday next for $1.50 and give a rebate of a glass of beer to boot." He chuckled softly. "Wonder how that will set with Mr. Latourette."

Matilda laughed. "Probably as well as it will with the other blacksmiths who all charge $2.00 a horse."

He grinned. "Probably. And heard that the rumor George McCauley is leaving for Italy turned out to be false. He says he has no intention of leaving America. At least not now, since his father is bad sick. They are moving him over to Alice's place to care for him. I guess it's getting too hard for Mrs. McCauley. Either that or he wants to spend his last days with his favorite."

"Poor George. Nothing he ever does pleases his father."

Lew laughed. "Well, his recent marriage certainly did nothing to endear him to either of his parents."

"Yes," Mary nodded. "Miss Crawford was not a wise choice."

"Lew," Matilda said the following Monday at breakfast, "Whitaker and Ray is having a sale and Mary and I would like to look at some of the calico they are offering. Can you take us to town this morning?"

"Sure," he grinned. "Chores are about finished. I'll hitch Ben up to the buggy. Maybe I can pick up a little gee-gaw for Media while we are there. She's always hinting I never bring her anything. Should talk to Mr. Latourette about this upcoming convention as well. He says he's looking for a partner to help him in his business." He gave his mother a sidelong glance. "Do you suppose you and Bill could get along without me if he makes me an offer?"

"Of course we can, Son," Bill said heartily. "Would be a good chance for you. Tinsmithing trade is a good one to learn."

"Hitch up the carriage instead of the buggy. Carrie wants to come too."

"Yes, Mother. I hear and obey." He wiped his mouth on his sleeve, a habit he picked up from his stepfather, Matilda thought with a patient sigh, and headed for the door, grabbing his hat off the rack on the way out.

As they passed the Methodist Church in Galt, on their way to the Whitaker and Ray Building, they passed Will Hicks on his horse and greeted him.

"Morning folks, ladies." He doffed his hat. "Fine morning for a drive." He grinned. "S'pose you're in town for Whitaker's big sale. Half the town is goin'. I suspect Mrs. McCauley is one of 'em. She wasn't at the ranch, and I got some business to discuss with her. As you probably know,

I'm rentin' part of her place on shares."

"We haven't seen her. Just got into town," Lew said. "But here comes her foreman, that Petre fellow, in her buggy. He might know."

As Matilda, Mary, and Carrie watched, Mr. Hicks pulled his horse next to Petre's buggy and posed the question. To everyone's astonishment, Petre began reviling Hicks, telling him it was none of his business where Mrs. McCauley was, and accusing him of mistreating that good lady. Hicks responded by calling Petre a liar, and Petre lashed Hicks across the face with his buggy whip.

To Matilda's horror, Hicks pulled his gun and began firing. All of the horses started at the sound of the shots. Lew struggled to get Ben calmed down, then urged him forward. "Let's get out of here, Mother! This is no place for ladies."

As the carriage pulled forward, Matilda looked back. Petre sat in the buggy, apparently unscathed by the fusillade of bullets. Of course, she thought, with a wry grin, it is hard to aim a pistol when your horse is jumping around in panic. Hicks had stopped firing, but continued to swear at Petre. She covered her ears and shook her head at such foolishness. Then she chuckled to Mary. "I wonder what is really behind all of that. Do you suppose Hicks really is trying to pull something on Mrs. McCauley?"

"I doubt it. I suspect it's just bad blood between Hicks and Petre. I'm sure glad none of those bullets hit anyone."

A week later, Bill told them the results of the trial in Justice Stringfield's court. "Had to postpone it until Kidder could get around again. Horse he was shoeing kicked him in the ankle and gave him a sprain that laid him up for a while. Guess when the whole story came out, the Court decided Hicks was justified in shooting at Petre, and since he didn't hit anything except the buggy, might just as well drop the whole thing. Let Mrs. McCauley sort it out."

"I'm sure she has other things on her mind at the moment, with her husband so ill."

"Yes, Mrs. Herbert was full of that as well. I guess the old gentleman is sinking fast. If you want to see him alive, I'd better take you soon."

"I've apple pies in the oven. Soon as one is cool enough, you can take me over."

"And she is also highly indignant because Lou ordered some printing from a salesman who came through a couple of weeks ago, and paid for the work ahead of time." He chuckled. "Now he's gotten two C.O. D. deliveries from two different Sacramento printers. Seems the fellow not only collected from the Herberts, he got a commission on the sales from the printing companies. Then lit out with the whole lot. So Lou wound up paying for two sets of printing, plus what he paid the salesman up front."

"I'll bet his wife had plenty to say about that," Matilda smiled, knowing Mrs. Herbert very well.

"I'll say she did. Says she told him all along to get his printing done by the *Galt Gazette*. Campbell's price may have been a little higher, but he's local, and can be trusted."

The visit to the Valensin residence was brief. Mr. McCauley had lapsed into a semi-stupor and really knew no one.

"Thank you so much for coming, Mrs. Frye," Alice said graciously, motioning to a servant to take the dish from Matilda's hands. "He's only able to sip a little soup, so I'm afraid he won't be able to enjoy your delicious pie, but the rest of us certainly will." She sighed. "You are going to have to let the neighborhood in on your secret recipe. You make the best apple pie!"

438

"I also can make a very good restorative chicken soup. Would that help?"

"I'm sure it would, Mrs. Frye." Mrs. McCauley entered the room in time to hear Matilda's last comment. "I've heard so much about your mother's healing wisdom, and if you learned the recipe from her, I'm sure it will help him retain his strength."

"Yes, my mother was very knowledgeable about herbs and restorative soups. I'll send it over with Lew as soon as it's ready."

"John won't know you, but would you like to see him? I know many have wanted to say goodbye to him, even though he is not aware of their presence."

"Thank you, I'd like that."

Mrs. McCauley ushered Matilda into the elegant room where the old man lay on a magnificent four-poster bed with satin sheets and a lace canopy. Matilda could not help comparing the luxury of the room with her simple home. As she stood looking down on the frail body, she thought of the power that man had wielded in his younger days. She wondered if Uncle Billy could see him now, stripped of his ability to wield that power. Somehow, there seemed to be a justice in it. She had to smile as she remembered how he even took on the State Government and won in the dispute over the San Quentin prison contract. And Mrs. Boone telling her and Alfred about the cobblestones in the streets of San Francisco McCauley had made a huge sum laying using convict labor for which he paid nothing.

His hand lay limply on top of the counterpane. Matilda touched it and found it cold. She stroked the wizened hand for a moment, then tucked it under the cover.

She left the room and returned to where Caroline McCauley stood. Hugging her warmly, she said, "Thank

you for letting me see him. I'll send the soup over as soon
as I can."

July struck with its usual vengeance, and heat swept over
them. Alf took his harvester crew and started on his rounds
of the West Side. Her nephew Sam returned for a visit from
Sulphur Creek and made the rounds of his old friends.

"Hear Charlie Quiggle and Joe Hunter had a row at the
Arcade. Guess Joe learned not to tangle with Charlie."

Matilda sighed. "That place is a disgrace. It should be
shut down."

Sam grinned. "Not as popular as it is among the young
bucks. They'll never let it be shut down."

"And how is your family?"

"Growing like weeds. Can't believe little Will is two and
a half already. And Ray is fifteen months. Keeps me busy
just putting enough food on the table. Thank goodness they
are all healthy. I'd hate to have doctor bills on top of bills
for food and clothes."

"And when is the next one coming?"

"No more in sight yet." He grinned. "But Carrie says
she is still waiting for her little girl."

"And how is Jack doing?"

He shook his head sadly. "He sold his land to Uncle Sam,
like he said he would. Guess he has just been living on the
$400 Uncle Sam paid him. He had Kidder draw up the
papers. Says he can't stand to be around Essie, for the older
she gets, the more she reminds him of Becky." He sighed.
"And poor little Essie adores her father."

John McCauley died on Monday, July 12, and the services were held the following day. Bill and Matilda attended, accompanied by Mary. Carrie elected to stay at home,

and Sammie stayed with her. The services began at the Valensin mansion, then the remains were transported to the Catholic Church in Galt. There Father Gualco officiated at the services, which, while beautiful, Matilda found lengthy and tediously repetitious. She had never attended a Catholic service before. She looked about the church as Father Gualco expounded on Mr. McCauley's generosity, as it was he who paid for the bricks used in its construction. Monsignor Capel was among those in attendance, along with most of Galt's important citizens.

After the church services, the coffin was lowered into a grave at the Odd Fellows Cemetery, next to the remains of John and Carolyn's two children who had died young of smallpox many years before.

Afterwards, Matilda spoke briefly with Mr. Latourette, who was there with his wife Eliza.

He beamed on Matilda. "Fine young man, your son is. He will be joining me for the Prohibitionist Party Convention in August." He winked at her. "And my daughter Media is quite taken with him. Wouldn't surprise me a bit if we have a wedding coming up in the not too distant future."

"Isn't Media a bit young, Mr. Latourette?" Matilda ventured.

"Sixteen, she is. And knows her own mind, believe me. Hasn't been able to see any young man except your Lewis since she met him."

"Yes," Matilda had to agree. "I remember the first day he came home after he met her."

"Am also glad to see he has decided not to hang out with that bunch at the Arcade. Bad influence, they are, drinking and carousing all the time."

"Oh, yes," Matilda had to laugh at the memory. "He

learned his lesson all right. And how is your mother? I hear she is growing more feeble."

Mr. Latourette sighed. "How she has managed to survive as long has she has never ceases to amaze me. She suffered a paralytic stroke several years ago and has been bed-ridden ever since. I know she suffers, but the poor old soul never utters a word of complaint, just patiently accepts whatever life deals her." He chuckled. "She was ill as a child, and promised God she would serve him all her life if she could only survive her illness. She grew up a Baptist, became a Methodist when she married my father, John Latourette. My father died young, only forty years old, never recovered from the war. When she married George Funderberg, she obligingly became a Dunkard, for that was his church. After he died and she and John joined me out here in California, she reverted back to Methodist."

Eliza chimed in. "Poor old soul says it doesn't matter what church you go to, they all worship the same God."

Matilda smiled. "It would be a much more tolerant world if more people subscribed to her philosophy. I'd really like to meet her. Could I come by and see her?"

"By all means. Lew has become such a regular visitor that we look upon you as family. Come by anytime." Eliza hesitated, then added, "But I would suggest you come soon. She grows frailer by the day, and each morning prays that this will be the day the Lord comes to take her home. I think she's tired of putting up with that paralyzed body."

"The poor dear. I will make it a point to come this Sunday after church."

Chapter 50

August to November, 1886

Elizabeth Funderberg died on August 3, and was buried in the Liberty Cemetery. As Matilda stood at her graveside, she could only think how bravely the woman had awaited death.

Lew stood beside her, with Media clinging to his arm. She had to smile at the sight. It did look like there would be a wedding in the not too distant future.

As family and friends gathered at the Latourette residence after the services, Matilda met P.H.s brother John, a quiet unassuming man, Willie, P.H.'s son, a lad of sixteen, and little Johnny, a boy of ten. "We had a daughter Minnie, just a year and a half younger than Willie," Eliza explained, "but she died at three years of age. Poor little thing took the scarlet fever. The doctors did everything they could, but we lost her anyway." Eliza's eyes filled with tears.

Lew and P.H. joined them. P.H. had his arm over Lew's shoulders. "Lew and I are thinking of going into partnership together. Will have some details to work out, but we'll have a chance to discuss them when we go to Sacramento on the 14th." He took Matilda's hand. "So glad we have an opportunity to get acquainted with you and Mrs. Douglass. Lew has spoken of you so often."

D.K. joined them. "Just got back from Tracy. Alf's crew is working away down there. Looks like he's got enough work lined up to keep him busy all season. Says he's got good prospects and lots of grain ahead."

"I'm glad. He invested all that money in that harvester. I know his wife was concerned they would not make enough off of custom harvesting to pay for it, so it looks like she did not have to worry."

D.K. grinned. "Just so he doesn't set the fields on fire like Quiggle's crew did over at the Marengo Ranch. Takes the profit out of it right quick."

P.H. shook Kidder's hand and said, "I understand your fame is spreading. Rumor says a gentleman from Stockton sent his thoroughbred up to Galt on the train to be shod by you and Sparks, saying your work is superior to what he could get done in Stockton. I'd say that's quite a compliment."

D.K. tried to look modest and failed completely. Matilda smothered a smile. "Yep," he admitted. "It was a beautiful horse. I can see why the owner was so particular about who worked on him."

Reverend Dyer approached to offer his sympathy and P.H. moved on.

Matilda turned to D.K. "Is it true that the Pattons have sold the Galt House and are moving to Stockton?"

"Yes. Say they have been here for nineteen months and don't care to live in Galt any longer."

Matilda smiled. "The fight with Monahan didn't have any influence on their decision?"

D.K. chuckled. "They didn't say, but odds at the Arcade say that's the main reason. Also, looks like George May will re-open the Galt House, so it will continue in business."

Lew returned from the Prohibitionist Convention in Sacramento grinning from ear to ear. "Mother, you are looking at the candidate for the 20th Assembly District on the Prohibitionist ticket."

She laughed. "Congratulations. It would never have occurred to me to vote Prohibitionist, were I allowed to vote, but out of loyalty to the candidate, I suppose we can get Bill to vote for you."

"And P.H. is the candidate for Supervisor."

The rest of August passed in reasonable quiet, with only a few incidents of note. An incendiary set fire to a large grain stack belonging to John Hicks. A son, Merritt, was born to James Hicks. The first week in September showed wheat at the unheard of price of $1.50 cwt. The steamer *Apache* collided with the plunger *Lizzie* in Three Mile Slough near Rio Vista, killing one crewman.

"P.H. is taking a two week vacation in the mountains," Lew reported. "He's asked me to keep an eye on the shop while he is gone. If it works out well, we'll set up that partnership he has been talking about." He gave her a sideways glance. "And I popped the question to Media. We've set the date tentatively for next June."

"That's wonderful. Congratulations. She is a lovely girl, and comes from a fine family." She hugged him. "You are just full of news today. Anything else?"

"Just that Mrs. McCauley is going to spend the winter in Missouri with her relatives." He grinned slyly. "And George is going with her."

"And leaving his bride?"

"And leaving his bride."

Bill joined them. "Wasn't there a preacher named McWhorter here some years back?"

"Yes," Matilda replied. "Milton McWhorter. Eight or nine years ago. Why?"

"Because he is the one who shot Robinson in Sacramento a couple of weeks ago. Robinson left a sickly widow and several children. Not exactly the behavior you would expect from a preacher."

"Well," Matilda said, with some hesitancy, "he was a good preacher, but he did tend to be a little impetuous."

"And the judge dismissed Alice Valensin's suit against her husband. He ruled there had been an agreement between them, and some of the money had come from Italy. The land should be worked as community property." Bill grinned. "And she had to pay court costs."

Lew laughed. "I'll bet she's mad about that."

"I'm sure. But I doubt we've heard the end of it. They've defaulted on a loan, and the property they gave for security is being auctioned on the 14th. "

The next major news to reach them was the surrender and capture of Geronimo on the fourth of September. Matilda sighed with relief to think that this event probably heralded the end of the Indian wars.

October brought the news that Dr. Montague planned to return to his practice in Galt in a few weeks.

"I'm so glad," Matilda sighed. "It will be nice to have him back. Dr. Patterson and Dr. Sanborn seem quite competent, but I just don't have the faith in them I have in Dr. Montague."

"And D.K. and Sparks are dissolving their partnership," Lew added. "Sparks will continue the business alone. D.K. is determined to move to Santa Barbara. Says since his brother A.M. died of consumption last September, his father needs him. When he was there for A.M.'s funeral he noticed how frail his father had become. Uncle Sevier has been living alone since Aunt Elizabeth died in '83. He can't expect his brother's widow to care for him. Poor Mina's busy enough trying to keep A.M.'s photography business going, and both of their girls live down in Arizona. Says he should be closer."

"He's probably right. I'm glad he feels he should take on the responsibility for his father's care. What does Maggie think about the move? And Lizzie and Bud? Are they going too?"

"Maggie says Santa Barbara is a beautiful area, and is looking forward to the move. Lizzie will go with them. Bud says he's going to stay here. He's old enough. Asked D.K. about him being on the ballot for Justice of the Peace, since he'll be leaving. He says he'll keep the job until he's ready to go, then resign." Lew chuckled and reached for another biscuit. "He may miss the job. Feller named John Brown stole Kidder's watch and Kidder sentenced him to a year in prison."

"Just for stealing a watch? Isn't that a little harsh?"

Lew shrugged. "Just goes to show, if you're going to rob someone, don't rob the Justice of the Peace!"

Mary looked up from the letter Lew had brought her with a smile. "Mary says Wes shot a huge bear right outside of their home in Placerville. Says the hide made a beautiful rug, but the meat was too tough to eat. She also says she would rather be back here. Bears scare her. Mining isn't paying much anyway, and it's already starting to get colder. She's not expecting another baby yet, but is hoping. She wants to come home for the birth."

"About time. Jessie must be almost eight."

"She was seven in April, and Chester is two years younger. At least Dr. Montague should be back before the next one comes, since she's not expecting yet. Got a lot of time." Mary grinned and folded the letter back into its envelope. "I suspect that's one reason she wants to come back." She added, with a chuckle, "And I suspect bears are the other."

The Hicksville school report came out in November, and Sammie was third in the school, with a 97, a figure he proudly reported to his mother. "Cousin Harry only had an 83. And Miss Dippel said I was not late one time."

"I would hope not," Mary said, a bit caustically. "You can see the schoolhouse from the front porch."

Sam appeared from Sulphur Creek for another visit with the news that the next Randolph would put in his (or her) appearance in July. "Belle is hoping for a girl this time. And she will be real happy to hear Dr. Montague will be back."

"Are you thinking of moving back here to stay?" Lew asked. "Are the mines doing anything?"

"Not much," he admitted. "Hear they are overhauling the bridges between here and Galt. If they fix them so a body can get across in the winter, I may consider it."

"Well, our big news here," Matilda told him proudly, "is that Mr. Latourette has invited Lew to be his partner in his tin shop in Galt."

"So they'd better get the bridges fixed," Lew grinned. "Otherwise I won't be able to get to work. And congratulations are in order. Media has agreed to be my wife."

"That's no surprise. We've known that was coming for a long time. When is the big day? We'll have to come."

"Next June."

As Mary, Carrie, and Matilda prepared pies for the Thanksgiving feast the next day, Lew came by with the mail.

"Letter for you Mary, from George's sister up in Montana. Why should she be writing you?"

"It must be about the children." Mary snatched the letter from her brother's hand and tore it open, tearing the letter itself in her haste. She hastily scanned the single page and met her mother's worried eyes. "It's about Mable," she said, her voice harsh. "She says she's begged George to bring her home. She had such a bad winter last year, and never fully recovered from her cough. Mary's afraid another winter in Montana will kill her, but George is doing so well in the mines he refuses to leave, or let Mary bring her to me." Her eyes hardened. "He's going to kill her, Mother. I'm going to talk to Grove Johnson. There must be something I can do to get her away from that horrible place. If he can't do anything, I'll go and get her myself."

Chapter 51

November,1886 to January, 1887

MARY CONSULTED WITH Grove Johnson, and learned she now had reason to file for divorce, since George had abandoned her, and had sent no money for her support during his absence,

"I didn't tell Mr. Johnson I'd have thrown it back in his face if he had," Mary told her mother on her return from the lawyer's office. "He says he'll start proceedings to get George to return Mable and Earl, since I can file for custody. He says the letter from George's sister will prove he has "shown a reckless disregard for her well being" as he says." Mary's face was grim. "I don't care what he calls it, just so I get her back before that awful place kills her."

But their efforts were too late to save Mable. A week later, a telegram arrived from Montana reporting that the child had died on December 3.

Mary's reaction frightened Matilda. She did not cry, or even speak to anyone of the death. She went about her day-to-day activities in haunted silence. Christmas was a grim one. Kidder and Maggie left shortly afterwards for Santa Barbara.

"Really hate to leave," Kidder said. "Sparks and I had a good business going. And I did enjoy being Justice of the

Peace. But Pa is getting feebler, and since Ma died, A.M. has been the one to look after him. Now that A.M. is gone. . . ." His voice caught as he mentioned the brother he had so recently lost.

Matilda patted his arm, and Bill said gruffly, "Good you feel the responsibility, Son. It speaks well for you."

"Be good for Maggie, too. She doesn't say much, but she still grieves for little Alfred. Complete change might help bring her out of it."

Bill chuckled. "Funny, we elect two Justices, you and Will Hicks. You're moving away and Will doesn't qualify. Guess the Board of Supervisors is going to have to pick someone. Will probably go for Meacham and Simons, since they're the two Republicans, and the Board is three Republicans and two Democrats."

"Yes," Matilda agreed. "Heaven forbid they would consider any qualifications other than political party."

On the first of January, Bill brought in the latest copy of the *Galt Gazette*, folded open, and placed it in her hands. She put down the dishtowel she held and took the paper. Her eyes fell on the article he indicated, and she read it through her tears.

In Memoriam

"Little Mable Douglass, aged 7 years, 10 months, and 26 days, daughter of Mr. and Mrs. George Douglass, departed this life on the 3rd of December, 1886, at the home of her aunt, in Butte City, Montana. Little Mable was a sweet child, loved by all who knew her. She was taken away in her early youth. God loved her and chose to take her soul to his Heavenly home."

Matilda's vision blurred and she could not read the poem that followed, dedicated to Mable. "What a sweet memorial to her," she whispered to Bill through her tears. "I hope it is a comfort to Mary."

"We'll hope so," he said gently, "but is it a comfort to Matilda?" He took her in his arms and she wept against his shoulder, thankful she had him. It was so hard being strong for Mary. It just felt good to be able to let go of her emotions.

When she had cried herself out, she smiled at him. "Thank you. I guess I needed that." She noticed him rubbing his side and felt a stab of fear, remembering that was the first symptom Alfred showed of the illness that killed him. "What's the matter?"

He smiled to reassure her. "Just a touch of wind in the stomach."

Lew came in a week later, the paper in his hand, grinning from ear to ear. "Paper says," he chortled, "that 'the departure of D.K. Stringfield from Galt is daily creating more and more anxiety among our fellow townsmen, from the fact that Mr. Stringfield was a little too familiar with 'means' that did not justify the 'ends.' Interesting."

"What are they talking about?" Mary demanded. Matilda echoed her question. Bill chimed in. "Has Kidder done something underhanded?"

"I have no idea," Lew admitted. "But I sure mean to try and find out." He handed the paper to Bill. "Guess Media's brother, young Willie, is in the hospital in Stockton. They say he has a cancer. Guess he's been sick a couple of weeks, and looks like its gone into spinal meningitis. Poor lad's not seventeen yet. Whole family is devastated. P.H.

says he's leaving the shop in my hands, as he and the missus want to spend every possible moment with the boy." He shook his head. "All Media does is cry. Says he's going to die." With a deep sigh, he added, "And I'm afraid she may be right."

"Poor Mr. Latourette. And so soon after losing his mother."

"That was a welcome release. This will be a major blow. Willie is the light of his father's life."

Media's prediction proved correct. Willie Latourette died on January 9th at the hospital in Stockton, of spinal meningitis, and was buried in the Liberty Cemetery next to his grandmother.

In the weeks that followed, Matilda tried to get life somewhat back to normal. Bill continued to have gastric upsets, and consulted with specialists in Stockton. She tried to convince herself the problem was minor, but the nagging fear never left her. The weather turned cold, with a number of days getting down to 30 degrees. She looked out over frost-laden fields day after day.

Word reached them that Dr. Montague, instead of returning to Galt as reported, was now living in New York City.

"He did say he planned to spend a year in New York catching up on the latest in medicine," Matilda mused when Bill told her. "But I wish he would come back. I'm sure he could fix up your stomach problems in no time."

Bill only laughed. "Your faith in Dr. Montague is admirable, but I'm sure the Stockton physicians are fully as capable." He placed the mail on the table. "Mrs. Herbert says Nigger Doc is ailing, has been for a couple of months. Seems his heart is weak, gets fainting spells. Says nothing the docs give him seems to help. Right concerned about him, she is. He's kind of a favorite around the neighbor-hood."

"Oh, yes," Matilda said. "I've known Nigger Doc for years. Such a polite gentleman, never married or had family that anyone knows about, just took in that one girl he raised." She laughed. "I suspect he was a runaway slave, and that's why he never said anything about where he's from or who his kin are."

"Does anyone know his real name?"

"It's William Wyatt, but that's all I know. He must be about sixty, although it's hard to say. He's kind of ageless. Alf says Doc was here in Hicksville when he bought his place in '58, so he has been here a long time. Got the name as he kind of set himself up as an herbalist, used to dose the neighborhood before any regular doctors moved in." She shrugged. "Still are some as swear by him, and I guess his record for cures isn't any worse than theirs." She thought of Alfred and Caroline and Becky, and how futile the current medical treatments had been. "We'll just have to hope for the best."

William Wyatt died January 23rd, and was buried in the Hicksville Cemetery. Matilda stood on the cold ground and watched his coffin lowered into the grave.

Mary visited Grove Johnson several times, determined to make George return Earl to her, and, finally, word came that George would be coming back to Hicksville as soon as the snow permitted travel from the remote area where he lived.

She reported the news grimly to her mother. "He's admitted that perhaps it was wrong to take the children up there. I think Mable's death shook him. He's always so cocksure of himself, always so convinced he's right. He wouldn't listen to me when I told him Mable couldn't stand those cold winters."

455

"Did he indicate when he would be back?"

"No, but it can't be too soon to suit me." She scowled. "And if he thinks I'm going back to live with him when he gets home, he's got another think coming. I've told Mr. Johnson to go ahead and draw up the divorce papers. He can go back to his mother. She can wait on him hand and foot, and iron his shirts just the way he wants them." Her face lighted and she smiled. "I saw Frank Walton the other day. He had come to Hicksville to consult with Mr. Hansen on some blacksmithing job he was working on. He's still single, you know."

"Mary!"

"Oh, nothing improper, Mother. He was very polite. His sister Penny has a little girl now. She's three years old already, and a bright little thing. Frank is crazy about her. And from what he says, his father is very active in the Elk Grove Odd Fellows Lodge. In fact, Frank says his father was one of the charter members. I told him Uncle Alf is a member of the Galt Lodge." Her eyes twinkled. "But if Mr. Johnson is successful in ridding me of George Douglass . . . ." Her voice trailed off.

"Just so you wait until he does," said Matilda firmly.

"Yes, Mother," said Mary demurely, and burst into peals of laughter.

Alf came bursting through the door, his face red, his hair disheveled, practically foaming at the mouth, so upset he was tongue-tied.

Matilda stared at him. "For Heaven's sake, what on Earth has happened to get you so upset? Somebody set fire to your barn? Emma decide to go back to Kansas? Here, calm down." She ushered him to a chair. "Have a cup of coffee and tell us what's the problem."

He sat and took several deep breaths. "It's that Count

Valensin."

"What's he done now?" Mary asked wryly.

"Remember when Mrs. Valensin brought suit against him to try and get back some of her money? Saying he had taken it from her for his own uses? Used it to buy race horses is what he did, so she had, in my view, a legitimate complaint."

Matilda hid a smile. She knew Alf strongly disapproved of horse racing as he did all other forms of gambling. Of course he would side with Alice in her suit.

"Anyways, me and Derby Cantrell posted bond for $6,000. When she brought the suit, she attached his property, so we went on the attachment bond as sureties. Now, after Sawyer, that Circuit Court judge, ruled in favor of Valensin, he's suing us for the $6,000." He ran his fingers through his hair and looked at her in despair. "What am I going to do 'Tilda? Where am I ever going to get the $3,000 if he wins the suit? Emma is all in a tizzy, telling me I was a fool to offer the bond in the first place. But how was I to know? I thought sure Mrs. Valensin would win. Who'd ever think a judge would be fool enough to rule in his favor?"

Matilda, her mind frantically trying to think of some way to calm him, finally said, "He's just filed the suit. It will be some time before it comes up in court. And then maybe it will be overturned. Let's not borrow trouble." We have enough, she thought, without worrying about something that may not happen. "If the judgment goes against you, I'm sure between all of us we can raise the money." And pray it doesn't come to that, she added in her mind.

Alf sighed heavily. "Thanks 'Tilda. I guess I just needed a good dose of your common sense." He sniffed in appreciation. "Is that apple pie I smell?"

She laughed, re-filled his coffee cup, and turned to Mary. "Please get your Uncle Alf a piece of pie."

The next complaint she heard about the Count came from Mrs. Herbert, about his attempts to close off the by-road from the County road to the Arno Station. "At least the Supervisors have some sense," she sputtered. "Last Monday they told Roadmaster Bryant in no uncertain terms to re-open that road, that taxpayer money had maintained it ever since the train went through, and Valensin had no right to close it off."

"Oh, yes," Matilda responded. Other events had driven the matter from her mind. "I remember both Bill and Lew signed the petition."

"Guess we showed that uppity Count, him as is neither an American citizen or a resident of the county." She smirked in satisfaction. "Yep, Supervisors told Bryant to re-open the road, remove all of the Count's obstructions, and keep the highway clear for "the general use of the public. So the Count can put that in his pipe and smoke it!"

Chapter 52

February to June, 1887

SPRING CAME EARLY in 1887. Matilda welcomed the warmer days after the cold of January. By the end of February, farmers were still sowing wheat, hoping the mild weather would lead to a bumper crop.

The partnership of Latourette and Baldwin flourished. Lew seemed to enjoy the change from farming, and the wedding plans continued.

She tried to hide her concern for Bill's health. He continued to travel to Stockton once a week to consult with doctors. Various medicines were tried, but none seemed to have any effect.

"Don't worry, Love," he tried to reassure her. "Can't be too serious. If it was, I'd think I'd be sicker by now. Just sort of seems to be there all the time." He laughed. "Don't worry about me. Save your sympathy for poor Mrs. Bottimore. I hear the Bottimore boy was striking two shells together to see how much it would take to set them off. Guess he found out. One of 'em exploded and gave him a nasty wound just above his eye."

"It's a wonder it didn't kill him," Matilda gasped. "How could he be so foolish?"

"Doc Nestell said the same thing when he treated him,

that it was a foolish stunt, and it was a miracle it didn't kill him." Bill chuckled. "Well, they say God looks out for fools and little boys, and it seems Charley Bottimore is both."

Grove Johnson continued on Mary's application for divorce. Mary reported with satisfaction that all the papers were ready to serve on George the moment he reappeared in Hicksville.

"And the Court has lowered poor Emma's claim down to $600. From the $3,000 Uncle Billy wanted to give her down to $1,800, and now down to $600," Mary reported. "Poor Uncle Billy tried so hard to do right by her, but the lawyers seem to be getting the lion's share."

"Maybe Shakespeare had the right idea," Lew muttered.

In May, Bill came home with the paper in his hand, grinning from ear to ear. "Well, George McCauley has filed for divorce from his Lizzie. Seems while he was in Missouri this past winter with his mother, his bride took up with a young man employed at the State Capitol, and they traveled together up and down the State until he grew tired of her and left her."

Matilda just stared at him.

"Yep, then she tried to commit suicide down on the Oakland mole, but some bystander stopped her."

"Too bad," Lew muttered. "Would 'a made it a lot easier for poor old George."

"Anyway, he accused her of adultery with seventeen different persons."

"Seventeen?" Matilda had difficulty grasping such a number. "Seventeen?"

"Seems so," Bill grinned. "They say she is now running a high class bawdy house in Fresno."

Lew laughed. "If she contests this divorce, Bill, it should be a very interesting trial."

Bill nodded, "That's what the paper says."

Plans for Lew and Media's wedding, scheduled for June 6, continued. The ceremony would take place at the Latourette's lovely home in Galt, and Reverend Dyer would officiate. Matilda felt a little guilty for not using Reverend Bauer, but the bride's family made the decision, and they attended the Congregational Church.

Bill finally gave up on the Stockton doctors. Matilda had felt he was wasting his time and money, but had said nothing, hoping for Dr. Montague's speedy return. Instead, he consulted with Dr. Sanborn in Galt.

"Wants me to go to San Francisco, he does, to that Hahnamann Hospital for an operation," he said. "Says I have a tumor in the epigastric region. Says their specialists should be able to take care of it."

Matilda felt the blood drain from her face. Stunned, she could not move. Not again, she thought. Please, God. Not again.

"When do you have to go?" she finally got her breath back enough to ask.

"The day after Lew and Media get hitched." He took her in his arms and she clung to him. "Told Doc Sanborn there's no way I'm gonna miss this wedding."

Memorial Day at the cemetery was the first hot day of the season. The men sweated profusely as they cleared the graves in their annual weed-cleaning ritual. The women kept them supplied with lemonade and fried chicken.

"Should have come yesterday, it was a lot cooler," Helen Putney remarked. Her eyes went to her husband, George, who faithfully cleared the graves of his first wife and their little daughter. Matilda never passed the grave without remembering sweet little Jenny.

Mary walked over to Earnest's grave. Tears sprang into her eyes. "I begged George to bring Mable home, Mother, so I could lay her to rest beside Earnest, but he said it "wasn't practical". So he buried her back there in that cold, lonely place where she won't have any family at all."

Matilda thought of Lewis and Baby John, buried at the Randolph Cemetery back in Kansas. Well, at least they were together. And Baby John had five little cousins buried there as well. She walked over to Alfred's grave. They were going to have to get a headstone before his death date was forgotten. A wave of fear washed over her as she thought of possibly losing Bill as she had lost Alfred. She forced it back, but it never completely left her.

Afterwards, Lew and Media joined the rest of the family on the front porch at Matilda's home to discuss the wedding. Matilda liked Media more and more each time she saw her. She was a charming girl, petite and pretty. Her family, she told them, had been in America for many years.

"The Latourettes came over when the French revoked the Edict of Nantes in 1685," she explained. "They were Huguenots, and they knew the Crown was getting ready to persecute them."

"Why would they want to do that?" Sam queried.

Media shrugged. "I guess they just wanted an excuse to take their property. Many of the Huguenots were fairly well off. Some old priest had a lot of influence with the Queen, and he hated Huguenots because they weren't Catholics. Funny thing is, they had moved to France from Italy to escape persecution in the 1500's.

"Anyway," she continued, "Count Henri of La Vedee, my ancestor, found out his name was on the proscribed list, and that they were being watched. So he made a deal with a British captain whose ship was in the port to leave at night as soon as they got on board. They gave this big celebration to fool the police. Under the cover of the party, the Count and the Countess snuck away, with their jewels, what gold they could carry, and the family Bible. They rowed out to the ship, and true to his word, the captain raised anchor as soon as they got aboard and brought them to New York."

"Wow," Sam exclaimed. "That must have been exciting."

Media smiled in her gentle way. "They had planned to go to South Carolina, but got blown off course and wound up on Staten Island. They bought land there with the gold they had smuggled out of France. Later, they sold it and moved over to New Jersey. When my grandfather John was four years old, his family moved to Clark County, Ohio. My Uncle John is out here, and my aunt, Mollie Mead, lives in Santa Cruz. But my aunt Sarah still lives in Ohio. She married a veteran of the War of the Rebellion, and I have a lot of cousins there."

She smiled shyly at Lew. "Maybe, after we're married, we could go and visit. I'd like that. When my mother went back a couple of years ago, she made contact with them. My father wrote to one, a Peter Latourette, and got a lot of information on the family from him. My father never knew any of the story, for he had never paid any attention when his grandparents talked about the family history."

Matilda laughed. "Your family has been in America almost as long as ours. The Randolphs came in 1635 and settled on Turkey Island, Virginia."

Media smiled. "My grandmother, Elizabeth, the one who just died, was a Rall. The Ralls were Dutch, and lived in

463

New York while it was still New Amsterdam. They came around 1640 or so. Grandmother could have told you. I forget the exact dates. The Dutch name was Jan Mangel. When the English defeated the Dutch in 1664, and changed the name of the colony to New York, he changed his name to John Rall." She giggled. "Guess he wanted an English name."

"Probably a good idea," Lew commented dryly.

June 6 dawned bright and sunny promising another warm day. Family and friends gathered at the Latourette residence to watch Reverend Dyer pronounce Lewis Gardner Baldwin and Armedia Latourette man and wife. The Latourette home was filled with flowers, and the punch was served in a magnificent crystal bowl. Matilda could not help but feel the tinsmithing business had been very good to Mr. Latourette.

Media shyly approached the bower set up by the fireplace for the ceremony. She wore a lovely silk gown of a soft ecru, her veil covering the blond curls. Lew looked so handsome in his best (and only) broadcloth suit. Matilda's heart swelled with pride as she looked at him. Lewis, my darling, she thought, her mind flying to the father Lew had never known, I wish you could see your son. You would be so proud of him.

The family of Henry Putney did not attend. Henry's brother George made their apologies. "My nephew, George, was kicked bad by a horse, a mean 'un I warned him to get rid of several times. Kicked in the breast and shoulder, broke three ribs, and bruised a kidney." George shook his head sadly. "Docs don't hold out much hope for his recovery."

"What a shame," Matilda cried. "And him just graduating from Sacramento Business College. Such a promising young man." She also knew George was Henry and Rhoda's only son, and the joy of his parents and sisters.

After the festivities, the new Mr. and Mrs. Baldwin took up residence in the home Bill Frye had purchased from Tom Randolph. Media had made it homelike before the wedding, with a number of examples of her crochet work on the furniture. Bill, as a bachelor, had kept it pretty stark. Lew's grandfather's chair, the one Gardner Randolph had brought across the prairie, stood at the head of the table

Matilda felt badly the young couple had no opportunity for a honeymoon, but Lew was needed at the ranch.

"It's fine, Mother," Lew reassured her. "Bill's health comes first. Media and I can take a honeymoon trip after you get back from San Francisco and Bill gets well."

So the following day, leaving Mary in charge of the household and Carrie and Sam, and Lew to run the ranch, Matilda and Bill took the morning train to San Francisco. Dr. Sanborn joined them at the Galt Station.

Under other circumstances, Matilda would have enjoyed the trip to San Francisco, through fields of ripening grain sparkling in the morning sun. At Oakland, the train car was mounted on a ferry for the crossing to San Francisco. Fog still hung over the city, and she remembered how cold it had been when she and Alfred had come on their honeymoon, so long ago. She thought of Mrs. Boone, now dead these past ten years. And Emperor Norton, who was also gone.

The city had matured in the twenty years since she had first seen it. They rode in one of the cable cars that had been put in after her last visit. As the operator gripped the cable and the little car began slowly climbing up the hill, she clung to Bill's arm, half in excitement, half in nervousness. These hills were as frightening as ever.

Bill grinned and patted her hand. "Relax. These cars are perfectly safe. Much safer than trying to negotiate these hills with a horse and buggy."

She gave a nervous laugh, remembering her feelings as Mrs. Boone's driver Charlie had driven them down the steep sides of Telegraph Hill. "I suppose so," she said, a little dubiously.

When they reached the hospital, perched on top of a hill, she had to admit it was an imposing edifice. She only wished they were there under more auspicious circumstances. Her heart raced as she realized Bill would soon see doctors who could, hopefully, cure him, or tell her there was no cure.

Several doctors met them, but the names did not register in Matilda's memory. Her whole being was with Bill as she watched them lead him away from her. He flashed her a reassuring grin as they whisked him out of her sight.

Unable to sit still, she paced nervously about the little reception room, waiting for the doctors to complete their examination. Nurses in immaculate white uniforms, with frilly starched caps, flitted busily to and fro. One offered her coffee, and spent a few moments trying to reassure her.

Finally, Dr. Sanborn emerged from the room. She rose to meet him and he took her hand. "They will operate tomorrow. Then we will know for sure what the problem is. Try not to worry. I will arrange a room for you in a nearby residence hall."

She attempted to thank him, but her vocal cords were so tight no words came out.

He seemed to understand. "Would you like to see him?"

She could only nod, and followed him to a long room with rows of beds. Bill was lying on the one next to the wall at the end of the room. In the bed, dressed in the white gown, he looked smaller, as though somehow diminished.

But his grin was as infectious as ever. He held out his arms and she flew into his embrace. "Doc tell you they want to cut into me tomorrow? Get out whatever this is that's been eatin' at me." He held her at arms length and shook her gently before folding her into his arms again. "Shoo, now, go ahead and cry. I'm gonna come through this just fine, you wait and see if I don't."

The next morning, she rose after a restless night. She did not know if it was the lumpy bed, the strangeness of her surroundings, or her concern for Bill, but sleep had eluded her in spite of her exhaustion. Probably a combination of all three, she thought, looking at her haggard face in the little mirror. Was it just her imagination, or were there actually more gray hairs now? How old am I, anyway, she thought, thinking back. She had turned fifty last July, and would be fifty-one in a few weeks. Heavens, she thought. I'm an old woman.

When she reached the ward, she was told Mr. Frye was with the doctors in surgery, and probably would not be out for several hours. The kind nurse who had brought her coffee the previous day now brought her another cup and a bowl of hot porridge. Matilda had no appetite, but knew she should keep up her strength, so she forced herself to eat. Afterwards, she could not recall what it tasted like, but a slight, medicinal smell hung over everything. .

The time dragged by. Matilda tried to keep her mind from dwelling on the fear that Bill would not survive the operation, trying to convince herself he would come through this and be himself again.

At last. after several endless hours, Dr. Sanborn appeared. At least he was smiling, so Matilda was encouraged.

"The problem was his spleen, not a tumor as I had feared.

The spleen was much enlarged, and had lost its attachments, so it moved about freely." He shook his head. "Must have been twenty doctors come to check it out. None had ever seen anything like it. They hope the inflammatory adhesions from the operation will hold the spleen in place."

She could only gape at him. "Will he recover?" she finally managed to gasp.

"We will hope so. Since there has never been a similar case, to anyone's knowledge, there can be no guarantees." He smiled gently. "We will just have to hope for the best."

Not very encouraged, Matilda asked, "When can I see him?"

"He should be awake in a few hours. If you wish, you can sit by his side and wait." He escorted her to the ward where Bill lay on the bed, silent and unmoving. A nurse stood beside him. She looked up and smiled as Matilda joined them.

Matilda sat down and took Bill's hand in hers. He did not respond.

She sighed. It was going to be a long day.

Chapter 53

July, 1887

MATILDA AND BILL returned home early in July, with strict orders for Bill to stay in bed for two more weeks. His rapid recovery from the surgery encouraged Matilda, and she was glad to be home.

Almost the first thing she learned was that George Putney had died on June the 12th, from his many injuries.

Mary told her she and Carrie and Sam had attended his funeral, as did Lew and Media. "Real sad, Mother. He rallied after a couple of days and the family was encouraged he might survive, but he slipped back and died." Tears flowed down her cheeks as she described her visit to the dying young man. "He was in such pain, Mother, and so brave."

"Seems to be the season for it," Carrie added. "Young Will Journay was kicked in the chest a few days ago. Took him to the hospital in Stockton. Haven't heard any more, but guess he wasn't hurt as bad as poor George." She smiled. "The other thing you missed, Mother, is that Celestia Johnson has filed for a divorce from Dick. Charges him with 'failure to provide, desertion, etc.' Says Dick will not contest the charges. I gather all has not been well in the Johnson household for some time."

"And Lack Quiggle and Dan McKenzie bought one of

those new combined harvesters. They were bringing it home when it overturned in front of Whitaker and Ray's." He chuckled. "Cost about thirty dollars to repair the damage they did to it. That's a lot of money, and it sure made Lack mad, and he blamed Dan for taking the corner too fast."

Matilda had to laugh in spite of her fatigue and her concern for Bill. "Sounds like it has been an exciting week." She settled into her favorite chair and took a sip of coffee from the cup Carrie placed in front of her. She smiled her thanks at her daughter. "It's so good to be home."

On Saturday, June 25, the closing exercises for the Hicksville School were held at the church. Bill, of course, could not attend, but he assured Matilda he would be fine alone for the short time she would be gone to the ceremonies. Miss Dippel had gone to a great deal of effort to put on a fine program. As usual, the girls out ranked the boys in scholarship, Blanche Dowzer and Mamie Keagle with 99, Mary McGuirk and Hattie Cottrel 98.

She applauded Sammie's performance of "The Lost Pantaloons", and enjoyed the rest of the program as well.

Miss Dippel spoke to her afterwards. "I'm so glad you came, Mrs. Frye. I know you have a great deal on your mind just now, but it means so much to the children to have an appreciative audience."

"I enjoyed it very much, Miss Dippel." She hesitated. "I have been so concerned about Bill for so long it was good for me to get out for an evening."

When June eased into July and Bill continued to improve, Matilda began to be encouraged.

Lew swung by on his way home to tell her Media's little brother Johnny had stepped on a rusty piece of iron, receiving a three inch long and very painful wound. "Doc Sanford cleaned it up and sewed it back together. Says if it doesn't suppurate he should be fine. I know Media is real worried. After losing Willie she has been so protective of Johnny."

"Just pray he does not develop lockjaw," Matilda said.

"Not even going to mention lockjaw to Media. She's worried enough already. Especially since her mother has been right sick. But she seems to be getting better." He grinned. "And they tell me Charlie Quiggle had an operation last week, but is recovering well. He has re-opened the Arcade Saloon."

"I hope you have no plans to attend his opening celebration."

"Not me." He shook his head for emphasis. "I don't ever want to feel like that again."

Matilda chuckled softly.

"And I see George McCauley was granted a divorce from his lovely bride, so he is again a free man."

Matilda smiled. "I hope he has learned something from the experience."

"I don't know. Bets are on at the Arcade as to how long it will be until he again subjects himself to petticoat government."

Lizzie Randolph, Will's youngest daughter, returned from Santa Barbara in mid-July for a visit.

"You really should come and visit us in Santa Barbara, Aunt 'Tilda," she exclaimed. "It's so beautiful. And none of this awful heat you have here in the summer. The ocean keeps us cool all year long. Britt's family moved over to Bardsdale, all of them, Sarah and Jim, Gardner, Chase, and Aunt Sarah. They have a beautiful farm there, miles and miles of orchards. Doing real well, they are. But it gets hotter there than in Santa Barbara. I'm glad Maggie and Kidder didn't go with them."

"You're sixteen now. You'll probably be getting married soon."

Lizzie blushed. "Well, Aunt Nancy and Uncle Joel Burnell's son Will has been hanging around. He's real nice, but I don't want to get married yet." She hugged Matilda. "I heard Uncle Bill had an operation, and I wanted to see him. How is he?"

Matilda heart lurched. Last week she would have said very well, but these last few days, her concern for him had increased. Instead of continuing to get stronger, he seemed to be weaker. She sighed. "Not as well as I had hoped."

Bill died on July 25, with Matilda at his side, holding his hand. Dr. Sanborn had left just a short time before, confessing he had nothing more to offer. Matilda was glad he had left, for she preferred to be alone with Bill for his last moments. He drifted in and out of consciousness, but did not seem to be in pain as Alfred had been. She watched his life ebb away.

He roused once and said, "Sorry 'Tilda. Sorry to leave you. They were . . . good, the years we had. . . .wish we could have had more . . . ." His voice trailed off, and he drew a long shuddering breath, and it was over.

She sat in silence, holding his hand. Mary and Carrie found her there. Mary gently eased her hand from Bill's and led her away, while Carrie drew the sheet over the still face.

The services were held at the Hicksville Cemetery, and Matilda added Bill Frye to the long list of loved ones buried there. After the services, the neighbors and family gathered at Matilda's home. She appreciated the support, but just wished they would all go home so she could be by herself.

At last she and Carrie were alone. Dear old Mrs. McGuirk, the last of the funeral guests, had departed and Sam had headed for the barn to start the evening chores. Matilda watched the McGuirk buggy wend its way around the potholes in the lane on its way out the drive.

"Well, Carrie," Matilda confided to the slender girl beside her, "I guess God did not intend for me to be married. Seven years with Lewis, nine with your father, and now only five with Bill." She sighed. "At least I was blessed with three good men, even if for so short a time."

Carrie nodded in sympathy. "I will always stay with you, Mother," she promised. When Matilda demurred, she added firmly, "Even if I do marry, you will stay with us. You will never be alone."

Matilda patted her hand. "You're a good child, Carrie. I only hope someday you will find love as I have." She stood in silence for a moment, then added, "Lewis and I shared young love. First love is special. I can still see the desperation in his face as he looked up at me from the well the day he fell." Her eyes brimmed with tears. "I thought I would never love so deeply again, but my love for your father matched or surpassed my love for Lewis." She sighed. "Bill was such a good man. He made wonderful company for me, even though I never felt as deeply for him as I did for Alfred." She smiled. "At my age, companionship is a good thing."

Tears threatened again, but she shook them off with determination. "Come, Carrie, we have work to do."

Carrie obediently followed her mother into the kitchen. The neighbors had brought in a good deal of food. They worked in silence, stowing dishes in the pantry, or the cool box, and a few things in the precious icebox. Carrie accepted the icebox as a convenience, but Matilda never ceased to marvel at being able to keep food from spoiling, especially the milk and cream. Perhaps had they been able to keep milk fresh, Baby John would not have died. She noticed far fewer babies took the second summer complaint now, especially in homes that had iceboxes.

Life had certainly gotten easier. All of these modern conveniences, lamps instead of candles, ice delivered, where would it all end?

"I wish I could come back a hundred years from now and see all the changes," she burst out suddenly.

Carrie, not having followed her mother's train of thought, replied with a startled, "What?"

Matilda laughed at Carrie's expression and explained what she had been thinking.

"Yes, Mother," Carrie agreed. "I even hear they are working on flying machines, of all things. But right now, I'd settle for an icebox that would make its own ice. Then we wouldn't have to worry about running out before the ice man comes." She picked up one of Mrs. Davis' egg white concoctions and popped it into her mouth. "We really should ask Mrs. Davis for her recipe for these. They're marvelous."

"Carrie," her mother interrupted, her mind not on Mrs. Davis and recipes. "I'm concerned about Mary." George Douglass had returned from Montana the day after Bill's death and persuaded Mary to go home with him for one more attempt at reconciliation. Mary had not spoken to anyone during the day, and had left almost immediately after the funeral. In fact, several people had commented on her behavior. "She's not happy. The only reason she went with George is because he wouldn't let her keep Earl here. She has no right to him until Mr. Johnson gets custody for her."

Matilda sighed and began pumping water from the pump at the sink to refill the teakettle. Putting the kettle on the stove, she spoke, more to herself than to Carrie. "If only she hadn't married so young." She shook her head sadly, "I just felt George Douglass was not right for her. He always had such a violent temper, even as a child."

Carrie said nothing, as Matilda seemed to expect no answer.

Matilda pressed her hands to her temples, as though holding her head together would keep it from bursting. She noticed Carrie watching her anxiously and pulled herself together.

"Come, Carrie," she smiled. "You'd better light the lamps. It's getting dark."

Chapter 54

July to September, 1887

MARY RETURNED the next morning, alone. "It's no use, Mother. I will not spend the rest of my life living with that man." She showed her mother the bruise on the side of her face. "He got roaring drunk last night, and when I refused to give him what he claimed were his 'husbandly rights', he hit me. I spoke with Mr. Johnson this morning. He agrees with me that I can get custody of Earl. He's drawing up the papers."

George appeared an hour later, sober and contrite. "Please, Mary, for the sake of the boy, won't you come back? I promise not to take too much whiskey again."

The blue eyes flashed. "It's for Earl's sake I'm filing for divorce and for custody. You killed Mable, taking her off to that God-forsaken Hell-hole. Do you think for one minute I'm going to take the chance of you doing the same with Earl, should you take another notion to go off somewhere?"

"I'll stay here. My mother wants . . . ."

"Your mother! I might have known. I've listened to your mother's criticism for the last time. You want your mother? You go right ahead and stay with your mother. But Earl and I are going to be here."

Matilda stood aside, watching them spar back and forth,

with the words getting more and more bitter. Just as she felt perhaps she should intervene, George turned on his heel and stalked out of the room.

"And here! Take your old ring. It's got your initials in it, not mine. I should have known better than to marry a man who would put his own initials in his wife's ring. Going to show the world she belongs to you?"

Taking the ring from her finger, she hurled it at his retreating back. Carrie and Sam both stood watching, mouths agape. Matilda saw the ring bounce off of George's back and disappear into the weeds in the yard.

George reached his horse and mounted. "You'll be sorry," he shouted. "You'll never see Earl again."

"We'll see what Grove Johnson has to say about that," she yelled after him, and stomped back into the house, Carrie at her heels.

Sam began a methodical search of the yard, looking for the missing ring. Matilda watched him for a moment, then followed Mary into the house

An hour later, he rejoined his mother and sisters where they sat discussing the morning's events over a cup of coffee. "I can't find it, Mother. I looked and looked."

"Don't worry, Son. It'll show up some day."

A few days later, Sam sat in Bill's usual chair and read to his mother from the newspaper, as his father before him had done, and as he had watched Bill do so many evenings.

Bless him, Matilda thought, he's trying to fill the gap left by Bill. She smiled at him, "Sorry, Son, my mind wandered for a moment. "What did you say about the Count?"

"Just that some fellows from Stockton took him to the Queen's taste. He's always up for any sporting event, and, as usual, had more money than sense. So a bunch of them got together and set up one of their own as a wealthy out-of-town businessman. They rigged a phony race down in Lathrop and got the Count to bet $5,000 on the outcome."

"And he fell for it?"

"Hook, line, and sinker. After the race was over, the supposedly wealthy man went back to his humble job as a driver of a coal and ice wagon. And he and his cohorts went back to town and divvied up the Count's $5,000. As the paper says, "the Count left Lathrop with a heavy heart and a light purse." I wonder how he explained that one to Alice."

Matilda laughed. "I'll bet he doesn't even try. I hear the Supreme Court has granted Alice a new trial. Maybe this time she can be shed of him." She sighed. "At least it will give your Uncle Alf and Mr. Cantrell another chance to get off the hook on this bond surety business. I'm sure your Uncle Alf will be relieved."

Sam nodded. "And should stop some of Aunt Emma's complaints."

"Poor Alf," Matilda sighed. "He can't seem to please her no matter how hard he tries. Too bad she doesn't have another baby. That would give her something else to think about."

August passed in relative quiet. Matilda tried to keep busy, which was not hard to do between the gardening and the canning and all of the daily chores. Lew and his new bride came frequently for Sunday dinner after church.

"Reverend Dyer and his wife have a baby girl," Media told Matilda. "He is so proud."

"And Mr. Hagel got $1.72 a hundred for his grain," Lew added. "Sure hope we get that much. Alf should be done harvesting here in another week. And I hear Jack got himself into a fight at one of the saloons down on Front Street," he continued. "Picked a fight with Will Young, which was a mistake. Will's a right good fighter, and Jack was pretty drunk. Witnesses say Jack brought it on himself, and no one was feeling sorry for him."

"I wish he had stayed over in Lake County.' Matilda shook her head sadly. "Sally and Sam would have kept an eye on him. He's just not been himself since Becky died."

Lew grinned, "Well, Latourette and Baldwin are flourishing. Did you see our notice in the last paper? Hardware, tools, stoves, ranges, pipe, you name it, we carry it. And will install it too, if you want. Have been even talking of hiring another couple of clerks."

"Maybe you should hire your cousin Jack. He needs something to give him a purpose in life."

"After his last little drunken episode? And Pa Latourette a staunch Prohibitionist?"

"I agree, Mother," Mary laughed. "I can't see Mr. Latourette hiring him."

It was Annie Herbert who told Matilda and Mary about Andy Shields. "Manager for Mrs. McCauley, he is. Has a lady here in Hicksville, and harnessed his best mule to his Petaluma cart and drove up here to see her. Hitched the mule to a fence and went in the house to spend an hour with the object of his affections."

"And who is this lady?" Mary asked.

Mrs. Herbert shrugged. "Didn't say, but was close around here. Seems while he was in the house, another would-be swain came by and recognized young Shields' mule. So, to get even, he unhitched the mule, took him to the other side of the fence, then poked to shafts of the cart through the fence and re-hitched the mule."

Mary's laughter interrupted her.

"Yep," she continued, " and Andy still declares he can't figure how that mule ever got through the fence without breaking a board."

Matilda still did not sleep well at night, so she was awake at midnight and saw flames out of the window. She donned her robe and went to Sam's room to rouse him.

"It's from the direction of Hicksville. You'd better go check. Celestia might need help."

She knew she would not be able to go back to sleep until Sam returned, so she went into the kitchen and stirred up the fire enough to heat the water in the teakettle to brew a cup of tea. She sat and sipped the tea while she waited.

When Sam returned, two hours later, he told her what he had found. "Was the Hicksville Hotel, all right. Started on the outside, away from any stove, so it had to have been the work of an incendiary. Just like the Arno Hotel a year ago. Lucky there were some fellows playing cards awake to sound the alarm. Otherwise, those sleeping might not have gotten out. They barely escaped as it was. Whole place was enveloped in flames in no time at all. By the time I got there, the whole building was one massive bonfire."

Matilda sighed. "I guess not everyone wants us to have a hotel at either Arno or Hicksville. I guess they've gotten their way."

"Not for long," Sam grinned. "Mrs. Johnson says she's going to rebuild as soon as possible. Says no low-down scoundrel of an incendiary is going to put her out of business."

"Good for her," Matilda muttered.

At church the next Sunday, Reverend Bauer announced

his last sermon would be on the 24th of September. He also suggested the congregation pray for Mrs. Johnson after her loss in the conflagration.

"He might also ask God to help us catch the incendiary," Sam muttered, half under his breath. Matilda shushed him.

At the conclusion of the services, Matilda spoke briefly with Reverend Bauer. "We're so sorry you'll be leaving us. We'll miss you. Could you not stay on for another term?"

He laughed dryly. "I can't afford it. I have been here for three years, and the congregation is in arrearage for nearly a thousand dollars. I have enjoyed the community, and have made many good friends here, but I fear I must also be able to support my family."

Stunned, Matilda could only gape at him. "But surely," she stammered, "I know I have not been able to donate very much, but . . . ."

"Please, Mrs. Frye. Do not feel you alone are responsible. I knew when I came that a farming community is frequently not a wealthy one, although some here could, no doubt, pay more."

Grove Johnson finally filed the papers for Mary's divorce from George, and Matilda served him the summons on September 23.

"I'm sorry it has come to this, George," Matilda said as she handed him the stack of papers. "But I'm afraid Mary is determined to follow through."

"It's not your fault, Mrs. Frye. I know I'm a hard man to live with." He grimaced. "God knows she's told me that enough. And my mother can be a bit exacting."

That's putting it mildly, Matilda thought, but she made no reply.

"Tell her I won't contest it. She can have Earl. He's

probably better off with his mother. I know she blames me for Mable's death, so I guess I owe her that much."

"Thank you." Matilda did not know why he had this change of heart. Whatever his reason, a wave of relief swept over Matilda as she returned to the buggy where Sam waited. They would be spared the expense and humiliation of a public trial. Charley snorted and stamped a foot, anxious to head for home. Sam helped his mother to her seat and climbed up beside her. As he jiggled the reins, to urge Charley forward, George had one parting shot.

"Maybe she'll be happier with Frank Walton."

Chapter 55

September 1887 to April 1888

AS SOON AS they were out of range of George's hearing, Matilda turned to Sam. "And what did he mean by that remark?" She eyed her son severely, for she knew the boy always enjoyed a good scandal. "Has Mary been seeing Frank Walton?"

Sam's face took on its most innocent look and he shrugged his shoulders expressively. "Guess you will have to ask Mary."

"Oh, I will, you can be sure. I intend to ask her just as soon as we get home."

Mary, of course, was the soul of innocence. "I can't imagine why he would say that, Mother. Frank and I have never exchanged more than a few words." Her eyes fell under her mother's scrutiny. "Well, we did have a dish of ice cream at the restaurant in Celestia's hotel before it burned down." She paused. "And he did give me a ride home from the Post Office in his buggy. I had walked down, and it was such a hot day."

Matilda started to laugh. "Your activities have obviously been noticed by enough people that they have come to George's attention. I advise you to be the soul of discretion until after your divorce is granted. No point in giving him any reason to contest your application for custody of Earl. Can't you imagine what your Aunt Emma and Uncle Alf would say if he accused you of not being a fit mother?"

Two fires a couple of weeks apart on the railroad bridge at Arno and the arrest of George Moore on the charges kept the gossips busy until after Mary's October 11 appearance in court. George, true to his word, did not contest the action, and Mary was free. Two weeks later, on October 28, she was granted custody of Earl.

The following Sunday, they held a celebration dinner after church. Lew and Media came, full of the news of the fires on the Arno bridges.

"They say Moore tried to blame it on Mexicans. Even identified one of them he says he saw setting the first fire." Lew grinned. "Only problem was, the Mexican fellow had an iron-clad alibi. The constable tricked Moore by putting up a young man he knew could not possibly have caused the fires. He's more convinced than ever that Moore is his man. They've got him locked up."

"Good," Matilda said. "Setting fire to that bridge could have caused a wreck and killed a lot of people."

Alf and Emma joined them. Alf had plenty of reason to celebrate. "You were right, 'Tilda," He heaved a sigh of relief. "The Court dismissed Valensin's suit against me and Derby."

"Oh, I'm so glad." Matilda had had tried to convince Alf the suit would be dropped, but she had not been so sure her-self.

"And he has deeded the last two tracts of land here at Hicksville to Alice. So I guess that winds up his business in Sacramento County."

"Is he moving? Are he and Alice really splitting up?"

"They say he bought land over in the Livermore area.

That's all anyone seems to know."

"Jim Hicks is offering a reward for the return of a sorrel horse, a bay mare and colt, and two mules that have strayed from his place," Alf added. "Anyone seen 'em?"

"Not yet," Sam grinned, "But will be glad to go look for 'em. How much is he offering?"

Alf grinned. "He doesn't say. And three horses have strayed from the Valensin ranch as well. Must be the season."

"Shame about that fellow from Elk Grove as fell off his wagon over on the Hicks Bridge. Say he was killed instantly. Fellows that are working on Mrs. Johnson's new hotel told me about it."

"How is the construction coming?" Mary's eyes sparkled. "Frank has asked to escort me to the Thanksgiving Dance she is planning to honor the grand opening."

"Sawyer says construction is right on schedule. So guess it'll be ready for the Ball." Lew sighed. "They say it will be two stories high, with thirty rooms. All hand finished. Should be real elegant."

"And I got a letter from Laura," Matilda announced. "Abe has finally remarried, up in Waputa to a young lady named Susan Theobald. Laura says she was born in Sacramento, so she's from around here. She says now she and Anna can finally get married. Guess she has a young man in mind."

"But the best news of all," Carrie announced shyly, "Is that Mary and I have decided to attend the Stockton School of Business."

Matilda gaped at her youngest daughter. "And you never told me?"

"We wanted to be sure we could attend before we told anyone. And our acceptance letter came yesterday." She

487

smiled. "We decided to tell everyone at once."

Earl settled happily into the little room that had been Sam's until his brother Lew moved out. "It's so good to be home, Mother," he said, "I just wish Mable was here." His eyes filled with tears. "She's waiting for me in Heaven, isn't she, Mother? She promised me she would be."

Mary took him in her arms and held him closely. "Yes, Darling, she is waiting for you in Heaven." Her arms tightened around him. "I just want her to wait a long time," she whispered.

Matilda watched the scene with an ache in her heart. She remembered the little girl who had been so heart-broken to leave, the blue eyes and red hair so like Mary's. She remembered Mary's prediction on the day they left for Montana, and the tears rolled down her cheeks.

Earl enrolled in the Hicksville School, and Mary and Carrie took the train each morning for their classes at the Stockton School of Business. They settled into a routine. The newly re-built Hicksville Hotel held the Thanksgiving Ball on November 21st as planned, and Mary did go with Frank Walton as her escort.

"Road between Hicksville and Galt in bad shape again," Sam reported after dropping his sisters off at the train one morning. "All the fellows at the Arno Station are complaining." He grinned. "They also told me Charlie Quiggle got into a fight with some hoodlums from Stockton. Wound up getting the worst of it."

Matilda sighed. "I'm not surprised. He encourages all of those no good bums to hang around the Arcade. Rumor says he plans to start having chicken and dog fights. Can you imagine what type of clientele he will get to those?"

Winter turned out to be one of the coldest in history. Reports came in of people dying in blizzards throughout the United States. The first week of January even brought an inch of snow to the community of Hicksville.

"Understand they got three inches of snow in Elliott. And they say they've got slush ice in the Sacramento River," Sam reported as he came back from his daily chore of delivering his two sisters to the train station at Arno. He rubbed his hands together, his breath making little clouds in the cold in the room. "Better get this stove cranked up. No point in taking a chance on getting a chill. They say it's the first time in recorded history there's been ice in the Sacramento River down this far."

"Just be glad we don't live in Kansas anymore. I understand it's terrible there. As bad as the winter your grandfather lost so many cattle." She remembered Lewis returning with the heifer he had rescued slung across White Star's pommel. It seemed so many years ago. But she never forgot that biting cold and the mounds of snow that melted the next spring. And the flood that followed.

She realized Sam had spoken and she had not heard a word. She pulled herself back to the present. "Sorry. What did you say?"

He grinned. "I said it's got one good side to it. The ducks and geese have been swarming down. Going to be many a goose dinner."

"Why don't you take the shotgun and see if you can get us some? Goose sounds real tasty. Just be careful." The thought of goose hunting always brought the death of her nephew Michael to mind, even after all of these years.

"And they say Birdie Andruss ran off and got married to a guy named Trueblood out of Stockton."

"Birdie? Why, she can't be more than fifteen!"

489

"Sixteen," Sam replied. "But she told the clerk she was nineteen, and I guess he believed her. Anyway, they're married."

Matilda sighed. "She always has been a flighty little thing. I hope it works out well for her."

Almost the first news to reach them after the holidays was that Billy Bandeen had died. Jane stopped by to visit Matilda and told her all about it.

"We knew his heart was bad, but he was only 62. Expected him to live a little longer than that. His temper probably was his undoing. He would get so violently mad about the silliest little things. Doctors always told him he was going to burst a blood vessel someday."

Matilda murmured a sympathetic sound, but Jane only laughed. "No point in me pretending to grieve, 'Tilda. It would be hypocritical. I have been so happy with Tom I have never looked back. I just feel sorry for Billy for separating himself from his family. Jane is married now and living clear down in Los Angeles, and Nancy lives with her, so I can understand not visiting them. But John is nearby and Will, Jr. lives right here in Hicksville. You'd think he would at least have wanted to meet his grandchildren. Gracie and Merrill are such nice youngsters."

It was on the tip of Matilda's tongue to ask about Billy's estate, but she hesitated. After all, it was really none of her business.

But Jane had already launched into the tale. "Left each of his four children just one dollar," she pronounced indignantly. "And the bulk of his estate to that Betty White person he had been boarding with. John said all along she was after his money. He's not going to let her get away with it. He filed to have the will overturned."

"I hope he is successful."

"I'm sure he will be. Billy had gotten so bitter these last few years any court will have to agree he was not in his right mind. And she was encouraging that bitterness." Jane laughed. "I can't tell you how much happier I am with Tom!"

Matilda rose to refill the teapot and bring them each a slice of pie. "Did you hear Charlie Quiggle is having dog and chicken fights at that Arcade of his? I heard he had plans, but never thought the town would allow it."

"They may stop it yet. John says there has been talk of issuing a cease and desist order to them for 'conducting a public nuisance'."

Matilda smiled. "I certainly hope so."

"How are Carrie and Mary doing at the Business School?"

"Very well. Carrie in particular is quite enthusiastic. I'm not as sure about Mary. I'm beginning to think she may decide life as Mrs. Frank Walton may be preferable to that of a secretary in somebody's office."

Jane laughed merrily. "Well I must say Frank is a charming young man. Bets are he is a confirmed bachelor, though. Mary may have a job convincing him to change his status."

"We'll have to wait and see. I hear Dr. Montague is really coming back this time. They say he should be here in a few weeks. His father died, and he is returning right after he goes to North Carolina for his father's funeral." Matilda did not say what she had in her mind. That if perhaps he had come back sooner, Bill might not have died.

Jane seemed to read her thoughts. "Don't dwell on it," she advised gently. "We'll never know. Perhaps even Dr. Montague might not have been able to save him."

Matilda only sighed. "You're probably right."

Dr. Montague did return in March, and opened his offices in the Whitaker and Ray Building on Front Street.

Alf reported a new Chinese treaty had been signed. "No new immigration to be allowed for twenty years. And those as leave won't be allowed back in unless they meet some real stringent requirements."

"Does that mean all of these people who have been harassing our Chinese will now leave them alone?"

"And can we keep our Chinese laundries?" Mary was more concerned with that, since she had finally found a way to avoid ironing.

"And Tommy Riley had to pay a $15.00 fine. He punched out Jimmy McGuirk and made some rather ungentlemanly references to McGuirk's ancestry. So McGuirk brought him up on charges in Judge Simon's Court."

"Aren't they both Irish?" Mary queried.

"Yes, but the references were not regarding the Irish in general. They were more specific."

"All right," Mary grinned. "I don't think I need to know any more."

"Probably not," Alf agreed.

When winter finally loosened its grip on the land and spring wildflowers began to make their appearance, Matilda decided she wished to speak to Mr. Herbert. He had repaired the pump in March for $3.50. She asked Sam to drive her to Hicksville.

They had barely alighted when a buggy driven by a woman came racing past and pulled up beside a cart tethered in front of the saloon. Shouts drew their attention, and Mrs. Herbert came racing from the shop.

"Who is that woman?" Matilda asked.

"Mrs. Ober, owns a small ranch out east of town a bit. Just married a plumber out of Sacramento name of Donnelly."

The yelling continued as a man emerged from the saloon, apparently in an attempt to reason with her. She reached into his cart and seized the shotgun that had been lying on the seat.

"Look out, Mother," Sam shouted. "She's got a gun!"

Chapter 56

May to August, 1888

SAM PUSHED HIS mother to the edge of the buggy, shielding her with his body.

Matilda watched in horror as the two struggled over the gun, the woman letting loose a string of epithets that blistered Matilda's ears, half of which she did not even understand. Among the accusations she flung at the man was of marrying her for her money and her ranch.

"I wish to God I'd never seen either you or your blasted ranch," he swore, wresting the gun from her hands and leaping into his cart. He headed the horse towards Sacramento, with his wife right behind him in her buggy. As the stunned observers watched, the two vehicles disappeared in dual clouds of dust.

"Are you all right, Mother?" Sam asked anxiously as he helped Matilda to her feet.

"I think so," she gasped. "Heavens, I've never heard such words from a lady before."

Mrs. Herbert, beside them, chuckled softly. "I think it would be a bit of poetic license to call Mrs. Ober a lady."

Spring also brought the birth of Alf and Emma's third child, a son born May 9, 1888, and named Clinton Alfred.

And the news that John Bandeen had been successful in getting his father's will set aside.

"He won't get a lot of money, by the time he pays the lawyers and court costs and shares with Jane and Nancy and Will," Jane chuckled as she told Matilda all about it. "But he has the satisfaction of knowing that woman won't get much either."

May also saw Carrie and Mary's graduation. Carrie proudly displayed the certificate, showing she was a graduate of the Stockton School of Business and Type Writing to her mother. "Now I just need to find employment."

"Your cousin Joshua says the school his daughter Della attends is in need of a teacher." Matilda hesitated. "But it's clear up in Garfield where he has his blacksmith shop. Are you sure you want to go that far away? He's on the School Board, and says you can live with him, which will be better than boarding with strangers. And your Uncle John and the rest of the cousins are not too far away."

"I'll write to Cousin Josh right away, Mother. It will be fun to see everyone again, and a small school will be a good place for me to start."

In June, Lew told his mother he and P.H. Latourette had dissolved their partnership. "We were doing fine, Mother, and I would have liked to continue, but with Bill gone, I've not only got your land to care for, I've got the 300 acres on his place as well. Too much for Sam, he's just a boy. And hired hands just don't take the interest in the place that an owner does. I'm needed here. Media agreed, and Pa Latourette says, much as he hates to lose my help, he can see why I'm doing it, and that it needs to be done."

Matilda sighed. "I hate to see you turn down such an opportunity, Son, but you are probably right. The place has been kind of neglected since Bill's health started to fail."

In June, young Raymond Gaffney died. Lew brought the news to his mother. "Only seventeen, he was," Lew said, hanging his hat on the hook by the door and taking his seat at the table. "Guess his mother and sisters are devastated. Had the measles, but refused to stay in bed, said he wasn't about to be laid low by anything as trifling as the measles."

"But measles can be very dangerous!" Matilda paused as she dished up a plate of stew for her son, the ladle poised above the kettle. "Mother always said how important it was to stay quiet in a darkened room."

"Sure proved to be so. He took a cold, and Doc says that drove the measles back inside. Went into convulsions, and nothing Doc could do to save him. He even called in Doc Nestell for consultation, but he couldn't add anything."

"I guess if Dr. Montague couldn't save him, he was beyond help."

Lew dug his spoon into the savory stew. "But the whole affair had its bright side. Folks around town are now saying Doc was quite smitten by the young Miss Gaffney."

Matilda laughed. "So our bachelor doctor may yet succumb to Cupid's arrow? Which one, Annette or Isabel?"

"My informant wasn't sure, but bets are on Annette, since Isabel is being courted by young Colin McKenzie from over New Hope way."

The next loss in the little community was Mrs. Derby Cantrell. A long time resident of Hicksville, she was the sister of Billy Hicks' wife Sarah Wilson, and aunt of Caroline McCauley.

At the funeral, Matilda was horrified to see how much her widower had aged. Poor Derby, she thought. He is taking this very hard. Of course, the death had been sudden, so he was probably still in shock. The last time she had seen him, not three weeks before, he had been in the bloom of health, strong and vigorous.

Mary had apparently noticed the change in him as well, for she murmured to Matilda, "They were married for 44 years, Mother. Clint says his father is not handling his mother's death well at all. He is really concerned about him. Says he can't get him to eat, or take any interest in what's going on around him."

Matilda sighed in sympathy. She could identify with him, knowing the feeling well after burying three husbands. "It's only been a few days. Tell Clint not to despair. His father may come around and start taking an interest in life again. Particularly with all of the grandchildren he has. Tell Clint to get Derby's attention focused on them." Think of the next generation, she told herself. Lives end and lives begin.

July also brought the death of Mammy Hoyt. As Matilda stood by her graveside at the little cemetery in Hicksville, her mind flew back to the scandals that had emerged back in 1874. Billy Bandeen, after his divorce from Jane, had married, briefly, to a woman from out of town whose name Matilda had even forgotten. Started with an L, she remembered. Louise? Liza? Laurilla? No, not Laurilla. That was George McCauley's folly. She sighed. The name escaped her. Anyway, she divorced Billy a year later, accusing him of various affairs with, among others, Mammy Hoyt.

She smiled as she thought of Jane's indignant report. "Why, she even accused him of carrying on with me! I told her in no uncertain terms that when the divorce was over, I was through with Billy." The divorce, Billy's second, had made a lot of ripples through the community at the time, even more than his first, from Jane. And now both Billy and Mammy were dead, and most of the people did not even remember it. Many had moved on or been born after the events.

Matilda pulled her mind back to the Reverend Pendergrast's words. She glanced over at Jane, and wondered if the same memories were going through her mind.

Water under the bridge, she thought. Maybe Mary was right. People do tend to forget even the most scandalous affairs after a short time.

The rest of the summer passed uneventfully, busy with harvesting and the ever present fears of fire. A wave of intense heat in mid-August killed a number of chickens. Disputes over the proposed routing of a new road through Hicksville drew large amounts of vitriol from both sides, but Matilda stayed aloof from the quarrels.

At the end of August, Mary, Earl, Sam, and Matilda saw Carrie off on the train to Washington to take up her new post as teacher in Garfield. Her cousin Joshua said the whole family looked forward to seeing her again, and his daughter Della was bragging to her friends that her "Aunt Carrie" was the new schoolmarm.

"Be sure and keep an eye on your reticule," Mary cautioned. "I've heard there are unscrupulous men who try to rob women traveling alone. And you are such a tiny little thing."

"I'll be careful," Carrie laughed, giving her mother a farewell hug. "Earl, you mind your studies. Your last report was very high in deportment; but pretty low in scholarship."

"Just like his mother," Sam grinned, and dodged the swat with the parasol that Mary aimed at him."

Earl solemnly shook Carrie's hand. "I promise, Aunt Carrie."

The whistle blew and the train pulled out. Little did

Carrie realize how many changes would take place before she returned.

Chapter 57

September, 1888 to December, 1889

THE REMAINDER of 1888 was relatively uneventful. Matilda's brother Tom came down from Oleta with a fine lot of mountain apples, and her brother Sam visited from Lake County.

Matilda greeted Sam with delight. She missed him more than any of her other brothers. "You look wonderful," she declared. "The climate over there must agree with you."

He grinned. "With both Sally and Essie fussing over me all the time, it's a wonder I don't weigh two hundred pounds."

"Good. I'm glad they're taking good care of you. How's the sheep business?"

"So-so," he shrugged. "Making a living."

Something in his expression made Matilda refrain from any more questions. She shifted the conversation to bringing him up to date on the latest neighborhood gossip, including an update on the ongoing road controversy. "I suppose they'll settle it one way or another pretty soon."

He laughed. "Yes, in typical County fashion, in their own good time."

James Short and his wife Marie moved back to his old

place, the one Matilda and Alfred had rented so long ago before they bought their home, and was reported to be remodeling it.

"I'm sure it needs some remodeling," Matilda chuckled when Sam reported the news to her. "It needed it when we lived there twenty years ago!"

"And his son Willie came up from San Francisco to cast his first Presidential vote. He'll be here until after the holidays, then he goes back to Cooper Medical College."

"I'll bet it was not for the Prohibition Party," Mary chuckled. "I understand the party got only one vote."

"And it wasn't Mr. Latourette," Sam said. "He already announced he was voting Republican."

Shortly before Thanksgiving, a barn burned on Mrs. McCauley's property near the Hauschildt Ranch, creating some excitement in the neighborhood. Speculation that it had been caused by an incendiary ran high.

"Too many fires of a suspicious nature have been happening," Lew declared. "Going to have make an example of some of these fellows."

"Have to catch them first," Mary observed with some cynicism.

"Mrs. Gaffney is moving to town. She's remodeling her home. Guess with both of her daughters being close to matrimony she figures she had better be closer to town."

Lew and Media hosted Christmas festivities in their small home, Media shyly playing gracious host to Matilda, Sam, Earl and Mary as well as her parents and brother John.

Matilda sat in the living room with Eliza while the younger women prepared the meal. "Seems strange not to have to do any cooking," Matilda laughed to Eliza. "Guess this is one advantage to being the older generation."

Eliza returned her smile. "Just enjoy it. How is your grandson adjusting to life back with his mother?"

"Very well. He has even started doing better in school, although his scholarship is not as good as I would like. At least he has stopped talking about joining his sister Mable in heaven. That worried me. A child that young should not be so pre-occupied with death."

"Agreed. Although Johnny still asks when Willie is coming back."

Matilda sighed. "I suppose it is hard to accept when two siblings were close. I know Earl and Mable were. Especially since they were so far away from all of their family and friends." She sighed again and changed the subject. "Did you hear Celestia Johnson's boy Vessie was wrestling in fun with a friend, and fell and broke two fingers and two bones in his right hand? Gave the doctors a real challenge to set it proper." She chuckled. "I bet he'll be more careful in the future."

Eliza laughed. "I'm sure. And one of the hired hands on Jim Hicks' place managed to chop off three toes with an ax while he was chopping wood."

"Speaking of chopping wood, I hear Mrs. McCauley has a hundred Chinamen chopping wood for her at her ranch. So much for boycotting Chinese workers!"

Eliza nodded. "That's because you don't see any white men clamoring to chop wood for a living."

Mary entered the room in time to hear the end of the exchange. She started to laugh. "That's right. Any more than you see them eager to do laundry." She held out her hand to her mother. "Come to the table. Uncle Alf and Aunt Emma and brood have just arrived and dinner is served."

1889 opened with a letter from Carrie saying how much she enjoyed teaching school.

"Little Della is a delight, Mother, and such a bright little girl. But it is much colder here than at home. I have trouble keeping warm, but everyone has been very kind. And they all send you their best regards. Did you know that Uncle John got his homestead up here by trading a horse for it? I always knew he had top quality horses, but never thought he had one worth that much."

Matilda smiled as she folded up the letter. She suspected the reason John got such a bargain was that the owner of the land just wanted to get away, and was willing to swap the land for a good horse. She handed it to Mary to read. "Your sister seems to be enjoying life as a school teacher. Have you given a thought to using your diploma from the school for a teaching job?"

Mary laughed. "Not me, Mother. No way would I be trapped in a school with twenty-five brats. If I go to work, it's going to be in an office using one of those new type writing machines. They are really amazing."

"And I suppose you'll want to ride to work in one of those new electric streetcars they have installed in Sacramento."

She laughed merrily. "Of course!"

In February, an earthquake jarred them at 8:00PM on Wednesday, and again at 4:00PM on Thursday, but seemed to do no damage. Remembering the mess she had when an earthquake had knocked her jars of canned goods off of the shelves, she had been cautious to always have a lip on the shelves from then on. She sent Sam to the cellar to check to be sure, but all was well.

In March, a heavy downpour for removed fears of drought. The crops had been doing poorly due to the lack of rain, but recovered quickly.

Sam continued to attend the Hicksville School. Mary felt he should stop going to school and help on the farm. "After all, Mother, he is seventeen years old. He should either go to work or we should see if we can get him into a high school program."

"I know," Matilda sighed. "But he does so love to read, and this is really the only way he can have such an access to so many books. He is beginning to feel a little out of place, with all of the other children so much younger, but Mrs. Johnson uses him as a sort of teacher's helper, hearing the younger children read, and drilling them in their spelling words. It's a help to her and he seems to enjoy it so."

In May, the quarrel over the proposed new road in Hicksville grew more virulent. Mrs. Johnson accused Mrs. Valensin of trying to ruin her business.

"Give Alice credit," Matilda exclaimed in some exasperation. "She did try to work out a compromise, by moving Mrs. Johnson's new hotel over to Arno. Wasn't her fault Mrs. Johnson had trouble getting the move financed."

"But when she did get it financed, Alice tried to back out," Mary retorted. "And Mr. Hansen's blacksmith shop will be affected too."

"Well," Matilda sighed, "I suppose they will eventually work out their differences. Did you feel the earthquake this morning? It woke me up, but I didn't bother to get up. It seemed a mild one."

"Didn't feel a thing," Mary laughed. "I must be getting used to them."

June brought the news that a daughter of a Galt couple, Solomon and Jane Kreeger, died in a fire in Sacramento.

"Threw coal oil on the fire to make it burn faster," Sam reported. "It burned faster all right. So fast it burned her too. Her two sisters got hurt as well, trying to save her, but they'll recover."

"What a shame! After all of the reports of people being injured doing just that, it amazes me that someone could be that foolish."

Sam shrugged. "I guess the world still has a lot of foolish people." He sat down and Matilda placed his supper in front of him. "Also heard Dr. Turner is taking his dental business to Lodi."

"Why? Not enough tooth problems in Galt?"

He grinned. "Either that or not enough people willing to pay him for the work."

Matilda laughed. "I suspect that is probably the reason."

"Mother, come quick." Sam had the buggy ready when Matilda came running at his call. "It's Caleb Dillard. He fell off the mower, and he's hurt bad. Columbus says he's dying. I knew you'd want to say goodbye, since he's been a friend for so long."

Matilda quickly climbed into the buggy, and they hurried to the Dillard ranch. Caleb's son Columbus met her at the door.

"I'm so glad you came while he is still conscious, Mrs. Frye. He always speaks so highly of you." He ushered her into the room where the old man lay. Dr. Montague rose as she entered and escorted her to the bedside.

"Hello, Caleb," she said, taking the hand lying on top of the counterpane. His daughter sat on the opposite side of the bed, holding his other hand, silent tears rolling down her cheeks.

His eyes opened, and he smiled faintly. "Thank you fer

comin', 'Tilda," he whispered. "Done a fool thing. I did. Leaned over to clear the wheel without stoppin'. Fell off the seat and the mower ran over me."

"Don't try to talk," she soothed. "Save your strength to get well."

His faint smile told her he knew better. As they watched, his breathing grew more ragged, and finally stopped.

The next excitement in Hicksville came early in July, when two boys getting ready to go to sleep by a haystack on James Clausen's property knocked over a lantern and set fire to the haystack.

"At least it was not the work of our local incendiary, whoever he is," Matilda said with relief when she heard the story.

"No, that's one good thing about it. And I heard Lack Quiggle and his wife lost their little boy. He only lived one day."

"What a shame. On top of losing little Johnny."

Mrs. Gaffney and her two daughters moved into their newly refurbished residence on Oak Avenue and 'A' Street, and the girls immediately became the center of the local society.

"But I suspect it will be short-lived," Mary laughed. "Colin McKenzie has become a regular visitor, and so has Doc Montague. Wouldn't surprise me if both of them marry within the year."

"They say Doc Montague is not quite as popular as he used to be since he got himself appointed Health Officer. One of his first orders was to remove any pig sties in the city limits." Matilda chuckled. "Lots of the folks as are used to keeping their own pig or two for ham and bacon don't much like being told they can't keep them in the city anymore."

"And he has quarantined some folks against their will. That hasn't set too well either," Sam contributed. "Good thing he is such a good musician."

"Yes, the Galt Orchestra is pleased to have him and his clarinet, pigs or no pigs."

"Also," Sam continued, "I hear J. Brewster and Company is about to pass out of receivership. Scott, the new owner will take over soon." Sam reached for another biscuit. "Pass the honey, Mary. And Scott is trying to collect on some of the money owed." He chuckled. "He probably won't have any more success than Brewster did."

The rains began in October, and were so heavy that by the end of the month, farmers began to have concerns for the survival of their crops

On November 6, Isabel Gaffney became the bride of Colin McKenzie in a very fashionable wedding. The nuptials took place in Stockton at the residence of the pastor of the Presbyterian Church there.

"Young McKenzie is foreman for the Shippee Ranch down at New Hope," Mary told her mother in reporting the news to her. "The young people of Galt will miss her from their circle. I understand it was a very small wedding, just family and a small circle of friends."

"I suppose they had such a small wedding because of Raymond's recent death." Matilda remarked.

"Could be," Mary shrugged. "I think we had better worry more about the rain. If it keeps on like this, we are going to have a lot of damage. Already the creeks and streams are booming."

In spite of the rain, the whole family attended the New Year's Eve Party Celestia Johnson and her son Vessie hosted at the Hicksville Hotel.

Matilda sat listening to the Galt Orchestra perform. Dr. Montague really did play well, she thought. And as young Annette Gaffney watched him, Matilda could not miss the look of admiration that lighted up her face.

Mary spent the entire evening with Frank Walton, and Matilda noticed, to her relief, that none of the Douglass family was in attendance.

When the orchestra broke for supper, just before midnight, Mary and Frank approached Matilda. Matilda knew what had happened from the glow on Mary's face and the grin plastered all over Frank's.

"Look, Mother," she told Matilda. "Look at this!"

She held out her left hand for Matilda's inspection. On the third finger sparkled a lovely ruby ring, surrounded by diamonds. The beauty of the ring took Matilda's breath away.

"And this time it will be because I want to be married. This time it will be to a man I really love. Oh, Mother! We are going to be so happy." She threw herself in her mother's arms.

"I'm so glad for you, Darling. So glad."

But as she looked out of the window, a shadow crossed the moon.

Chapter 58

January to April, 1890

1890 BEGAN ON A positive note. Alf announced he had increased his holdings to 250 acres by purchasing a neighbor's property.

"How did you get the money?" Matilda asked.

"Borrowed it from McFarland. $9722.00. Put up the land as collateral."

Matilda felt a stir of dismay in her breast. So many had lost their land through just such an arrangement. She stood at the kitchen window and watched the water pour off the eaves and run in little rivulets down the hill towards the creek, a creek already full. "We are getting a lot of rain this year." She wanted to think of something other than the possibility that Alf could lose his land.

He crossed the room to stand beside her at the window. "Over twenty inches so far. Creeks rising fast. Probably gonna lose some bridges again. Lots of snow in the mountains, too. We'll get a lot of runoff this spring."

"The road between McConnell and Hicksville worries me." She brushed a stray lock of hair back into place. "That big hole in the middle should have been fixed before the rains started. It will only get worse now."

Alf shrugged. "County keeps talking about fixing it, but

511

so far all I've heard is talk. No one says anything about when and how."

The following morning, Mary approached Matilda as she stirred up the fire preparatory to making breakfast. Startled to see worry written all over Mary's face, she asked, "What's the matter?"

"Earl has a fever, and says his throat hurts."

Matilda's heart contracted. Diphtheria had forced the closure of the school just the week before. She turned to her daughter and saw the fear in her eyes.

"I'll send Sammie for Dr. Montague."

Dr. Montague came and confirmed the diagnosis. With a quill, he blew a mixture of powdered sulphur and alum into Earl's throat. He followed that with a light purge of syrup of rhubarb. "Keep his throat clear and give him the fever medicines. This seems to be a light case. If his heart is not affected, he should come through just fine." He took Matilda's hand. "Try not to worry. He's a healthy little boy. God willing, he should survive this."

He returned the next day and cauterized the false membrane that had begun to form on the boy's throat with lunar caustic, and demonstrated to Matilda how to repeat the treatment. "We must keep his throat clear, or he will suffocate. Come, we will make up a solution that I want you to have him gargle every fifteen minutes while he is awake." To a teacup of hot water, he added ½ teaspoon of cayenne pepper, a pinch of salt, and a spoonful of molasses. Stirring this, he added a little cider vinegar. "You can make up more of this as it's needed."

Matilda's hands shook as she copied his actions.

"Just keep his throat open," he repeated, "and we will pray it does not affect his heart."

A week later, Dr. Montague took Miss Annette Gaffney as his bride, but the affair went unnoticed in Matilda's household. Their whole efforts were concerned with keeping Earl alive.

The child retained his cheerful positive attitude. As Mary sat beside him with tears streaming down her cheeks, he patted her hand and said, "Don't cry, Mama. I'm going to get well."

Alf came by to see how Earl fared, and brought the local news. "Johnny Kohler, barber in Galt, died of Bright's Disease. Shame, young man as he were and all. Say he swelled up like a poisoned pup afore he died."

Matilda grinned wryly. "Thank you for that graphic description. Don't you have any good news? We could certainly use some. I worry so about Mary. She just sits there by Earl's bedside with the tears flowing." Poor Mary, to lose Earnest, then Mable, and now, in all likelihood, she was going to lose Earl as well.

Alf took her in his arms and awkwardly patted her on the back. "Shoo, now, you go on and cry, little sister. You're entitled to a good cry. You been through a lot." When she took a deep breath and gave him a shaky little smile, he asked, "And how is the little fellow?"

Matilda shook her head. "Not good. His throat is clear now, but he has been lapsing in and out of consciousness for the past two days. He just wakes up long enough to tell Mary not to cry, and promise her he will get well."

Alf shook his head sadly. He had no words of comfort to offer.

George Douglass spent more and more time with them as it became apparent Earl would not recover. Even Dr. Montague ceased to be optimistic.

"Gone to his heart, it has," he said sadly. "He grows weaker and weaker."

On the morning of February 11, Earl roused for a few moments from his stupor and whispered, "I'm going to see Mable now. She's waiting for me." He lapsed back into unconsciousness. Matilda, Mary, and George sat in silence by the bedside until the breathing stopped.

The following day, they buried Earl in the Hicksville Cemetery next to his grandfather Douglass.

Two weeks after Earl's death, Lew came by to tell her of a strange accident on the Gaffney place, about eight miles east of Galt.

"Seems this lady left her ten month old baby in a baby buggy and went out to milk the cow. The four year old was in the house with him. Guess he got tired of watching the baby and went outside to play. When the mother got back into the house after finishing milking, she found the buggy had rolled up against the stove and the baby was burned. Say his little feet were burned to a crisp. Poor mite only lived a few hours."

"How dreadful!" Matilda exclaimed. "How could the buggy have gotten to the stove?"

Lew shrugged. "No one knows. Some speculate the four year old pushed it there. Others say maybe the little one's movements made it roll. Guess we'll never know."

Matilda sighed. "Goes back to what I have always said. Never leave a baby alone."

On Thursday, March 13, Will Bandeen rode into the yard, pushing his horse in spite of the rain, splashing through the puddles. Matilda heard the horse and hurried to the door to meet him, wrapping a shawl around herself as she ran. Instinct told her something was wrong.

"What's the matter?" she cried, recognizing Will. Fear for Jane ran through her.

"It's Tom. He just collapsed. Vessie Johnson rode for the doc, and I come to get you, seein' as how you're Ma's best friend." His voice choked. "I'm sure he's gone. Couldn't rouse him, or feel no heartbeat. Ma jest sits there on the floor beside him, holdin' his hand and wailin'. I don't know what to do or say." He took a deep breath. "You know how Ma feels about Tom. I fear for her. Can you come?"

"Of course. Sam will bring me as soon as he can get the buggy hitched. Go on back to Jane now, and we'll be right behind you."

Sam, who had followed his mother to the door, slapped his hat on his head and headed for the barn on a run. Matilda returned to the house to push the pot of stew to the back of the stove so it would not burn and hurried to pull on her boots.

When they arrived at the Mahin household, Jane still sat as Will had said. Matilda knelt beside her and took her in her arms.

"Oh 'Tilda." Jane sobbed against her friend's shoulder, "He's gone. He's gone."

Matilda held her and rocked her until the sobs subsided.

Two days later, the *Galt Gazette* printed a lovely poem in Earl's memory. Matilda, who had hung on to her composure all through the days following his death and funeral, lost the battle, and burst into sobs.

The following week Media showed Matilda the school report from Galt. "Look, Mother Matilda," she cried. "My brother Johnny made the Honor Roll."

Matilda smiled. "You have a right to be proud of him,

my dear. He's a bright little boy."

Media's eyes filed with tears. "So was Willie. I'll never understand why God takes boys like Willie and Earl so young." She lifted her chin in defiance. "Reverend Dyer says it's blasphemy to question God's will, but I can't help it."

Matilda, remembering having such thoughts herself, patted Media's hand. "I know. I'm sure God will understand."

The road situation continued to deteriorate. By the end of March, the paper wrote lengthy articles on the disgraceful conditions that were allowed to remain with no evidence of plans to repair them.

Frank Walton became a frequent visitor. Matilda was glad he showed such understanding and patience with Mary after Earl's death. If anything could bring Mary out of her depression it would be Frank's devotion.

He came by one evening to report Count Valensin had returned from the East where he had been selling his Sidney colts.

"Got an average of $2800 for 'em. Guess he's trying to earn enough to pay back his mother."

"What?" Matilda had not heard that before. "Did he use his mother's money as well as Alice's?"

"Yep," Frank grinned. "When his father died, he left Guilio $100,000. When the mother dies, she is to leave him another $100,000. Seems after he went through the money from his father, he got his mother to advance him the $100,000 she would eventually leave him."

"And now he'll go through that." Matilda shook her head at such foolishness. She could not conceive of going through that much money in a lifetime. "Is he back at his place down in Livermore?"

"That's what they say." He smiled at Mary and patted her hand affectionately. The love that sprang into his eyes as he looked at her gladdened Matilda's heart. Mary so deserved a little happiness. "And I also hear he has an inamorata in Sacramento."

"But he's still married!" Matilda gasped.

"That's okay," Frank grinned. "So is she."

Mary giggled. Matilda only shook her head.

In mid-April, Lew and Media came for Sunday dinner after church, full of news.

"Dr. Montague is renovating his residence on Fourth Street," Lew reported. "Guess now that he has a bride he decided the old homestead needed sprucing up."

"If his wife is going to be our leading milliner with the most prestigious shop in town I guess he feels the house had to match," Mary said caustically.

"And Willie Short's dog is missing. He has offered a reward."

Mary laughed. "You mean Doctor Short. Let's not forget he's not just our Willie anymore. Did you see where a Shoshone Medicine Man has predicted a flood that will drown all white men and half breeds?"

"This would be the year for it," Lew added. "Haven't had this much rain in a long time."

"Does the article say how the flood can be so selective?" Media asked. "My experience with floods has been that they pretty much take everything in their path."

Lew laughed. "Doesn't say, but who are we to question the Medicine Man?"

Chapter 59

April to May, 1890

APRIL 25 DAWNED bright and sunny after so many days of rain. Lew and Media arrived in the buggy shortly after Matilda had finished the breakfast dishes and was setting the milk she had pasteurized in pans to cool so she could skim the cream to make butter. Sam had finished his morning chores and sat at the table having a second cup of coffee when they heard the crunch of buggy wheels in the driveway.

"Good." Sam looked up at the sound. "Lew is here. I need his help to get the hog pen fixed. The ground has been so soft from all the rain that those wretched hogs have burrowed underneath. The two that got out followed me right back in when I brought them their breakfast. I stuck in a couple of planks to block the hole, but it needs more work.

"And we need to work on the mower," he went on. "After we finished last summer, I noticed the blade had lost a bolt. I'm sure it needs to be sharpened, too."

Lew came in the door, and they heard the buggy leaving. "Media wants to spend the day with Rose and Anna McConnell, so she's taking the buggy on over." He beamed proudly. "Independent, she is. I offered to drive her, but she said Sam here needed my help, and she could manage just fine."

"She'd better be careful," Mary warned. "The last time Frank came down he said the road between McConnell and Hicksville is really bad. There's a big hole you have to drive around, and it takes you close to the edge of the levee."

Lew shrugged. "Headstrong, she is. We'll see what she says when she gets back. Blaze is a good horse."

Matilda laughed, remembering when Blaze brought Lew home after his night at the Arcade. "Well, he certainly took good care of you."

The day passed quickly. At dinner, Sam reported the pigs were secure. "We drove some stakes down into the mud. Like to see them get through that."

After dinner, they went out to look at the mower. Matilda washed up the dishes with Mary's help, and they began to skim the cream.

"Going to get a fine batch of butter out of this," Mary remarked. "That old cow really outdid herself this time." She looked at the watch pinned to her shirtwaist. "Three o'clock. Shouldn't Media be getting back? Frank really was concerned about that road."

Matilda nodded, pouring the skimmed milk from the pans into the pail to clabber to feed to the hogs. "Yes, if she's not back by four o'clock, we'll have to send the boys after her."

They looked up at the sound of hoof beats in the drive. Matilda looked at Mary. "Who's coming? I don't hear any buggy wheels."

They raced to the door to see three horses. Blaze carried Media, wrapped in blankets. Vessie Johnson and Will Bandeen accompanied her, one on each side.

Lew came running from the shed to help Media down

from the horse.

"What happened?" Matilda cried.

Mary grinned wryly. "Pretty obvious. Just like Frank said. She dodged the hole and got too close to the levee."

They hustled Media into the house and out of her wet clothes. Her eyes blazed. "That road is in despicable condition. The wheels got too close to the edge and over the buggy went. Threw me right into the water. I guess I screamed, for the next thing I knew Will and Vessie were helping me out."

"And Blaze?" Mary asked. "Obviously he wasn't hurt."

"No, bless him. He stopped the second the buggy tipped. That's what saved me. If he had run, as so many horses would have, he'd have dragged me in deeper. But they'd better fix that road." Her eyes narrowed. "Or I'll get myself a horsewhip and go after those Commissioners myself."

Fortunately, Media recovered quickly from her ducking, and suffered only a few bruises "in places that don't show," she laughed.

Lew filed a formal complaint with the Board of Supervisors, and they promised to make repairs as soon as the water went down.

"They're just waiting for someone to get killed," Lew grumbled. "Media's accident is the talk of Hicksville and Arno both." Then he grinned. "Word is Hiram Rattan has run off and left his wife and young-uns."

"Just left them? But he has six children. Who's going to feed them?" Matilda stared at Lew, aghast.

"Just up and loped off, he did. Guess listening to six was more than he could take."

Matilda grinned wryly. "Six can't be much worse than five, and that's what I had."

"Yep, but Carrie and Sammie were quiet. That's not what I've heard about the Rattan bunch."

Matilda sighed. "I suppose that means the neighborhood will have to see they are fed."

Lew nodded. "I suppose you're right."

Five days later, as Mary prepared her basket to take to the Granger's picnic at Elk Grove Park, Matilda felt a flash of fear as she thought of Media's recent narrow escape from drowning. There had been no more rain, for which everyone was thankful, but the water remained high.

"Mary," Matilda began. Mary turned to her. "Do you - - do you really think you should go to the picnic today?" She hesitated to say it, for, as usual, her beautiful, headstrong daughter laughed off any attempts to curb her activities.

"Mo - - ther!" Mary's amusement showed in her voice. "I can hear Aunt Emma now." The laughter danced in her blue eyes as she mimicked her aunt's voice, "Matilda, do you really think Mary should go to the dances at Arno?" Alf's wife was a staunch Methodist, even more so than Alf himself, and very concerned with propriety. "Or go riding in that fancy buggy with that rich young man, as if being rich is somehow evil. Why can't she ever call Frank by name?"

Mary did not mention it, but her Aunt Emma had been scandalized when Frank gave Mary the expensive ruby ring. Matilda had been amused at Emma's attitude. Frank and his father owned a blacksmith shop in Elk Grove. She wouldn't exactly call them rich, not like the Valensin's.

"No, no, Mary," Matilda interposed when Mary stopped for breath. "It's just that the river is so high. What if the road washes out? You could be trapped on the other side.

Then what would your Aunt Emma say?" She had to laugh to herself when she thought about it. Little Emma, who had scandalized everyone by marrying Alf, twenty-five years her senior, had turned out to be the most prudish member of the family.

"Oh, Mother," Mary began.

"Or worse, you might have to spend the night in the buggy. What if you took a chill?" She did not voice her worst fear. The road was still in very bad condition. After all, Media had almost drowned just last week. "Remember how Frank said there is a huge hole by Cantrell's, in front of Billy Hicks' old place? The road is probably worse now than when Media went in." She felt fear like a cold lump in her chest, but said nothing more, knowing Mary was completely convinced of her own personal invulnerability.

Mary, as Matilda expected, laughed at her mother's fears and gave her an affectionate hug and a quick kiss on the cheek. Frank's buggy had turned into the lane.

"Don't fret, Mother. I can take care of myself. I am thirty years old. And Frank knows about the bad spot. He's been by it many times, and he's a good driver." She picked up the picnic basket. On her finger the lovely ruby ring with its circle of diamonds flashed in the morning sun.

As Matilda watched them drive away, she tried to reassure herself. Surely Mary would return safely. But she looked uneasily at the sun sparkling on the vast lake created by the flooding waters of Willow Creek, south of the house. The water stood at the highest level she had seen in years.

The beauty of the scene held her. Wildflowers covered the fields with color. Blue lupine, bluebells, yellow mustard, pink and lavender wild radish. Snow-covered peaks stood in the distance. She smiled. California was so lovely in May. She remembered Kansas with a shiver.

But all that lovely snow on the California mountains melted every spring, raging down into the valley with a vengeance. The Cosumnes River, a mile north of the house, topped its banks in many places, racing towards the bay with frightening ferocity. One misstep by the horse, a little weakening along the levee . . . . She remembered Frank's description of the hole in the road and shuddered.

That evening, as the room began to grow dark, Matilda lighted the lamps. Uneasiness crept over her. Mary should be back by now. The memory of the soaking wet Media being dragged from the water would not leave her. She tried to reassure herself. Frank knew the road well, but still she felt a tug of fear.

Sam clumped onto the porch, having finished his evening chores. Pulling off his muddy boots, he joined her in the kitchen.

"Your sister isn't back, Sam. How late did they expect to be?"

"She's not back?" A lock of blond hair flopped over his forehead as he shook his head. "I know Frank planned to be back before dark. But there is a good moon. Should be light enough to drive. Did the buggy have a lantern?"

Matilda tried to think but could not remember. The thought of Mary being caught on that narrow levee road in the dark made cold chills run up her spine.

"Sam, we have to do something."

Sam grimaced. "Relax, Mother. Mary has gotten herself in and out of scrapes before." Sam shared his sister's conviction that she was indestructible.

Matilda said nothing, trying to stop the visions running through her mind.

"Okay, okay, I'll throw a saddle on old Blackjack and try

524

to find her for you." He shrugged into his coat and went to find his riding gloves.

Ten minutes later she heard the horse gallop out of the lane. She watched the lantern glow in the gathering gloom until it vanished. She stood bathed in the bright moonlight for a few moments. Bright enough to drive by on a good, level road, but would Frank be able to see if a portion of the road had washed out? Would Sam? Fear stabbed her again. Sam was only eighteen. Had she sent him into danger? Should she have sent him for Lew instead?

She could do nothing but wait. The minutes dragged by as she sat alone by the lamp on the table, trying to concentrate on her mending. She told herself surely they must be spending the night with friends. They probably lost track of time and realized they would not have time to get back. She gave up on the mending and just sat and waited.

In less than an hour, Sam stomped back into the house. "No point in looking any farther," he reported. "They aren't on the road. They probably stopped at Davis' or McConnell's, or maybe even decided to stay with Frank's folks." He pulled off his coat. "Go to bed, Mother. We'll find her in the morning."

Matilda realized the wisdom of his words, but it took her a long time to fall asleep.

Matilda woke early the next morning. Jumping out of bed, she quickly dressed and ran into Mary's room. Mary's bed remained empty. Trying not to be frightened, Matilda told herself there were a dozen possibilities. She would even be glad of a scandalous one if she could only be sure of Mary's safety.

She had been up only a short time when she heard a horse coming down the lane. She looked out of the window, but could not identify the horse. It took her a moment to recognize the rider. Ezra Walton, Frank's father. She ran out of the door to meet him.

He did not dismount. One look at his face told her something was wrong.

"Did Mrs. Douglass get home last night, Mrs. Frye?" He had not shaved, and he looked disheveled.

Matilda's voice left her as fear gripped her throat in a vise.

"Did she?" he cried hoarsely.

"No," she finally whispered. "And I have been so worried. Has something happened to them?"

With a wild cry, Mr. Walton turned the horse and raced back up the lane.

Matilda turned to Sam standing agape beside her. "Something has happened to Mary, Sam. Follow him and find out."

Sam ran to the barn and in moments was galloping after Mr. Walton in the direction of Hicksville. Matilda stood rooted to the spot.

Jake seemed to sense her fear, for he crept up beside her and huddled next to her skirt. She reached down and stroked the old dog's head. She took a deep breath. Nothing to do now but wait and pray.

She had to wait several hours, but at last a wagon turned-into the lane. She recognized George Hicks and Sam on their horses. Mr. Linnell drove the wagon, with Mrs. Poston beside him on the seat.

Matilda's heart missed a beat. She knew now what she had been trying for so many hours to deny.

Sam dismounted and embraced her. "They were about a mile north of Hicksville, Mother," he told her gently.

"Right by where Media went in last week. Frank must have gone around that hole and gotten too close to the edge. It's harder to judge in the moonlight. The buggy went over the side and the horse fell on top of them, so they couldn't get out." He put his arms around her and kissed her gently on the forehead. His eyes filled with tears. "I went right past them last night, but since only the horse's hooves were above the water, I didn't see them. Mr. Walton spotted them when he came looking for Frank this morning, and recognized Frank's horse."

Matilda shuddered, thinking of the muddy water closing over Mary's head, her old horror of water returning. Mary, whose sparkling eyes were so full of life, who had risen above the loss of all of her children. Mary, who laughed at so many of society's restrictions. Mary, so full of plans and dreams, who had finally found the love she had sought so long.

Matilda lost her struggle to control the tears, and wept against Sam's shoulder.

The neighbors rallied to her support. Media cried as she combed Mary's beautiful red-gold hair, preparing her body for burial. She took the ruby ring from Mary's finger and gave it to Matilda.

Matilda held the ring to the light. The color sparkled. "Maybe we should bury it with her, she loved it so much," she told Media.

"Oh, no, Mother Matilda," Media cried. "It's too beautiful and much too valuable."

Matilda hesitated. Maybe Media was right. It hurt to look at it, so she put it in her jewelry box. Maybe later she would wear it. Not yet.

Sam brought her a copy of the *San Francisco Call Bulletin*, turned to the notice.

"Frank Walton and Mrs. Mary Douglass lose their lives in the Cosumnes River," she read through her tears. "Galt, May 2, Frank Walton, a young man living at Elk Grove, and Mrs. Mary Douglass, who lives with her mother near Hicksville, were drowned in the Cosumnes River while returning from a picnic last night. The parties were well known in this community. The bodies were found near the place of the accident.

"It seems the buggy was upset and rolled into the ditch, the occupants falling beneath, with the horse's hooves protruding from the water."

Matilda's eyes blurred and she rubbed them vigorously to clear them before reading the last sentence. "Walton and the young lady were soon to be married." She looked at Sam, who smiled gently.

"I knew you'd like that last line," was all he said.

They buried Mary in the Hicksville Cemetery, next to Earl. Matilda wanted to bury Frank beside her, but his father decided to bury him in the Odd Fellows Cemetery by Elk Grove.

After the service, as she stood alone at Mary's grave, Matilda looked across at the graves of others she had lost. Sinclair, Minerva, Michael, Alfred, Bill, Earl, her parents. She thought of Lewis and Baby John, buried far away in Kansas.

She remembered her mother's calm acceptance of whatever blow life dealt her, whatever happened, and began to understand it. If you try to find a reason for every tragedy, she thought, you will only drive yourself mad.

How much more to I have to bear, God? she silently asked. How many more are you going to take before you take me?

Chapter 60

May, 1890 to February, 1891

FOUR DAYS LATER, on May 6, Alf and Emma's baby son was born dead. Alf rode over to bring the sad news to Matilda. "Real upset she was, by both Media's accident and then losing Mary. Right fond of Mary, she was, in spite of all her complaining about her behavior. And she wan't carrying this one well. Said she didn't feel him moving at all the last couple of days. And he wasn't due for another month. Just a little mite he was, and never breathed a gasp."

"Probably been dead for two days, if she couldn't feel him move." Matilda nodded. "That's why he came early. Good thing, too. I remember Mother talking about a couple of her patients where the baby died and turned septic before being born. Mother died as well as the baby."

"She blames me. Said if she hadn't been frettin' so about how I was to pay off McFarland she wouldn't have lost him." He sighed. "Guess you've got enough grief on your hands without me adding to it. You told Carrie about Mary yet?"

"Yes, Sam sent her a telegram. She's coming home as soon as the school year finishes." Matilda sighed. "She so enjoys it there. I hate to see her leave, but I do need her."

The paper on May 10 carried a beautiful memorial poem

531

dedicated to Mary's memory. Matilda read it through tears in her eyes.

"The loved and lost! Why do we call her lost
Because we miss her from our onward road
God's unseen angel o'er our pathway crossed
Looked on us all, and loving her the most
Straightway relieved her from life's weary load."

The tears blurred her vision and she had to clear them before she could finish. She knew it was not her place to question God, but she could not help but feel some resentment. Her feelings must have shown in her face, for Sam, seated across from her at the table, patted her hand gently. "She and Frank are together, Mother. And she's gone to be with Earl and Mable. Maybe she'll find the happiness she sought where she is now."

Matilda smiled through her tears. "You're right, Son. I'm being selfish." A deep sigh escaped her lips. "Mary went through so much, between her unhappy marriage to George, and then losing all three of her children. It just seems a shame she didn't get a chance to have a little joy with Frank."

Alf came by a few days later with some papers for her to sign. She had decided to deed Bill's property over to Lew, since he had bought it from Tom with Lew and Media in mind. Alf had done the paper work for her.

"Are you sure this is what you want to do, Sis?"

"Yes, he should have his own place. He has worked so hard. And I am 54 years old. If something happens to me, he won't have to wait for the courts to decide what to do. He'll have it free and clear." She smiled. "Henry will always take good care of Elizabeth. He is such a fine man. And I can leave this place to Carrie and Sam."

"Okay, just so you're sure." He placed the paper on the table in front of her. "Went by Walton's place to see how Ezra was holding up. Talk is he's about out of his head with grieving. Mrs. Walton is worried sick about him. And Jim Chinnick says his daughter Ethel keeps asking when her uncle Frank is coming back. She's only seven, and I know Frank doted on her. Even drove her to school each day in that fancy buggy of his while all of the other young-uns had to walk."

Matilda sighed. "How sad Mary and Frank never had a chance to have babies. He would have made a wonderful father."

"Penny says it would mean a lot to her mother if you would stop by and see her."

"I'll do that. Right after church this Sunday. I'll have Sam drive me over. I haven't seen her since Frank's funeral."

Alf grinned. "Did you hear about Mabel Donaldson and Zoe Bailey's little mishap?"

"No. What happened?"

"Horse spooked at a hole in the bridge over the Laguna, down by Riley's place. Tossed 'em both out. Mabel managed to scramble onto the bridge, but Zoe went into the water."

"Is she all right?"

"Oh, yes. Riley's hired man heard all the commotion – I guess Mabel was screaming like a banshee – and fished poor Zoe out of the water. But it's the talk of Hicksville and Arno. People are after the heads of the Road Commissioners."

By mid-June, the water had receded and the land began to dry out. Matilda had Sam take her in the buggy to the spot where Mary had drowned.

"Look at the size of that hole!" she gasped. "No wonder there have been so many accidents here. I certainly hope they fix the road this summer so we don't have another spring like the one we just had." With Sam's help, she descended from the buggy and placed the bouquet of Cecil Bruner roses in a makeshift memorial by the side of the road. She had cut them from the bush in the front yard. Mary had loved the small fragrant pink roses, and had nurtured the little bush until it flourished.

She rose and smiled faintly, holding back the tears. "Let's swing by the Post Office on the way home. We should have a letter from Carrie telling us when she will arrive."

At the Post Office, Celestia Johnson told them she and Vessie had sold the hotel.

"Getting too old to fight it anymore, between Alice Valensin trying to take everything to Arno, and being burned out twice. Find myself wondering if I'm going to make it out alive the next time it happens. Going to take it easy for a while. Will Hicks wants to try his hand, so we sold it to him. After all, it was his Uncle Billy as started the town."

Vessie grinned. "And I told him I'd stay on and help him out."

"And construction has started on that new hotel Alice is building at Arno." She sighed. "She says it's going to be a 'family hotel', implying this is not a good place for families to stay. She seems determined that Arno is going to replace Hicksville. Poor old Uncle Billy would turn over in his grave. Her father took his land, and she is bent on wiping out his town."

Matilda had heard such rumors before. "Is she really going to get the Post Office moved to Arno as well?"

"Yes, she should have that done by the end of the year." She chuckled, "And Will's brother John's wife is suing him for divorce."

"Viola?" Matilda looked up in astonishment. "I thought they were quite happy."

"Not according to Will," Vessie chuckled. "John wants to move to Mexico. Says he can get a lot of land in Sonora for next to nothing. But she won't go."

"He also says Alden Ames has been coming around." Celestia clucked her tongue. "Such goings on."

"I suspect that's one reason John wanted to move to Mexico," Vessie added. "And also why she refuses to leave."

Matilda only shook her head and opened the letter from Carrie. "Carrie will be here Saturday," she told Sam after scanning the one page the letter contained. "Let's go home."

The remainder of the summer passed quickly. Dr. William Short, to his father's disappointment, moved his practice from Galt to Knight's Landing.

"Had hoped the boy would stay here and practice," he told Matilda sadly. "Since his mother died, he's all I've got."

In August the papers reported a riot between Chinese and whites near McCracken's Wire Bridge on the Cosumnes. Matilda received this news with exasperation. "I thought this was all behind us. What do they hope to accomplish by fighting?"

Carrie could only nod in sympathy.

September brought the news that Matilda's uncle, her mother's brother Sevier Stringfield had died in Santa Barbara on September 26.

"Ninety years old, he was," Alf reported. "And still preaching at the Methodist Church."

"Good thing D.K. went there when he did," Matilda said. "Melvin and Sarah are both clear up in Humboldt County. I think Nancy is too. Nancy's son Will is courting our Will's Lizzie."

"Keeps all the blood in the family," Alf chuckled.

Sam came by briefly from Lake County, with a report that Sally had a beau. "About time," he chuckled. "Gettin' to be an old maid, she is. Told her she shouldn't have to spend her whole life taking care of an old bachelor uncle."

"And what brings you over here if you can only stay until tomorrow?"

He hesitated before replying. Matilda waited. Finally, he took a deep breath and said, "Sheep business not as good as I'd hoped. Came over to borrow some money from Whitaker and Ray." He chuckled. "After all, they got me into the sheep business, thought they would be the logical ones to help keep me in it."

Yes, she thought, after swindling you out of your land here, it's the least they can do. Aloud, she said, "And they were willing to give you a good interest rate?"

"Well," he paused and sighed. "Ten percent."

"And I suppose a demand note?"

"Yes," he admitted.

"Well," she said, a bit caustically, "I suppose you can always move back here and help me."

He laughed. "It's a promise."

In November, John Sawyer began construction on the new Post Office Alice Valensin had ordered built at Arno, with plans to move the facilities from Hicksville into the new building. Annie Herbert told Matilda all about it when she went to Hicksville to pick up her mail.

"Determined, she is," Mrs. Herbert said. "Wants to appoint Metzner in charge, and is telling everyone what a fine building it will be, much better than the one here at the Hotel. At least my Louis has been named road overseer, so she won't be able to shut off any roads like she's tried before."

"I certainly hope he can get the County to keep the roads in better repair," Matilda said. "We don't want to go through another winter like the last one."

"We sure don't," she vowed. "If anyone can whip those Road Commissioners into shape, it'll be my Lou."

Matilda laughed. "I believe it. Did you hear that John Hicks' ex-wife has married that Alden Ames?"

"Disgraceful, I say," Mrs. Herbert clucked. "I guess John did go off to Mexico. Some say he did it to get away from the gossip. Poor dear."

On Wednesday, December 6, the Post Office was officially moved to the new building at the Arno Station and Mr. Metzner put in charge. The Hicksville Post Office was a thing of the past.

Christmas was a solemn affair. Lew and Media tried to instill a little Christmas cheer without too much success. Even the little tree seemed to droop, and the candles refused to stay lighted. Matilda sensed all was not well with Alf and Emma, for Emma maintained a grim silence the whole day and Alf's cheerfulness was obviously forced.

Finally, Matilda could stand it no longer and pulled Alf into the pantry where they could be alone. "What on earth is the matter?" she hissed. "Emma hasn't said a word all day. Have you two quarreled again?"

Alf hung his head and said nothing. Matilda waited.

"It's the loan to McFarland," he finally whispered. "It's due in January and I can't pay it."

"Will he give you an extension?"

"No. He wants the land."

"Of course," Matilda nodded. "That's how McCauley and Whitaker and all the rest got so much. Believe me, you are not the first to lose everything to those loan sharks." Her thoughts flew to poor Uncle Billy.

"But what am I gonna do,'Tilda?" he finally blurted. "And we just got the house fixed the way Emma likes it. She keeps telling me I was a fool to borrow money from McFarland."

Matilda remained silent, for she, too, had thought her brother had made a mistake. She watched him for a long moment. "I suppose you're going to have to give him the land. Does he have any claim to your equipment?"

"No, just the land and buildings."

"Then I suggest you look into a place to rent. You can continue your custom harvesting from there. I understand there is a place up on Taverner Road that may be available."

Hope sprang into his eyes as he looked up. "You're right. He takes the land and I'm free and clear. I can go on doing business, just from a different place. Thanks, Sis. I should have talked to you sooner." Then his face fell. "That will take care of McFarland, but I still have to deal with Emma."

"Talk to her when you get home. You had better go soon." She looked out the window. "It's getting thick again." The fog had been a major problem for the past two

538

weeks, day after day of grim grayness, with the sun seldom managing to break through for even a few hours in mid-day. "See you at Lou Herbert's birthday party in a couple of weeks."

In spite of the fog, a gala crowd gathered to congratulate Mr. Herbert on the occasion of his sixtieth birthday. Carrie and Sam circulated among the young people. Matilda settled in a comfortable chair, plied with fried chicken and a glass of punch, and listened to the neighborhood gossip as it flew around her. She chuckled softly. No need for newspapers. Just come to a neighborhood gathering and you will hear everything.

The big news, of course, was the closing of the Hicksville Post Office. Feelings seemed divided between those that thought the new facility an improvement and those who hated to see the old one abandoned, as it seemed disloyal to Uncle Billy's memory.

"Jim Hicks ever recover that horse and saddle as got stolen?" Jim McGuirk asked Tom McEnerney.

"Nope. Disappeared without a trace. Probably a hundred miles away by now. Doubt it was a local thief, just someone passin' through and saw his chance." Tom shook his head sadly. "Nice horse, too. And an expensive saddle." Then he grinned. "But I did hear Jim's talking about selling off the cattle and raising sheep instead. Says there's more money in sheep."

McGuirk shrugged. "Leastways never have a problem with coyotes runnin' off with a cow."

They moved beyond Matilda's hearing, and Helen Putney approached her. "Have thought of you often this past year, been a bad year for you. So sorry."

Matilda just nodded. She did not wish to talk about Mary

and Earl. It still hurt her too much.

Helen rattled on, in her usual fashion of jumping from one topic to another. "Hear that sister of Doc Montague's wife, the one as married the young man from New Hope, says they are thinking of moving to Walnut Grove. Mark my words, they won't like it. And I hear their brother Vin as lives up in Vina has been ailin' with consumption. Right worried about him, they are, especially after losing young Raymond like they did. Foolish, he was, not takin' care with the measles. And I hear scarlet fever is goin' through Galt. They say Etta Planalp got it, but Doc Montague treated her and she's recovering."

Before Matilda could reply, Helen was on to the next subject. "Now that Mr. Herbert is the Road Overseer for Hicksville, he has got to get them busy fixing the road again. George said the last time he came from Galt to Hicksville he noticed several bad spots. Sure don't want any more accidents like happened to poor Mary and Frank."

Matilda wholeheartedly agreed, but said nothing. Helen rambled on. "And wasn't that fire at Clausen's a shame? Lost not only the house and barn, but 25 tons of hay as well. No question but what it was an incendiary. The dreadful man pulled burning hay from the barn and dragged it to the back porch so the house would catch fire as well." She shook her head. "Just lucky no one was killed. Wasn't anyone at the house at the time. Mrs. Valensin owns it, Clausen just farms it, so he wasn't living in the house."

She looked over her shoulder and lowered her voice. "There are some as say whoever did it was tryin' to get back at Mrs. Valensin, her as has been runnin' kind of roughshod over the neighborhood, so to speak."

Matilda demurred at that. "Now, Helen, I'm sure Alice has only the best interests of the community in mind."

Helen nodded, skepticism all over her face. "Mark my words," she said ominously. "Mark my words."

The next event was the marriage on January 26 of Will and Mary's son Bud to Agnes Lawton. The girl had been working for the Randolph's and evidently caught Bud's eye. Matilda could not help but remember what Annie Hurd had told her about the girl as she watched them exchange their vows.

At the end of February, Will Hicks held his first social as proprietor of the Hicksville Hotel. The prime conversation was how people were using the newly installed long distance telephone service. One young man reported he played his guitar over the line while his girl friends along the route did the singing. Another amused his girl in Clements by playing his guitar over the wire. George Need claimed he could now talk with his lady friends without detection. Fred Bradshaw reported he had a different cipher for each girlfriend.

Matilda listened to these reports with amusement. "Charley Quiggle is figuring out how he can use the newfangled device to improve his real estate sales."

"Judge Ferris has said now he can consult with legal experts in Sacramento in technical points." Sam grinned. "I don't know if that's good or bad."

Matilda's Story: The California Years

Chapter 61

February to November, 1891

AFTER SAM DRIFTED off to talk to others, Jim and Benecia Chinnick came by to greet Matilda. She greeted them warmly. "And Penny, how is your father doing?"

Jim only shook his head. Tears sprang into Benecia's eyes. "My mother is very concerned about him," she said with a heartfelt sigh. "He keeps saying that life isn't worth living without Frank. We try and point out that he has me, and Mother, and little Ethel adores her Grandpa. In fact, since she lost her Uncle Frank, she clings to him more than ever."

Jim nodded. "We just can't seem to bring him out of it. We know Frank was the light of his life, but no one seems to be able to console him." He took a deep breath. "I've found him several times just sitting out by Frank's grave. He doesn't say a word, just comes home with me when I go after him, but . . . ." His voice trailed off.

Matilda could only sigh.

McFarland foreclosed on February 2, as Matilda feared he would, and Alf was forced to move. He did manage to rent the property Matilda had referred him to, up on Taverner Road in the Alta Mesa Colony.

He seemed resigned. "Emma likes the house, and has met a couple of the neighborhood ladies, so she has some friends. Should work out." He grinned ruefully. "But you were sure right, 'Tilda. I've learned my lesson. Stay away from folks as want to lend you money."

The community of Hicksville became more and more concerned with the actions (or lack of actions) by the Road Commissioners. Mrs. Herbert told Matilda all about it.

"Mrs. Valensin claims the culverts are too small to carry away the water when the spring floods come. Lou tried running it along the road, but that don't carry it away fast enough to suit. Says the levee dams the water up and makes it flood her place." She grinned. "Even that big fancy mansion can't stand up to being flooded year after year."

"And is Lou going to get them to do it?"

Mrs. Herbert nodded. "He's sure going to try. But right now, he's more concerned with getting them to replace the bridge over the Laguna, down by Judge Donaldson's place. Says someone is going to fall through and get killed if they don't get it fixed soon. He's presented the Commissioners with a petition all the neighborhood has signed."

"I hope it has some effect. Those bridges have been allowed to deteriorate to where they are a disgrace." Matilda fanned away a persistent fly with a little more energy than was really required.

"Gonna have to build the new one before the rains start again. They made a temporary road through Judge Donaldson's field to a low place that's fordable now, but sure won't be if it rains."

Mrs. Herbert panted a little as she carried the tray with the pot of tea, cups, and sugar to the little table where she and Matilda sat. "And did you see," she added, pouring them each a cup of the steaming tea, "the latest article in the *Gazette* bragging about how Arno is developing? New road, new Post Office, new telephone connection." She snorted. "And praising Alice Valensin for all the trees she's planting along the road."

Matilda had to laugh at Mrs. Herbert's indignation. "It also said Mr. Sawyer is building a fine, two-story house for all of the McEnerneys. Do you realize there are nine of them now?"

Annie Herbert grinned wryly. "Probably be ten by the time the house is built." Then she chuckled. "See where the W.C.T.U. has taken it upon themselves to drive Georgia Lawrence out of town?"

"Georgia Lawrence? Do I know her?"

"Probably not. She runs a bawdy house on Fourth, between A and B. Not a stone's throw from the schoolhouse. Campbell calls her the siren mistress of the Red Lights. When the ladies showed up at her door, she cordially invited them in. They refused and told her they were there to tell her to be out of town by Saturday."

"And did she agree to go?"

"Not at all. She told the ladies to go home and tend to their household duties and take care of their own husbands. As they left, she defied them all and told them she had come to stay the summer, and ended up by implying the husbands of four local households had already been clients of hers."

Matilda laughed. "I'll bet that did not set well with the good ladies."

"Not at all. They're hauling her into Court."

"Where the judge and all of the jury will be men?"

"You're right, 'Tilda," Mrs. Herbert laughed heartily. "The ladies have already lost, for all the *Gazette* agrees with them. Actually, his main objection is she's so close to the school. Didn't complain much about her activities. "

Mrs. Lawrence's trial came up in May and, true to Matilda's prediction, she was acquitted. Caroline Clough, in spite of being 82 years of age, took the lead in the prosecution, but to no avail, in spite of one witness describing the defendant as a "typical cigarette-smoking, whisky-drinking San Francisco hoodlum".

May also brought the unexpected death of James Short's wife Marie, a shock to the whole community, for she had been very popular with the denizens of Hicksville, in addition to being the wife of one of the little community's most prominent citizens and mother of Dr. William Short.

At her funeral, at the Hicksville Cemetery, Matilda noticed young Dr. Short did not look in the bloom of health. She commented on his pallor and the feverish look in his eyes to Carrie.

"Hush, Mother. Mrs. Short was so worried about him. She feared for some time that he's consumptive. Wouldn't surprise me a bit to find worrying about him brought on her collapse."

"Poor Jim," Matilda murmured. "I hope, for his sake, that we are mistaken."

The concern over Ezra Walton came to a head on the 29th of May. Lew and Media came by in the buggy. One look at their faces told Matilda something had happened.

"It's Mr. Walton, Mother," Lew said gently. "He's gone. We came to get you to take you over to see Mrs. Walton. She seems to take comfort from you."

"Well, he is seventy years old, after all, and he has been under a strain. Did his heart give out?" Matilda asked as Lew helped her into the buggy.

Lew hesitated. He glanced at Media, who nodded. "No,

Mother, he took his own life."

"Oh, no! His poor wife. And poor little Penny. And Ethel will be devastated. She adored her grandfather. What happened?"

"All I know is they found him lying with his head on Frank's grave with an empty laudanum bottle beside him. He left three notes. One for the Coroner, one for the Odd Fellows Lodge, and the third addressed to Jim Chinnick." He urged the horse into motion. "I guess the one to the coroner made it plain he took his own life, and the one to the Odd Fellows was about some unfinished lodge business." He paused and took a deep breath. "In the note to Jim, he said to make sure Ethel never forgot her grandpa, that he would always love her." He sighed. "And he said he wanted to be buried next to Frank in the Odd Fellows Cemetery there in Elk Grove."

In June, Dr. Montague's wife left hastily for Vina on the report that her brother Vin had taken a turn for the worse, and he died a week.

"Guess she went alone because her sister Isabel just had a baby girl, born on May fifteenth," Carrie told her mother as she reported the news. "Too soon for her to travel. They say her mother has been staying with her, so poor Nettie had to make the sad trip by herself." She smiled. "I hear Isabel named the baby Nettie, after her sister"

"Poor Mrs. Gaffney," Matilda sighed. "First her husband is killed by a horse and now she has lost both of her sons." Some day, she thought grimly, remembering the frustration as she lost Temperance and Caroline to consumption. Some day we will be able to defeat that dreadful disease. She forced her thoughts from the sad news. "Look, Carrie. Arno is going to have a hotel and a restaurant with a French cook. Mr. Viano is not only a cook, but an accomplished musician as well. He even tunes pianos. He can tune this lovely piano you bought with the money you saved working up in Garfield.

"And I guess being Postmaster doesn't keep Metzger busy enough. I see he is opening a carpentry shop, and has brought in a horseshoist for an adjoining blacksmith shop." Matilda chuckled softly. "The paper also says all of these developments are due to the "intelligent energy of Mrs. Valensin". I wonder what Annie Herbert will have to say about that!"

"Plenty, I'm sure," Carrie said with her soft laugh. "And did you see where Edison has invented an electrical contrivance which allows people to see a dramatic or operatic performance in their own house?" Carrie looked at her mother with awe in her face. "Can you imagine that?"

"Humph." Matilda was skeptical. "I'll believe it when I see it."

On the following Wednesday, as she put a kettle filled with jars on the stove to boil, preparatory to canning some of the tomato crop, Matilda smelled smoke.

Sam, seated at the table having a second cup of coffee after the morning chores, evidently smelled it as well, for he jumped to his feet. Carrie came running in, her basket half full of ripe tomatoes. "It's in Valensin's field," she told her brother and mother. And it's already big."

Sam jammed his hat on his head. "I'll get the buggy and the gear. Back in five minutes."

Matilda shoved the kettle to the back of the stove and hastened to fill the jug with drinking water and the basket with biscuits and cold chicken for the fire fighters. When Sam returned with the buggy, full water buckets clattering about in the back, a stack of burlap sacks on top, they met him at the door.

The fire had started at the railroad. "Those trains again," Matilda muttered, half under her breath when the origin became apparent. "Maybe my father was right."

Sam pulled the buggy to a halt in front of the hotel porch and several men ran to help him unload the buckets of water and the sacks. As the men took off on a run towards the fire line, Matilda handed the basket of chicken to Carrie and climbed down.

Annie Herbert greeted her. "Just barely got a back fire started in time to keep it away from the buildings. But it's raging through Moroney's wheat fields, and gonna take Alice's as well. Lucky for Denis, he's about half way through harvesting, so he won't lose it all."

As Matilda watched the skyline, great billows of light brown smoke rose into the air.

"It's no wonder we have such a fire going," Matilda murmured. "The weather has been so hot lately. Everything is dry as tinder."

"Yes," Annie nodded. "They say they've even had several folks die of the heat in Sacramento. Gets hotter there. They don't get our cool breeze."

Sam returned to the porch of the hotel, Will Hicks beside him, and both gratefully drank some of the cool lemonade Matilda had brought.

"Thank you, Mrs. Frye." Will wiped his sooty face with a grimy sleeve. "The fire has reached a swampy area east of Alf's old place, and seems to be dying down." He hesitated, then said, "But I'm afraid it went through the cemetery. Some of the graves only had wooden markers, and most of them burned."

With a sigh, Matilda thought of Mary and Earl. She had not been able to pay for a stone marker yet. She thought back to her discussion with Carrie, who had wanted to use some of the money she had earned teaching in Garfield to buy markers, especially for Mary, but Matilda had persuaded her to buy the piano and the sewing machine instead.

Her eyes met Carrie's and she saw Carrie thought the same thing. With a smile, she reassured the girl. "The piano and the sewing machine are for the living, Carrie dear. We'll put up another temporary marker until we can afford a permanent one."

In August, Alf told Matilda he and their brother John were suing a neighbor named Isaacs for damages.

"Lets those hogs of his run all over," Alf declared indignantly. "Got into that field I'm rentin' on shares with John, on the Hudson place, and ruined a whole field of corn. Five hundred dollars is a small price for him to pay for all the damage those wretched hogs of his done. By rights, we should ask for more, but John, him being a lawyer, says that's enough. Says we'll have a better chance of getting what we ask for."

"Well, I wish you luck," Matilda said with a smile. "I'm sure you can use the money. Have you heard we are going to have a brand new school here in Hicksville? The paper says we are more enterprising than Galt. They are trying to get the State to pay for a new school. Here, the people decided to just raise the money. A Benefit Ball is scheduled early in September."

"I wish the good ladies the best. Did you hear that Doc Montague's brother Alpheus was in a buggy accident? Guess he lost a wheel and the buggy overturned."

"No!" Matilda gasped. "Was he injured?"

"Just bruised a bit. There are some as are saying someone loosened the wheel to get even with Doc. Guess he's finally put some teeth into his rule about no more pig sties in the town limits, and some folks are upset. Probably the ones who have ignored his orders."

"He's been trying to get rid of those pig sties for quite a while now," she chuckled. "Guess he decided the only way he'd ever succeed is to put his foot down."

"Well," Alf grinned, "we'll see what happens."

In September, Sawyer created a sheltering shed for buggies at the new Arno Refreshment Room, to add to Metzner's new carpenter shop and blacksmith. Matilda could not repress a sigh. The encroachment on Hicksville continued.

Also in September Matilda, with Carrie and Sam, attended the Benefit Ball for the funds for the new schoolhouse.

Carrie returned to where her mother sat with a dish of ice cream for her. She laughed softly. "Some of the ladies are complaining some of the Galt Merchants refused to buy School Benefit tickets. They are furious, and talking about putting out a list of those merchants and passing it around so all Hicksville people can boycott them."

Matilda laughed. "I'll bet that would not set well with the merchants. Perhaps they should have threatened that earlier."

"Probably." Carrie sighed. "Did you hear that Fred Harvey is taking Genevieve back to Philadelphia where she will go to school? He's continuing at the Boston School of Technology."

"Must be nice to have a rich father," Sam commented dryly.

Celestia Johnson joined them. "Quite a successful benefit," she remarked. "Have netted over $100. Now just have to get enough to buy some new desks."

"Would have been nice if they could have gotten enough

to build a porch," Carrie sighed.

Celestia nodded. "Maybe when they sell the old building at auction they'll get enough. I understand they've delayed the sale for a week."

Helen Putney strolled up and greeted the group. "Did you hear Henry Hauschildt is getting ready to purchase the Beckwith Ranch? Watch that man. He's going to be one of our wealthiest ranchers."

"Good for him," Matilda smiled. "I'd like to see him do well. I understand he is an honest man and a hard worker."

"Got a new druggist at Whitaker and Ray's," Celestia announced. "Name of Archibald. Mr. McIntyre has decided to return to New York. Something about family responsibilities."

"Sorry to see him go," Matilda murmured. "Always found him helpful and obliging." She smiled at them. "You ladies coming to the Sunday School picnic at Keagle's Grove? I know the girls have been working very hard on the 'Wheel of Fortune' quilt they plan to auction off."

"Planning on it," Celestia said. "After all, only fifteen cents for lunch and fifteen cents for a dish of ice cream is a pretty good price."

"And we are going to present both literary and musical entertainment," Carrie offered shyly. "We'd be very pleased to see you ladies there."

At the end of October, her brother Tom and his wife Mary visited from Oleta, bringing a load of fine mountain apples.

Matilda greeted them warmly. "Reminds me of the barrel of apples our sister Sarah sent from Illinois when we had that dreadful drought in Kansas in '60. You missed that. You and Abe and Minerva had left Kansas by then."

Tom hugged her and grinned. "And never regretted it for

a moment."

"So how is mountain life agreeing with you?"

"Dull. Can't compare the company up there to here. Sure do miss all of our old friends."

"You'll just have to move back," Matilda laughed.

"We may do just that. I hear a couple of my neighbors are dickering to buy the Hicksville Hotel from young Will Hicks."

Matilda sighed. "I did hear that he's sold it to some Amador County people. Such a shame. And the *Galt Gazette* predicts Hicksville will soon be a thing of the past, that Arno will be the place of the future."

"Too bad." Tom sighed. "Poor old Uncle Billy. Swindled out of his land by Alice's father, and now Alice is going to wipe out his town."

True to Annie Herbert's prediction, the tenth McEnerney put in his appearance on the 4th of November. And on the 20th, Miller and DeVore, the new owners of the Hicksville Hotel, gave a ball to celebrate their grand opening. The neighborhood reported it a rousing success, and hopes the hotel would thrive under its new owner were high.

Matilda could only sigh when she heard this. "I certainly hope so," was all she said.

Sam rode home from the Post Office the next day grinning from ear to ear. "Jim Hicks almost blew off his foot. He was rubbing a sore corn with the muzzle of his shotgun when the gun went off."

Matilda gasped in horror. "Will he lose his foot?"

Sam grinned. "Doc says no, but he did succeed in shooting off the corn!"

Chapter 62

January to May, 1892

1892 OPENED WITH a Bonbon Party at the Hicksville Hotel. Matilda, Carrie, and Sam attended along with Lew and Media and most of the neighborhood.

The hostess Mrs. Miller greeted Matilda and her party warmly. "I'm so glad you could join us, Mrs. Frye. We missed you at the last dance."

Matilda smiled. "Thank you. We were all suffering a touch of la grippe, and I'm afraid would not have been very good company."

"I understand Dr. Montague has been treating Mrs. Valensin and Pio for the same thing. It must be going around. I know a lot of folks have been down with that achy fever. That's probably why attendance in December was so light."

"But I understand everyone who did come had a wonderful time," Matilda reassured her.

Mrs. Miller smiled and turned to greet Tom Riley and his wife. Matilda and her family moved on into the hall.

"Did you hear the steam carriage has a new rival in the gasoline quadruped of Mr. Peugeot?" Lew said with a grin.

Matilda shook her head. "What will they think of next?"

Later in January, on a clear, cold day, Matilda had Sam

drive her and Carrie to Galt. "Whitaker and Ray's Department store has a special on calico. Your sister is sadly in need of a couple of new dresses, now that she has that fancy new sewing machine."

"She just wants an excuse to practice with her latest toy," Sam chuckled. "If she had to sew them by hand, I'm sure she would be happy with the dresses she already has."

"You're probably right," Carrie laughed. "Sewing a long seam by hand is pretty tedious. The machine does it in a few moments. But he's also selling white wool blankets for only four dollars. That's two dollars off the regular price.

That afternoon, with several bolts of calico, numerous spools of thread, and two of the new blankets in the back of the buggy, the three of them stopped at the Post Office in Arno. Every time she went by Matilda felt a twinge of regret for the loss of the Hicksville Post Office. Poor Uncle Billy.

Sam pulled the buggy to a halt in front of the hitching post and assisted his mother and sister to alight. Sam stayed with the horse while Carrie and Matilda entered the building.

Mrs. Metzger greeted them from behind the counter. Her baby slept in a small bed beside her. "Mrs. Poston has been watching the mail for me, but she took the train to Los Angeles yesterday. Seems her brother as lives down there has passed on. And I hear John McFarland's brother Duncan has died up in Canada, so he's headed up there."

"That's too bad. Is Mary going to go back with John?"

Mrs. Metzger shrugged. "She's got all those babies. Be right hard for her to - -."

"Look out!" The shout from Sam interrupted them and all three scurried to the door. As they watched in horror, the tower on which the two water tanks rested seemed to crumble.

Matilda stared, mesmerized by the scene, which seemed to be happening in slow motion. Plank after plank popped loose from the supporting towers, then the northwestern leg folded in on itself. As it tilted more, one of the water tanks tumbled to the ground with a shattering of wood, a cloud of dust, and splashes of water.

The fall of the first tank settled the fate of the second one. In eerie silence, it came straight down, landing with a crash that sent wooden fragments of the tank and water in a wide circle.

Men came running from every direction. Sam hurried to Matilda, who clung to the porch upright, her knees refusing to hold her. "Was anyone underneath that?" she finally managed to gasp.

"No," Sam assured her. "Luckily, no one was hurt." He grinned suddenly. "But it sure made a mess of those towers. Trains aren't going to be taking on water here for a while."

Matilda took a deep breath. "I think I've had enough excitement for one day. Let's go home."

The next major event to catch their attention was the fire at the Arcade Livery Stables.

"Began about midnight last Saturday," Lew reported to Matilda, Carrie, and Sam. "Reduced the whole block to a pile of ashes within two hours."

"Was anyone killed?" was Matilda's first question.

"Luckily not. Joe Angrave was sleeping in a room in the stable on the first floor. He heard the fire roaring overhead in the hay loft and raised the alarm. He managed to get all of the horses out. The buggies are a total loss."

"Oh, I'm so glad none of the poor horses were burned,"

Carrie cried.

"Everyone is saying it was the work on an incendiary except Charlie Quiggle." Lew chuckled. "Charlie got everything out of his house, so he didn't lose much, leading some to believe maybe he set it. His theory is some tramp spent the night in the loft and started it by accident. McKinstry, on the other hand, insists it began at the torch of a fire fiend. He even claims to know who it was, although he admits he has no proof."

Matilda sighed. "I guess we will just have to wait and see."

On February 5, Caroline Clough died in her home at the age of 84.

"They say she never got over her rage at the men who acquitted Mrs. Lawrence," Sam chuckled as he reported the news to his mother and sister. "Her daughter says that was all her mother could talk about. Says that brought on the attack of apoplexy that killed her."

Matilda sighed. "Just goes to prove what I've always said. Don't ever let your anger take control of you."

"She lived to be 84," Sam nodded. "That's long past the biblical three score and ten."

"Yes," Matilda agreed. "Not even my mother lived that long."

"And one of the Hanson girls down at the blacksmith shop was chopping hay with a hay knife and managed to cut off the ends of two fingers."

"Oh, dear, will she be all right?" Matilda gasped.

"Doc Montague says she'll recover, but will have two short fingers." He reached for another biscuit and slathered on a spoonful of elderberry jelly from the glass on the table. "And I hear Count Valensin has taken his new wife and gone to spend the summer in Cleveland showing his horses."

"Did he marry that woman he ran away with?" Carrie asked.

"Well," Sam grinned, "she went with him. That's all I know."

On a fine day in April, Matilda asked Sam to give her a ride over to see Jane Mahin.

"I haven't seen her all winter, the weather has been so dreadful."

Jane greeted her friend with enthusiasm. "I've missed you, 'Tilda. You look wonderful. How you always manage to look so healthy is a wonder."

Matilda laughed and returned her friend's embrace. Jane hustled her into the kitchen where she scurried about making them a pot of tea, and set a plate of gingerbread on the table between them.

"My family is almost as scattered as yours," Matilda said. "Sam over in Lake County, Sally and Essie with him, Tom still in Oleta, John clear up in Washington, and I hear he is planning to move to Idaho. Carrie has applied for a teaching position at the Alabama School." She smiled, "And I suppose you've heard that the Millers who have the hotel now have a new baby girl."

"Yes, I heard that." Jane took a deep breath. "Gracie has diphtheria. John and Mary are quite worried about her. That new doctor, Dr. Morgan, , had some new kind of treatment, and she seems to be getting better, but she's not out of danger yet."

Matilda's thoughts flew to Earl. "Has it affected her heart?"

"We don't know," Jane sighed. "Poor John had a hard

time getting to town to get the doctor. He's had a petition for a road to his property before the Board of Supervisors for a long time. His neighbor, Presbury, had put a fence across the way. John's attorney advised him to cut the fence to get through, so he did."

"Sounds pretty un-neighborly of Presbury."

"Wasn't it? And when John returned with the medicine, Russell, the other neighbor stopped him, and said he would only get through over his, Russell's, dead body."

Matilda chuckled, "I'd think twice about issuing such a challenge to a man who has a sick child waiting for medicine."

"I guess Russell had second thoughts as well, for John said that could be arranged, and waved his shotgun under the fool's nose, so he let him pass." Jane shook her head. "A fine thing, when a man's family is sick and he can't get to town to the doctor. Anyway, it's supposed to come up before the supervisors soon, then it will be settled."

"I hear Count Valensin is ill, back in Cleveland where he is showing his horses. They say he is suffering from paralysis of the stomach."

"I assume his new wife is with him?" Jane grinned wryly. "I hear her husband finally got a divorce, so I guess the Count married her."

"Annie Herbert thinks so, but she couldn't say for sure."

Gracie Bandeen died on April 18. Sam reported the sad news to his mother.

"So I guess Dr. Morgan's medicine was no more effective than Dr. Montague's."

Sam shrugged. "Sawyer's wife recovered, so I guess some people survive. I came to get you because I knew you would want to go see Jane."

"Let me get my shawl."

Early the next morning, an earthquake struck with such intensity the whole house shook, even knocking over some plates in the cupboard. Matilda jumped out of bed, meeting Carrie emerging from her room.

"That was a strong one," Carrie gasped. "Is anything broken?"

Matilda scanned the shelves, replacing some plates in their stacks. "Not here, anyway. Let's check the basement." Visions of the '68 quake which had knocked so many things off the shelves rose in her mind.

They hurried to the basement, where she discovered her foresight in having the lip built on the shelves in the basement had paid off. Most of the jars of canned goods and glasses of jelly and jam survived intact. Carrie stooped and picked up one broken jar.

"Looks like we were luckier this time." Carrie set some more jars upright that had fallen over but not broken.

"Not lucky," Matilda chuckled grimly. "I had your father put that edge on the shelves for this very reason."

The next afternoon, as Gracie Bandeen was laid to rest in the Hicksville Cemetery, an aftershock struck, shaking the ground beneath the crowd of mourners, causing some consternation among them. One woman screamed and all clung to one another. Fortunately, the tremor passed quickly.

"Just a little aftershock, folks." Reverend Hyden reassured the crowd. "Please join us in the church for refreshments.

As the group filed off to the church where the ladies prepared the funeral repast, Matilda and Jane paused by little Henry Bandeen's grave, then stood a moment by Tom Mahin's.

Jane sighed. "He was such a good man, 'Tilda." She took two small sprigs of flowers from the offerings at Gracie's site and placed one by Tom's headstone. "I'm sure he will take good care of Gracie, wherever they are now." She walked back over to little Henry's grave and placed the second bouquet there, then broke into sobs against Matilda's shoulder. Matilda held her while she cried and slowly led her back towards the little church. They stood outside while Jane blew her nose and wiped her eyes. Then she smiled. "Thank you, 'Tilda. You're a good friend. I'm ready to face people now. Let's go in."

Another aftershock struck on Thursday, then the earth seemed to settle down.

"Hear they had a lot of damage to buildings in Sacramento," Sam reported. "They got it a lot worse than we did."

"Well, I'm certainly glad we didn't have any major damage here. Did you hear George McConnell is building a new house on his father's place? Does that mean he's planning to get married?"

Sam shrugged. "Haven't heard a word. But the big news is that Count Valensin died. Died April 15th, he did, but the news just reached us. Guess the body is being shipped to Florence for burial. His mother and sister live there."

"A shame," Matilda murmured. "He was still a young man."

"Forty, as I understand." Sam said. "Will be interesting to see what comes out in the paper."

The next day, Sam returned with a copy of the *Galt Gazette*, turned to the article on Giulio Valensin's death.

"Says his principal mourner is the valet who was with him since his childhood." Sam grinned. "Guess his valet misses him more than his wife or his mother and sister.

562

Also says he was not a Count, and objected to being called one, since he 'expressed the greatest dislike to that cognomen, because he did not wish to be accredited with any false rank'. Never bothered him when he lived here, as I recall."

Matilda laughed softly. "I suspect it was Alice who liked it when he was thought of as a Count. She has always considered herself royalty."

"Says his wife and her mother, Mrs. Paine, will take the body to Italy as soon as Mrs. Paine gets from Sacramento to Ohio."

"Does it say much about Alice?" Carrie wanted to know.

"I quote: 'Happiness reigned supreme for a few years, but finally Mr. Valensin tired of rural life and neglected his family. He became anything but a model husband.'"

Carrie giggled. "Go on," she urged.

"'For a long time, Mrs. Valensin suffered the indignities heaped upon her by her husband.'"

"I remember many of them," remarked Matilda dryly.

"'But finally she appealed to the Court and was given a legal separation from her husband and was awarded custody of her son Pio. The unfaithful husband next eloped with a married woman in Sacramento. The husband of the latter in due time secured a divorce and Valensin married the woman.'" Sam looked up from his reading at the two expectant faces before him.

"Is that all?" Carrie asked.

Sam grinned. "Essentially. The only other thing he says is 'Here we drop the veil with charity toward the dead man, who is now before his maker and can best answer all questions.' And yes, that's all."

"Thus ends an era," Matilda murmured.

"Yes, looks like it." Sam put the paper down on the table

and rose to refill his coffee cup. "Did hear one other thing in town," he commented. "Viola Briggs is filing for an annulment."

"Annulment? Why? I thought they were quite happy." Matilda shook her head. "They've only been married for a couple of years."

"Because," Sam grinned, "it seems that Bill has a wife in Missouri and he never legally separated from her. He forgot to mention that little detail to Viola. When she found out, she was upset, to say the least."

Matilda laughed merrily and quoted. "Oh, what a tangled web we weave!"

"And the C Street Hotel, formerly the Galt House, will re-open on the 23rd of May. Beckman has completely renovated it into a first class hotel, with forty bedrooms, parlors and sitting rooms. Should be real nice. George May is going to manage it."

"Well, I wish him well," Matilda sighed. "Past experiments with hotels in Galt have not been too successful."

"Well," Sam said, "At least he doesn't have some determined incendiary trying to burn him out, like Hicksville and Arno."

"Hush!" Matilda shook her head. "Don't even mention incendiaries."

Two weeks later, on Monday evening close to midnight, the smell of smoke wafting in through the open window woke Matilda from a sound sleep. Startled, she sat bolt upright in the bed. Had their fire fiend struck again?

Chapter 63

May to November 1892

SAM WAS UP and dressed when Matilda entered his room. "I smelled it too, Mother. Look west. You can see the flames. It's either Arno or Hicksville."

"And Mrs. Miller has a young baby. I do hope it's not Hicksville."

Carrie joined them, her worried face reflected by the light of the lamp she carried. "Are the fields dry enough to burn? Will it reach us?"

Matilda hastened to reassure her. "We just had a good rain. Everything is still pretty green."

"I'll be back as soon as I know." Sam pulled his hat onto his head and ran for the door. "Put on the coffee."

Matilda and Carrie sat in the kitchen and awaited Sam's return. Time passed slowly. One or the other would walk to the window every few minutes to check on the progress of the fire.

Carrie sat down again after her latest check. "Seems to be dying down. They must be getting it under control."

"I do hope it wasn't the Hicksville Hotel," Matilda sighed. "Poor Mrs. Miller. And Mr. Miller is up in Reno, so she's all alone."

"We'll know soon," Carrie replied. Then she giggled. "Did you hear that man Smith, one of Sheriff Stanley's deputies, is up to his old tricks? He's been collecting the rent on Mrs. Dr. Patterson's house in Galt. Since Dr. P. moved his practice to San Francisco, she's been renting to a fellow who's been paying rent regularly to Smith, as her agent, but Smith has been neglecting to send the money on to her."

Matilda shook her head. "Fine goings on for a deputy sheriff. Surprised Stanley keeps him on."

Carrie shrugged. "Guess Sheriff Stanley figures Smith has his uses. But Mrs. P decided it wasn't worth it. She sold the house to Don Ray."

"I'd like to see Smith try and swindle Don Ray," Matilda chuckled.

"No way." Carrie shook her head. "He's met his match. No one can out-swindle Don Ray."

Matilda rose and checked the fire. "Seems to have died down. Sam should be home soon."

"Hope it was not the Arno Post Office. Metzner is already talking of leaving Arno and moving to Galt." Carrie laughed softly. "I guess Alice Valensin is a tough landlady. Mrs. Metzner was telling me just the other day that she thinks Alice is trying to drive them out to take the job of Post Master for herself."

Matilda could only sigh.

Sam returned half an hour later, his face sooty, his clothing reeking of smoke. His mother and sister looked at him expectantly.

"Was the Hicksville Hotel." He shook his head sadly as he poured himself a cup of coffee and joined them at the table. "But everyone got out safe, just in the nick of time."

Matilda heaved a heartfelt sigh of relief. "I was so worried about Mrs. Miller and the baby."

"Place burned fast, all the way to the ground in under thirty minutes. It was almost all over by the time I got there."

"And an incendiary again?" Matilda knew the answer before Sam replied.

"Yep. Started in the kitchen and back porch. Smelled coal oil all over."

"Three hotels burned in the space of as many years," Matilda murmured. "Looks like someone does not want a hotel at Hicksville."

The summer passed quietly. As suspected, Alice Valensin got herself appointed Postmistress of the Arno Post Office, and named her son Pio Deputy Postmaster.

"Nepotism is alive and well," Matilda commented to Annie Herbert, who had related the news to her.

"What's that?" Annie looked blank.

"Nothing, just something that came into my head. What's this I hear about Maud Theobold from up Sheldon way eloping with a married man?"

Nothing loathe, Annie launched in to the tale. "Only fifteen, she is, and fancies herself in love with George Kelly, him as is not only a married man, but forty-two years old as well. Must be in his second childhood. Poor Mr. Theobold tried to stop it and Kelly hit him with an axe."

"No!" Matilda gasped. "Did he kill him?"

"By some miracle it was a glancing blow and just knocked him out. Doc Nestell says he'll recover." Mrs. Herbert shook her head. "And can you believe Maud took off with that man, with her father lying there unconscious? Such goings on. Disgraceful."

Matilda's mind flew to Abe's new bride, Susan Theobold. She had come from Sacramento, according to Laura, and Sheldon was not that far from the city. Could it be the same family? She would have to ask Laura.

Mrs. Herbert was on to the next subject. "And Celestia, bless her heart, has taken back the Hicksville Hotel. Says she's going to rebuild."

"After being burned out three times?" Matilda stared at her friend in wonder. "She's got more courage than I have, I'm afraid."

"Oh, yes, Celestia's got gumption, all right. Enough to get rid of that husband of hers. Take more than an incendiary to drive her off. And did you hear George McConnell got married?"

"Oh, yes, at the bride's parents' home at the Union House. Carrie, Sam, and I went to the wedding with Lew and Media. We suspected he had plans when he built that lovely new home on his father's place. Hattie Sims made a charming bride."

Annie Herbert sniffed. "Well, they never invited me and Lou." She dismissed the McConnell nuptials with a wave of her hand. "And a feller name of Meyers got a horse-whipping from his landlady. Seems he made some comments about her character she didn't take kindly to."

Matilda laughed heartily. "Serves him right. I trust he will hold his tongue in the future."

Elk Grove was the next community to feel the incendiary's wrath. Carrie and Matilda heard all about it when they visited Ezra Walton's widow.

"Started about 10 o'clock at the Toronto Hotel, it did, and immediately took the hotel, the depot, the Post Office, and Mr. Andrews' fine general merchandise store." She clicked her tongue in dismay and shook her head. "Railroad fire engine got there about 11 o'clock with two water tank cars and managed to save the Elk Grove House. Got there too late to save Everson's house and store." She sighed and her eyes filled with tears. "And the Odd Fellows building burned to the ground. Ezra would be heart broken, were he alive to hear it. He worked so hard to get that building erected when they chartered the Odd Fellows here in Elk Grove."

She rose and refilled the plate of cookies. "And I hear tell Tom Loughran is selling his place over there at Arno. Good rich bottom land, it is. Should get a good price for it. Why's he selling?"

"Says he's tired of farming, feels it's time to retire and take it easy," Matilda laughed. "Some are saying it's because that son of his will never be a farmer."

"Shame. Means a lot to a man to have a son to take over." Mrs. Walton emitted a heartfelt sigh. "I know that's one reason Ezra took it so hard when we lost Frank. They had worked the blacksmith shop up to such a good business . . . ." Her voice trailed off and she fell silent.

Matilda felt it time to change the subject, so she said brightly, "Did you hear Lack Quiggle proposes to introduce kangaroos? Says they are a good source of both fur and hide. Easy to domesticate and breed well in captivity."

"Kangaroos!" Mrs. Walton exclaimed, "What will they think of next?"

"And Carrie Mason, wife of Joe Mason who has the butcher shop in Forest Lake, left her baby with a friend in Sacramento and loped off to San Francisco. The grandmother picked up the baby, and Joe is still looking for his wife."

On August 16, Alf rode over to bring Matilda the news that he had received a telegram from Sally in Lake County. "She says she found Sam dead on the floor," he told Matilda and Carrie gently. "Guess his heart gave out."

Matilda felt as if the floor had dropped from beneath her feet. Sam. The one she had always turned to. Her rock. She must have turned pale, for Carrie hurried to her side.

"Mother!"

Matilda smiled wanly into Carrie's worried face. "I'm all right. It just took my breath away for a moment. We had no idea he had any health problems." She remembered her concern for him on his last visit, when he was trying to borrow money from Whitaker and Ray. Could financial worries have brought on his death? They would probably never know.

"I'm on my way over there. I told Sally I'd come," Alf told them. "No need for you to join me. Essie and Sally are there. I'll try to find his will and make all of the necessary arrangements."

Matilda nodded mutely. Three of my sisters gone, she thought, and now four of my brothers.

Alf returned a week after he left, and Matilda rushed to the door to meet him. "We've been wondering when we'd hear from you. Did you bring Sam with you? Did you find his will?"

Alf took her in his arms. "We buried him there, me and Essie and Sally and a host of friends he had made in the area. It was what he would have wanted. The expense of trying to bring him back to bury in Hicksville was just too great. He left the place to Sally, and she wanted him near."

Stunned, Matilda stared at him. "But I never got a chance to say goodbye," she cried.

"He knew you loved him, that's all that matters," Alf said gently. "And I found his will. He had hidden it in a secret drawer in his dresser."

"Couldn't have been too secret if you found it so easily,"

Matilda remarked dryly.

"Oh, it wasn't easy. It took me some time to find it." He hesitated. "Sam meant to leave a lot to everyone, for he names all of us in his will, but I'm afraid by the time Whitaker and Ray are paid off, there won't be much left. I just hope we can hang on to the place for Sally. She wants to stay there."

Matilda sighed. "I feared something like this would happen. Once those vultures got him in their clutches . . .." Her voice trailed off.

"Sally will be all right, and she'll take care of Essie." He grinned. "Met her gentleman friend. Name of Jimmy Brennard. He's a little older than she is, but is besotted with her. Fine man, he is."

The next story to circulate through the little community was that the Reverend McCallum of the Methodist Church in Elk Grove had disappeared.

On Matilda's next visit to Mrs. Walton, it was all she and Benecia could talk about.

"Word was goin' around that he'd been kidnapped and murdered," Mrs. Walton chuckled. "Then it turns out a married lady from his congregation disappeared at the same time."

"Leading to a lot of speculation that he hadn't been kidnapped at all," Penny chimed in.

"And then his wife gets this letter from him mailed in Omaha. He gives her this cock and bull story about how two men seized him, drove him around for a while, then gave him forty dollars and a railroad ticket and told him to get on the first train." Mrs. Walton shook her head in disbelief.

"And if that wasn't enough," Penny added, "he said they

told him they'd murder him if he ever came back to Elk Grove."

"And did he suggest his wife join him in Omaha?" Matilda asked.

"Not one hint," Penny responded. "Didn't even tell her exactly where he was located. All she knows is the letter was postmarked Omaha."

Matilda shook her head. "Such goings on for a minister of the gospel."

Penny grinned. "Mrs. McCallum didn't buy the tale either. Word is she's already talked to Grove Johnson about a divorce on grounds of desertion."

On Thanksgiving Eve, Matilda, Carrie, and Sam attended the Thanksgiving Ball hosted by Celestia Johnson celebrating the grand opening of the newly re-built Hicksville Hotel.

One of the main topics of conversation was the fire at H.C. Bell's place on the Laguna, about a mile and a half from Hicksville.

"Lost not only the barn and the baled hay, but two fine horses and his new harvester," Tom Riley told Matilda.

"Did they ever find out how it started?" Matilda asked, ever fearful that the local incendiary had struck again.

"No, but there's no evidence it was set deliberate. Probably someone knocked over a lantern."

Tom Riley moved on and Helen Putney joined Matilda. She settled into her chair with a sigh of relief. "Feels good to set a spell. I hear John McClanahan's wife had a twelve pound baby boy."

"Twelve pounds! Oh, my. That's pretty big," Matilda gasped. "Is she all right?"

"Just fine. They say the Irish are born to have babies."

She chuckled. "I guess they're right." She ate in silence for a moment, then said. "I hear Gus Hauschildt married Ruby Hatton. And I hear his brother George is thinking of tying the knot as well."

"How is Ruby's health?" Matilda asked. "I understand she's consumptive."

Helen shook her head. "Doc Montague has been treating her. I guess she's doing fairly well. They say Cora Quiggle married one of the Bottimore boys. And didn't Will and Polly's boy Bud just produce his first?"

"Yes," Matilda nodded. "Agnes delivered a beautiful baby boy October 12. They named him William Michael after his father and grandfather." She smiled "He's an adorable baby. I'm just sorry Polly didn't live to see him."

"Shame about your brother Sam. Right sorry to hear it, him always being so healthy and active. Knew traipsin' off to Lake County was a bad move. Should'a been suspicious of anything Don Ray and Andrew Whitaker have a hand in"

"Yes," Matilda sighed. "Like my Sammie says, Don Ray sure got his hooks into poor old Uncle Sam. Looks like they won in the end. Sam tried to leave his estate to his surviving family members, but Whitaker will get most of it."

"I hear Whitaker's under a doctor's care. Some are sayin' his heart is real bad."

"Really?" Matilda had not heard that. Then she chuckled softly. She knew it was a wicked thought, but could not help feeling there was perhaps some justice in the world after all.

Chapter 64

December 1892 to July 1893

CHRISTMAS CAME and went amid a spell of dreary fog that continued into January. Day after day of relentless gloom passed with the sun never managing to break through even for a few minutes during the day.

Matilda shivered from the cold and damp. Her knees pained her, and the joints in her hands swelled. She remembered how her mother had suffered so badly with rheumatism, and hoped the aches would pass when the sun returned.

One bright spot in her life that dismal winter was the anticipated birth of Elizabeth and Henry's third child. Since Pearl was eleven and Henry Junior, eight, Matilda had begun to think there would be no more. She smiled at the thought of another baby.

In March, news reached them that D.K. Stringfield had died of consumption at the age of 41 in Bucoda, Washington where he had moved his family to be nearer his brother and sister after his father died in Santa Barbara.

Matilda read his obituary, copied by the local paper from the Washington papers. Her heart went out to poor Maggie, to be widowed so young. Matilda certainly knew how that felt. And she knew Gussie and Alice adored their father.

She had to smile at the memory of the comment in the *Gazette* when D.K. left Galt, about the ends not justifying the means. Lew and Sam had tried and tried to learn what Campbell had meant by that cryptic remark, but were never able to find out anything, and Campbell would never say.

Alf came by and told them that someone had broken into Tommy Riley's smokehouse and robbed him of thirteen porkers he had just butchered and hung.

Sam chuckled at the news. "Sure Judge Donaldson didn't have a hand in it? Our expounder of Blackstone has been threatening to sue Tommy. Says it's Tommy's fault his wife left him."

Matilda, shocked, had to gasp. "Surely he would never stoop to common thievery."

Alf grinned. "Hard to say. I know he's furious. Been sayin' some pretty harsh words about our boy Tommy."

"But Tommy has a wife and four children. Why would he want Donaldson's wife?"

Sam shrugged. "No one said she left Donaldson for Tommy, only that he encouraged her to leave."

"I suppose that is a fine line to draw," Matilda remarked caustically. "How is Mrs. McGuirk? I hear she has a terrible abscess on her jaw, and that they took her to the hospital in Sacramento."

Alf shook his head sadly. "Not well. She's probably have been better off with some of Mother's herbal poultices instead of all of those doctors cutting on her."

Matilda could only sigh. Alf was probably right. "And I suppose the roads are in terrible condition again. Thank heavens this dreadful fog has finally left us. I was beginning to think we would never see the sun again!"

On March 28, Elizabeth presented Matilda with another

granddaughter, a child they named Virginia. Matilda, who had been present at the birth, cuddled the precious bundle. No matter how many times she held a newborn, she never ceased to marvel at the miracle of birth, at the wonder of holding a new life in her arms.

Pearl stood beside Matilda, her eyes wide in wonder as she stroked her baby sister's silky hair. "Isn't she beautiful, Grandmother? Isn't she the most beautiful baby you've ever seen?"

The baby, totally oblivious to all the attention, yawned and stretched her little arms above her head. Matilda smiled at Pearl. "Yes, you have a lovely little sister. And she's going to have your father's blond hair and your mother's dark eyes. She will be a beauty."

A week later, after church services, Annie Herbert spoke with Matilda over coffee and cookies, and congratulated her on her latest grandchild.

"Land sakes, was beginning to look like she and Henry were only going to have the two. Henry, Junior, now, he must be seven or eight."

"He's eight," Matilda said. "I guess Elizabeth has been so busy helping Henry run the cattle every summer she never had time for more babies. But after the buggy upset and threw them all in the ditch, she felt she should stay home with the children, not wanting to risk them like that again. They were fortunate no one was seriously injured, but it frightened her."

"Wise of her," commented Mrs. Herbert. Then she chuckled. "Remember Helen tellin' you young McKenzie would regret moving to Walnut Grove?"

"Very well," Matilda laughed.

"Guess he's been having all sorts of problems. He had one neighbor arrested for stealing some hay, another for malicious mischief, and a third, a woman, for foul language and disturbing the peace."

"Oh, my. Doesn't sound like he's made himself very popular."

"That's putting it mildly," Mrs. Herbert said wryly. "One of 'em got even by setting fire to his barn."

"Oh, no!"

"Oh, yes. I hear he's plannin' to move to Galt. Has put in a word to rent the Beckwith house, him movin' out as he is."

May brought sunshine and warm weather. Matilda's knees continued to pain her, but at least her hands stopped hurting, and she was able to help Carrie get the garden planted.

Sam helped her to her feet as she finished tamping the dirt around the last tomato plant in the row. One look at his face told her he was bursting with news.

"What is it?" she asked.

"Birdie Andruss. Remember her?"

"Yes, the flighty one that ran off at fifteen and married that Trueblood fellow."

"She's filing for divorce, on grounds of desertion and failure to provide. Seems her swain loped off without her to parts unknown."

Matilda shook her head. "Let that be a lesson to her."

In June, a tong war in Sacramento exposed plans to blow up buildings. "The Chee Kong Tong says they are in a highbinder war," Sam reported to his mother.

"Highbinder? What on earth is that?"

"A member of a secret Chinese band. Anyway, some of the fellows are saying we should take a bunch of men and clean out Chinatown."

"Oh, I hope it doesn't come to that," Matilda exclaimed. "Surely there are many innocent Chinese who don't want problems either."

"I guess saner heads have prevailed," Sam grinned, "but I don't plan to go down there until I'm sure it's settled."

"Look, Mother," Carrie cried, pointing west. Busy picking apricots from the tree in the back yard, Matilda followed Carrie's arm with her eyes and saw black smoke rising in a column.

"Get Sam," she told Carrie, climbing down the ladder and putting the bucket in the shade of the tree. "Dear God, don't let it be Celestia's hotel again."

They arrived at Hicksville to find Rose Johnson's blacksmith shop engulfed in flames. Rose herself was passing buckets in the line when Matilda arrived.

"Come," Matilda soothed, leading the distraught woman away. "Let the men fight it." She led Rose to the porch where she stood watching the men's efforts, wringing her hands, tears flowing down soot stained cheeks.

"Both mowing machines," she wailed, "my new hay rake, the fancy seed sower I bought at your brother Will's estate sale - - "

"Just be thankful no one was killed. They got the horses out?"

"Yes." Rose swallowed her sobs and took a deep breath. "Mr. Major got them out right off. But I had over 700 bags of grain in there. The main portion of my crop and the seed for next season." The tears flowed again. "My poor husband will be turning over in his grave, God rest his soul."

"Do they know how it started?"

"Must have been a spark from the forge. Jim and Sam Donaldson were doin' some work o' their own." She sighed heavily. "Mr. Major came into the house for a glass of lemonade, and when he got back, it had a good start. The Donaldson boys had just run, so Mr. Major, he scurried back in to save the horses. He had two of 'em in there for shoein', two as belonged to Mr. Short, so he got them okay. By then, it was too late to save anything else."

They watched in silence as the roof collapsed in a shower of sparks.

Sam joined them on the porch. "Gonna smolder for days, with all those bags of grain," he said solemnly. "But it looks like it's under control now. Won't spread to the rest of the buildings, long as someone keeps an eye on it."

Shouts attracted their attention. "What's going on?" Matilda asked Sam.

"The blacksmith, Mr. Major, he's accusing the Donaldson boys of starting the fire. Said if they'd got onto the sparks right off, instead of running, the fire wouldn't have spread. Also told them they should have had better sense than to let a spark get away from them."

The shouting intensified and, to Matilda's horror, one of brothers struck the blacksmith. The other brother, not to be outdone, took a swing at him as well.

It bid fair to become a real melee when several men jumped the two brothers and told them to cool down. Major wiped the blood off his cut lip with a not too clean handkerchief. His right eye swelled rapidly.

Matilda shook her head in disgust. "He'd better get a compress on that eye."

Three days later, Sam came to tell Matilda that Mr. Major had filed charges against the Donaldson brothers for assault and battery. "They pleaded guilty," he chuckled. "With all those witnesses, no point in paying a lawyer. Judge Simon fined Jim $35, since he started the fight, and Sam $25."

Matilda sighed. "If men would only learn to keep their tempers. All those cases of assault and battery, drunkenness, even two murders. Our community is going to get a bad name."

"To say nothing of our hotel being burned to the ground three times," Carrie added.

On Sunday, July 16, Matilda attended the little Methodist church on the cemetery grounds, as usual. During the social hour after the services, Media approached her mother-in-law.

"Mother Matilda, I'm so worried about my mother. Her kidney is bothering her again. She is in such pain." She sighed deeply. "Nothing Dr. Montague does helps. The laudanum takes the pain away for a little while, but it comes right back."

"Has she tried sassafras tea?" Matilda asked. "I know Mother always swore by it for kidney disorders. And plenty of good, fresh water to flush out the poisons."

"What did she do for the pain?" Media asked.

"Lobelia poultices." Matilda smiled at the memories of her mother's many remedies.

Even Lew laughed at that. "Yes, I remember Grandmother and her lobelia poultices. Everything from rattlesnake bites to back pain. And if anything was broken, comfrey poultices."

"Don't laugh, young man," Matilda smiled. "Her cure rates were as good or better than many of our modern doctors." She turned to Media. "Have your mother try the sassafras tea. It can't hurt, and it might help."

Celestia Johnson approached Matilda. "Did you hear our local fire fiend tried to burn me out again?"

581

"Not again!" Matilda gaped at her friend. "What happened?"

"Friday night, about 11:30, I had gone to bed, but had not yet blown out the lamp. A flash of light startled me. I ran downstairs and found the back of the kitchen ablaze. Someone had thrown coal oil on the wall and ignited it."

"Good Heavens. You apparently got it out in time?"

"Yes, I roused all of my lodgers and they quickly extinguished it. Gave us all a bad fright, it did." She chuckled grimly. "Almost hesitate to tell Mrs. Kruzenberg. She put up two-thirds of the money to help me re-build this time. She won't be happy to learn our local incendiary is still trying to burn me out."

In the buggy on the way home, Sam remarked to Matilda. "Sure looks like someone is determined to see we don't have a hotel in Hicksville."

Matilda was silent, thinking. Who would benefit from destroying Celestia's hotel? Her ex-husband had died several years before, and the first fire had occurred while he was still an owner. Alice Valensin? But the Arno Hotel had felt the incendiarist's wrath as well. Could Celestia have an enemy not even she knew about? But the third fire had occurred while the Miller's owned the hotel.

She shook her head. If the Sheriff couldn't find the villain, it was unlikely she could.

That night, she lay in bed unable to sleep, thoughts of Celestia's story running through her mind, when the unmistakable smell of smoke roused her to full alertness. Jumping from the bed, she ran to the window and stared in disbelief at the flames leaping skyward from the direction of Hicksville.

Chapter 65

July, 1893 to July, 1894

SAM RETURNED from the conflagration and confirmed Matilda's worst fears. "It was the Hicksville Hotel," he reported to his mother and sister. "Looks like whoever tried on Friday was determined to succeed. Threw coal oil all over the front door and set it on fire. Mrs. Johnson and her lodgers were lucky to get out with their lives."

"Poor Celestia," Matilda sighed. "What is this world coming to?" She shook her head. "I'm glad no one was killed. Where is Celestia now?"

"With Mrs. Herbert."

"I'll go and see her tomorrow."

The first thing Matilda learned when she arrived at the Herbert residence the next morning was that a suspect had been arrested.

"Lou swore out a warrant on Gordon Raphael, that Injun boy as hangs around the hotel. Hauled him into Judge Simon's Court, they did."

"They'll release him." Celestia spoke up. "I've been like a mother to Gordon and his half brother. Why would they burn me out? Now he doesn't have any place to stay either. That new fellow, Clifford, he's the one as put Lou up to it.

He makes no bones about not liking Indians, and he and Gordon have had a few words. I'm sure he saw this as a chance to get even."

"What are you going to do now, Celestia?" Matilda asked her friend gently. "Are you going to rebuild again?"

Celestia sighed. "It's been hard, running it by myself, even with Vessie's help. And after being burned out four times . . .." her voice trailed off. "I don't know," she finally whispered. "I just don't know."

A few days later, Sam brought the news that Gordon had been released. "Never should have been arrested in the first place," he declared. "Not one tittle of evidence against him. Just that Clifford fellow's personal prejudice."

Media's concern for her mother deepened, and Mrs. Latourette spent the summer in bed with severe pain in her right kidney. Nothing seemed to help.

In September, Carrie began teaching at the Alabama School, and word spread through the little community that Alice Valensin was challenging her ex-husband's will.

"Says he was insane when he wrote it," Annie Herbert chuckled when reporting the news to Matilda. "He may have been insane to run off with a married woman, but I can't see how she can get the Court to say he didn't know what he was doing when he willed everything to his widow."

"Didn't know he had much left," Matilda remarked dryly. "I thought he was going through it pretty fast."

"He was," Annie laughed, "but I guess Alice figured if he hadn't spent it all, young Pio is entitled to something."

"We'll probably never hear for sure, him dying back in Ohio and being buried in Italy. Alice surely won't tell anyone if she loses."

"You're probably right," Annie nodded. "Oh, well, I wish her luck." She rose and refilled the teapot. "Word is Colin McKenzie's moving to Galt next week. Did go ahead and rent the Beckwith house."

Harvest over, time drifted into fall. Word reached them that Colin McKenzie's wife had produced their second child at the end of October.

"Weighed in at eleven pounds," he chuckled. "Big boy. And I hear he's dickering to rent that 1260 acres just east of you, Mother," Lew added. "Should make good neighbors."

"And how is your mother doing, Media?" Matilda asked.

Media shook her head. "Not well. They want to take her to the hospital in Sacramento and take out the kidney that's causing her so much grief." Media's eyes filled with tears. "Just the thought of those doctors cutting on her frightens me." She rose abruptly and began carrying plates from the table to the sink in the kitchen.

"Bothers her to talk about it, Mother," Lew whispered as the girl left the room.

Matilda nodded in understanding, remembering her reluctance to have the doctors operating on Bill and the outcome of that procedure.

"Alice Valensin is providing the materials to make the repairs to the Arno Bridge," Media put in when she returned for the second load. "Sit, Mother Matilda. Carrie and I will do the dishes. You and Lew can visit."

On Sunday, December 10, Eliza Latourette was taken to the Sacramento County Hospital.

Media begged Matilda to persuade her mother to refuse the operation. "I know it will kill her, Mother Matilda. I just know it. I don't trust doctors. They are always so sure of themselves."

"The decision has to be hers, Media," Matilda soothed. "She's the one who's suffering."

On Tuesday evening, the surgeon removed the offending kidney. The following morning, Matilda watched as her good friend Eliza, with her husband holding one hand and Media the other, slipped away from them.

As Media sobbed in her arms, Matilda could only think that now the poor woman was finally out of pain. The decision to have the operation had been hers, and hers alone. She had told Matilda she would rather die than continue as she was. Matilda thought back. Eliza had suffered for so long with that diseased kidney. Seven months, yes, it was last May when the pain began. Seven months is a long time to suffer.

After Eliza was laid to rest in the Liberty Cemetery alongside of her beloved son Willie, Matilda tried to get her life back to normal. Carrie looked tired all the time, and Matilda was concerned. "Are you sure teaching school every day along with all of your other work here isn't too much for you?" Carrie was such a tiny little thing.

Carrie sighed and helped herself to another biscuit. "Maybe. I think I'll finish this year and then stay here with you. All the work here plus teaching is, I think, what is wearing me out."

"Good," Matilda nodded. "I didn't want to stand in your way if you really wanted to teach, but I do need your help here."

Sam interposed, "Kelsey Hobday's wife had another boy. Named him Bill."

"That's good news," Matilda smiled. "And how is Tommy Riley? I guess all the fuss about him and Judge Donaldson's wife has dissipated. But Annie Herbert says he is in bed with pneumonia. That can be dangerous."

"Haven't heard how he's faring. Did hear he had two more horses killed by trains. That makes five so far. But he'd better get well. He's got a wife and four little ones." Then he grinned. "And they say Hiram Fugitt tried to get out of jury duty by claiming to be deaf."

Carrie and Matilda laughed. "And did it work?" Carrie asked.

"Nope," Sam grinned. "Judge just told him he could sit near to the front of the jury box, and he'd tell all the witnesses to speak louder."

1894 opened with Tom and Mary Randolph moving back to Galt from Oleta.

"Just couldn't stay away, could you?" Matilda teased him. "What's the matter? Apple market not so good?"

He hugged her and grinned. "Getting too old to handle all the work. Heart's been giving me some palpitations, so came down to see Doc Montague. He said to lay off such strenuous work as climbing trees to pick apples, so we sold the place and I'm going to retire. Have rented a house in Galt and plan to sit back and relax. Got enough money from the sale we should be able to live comfortable."

"Well, take care of yourself." He did look tired, Matilda thought. After all, he is 67 years old. Sometimes she had to stop and think to realize he was ten years older than she. "What did he recommend you take for your heart?"

"He just said take it easy, see if that took care of the problem." Tom took off his hat and coat and settled into a chair. He accepted the steaming cup of tea Carrie handed him. "Thank you, Carrie. And I do feel better already," he told Matilda.

"Mother always recommended Indian Hemp Root for

heart palpitations."

"I tried to give him some," Mary declared, "but he said it tasted too vile."

Matilda laughed. "Most of Mother's remedies tasted vile, as I recall. That's why she always added sugar."

News of the death of Obed Harvey on January 17 quickly spread throughout the community, for he was held in high esteem as the founder of the town of Galt. He even rated two whole columns in the *Galt Gazette*.

"Paper praises him to the skies," Sam reported with a grin. "Nothing about how he contributed to the demise of Liberty. Only all of the good he did for the community of Galt. And his experience when the Central America sank. And his medical and legislative background. Going to bury him in Sacramento as soon as his daughter Genevieve gets here from Boston. Guess she's in school there."

"Sacramento?" Matilda gaped at Sam. "They aren't going to bury him in his town?"

Sam grinned. "Apparently not."

Matilda shook her head. "And I guess he died of apoplexy. Died right in the Post Office."

"Yep, only lasted two hours. They got Doc Montague right away, but there was nothing he could do."

A few weeks later, Sam looked up from the paper he read and grinned. "April 14. Women of Colorado now have the elective franchise."

"It's about time," Carrie exclaimed.

"Wonder what Uncle Alf will have to say about that?" Sam added with a chuckle.

"Plenty, I'm sure," Matilda said, thinking of the many arguments that had gone back and forth between herself and her brother in the past. "How's the wheat crop doing?"

"Coming along. That last rain really gave it a boost. Swear it grew an inch overnight."

"Wonderful, we could use a good crop." Matilda sighed, thinking of the many times they thought the crop would be successful only to watch an early drought or a late rain shatter their hopes.

"Dr. Short is ailing," Carrie said. "I overheard Mr. Short telling Reverend Roberts last Sunday that he fears for him."

"Been a sickly young man ever since he had that tumor in his side." Matilda shook her head sadly. "He's done well to finish medical school like he did. I recall his mother being so worried about him." She shook her head. "Docs say it's a collection of diseases, but for my money, he has consumption. I think Marie thought that was what ailed him."

On Sunday, April 15, Dr. William Short was laid to rest in the Hicksville Cemetery, next to his mother, following services at the Methodist Church there. A shame, Matilda thought. Not yet thirty years old and with a young wife, and such a bright future in front of him.

In April, the Hicksville Road was closed again at the order of Alice Valensin.

"Just up and fenced it off, she did," proclaimed Annie Herbert to Matilda. "Said this has been going on since '88, when she gave the land for the new road to the County. Says she even paid the $700 to improve the new road."

"But didn't Lou and Celestia protest closing the old road?" Matilda asked.

"Yep, so did Mr. Hansen. So the old road was kept open. Alice just notified the Board that since they wouldn't give her no order to close it, she had taken full possession and fenced it off."

"And so?"

"And so now the fence was taken down and the whole thing started through the Courts again."

"Well, no one can say Celestia hasn't got gumption."

"I'll say," Annie chuckled. "After her rebuilding that hotel again after being burned out four times. Thought for sure the last time she'd throw in the towel."

"Not Celestia," Matilda smiled.

At the end of May. Matilda awoke to the sound of rain on the roof. Startled, she sat up in bed and listened as the rain pour off and down the eaves. Not a light sprinkle, but a downpour. The wheat, she thought. Just when we thought we were going to get a good crop, we have to get a heavy rain in late May. She sighed. Nothing she could do. What would be would be. She snuggled back under the covers.

The rain did do a lot of damage to the hay crop, but the wheat seemed to come through fairly well. "We'll see," was all Lew said.

In June, all the Randolphs gathered at the Methodist Church for a benefit performance for the Reverend Roberts.

"I see both Carrie and Sam are performing," Celestia said with a smile. "They are both so talented."

"Yes, Carrie is reciting a dialogue called 'Who on Airth is it?' which is very comical. Sam is in several. One is 'The Gypsy's Warning', along with Zoe Bailey and Ham Davis and 'The Fogg Divorce Case' with Mattie Moore and Ham. Also, he's in a couple of the tableaus."

"I guess Zoe has recovered from her soaking in the Laguna."

Matilda laughed. "She wasn't injured, but she still talks about how frightened she was."

Her brother Tom and his wife joined them. Tom hugged

her and grinned. "Sure glad I got out of the apple business. Gonna be a railroad strike. That Debs fellow back in Chicago is creating all kinds of problems. Trains don't run, no one'll be able to ship. Gonna ruin the fruit growers, it will."

"Even some talk of the Government taking over the railroads." Celestia said.

"That'd go over big with the railroad magnates," Tom grinned. "Even hear Huntington is pleading poverty and asking Congress to pay his debts."

The railroad strike did raise havoc. Even wheat fell to ninety cents per hundred-weight, and many fruit growers were ruined.

Then, on August 4, the County Board of Supervisors voted three to two to close the Hicksville Road. Alice Valensin had won, but the residents of Hicksville would not give up their road without a fight.

Chapter 66

August to December, 1894

THE DISPUTE OVER the Hicksville Road continued, to Matilda's dismay.

Sam, at supper Tuesday evening, told his mother and sister all about it with great relish, "Monday, after the Board of Supervisors gave the decision to abandon the old road, Alice fenced off each end." He chuckled and reached for another biscuit, slathering it with fig jam.

"And?" Carrie and Matilda asked together.

"Eight last night, just before dark, Celestia and those two young nieces of hers took an ax and chopped it down."

"Just the three of them?" Matilda stared at Sam, then laughed. "I always knew Celestia had spunk, but I didn't think she would go that far."

"Yep. But by this morning, Alice had gotten the fence up again. Young Pio admitted she told him to re-build it. Not to be out done, this afternoon, Henniker, the blacksmith who works at Hansen's shop, took Dan Fox and destroyed the north section. Lou Herbert paid a tramp fifty cents and three glasses of beer to cut down the south end. Lou loaned Fox that Winchester repeating shotgun of his and told him to stand guard while the tramp did the work."

"And is that the end of it?"

"I doubt it," Sam grinned. "Alice is a pretty determined lady. Some are saying the fence will be up again tomorrow. Lou and Celestia are headed for Sacramento first thing in the morning to get an injunction against blocking the road. Soon's I get the chores done tomorrow I'm going down there to see what's happening."

"We'll go with you," Matilda said firmly.

"Okay. And I hear Andrew Whittaker died," Sam said.

"About time," Matilda sighed.

"They say his heart just quit," he added.

"Didn't think he had one," Carrie muttered, half under her breath.

"Now, Carrie, we mustn't speak ill of the dead," Matilda admonished her. No matter how glad we are to hear it, she thought.

The next morning Sam hitched Blackjack to the buggy, and the three of them went to Arno for the mail. They swung by Hicksville on the way back and met Lou Herbert and Celestia Johnson as they returned from Sacramento in triumph.

"She had those fences up again," Celestia declared. "So Lou and I cut the north end on our way back from getting the injunction."

"She sure got them up fast," Matilda murmured.

"Yes, but now that we've got everything legal we need, I'm going to cut down the fence across the south end right now, and Sheriff O'Neil is going with me."

Followed by the Sheriff and several men, she strode off, ax in hand.

"Want to go watch her chop, Mother?" Sam asked. He urged Blackjack into motion as soon as the three of them were settled in the buggy again.

Matilda shook her head. "No, let's go home." She held

herself back until they were out of sight of the combatants and could restrain herself no longer. She started to laugh.

Sam chuckled along with her. "And they tell me you should have heard the language they used!"

Matilda continued to laugh, and finally managed to gasp, "Oh, I'm glad I didn't."

The three of them, accompanied by Lew and Media, joined Alf and his family for Sunday dinner after church on the last weekend of September. Essie had come over from Lake County to spend some time with her fifteen-year-old cousin Stella.

Matilda greeted Essie with a warm hug. "You are getting to be quite the young lady," She smiled at the girl. "How old are you now?"

"Seventeen, Aunt 'Tilda. And Stella and I have been having a wonderful visit. We went to the housewarming for Will Hauschildt and his wife and had a most enjoyable evening. They had music and dancing and a really good supper." She laughed. "Not much goes on over in Lake County. In fact, Sally is talking about moving back here."

"Is she going to marry that nice Mr. Brennard?" Carrie asked.

"Oh, I imagine she will eventually. He's over all the time."

"She'd better hurry and make up her mind. She is pushing forty, after all," Matilda said. "Was the housewarming well attended?"

"Oh, yes, everyone was there. All of the Hauschildts, the Orrs, the Cains, Kittie Brewster and Annie Ferguson, and ever so many single young men!" She giggled. "I danced every single dance. Of course, poor Mrs. Hauschildt had to take it easy because her baby is due any day now."

Matilda glanced at Alf, who scowled. The Methodist Church had long since given up its prohibition on dancing, realizing the young people enjoyed it so, but Alf clung to the old ways.

She worried about him. He looked old and tired. Losing his ranch to McFarland had changed him, seemed to have taken all of the life out of him. The way Emma acted around him bothered her too. Emma seemed almost to hold him in contempt. Matilda feared the 25 year age gap, which had not seemed so marked when they were 44 and 19, became more obvious now that they were older.

With a sigh, she turned her mind from it, saying, "And has everyone heard of Mr. Short's upcoming wedding to Augusta Sawyer?"

"Of course," Emma laughed. "It's the talk of the town."

"Reverend Roberts will perform the ceremony," Matilda said. "I'm so happy for Mr. Short. He's been so alone, losing first Marie and then Willie. And Augusta is a fine woman. They'll get on well together."

"Better than John Rae and his new wife," Stella giggled. "I hear they fight all the time."

"Now, Stella," Alf admonished his daughter. "You shouldn't listen to gossip."

"Might have known," Matilda sighed, "him marrying so sudden after Alice passed on. She was such a good woman, and there was a lot of talk about his new wife at the time." Then she added, "Maybe we need to introduce Derby Cantrell to a local widow to bring him out of his doldrums. I saw Clint at the Post Office the other day and they've been real concerned about his health for several months now. Seems to have lost all interest in living since his wife died, poor man. They had been married for so long, and been through so much together. She meant the world to him."

The dispute over the Hicksville Road took over the conversation for a while, until the fried chicken, biscuits, and mashed potatoes disappeared and Emma and Stella served the apple pie. Then Media volunteered the information that her brother John had moved to Sacramento.

"Got a job there as a plumber. Decided he didn't want to go into business with Pa as a tinsmith." She frowned. "They don't get along all that well. Pa wants Johnny to be like Willie, and he's not like him at all." She giggled. "Willie was very gentle and easy going, like Mama was. Johnny is headstrong, like Pa."

"Yes, being brothers doesn't mean they are the same in temperament," Matilda said, thinking how different Elizabeth and Mary had been.

Lew interrupted her musings. "Did you read where a Philadelphia dealer in antiquities is offering a revolver for sale he says once belong to Julius Caesar?"

On Saturday night, October 6th, the Hicksville Hotel was again burned to the ground by an incendiary.

"Midnight last night," Annie Herbert told Matilda the next day after church. "Poor Celestia barely got out again. Did have some insurance, $400 on the building, $100 on the contents, and $300 on the piano." Annie shook her head. "Sheriff O'Neil says he's coming out tomorrow to start an investigation, but I'll bet my last dollar he doesn't have any more luck than his predecessors in ferreting out the culprit. Five times in as many years. Absolute disgrace, it is."

"And Celestia?"

"She says she's going to take the insurance money and retire."

Matilda had to laugh, as sorry as she felt to hear the sad news. "I can't say as I blame her." But that means the end of a hotel in Hicksville, she thought sadly. One more nail in Uncle Billy's coffin.

"Cupid has bitten the esteemed editor of our local paper," Sam reported one evening n December. "Campbell plans to marry Nettie Montague's partner Belle Carty next month."

"It's about time," Carrie remarked. "He's been courting her for a long time."

"And the trial in the Hicksville Road dispute has begun."

"Thank goodness," Matilda sighed. "Now maybe we can finally put that endless squabble to rest."

"Had another fire started by an incendiary," he added. "Commercial Hotel in Galt. Started by igniting a bundle of clothes in the rear of the building."

"So there's no question? It was deliberate."

"Oh, yes. But this time they caught someone. The sheriff arrested that William Callaway as has been washing dishes at the hotel. Shifty kind of fellow." He frowned. "They let him go for lack of evidence, but everyone is sure he's the one, so the sheriff is continuing to investigate."

Chapter 67

January to June, 1895

1895 OPENED with the worst storm Matilda could remember. The wind roared out of the south and pounded the rain against the kitchen window with such ferocity she almost expected the glass to come flying in. After it passed, Sam and Lew spent two days replacing shingles and clearing away one downed tree.

"Lucky we didn't lose the whole roof," Sam said with a sigh. "One of those trees falling the wrong way could have been bad. I hear the Methodist Church in Galt got wrecked."

"Really? We have to go see," Carrie said.

The following day, Matilda stood between Carrie and Sam and viewed the destruction. The pinning under the north side had collapsed, allowing the strong southerly winds to careen the building almost onto its side.

"Wow," was Sam's only comment.

Reverend Roberts joined them. "Yes, really sad. This was Galt's first Church, and the interior is demolished. After the wind did its damage, the rain got in and completed the destruction. The ceiling has collapsed. I'm afraid the building is totally unusable, and probably irreparable."

Matilda finally found her voice. "What are you going to do?"

"I've spoken to the Congregational Church. They will

allow us to hold services there until we can decide."

On February 10, they attended the wedding of the daughter of their good friend and neighbor, Columbus Dillard. Maggie Dillard and Louis Greeno at her parents' home on Dillard Road.

The road was in its usual dismal condition. Many times on the ride over Matilda held her breath as Sam negotiated the buggy around a particularly precarious spot.

"Don't worry, Mother," he assured her with a grin. "We're not going to drown. Blaze is very sure-footed."

Matilda said nothing, merely held tightly to the side of the buggy, her eyes on the raging water. When would the County ever make this road safe?

"We almost didn't make it," Matilda declared as Columbus greeted them at the door when they finally arrived. "That road is bad again."

"Yep," he agreed. "That hole down by Clausen's place is so deep it makes the road almost impassable."

"Are they ever going to keep our roads in good repair? Do we have to have another accident like Mary and Frank?"

He sighed. "A number of us have complained and complained." Then he smiled and offered Matilda his arm. "But you're here safe and sound. Please, come in, come in. Maggie and Lou will be so glad you could join us for this happy occasion."

Matilda accepted his arm and returned the smile. "Do you think a little thing like a bad road could keep me from witnessing the union of two of our most prominent families? I just wish Caleb were still here to see what a beautiful young lady his granddaughter has become."

"Speaking of grandchildren, I understand you have another one of your own."

"Yes, January 27. Elizabeth and Henry now have another little boy. They named him Richard at his big brother Henry's insistence. Henry is ten, and he has announced it's about time they had a boy, that they already had too many girls in the family."

"And I hear Judge Prewitt removed the injunction Celestia Johnson had filed against Alice Valensin. He ruled in favor of Alice," Columbus chuckled. "But said it only frees her to remove the fences along the sides of the road so she can make it one field. She can't block it with a fence or plow it. It has to be available for passage."

"Does it really matter any more? Since Celestia no longer has the hotel?" In the back of her mind nagged the thought that someone did not want a hotel in Hicksville.

"Not to Celestia. But Hansen's customers still use it to get to his blacksmith shop, and the rest of us use it too."

Annie Herbert was full of the story when Matilda went to see her. Annie filled Matilda's teacup. "She can go ahead and do what she wants on the sides. Just so's we can get across it. It's a lot longer to go down to Arno before turning north if a body is going to Sacramento.

"Hear they got diphtheria going again," Annie went on. "Lou said he was reading the *Scientific American* and they claim a sure way to cure it. Say you close up the room, fill a tin cup with a mix of half tar and half turpentine and hold it over the fire. Fills the room with fumes, it does, and when the sick person inhales the fumes, he'll cough up the diphtheria membrane over his throat and the disease will disappear."

"If the fumes don't kill him first," Matilda remarked caustically.

Early in March, Sam returned from a trip to Galt full of news.

"John Fugitt and his cousin Will were watching for fire bugs at the Dance Hall in the Whitaker and Ray block when John's gun apparently went off accidentally. Killed him straight off."

"John Fugitt!" Matilda gasped. "Oh, no! Poor Ida, and her with four little ones. How in the world did it happen?"

"From what they tell me, it looks like he was moving the gun so he could roll over. Will heard the shot and found him lying on the floor. He ran for Doc Montague. Shot went through John's neck and up into his head. According to Doc, he died instantly."

Matilda could only sigh. "We must go to the services. I suppose they'll be down at Liberty. It'll be harder, with Lew having to go to Sacramento every day to serve on that Grand Jury. I hope that session is over soon."

"On the bright side," Sam added, "I hear Will Callaway has confessed to the arson fires. Now maybe they'll stop."

"So Sheriff O'Neal was right after all," Carrie interposed. "He was so sure Callaway did the deeds, evidence or no evidence. How did he get him to confess?"

"I didn't ask," Sam grinned. "He's implicated someone named Haller, but no one seems to know who he is or where he's located." Sam pulled on his boots and reached for his hat. "I'm off to do Lew's chores. Sure be glad when he gets off this jury business. Doing chores at two places is getting me down."

"We need a hired man," Matilda murmured. "I wish we could afford one."

"Hope he gets off before April 12. I want to see the Indian Club Swinging at the Hicksville Hall."

Lew was released from Grand Jury duty in time for all of

them to attend the entertainment benefit for Reverend Roberts, held, as Sam had said, on Friday evening, April 12.

Alice Dipple greeted Matilda warmly. "I'm so glad you could come, Mrs. Frye. I know you always enjoy my little exhibitions of elocutionary talent. Every performer enjoys having an appreciative audience. The one I am performing tonight is a young man teaching his mother to ice skate and she keeps falling down. It's really funny."

Matilda returned her smile. "I'm afraid Sam is here more for the Indian Club Swinging and the fencing drill, but I am looking forward to your performance."

Alice turned to greet another arriving guest. Matilda moved on into the hall and took a seat beside Celestia Johnson. She admired the decorations in the hall. Ribbons hung along the wall, and flowers were everywhere.

"And how are you enjoying your retirement, now that you no longer have a hotel to run?" she asked her friend.

Celestia laughed. "I should have done this three fires ago. No more lying in bed at night wondering if I am going to have to get out fast or be incinerated. Did you get to see Reverend Anderson when he was here last week?"

"Yes, I try to see him whenever he's in town," Matilda smiled. "He still talks about marrying me and Alfred. I don't know why our wedding was so memorable to him. Surely he has performed many marriages before and after ours."

Celestia squeezed Matilda's hand with affection. "It's because you are such a special person."

"Is it true that Jim Hicks is moving to Galt? Is he going to sell the place Uncle Billy left him?"

"Apparently so. Says farming's getting to be too hard for him. Plans to retire on the money he gets from the place."

Matilda laughed. "He'll get bored doing nothing. He's

603

too young a man to sit and whittle on the front porch."

Mrs. Cain joined them. Matilda thought Lem's new bride was a charming young lady. Pretty blond curls bobbed as she talked with great animation. "Wasn't that something about that crazy man who jumped off the train?"

"I hear he thought he was attacked and threw his money out the window, then jumped."

"Yes. Wonder is the fall didn't kill him," Mrs. Cain said. "Lucky for him he landed in that marshy spot up by McConnell's. He came running into Lem's saloon, saying he'd escaped the clutches of seven highwaymen, and jumped out the window of the train. He ran all the way in his stocking feet, no hat or coat. Must have run over two miles. Said he had bullets flying all around him."

"What did Constable Quiggle do with the poor man?" Celestia asked.

"Took him to Sacramento. Judge Catlin sent him to Dr. White, who held him at the County Hospital. Looks like they'll probably declare him insane and send him to the State Insane Asylum in Stockton."

"Shh," Carrie whispered to her mother. "Miss Dipple is getting ready to perform."

The next news to reach them was that John McFarland had sold the property he took from Alf to a Thomas Stephens of Placerville.

"They say he's planning to move in immediately, so at least the old place won't sit there vacant anymore." Lew told Matilda all about it when he and Media came to Sunday dinner after church.

"Poor Alf," Matilda sighed. "I don't know which is harder for him, seeing the home he built with his own hands lying empty, or seeing someone else living in it."

"Alf may have more to worry about than that," Lew muttered.

"Why?" Matilda demanded.

But Lew and Media exchanged glances and he would say no more. Instead, Media changed the subject.

"Mother Matilda, my father is getting married again. Alice Henley's daughter Dora has set her wedding date for May 5, and so they have decided to make it a double wedding."

Matilda's eyes met Media's. "And do you like the idea of a stepmother?" Matilda knew Mrs. Henley slightly, for she had been the landlady of the Union Hotel in Galt since moving down from Elk Grove a few years back.

"Oh, yes, Pa has been so lonely since Mama died and Johnny moved to Sacramento. And she's a very nice lady. It will be good for him to have someone to fuss over him again." She laughed. "It'll be a big social affair. Everyone will be there."

"We'll look forward to it," Carrie smiled. "And of course, it will be at the Union Hotel."

"Of course," Media nodded. "They have already started decorating."

"I hear the Methodist Church Society in Galt has purchased the lot where Iler had his blacksmith shop. They hope to build a new church there in the near future, since the old one blew down."

On April 21, Lew rode in, his face grim. "Come quickly, Mother. Ethel Chinnick's been in an accident."

"Oh, no! Not dear little Ethel." Matilda knew she was their only daughter, and the light of their lives. "Is it serious?"

"I only heard she was hit by the train. But Penny has

always taken comfort from you, Mother, especially since Mrs. Walton passed on. So she needs you now."

They reached the Chinnick residence in a remarkably short space of time. Many friends and neighbors milled about. Jim saw Matilda and hurried to help her down from the buggy. His eyes were red, and she knew then that the accident had been fatal. Poor little Ethel, and her only twelve years old.

"Thank you for coming, Mrs. Frye." Jim's voice was husky with unshed tears. "It will mean so much to Penny. Since she's lost her mother, she looks to you."

Matilda did not trust herself to speak and allowed him to lead her into the house. Benicia saw them come in and threw herself into Matilda's arms. "Oh, Aunt 'Tilda, Aunt 'Tilda," she sobbed. "How could God be so cruel as to take my little girl?"

Matilda had no answer. She just held the weeping woman closely. Yes, she thought, as she had so often before, how could God be so cruel? Poor Penny. To lose her beloved only brother in the tragic accident that had taken Mary's life as well, then her father by his own hand, and, just recently, her mother. And now this.

Her eyes met Jim's over Penny's bowed head. "She had gone for the mail," he said. "On the way home, she ran across the tracks in front of the eastbound Overland Express." He took a deep breath to get his voice under control and continued. "Gray, the Wells Fargo agent, yelled at her not to cross, that the train was too close and coming too fast. But either she didn't hear or didn't heed." He sank into a chair beside her and put his face in his hands. "The engine struck her and crushed her skull," he whispered. "She was dead when they reached her." His shoulders shook with silent sobs.

Matilda continued to hold the weeping Penny. She put a hand on Jim's shoulder, and the tears she had been trying to hold in check now ran down her cheeks. Some day, God, she thought, some day we will understand.

Two weeks later, the whole family attended the wedding of P.H. Latourette to Mrs. Alice Henley, along with that of her daughter Dora to Mr. H.S. Clark of Lodi.

"Look, Mother," Carrie whispered as they took their seats on the groom's side of the aisle. "Isn't it lovely?"

The parlor of the Union Hotel had been gorgeously decorated with flowers and evergreens. The marriage bell was made up of white and red roses suspended from the ceiling. That and many other floral arrangements adorned the room.

When the Reverend Mr. Feller stepped into place, Matilda wondered which couple would go first, but Mr. Clark settled it at once. He led Dora under the bell of roses and announced, "Since I was the one who started this whole business, I claim first place."

Everyone laughed, and that ceremony was the first to be concluded. After the new Mr. and Mrs. Clark retreated back up the aisle, Mr. Latourette led his bride forward under the bell, where Mrs. Alice Henley became Mrs. P.H. Latourette.

Refreshments of punch, cake, and coffee were served, and congratulations pressed upon both couples. At the conclusion of the festivities, they departed for their honeymoon trip.

"Where are they going?" Matilda asked Media.

"They're taking this evening's train to San Francisco," Media replied.

"Lovely place for a honeymoon," Matilda agreed. She was not thinking of the two happy couples. She was thinking of a memorable trip by steamer to San Francisco and another honeymoon many years before.

Chapter 68

June 1895 to March 1896

FOG SWIRLED around the house as Carrie and Matilda put the last touches on the Christmas tree. Elizabeth's daughters Pearl and Virginia helped. Virginia, who would be three in March, kept eating the popcorn her mother made almost as fast as Pearl could string it.

The last six months of 1895 had been eventful ones for the little community, but none touched Matilda too directly. The death of her mother's brother A.M. in Bloomington had not affected her very much. She had not seen him since the Randolph wagon had left Randolph's Grove en route to Kansas back when she was only 18.

In September, the neighborhood buzzed with the news that Jay Miller, nephew of J.H. Sawyer, had been murdered in Arizona. She knew there were some suspicious circumstances surrounding the killing, but as she had never met him, she was not too concerned. She did feel a twinge of pity for the young man's mother, who had been just about to set out on a trip to visit him.

Mr. and Mrs. Stephens moved into Alf's old place, which they had purchased from McFarland, and the neighborhood greeted them cordially.

"After all," as Annie Herbert put it, "Can't blame *them* for McFarland taking Alf's land."

"Gramma, Ginny's eating all the popcorn." Pearl's voice brought Matilda back to the present just as Lew and Media joined them.

There was still no sign of a baby from Media, but neither of them ever mentioned it, and Matilda did not feel it was her place to pry. But she did wonder. Usually the first baby put in its appearance within a year. But Lew and Media had been married - - she thought back - - since 1887. Over eight years.

Of course, maybe it was just as well. Media was such a tiny little thing. Having a baby could kill her, as it had poor little Belle Carty, who died the day after her son was born. She felt sorry for Mr. Campbell, after courting Belle for so long to then lose her after only ten months of marriage.

Lew greeted her with a warm hug. "Did you see where the transmission of electric power for long distances over wires was demonstrated in Sacramento? Power generated in Folsom by water from the America River has reached all the way to Sacramento."

Matilda, mounting the candles on the tree, said to Carrie, "Wouldn't it be nice if we could put electric lights on the tree instead of candles? Then we wouldn't have to worry so about fire."

Carrie laughed. "Yes, it would be. But just because it's in Sacramento doesn't mean it will be here soon."

"You're probably right," Matilda sighed. "Oh, well, it was just a thought. Pearl, how are you doing with the popcorn strings? Getting ahead of Ginny's appetite yet?"

"Mother just made another batch, and I think Ginny is finally getting full."

Alf and Emma arrived, accompanied by Harry, Stella and little Clinton, and laden with pies and gifts. Matilda greeted her brother warmly. He looked older every time she saw him, but Emma looked positively radiant.

He said morosely, "I hear they're circulating bogus silver half dollars in Stockton. Man has to be so careful these days. Didn't used to have to worry about getting cheated at every turn."

Matilda, remembering some of the stories she had heard of early California days, made no comment.

Alf hung up his hat and greeted Henry and Elizabeth. "My, Lizzie, I do declare you get prettier every time I see you."

She laughed and hugged him. "You old flatterer, I love you. Come and sit down."

He greeted Lew, and took the seat beside him. "Hear they say Lt. Governor Reddick died because the skins of green peppers lodged in his intestine. Always said those things weren't fit to eat. Now seems they can even kill a man.

"And disgraceful about poor Sam Prouty. Still in the hospital in San Francisco, from what I hear. Imagine your own son-in-law beating you to within an inch of your life because you refused to cancel a $4000 debt!"

"George Conner has always been an impulsive man, and I hear he's in some bad financial straits. Not that I excuse his behavior," Lew added hastily, "but I think there's more to the story than we've been told. What I can't understand is how George's brother could just stand by and witness the attack and make no attempt to stop it."

"I guess Prouty's court battle with Charlie Quiggle is still going on, even with Prouty in the hospital." Carrie added. "With all of the money Prouty has, you'd think he could forgive a debt to his own daughter!"

Lew grinned. "That's why I said I think there's more to the story than we've been told."

"Enough," Matilda said. "Come and eat before the ham

gets cold. Alf, as senior member of the family, you have to preside."

"Where's Tom," he grumbled. "Tom's older than I am."

"They went up to Carbondale to spend the day with Bud and Agnes, since Frank and Annie are clear up in Vina. Annie is expecting another baby." Matilda sighed. "And in her last letter she said she fears Frank has consumption. He's been losing weight, and has a persistent cough."

"I did hear Frank's been ailing," Alf said solemnly. "We should remember him in our prayers." Then Alf gave his usual lengthy grace. Matilda almost laughed when he asked God to protect Mr. Prouty's interests in the affair with Quiggle, and to motivate the County to fix the bridges, but it ended at last and they began to eat.

"And what do you think of our new minister?" Matilda asked Alf. She still missed Reverend Roberts.

"City feller. He won't last," Alf predicted. "Wish we could get Eli Robertson back. Hear he's riding circuit up around Red Bluff. Not good for him, in his poor health."

On January 5, a brilliant meteor lighted up the sky over Arno, as bright as an electric searchlight. It was only seven in the evening, but a pitch-dark night with no moon emphasized the brilliance. Matilda had visited the outhouse and was walking back to the house when the flash of light lit up the whole sky.

Stunned by the spectacle, she stood and stared. She had never seen one so large before. For a moment, she wondered if it were a comet.

Carrie, on the back porch, had seen it as well and could only gape. Sam came bounding in from the barn a few moments later. "Did you see that?" he gasped. "Wasn't that spectacular?"

The month of January also saw the Cosumnes overflow its banks once more.

"Again," Matilda sighed. "Do you suppose some day they'll figure out a way to stop these constant floods?"

"Maybe," Sam grinned, "but I doubt we'll see it. I hear Jane's grandson, John's boy Merrill is in Sacramento for an operation for his appendix. Seems he's coming along okay. They say he'll be able to come home Thursday."

"I know Jane will be relieved. She's been so worried."

"And I guess Mr. Loughran's son Jim finally got drunk one time too many. Picked a quarrel with a fellow named Costello and Costello shot him dead."

"Killed him?" Matilda gasped. "Poor Mr. Loughran has had so many problems with his son's drinking. And he was so disappointed Jim had no interest in farming, after the poor man built up his farm so nicely with his son in mind. Is Tom still in San Francisco?"

"I hear he's staying with the daughter that lives in Sacramento. Anyway," Sam chuckled, "Campbell is pretty blunt in his article in the paper." He put the paper in Matilda's hands and as she scanned the page, he added, "I guess they're going to bury him in San Francisco."

Matilda looked up from the paper. "Oh, my, 'black sheep, wayward son, holy terror.' That won't set well with Mr. Loughran."

March opened with a furious rainstorm, with strong winds and even a sprinkling of snow. The wind whistled through cracks in the walls, making it impossible to keep warm except close to the stove.

"Whoosh," Sam exhaled as he struggled to hold the door against the wind. Carrie hurried to take the pail of milk from his hands. Steam rose as the cold in the room reached the warm milk.

Matilda stayed huddled by the fire as Sam helped himself to a cup of coffee and a bowl of porridge. I must be getting old, she thought. I don't remember cold days bothering me so much before.

Carrie bustled about pouring the milk into pans so the cream could rise.

"I hear they caught that Russian tramp as killed the two Japanese fellows down by the trestle on the Laguna," Sam told his mother and sister. "Name of Simon Raten."

"Oh, I'm so glad," Carrie exclaimed. "Everyone has been so worried, to think of him being on the loose. Poor Mrs. Riley was really upset, her being alone with the four little ones since Tommy died. She said the tramp that found the poor men was so excited when he got to her place he was incoherent. Scared her half to death. Lucky Hugh McGuirk came over from Alice's store and took charge."

"And I also hear burglars stole a thousand cigars from the Southern Pacific Railroad Station in Elk Grove," Sam added.

Carrie laughed. "Is that why the watchdog was poisoned last week? So the way would be clear to steal the cigars?"

Matilda could only shake her head. "A thousand cigars. Of all of the things in the world to steal!"

Chapter 69

April 1896 to January 1897

CARRIE AND MATILDA attended the Arbor Day ceremonies at the Hicksville School, and watched as the Elm and Blue Gum trees were planted around the new school building.

The ceremonies opened with the children singing "America" and the Arbor Day song, followed by recitations, dialogues, and songs by the students. Demonstrations of maps and drawings cover the blackboards.

"Look," Carrie murmured to her mother. "There's enough McEnerneys to have one in almost all of the eight grades."

"I was noticing how tall Frank Blue has gotten. He's a head taller than all of the other boys."

As Alice and Mrs. McEnerney served the cakes, candies, and coffee, Matilda spoke to Miss Hicks, the teacher. "Weather certainly has improved over two weeks ago."

"Yes," Miss Hicks laughed. "Would have spoiled our tree planting efforts to have it snowing! Did you know Mrs. Valensin grew the Blue Gum trees from her own seeds? Forty-two of them. Enough to go all around the grounds. Quite the horticulturist, she is."

The following Sunday at church, Matilda learned that Reverend Van Derventer had unceremoniously departed for Los Banos, leaving no replacement.

"I told you he wouldn't last," Alf said to Matilda as she registered her astonishment at his precipitous departure.

"Yes, I know, but to just up and abandon his post? I'd have thought he would at least arrange for a substitute."

Alf shrugged. "Guess he decided to just leave." He offered her his arm to help her down the steps. "Emma says you and Carrie and Sam are joining us at Lew's for dinner?"

"Yes, Media decided since they have been having Sunday dinner at my house so often it was her turn to cook."

After a lovely fried chicken dinner, for which Media shyly accepted compliments, the men sat down to gossip while the women washed the dishes.

Their conversation drifted into the kitchen and Matilda heard Lew say, "I read where 5000 Italian soldiers and 500 officers were killed in Abyssinia. Don't know what they were doing there in the first place. They should have stayed home."

"Bunch of free-booters, I'll bet," Alf said. "Serves 'em right."

Matilda wondered vaguely where Abyssinia was. Someplace in Africa?

"And," Lew continued, "They say Raten is going to try and get out of being hung for murder by claiming to be insane when he murdered those two poor fellows."

"Disgraceful, I say," Alf muttered.

"And Colin McKenzie has rented that 1260 acres just east of Mother from McCauley. Be good to have someone living there again."

Summer brought the news that Frank Randolph, Will's son, had died in Vina. "Guess he did have consumption after all," Matilda sighed when she heard the news. "And poor little Annie expecting her next baby any day now.

Mary brought her down here after the funeral. Reckon she'll stay here at least until after the baby is born."

"Poor girl," Carrie sighed. "She has had a hard life, and she's still so young."

Simon Raten was ruled insane, and sent to the Stockton Insane Asylum.

"Folks are saying he's faking it, but I guess he's pretty convincing," Sam grinned. "At least they sent Costello up for ten years for killing Jim Loughran."

"I guess there is some justice in the world," Carrie mumbled. "I'm so glad summer is here. Maybe this miserable winter is over and we can drive to Galt without risking our lives crossing the bridges. They say the bicycle path from Sacramento to Galt is open except for the stretch between McConnell and the Laguna."

"At least it's warm enough we can have a picnic without freezing," Matilda laughed, remembering how the Queen of May had worn her sealskin bloomers under her gown at the Maypole Dance.

"And Jane's real proud of John," Sam said. "Papers say his farm is the garden spot of Sacramento County."

"Even though he lost his whole crop of alfalfa in the April rainstorm?"

Sam grinned. "The article doesn't mention that."

Colin McKenzie and his family moved in over the summer. Delighted to have a close neighbor again, Matilda welcomed them with one of her apple pies.

"Thank you so much, Mrs. Frye. Your pies are legendary." Isabel greeted her with enthusiasm. "We are so glad to be here. Was hard on Colin, trying to farm living in town. And our move to Walnut Grove was certainly less than a success."

Matilda took off her bonnet and returned the girl's smile. "Yes, we heard some of the problems you had."

"That woman! You should have heard her! Couldn't have little Nettie around language like that! She's five now, and was beginning to understand what that woman was saying."

"Can't say as I blame you," Matilda laughed. "You won't have that problem here."

Nettie came in and solemnly shook hands. Her little brother peeked around her shoulder shyly. Matilda realized this must be the boy that had weighed eleven pounds at birth. He certainly was a stout little fellow.

She returned Nettie's handshake and said, with a smile, "Welcome to Hicksville, Miss McKenzie."

In July, news reached them that Reverend Van Derventer had died in Los Banos..

"I guess that's why he left so sudden. He wanted to go home to die." Alf shrugged. "Guess he didn't want anyone to know he was dying."

July also brought the birth of Annie's daughter, shortly after Frank's death.

"Hear she's staying with Tom and Mary in Galt," Lew told his mother. "Got a fellow managing their farm up in Vina."

"Babe's not thriving as it ought." Sam shook his head sadly. "Looks like the poor little mite may join her father soon."

Matilda murmured in sympathy. "Such a shame. And how is Mr. Latourette's sister doing?" she asked Lew. "I hear she's taken a turn for the worse."

"Yes, Media says she's got a cancer eating away inside of her, and she knows nothing can be done. She's a brave soul,

618

and has accepted the knowledge that she won't live much longer. She says it's time she joined Mr. Mead, who died two years ago. Says they've been parted too long. Guess they were real close, not having any children, it being just the two of them." He shook his head. "I think it will be a relief to her when it is over."

The end came on October 21, and Mollie Mead was laid to rest in the Liberty Cemetery next to Eliza and Willie Latourette.

She was followed eight days later by Annie's three month-old daughter. Shortly after burying the child in the Hicksville Cemetery next to her father, Annie returned to Vina.

"That's the home Frank built for me," she told Matilda, "And that's where I'll stay. We've made a good living off the fruit trees, and the children are happy there. That's the only home they've really ever known."

Christmas again found them all gathered at Matilda's. As she looked about at her loved ones gathered there, she realized another year had flown by. Where did the time go?

Whitaker and Ray had a sale on books, so this Christmas she decided to give books as gifts. Pearl would receive a copy of *Gulliver's Travels*, which cost Matilda $1.25, and for $2.00 each, she had purchased a collection of Longfellow's poems for Carrie, and one of Whittier's poems for Sam. All three of them loved to read, and she looked forward to the joy she knew the books would bring.

The men, as usual, talked of world affairs. "I see Russia, England, and France want to take control of Turkey," Alf said. "I guess that means the Dardenelles will stay open."

"We should stay out of it," Lew said firmly.

"At least if they take over, it should help the poor

Armenians," Henry put in. "Then it should stop the plans to make an Armenian colony here in the U.S."

Lew sighed. "I suppose. I just don't think all these European countries have a right to go carving up territories where they don't belong."

"I guess Italy learned that lesson after their debacle in Abyssinia," Henry laughed.

"Yes, but I'll bet they don't remember it for very long. They'll be back with a stronger force."

"Speaking of futile wars," Lew added, "I see Scarface Charlie, of Modoc War fame, has died of consumption. Poor man. All of the Modocs on the Quawpaw reservations are in mourning."

"But on the bright side of the news," Henry said, "I hear wheat prices are expected to be higher."

"Enough politics," Matilda ordered. "Come and eat. Elizabeth, you sit down. Close as you are to your time, you shouldn't be on your feet so much."

Elizabeth laughed and sank into a chair. "I must be getting older. Didn't seem to me I got this tired with the rest of them." She looked fondly at little Dick who, at almost two, scampered around the room.

Matilda watched his antics and smiled. "I suspect it's because you're trying to keep up with that active little fellow. He wears me out just watching him!"

On January 11, 1897, a wire from Anderson, in Shasta County, informed them that Eli Robertson had passed away, and his body was being shipped to the Arno Station, at his request, for burial in the Hicksville Cemetery next to his beloved Caroline.

"He waited twenty-five years to join her," Matilda murmured as the clods fell onto the coffin with that all too familiar dull thud. "And in all of those years, he showed no interest in any other woman. How he must have loved her."

On January 30, Pauline Wade was born, to the delight of Pearl and Ginny and the disgust of Henry, who had hoped for another boy.

"She's healthy, and all of her fingers and toes are in the right place," Elizabeth laughed when settling the dispute. "That's all we care about."

At the end of January, Matilda received a letter from her friend Sarah Williams. The image of the beautiful Sarah immediately rose in her mind, and she wondered if the years had been kind to her. She imparted the sad news she had lost her mother, but the rest of the letter sparkled with the same Sarah she had known as a child.

My Dearest 'Tilda,

"My mother finally slipped away from me, but I am happy I can report that the last thirty years of her life were much happier than the previous thirty.
"Our efforts to get women the vote have been successful in several States, but I'm afraid Kansas is going to be one of the last. Would you believe they have passed a law in Kansas forbidding women to wear bloomers? And making it a misdemeanor for a woman to appear in public riding a bicycle astride! I suppose they mean we should have a man pedaling for us.
"Representative Lambert even goes so far as to say "emi nent physicians" (he doesn't name them) say women are ruining their health by riding bicycles. Says riding makes them unfit for motherhood and could lead to the extermination of the race.

"I thought I had heard all of the ridiculous nonsense men could come up with to keep women down, but this one is a real prize.
"Is Alf as Anti-suffragette as ever?"
> *Love to all,*
> *Sarah*

Chapter 70

February to July, 1897

ON FEBRUARY 24, the whole family took the train to Sacramento to witness the marriage of Media's brother John to Miss Etta Larned. The nuptials took place at the beautiful old home of Miss Larned's parents, not far from where Matilda and Alfred had married.

As the guests mingled after the ceremony, Matilda found herself seated next to P.H. Latourette's new bride.

"So nice to get a chance to visit, Mrs. Latourette. We've had so little time to get acquainted."

"Please, call me Alice, Mrs. Frye. And may I call you Matilda?"

"Call me 'Tilda," Matilda replied with a smile. "We are all so pleased to see Mr. Latourette happy again. Poor Eliza suffered for so long, and losing Willie was a real blow to him." She glanced at the new bride and groom. "And I know he was disappointed that Johnny refused to go into business with him."

Alice laughed. "It would never have worked. Those two are so much alike they'd have fought all the time. Both would have insisted on being boss. Much better John is making his own way. In fact, he's talking about selling insurance. Guess plumbing isn't what he's cut out for, wrestling with pipes every day."

"He's a good talker," Matilda agreed. "Should do well as an insurance salesman." They sat in silence for a moment watching the new bride greet her guests.

"Disgraceful about John and Catherine Rae," Alice said abruptly. "They say the divorce is going to be a real scandal."

Matilda smiled faintly. "I know. I'm afraid many are looking forward to it." Including Lew and Sam, she thought, but did not tell Alice,

"There's talk of moving the venue to San Francisco, to get away from all of the curiosity seekers."

"Might be for the best," Matilda sighed. "Poor Mr. Rae. He is such a nice man. I always felt he re-married too hastily. Alice was such a good woman. I think he was hoping to get someone like her."

"Which Catherine is definitely not," Alice laughed. "Understand young McKenzie lost their little boy."

"Yes, last month. Pneumonia. Just over three years old, he was." Matilda sighed. "We tried so hard to save him, but he only lived a few days."

Alice clucked in sympathy. "And wasn't it a shame about the Commercial Hotel burning down? Guess it started in the kitchen. Someone must have left something too close to the stove."

"They don't suspect an incendiary?" Matilda's mind flew to Callaway's confession.

"No, they seem to think it was just carelessness on somebody's part. Lucky the breeze was from the south, or the Phoenix Saloon would've gone up too."

Matilda thought of Chism Fugitt. "You know, that hotel was built in Liberty in 1859, long before there was a Galt. Judge Budd of Stockton ran it for a time."

"You mean the Governor's father?"

"Yes. Then in '69, when the railroad came through Harvey's land instead of by Liberty," and destroyed Chism's town, she added in her mind, "they moved the building to Galt and Harvey opened it as the Harvey House."

"My," Alice laughed. "You sure know the history of the town. When did you come?"

"Oh, I didn't come out until '64, but between Chism Fugitt and my brother Alf, I heard every word of it!"

"I hear Whitaker and Ray are planning to build another hotel in town, to replace the Commercial," Alice continued. "I guess old Andrew's son is determined to follow in his father's footsteps."

"If Don Ray is teaching him, then he's learning from the master."

Matilda's next trip was to San Francisco for the wedding of Alf's daughter Stella to young Arthur Wells of Franklin. Stella decided she wanted to be married at the home of her uncle, W.F. McFadden, Emma's brother.

The ceremonies were scheduled for April 8. On April 6, Matilda and Carrie took the morning train to San Francisco from the Arno Station. As the train rumbled along the tracks, she could not help but think of the last time she had made this journey, when she and Bill took the ill-fated trip to Hanrahan Hospital for Bill's surgery. Tears filled her eyes as she thought of how bravely he had faced that ordeal. She forced her thoughts to brighter things. She turned to Carrie and said, "I'm going to take another ride up one of those famous hills in a cable car. I won't be so frightened this time." She sighed. "I wish Sam could have joined us, but someone had to stay and do the chores."

"Lew didn't come for the same reason, Mother, and Media wouldn't leave him. And only Art's mother and father will be present from his family. If Stella wanted the whole family present, she should have gotten married closer to home."

"I know, Carrie, but she had visited her uncle before and decided his home would be a lovely place for a wedding. I understand it's up on Telegraph Hill, with a spectacular view of the bay and the Golden Gate." She thought of the view from the room in Mrs. Boone's house she and Alfred had shared on their honeymoon, so many years before.

In May, the road between Arno and McConnell became very dangerous again, resulting in many vocal protests by the local residents.

"Never going to do anything about those bad spots," Annie Herbert grumbled to Matilda. "You'd think after all the problems they've had with that stretch they'd do something."

But concerns over the road were dwarfed by the news that her sister Sarah was coming for a visit in June.

"She says since Albert is gone now, and her family is grown, it's time to visit her relatives in California, since it's so easy to travel by train," Matilda told Carrie as she read her sister's letter. "I guess since John, Tom, Alf, and I are her only siblings still living, she feels she had better come and see us. But she has never laid eyes on any of you. She's right, it's time she came. She's going to spend a week with us, then go on to Washington to visit John and Mary Ann." Matilda laughed. "An ambitious plan for a woman of her years. She'll be 73 in October."

"I'll be glad to meet her. Are we going to Helen Putney's funeral tomorrow?"

"Of course. George needs our support. Poor Helen. She was so sick for so long. We'll all miss her, and the lovely cakes she baked for all the neighborhood parties."

Sarah's visit was everything she wanted it to be. The weather turned perfect, the river receded, and the road dried.

"Sarah Welch, you look absolutely radiant, even after that long trip." Matilda hugged her sister. "And you twelve years older that I am. I swear you look younger."

Sarah laughed. "It's an illusion. I have to admit I am more than ready for a good night's sleep on a bed that doesn't move or clack."

"We're going to give you a whole day of rest before subjecting you to all of the family. The only one you'll see tonight, besides us, is Alf. On Sunday, after church, all of the children and spouses and grandchildren will come for dinner."

On Sunday, the family gathered. Tom and Mary came with George. Tom looked tired, and Matilda was concerned. Perhaps his heart had not recovered as much as he said it had. Alf and Emma arrived with Harry and Clint.

"Stella and Art will be along later," Alf said, giving Sarah a hug. "I can't get over how great you look. Guess life has been good to you."

"Can't complain," Sarah laughed. "Albert was a wonderful man, and I have four lovely children. Although I can't really call them children anymore. Lawton is fifty years old."

Next to arrive were Bud and Agnes with their family, with their three boys, five year old Will, George, almost three, and fifteen month old Erald, who scampered about after his bigger brothers.

Henry and Elizabeth arrived with their five. Pearl was already becoming a young lady. Baby Pauline looked feverish, and Matilda did not like the sound of her cough. Hopefully, she thought, now that summer is here the warm weather will dry out her lungs. Elizabeth said nothing. Neither did Matilda.

The afternoon passed quickly, with everyone talking at once. Matilda looked forward to having Sarah to herself the next day. Then she would spend a day with Alf and Emma, and the following with Tom and Mary. After that, she would board the train for Washington to see John and Mary Ann.

After Sarah retired for the night, Matilda and Carrie finished tidying up the kitchen. "Carrie," Matilda said with a frown as she replaced the last teacup in the cupboard, "I don't think Agnes watches those children closely enough."

Carrie laughed. "Yes, that little Erald was into everything, wasn't he?"

"And she did not seem concerned when he went off by himself." She sighed. "I keep remembering that baby on the Gaffney place who burned to death because his mother left him with the four-year-old while she milked the cow." She sighed. "Oh, well, what will be will be. Let's get to bed. We have a busy day tomorrow."

Matilda and Carrie joined Tom and Alf as they saw Sarah off at the Arno Station four days later. They parted with hugs and promises to write. It was a bittersweet moment, for both knew they would probably not see each other again.

Matilda waved until the train disappeared into the distance.

Lew appeared on her doorstep two weeks later shortly

after she, with Sam and Carrie had returned from church. She had just removed her bonnet, put on her apron, and was removing the chicken from the icebox preparatory to starting Sunday dinner.

"Why Lew," she said, "you're early. I've not even had time to get the chicken on to - - " She looked at his face and stopped. "What's the matter?"

"There's been an accident at Bud's, up on the Prouty Ranch where they live. Something about one of the children. I've come to get you."

"What happened?"

"I'm not sure. All I heard was come at once."

Matilda quickly replaced the chicken in the icebox and climbed into the buggy beside him. Carrie scrambled into the back. Sam waved as they drove off.

When they arrived at the house, Matilda smelled burned flesh as soon as she entered the building. Bud, his eyes red, greeted her. "It's Erald," he whispered. Agnes threw herself into Matilda's arms, weeping.

She waited until they were ready to tell her what had happened. Finally Bud took a deep breath and said, "We built a Dutch oven in the ground outside to bake a batch of bread in a big iron kettle." His voice broke and he paused a moment. Matilda said nothing, but realized what had probably occurred.

"Guess he wandered back outside by himself after Aggie brought the bread in and –and . . .." His voice trailed off. "Sheep herder heard him and pulled him out. Figure he was in the pit for three or four minutes." He broke down and wept, unable to continue.

Still holding the weeping Agnes, Matilda approached the little bed where the pitiful body lay crying in pain. She lifted the blanket and wished she hadn't. His legs were so badly burned the flesh was peeling off, and the toenails had been burned to crisps. The smell of burned flesh sickened her. She replaced the cover and turned away. "We should give him laudanum to ease the pain," she said gently. "I'm afraid there's nothing else we can do."

"That's what the Doc said," Bud whispered.

The baby died the next afternoon, and was buried Wednesday in the Hicksville Cemetery. As the little casket was lowered into the grave, Matilda could not help remembering what she had said to Carrie after Sarah's visit. She felt a twinge of guilt. If only she had said something! She shook her head. Agnes would probably have felt it was none of her affair. But still, she knew Agnes had never had a real mother to help her. She sighed. Nothing she could do about it now.

Chapter 71

July to December 1897

"HEAR JOHN Bandeen lost 250 tons of alfalfa. They say spontaneous combustion. Put the hay in the barn before it had a chance to dry."

"Well, Sam," Matilda sighed, "at least it wasn't an incendiary."

"And I guess Lulu Coulson is a widow."

"Already?" Matilda gasped. "She was just married a couple of months ago."

"I know." Sam shook his head sadly. "They say the emery wheel in her husband's blacksmith shop exploded and blew off the top of his head."

"How dreadful. Poor Lulu."

He shrugged. "I'm off to the Post Office to get the mail. Need anything from the store?"

"Pick up some saleratus. I'm almost out."

"And I hear Whitaker and Ray plan to put those fancy new-fangled acetylene gas lamps in their new hotel." He pulled his hat on his head.

Matilda finally had to laugh. "You're just full of news this morning. You must have had a busy evening last night. No wonder you got home so late. Anything else I should know?"

"Just that Jim Hicks is talking about going to the Klondike for the gold rush."

Matilda smiled. "I knew he was too young to retire. He just got tired of farming."

In August, Matilda received a letter from Minerva's daughter Laura in Washington.

"Seems I have a new little sister. Pa and his new wife have a little girl. They've named her Goldie. He is besotted with her. Imagine him a new father at his age!
"My boys are growing like weeds. John is 13, Charlie 11, Ralph 10, and my baby, Earl, will soon turn six. Charlie is as charmed by little Goldie as Pa. He says we should have another baby so we can have a little girl of our own. I told him absolutely no. If he wants to coo over a baby girl he can coo over Goldie."

Matilda laughed and folded up the letter. Sam, who had returned from the Post Office with the mail, waited until she had finished, then said, "Jim Hicks and Dorr Phelps left for the gold fields of the Klondike last Thursday."

"Good heavens, isn't that a long trip?"

"Train to Seattle, then by boat to Skagway. That's the easy part. Once they get to Skagway, they have to pack in to where the gold is supposed to be. Imagine we'll hear more. All the family told him to write and tell everyone all about it."

"Well, "Matilda sighed, "it sounds like a dreadful trek, but I wish him well." Then she laughed. "I guess it's no worse than traipsing across the prairie like we did in '64. At least he doesn't have to cross any deserts."

"No," Sam grinned. "Just snow fields. I don't know which is worse."

"Sam," Matilda said the following Saturday, "Can you drive me over to see young Isabel McKenzie? I made apple pies yesterday and I want to take her one. She's expecting another baby any day now, and I'm sure she has her hands full."

Isabel greeted Matilda cordially and invited her in for a cup of tea. "Colin has taken a load of hogs to Sacramento. Should get good money for them. He had 21 fine ones." She placed the cup in front of Matilda and poured the steaming tea into it. "I'm so glad you came, Mrs. Frye. I'm used to living in town, where neighbors popped in all the time. I get lonesome for company out here." Then she laughed. "But it's certainly a better place to live than Walnut Grove! We had nothing but trouble with the neighbors there. Here, everyone is cordial, even if they are too busy to visit much."

They chatted about neighborhood gossip and the achievements of six-year-old Nettie, who shyly offered her hand to Matilda. While they visited, they heard a wagon pull into the yard. Moments later, Colin strode into the parlor, Sam right behind him. One look at Colin's face told Matilda and Isabel something had happened.

Isabel jumped to her feet in spite of her advanced state of pregnancy. "What's the matter?"

Sam, following Colin in, was chuckling, telling Matilda the event could not have been too tragic. The agitated Colin took a deep breath and began. "Left early this morning, as you know," he said.

"Yes," she nodded. "Before dawn."

"Got almost to the city when a hobo stopped me and tried to sell me a whip. I kept telling him I didn't need one, and he lowered the price, but I told him again I'd no need for a whip." He paused for breath. "Then he persuaded me to give him a ride into town, so I agreed."

"He'd probably stolen the whip," Isabel remarked caustically.

"Probably. Anyway, we got into town about ten o'clock, and since I'd had no breakfast, I headed for the first hotel I saw to get something to eat. I hitched the team to a nearby rack and went in to get a bite. The hobo took his whip to trade for a beer.

"Anyway, when I finished breakfast, I found the team, with the wagon and the porkers, was gone. Feller at the restaurant directed me to the police station to swear out a complaint, and I headed for the station. But when I got to Second and I, there was my wagon."

"Your hobo 'friend' had stolen it?"

"Yep, and had just concluded a sale with the Chinaman and was about to collect his money when I came into sight."

"I'll bet that sent him running," Sam commented.

"I'll say. He scooted down the alley between Front and Second and was out of sight in no time. Then I had to argue with the Chinaman. He wanted to buy the hogs from me at the price he had negotiated with the hobo. His English wasn't very good." He grinned. "And neither is my Chinese. So it took a while before I got through to him that the hobo had stolen the hogs and they were not his to sell."

"So did you file the complaint?" Isabel asked.

"Sure did, as John Doe, but I gave them a real good description." He grinned and hugged his wife. "But I've learned my lesson. No more letting hobos talk their way into my good graces."

Alf and Emma joined them for Sunday dinner after church early in September. Alf was full of the news of a possible Hebrew colony to be founded at Conley Station.

"I hear a prominent Hebrew scholar is looking to buy Samuel's Tract for Russian families. That's about 1100 acres."

"The poor souls are trying to get away from Russia because that horrid Czar is killing them and driving them from their homes," Matilda declared. "That's a terrible thing for him to do."

"Yep," Alf grinned, "But some of the good Christian folk are up in arms."

Matilda only shook her head. "I hear you and your fellow jury members found in favor of McKenzie when Donaldson refused to pay him for the return of the horses that strayed onto McKenzie's land."

"Yep," Alf grinned, "But by the time they all got done paying court costs and attorney fees, they'd have done better to settle it between themselves."

"What did you give him?" Sam asked.

"A dollar for damages and fifteen cents a day for the care and feeding of each of the horses." He grinned. "And Donaldson is out over $100."

"Such goings on between neighbors," Matilda sighed. "Has anyone heard from Jim Hicks since he took off on that frightful trip?"

"Annie Herbert says his wife got a letter saying they had arrived in Skagway, and were outfitting to head inland. That's all we know."

"I'm sure he'll encounter all kinds of hazards, going out into that wild country," Matilda sighed. "I know his wife is worried."

"Speaking of hazards, we had our own right here," Emma said. "It's wonderful that the County is putting in a new bridge across the Cosumnes there by McConnell's. I was always afraid to cross that rickety old bridge. I felt it was going to fall down at any time."

"Yes," Alf agreed, "and Supervisor Jenkins has said they should go all the way and put the road in first class shape as well. Bids will go out next week. Clint Cantrell has promised to donate the land for the right of way."

"Good," Sam said. "Clint won't change his mind and take the road back. His word is as good as his bond."

"I suppose we will be at war with Spain soon, " Alf said morosely. "Over this Cuban problem. Have a battleship down there already."

"Oh, I hope not," Matilda replied with a sigh.

On September 22, a son was born to Isabel and Colin McKenzie. Matilda went to see the new baby. Six-year-old Nettie proudly led Matilda into the room where her mother and new baby brother lay.

Matilda smiled and took the infant in her arms. "He's a beautiful baby, Belle. Have you decided on a name yet?"

She laughed. "Finally. We've named him Montague, after Alex, since it looks like he and Nettie aren't going to have any babies. Colin has been so busy with his disputes with Judge Donaldson that a name for his son was the farthest thing from his mind. At least they agreed to arbitration this time. George Stamp and Lack Quiggle agreed to have Donaldson pay five dollars for those sixteen hogs and be done with it. No court costs and no lawyer fees. I'm so glad they've come to their senses."

On October 7, the Union Hotel in Galt burned to the ground. Since Media's step-mother had been the manager there, and everyone had attended her wedding to Mr. Latourette at the Hotel,. Matilda was shocked when Lew and Media told her the news.

"Tried to burn it down last Tuesday, but the fire was found and put out. Then Thursday, the incendiary was successful."

"That lovely hotel! What a shame. Do they know who did it?"

"Suspicions run high that it was the owner, a Lodi farmer. Building was insured for $1000 and the furnishings for $500." Lew grinned wryly. "Looks like he did it for the insurance money. Surrounding property owners jumped him pretty hard. Accused him to his face of setting it. Seems he was in both rooms before the fires started and left just before the alarm was given."

"And poor Mrs. Botzbach rented the building for twenty dollars a month, and was supporting a sick husband and five children," Media cried indignantly. "And now the poor soul has no place to live and no income."

"Paper is calling for the townsfolk to come to her aid," Lew said. "So maybe she will get some help. But it's a shame a man's greed would drive him to put the poor woman in such a situation."

At Thanksgiving dinner, the Russian Hebrew colony was discussed at length.

"Will locate in the spring, on the Samuels Tract like they said," reported Alf.

"And the wheat market is moving up. Those who held on to their crops have been getting a better price."

Matilda sighed. "I certainly hope so. We could use a good year. Come on, let's eat. Alf, please offer thanks." She paused, then added, "And you might include a request for the price of wheat to go higher."

Chapter 72

January to September 1898

1898 OPENED WITH the news that the colony of Russian Jews slated for Conley Station chose instead to locate in Lyon County, Nevada.

"Guess they got 5300 acres in the Sagebrush state for less than they would have had to pay for the Samuels Tract. Good deal for them, and no one in Conley is complaining."

In February, the news that the battleship *Maine* had been blown up in Havana Harbor caught everyone's attention.

"They say the sailors claim a torpedo was directed from shore," Lew reported. "254 of a crew of 350 were killed."

"Oh, the poor men!" Carrie cried.

"McKinley is trying to hold Congress in check until a full inquiry on the *Maine* incident can be made," Lew continued, "since it could have been an accidental explosion. But many are pressing for war. They say not only have we been attacked, but we have to save the Cubans, since Spain's policy seems to be the extermination of the whole population of Cuba."

"Hear there is trouble over the boundary between Costa Rica and Nicaragua," Sam said. "Might be war there, too. If so, it would probably involve all of Central America."

Matilda sighed. "Why do men always think the only solution to a dispute is to kill each other?"

In the middle of March, Arbor Day was again celebrated

639

at the Hicksville School. Carrie and Matilda attended. The teacher, Louise Need, opened the ceremonies and introduced Monsignor Capel, who made a long address.

During his lengthy dissertation, Matilda found her mind wandering. She looked at the chalk paintings on the blackboards executed by the Antwerp boys. She nudged Carrie and indicated the artwork.

"Lack the quality of the great masters," Carrie whispered, "but do show budding talent."

Monsignor Capel finished his talk with a reference to the ceremonies two years previously, and recitations were given by a number of students, followed by reading demonstrations.

After the ceremonies, everyone went outside to plant trees, but a cold wind necessitated an early retreat to the classroom.

"Brr, that wind is freezing," Carrie shivered as they scurried back to the warmth of the schoolhouse.

"Typical March," Matilda chuckled. "Have some cake and a cup of coffee. Ice cream after the coffee warms you up. Alice supplied plenty of ice cream for the occasion, and I think every parent here brought a cake."

"I hear Alice is trying to get them to change the name of the school from Hicksville to Arno," Carrie said.

Matilda laughed, a little grimly. "Poor Uncle Billy. She'll probably succeed. She's going to be a trustee, and she is a very determined lady once she makes her mind up to something."

Carrie looked at the diminutive lady serving ice cream and smiling, charming everyone around her. "Yes," she said, "You're probably right." Then she smiled. "Did you hear that Charlie Quiggle had to pay what he owed to Lack? He actually tried to get out of it by saying Lack had no right to bring the suit because he lives in Alabama township, not Dry Creek!"

Matilda nodded. "Yes, and all over sixty dollars."

Mr. Hansen approached and greeted them. "Lovely day, ladies, if a bit chilly. Did you enjoy the performance?"

"Oh, yes, Mr. Hansen. Both Emma and Eleanor performed very well," Matilda replied. "We enjoyed it so much."

"Terrible, all this talk of war. Hear we are going to just take over Cuba. Good thing, in a way. That revolt has been going on for thirteen years. Time someone stepped in and stopped it. And war fever is affecting the whole world. I hear Italy wants to take over Haiti, and Japan and Russia are squabbling over China."

"Terrible," Carrie agreed.

"I notice war fever runs very high," Matilda remarked caustically to Carrie after Mr. Hansen had moved on. "Especially among those who plan to remain at home."

On May 28, Carrie and Matilda, escorted by Sam, attended the social at the Hicksville Methodist Church. War news dominated the conversations.

"Hear Commodore Dewey has annihilated the Spanish vessels in Manila Harbor, so the Philippines are ours," reported Lou Herbert with satisfaction. "Porto Rico will be next. And five thousand U.S. troops have landed in Cuba."

"Yes," Sam agreed. "Spain has been trying to get help from other European countries, but I guess none of them are willing to fight to pull Spain's chestnuts out of the fire."

"They say Spain now wants to sue for peace," chimed in Mr. Hansen.

Matilda half listened to the conversation among the men. What concerned her more was the drastic drop in the price of wheat, just as the grain was about to be harvested. She sighed. Maybe Jim Hicks was right. Maybe farming is too hard a life. Maybe we should switch from wheat to oranges and lemons. Ed Riley is doing well raising citrus fruits. Or maybe use the wheat to feed chickens instead of selling it on such an unreliable market.

Media interrupted her musings, having listened to the war talk as well. "My step-mother has helped organize the Red Cross in Galt. They have ordered a bolt of flannel and are busy making bandages."

Matilda sighed. "I just hope it's over before they are needed."

The whole family celebrated Pearl's sixteenth birthday at Henry and Elizabeth's new home in Galt. Matilda picked up little Pauline, horrified to realize how thin she had become.

"Is she still coughing?" Matilda asked Elizabeth. "I had so hoped the summer heat would clear up her lungs."

Elizabeth's eyes filled with tears. "No, the cough is no better, and she's feverish all the time as well. Dr. Montague fears she may be consumptive."

"Oh, no," Matilda whispered, holding the child closer. Please, God, she thought. Please don't take another grand-child from me. Not precious little Pauline.

"Henry didn't help take the cattle to the foothills this year. He wanted to stay with us in case - - in case . . . " her voice trailed off. "He's such a good man, Mother. I'm so fortu-nate. When I think of what poor Mary went through with George - - well, I realize how lucky I am."

"I hear there's a Chicago doctor who claims to cure con-sumption by compressing the lungs with nitrogen," Carrie said. "Supposed to allow the lung to heal by letting it rest."

"And how does the patient breathe?" Matilda demanded.

Carrie laughed. "Well, I'm sure he doesn't compress both sides at once!"

"Enough talk of consumption," Henry interrupted, his voice gruff with emotion. "Pauline is going to get well." He took the baby in his arms, eliciting a smile from her that wrenched Matilda's heart. "Come, dinner is served. Did you hear about the terrible fire in Tracy? Wiped out the whole business district."

In July, Matilda attended the funeral of a good friend and neighbor from Siwash, Benjamin Wilder. He had died July 28 after a long illness.

As she listened to the eulogy, Matilda thought how long the poor man had suffered with sciatica, and all the treatments he had tried to no avail. At least, she thought, he's no longer in pain. She looked at Elitha, who sat between her two sons, Allen and George, her face set. Poor woman, Matilda thought. She has been through so much in her lifetime. At least she had gotten a good man in Ben. Then she thought, with a faint smile, Elitha is a survivor, like all good pioneer women had to be.

I'll go over and see her, she thought, as soon as things settle down. I can certainly understand how she feels.

At the gathering after the ceremony, the talk, of course, turned to the war.

"Hear Santiago has surrendered," announced Columbus Dillard. "Should have the whole affair wrapped up soon." He chuckled. "And they say it was the colored troops that saved the rough riders from extermination. A brave dash by them at the critical moment made the difference. Wonder how that will set with some of those rabid Southerners."

"Philippines are not going to be as easy," Sam said.

"They wanted the Spanish out, but are not sure they want the Americans instead. I understand they plan to fight."

Will it never end, Matilda thought with a sigh. She said nothing.

In September, word reached Matilda that Frank's widow, Annie, had re-married on September 19, to a man named James Blythe South.

"Stockton man," Carrie said. "Guess he's going to move onto her place and help her with the farm."

"Good," Matilda said. "She's a nice girl, and deserves another good man."

The ladies auxiliary of the Galt Methodist Church raised funds to erect a new church building on the site of the Iler Blacksmith shop, where they had been holding services.

"They held their first meeting in the new church last Sunday," Carrie told her mother, "Even though it isn't finished. They were so anxious to be in their own building again."

"I'm glad," Matilda said. "The ladies have worked so hard to raise the funds."

Sam chuckled. "Also hear rumors are running around saying there is a gold strike in the Philippines. Find it hard to believe, myself."

"Heavens, yes," Matilda responded "The Spanish have been there for years. If there had been any gold, I'm sure they would have found it."

"I don't know," Sam laughed. "Look how long they were in California, and it took an American to find the gold."

"Yes," Matilda answered tartly, "Because the Miwoks hadn't dug it up for them to steal like the Aztecs and the Incas."

By fall, they could no longer deny that Pauline was seriously ill. Matilda spent more and more time with her, reluctant to leave for even a short time. So on the fifteenth of October, 1898, three months short of her second birthday, Pauline died in Matilda's arms.

Chapter 73

October 1898 to April 1899

PAULINE'S DEATH cast a pall over the whole family. Not since they lost Mary had Matilda felt so keen a loss. Elizabeth was inconsolable.

"I worry about her health, Mother Matilda," Henry confided two weeks after Pauline's funeral. "She won't eat, I know she hasn't slept. I find her holding one of Pauline's toys or one of her blankets and staring off into space. I talked to Doc Montague, but all he could do was give her some laudanum so she would sleep." He paced around the room. "Dickie can't understand. He keeps asking when the baby is coming back, and why his mother doesn't read to him any more."

"Time," Matilda said, remembering how devastated she had been when Baby John had died at about the same age as Pauline. "Only time." Even another pregnancy had not removed the ache, removed the feeling that her arms were empty all the time. Matilda thought how supportive Lew had been when they lost Baby John. "Time and love. She's fortunate to have you, Henry. Your love and support is what she needs now."

At the end of October, a letter arrived from Jim Hicks.

His brother Will could talk of nothing else the following Sunday after church. Matilda heard him expounding to anyone in hearing range.

"Had to move out of Canada and over into Alaska Territory. Seems those Canadian officials are real sneaky. Jim says in Dawson, everything is run by the Canadian Police, and they get the best of everything. Outsider can't get a claim registered. Man tries to register one, they send out a recorder. If the claim looks good, they send out one of their own to make the discovery."

"Don't they have any mining laws?" Lew asked.

"Only as the Commissioners make them. So Jim moved to Eagle City, twelve miles beyond the Canadian border and has located a claim there. Says he's even building a house."

"Real sneaky. Amounts to claim jumping," someone in the audience said.

"I guess they figure Canadian gold is for Canadians," Tom Riley put in. "Plenty of space in Alaska, so Americans should stay in American territory."

Will grinned. "He plans to do just that."

The rest of the year passed quickly. It seemed to Matilda that the older she got, the faster the years passed. A letter from her sister Sarah back in Illinois told her Temperance's daughter Sarah had died in De Witt County, Illinois, at the age of fifty. Memories of her sister Temperance flooded Matilda's mind, of the wonderful stories she had told, of leading little Sarah by the hand to gather blackberries, of Temperance's tragic early death, of poor Josh dying of the wound he received at the Battle of Shiloh. And their poor son Henry dying at just sixteen, far from home and loved ones in that battle in Georgia.

She sighed. And now Sarah was gone as well. Since

Sarah left no children, her death meant the end of Josh and Temperance's line. She folded up the letter and returned her mind to the problems at hand. Anthrax was making its way through the cattle. Already several neighbors had suffered losses. A specialist from Sacramento had visited just the day before and cautioned them to watch for the disease.

With a smile, she recalled the visit. He had been accompanied by that charming young doctor who had just opened his practice in Galt, Doctor Harms. He seemed a pleasant man. She hoped he planned to stay. Dr. Montague could certainly use the help, Galt's population had grown so much lately.

As the family gathered for Christmas, at Matilda's home again, she sensed all was not well between Alf and Emma. Even ten-year-old Clint seemed subdued. One of the reasons for her suspicions was that Alf was more garrulous than usual. He rambled on about the election of young Will Hicks as constable.

"Won the election, he did, but looks like he'll fail to qualify in time."

"Why on earth not?" Matilda demanded.

"Didn't file papers as he should. Guess he was so concerned about that young-un of his that he forgot everything else. And then the poor little mite died anyway."

"But everyone wanted him. Can't they work something out?" Matilda cried, appalled to think Will's baby's illness would cause him to lose the position.

"Law's the law," Alf shrugged. "Maybe the supervisors can appoint him, but not likely. Just be glad we got Simons as Justice of the Peace. McKinstry won in Galt by three votes, but Simons got a good enough showing here in Hicksville to win."

"I'm gone get me a gun and shoot some coyotes, Aunt 'Tilda," Alf's twenty-two year old son Harry announced. "Did you see where a bunch of fellows have founded the Alabama Coyote Club? Gonna raise money, they are, to pay a bounty on every coyote killed. Jim Rice was the first to collect. Five whole dollars just for shooting a coyote."

"You may have to earn that five dollars," Matilda laughed. "Coyotes are wily creatures. They seem to know just how far away they have to stay to be out of range of your gun."

"Probably why they only pay half as much for pups, because the pups haven't learned yet and are easier to kill," Harry grinned. "But I'm sure going to try."

Carrie announced dinner was on the table, and they all gathered. Alf droned on and on saying the Grace. Again Matilda wondered what was going on.

After the guests departed at the end of the festivities, Matilda remarked to Carrie. "All is not well in Alf's household."

Carrie shrugged. "Losing his land probably still bothers him. And Emma is not letting him forget she told him not to borrow money from McFarland."

Matilda frowned. "No, it's more than that. Something is bothering Clint, too." With a sigh, she straightened a chair and put the last stack of her good dishes under the sideboard. "I guess we'll find out in good time."

January blew in with the usual cold and fog. Matilda stood in front of the sink each morning and watched the cows grazing on the hill south of the house fade and reappear as they moved about through the mist. She shivered in the morning chill and held her hands in front of the stove to warm them, thinking how she did this every morning.

After getting no rain at all until the end of December, in the middle of January, a huge storm blew in and the rain poured down for two days without relief. Water poured off the eaves. The whole garden was one soggy mess. The cattle plodded in mud up to their knees. Sam came in from doing the chores with rain dripping off him.

By the end of the second day, as Matilda began to feel the rain would never end, it finally eased off, to everyone's relief.

"Paper says Galt got 2.63 inches of rain in this storm," Sam reported, "but I swear we got more than that."

Toward the end of January, when the sun broke through the gloom for a short time after mid-day, she had Sam hitch up the buggy and take her to the store in Arno. Since young Will McEnerney was now running the store for Alice, they carried a good stock, and her supply of flour and coffee was running low.

Several of the neighborhood young men greeted Sam with enthusiasm as he helped Matilda alight from the buggy.

"Hey, Sam," said Tom McEnerney, "Did you hear Fred Wilson, that foreman of McCauley's loped off with the money he collected for some wood a fellow in Lodi owed McCauley?"

"Isn't he the one McCauley posted bond for? The one charged with assault to commit murder?"

"Yep, the very one. McCauley sent him to Lodi to collect on the bill for that load of wood. Feller was last seen in Lodi on a spree with $80 in gold coin, apparently what he collected, and hasn't been seen since."

"So," young Jim McGuirk chuckled, "McCauley is out not only the $500 bond money, but the money owed him for the wood as well."

Matilda, overhearing the conversation, could only think yes, and an accused murderer is never brought to trial.

Sam came home from Arno one evening towards the end of February grinning from ear to ear, and waving a five dollar gold coin.

"They paid me, Mother. All I had to do was show the tail of that coyote I shot when I caught him trying to get into the chicken pen." He tossed the coin in the air and caught it on its way down. "Will Hicks says the Alabama Coyote Club has paid bounty on 29 coyotes so far."

"Where on earth are they getting the money?" Matilda demanded, figuring up the total in her head. "That's $145 already."

"They're planning another benefit dance, and the ladies are talking about a supper and entertainment."

Matilda sighed. "It just seems like a lot of money. But if you can get five dollars for every coyote you keep from eating our chickens, I'm all for it."

On the last Friday in February, Matilda and Carrie accompanied young Isabel McKenzie to the festivities at the school to celebrate the birthday of the Father of the Nation, primarily to watch young Nettie McKenzie perform.

As they walked up to the front of the school, Matilda read the sign above the porch roof reading "Arno School" with the same twinge of regret she felt when the trustees voted to change the name. Poor Uncle Billy, she thought, has lost again. She glanced at Alice Valensin, very much in the forefront, and murmured to Carrie, "I suppose next she'll want to change the name of the cemetery,"

"Oh, no, Mother," Carrie laughed. "She has no interest in the cemetery. None of her family will ever be buried there."

"Maybe, maybe not," Matilda murmured as they took their seats. Monsignor Capel opened the ceremonies as usual. Never the Methodist minister, Matilda could not help thinking. He congratulated Miss Need for the children's accomplishments, then the students presented their essays, poems, and songs.

"Nettie did very well, for one only eight years old," Matilda said to Isabel, who tried to keep a squirming two-year-old Monty on her lap. "And Emma and Ella Hanson are becoming quite mature young ladies."

Afterwards, everyone rose and sang "America" with great enthusiasm, if slightly off-key.

Following the singing, candy and fruit were served. Miss Need announced that the refreshments had been donated by Mrs. Valensin, "one of our Trustees".

"Probably trying to soothe some of the feathers that were ruffled when she insisted on changing the name of the school."

Matilda heard the murmured comment from someone behind her. She did not try to identify the speaker, but knew the sentiment was widespread Next she'd try and get the name of the road changed from The Ione Road to Arno Road.

Early in April, Matilda received a letter from Minerva's son Will up in Spokane, Washington reporting his brother's death.

"Too Tall Charlie died of consumption on April 2. I went back to Kansas for his funeral. He had been ailing for some time, so it was not unexpected. He died in Belleville where he had been working at the Post Office until his health

failed. Poor Emma is devastated. They just have the one daughter, Rachel. She is a pretty little girl. I had never met her before her father's funeral.

"Poor man was only 35. Consumption is such a terrible disease, and takes so many of our young people. He was buried in the Carnahan Cemetery in Olsburg."

Matilda folded up the letter. Tears sprang into her eyes as she thought of Charlie. They called him "Too Tall Charlie" because he stood six feet four inches tall, but she remembered him as a little boy.

Her thoughts went to when Minerva died, and Mary, child that she was, had taken the confused and frightened little boy away from the chaos and grief in the house. And now they were both gone. She sighed as the tears spilled over and rolled down her cheeks.

Her concern for her brother Alf deepened. He continued to evade her inquiries as to what bothered him. Questions to Harry were met with a blank stare and a denial that anything was amiss.

Finally she cornered Lew one Sunday after church and demanded he tell her. She knew he was aware of something.

He hesitated, but finally drew a long breath and said, "Emma has a lover over in Walnut Grove. She's been seeing him for months."

Chapter 74

April to December, 1899

MATILDA HEARD Lew's announcement with horror, yet, somehow, she had seen it coming. Alf had aged so in the past few years, especially since he lost his land to McFarland. Emma was still a young woman. It was kind of comical in a way. Emma, who had been so scandalized by Mary's behavior leaving her husband and taking a lover.

As she looked back, perhaps some of Emma's criticism of Mary was based not so much on indignation as on envy. Perhaps Emma had regretted her marriage to Alf as much as Mary had regretted hers to George. Mary had the courage to defy George and find a new man, one with whom she could find happiness. Emma had wished she could do the same. And now it looked like she had.

Matilda's heart ached for her brother, for she had sensed his unhappiness for some time. She knew he loved Emma deeply. With a sigh, Matilda realized all she could do for Alf was continue to love him.

The big news to hit the community in April was that John Bandeen had been forced to kill a former employee to save his own life.

"Fellow named Pierson," Jane told Matilda. "Ugly fellow he was, when he got to drinking. Four years ago, when Merrill was only seventeen, he threatened to kill the boy.

Pierson was angry because Merrill had gotten the Sunday paper and he had not. Merrill was still kind of weak, for it was just after he got over that operation for his appendix. Anyway. They were fighting over this paper like two children, and Pierson threatened to kill the boy. Pulled a knife on him, he did. That's when John fired him and told him to stay away from Merrill. Pierson threatened vengeance. Even threatened John with the knife."

"Over something as foolish as a Sunday paper?"

"Apparently."

"And why did it take him four years to try again?"

"John rented his place to Marty Brothers when they moved to the new ranch about five miles east. Mr. Brothers re-hired Pierson. I guess he's a pretty good worker when he's sober. John would see him from time to time, and he would always repeat the threats, but John always managed to evade him. Until last Tuesday."

"And what happened last Tuesday? Why couldn't John just evade him again?"

"Guess what set him off this time was John made some repairs to a fence and left a roll of barbed wire in the field where Pierson was working. He ran into it and became very angry. Accused John of leaving it there deliberate for him to hit. He was working in one field and John in the next when Pierson found the wire. He climbed the fence and threatened John then. John told him he didn't want any trouble and went on plowing."

"How terrible for John!"

"Yes," Jane agreed. "There was a pile of kindling by the corner of the house, and an axe was lying there beside the chopped wood. When John came around the corner of the house, Pierson came at him with the axe. John drew his gun and shot him."

"Did he kill him instantly?"

"John didn't even check. He jumped on a horse and raced to town to send a doctor out to the ranch to tend him and rode up to Florin to turn himself in to the Sheriff."

"Surely they won't charge him!"

"I doubt it," Jane said. "The coroner's inquest ruled John fired in self-defense, so that should be the end of it." Then she grinned. "Bullet went right through Pierson's head. Pretty good shot, I'd say."

Matilda laughed. "Yes, a pretty good shot."

On April 29, Matilda lost her good friend Celestia Johnson at the age of 59.

"Veso found her dead in her bed," Annie Herbert reported sadly to Matilda. "Good woman, she were. Fought a good fight. Her bein' burned out five times, and all that bickering over the road had to've put a strain on her heart. Veso run for Doc Montague, o' course, but wa'n't nothin' he could do."

Matilda could only sigh. "Poor dear. She had a hard life. I hope she has found peace now."

"Hear the Sawyer girl died of heart trouble too."

"No!" Matilda gasped. "She was so young."

"Twenty-nine. They say it was induced by gastric troubles. Family's devastated."

"Poor thing," Matilda murmured.

Annie reached across the table to swat a fly that had landed. "Any of you folks goin' to the Grangers picnic next Saturday in Elk Grove?" She grinned. "They're sayin' it's gonna be the picnic of the season. Guess they got all kinds of stuff planned."

"Carrie and Sam plan to go. Sam has a lady friend from over Lockeford way. He says he wants to bring her so we can all meet her."

"Oho!" Annie chortled. "So the love bug has bitten him at last! And Carrie? Still no young man in sight?"

"Not yet," Matilda chuckled. "She keeps saying she's going to stay with me. But I suspect if the right young man comes along, she'll change her mind."

Sam did take his sweetheart to the picnic, and en route stopped by the house to introduce her to Matilda.

"This is Phoebe Reynolds, Mother. Her father owns a farm over in Lockeford, but she has friends in Galt where she stayed last night. I'll take her back there after the picnic."

Matilda took Phoebe's hands in hers and kissed the girl on her cheek. "So nice to meet you, my dear. It's about time our Sam had a lady friend. I guess he's been waiting for you."

The girl blushed. "I've looked forward to meeting you as well, Mrs. Frye. And I do enjoy Sam's company. He talks so educated, and reads so well."

Matilda laughed. "That's our Sam. Enjoy the picnic. At least with the new bridge the crossing should be safe in spite of the high water."

Carrie climbed into the back seat. Sam turned the horse, and they were off. As she watched them go, Matilda could not help but remember how she had watched Frank and Mary go off to the Grangers picnic on that ill-fated day nine years before.

A week later, Sam read her an article in the paper. "Says the Sultan of Turkey will pay claims of $100,000 to American citizens who suffered damages during the Armenian massacre."

"So he's admitting to the massacre?"

"In a way," Sam grinned, "But he only offers reparations to American citizens."

Matilda shook her head.

After church the first week in June, Alf came alone to dinner at Matilda's. He looked more morose than ever. "Got the papers June 4. James Keefer served me. Emma's filing for divorce, charging desertion."

Matilda put her hand on his as it lay on the table. 'I'm so sorry," she murmured.

"You knew, didn't you? That she has another fellow?"

"Yes," she admitted. "Lew told me."

He sighed. "I don't know how Lew found out, but he's known for some time. I guess Mother was right when she said Emma was too young for me." Tears filled his eyes and overflowed down his weather-beaten cheeks. "But we were so happy for so long," he said, his voice so low Matilda had to lean forward to hear him. "At least I was, and I thought she was, too."

"Remember the happy times," Matilda murmured. "And you have two fine sons and a lovely daughter."

He blew his nose and attempted a smile. "Thank you, 'Tilda. At least I can always count on you."

On July 1, Veso re-opened the Hicksville saloon. Sam reported the news to his mother.

Matilda could only sigh, thinking of how many who had tried to make a living in Hicksville. She feared the *Gazette* was right, that Arno would be the place of the future. That Hicksville was doomed to oblivion by the railroad, like Liberty had been.

"And," Sam continued, "Jim Hicks' wife got another let-

659

ter from him up in Alaska. Says he run into that Moseley fellow as loped off with the money from Stockton folks and lost it in real estate speculations."

"I'll bet he has no plans to come back," Matilda chuckled.

"None whatsoever. In fact, he told Jim some of the folks he dealt with don't want him to come back, as some of the things he did they'd just as soon never came to light."

"Well, that should end the speculation that he's in Mexico."

"Yep, he's in Alaska, no question about it."

The remainder of the summer passed quickly. Her brother Tom's heart gave out at last and he slipped quietly away to join his brothers and sisters. After the funeral, his widow Mary announced plans to move to El Dorado County. "George and I both liked living in the hills. The heat here in the valley bothers me. I've found a lovely cottage in Placerville that will be perfect for us."

"We'll miss you, but I can't say as I blame you," Matilda said, wiping her overheated forehead with a handkerchief already soggy. "This heat can be really miserable."

August brought a terrific thunderstorm and concerns about a neighbor girl who worked for Isabel McKenzie.

"I'm worried about Maud," Isabel confided to Matilda and Carrie over the cup of tea the hired girl had brought them on their next visit. "Colin hired her so I would have some help around the house." The three sat in Isabel's parlor. Isabel lowered her voice. "She's just a child, barely eighteen. A year ago she married young Barnhart, but he hasn't been around in an age. They never have lived together. She's crazy about him, and mopes all the time."

"Didn't Mr. Fleming insist on the marriage?" Carrie

asked. "I heard the Barnhart boy was forced into it."

"Yes, I've heard the same thing, but I can't help but pity the poor child. She's so unhappy. She's even talked of killing herself."

"Oh, I hope not," Matilda exclaimed.

Isabel nodded. "I know. Colin and I both have tried to tell her she has a lot of years in front of her, that she may meet someone else, someone who does love her." She shrugged. "Not much else we can do. She's such a mousy little thing. I don't think any of the other boys have ever taken any notice of her." She sighed and refilled the teacups. "Have a cookie. Maud is a pretty good cook, I will say that for her. You folks have any problems with that thunderstorm?"

"No, but I understand the lightning took out a number of telephone fuse boxes," Matilda smiled. "Since we don't have a telephone, it didn't affect us."

"We may have one soon, though, Mother," Carrie said. "A number of farmers around here are talking of forming our own line."

"Could be handy sometimes, I suppose," Matilda shrugged. "To be able to call the doctor instead of having to send someone riding for him would save a lot of time. And maybe some lives. You and Colin planning to go to the Harvest Ball?"

"Of course. How else can we keep up on the neighborhood gossip?" Isabel laughed. "Have another cookie. Do you suppose the French Court will find Dreyfuss guilty again this time?"

"Probably," Matilda remarked dryly. "With a prejudiced court backed by a corrupt army, what else can you expect?"

"Colin says they'll find him guilty and give him a light sentence so they can save face. He's just lucky Mr. Zola wrote that book about his case. Otherwise the army would have just left him in prison and forgotten about him."

"Did you hear George McCauley bought a whole lot of land just east of here? Says he's going to divide it into five and ten acre parcels for truck farming, and to encourage settlers. Says he's not doing it for the money, but for the good of the community."

Matilda grinned wryly. "I'm sure the money was part of the appeal of the plan."

Isabel laughed merrily. "I suspect you're right. Anyway, Colin is dickering to buy about 300 acres not far from here. Then we will have our own place. No more struggling to pay the rent."

"No," Matilda chuckled. "Then you'll just have to struggle to pay the taxes."

Sam roused Matilda the following Monday morning. "You'd better get over to Isabel's, Mother. I guess she's almost beside herself. That girl that works for them took a dose of Rough-on-Rats, which, as you know, is almost pure strychnine. Seems yesterday was the anniversary of her marriage, and Barnhart had said he would come by and see her. When he didn't show, she took the poison. When she went into convulsions, Colin raced for Doc Montague."

"Was he in time?" She immediately thought of her remark just last week that having a telephone could reach the doctor quicker.

"They thought so. He gave her the antidote and the convulsions stopped. But she took a turn for the worst just before dawn. As I was getting the cows in, Colin came by and said he was going for the doc again, and asked if you could stay with Isabel."

"Of course." Matilda hurried to dress, as did Carrie, and

they reached the McKenzie residence before Colin returned with the doctor. It was apparent to Matilda the girl was near death.

"We thought we had caught it in time," Isabel sobbed in Matilda's arms. "She was so heartbroken when that rat of a husband didn't come as he had promised."

The arrival of Colin and Dr. Montague ended the conversation. The doctor examined the limp body and shook his head sadly. Isabel took the girl's hand, tears streaming down her cheeks.

"Don't cry, Miz. McKenzie," the girl whispered. "I did it myself, and I'm glad. Life ain't worth living." She drifted into unconsciousness. The breathing gradually slowed, and finally stopped.

Two weeks after Maud's funeral, Matilda again found herself at the little cemetery, this time to honor long-time friend and neighbor, David Davis. He was laid to rest in the plot where many of the Davis children had been buried. His wife and nine living adult children were present.

"Guess he didn't recover quite as well as everyone thought," Carrie murmured in her mother's ear, referring to his recent illness.

"I was thinking, since he has all of these living descendants, and all of those little ones buried here, how many babies Elizabeth must have borne!"

Carrie laughed softly. "Guess he didn't want Tom McEnerney to beat his record."

September saw Dreyfuss found guilty, as expected, and, also as expected, pardoned a week later.

On September 25th, Emma's divorce from Alf became final. Alf did not contest the action.

"But she left you," Matilda exclaimed. "How could she

claim you deserted her?"

"It was what she wanted, 'Tilda," he said sadly. "It's the least I could do for her."

"And Clint?"

"He'll stay with me half the time and with his mother the other half."

"And how does he feel about the arrangement?"

Alf shrugged. "He wants to stay with me. Says he hates his mother's new beau. But the Court felt he should spend some time with his mother."

Matilda could only shake her head.

On December 9, 1899, Emma became Mrs. John Richie, and moved to Walnut Grove.

Chapter 75

April to December, 1900

THE LAST YEAR of the nineteenth century began with the usual bout of dismal fog. The paper reported in February that it seemed a year since the sun had been seen. It also said that the rebellion in the Philippines was over, and that the British were defeating the Boers.

Sam's romance with young Phoebe Reynolds continued to flourish, and Matilda began to have hopes for a wedding in the near future. Caroline's daughter Sally did marry her suitor, Mr. Brennard, and they continued to farm Sam's property in Lake County.

Easter saw the family gathered at Matilda's home. Alf seemed to be adjusting, although whenever he thought no one was looking, the sadness washed over his face again. Clint was with him for the festivities.

Another baby girl, named Elizabeth for her mother and great-grandmother, and called Bess, had arrived on October 11 and brightened some of the pall cast by Pauline's death. Little Dickie immediately fell in love with the new baby, and carried her around as much as her doting mother would allow.

Media laughingly related her stepmother's trials and tribulations with the County Board of Supervisors. "She's

665

not at all like my mother, who was quiet and happy to stay at home most of the time. Alice is always in to some project or other, like when she was organizing the ladies to make bandages for the Red Cross during the war with Spain."

"Has she found a new cause?" Carrie asked.

"Oh, yes, she has taken the Salvation Army Rescue Home over in Alameda County under her wing. Seems four or five young women from this County are residents there, where they are receiving moral and physical training. She went to the Board to ask for an appropriation. Morris moved to send fifty dollars, Curtis lowered it to twenty-five, then Gillis and McLaughlin voted against it. Jenkins chose, wisely, to be absent that day. He's frightened to death of my stepmother. He knows what a force she can be when she gets her dander up."

"They turned her down?" Matilda asked, appalled.

"They sure did. And she is livid."

Spring also brought the news that Colin and Isabel had purchased their home as planned and would be moving.

"I'll be glad to leave this house," Isabel confided to Matilda. "Since Maud's suicide this place has a bad aura."

Matilda hugged the girl warmly, "I'll miss having you as a close neighbor, but do hope we can keep in touch."

"Oh, yes, we won't be that far away, only about a mile. You have been such a help to me."

In May, Rawson's Pacific Shows performed a trained animal exposition and children's carnival under a mammoth tent. Carrie and Matilda went with Elizabeth to take the children to see it.

"After all, Mother," Elizabeth explained, "It's right here

in Galt. The children have never seen sea lions and tigers and monkeys before. The seats are only twenty-five cents."

"Unless you want to sit where you can see something," Carrie laughed. "Then it's fifty cents."

They had a wonderful afternoon. The children were thrilled, and returned home sated with caramel corn, their faces sticky from candied apples. Even little Bess, though far too young to understand any of it, caught the excitement and, sitting on Matilda's lap, clapped her little hands together and bounced gleefully when the others applauded.

A week later, Sam announced that Pio Valensin had been named census enumerator for the Dry Creek and Alabama townships. "Census to be done June first."

"And I wonder how he got that appointment," Carrie remarked dryly.

Sam only grinned. "I didn't ask."

In September, the ladies of the Hicksville Methodist Church held an Ice Cream Social. As usual, the neighborhood gathered for ice cream and catching up on the latest gossip.

"Rumor says your father is planning to sell his tin shop," Lou Herbert said to Media.

"Yes, he has it up for sale. Says there's no point in keeping it, with Willie gone and Jack planning to sell life insurance. Is talking of moving to Loomis, although I can't imagine why. A fellow by the name of Orvis has been looking at it."

"And did Carrie's girl finally marry that nice man from over in Lake County?" Annie continued

"Yes, but I've never met him. They are talking of moving over here, but so far have made no plans. Lew will meet him next week, for he and George McGuirk are taking a two week hunting trip over there, and plan to spend some time with them."

"They say oil discoveries in Southern California will mean the end of coal as heating fuel," Annie went on, with her usual ability to jump from one subject to the next. Sometimes Matilda had trouble keeping up with her.

"That will be nice," murmured Matilda. "Coal is so messy. And to use wood means someone has to be chopping all the time. Do they say how we are supposed to use it?"

Annie shrugged. "I guess it requires some kind of special stove. You can't just pop it in like you do coal."

"No," Matilda agreed, "probably not."

"And I also read that squabbling among the Sutro heirs will result in the break-up of his library. The 280,000 volumes will be scattered among them."

"Oh, my," Matilda gasped. "Don't tell Sam. His life's ambition has been to spend a week or more at the Sutro Library browsing among the books."

"Yes, Sam's the bookworm, all right," Annie agreed. "Real shame to bust up that collection. They say it's the finest in the State."

In October, P.H. Latourette did sell his tin shop and hardware store to J.I. Orvis, with plans to go to Loomis. "But," Media laughed, "they wound up in Oak Park, and my stepmother says she likes it there, so they'll probably stay. She's a pretty strong-willed lady."

Also in October, Matilda had both Sam and Lew to feed and look after. Media went to visit friends in San Jose, and Sally Brennard had come over from Lake County and she and Carrie went to Lockeford to spend some time with friends there.

"I declare," Matilda laughed as she put the food in front of them, "If there wasn't a woman around you men would starve."

"Now, Mother, George and I managed to survive a two week hunting trip."

"And how many meals did you eat at Sally's?"

Lew laughed. "You win. Quite a few. There's nothing like a woman's cooking."

Sam grinned. "Did you hear a famous scientist has predicted the world will end in 1914?"

"Humph," Matilda said. "And how did he come to that conclusion?"

"Says he based it on a Biblical calendar. Since any Biblical calendar I've ever seen has been pretty ephemeral, I've no idea how he can be so certain. Must have used a different Bible."

"Well," Lew grinned. "Time will tell."

"Yep," Sam said. "Just have to live fourteen more years and we'll be able to prove him wrong."

"Or right," Matilda said with a touch of skepticism. "But I doubt I'll live to see it."

"Of course you will, Mother," Lew said, helping himself to another boiled potato. "You're indestructible. Gram lived to be 81. I can see you doing the same."

Matilda laughed. "We'll see."

Christmas was a small one. On Christmas morning it was just the three of them. Sam presented Carrie with a small book, of Tennyson's poem "*Marmion*". In it, he inscribed:

"Jan 1, 1901, Dear Sister: On this the birthday of the Twentieth Century, I present to you this little volume as a token of a brother's love. Within its pages are some of the noblest thoughts ever expressed by man, and a perusal of them cannot help lifting one above and beyond earthly feelings thereby making them near the goal of perfection. Your affectionate brother, S.A. Wheelock."

When Carrie finished reading the inscription, Matilda had a lump in her throat. Carrie smiled at her brother with tears in her eyes. "Thank you, Sam. What a lovely sentiment. I'll treasure this little book for the rest of my life."

Chapter 76

January to December 1901

1901 OPENED WITH the papers reporting the death of Queen Victoria.

"Heavens," Matilda shook her head, "she ruled for sixty-four years. She was an institution."

"Yes, and she was opposed to Chamberlain's aggressive policy in bringing on the South African war. And it looks like she was right. Chamberlain said the war would be over in three months, and it's been almost three years already. She didn't deserve the burden of that." Sam slathered another biscuit with elderberry jelly. "I wonder if it will mean any changes in England."

"Probably not," Matilda remarked with a touch of sarcasm. "Chamberlain got them into that war and he has to be the one to get them out."

"Shame," Sam remarked. "Many fine young men have died, and for what?"

"That's what war always is," Matilda sighed, thinking f Josh and poor Henry. "Old men make wars and young men die."

"Well, I guess it's still going on." Sam rose and carried his plate out to the sink. "I'd better check on that cow with the new calf. Water is pretty high, and I don't want it to get stranded."

671

"Guess the water's high all over. At church last Sunday I heard they have a lot of flooding south of Galt."

After church services at the end of February, Will McEnerney reported George McCauley had a lot of trouble with the flooding.

"Sent one of his milkers, name of Emmons, out to hunt down a missing cow. Couple of fellers out rabbit hunting saw him and his horse disappear. Had to have gone into the river to vanish that quick."

"Fast as that river's moving, they'll be in San Francisco Bay by now," remarked George McGuirk.

Matilda moved away from the speakers. Even though it had been ten years since Mary and Frank drowned, it hurt her to hear of it happening to anyone else.

Sam followed and helped her into the buggy. "Gonna get worse before it gets better," was all he said.

Flooding continued into March. Matilda stood at the window and watched the water race past. Both the Sacramento and the San Joaquin Rivers had several breaks in their levees.

Carrie came up beside her and they watched the water in silence for a moment. "I hear over seven thousand acres are flooded by Tracy. And they found the horse Emmons was riding. So the horse got out okay, but no evidence yet of Emmons."

Matilda sighed. "Poor man. He must be drowned."

"Is Sam taking his sweetheart to the dance at Hicksville next Friday? The Alabama Coyote Club is trying to raise money to pay the bounties."

"Oh, yes," Matilda laughed. "I suspect we will be having a wedding soon. He's really smitten."

"I'm sure that new minister, Mr. Frazer, will be happy to oblige them." Carrie took the teakettle to the pump in the sink and filled it with water. "Did you hear that man Tesla is testing a wireless telegraph?" she added as she put the teakettle on the stove.

"My heavens, what will they think of next?"

Sam popped the question to Phoebe at the Hicksville dance. The Reverend Frazer announced the news to the church congregation the following Sunday. The newly engaged couple was surrounded by well-wishers as soon as the services concluded.

"You gonna be married here or in Lockeford?" Sam was asked by one of his friends.

"Neither one," Sam replied with a grin. "She wants to get married at her grandmother's home up in Tigardville. Guess the old lady can't travel, and Phoebe feels she should go there. Since her own mother is dead, she wants her grandmother at her wedding."

"Tigardville? Where on Earth is that?" George wanted to know.

Sam shrugged. "Up in Oregon someplace."

"So we don't get to go to your wedding?"

"You can come to Tigardville," Sam grinned. "But my mother is already planning a reception for us when we get back, and you're invited to that."

Annie Herbert congratulated Matilda on Sam finally choosing a bride.

"Yes," Matilda agreed, "She seems to be a fine girl, if a little flighty. I know her father is pleased. He wants Sam to come and take over running his farm in Lockeford. Guess he's getting up in years, and with no son, he needs someone."

" But what will you do without him?" Annie asked.

"Lew says he can help me for a while. Media has a cousin back in Ohio with a hankering to come to California, so I suspect I'll hire him on as a hand. Like to know who I'll be hiring, since I don't have a bunkhouse and he'll have to stay in the house with Carrie and me. And I've been talking to the trustees about boarding the schoolmarm, since I have space."

"Good. That'll give you a little extra income, which I'm sure you can use."

"Oh, yes, I certainly can." Matilda laughed. "I hear President McKinley is planning to tour California. Are you going to come to town to see him as he goes through?"

Annie shrugged. "Maybe. Depends. I hear that Ag - - - Ag - - - Ag, whatever, was captured in the Philippines, so maybe that will settle things there."

"Aguinaldo," Matilda laughed. "Time will tell." She rose to leave. "Carrie and I went to hear Miss Harvey's performance on the harp at the Congregational Church. She's very talented. And such a gracious young lady."

"Yep, understand old Obed Harvey thought the sun rose and set in her."

Spring blossomed in its usual glory. Matilda found working in the garden harder now, and she found herself getting a little short of breath.

"Getting what Mother used to call 'a touch of the rheumaticks' in my knees now," she laughed to Carrie as she struggled to her feet.

"I understand McKinley's train is coming through Galt tomorrow afternoon about two. Sam said he'll take us."

"Good," Matilda responded. "And maybe we can catch a glimpse of that fancy eight hundred dollar automobile that Fred Harvey has been tooling around town in."

Carrie laughed. "I understand he has an exclusive right to market them in Sacramento and San Joaquin Counties.

I'm sure he'll be happy to sell you one."

"Not yet. They seem a little scary to me." Matilda thought of Sinclair, of Will, of Britt, all killed by horses. "But I guess they've got to be less dangerous than horses."

The following day Matilda stood on the crowded platform in the Galt Station waiting, with hundreds of others, for President McKinley's train to come through.

"Don't see why he can't stand on the platform as he comes through Arno, then we could have seen him from there," Lem Cain grumbled.

Matilda laughed. "Guess he'd be on the platform for the whole trip if he greeted every station."

A whistle sounded in the distance. "Here he comes," someone shouted.

The train bore down on them, slowing a little, and bounded through. At the end of the train, President McKinley stood on the rear platform and bowed and waved.

Matilda waved back, standing on her tiptoes as she did. She never forgot that one brief glimpse of President McKinley.

In September, she was devastated by the news that the President had been shot.

"By an anarchist with some outlandish foreign name," Lew told her. "There are those who are saying the whole anarchist movement should be stamped out if they call for assassination of government officials."

"I'm inclined to agree," Matilda nodded, recalling their attempt to blow up the City Hall in San Francisco some years before. 'Too bad they didn't do it before this monster had a chance to harm our dear President."

At the end of September, accompanied by Phoebe's father, J.A. Reynolds, Sam and Phoebe boarded the train for

Oregon for their wedding. Carrie and Matilda saw them off from the Arno Station.

"Hurry back," Carrie told Sam as she gave him a farewell hug. "Your reception is scheduled for October 12, and the whole neighborhood is planning to come. It would be a shame if you weren't there!"

"Don't worry," Sam laughed. "We plan to head back the day after the wedding. The hired man is tending the place while we're gone, but Mr. Reynolds doesn't like to leave him alone for too long."

"That's because he's too fond of his whisky jug," Phoebe added. "He just might take a notion to finish the bottle instead of milking the cow."

"Then you'd better hurry back," Matilda remarked dryly.

On the drive back home, they passed the church, and Carrie commented, "It's probably just as well they're marrying in Oregon. I see the carpenters have started on the renovations."

"Yes," Matilda agreed. "A wedding with sawdust all over the pews and the smell of paint all around is, I'm sure, not what they had in mind."

"It is sweet of Phoebe, to think so much of her grandmother that they take that long ride just so she can witness her wedding."

True to his word, Sam was back the day before the scheduled reception, his bride on his arm. Mr. Reynolds looked worn out, but Sam and Phoebe were radiant.

The reception was a great success. All of the family members living in the area were present, as well as friends and neighbors for miles around. McEnerneys, Dillards, Moroneys, Cantrells, Rileys, McGuirks, Hansens, McKenzies, and, of course, Lou and Annie Herbert.

Matilda was sorry Jane could not be present, but since she had married Dr. Bainbridge and moved to Lathrop, she did not see much of her, although they still kept in touch by letter.

Young Eleanor Hanson had turned out to be quite a pretty girl, as Alf's son Harry seemed to notice, to Matilda's amusement. Matilda was thankful the weather had remained mild, so the crowd could mill around outside as well as inside. While the ham and chicken and deviled eggs disappeared, laughter and conversation floated around the room.

"Hear there's an insurrection on the Island of Samar," Ed Riley commented to George McGuirk. "Guess the Philippines are not as quiet as we were led to believe. Kind of felt they were being a little optimistic."

"Sort of like the Brits and the Boer War," George chuckled. "The war they predicted would last three months has cost them over $700,000,000, and 18,000 men have been killed and over 75,000 wounded."

Matilda, overhearing the remarks as she carried another platter of fried chicken to the table, could only shake her head at such a tragic waste of money and lives. When she reached the table, Lew joined her and helped her clear a space by removing an empty plate.

"Sure can eat, these folks," he grinned as he handed the empty platter to Media to return to the kitchen. "Did you hear there's talk of putting oil on the roads to improve them? Supposed to keep them from making so much dust in the summer. Maybe even help keep them from becoming such a muddy morass in the winter."

As the afternoon wore on and the food disappeared, Carrie and Media cleared the table and Lew and Sam carried the cake from the kitchen and placed it in the center of the newly cleared table. As the beaming young couple cut the first slice, George raised his glass of punch and proposed a toast.

"Long life and happiness to Sam and Phoebe."

Cheers went up throughout the room.

"And may you prosper and have many children."

Phoebe blushed.

As they cleaned up after the last of the guests had departed, Matilda collapsed onto her chair with a sigh of relief.

"Put your feet up and rest, Mother," Carrie said. "Media and I will clean up."

"Thank you. I'm ready for a little rest."

"I guess the next wedding will be Pio Valensin and Lily Moroney." Carrie tucked a blanket around her mother's legs. "It's set for the end of November, and if I know Alice Valensin, it'll be the wedding of the century. I even hear Lilly is going to wear a white satin gown!"

Chapter 77

January to May of 1902

THE FIRST NEWS they heard in 1902 was rumors of a smallpox epidemic.

"Said to have begun down in Stockton," Lew reported. "Guess it came up the river on one of the boats. First outbreak was in one of the schools." He poured himself a cup of coffee.

Matilda sighed. "When will people learn to get vaccinated? Smallpox should be a thing of the past. I just wish it was as easy to prevent cholera."

"Grandmother Betsy Ann was right," Lew grinned. "Boil the water. Just think. She knew to do that forty years before the scientists figured out what causes diseases like cholera."

"She was wise beyond her years," Matilda agreed, "I can remember people laughing at her as she boiled the water 'to get out all of the deleterious properties'. She didn't know what she was getting rid of or how, but she knew it worked." Matilda sighed. "The only thing she couldn't defeat was consumption."

"And horses," Lew grinned. "Did you hear that Reverend Staton died at his home down in Gilroy?"

"No! What happened?"

"They say he died of heart disease brought on by exhaustion from a long bicycle ride."

Matilda shook her head. "Maybe the doctors that say riding bicycles is bad have a point."

"No more dangerous than horses."

With a sigh, Matilda had to agree.

The opening ceremonies for the newly renovated church at Hicksville were set for March 23.

"Will the building be ready in time?" Matilda asked Rev. Frazer the week before. As she looked around, it seemed there was a lot left to do.

"Miles Stevens is going to be busy painting the inside, starting tomorrow. He has promised it will be ready." He shook his head. "I'm just sorry I'm scheduled to be in Elliott. Presiding Elder Moore will get the honor of giving the first sermon under the brand new ceiling."

"And you'll miss the basket dinner as well. The ladies have promised it will be special."

Matilda and Carrie attended both the 11 AM and 2:30 PM sessions, and enjoyed the basket dinner in between.

Columbus Dillard greeted them. "The new ceiling is real nice, isn't it? And Miles really outdid himself painting the interior. It's very artistic. He's so talented."

"Yes. He certainly is," Matilda agreed.

"Did you hear the Post Office wants to start rural delivery throughout the county?" he went on. "Imagine not having to go to the Post Office for mail."

Carrie laughed. "Then how would everyone keep up with the latest gossip?" She lowered her voice. "Like Doc Harms is interested in one of the Galt school teachers?"

Columbus joined her laughter. "Or that those fellows who built the airship in Ione plan to fly it to San Francisco the first week in May, and they plan to hover over Galt. Philips says they're going to lower a line and he'll be sending up fried chicken and liquid refreshments."

Matilda laughed. "That I've got to see."

May saw Columbus Dillard and his family quarantined by Dr. Montague, for his wife and daughter were stricken with smallpox.

Matilda was shocked when Carrie told her. "You mean as enlightened a man as Columbus didn't have his family vaccinated?"

"He was, several years ago, but his wife was afraid, and he didn't insist."

"I'll bet he's sorry now," Matilda said caustically.

Carrie laughed. "Yes, I'm sure he is."

Two weeks after he quarantined the Dillard family, Dr. Montague himself was taken seriously ill and transported to the hospital in Sacramento.

"They say it's his appendix," Lew reported to his anxious mother, "They operated, but it was all full of pus. I guess he came though the operation all right, but now they are afraid of peritonitis because gangrene had set in."

"Oh, no, poor Nettie," Matilda cried. She knew only too well what would happen if he developed peritonitis. "Is there anything we can do?"

"Pray," Lew said tersely. "That's all even the doctors can do."

Carrie told her the next day that Mount Pelee on the Island of Martinique has exploded.

"Oh, no," Matilda gasped. "And after all of those scientists said there was no danger?"

"Goes to show scientists don't always have all the answers," she replied grimly. "First guess is that about

40,000 have died."

"What a shame." Matilda smiled wryly. "That's news, 40,000 dying from an exploding volcano. The fact that we may lose our one beloved Dr. Montague, that's a tragedy."

Dr. Montague's death came on the following Wednesday, and all attended his funeral on Saturday at the Congregational Church. As Matilda watched his body lowered into the grave in the Odd Fellows Cemetery, she could only think that his death was a tragic loss not only to his family, but to the whole community.

Why, God? she asked silently. Why? Such a fine man, who had done so much for so many people, and still had so much left to offer. She looked over at Nettie, standing alone, and her heart ached for her.

As spring drifted into summer, Lew and Media came to dinner after church one Sunday in June and Media announced her cousin was on his way to California.

"I told him you needed a hired hand, Mother Matilda. And it will be wonderful to see him again. I was only six when my father decided to bring us to California, so all I can remember of him was thinking what a handsome boy he was. He's two years older than I am."

"Oh, good. It will be wonderful to have help."

"But here's our big news, Mother Matilda." She paused.

"You're going to have a baby at last," Matilda exclaimed. "I was wondering when that was going to happen."

Media laughed and Lew chuckled. "Not quite like that," she said. "We're going to adopt a little girl."

Matilda only stared.

"She's a year old," Lew explained. "The friend I went to school with at Pacific Methodist, the one who's a judge in Sacramento, found out this family of three little girls was abandoned by their mother. She ran off and left them all alone."

"But their father?" Matilda asked, aghast to think any mother could ever do such a thing.

"Cowboy, he is, up Williams way. He was away on a job. Came home to find the girls alone."

"But they were just babies," Matilda cried.

"Guess the oldest girl kept them all alive by cracking walnuts for them to eat. The littlest is only a few months old. Judge and his wife are taking her. No way the father can take care of the two littlest ones. We're going to take the middle one. Her name is Myrtle Alvey, but," he grinned, "only until we get the paper work done. Then she'll be Myrtle Baldwin. She's a beautiful little girl, Mother. You'll love her."

Matilda smiled. "I love her already."

Chapter 78

June to December, 1902

EARLY IN JUNE, Media's cousin, Martin Luther Shellenbarger, arrived on the train. Lew and Media met him at the station and brought him to meet Matilda.

Matilda noticed he was indeed a very handsome young man. She extended her hand. "Welcome to California, Martin. Media has told me so much about you we feel we know you. And we can certainly use your help."

He took her hand in a firm grip and said, with a smile that went straight to her heart, "Please, call me Mart, Mrs. Frye. And I have heard many good things about you from Media. And about California weather from Uncle P.H.!"

Carrie entered the room at that moment, and stood as though stunned. Matilda saw the light leap into Martin's eyes and she chuckled softly to herself. Carrie had never shown any interest in the neighborhood swains, but somehow Matilda suspected this young man would be the one to break through that reserve.

Martin settled in quickly, and proved not only a charming young man, but a good worker as well.

June brought a swarm of locusts that threatened crops, leading to the burning of pasturelands in hopes of keeping them from grain fields. It also brought the welcome news that the Boer War had come to an end at last.

"It's about time," Matilda said with a sigh when Martin reported the news.

"A ranch hand over in Siwash got drunk, and when they locked him up in a cell, he set fire to his bedding. Like to suffocated himself, he did."

"The poor man," Matilda murmured. "Must have been too drunk to realize what he was doing."

"Serves him right," Carrie muttered.

Matilda had to smile. The normally very patient and tolerant Carrie did not hold with drinking, and had no patience with those who drank to excess.

"And I hear Doc Montague's brother Alpheus is contesting his will."

"How can he do that? Doc left everything to Nettie, as is proper. Surely they can't try and say he was insane when he wrote it!"

"Guess he owned a lot of property, both here and in North Carolina, from what they say." Martin chuckled. "Been my experience, when a lot of money and property is involved, folks tend to think they have a right to a share of it."

"I suppose you're right," Matilda sighed. "It just seems a shame that poor Nettie has to go through this on top of losing her husband."

"Never met the lady or her husband, but I agree it is too bad she has to deal with a bunch of hostile in-laws," he nodded and rose. "Better get on with the chores. Lew's coming tomorrow to help me and we're going to butcher that fattest hog. I filled the scalding kettle and piled a lot of wood under it. I'll get it lighted early tomorrow so the water will be hot when Lew gets here."

Matilda nodded. "Be good to get the rendering done before summer sets in. And we are running low on soap.

Time to make another batch."

He grinned. "And I can taste the cracklings already." He pulled on his hat. "Carrie's due back. Got to get the gate open for her." He headed out the door on a run.

Matilda smiled at his eagerness. Carrie gave no hint of a budding romance, but it was certainly obvious to Matilda that Martin was smitten.

When Lew and Martin came in for dinner, after they had butchered, scalded, and scraped the hog, Lew voiced his concern for fire. "Been several already, around Elk Grove. Freight trains ignite 'em. Columbus lost a wheat field, and so did McCauley. Hope they miss us until we get that wheat harvested." He grinned. "That little Myrtle is the cutest little thing you ever saw, Mother. She's got the prettiest smile, and she's getting this walking business down real good."

Matilda laughed. "Enjoy her while she's little. They are babies for such a short time. I'm just glad she's such a healthy little girl."

"You're not half as glad as we are. Wonder is she survived at all. She must be tough." He rose. "Come on, Mart. Let's get that hog cut up. Got your rendering pot ready, Mother? This one's got enough fat to keep you in soap all year."

In August, Martin returned from taking a load of wheat to the rail station at Arno full of news.

"You know the Wilders, don't you, Mrs. Frye?"

"Of course. Elitha and I have been friends for years. Poor dear has been through so much in her life, and losing Ben was a real blow to her. Has something else happened?"

"Seems there was a fire where her son George and his family have been living, and the house was destroyed. George's wife and the three children died."

"Oh, no," Matilda cried. "Poor George. And poor Elitha, to lose her three grandchildren. She was so proud of them." Matilda could not take it all in. To lose three at one time! "Hitch up the buggy. I must go see Elitha at once."

When they arrived at the Wilder ranch, many people milled about. Allen was trying to keep some semblance of order. He greeted Matilda warmly. "You are just the person Ma needs now, Mrs. Frye. Everyone keeps asking her what happened, and they are driving her to distraction. Poor George is beside himself. I brought him home to be with us. Felt he should not be alone, especially as some fools are saying he set the fire himself, to kill his wife."

"But surely no one believes he would deliberately kill his own children!"

"No one who knows him would think it for a moment. Those three babies were the light of his life. He carried little Bertie everywhere he went. And poor little Frankie was only three months old."

"I never really knew Katie very well. Was she at all unstable?"

"Her father died of cancer a few years back, and she was sure she had cancer of the breast. Had pain all the time, she said. She had a real fear of dying in agony like her father did. The night it happened, she kissed George goodbye, said she was going to take the children and go to a better place. He begged her to get medical care, but she refused." He sighed. "So George went to sleep in the next room, and when the smell of smoke woke him up, it was already too late. She must have set fire to the room as soon as Bertie, Dickie and the baby were asleep."

"Why didn't he stay with her, since she was so obviously upset?"

"That's what the Coroner wanted to know, and why a lot

688

of suspicions have been cast. But poor George is so distraught, blaming himself for not being more aware of her state of mind, and berating himself for not insisting on staying with her that anyone should be able to see he is totally innocent."

"The poor dear," Matilda sighed. "Your support is what he needs now. Let me go to Elitha and give her what comfort I can."

A week later, as Matilda and Carrie put the finishing touches on another batch of dill pickles from the cucumbers in the garden, they heard buggy wheels crunching the gravel of the driveway.

It was one of the hands from the Wilder place. He pulled the buggy to a stop and called to Matilda, "Come quick, Miz Frye. Allen says his mother needs you. Seems her son George up and hung himself this morning."

George's suicide ended any talk of prosecuting him for the deaths, and life drifted slowly back to normal. The suit contesting Dr. Montague's will continued.

"I agree with Campbell on the business," Lew declared. "He says the whole thing is trumped up to scare Nettie into sharing the estate with her in-laws. The whole thing is ridiculous, and will probably be thrown out of court."

"Well," Matilda sighed, " for Nettie's sake I certainly hope so."

"Hear Mt. Pelee erupted again. They say ash blocked the sun for five miles out to sea."

Matilda laughed. "I'll bet the scientists will be a little more careful in the future about telling people there is no danger from a volcano!"

Chapter 79

January to May 1903

MART RETURNED from a trip to Galt chuckling over Lack Quiggle's plans to turn Midway Station into a major resort.

"Says he's gonna have zoological and botanical gardens as well as piped in water from the Hatselville Springs. Water's supposed to cure everything from arthritis to bunions. Even says his 'gold cure' removes the craving for alcohol. Several people say they have no desire to drink after using the water. Lack says he'll keep a quantity of the 'Golden Liquid' on draught all the time to allow chronic imbibers a chance to break the habit."

Matilda shook her head. "Some folks will believe anything. You get those canning jars Whitaker and Ray had on sale?"

"Yes, and the stove polish you wanted. Only a nickel for two boxes, and the letter size tablet of onion skin was only a quarter." He slathered another biscuit with jam and took a big bite. "Got myself some wool socks, too. Only wanted fifteen cents a pair, and all of mine got holes in 'em."

Matilda laughed. "Give them to me or to Carrie and we'll darn them for you."

He grinned. "Okay, thanks. And they say smallpox is

691

making its way around Galt again."

"Again? When will people realize the advantage of being vaccinated?"

"Guess not even the docs have learned it. They say Doc Browning came out from Lodi to treat Will Hicks' family and he took it from them. Doc Hanna came down from Sacramento to investigate, and put Doc Browning in the Pest House."

"A doctor?" Matilda gasped in dismay. "Of all the people who should be vaccinated it would be doctors!"

"Well," Mart grinned, as he reached for another biscuit, "Guess that one had to learn the hard way." He finished the biscuit and shrugged into his coat. "Better get those cows in. Gotta get 'em in before dark. Rounding 'em up by lantern light is no fun."

He headed out the door and Matilda turned to Carrie with a sigh. "A doctor not vaccinated. Can you imagine?"

"No," Carrie admitted, "But did you hear John McFarland's nephew, the one who lives up by Forest Home, is challenging his uncle's will?" John McFarland had died the previous December and left his property to three nieces, Mary, who lived in Galt with her husband and three daughters, and two others who still lived in Canada.

Matilda laughed. "Taking a lesson from Doc Montague's relations, I guess."

At the end of February, Matilda received a letter from Minerva's daughter Laura telling her that Will's daughter Susie's youngest girl had died.

"Only fourteen, she was," Laura reported. "Doctors say it was cerebro-spinal meningitis complicated by heart trouble."

Matilda read the note to Carrie and sighed. "Susie said

poor little Jenny was never strong. Guess her heart was bad from the time she was born. But Laura certainly has four fine boys. Min would have been so proud of them. It's such a shame Laura's sister Anna died so young."

"Yes," Carrie said, "and Uncle Josh just had the one girl, and Too Tall Charlie had only Rachel. Laura must be very proud of those four boys."

"But Abe's little girl with Susan Theobold is growing well. Maybe she'll have some sons when she is old enough."

"Yes, Abe is very happy to have another little girl, and loves Goldie to death. Laura says he spoils her rotten. I know he was devastated to lose Anna. She looked so much like Min."

In May, Carrie, Mart, and Matilda, with Lew and Media and little Myrtle, attended the Lockeford Picnic at the invitation of Sam and Phoebe. The day was a fine one, and the food abundant. Phoebe's father invited her to sit with him to watch the races.

"Thank you, Mr. Reynolds. I'll be happy to join you. We've not had much chance to visit since the reception for Sam and Phoebe last fall. How are things working out for you?"

"Fine, fine," he enthused. Matilda noticed he was a little short of breath, and felt a twinge of concern. The short walk from the picnic tables to where seats had been arranged to watch the races should not have over-exerted him.

But he recovered quickly, and went on, "Sam is a fine young man. Reads to Phoebe every night." He chuckled softly "Phoebe listens patiently, but she has never been much of a scholar. However I certainly appreciate it. My eyes have gotten bad of late, so I can't read too well any more." He paused to catch his breath. "And Sam's a good worker, if a bit absent-minded." He grinned. "Between him with his nose in a book half the time and my hired hand with his nose in his whiskey bottle, I've got one whole worker between 'em."

Matilda laughed with him. "Yes, Sam has always had his head a bit in the clouds."

A blast from the trumpet signaled the start of the first race, and everyone's attention focused on the contestants.

She noticed Reverend Frazer, with his little girl in his arms, had edged close to the route the horses took. She commented on it to Mr. Reynolds.

"Is a bit close," he agreed. Then he laughed. "Maybe, him bein' a preacher, he figgers God'll protect him."

The first race concluded, and the winners were appropriately cheered. Then the second race began, and as the outside horse rounded the corner where Reverend Frazer stood, Matilda saw him reel backwards and land on his back, the baby flying from his arms. With a cry of horror, she started forward, but the crowd surged in front of her so she could not see. Her heart leapt into her throat.

She turned to Mr. Reynolds and saw him clutch his heart, his face gray.

"Mr. Reynolds! Are you all right? Here, sit down. Can I get you a drink of water? Do you want me to call the doctor?"

"No, no," he gasped. "I'll be fine. Just need to catch my breath a bit. Startled me, is all." He seemed to recover his color, and smiled into her anxious face. "Doc has told me I should avoid over-straining and over-excitement."

In her concern for him, Matilda had almost forgotten Reverend Frazer. As the crowd dispersed, she saw him on his feet, so he did not appear to be badly injured. The little girl, in her mother's arms, clung to Mrs. Frazer's neck, but seemed uninjured.

Carrie reached her mother's side and reassured her. "Baby's fine, and Reverend Frazer doesn't seem to be injured." Then she laughed. "But he'll be plenty sore tomorrow. I'll bet he has a lot of bruises!"

Summer burst upon them with the usual spate of activity. Between tending the garden, canning the garden produce, and preparing meals for the harvest crews, day swiftly followed day.

Matilda and Carrie did find time to visit young Isabel McKenzie in her new home on the 364 acres Colin had purchased about two miles from the previous home. Almost the first news Isabel told them was that the challenge to Dr. Montague's will had been dismissed.

"Oh, I'm so relieved," Matilda said, "And it must be such a relief to Nettie as well."

"I'll say," was the heartfelt reply. Then she laughed. "I don't think she realized just how vast the estate was. She's really quite a wealthy woman."

"With no children of her own, some of it will probably go to your children."

"Yes, or to my brother Vin's." Isabel smiled. "She's grown quite fond of my Nettie. Nettie is twelve now, and my sister takes her to Sacramento on her buying trips, and is teaching her to trim hats and help out in the shop."

"Nettie certainly performed well at the last school presentation. She did 'An Order for a Picture' very well. She is getting to be quite the young lady."

Isabel laughed. "And Monty practiced so hard for his dialogue 'Four Things to Learn'. He feels that now he is six years old he is all grown up." She poured tea into the dainty cups and placed a plate of sugar cookies in front of them.

"You folks lose any hogs?" Isabel asked. "I understand hogs have been dying by the thousands all up and down the Cosumnes."

"Not yet," replied Matilda with a relieved sigh, "but Columbus Dillard has, and so have the McEnerneys, so it's all around us. We have our fingers crossed."

"And such a shame about the Howard girl drowning in that boating accident."

"Yes, really sad. And her father was up in the hills with his sheep and didn't know about it for several days. No one knew exactly where he was." Matilda sighed, her old fear of water re-emerging. "Guess that's why I never get into boats." She reached for another cookie and took a sip of tea. "This tea is delicious." She glanced at Carrie, then faced Isabel. "Rumor says Nettie has a beau."

Anger flared in Isabel's eyes. "That Tom Patton has been coming around. I don't like him and I don't trust him. If you ask me, he's just after her money."

The big news to go through the community in August was the death of Dr. Charles Gordon, former husband of Laura DeForce, and present husband of a prominent lady in Lockeford.

Phoebe could talk of nothing else when she and Sam came to dinner the last Sunday in August.

"Turns out he was married all along to a lady as lives in England. He married her before he left the Old Country, and never divorced her."

"You mean his marriage to Laura DeForce was a bigamous one?" Matilda could only stare.

"Yes, as was the one he entered into after Laura left him.

They've got to try and straighten out his estate and that is going to take some doing."

Summer drifted into fall. Matilda, with Carrie, Mart, and Lew, attended an auction at Pio Valensin's. Although she had no intention of buying either horses or cattle, she enjoyed the action and the camaraderie of the scene. She found herself seated next to Mrs. Shields. She had come down from Sacramento, she said, with her son Robert who was buying stock for his farm.

"That's my Robert, over there." She motioned to a young man actively bidding on a beautiful sorrel. "My other son studied law," she boasted, "And was just named judge of the Superior Court in Sacramento."

"Oh, yes," Matilda nodded. "Peter Shields. My son Lew knows him. They have a mutual friend who is also a judge."

They passed a pleasant afternoon together, and when they parted, Mrs. Shields handed Matilda her card. "When you come to Sacramento, you must come and visit me."

Matilda accepted the card and promised. But as she watched the buggy drive away, she had a strange feeling she would never see Mrs. Shields again.

Chapter 80

September 1903 to August 1904

Lew brought her the news the next day. "Mrs. Shields was killed on their way home. She and Robert were driving through Sacramento and their buggy collided with an electric streetcar."

Memories of the pleasant afternoon spent with Mrs. Shields flooded back. "Oh, no what a shame. And her son? Was he injured?"

"Bruised and shaken, but the doctors have assured Peter his brother will recover. Their mother was thrown from the buggy and her neck broken. Poor Peter is distraught. His mother meant the world to him."

"Find out when the services are. We must attend."

At Thanksgiving, held at Matilda's house as usual, Phoebe could talk of nothing else but the scandal surrounding Dr. Gordon's death. "It's the talk of Lockeford, Mother Matilda. The man was married to Laura DeForce for eighteen years and to his present wife for over twenty. He married her four or five years after Laura divorced him. He left a fair-sized estate, according to all I hear. And it turns out he married this woman in England some 45 years ago, and she's still alive and plans to file a claim for the money as his widow."

Sam grinned and quoted, "Oh, what a tangled web we weave."

"It's very embarrassing for poor Mrs. Gordon. Neither she nor Laura had any idea he had been married before."

"And I hear Doc Montague's widow has remarried," Lew announced.

"No!" Matilda gasped. "When? Not to that Tom Patton, I hope."

"Last July, and yes, to Tom Patton. He's been chasing her ever since Doc died." Lew grinned, "Some are saying he's after her money."

Matilda sighed. "Isabel doesn't like him. She felt the same thing, that he's only after Nettie's money. She says he pulled back for a while, when the will was challenged, then re-doubled his efforts after the court dismissed the suit."

"Sounds suspicious, all right," Mart agreed, entering the room with a platter full of turkey he had carved into tempting slices. "Where do you want this put, Mrs. Frye?"

She moved a dish of green beans to make room for the platter. "Thank you, Mart. I think we're about ready to eat. Tell everyone to gather for Grace. Do Media and Carrie have the table set up for the children?"

As Matilda moved to her place at the foot of the table and Alf took his at the head, she felt her heart flutter, then miss several beats. Startled, she placed her hand on her heart and took a deep breath. The normal rhythm resumed. Reassured, she took her chair. If her heart did that again, she'd have to talk to Dr. Harms. She again regretted Dr. Montague's death. No other doctor instilled as much confidence in her as he had.

She dismissed her concerns and smiled at Alf. "We're

ready."

January of 1904 saw Lewis installed as an officer of the Masons. A joint installation of Masons and Eastern Star was held at the Odd Fellows Hall. Carrie and Media were two of the five points of the Star.

During the splendid repast that followed the ceremony, Matilda overheard Mr. Brewster remark to Dr. Harms that it looked like the Panama Canal would be built after all.

"Democrats tried to block it, but think what it will mean for California. Ships from Europe can make it here in half the time. And no more having to off-load in the East to ship by rail."

"And they say war is imminent between Russia and Japan over Korea and Manchuria," Dr. Harms added.

Matilda moved away. She was tired of hearing about politics. One of the young ladies present (whose name escaped Matilda at the moment – she'd noticed that more lately, there were so many of them, and they grew up so fast) asked rather breathlessly, "Oh, Mrs. Frye, I saw Harry Randolph at Ella Hanson's 18th birthday party. He seemed so interested in her. Do you suppose they'll get married?" She sighed. "He's *so* handsome."

At the end of February, word reached Matilda that her friend Jane Bandeen Mahin, now Bainbridge, was ill at her home in Lathrop, so she and Carrie boarded the train to go and see her. John Bandeen's wife, Mary accompanied them.

"John is sending me to find out if she needs any help," Mary laughed to Matilda as they settled into their seats. "He's afraid if he goes, she'll be stoic and say everything is fine."

"Well, her husband is a doctor, after all," Matilda said.

"He should know."

Mary nodded. "John has no faith in doctors since we lost Gracie. He says if they knew how to cure people, she would have lived."

Matilda laughed. "John and my mother would have gotten along very well. She was completely convinced they were all useless, and disagreed with every one of them."

At the Lathrop Station, they hired a buggy to take them to the Bainbridge home. The housekeeper greeted them at the door.

"Oh, Miz Mary, I'm so glad you come. Miz Bainbridge, she been down in the dumps all week. Dr. B. finally had to go back to seeing some of his patients. He's been doin' all he can fer her."

"Thank you, Mrs. Bates. I've brought two of her friends from Hicksville to see her as well. Mrs. Frye," she indicated Matilda, "has been Mother Jane's closest friend for many years."

Mrs. Bates ushered them into the bedroom where Jane lay, her right hand lying motionless on the counterpane. Her face lighted at the sight of Matilda, and she tried to speak, but could not make the garbled sounds into understandable words.

"Paralyzed on her right side, she is," Mrs. Bates nodded. "Poor soul. Tries to talk, but can't form no words. Just makes them sounds."

"Poor Mother Jane," Mary told Matilda. "She fretted so over Merrill and Lola's divorce last summer. Dr. Bainbridge says that's probably what brought on the apoplexy."

Matilda hugged her long-time friend, her heart aching to see her in such a condition. Jane made several unsuccessful attempts to talk, then just clung to Matilda's hand while the tears rolled down her cheeks.

On the return trip home, Matilda's thoughts were filled with her friend's plight. Poor Jane, to be trapped in a body that no longer responded. And so frustrating to want to speak and to be able to make only uninteligible sounds.

She thought of Mrs. Funderberg, Media's grandmother, who had lived in such a condition for a number of years. No wonder she prayed each day for God to free her and take her home.

She sighed. Carrie nodded in understanding. "I know it's hard for you to see her like that, Mother, but Jane will cope."

In March, a terrific rainstorm lasting over two days unroofed houses and blew down trees. More episodes of missing heartbeats drove Matilda to consult with Dr. Harms. He assured her the problem was not serious, and prescribed an iron tonic every morning to strengthen her blood, and urged her to get enough rest.

Matilda found herself wishing she had been able to see Dr. Montague. She felt he would have been able to tell her what was wrong, why she kept having these spells of faintness and missing heartbeats.

Carrie, who had accompanied her mother to the doctor, tried to get her to let her and Mart handle the workload.

"Mother, you shouldn't be on your feet for such long hours." She took the skimmer from Matilda's hand. "Let me skim that cream. I'll make the butter. You sit down."

Matilda laughed and yielded the skimmer to her daughter. "You win. I wanted to read that latest information I got on raising chickens. I just wonder if maybe we should switch from selling our wheat on the market to using it to feed chickens. We get twenty cents for every dozen from Whitaker and Ray." And five dozen paid for a bottle of the iron tonic Dr. Harms wanted her to take. She settled in her favorite chair and picked up the newspaper article she had saved. "I'll have to discuss this with Alf the next time I see him."

Her opportunity came when the family gathered for Easter. He arrived while the grandchildren eagerly hunted for the boiled eggs she and Carrie had dyed the evening before and Mart had hidden in the grass around the house. She looked closely at Alf, and for the first time he looked old, really old.

She hugged him. "Are you well?"

"They sold my ranch at auction." He still referred to the land McFarland had taken from him as his ranch. When Mr. Stevens had returned to Placerville on the death of his wife, the property had reverted back to McFarland. "His nieces are selling his estate, all except the home place. Guess George and Mary have to pay off the two nieces up in Canada."

"I know," she said softly. "I heard." When Mart brought her the news, she had thought how devastating this would be to Alf. "And has the nephew at Forest Home given up his attempt to break the will?"

"Guess so," he shrugged. "Fellow named Allen bought the place for his mother. They say he paid $7000 for it, even though the appraisers only valued it at $4500." He sighed. "Seven thousand. And I lost it for owing $2800," he said bitterly. He sank into a chair and put his head in his hands. "Makes a man wonder why he works so hard all of his life. To wind up with nothing."

The last words were whispered so low Matilda scarcely heard them. She put her arms around him and placed her cheek against the top of his head. She could think of nothing to say.

Chapter 81

April to October, 1904

CLINT ENTERED the room as Matilda brought Alf a cup of coffee. He carried his cousin Bess's Easter basket for her, grinning happily. Bess adored her sixteen-year-old cousin, and he seemed to return her affection.

"Look, Gramma," Bess beamed. "Clint helped me find all these eggs!" She proudly held up her basket. "He says we found more than anyone else."

"And how many did you find, Dear?" Matilda asked. She and Carrie had been teaching the child her numbers.

Bess bit her lower lip in concentration as she counted. "One, two, three - - ," she scowled, then added, "four, six - - no, five!" She looked up in triumph. "Five eggs, Gramma."

Matilda laughed and hugged her. "Very good, Dear. Now run along and wash up. Dinner will be ready soon." She smiled at Clint as the girl ran from the room. "Thank you for your patience with her." It reminded Matilda, with a twinge, of how Mary had adored her Uncle Michael, and how devastated she had been to lose him. She pulled Clint from the room, out of his father's hearing, and murmured. "I'm worried about your father."

"So am I. I told my mother I'm going to stay with him all the time now. He needs me and she doesn't. Besides," he scowled, "I don't really like Mr. Ritchie very well. And I don't think he likes me above half either."

"I'm glad your mother agreed. Your father does need you."

The rest of the children came running in, so they had no further chance to talk in confidence. Instead, Clint said, "They're restarting the Coyote Club, only now they're calling it the Farmers Coyote Club." He grinned. "Only going to pay $2.50 for adult coyotes and $1.50 for pups. George McGuirk is President and Frank McEnerney is treasurer."

"I guess they were running out of money at five dollars a coyote," Matilda laughed. "I thought that seemed like an awful lot to pay."

As everyone gathered for Easter dinner, Bud and Agnes' little boy Walter began to cough. Elizabeth looked at him in alarm. "He doesn't have whooping cough, does he? It's going though the Galt children. I hear the Pearson's lost their little girl."

"Oh, I don't think so, Lizzie. He doesn't have any fever, and I haven't heard of any cases around Carbondale."

Matilda thought it time to change the subject. "Has anyone given any thought to my suggestion we use our wheat crop to feed chickens instead of selling it? I've read that a living can be made with only about five thousand."

"Where would we get that many chickens?" Lew asked.

"We could hatch them ourselves. I understand they are now making incubators just for that purpose."

"Well, Mother, since you've got your heart set on it, I guess Mart and I are going to have to look into it further," Lew laughed. "For now, let's just settle for eating all of these eggs the children found."

Towards the end of May, Matilda and Carrie paid a visit

to Isabel McKenzie. She greeted them with enthusiasm, and her big news.

"We're going to have another baby in January. Colin is thrilled, and so is Nettie. I'm not so sure the boys are as enthusiastic. Monty ignores the whole subject, and little Jim may not understand. He's only three."

"That's wonderful news," Carrie beamed. "And I hear they've formed the Sunset Rural Telephone District. For fifty cents a month we'll be able to hook into Central and be able to call all over."

"And Colin has almost finished the new barn to replace the one that burned down last year. Never did figure out why, but probably spontaneous combustion."

Matilda sighed. "Yes, all of those incendiary fires we had for so many years seem to have stopped, thank goodness."

Isabel laughed. "Did you hear Will Bottimore tipped over his fancy new automobile? He was squiring a group of young ladies around Galt and hit a culvert. Dumped them all out and left his machine pretty badly used up."

"Yes, Mart came home full of that. Thought it was real funny, for Will was so busy showing off he didn't notice that broken culvert." Carrie chuckled softly. "Fortunately, the only injuries were to the automobile."

"And, not to be out-done, Lack Quiggle has purchased a beautiful roadster for his daughter Maud." Isabel laughed. "Guess he didn't want the Bottimores to get ahead of him."

By the middle of June, the fancy new telephone box hung on the wall of the kitchen. Matilda was not sure if she liked the contraption or not. The barbed wire strung on fence posts between Herbert's place at Hicksville and Matilda's continued on over to Lew and Media's, and down the road to Colin and Isabel's. The sound of the ringing startled

Matilda every time, somehow thinking it had to be an emergency, but soon learned many of the ten families along the line merely viewed it as a way to chat "without having to hitch up a buggy or saddle a horse" was how Carrie put it.

Later that month, one long ring followed by a short one caught their attention. Matilda waited to see if another long – the signal for Lew and Media – would follow, but it did not. Carrie answered. "Yes, yes, we'll send Mart at once. Media, are you there?" She paused. "Good. Tell Lew." She hung up and turned to Matilda, agape beside her.

"That was Isabel. There's a big fire over by Squire Short's place. Started in the oats Colin is growing on the land he rents from McCauley." She ran out the door, calling for Mart. Matilda followed and looked to the southeast. Yes, a large column of smoke rose high into the air. She sighed. Would they ever be free of fire?

Mart returned several hours later to report. "Colin was harvesting his field when it started, so he and his crew managed to save all but about 15 acres of oats. Real lucky. He could have lost the whole 800. Spread into Short's and took the whole field." He grinned. "And about a mile of fence. Lucky none of the fence burned carried our new telephone lines."

"Do they know how it started?" Matilda asked.

"Colin says a couple of fellows hauling hay passed them a few minutes before it started. He suspects one of them tossed a lighted stump of a cigarette into the field. Pure carelessness."

"My mother was right," Matilda muttered. "Smoking is bad for the health."

Mart laughed. "Well, it certainly is bad for farmers." Then he grinned. "Did hear they are trying to take action to close the Conley Saloon. Want the place declared a nuisance, saying Charley is selling liquor to minors.'

"Good," Carrie declared. "It should be shut down."

On August 20, their old friend and neighbor, Joseph Hicks passed away in his home at the age of 81. Matilda and her family attended his funeral at the Odd Fellows Cemetery in Galt.

"Poor old fellow," Carrie murmured to her mother. "Will says he was as childish as a baby for the last year or so, and no longer knew anyone. So his death is actually a relief. He started his decline after Jim died. Seems that Jim was his favorite, and the one he always looked to . Will, John, and George all agree. Even the girls."

"He certainly has left a legacy, with all of those children and grand-children, even great-grandchildren. I don't even know how many there are." And so, Matilda thought, another pioneer is lost. Soon all of the old-timers will be gone.

Her heart gave another of its little flutters and missed several beats. She took a deep breath. The iron tonic she faithfully took every morning did not seem to help very much. She sighed. Perhaps her time would be coming soon as well.

Sam and Phoebe joined them when the services were over. Sam grinned. "Did you hear Doc Harms married the schoolmarm after all?"

The unexpected death of John Bandeen after an illness of only a week stunned them all.

"Oh, poor Jane," Matilda cried when the news reached her. "What did he die of?"

"Pleural pneumonia, according to Doc Harms," Mart told her. "Seem he got caught out in that late storm we had a couple of weeks ago and took a bad chill. Got a cold and it went into his lungs."

"Get that last pie out of the pie saver. We'll take it with us."

When they reached the Bandeen residence, Jane sat in a chair by the stove, her face swollen with grief. Tears poured down her cheeks, and she burst into sobs as Matilda put her arms around her old friend.

Dr. Bainbridge stood beside his wife, his hand on her shoulder. "We came up yesterday when Dr. Harms called me to say he feared John would not recover. We were in time to say goodbye."

Jane, still unable to talk, nodded and clung more closely to Matilda.

"Services will be later this week. Will is making the arrangements, but we are waiting for Jane and Nancy to arrive from Los Angeles."

Matilda just held Jane and stroked her hair. She could think of no words of comfort.

Chapter 82

July 1905

MATILDA WOKE TO bright sunshine, heat already beginning to permeate the room. She rose and dressed, smiling in anticipation. Today was her 69th birthday, and Mart and Carrie, in collaboration with Lew and Media, had a big affair planned. Carrie and Media had spent most of the previous day cooking and baking, and sending Mart to the Arno Store for additional needed items.

Carrie entered the room as Matilda put the finishing touches on her hair and smiled. "Happy Birthday, Mother." She hugged her warmly. "Would you believe Henry and Lizzie have already arrived? They must have left Galt at daylight. But I'm glad she's here. She can help us get ready for the crowd."

Matilda sighed. "Are you sure we should have invited the whole neighborhood? It's made a lot of work for you and Media. A quiet family party would have been enough."

"Oh, no," Carrie laughed. "We decided it was time you had a royal celebration."

By noon, most of the guests had arrived. Carrie and Mart had settled Matilda on the section of the porch shaded by the big locust tree in the front yard. A lovely breeze wafted over her. Maybe the day would not be as hot as she feared.

Allen Wilder arrived with his wife Mayme and mother Elitha. Elitha looked well, in spite of all she had gone through, first losing Ben, her rock and anchor, then to have her son George hang himself in response to the tragic deaths of his family.

"Did they ever find who stole your trousseau, Mayme?" Matilda asked. She had attended the wedding last fall when the bride's trunk had been stolen out of the back of the buggy, forcing her to be married in her traveling dress.

"No," she laughed, "and probably never will. Brazen, they were, to just up and grab that trunk with me and Allen sitting in the buggy!"

"And you never saw their faces?" Mart asked.

"No," Allen said. "They were so quick they were running down the street by the time we turned around. All we saw were their backs. Two of 'em."

"I'll bet they thought they were getting something valuable," Mayme chuckled. "I'd like to have seen their faces when all they had was my wedding dress and petticoat, and a couple of chemises and drawers. And my new nightgown," she added mournfully.

Next to approach her were Annie and Charlie McKean, with baby Charlie.

"My, he's grown," Matilda declared. "Let me see, he must be six months old by now."

"Seven, Mrs. Frye," Charlie grinned. "He was born December 4."

"And such a beautiful little boy. His grandfather must be very proud of him."

Annie laughed. "Oh, yes, all of the Blues say he's the

handsomest of the babies." She gave her husband a merry glance. "I tell them it's because he has such a handsome father."

Lou Herbert and several of his daughters were next to greet her. She looked at Lou with some concern. He had aged since his wife had died the previous January. Of course, she thought, Annie had been 84, so Lou has to be somewhere around that age. Figures he would start looking older. Somehow, Annie had never seemed that old. . .

"Congratulations, Mrs. Frye, and many happy returns of the day." He bowed gallantly and kissed her hand.

"Thank you," she laughed, "And thank you for coming. Do get a plate and get something to eat. Carrie and Media have been cooking for two days. Nothing as fancy as the tongue with parsley sauce or the leg of lamb they served for Christmas at the Galt Hotel, but good solid food." Lew, Media, Carrie, and Mart had taken her to the Galt Hotel for the Christmas banquet, and she still marveled over the menu that had been presented to her.

"Then by all means we must show our appreciation for their hard work." He moved on, towards the tables set up at the end of the porch.

Isabel and Colin were the next guests to greet her. They were accompanied by Monty, four-year-old George Stuart (though they always called him Jim), and baby Isabel, born the previous January.

Matilda hugged Isabel warmly. "I thought you might not be able to come, Nettie sick the way she is. Is she better?"

"Yes, she gets better every day. Dr. Mason says she should be up and about in a day or so. We left her in my sister's care. She fusses over the child more than I do."

"That's a relief, to hear she's recovering," Matilda sighed. "When I heard she had been ill for two weeks I feared it

713

might be diphtheria or consumption."

"No, just seems to have a bad cold and it has taken her a long time to recover. Dr. Mason says her blood is poor, and has prescribed a tonic." She shrugged. "Whether it's the tonic or the attention she gets from my sister, she does seem to be getting better."

Matilda thought of the tonic she faithfully swallowed every morning, but seemed to have no effect on the missing heartbeats she still suffered almost daily. She hoped it would be more beneficial to little Nettie.

Her nephew Harry arrived with Ella Hanson, his brother Clint in tow. Since Alf's death on February 11, Harry had filed for custody of Clint, and his mother had offered no objection. Matilda had also signed papers approving the action. She thought of poor Alf, whose last years had been so sad. She could not help but feel he had to be happier now.

She sighed. I've outlived all of my brothers and sisters except Sarah and John. Her heart gave another of those funny little flutters. She should be grateful she had lived this long. Doctor Harms had said the flutters should not be any cause for worry.

As Harry and Ella spoke to her, she suspected there would be another wedding in the not too distant future. She knew Ella planned to go to school in San Francisco in the fall.

"Happy Birthday, Aunt 'Tilda," Clint beamed. "Harry and I have been having a great time together. Except, of course," he scowled, "when he thinks I should get better grades in school."

Matilda laughed. "He's just being a conscientious father, Clint. Be patient with him."

They moved on. Alone for the moment, Matilda looked about her at the happy faces. Elizabeth, six months pregnant with her next child (and which she vowed would be her last, claiming to be too old to have babies), surrounded by Pearl, Henry Jr., Dick, Virginia, and Bess. The devoted Henry hovered nearby. She could not help but compare Elizabeth's happy marriage to Henry with Mary's turbulent one with George. Pearl, at 23, already taught at a Stockton school and enjoyed it so much she vowed she would never marry, and would spend her life teaching. Henry, at twenty, bid fair to be just like his father. Virginia, at twelve, was turning into a charming young lady. Dick, at ten, hovered over little Bess, who would be six in the fall.

Bud and Agnes had come down from Carbondale for the occasion, and were surrounded by their whole brood. Willie, thirteen, George, ten, Earl, seven, little Walter, who had just turned four, Frank, who would be three in November, and Viola, just nine months old. Matilda had to smile as she watched Agnes hover over the younger children She had become such a careful mother after losing poor little Erald in that dreadful accident.

Sam and Phoebe had come from Lockeford alone, poor Mr. Reynolds having died the year before. So far, she saw no signs of another grandchild from that direction.

Lew and Media were there, of course, with three-year-old Myrtle. Myrtle had blossomed into a lovely child under the tender care of her adopted parents. She chuckled softly as she saw how Mart solicitously insisted on carrying any burden he saw Carrie trying to lift. Mart had taken Carrie to the dance at Hicksville last month and, watching them together, she could see a romance blossoming there as well. She nodded. Carrie was getting up in years. Time she married.

Matilda smiled. Life had not been easy, but it had been a full and rich. She had known the love of three good men.

Few women were so blessed, remembering what her friend Jane had gone through with Billy Bandeen, what Celestia Johnson had tolerated from Dick (they were even buried in separate cemeteries), and Mary's turbulent marriage to George Douglass. And although she would forever regret losing Baby John and her beautiful Mary, she was grateful she had Elizabeth, Lew, Carrie, and Sam.

She remembered her thoughts when Sinclair had been killed, so many years before, how she wondered why we worked so hard to survive, then gathering little Lewis in her arms, thinking that was why, for the children. She smiled. Now Lew was a grown man with a family of his own.

Little Bess ran up to her with a small bouquet of wildflowers in her chubby hand, the colorful blossoms already wilting in the summer heat.

"These are for you, Gramma," she cried, holding up her little offering. "Happy Birthday."

Matilda hugged the child and accepted the flowers. Yes, she thought, I have had a good life.

716

Epilogue

January, 1906

GALT GAZETTE, January 20, 1906
"The many friends of Mrs. Frye of Hicksville will regret to learn of her death which occurred Monday of this week from heart disease. Deceased was a native of Illinois and was born July 19, 1836, and she came to California in 1864. Mrs. Frye had been quite ill for some little time, was under the doctor's care, but it was not supposed she was in any immediate danger. Sunday night she retired as usual and died without awaking about 1 o'clock in the morning. The funeral took place Wednesday from the Hicksville church, and the interment was in the cemetery at that place."

On January 21, 1906, at the home of Mr. and Mrs. Lewis Baldwin, Carrie Belle Wheelock and Martin Luther Shellenbarger were united in marriage.

On January 10, 1907, John Alfred Shellenbarger was born.

APPENDIX A

Descendants of Gardner and Elizabeth Ann Randolph

James Brittain (Britt) 18 Oct 1818 to 31 Dec 1876
    Married Sarah Evans 23 Jul 1838
    Sarah Elizabeth 1840
        Married James Morrison
    Minerva, died 1843
    William Chase 1844 to between 1914 and 1916
    Gardner born 1846
    Owen, born 1849, died before 1880

Temperance 14 Feb 1820 to 4 June 1851
    Married Josh Tovrea 18 Nov 1838
    Sarah Rebecca 08 May 1841 to 11 Nov 1898
    Henry born 1848, died 04 Aug 1864

William 10 Dec 1822 to 09 May 1875
    Married Mary (Polly) Cottrell August 1846
    William Jr born 1848
    Michael 15 Dec 1850 to 17 Dec 1866
    John Sinclair (Jack) 1855 to 15 Aug 1925
        Married Rebecca Evans
        Maud Estella (Essie)
        One child stillborn
    Frank died between Oct 1895 and Oct 1896
        Married (1) Clara Maxfield 3 Aug 1879

Married (2) Annie Hurd
Edward Franklin 1883-1918
Son born 26 Jan 1885
Clara Osborn born 20 May 1887
      M (1) Jesse Clark
      M (2) Derry
John Clifford 1893 to 02 Nov 1919
      M Daisy May Derby
      Son June Clifford b&d 1916
Daughter died 29 Oct 1896 age 3mo.
Mary C born 1858, died Jan 1925
      M. Wesley Overton 05 May1878
      Jesse, born 1879
      Chester
      Another girl
Susan Harriet 15 Feb 1860 to 06-Oct 1914
      M. John Jacob (Jake) Davis 1878
      Roy Elmer 02 Dec 1879-28 Nov 1955
      M Essie Bell Rhodes
      Della, born 1881
      M Bill Swant (Schwant)
      Dora L, July 1888 to 06 Jan 1922
      Jenny J, Oct 1889 to 28 Feb 1903
      Susie, born Feb 1891
      M. DeMaster
Margaret Ann born 11 Feb 1862
      Married D.K. Stringfield
      Gussie Elizabeth born 11 April 1878
      Alfred born 1879? Died young
      Mary Alice born 14 May 1888
Samuel Thomas (S.T.) 16 June 1865-17 Apr 1916
      M. Carrie Belle Robertson 31 May 1883
      William H 27 Mar 1884 -19 June 1970

Raymond Lester 06-Apr1885-01 Feb 1950
Clifton H 12 Jul 1887-13 Oct 1960
Cora M, born Fen 1889
Emma Alene 25 Jan 1891-27 Apr 1985
    M. Cleve Allen
Ansel Samuel 01 Apr 1892-04 Dec 1940
    M. Charlotte Mae Grigsby (Div)
        Samuel T born 02 May 1916
Stella May 01 Apr 1895-17 Sep 1991
    M. Crawford
Bessie Adella 01-Apr 1895-10 Jul 1987
Michael Brittain (Bud) 29 Apr 1867-20 Dec 1939
    Married Agnes Lawson 26 Jan 1891
    Elizabeth (Lizzie)
    William Michael 12-Oct 1892-1934
    George 1895-1929
    Harold (Erald) died 07-12-1897, age 17 mo
    Stillborn P.H. born 1896 (same as
    Erald/Harold?)
    Walter Lawson 07-Sept 1901-1956
        M. Annie Marcella Taylor 1925
        Son Leonard
    Franklin Edward 06 Nov 1902
        M (1) Ethel Woodford
        M (2) Celeste Wilheim Boshaw
    Viola Marie 27-Oct 1904
        M Bernal Gold
    Alice A. 11 Aug 1907
        M Roy Combs
    Clarence H, born 1909, died 1928
    Edna 20 Oct 1910
    M Melvin Tripp
Sarah Elizabeth born 1871, died 1922

M. Will Burnell
Fred

Sarah Boydston 11 Oct 1824 – 09 Aug 1910
Married Albert Welch 22 Oct 1846
Lawson D.02-Dec 1847
    Married Arabella Lerner
    William P, died 05-Oct 1879, 4y9m14d
Elizabeth born 1849, died young
Caroline Matilda born 1850
    M. Orrie Brown (Brun?)
John G born 1851
Rachel
    M. Henry Raley

Thomas C. 28 Jul 1826 died between 1894 and 1900
Married Mary Dooley in 1878
Adopted Annie Hurd, born 19 Feb 1868
    M. Frank Randolph 07 Sep 1882
Adopted George Jones (takes name of Randolph)

Samuel Thomson 22 Mar 1828 – 16 Aug 1892
Never married

Alfred 15 Jul 1830 – 01 Feb 1905
Married Emaline McFadden in 1876
Henry Marvine (Harry) May 1877 - 1970
    M Eleanor (Ella) Hanson
        Son Henry
Stella born 1879
    M (1) Arthur C Wells 8 April 1897
    M (2) Black
        Grandson Jack Niles

Clinton Alfred 09-May 1888
Son stillborn 6 May 1890

John Sevier 15 June 1832 – 1908
    Married Mary Anne Tate 6 Nov 1861
    William 01-Sep 1862-26 May 1862
    Joshua Alfred 15 Apr 1864 – 10 Nov 1944
        Married Lily
            Della born 1885
    Matilda Belle 24 Sep 1865 – 18 May 1930
        M. William Muncy in 1883
        Edwin Francis 21 June 1884
        Meda Mable 12 Nov 1885
        Millie Ettie 25 May 1889
        Vina Ann 09 Jan 1891
        Lawrence Severe 04 May 1893
        Fred Allen 8 Aug 1896
        Ada Delina 05 Sep 1900
    George Thomas 02-May 1867-09 Aug 1870
    Nora 13 Jan 1869-11 Aug 1870
    Edwin 13 June 1870 – 13 Aug 1871
    Lily May born 8 June 1872
        M. Charles Berry 06 Dec 1900
    Eva Edith, born 8 June 1873
        M. (1) Lucius Corbett 21 Jan 1890
        Ora Letha born 04 Apr 1885 (?) prob 95
        Delbert S
            M Catharine
        Elvin Emery born 13 June 1891
            M Myrtle Haviland 13 Jun 1912
        Estelle May born 14 Aug 1896
            M George Mortimer Keribel 1918
        M.(2) Alex Simpson 25 Dec 1917

723

Ora born 29 Oct 1876
    M. Ford
Britten Wesley born 9 Apr 1879
Anna Estelle born 17 May 1886
    M. Kellogg

Caroline 03 May 1835 – 12 Feb 1872
    Married (1) Tommy Evans 22 Aug 1854
    Rebecca born 1855, died 17 Mar 1885
    Sarah Morris (Sally) born 1857 - 1936
    Anna Thomas born 1858 died 15 Dec 1863
    Married (2) Eli Robertson
    Carrie Belle born 24 Oct 1864-31 Oct-1935
        M. S.T. Randolph (see his)
    Minnie Marian born 1867
    Fannie C Born about 1868,dead before 1872
    Matilda Lavina (Till) born 1870
        M. Grigsby

Matilda Virginia 21 Jul 1836 – 14 Jan 1906
    Married (1) Lewis Clark Baldwin 01 Sep 1856
    John O. 27 Jun 1857-27 Jan 1857
    Mary Jane 06-Oct 1859-01 May 1890
        M. George E Douglass 17 Jan 1876
        Earnest, died in infancy
        Mable 07 Jan 1879-03 Dec 1866
        Earl 19 Apr 1881-11 Feb 1890
    Elizabeth Anne 07 Dec 1861-17 Mar 1939
        M. Henry Marshall Wade 11 Dec 1879
        Pearl born 1882
        Henry Jr, born 1885
        Virginia 28 Mar 1893 – 23 Jan 1983
        M. Bert Neville

                 Patty died at age 4
        Richard Lewis 27 Jan 1895-29 Mar 1917
        Pauline 30 Jan 1897-15 Oct 1898
        Elizabeth (Bess) 12 Oct 1899-18 Sept 1993
        Robert Lee 24 Oct 1905-17 Feb 1959
    Lewis Gardner 28 Oct 1863-1917
        M. Media Latourette 06 Jun 1887
        Adopted Myrtle born 27 Oct 1901 in 1902
    M. (2) Alfred Wheelock 17 June 1867
    Carrie Belle 01 Mar 1869-Nov 1936
        M. Martin Luther Shellenbarger 21-Jan
1906

        John Alfred 10 Jan 1907-7 Dec 1977
        Twin boys, stillborn 1908
    Samuel Alfred 04-Oct 1871-24 Dec 1959
        M. Phoebe Reynolds 08 Oct 1901
        No children
    M. (3) William Frye 02 Nov 1882

Sinclair 27 Jan 1839-09 Aug 1865
    Never married

Minerva Elizabeth 23 Aug 1841 – 27 May 1866
    M. Abraham Oakes Dyer 07-Dec 1856
    Stillborn, 1857
    Laura, born 1859, died 17 Nov 1948
        M. Charles Arnold
        John, May 1884
        Charles, Feb 1886
        Ralph. 1887
        Earl 1891
            Married Maud
            Two sons

Anna born 1861, died before 1893
   Married Banks (?)
James William 16 Sep 1862
   M. Edith Murray
     Inez, married Hood
Charles H. 13 Mar 1864 – 02 April 1899
   M. Emma Thompson
     Rachel, m. Herbert Huston 1916
     Son Stuart

Andrew born 1843 or 1844. Probably died close to April of 1844, as family took in Weldon Crose, born 06-April 1844

APPENDIX B

Decendants of James Latourette, 03 Nov 1794-07 Nov 1877 and Mary Roll 06 Dec 1791-Nov 21 1887

John Latourette died 26 Aug 1859
    M. Elizabeth Rall (she m 2nd Funderberg)
        M. 25 Dec 1838
        Died 03 Aug 1886
        James Emory 10 Oct 1839-2 Dec 1865
        William Henry 18 June 1841-18 Sep 1842
        Mary Elizabeth 23Nov 1843 - 21 Oct 1896
            M. Mead
        Paredes Hamblin 16 Feb 1846-15 Apr 1929
            M (1)Eliza Smith 2 Mar 1867
                09 Apr 1845-12 Dec 1893
            Armedia 07 July 1868
                M. Lewis Baldwin 6 Jun 1887
            William 22 Feb 1870-09 Jan 1887
            Minnie 13 Oct 1871-19 Feb 1875
            John 18 Feb 1876-
                M Harriet Larned 24 Feb 1897
            M. (2) Alice Henley (Jones) 5 May 1895
        Sarah Louisa 7 Apr 1848 –19 Dec 1906
            M. Jonas Shellenbarger
            Martin Luther, born 1877
                M Carrie Belle Wheelock
            John Alfred 10-Jan 1907

John
Three daughters
John Durben Fletcher 26 Mar 1850-22 Oct 1931
Annie Miller 10 Jul 1852-7 Nov 1852
Harriet Newel 21 Sep 1853-30 Oct 1853
Emma Jane 22 Oct 1855-9 Dec 1859

BIBLIOGRAPHY

Galt Gazette. August 1882 to January 1906, Courtesy of California State Library. Microfilm

Daily Bee (later *Sacramento Bee*) June 1867 to August 1882, Courtesy of Sacramento City Library Microfilm

Clark, William B *Gold Districts of California, Bulletin 193* (California Department of Conservation, Division of Mines and Geology, 1998)

Dick, William B. *Encyclopedia of Practical Receipts and Processes* (H .Keller & Co., 1872)

Gerson, Noel B. *Harriet Beecher Stowe* (Popular Library, 1976)

Grunsky, Carl Ewald *Stockton Boyhood* (The Friends of the Bancroft Library, 1949)

Gudden Erwin G. *California Place Names* (University of California Press, Bekeley Third Edition, 1969)

Hertzler, Arthur E., MD *The Horse and Buggy Doctor* (University of Nebraska Press 1938)

Holden, William M. *Sacramento, Excursions into its History and Natural World* (Two Rivers Publishing

Company, 1988)

Kloss, Jethro *Back to Eden* (Back to Eden Publishing Company, 1988)

Lewis, Oscar *The Big Four* (Alfred A Knopf, New York, 1941)

Reed, G. Walter *History of Sacramento County* (Historic Record Company, 1923)

Richardson, Joseph G, MD *Health and Longevity* (Home Health Society, Phildelphia, 1914)

Sperry, Baxter *The City of Galt* (The Laurel Hill Press, Galt, 1970)

Taylor, Henry S, MD *The Family Doctor* (The Keystone Publishing Company, Philadelphia, 1860).

The Gold Rush Letters of J.D.B. Stillman (Lewis Osborne: Palo Alto, 1967)

Thompson & West *History of Sacramento County* (Thompson & West, 1880)

Thompson & West *History of San Joaquin County* (Thompson & West, 1879)

Upton, Charles Elmer *Pioneers of El Dorado* (Charles Elmer Upton, Placerville, 1906)

Warp, Harold *A History of Man's Progress* (Harold Warp Pioneer Village, 1978)

ABOUT THE AUTHOR

Jacquelyn Hanson, great-granddaughter of Matilda Randolph, grew up on the ranch where Matilda spent the last thirty years of her life, surrounded by family stories. She decided to write them down so the stories would be preserved for future generations. As a result, her first novel, *Matilda's Story*, was published in 1997.

She went on to write two historical romances, *Susan's Quest* and *Katlin's Fury*, both based on the extensive research done for *Matilda's Story*. *Matilda's Story* ended in 1867 with Matilda's marriage to Alfred Wheelock, the author's great-grandfather, but demand from her readers to know what happened to Matilda after 1867 led to *Matilda's Story: The California Years*, which follows Matilda to her 69th birthday in 1905.

The author, a graduate of Stanford University School of Nursing, lives in Southern California with her youngest son, and recently retired from business with her oldest son. She has been published in professional journals, and several of her short stories have been published or won awards. This is her fourth novel.

She has been active with Liga International, Flying Doctors of Mercy for over twenty years, and goes to Mexico one weekend a month to operate a free clinic there. She is on a DMAT (Disaster Medical Assistance Team) and a volunteer with the Red Cross. She is also on the Board of Directors for the Orange County Natural

History Museum, and a member of the Laguna Hills/Lake Forest Rotary Club.

She has not decided what her next project will be, but is considering telling the story of her great-great grandfather, Gardner Randolph.